ACADIA EVENT

A Novel by M.J. Preston

ACADIA EVENT

All artwork and photography including cover image
By M.J. Preston

ISBN-13: 978-1507686102

Edited by Sara Kelly

This book is dedicated to

Robert James Steel

Historian and Author

Jim, without you I would have never found my Muse.
Bastard that he is.

Foreword

The novel you are about to read is a work of fiction, and for the most part, any resemblance to persons living or dead is purely coincidental; however, I have taken the liberty of using historical characters and made mention of living individuals to enhance the reader experience.

The instances where I make mention of actual people is done so with the permission of the individuals. For the record I would like to acknowledge those people now, and thank them for allowing me to use them in this work of fiction. They are: R. Bradford (Brad) Hardy, Heath Crane, and Kenneth Meade. All three of these individuals have been involved with the ice roads over a number of years. Only their first names were used in the telling of this story, but it is worth mentioning them in full as they not only played a part in the inspiration of this book but remain lifelong friends.

I would also like to acknowledge Michael B. Steward (Big Mike) who served as an inspiration for the character: Big Garney Wilson. Wilson's bigger than life persona is a reflection of my pal Big Mike, but not a mirror reflection. Certain aspects of Garney's personality and certainly mention of his family is complete fiction. Anyone who has heard that booming voice over the radio, be it in the NWT, Alberta, the Yukon, and even Inuvik will immediately recognize the traits upon which I latched in the birth of Garnet Wilson.

Finally, Merv Pink, who was an inspiration for the character Merv White. Merv Pink and I have been friends for damned near two decades. We met after he inadvertently backed me into a brand new Freightliner, scraping up its bumper outside of Buffalo, NY in 1999. At least that's how I remember it; he might have a different recollection of events. Anyway, Merv asked if I could write his character into this book and I obliged, with the understanding that I would fictionalize all other aspects of his life including mention of his family.

Since the conception of this book there have been a number of changes to the infamous Ingraham Trail, which snakes northward from Yellowknife to the world's longest ice road. The Ingraham trail has been upgraded with a by-pass which now routes northbound traffic around the landmark known as Giant Mine. I decided to leave that particular route intact as it plays a significant backdrop to two set pieces within the storyline. The Inuksuk Trail, Meanook and Acadia Mines, as well as Corbett Lake Camp and Targus Lake Meteorological Outpost are pure fiction. These places are inspirational reflections of diamond mines and outposts in the region. I have used the real mines, Ekati, DeBeers, and their outlying outposts as a template for this story.

Technical aspects of this novel have also been enhanced for storyline purposes. While there are many facets of this story which relate to my own experiences as a winter road driver, it should be noted that some parts are complete fiction and are a figment of this author's imagination. Any oversight, error or omission falls with the author.

M.J. Preston
Fort Saskatchewan, Alberta
December 24, 2014

Table of Contents

ACT III – JUST IN CASE

EXTRA – ART AND PHOTOGRAPHY

The above map illustrates the route to the Acadia and Meanook Mines from Yellowknife, NWT.

Before the Harvest

"The creatures outside looked from pig to man, and from man to pig, and from pig to man again; but already it was impossible to say which was which."

— George Orwell, Animal Farm

***

"And before we judge of them too harshly we must remember what ruthless and utter destruction our own species has wrought, not only upon animals, such as the vanished bison and the dodo, but upon its inferior races. The Tasmanians, in spite of their human likeness, were entirely swept out of existence in a war of extermination waged by European immigrants, in the space of fifty years."

—Herbert George Wells, War of the Worlds

***

"Harvest yes. Skent! Harvest!"

—The Collective of Skentophyte

***

ACT I
GHOSTS FROM THE PAST

"Ride the snake, Marty, ride the snake and get ready to race with the Devil because he'll be out there waiting for us."
— Big Garney Wilson

Chapter 1—Red

1

January 14th, 2015
Niagara Escarpment
26 Miles South of Hamilton

He rolled over on the bed—a dull throb behind his right temple gave warning of an impending migraine. She had already gotten up, the rush of shower water filtered down the hall into the room.

Better get up, he thought. *Better grab some Advil before this baby turns into a monster.* He rubbed his right eye, flung back the covers, and swung his feet onto the floor. The hardwood was cool against his soles. At a glance in the dresser mirror, he could see fresh snow flurries blowing at an angle against the window. Standing up, he felt the distant ache of arthritis under his knee cap and wondered if the pills he took would be compromised by the pain. "Fuck it," he muttered. "Better take four just in case."

Walking down the hall, he could hear her humming in the shower. The temptation to detour that way and have a little water play was barely trumped by the throb, which was making good on its threat. He turned left down the stairwell, holding the banister as he went. The old post-war house creaked under the weight of the snow, groaning a bit, as its ghosts listened intently to the silence of winter. The place had been his parents'; it had been willed to him after his father died only a year ago.

At the sink he reached and took a glass out of the dish rack and ran the water. He opened the cupboard to the left of the sink and grabbed a bottle of Advil as the water filled his glass. He decided on five, popped them into his mouth, crunched them between his teeth, then brought the glass to his lips and drank the icy water. As he swallowed, a pipe inside the wall shuddered and thumped twice. Maggie had shut off the shower. He heard the curtain rings scrape across the aluminum rod and pictured her naked form exiting and reaching for a cotton towel.

She'd made a fresh pot of coffee before hopping into the shower and its aroma filled the room. He looked at the toaster—the loaf of bread next to it, fresh from the freezer, still a hard rectangular block.

Peanut butter and toast might get these babies to work a little faster, he thought and undid the bag.

"You in the kitchen, Hon?" Maggie called.

"I am, and yes I will," he snickered, removing two mugs from the cupboard.

"Thank you!"

"Anything for you, me lady," he said in a terrible English accent and poured them each a cup. He heard the bathroom door creak, imagined her floating down the hall wrapped in a towel, rubbing her short hair with another. She was all legs, covered in creamy soft flesh that true redheads sported. Her hair was almost rusty red. She kept it short and sassy, which made her look incredibly sexy.

The toaster popped, breaking his thoughts and he absently stirred the coffees, unaware that his impending headache was beginning to retreat. That was because he was aroused thinking about her. She'd never let him run her back to the bedroom now, not after a shower. She had to get to work. Last night had been hours of playing around; Maggie was unstoppable in bed.

The floor creaked and he could smell the soapy clean scent even before she came from behind and wrapped her arms around him. "Not done that coffee yet, sweetheart? What's the hold up?" she purred and ran a hand down over his stomach and to the area she had been so many times before. "Ohhh, what's this?"

"That? That is going to get you dragged back into the bedroom and make you late for work," he answered, bringing his own hand around to caress her thigh.

"Why wait 'til we get all the way to the bedroom, we could go for it right here," she teased, her hot breath pushing into his ear, arousing him even more. He spun around to face her, she realizing her bluff had been called. "The hell with it, I'll take another shower," she laughed, ready to drop the towel and then the phone rang.

"Shit," he cussed.

She giggled and went for the phone, catching it halfway into its second ring.

Placing the receiver against her ear she smiled, her eyes wide, revealing the future etchings of crow's feet. She was so beautiful, and he loved her so much. "Hello?" There was a muffled voice he could not identify. "This is Maggie?" More inaudible language. "Yes. Yes, Marty lives here. Who is this?" She was still grinning, her left hand clutching the towel—a playful look on her face. "I'm his wife."

He put out his hand. Maggie was such a flirt, even on the phone. If he didn't make a move, she would joust with this unknown person forever.

"Well, it's nice to talk to you too."

He made a beckoning gesture.

"Yes, he's right here."

He rolled his eyes, but it was theatrics, nothing more.

"Okay, here you go." She passed the phone over, placing a hand over the mouthpiece and whispered into Marty's ear. "I was going to fuck you blind, baby, be sure to thank your old friend for that." He took the phone from her and she kissed him and turned. As she exited the kitchen, she lifted the towel, revealing her firm round bottom.

Sassy bitch, he thought and placed the telephone to his ear. "Hello?"

"Hello, Marty." The voice on the other end was raspy, sounding congested like a man with a cold or stuffed up nose. "Your wife sounds very pleasant."

Was there a hint of sarcasm in that voice?

"It's been a long time."

Oh my God! Marty Croft felt his chest tighten.

"Are you there, Marty?"

Get a grip on yourself, he scolded himself and said, "Yes, I'm here."

"You know who I am?"

"Yes," he answered, but he didn't want to say it. Not out loud, not ever.

"How have you been, Marty? I saw some of your work in Heavy Metal. You are really quite good. Of course you were always artistic, weren't you? Is that all computer generated work or do you use a conventional paint brush?"

"I'm fine, thank you. I use a mixture of photography and computer rendering." He looked down the hall, watched a half dressed Maggie cross, looking for something. *Probably her purse*, he thought.

"Say my name, Marty."

"Why?"

"Because I need to hear you say it."

He shivered, then whispered. "Gord. Gord Shamus."

"Aren't you going to ask me how I've been doing?" Shamus asked. "It's been over 10 years. A lot has happened."

"How are you Gord?" he asked while watching for Maggie. His knees were vibrating. "What can I do for you?"

"I'm okay, Marty, but we need to meet face to face."

"I can't do that, Gord."

"Oh yes you can."

"No, I'm sorry, I won't. That was another life, I've moved on."

"She doesn't know, does she?"

"What?"

"About us, about the old days. She doesn't know anything about it." Shamus released a loose echo of cackles. "Oh, this is sweeter than I thought. How did you manage that, Marty?"

He wanted to hang up, instead opting to stay silent.

"There's a small pub called Bradshaw's, used to be The Jolly Time when we were younger, meet me there after lunch."

"I'm sorry, Gord, I won't be there."

"Yes, you will." His voice was confident.

"Gord, I will not be coming and you are not to call here again." He was about to hang up when two things happened. First, Maggie came back into the kitchen and grabbed her travel mug off the counter. She was dressed for work; ready to roll. She leaned down and kissed him as he held the phone dumbly to his ear.

"See you at five, sweetheart," she whispered and hugged him. "I'll bring home some Chinese food for supper." He faked his best smile. She appeared not to notice, leaving him there in his seat—phone pressed hard against his ear.

"Red," Shamus said.

"What?"

"Her hair is red. She works for Fowler Insurance."

The front door closed. He wanted to drop the phone, chase after her, but what could he possibly say?

"Bradshaw's at noon, Marty. I'll be waiting."

The phone clicked.

***

Chapter 2—Doctor Hook

1

When Marty entered the dimly lit pub he spotted Shamus already waiting in a corner booth set away from the front. The older fellow working the bar pointed him to the back; the place was a tomb. No need for gangster discretion, they could have had any seat in the place. Shamus was as he'd remembered him, except for a few subtle changes. He was still thin, his blond hair now streaked with grey and the scar on his face which ran from eye to lip was hard and pronounced against the pocked landscape of his face. Marty remembered that scar well. Worse, he remembered what happened to the individual who had caused it, although no one ventured to speak about it. It looked as though Shamus was talking to someone and hadn't noticed him, but that illusion was broken when he raised his hand to wave Marty over. As Marty approached the booth he saw a bald head cresting the seat back.

"Marty! So good of you to come." Shamus stood up, a toothy carnivorous smile accompanied the welcoming handshake.

Marty considered saying, 'You didn't give me much choice,' but thought better of it. Gordon Shamus was a dangerous man with the temperament of a psychopath. "Hello, Gord." He shook his hand and peered toward the bald man.

Shamus's grin widened. "This is an associate of mine. Phil Crane." Crane didn't say anything, just nodded and watched the two men. "Phil is my security man, he oversees my operations and business dealings. He does it well. Phil, stand up so Marty can slide into a seat and we'll get right down to business."

The bald man slid out and Marty felt that same unsettling anxiety in his belly. Sliding in before this bald gorilla would mean no way to escape from Shamus's mad proposal—not that there would be any means of escape. Shamus would have his way, he wouldn't take no for an answer.

Marty slid into the seat wondering what the crazy bastard had up his sleeve. He thought he'd left this life behind. He knew that the old man was gone, but he'd hoped that he was a passing memory for the prodigal son. It wasn't enough to for Gordon to inherit the family business, he wanted Marty back and worse, he was using Maggie as leverage. This made his blood boil, if not for the gorilla sliding in next to him, he was half tempted grab the half-empty bottle of scotch sitting on the table and beat a new scar into the maniac's face.

Do that and they'll find your body in the spring, he thought.

"Jack, bring us over another bottle," Shamus called to the bartender.

"Alright Mr. Shamus," came the call from behind the bar.

Marty watched the man behind the bar disappear, then resurface with a fresh bottle and another tumbler. Marty hated scotch, especially served up by the likes of Gordon Shamus. Scotch meant one thing: he, Marty, was about to be on the end of a hard bargain. The bartender walked over to the table and set down the bottle, then pushed the empty tumbler toward Marty.

"Anything else, Mr. Shamus?"

"Nope, that will be it for now, Jack. Why don't you leave us here to talk some business and get a hand on your stock." Shamus wasn't asking, it was an order.

"Uh, okay." Jack the bartender got the message and walked on. He likely didn't want to know what Gordon Shamus had to say or anything about his business. That kind of information got you killed.

Marty watched the bartender disappear down the hall and wished he could follow him, but he was in it now. In it with this fucking psychotic gangster who had killed his fair share of men.

"Phil, do you know what Marty's talent is," Shamus said.

This was the preamble to the fuck-over that was coming.

"You said he's some kind of artist," Phil responded as if reading from a previously rehearsed script. The bald man's eyes were fixed on Marty, studying him the same way a snake might study unsuspecting prey.

"Oh, that's just one of Marty's talents." Shamus poured three fingers of scotch into his tumbler and set the bottle down. "Marty used to be a hook man, he could get in and out before you knew your trailer was gone. He made my Dad a lot of money." Without looking he asked, "How many times, Marty?"

Marty turned from Shamus Crane. He didn't want to say, but if he didn't, it might send Shamus into a crazy tantrum and that was something Marty didn't want to deal with. So he turned to Crane and said, "674."

Phil Crane's eyes widened. He switched from Marty to his boss, who nodded with that same smile. "You're serious."

Marty said nothing, he didn't need to.

"Six-hundred-and-seventy-four trailers, carrying every type of cargo imaginable. Cars, guns, tobacco, liquor, Marty was a mover and a shaker. My Dad used to call him 'Dr. Hook' but that isn't what makes Marty unique. Tell him why you're unique, Marty."

"Zero," Marty responded and though he didn't want to admit it, there was a certain amount of pride in that admission.

"You've never been pinched?"

Marty shook his head.

"The legendary Dr. Hook has a clean slate and that is why he's sitting here with us today, Phil. Do you know, Marty, I actually ran a pool on you back in the day. We were betting on the number you'd get nabbed and you never did." Shamus smiled and then added, "I had a G note on 544, but you cost me that." His face soured a bit, the grin faltering slightly. Not enough for Crane to notice, but Marty saw it. He could see the psychopath that lingered beneath Gordon Shamus's jovial exterior, had in fact seen it before.

Marty wanted to cut to the chase, but knew better. Gordon Shamus would not be pushed or prodded; doing so would be foolhardy, even dangerous. Instead he just sat there and waited for the gangster to work through his sermon and onto his pitch. Meanwhile he was thinking about Maggie; he was going to have to tell her something and he had no idea where to start.

"What do you know about kimberlite, Marty?" Shamus asked.

"Kimberlite?" Marty shook his head. "Nothing."

Shamus smiled, relishing Marty's ignorance of the subject. He stared into the eyes of the man who had won the affection of his gangster father thinking, *I'm smarter than you, Doctor Hook. You are just a drone, a worker bee, nothing more.*

Marty could see the jealousy in Shamus's face; he had in fact seen it many times before. Jude Shamus was pretty vocal about the shortcomings of his son Gordon. Had in fact called him "stupid" in front of the hired help. "Ye'd fuck up the lord's prayer if yay knew it," the old man would bark at his only son. "How the fuck did I end up with such a fuck-up for a kid!"

In the face of these verbal attacks the younger Shamus would say nothing, a smirk would crease his lips, signaling to Marty that there was a storm of psychosis spinning behind those lifeless hazel eyes.

"What is kimberlite, Gord?" Marty asked.

Shamus's smirk lessened and he seemed to come back. He turned to Crane and said, "Tell him, Phil."

"It is a deposit in the earth where diamonds are formed," Crane said. "In the deep…"

"Is your license up to date, Marty?" Shamus interrupted.

"Yes."

"Good, you will be heading for Yellowknife in a few days to start orientation. I have signed you on with a northern trucking company that does resupply to one of the mines in the deep North. You'll be hauling fuel. Give him the package, Phil."

Crane pulled out a large dossier, approximately four inches thick, and slid it across the table. Marty glanced down, not wanting to touch it. Doing so meant accepting Shamus's job and he didn't want that.

What the fuck else do I do, he thought. *If I say "No," this crazy head case might hurt or even kill Maggie.*

Reluctantly, he slid his fingers over the dossier, hooking its edge and pulling it toward him.

In bold letters: **WINTER ROAD 2015**

"Gord, this is the ice road. I've got no experience doing this sort of thing."

"In there you will find all the information you will need. We have already secured you a criminal background and an abstract on your license," Shamus said.

"Did you hear what I said?"

Shamus ignored him and continued. "You will need to pass a drug test. I'm guessing that won't be an issue for you, Marty. In the envelope you will find names that are highlighted in green, those are people that will know who you are and can assist you in getting ready. Phil will be working security on the ice."

"Gord, I'm the wrong guy for this."

Shamus stopped, lifted his drink, and sipped. "No, Marty, you are exactly the right guy for this. You can drive almost anything that has 18 wheels, you've pulled fuel trailers, and you are squeaky clean and…."

"I've never done this before, Gord," Marty said.

"You have a beautiful wife to give you incentive." Shamus grinned. And there it was, the king of all fuck overs. Marty's face tightened, his heart tightening like a soaked dishrag dispensing adrenaline into his veins, causing the muscles in his back to bind up. At this moment he was ready to lunge over the table and take his chances. Shamus continued,

"Simple job, Marty, you run the ice like any other driver and after the second run you are going to meet a lady who will give you a package to bring back."

"What package," Marty hissed fighting back his temper.

"Diamonds. After you leave the mine you will meet up with Phil at the halfway point. Corbert Lake and he will take the package. For this I will pay you $200,000.00." Shamus put out his hand and Marty stared, trying to decide whether or not to take it. Beside him, Phil Crane watched with interest—Marty guessed his next move would determine what Crane did. There really was no choice, he had to take the deal. From this point on it was all about Maggie and keeping her safe.

Marty took the gangster's hand and said, "After this, we're done. Your father gave me my retirement. I don't even want to do this, Gord, but if I do, this is it. I want your word that I'm out or it's no deal."

Shamus grinned, making the scar beside his nose push to the right and fold over. "Sure, after this I'm going to retire too, Marty." Then his grip tightened and his smile widened. "FYI, Marty, my Father is dead, you don't have pull with him anymore. I will cut you loose after this, but you best check your attitude and mouth or I will show Phil here my special talent."

Crane smiled. Marty couldn't help but think they were working from a script. "I've never disrespected you, Gord, I'm not about to start now."

"Good. Take the file and go through it. Pretty basic stuff and tonight after you get acquainted with the particulars you can call Phil for the rest of the details." He nodded to Crane, who produced a cell phone and slid it across the table. "From this point on, you only make calls on this phone and in a few days Phil will get you a new one. No talking about the job on air."

"My number is already programmed into the phone," Crane added.

Marty looked at it absently, trying to figure out a way to keep Maggie out of this and get her as far away from Shamus as he could put her. He'd have to tell her, it was the only way. Anxiety coupled with fear swirled in his lower belly and he thought he might vomit.

Damn you! I'd cut your throat right here if I knew I could pull it off!

"Okay, I am going to leave you with Phil to iron out a few other things, but I will be in the loop. If you need anything, let me know." Shamus got up and smoothed out his trousers and started for the door.

Crane slid out and stood up. Marty got out and stood beside him.

"What now?" he asked.

"You heard him. Go home, study the package. In it you'll find an envelope containing $2000.00. You can use that to buy the gear. After you've given it a full read, call and I'll fill in any blanks."

"How long ago?"

"How long what?" Crane questioned, but he knew what Marty was asking.

"How long ago did you stop being a cop and get onto Gordon Shamus's payroll?"

"None of your fucking business," Crane growled and began walking out. "Call me once you've read the file." Marty watched him leave the dank pub and wondered what he would tell Maggie, if anything at all.

***

Chapter 3—Dark Harvest

1

January 7th, 2015
ACADIA DIAMOND MINE
105 Miles South of the Arctic Circle

It was a closed meeting, only four of them, and all men. At the head of the table sat Damien Lars, the President of the Acadia Mine. He was watching the Chief Operations man, Chase Fenwick, who was doing the presentation.

"Four days ago, at approximately 18:20 hours, shift supervisor, Alden Roper, was overseeing an expansion of tunnel number #3 when there was a minor collapse. After clearing the debris and ensuring the area was safe, Roper made a discovery." Chase motioned for his assistant working the laptop to flip to the next page. Before them, still photographs of the tunnel accented by a computer rendering. The others followed along on their own laptops as he continued. "We have been getting regular deposits out of the main pipe, but what that collapse has revealed is a dual funnel of kimberlite."

Lars looked up from his laptop and directly at Chase—he didn't say a word—but Chase knew he had the old man's undivided attention. What they were viewing was a computer generated picture of the pit mine and the subsequent deposits that ran into the earth. The kimberlite pipe was an ice cream cone shaped deposit running through the Earth's crust and into the mantle, but that wasn't what Chase was referring to. They'd found a second deposit, a sister cone and that was the reason for this emergency meeting. This was something new altogether. "We took samples from the second pipe and at first we thought it was carbonado..."

"Black diamonds? Here," the Vice President sitting next to Lars interrupted. "That's ridiculous."

"Sally," Lars said, "if you want to find yourself sitting this one out, interrupt Chief Fenwick again."

Chase looked from Lars to Sal Godwin, whom Lars often referred to as "Sally" and waited to see if the exchange would go any further. It didn't, so he cleared his throat and continued. "We thought it was carbonado, but it's not; in fact our analysts have never seen a gem stone like this. Next page, Ronny."

Ronny Fraser clicked the mouse and a picture of an uncut stone filled the monitors. It was a jagged football shaped piece of glass that was smoky blue and a little bigger than a golf ball.

"Jesus Christ," Lars muttered, then looked from his monitor to Chase. "We have determined that this is in fact an allotrope." He paused, pushed his glasses up his nose and added, "I already know the answer, Chase, but I have to ask anyway." Chase didn't clear his throat, in fact he didn't say anything. He just smiled. Lars studied him for a moment, feeling the exhilaration building. "Holy Jesus Christ! Are you saying what I think you're saying?"

Chase held back, kept smiling.

"Damn it, Chase, don't fuck around here!" Lars was grinning ear to ear, because he already knew the answer.

"I can say with 100% certainty that Lupania Corporation has discovered a new gemstone in the allotrope family that is likely the most flawless diamond on earth to date," Chase proclaimed. His smile etched early age lines into his cheeks. He stood motionless waiting for the old man to have a coronary.

"How much have you yielded from the pipe so far?" Lars asked.

"We have removed 14 kg of uncut material, but there's something else."

"Did you say 14 kg? Fourteen fucking kilograms?" Lars looked like a kid ready to pee himself, and then he remembered. "Wait, you said there was something else. What was it?"

"I would prefer to show you."

2

The section of tunnel they were standing was cordoned off. A heavy tarpaulin grand as a theatre curtain hung in front of the shaft and as an added deterrent the area had been roped off with danger signs. After the analysis confirmed that they had discovered a new allotrope, Chase shut the operation down and closed the area off.

"Where are the workers from this section?" Lars asked.

"All are on paid leave with non-disclosure bonuses," Chase said. "$10,000 each delivered in 90 days."

"Shit, Chase, you're pretty loose and fancy with Lupe's money."

Chase smirked, knowing full well that the old man had signed the authorizations for the bonuses himself, but he played along. "Mr. Lars, Lupe's going to be authorizing a bonus a hell of a lot larger than that for its Chief Operations Engineer when I pull back this curtain."

Lars also grinned, showing off teeth that were too white, straight, and perfect for a man in his mid-sixties. It was the one thing Chase found unnaturally creepy about the old man, but he overlooked it after getting to know him. Damien Lars was smart and knew how to treat people who delivered. Chase Fenwick delivered. "Alright, pull the fucking curtain then."

Chase reached ceremoniously up, paused for dramatic effect, and then pulled the tarpaulin back. What it revealed was a black tunnel carved out of stone that looked like a poorly lit cave. For Sal Godwin and Ron Fraser it seemed let down, but then Chase removed a remote from his pocket and turned on the lighting.

There was a collective gasp of awe.

"Oh my god," Fraser said like a man viewing a naked woman for the first time, and in essence it was his first viewing of the dig. He was a geologist, but his work was almost exclusively in a laboratory setting.

Set into the hard deposit of kimberlite were multiple veins of the yet unnamed gem, which sparkled under high intensity lighting. The veins were as large as Chase Fenwick's forearm spiraling through the pipe in a crisscross fashion. On a good day, Lupania Corporation yielded a coffee can of raw polar diamonds from the Acadia mine; what they were looking at was three years' worth of gemstones that could be extracted in a few hours.

"Chase," Lars said without looking at him.

"Yes, Mr. Lars?"

"From this point on you can call me Damien."

Chase beamed.

"You said there was something else?" Sal Godwin asked.

Lars turned toward Sal. Chase half expected him to chastise his Vice President; instead he laughed and slapped the skittish man on the shoulder. "Sally, that's right. I almost forgot. What else was it, Chase?"

"There's a source of kinetic energy we've been picking up."

"Volcanic?" Sal asked.

"No, it's in the pipe, possibly in the deposit."

"The deposit," Lars puzzled. "I'm not getting you, Chase."

"I'm going to let Ronny explain that," Chase said and stepped aside.

Aware that this was his cue, Fraser stepped forward, but he was still uncomfortable with it. The Chief Geologist only felt comfortable in the confines of his lab, not doing presentations before the upper echelon of the corporation. When Chase insisted he be at this presentation, Fraser had tried to squirm out of it. He hated public speaking; in fact with the exception of his wife and Chase, he didn't care much for people.

"Alright then, I'm all ears, Ronny, spit it out," Lars prodded.

"Mr. Lars, Mr. Godwin, there is a source of kinetic energy in the pipe, but we are not sure yet if the source of the energy is from the kimberlite or from the allotrope deposit or even something else."

"You said kinetic. Are we talking seismic?"

Fraser scratched his temple, weighing the question. "We are not looking at anything seismic like shifting tectonic plates, but there is an energy that is not stationary. An energy that is almost magnetic in nature."

"And you're saying that it is in the pipe," Lars asked.

"Yes and no."

"Ronny, thanks for committing to vagueness. Chase, you want to help out here."

Chase urged Fraser to continue with his eyes.

"I'm saying that we haven't been able to isolate the energy source. We don't know if it's in the pipe or the deposit and it isn't stationary. It moves, Mr. Lars." There was an edge of irritation in Fraser`s voice; he didn`t like being pushed around.

"What do you mean it moves?" Sal piped up.

"I mean it moves. We've had kinetic anomalies in different parts of the pipe and it seems to move up and down and, as I said, it has magnetic properties."

"How do you mean magnetic, Ronny?" Lars asked, his voice less provocative.

"The samples we took held some of that energy after extraction in a similar fashion to which a piece of metal will magnetize."

"Is there any sign of radium?" Sal interrupted.

"Sally, you know better than to ask that," Lars barked.

"Mr. Lars is right, we have monitored this area extensively and there are no uranium deposits in the pipe. I can only speculate at this point, but I don't think the energy source is like anything we've seen before and as far as I can tell it is as innocuous as a radio wave."

"Any ideas?" Lars asked.

"Too early to tell, Mr. Lars, what I would like to do is take some core samples without digging further. Isolate the energy source if possible and run tests before extraction begins." Ronny sounded more confident.

"How long? A ball park figure will do to start, Ronny."

Fraser looked from Lars to Chase and then to the ceiling of the tunnel where Chase presumed the answer lay. He pulled in a deep breath and settled on the Mines President, his gaze confident and filled with resolve. "I think two weeks at the earliest, but you have to understand that it might take longer, Mr. Lars. I cannot commit 100% to a deadline."

"Fair enough, Ronny, the dig is your domain. You can have full access and pick an assistant, but be sure you know who you want, because you're stuck with them until you're done." Lars reached out his hand and Ronny took it. The old man's grip was firm and tight. That was Damien Lars, neither patronizing nor insincere. To shake this man's hand meant taking on great responsibility. Ronny turned this over in his head as he focused on the Chief Engineer. What was Chase thinking? Were they in over their heads? Then he heard the old man again.

"What I told Chase goes for you too. If this is as big as I think it is going to be, both of you will be set for your retirement."

Or fucked for the rest of our lives, Ronny mused and released his grip.

"Sally, get these men set up with whatever they need. I've got a meeting at noon, so I trust you'll get this ball rolling as quickly as possible." Lars turned and began walking away, barking orders as he went. "Chase, I want an update by supper and Ronny, you isolate the source of that energy."

"Yes, Mr. Lars," Fraser replied, "we'll get right on it."

"I know you will, gentlemen. I wouldn't have it any other way."

Chase, Godwin, and the rather meek Fraser watched the old man walk up the corridor to the waiting vehicle. Of the three, Ronny felt the pressure begin to build, not just from the old man, but from Chase as well. When the anomaly had first reared its ugly head, he could feel Chase's angst and knew that he was counted upon to find a solution to that angst.

He only hoped he was up to the job.

***

Chapter 4—Confessions and Light Reading

1

She'd gotten home around 5:30 pm, carrying her briefcase and a plastic bag that was marked **KIM WONG'S FINE CHINESE**. He helped her set the plates and they sat down to eat. Halfway through the meal as she lifted an egg roll from her plate, ready to take a bite, he looked solemnly across the table and said, "I have to tell you something."

For Maggie, the seriousness of those words sent a flurry of butterflies into her stomach. She wasn't expecting him to say that there was another woman, but as Marty unveiled his dark secret, a surreal disconnect melted over her. She remembered when she first met him, the awkwardness that came with someone new and she harkened this moment back to that time. The man sitting across from her, that she loved and made love to, was not there. Marty the artist, the deliberate and methodical man, had left the room and here sat this stranger. It was as though she was meeting him all over again.

He told her everything—about his former profession, Old Man Shamus, his psychotic son Gordon, and about the threat on her. She sat open mouthed, trying to grasp what he was saying, feeling a mix of disbelief and curiosity. She considered lashing out at him, calling him a "bastard," a "liar," or even a "prick," but she didn't, because she loved him.

Him? She scolded herself. *This isn't Marty, this is someone else.*

"We can call the police," she insisted.

"No, Maggie, we can't! Gordon Shamus has a number of cops in his pocket."

"Well, what are we supposed to do? I'm scared." Her voice hitched and she brought her hand up to her mouth to stifle the cry. "I don't even know this man. Why would he hurt me?" Her green eyes glistened with fresh tears, her cheeks reddening.

He stood and came around the table just as the tears began to spill down onto her cheeks and he could see the mounting terror. Her right hand still cupping her mouth, she was fixated on the seat where he sat. He wondered if she'd even seen him stand.

"Maggie." He reached out to touch her, but she blocked his hand.

"No, I can't. I won't. Oh, fuck!" She got up and bolted from the room.

He followed her into the kitchen where she retched into the sink in two great gluts. Chinese food mixed with the wine she had been sipping splashed against the stainless steel basin, and he heard her weep.

"Who are you," she stammered and reached for a piece of paper towel to clean up.

"I've gotta go do this. And you need to get out of here for a while, until this is done."

"Really?" She turned to face him, her eyes puffy, her hair now a tangle of chaos. "Why didn't you tell me, Marty? You say you love me. But you kept this from me. You're a fucking asshole!" She tried to slap him, but missed and rather than taking another swipe she leaned back against the sink and whimpered, "Damn you."

They stood like that, a long uncomfortable moment that spanned minutes until she finally gathered herself, using the back of her hand to wipe the stinging tears from her cheeks. Before her, Marty was ram-rod straight, robotic looking, careful not to touch her. She'd never talked to him this way, never raised her hand. He had hurt her terribly and now he was as purposeful as a man about to disassemble a bomb.

"What else don't I know, Marty?"

"I've told you everything." He was calm and meaningful.

"Why didn't you tell me? I love you, I would have understood."

"Maggie. I couldn't. I didn't want you to know about that life. I didn't want anyone to know. I walked away! Old Man Shamus let me go. I'm not proud of it!" He leaned forward again, trying to get her to look into his eyes, but she would have none of it and averted them to the floor, so he said, "I'm sorry."

But was he? He considered the conceit he felt when telling Crane of his conquests. Doctor Hook had been a cocky bastard who got high on stealing and cared less about who got hurt along the way. He thought he had buried that ghost a decade ago, but Gordon Shamus had dug up the corpse and here he was again. He told himself that he didn't want to do this job. But he wondered if that was entirely true.

He could debate that at a later time when she was safe and he was on the road. He reached out and touched her hand. "I do love you, Maggie, and I am sorry."

She studied him, staring at the dimple in his chin, tracing the stubble that peppered his cheeks, eventually coming to rest on his eyes. She held them unblinking and watched for even a hint of insincerity. Marty waited, feeling her probing—holding her gaze. Her right hand came up and touched his left cheek; it was cool, still damp from the sink.

2

In the study lay the envelope Crane had given him. He intended on opening it earlier, before Maggie got home, but had put it off. Maybe he had hoped that she would talk him out of it, or maybe it was that inner voice that nagged away at him. *Once you start down this road you are committed.*

He thought, *I'm already fucking committed.*

The voice fell silent.

From behind him he could feel her gaze upon him, not close enough to look over his shoulder, but still there. He had wanted to do this alone and was now cursing himself for procrastinating.

"Maggie," he tried, "I really don't want you involved in this."

"I'm already involved, thanks to your former boss."

He considered correcting her that Gordon Shamus was not his boss, then decided against it. She needed to be involved, it would be the only way she would able to trust him, if that was ever going to be possible.

For a long moment Marty looked from his wife to the envelope, and finally he let out a long bewildered sigh and picked it up. With his eyes, he considered the title: **WINTER ROAD 2015,** below that in smaller print: **Joint Exploration Meanook/ Acadia/Lupania Corporation.**

One last glance, and then…

"Fuck it!"

He tore the envelope open and began to go through the contents. The first item he removed looked like a novella. It was a photocopied manual laid out on legal paper that was about an inch thick. He flipped through it, absorbing minor details as he went. Setting that aside, he pulled out another smaller envelope containing the expense money Gord mentioned. Or was it Crane? He couldn't remember. What did it matter anyway? He set that beside the manual and pulled out a single piece of paper. It was a contact list.

At the top in bold print: (**Chinook Tundra Transport: A Northern Company**)

Just below that, a list of names, occupations, and numbers. He mouthed the names, following them down the page.

Anita Banner – Safety and Compliance,

Keith Akerson – Operations Manager,
Lester Busman – Sales and Acquisitions

And then he came to the first highlighted name on the list.
Robert Stewman – Logistics.

Probably a small fish with limited information, Marty thought.

Below that another sub paragraph with the heading: **Security**

Philip Crane – Roving Security – Corbett Lake Camp
The last name on the list was a surprise, because it was a woman.
Kristy Greenflag – Hydro Carbons – Meanook Mine.

"What is it that they want you to do?" she asked.

Glancing up, he saw that she was now standing directly over his left shoulder. Her tone had lightened, the knot of discomfort between them loosened slightly. "It looks like they want me to move stolen diamonds from the mine," he started, and considered leaving it at that, then decided that if something happened to him that Maggie would need to know. He waved for her to come in closer. "This guy," he said pointing to Stewman's name, "is connected to the transport company. My guess is, he was the one they used to get me on this job." He then pointed to Crane's name. "This guy is Shamus's right hand, he is the muscle. I met him at the bar this afternoon. He's a real thug, but he's also an ex-cop, which means he probably has a few friends on the force."

"What about the woman?"

"Hydro carbons. She works at the mine, she'll be handing off the package."

She moved in even closer, almost brushing against him, but stopping short.

"The package? That sounds like something out of a bad movie, Marty." She was still cold, but her anger had retreated and there was an undercurrent of fascination in her tone that told him that she was coming to terms with it. By nature Maggie was a pragmatist; her profession as an insurance adjuster demanded it. Often she would meet people on the worst day of their life—after a house fire, a car accident or even death. This led to situations where the victims of these circumstances would be at opposite ends of the spectrum. Hostile or immersed in grief, she often found herself the focus of clients. One woman had referred to her as an "insidious cunt" sent by the vultures to feed on her sorrow after her husband was killed in a traffic accident with a train. Another client called her an angel of mercy when his child was burned horribly in a barn fire. In truth there were two Maggie's, the professional calculated adjuster, seemingly devoid of emotion. And then there was Mrs. Maggie Croft, outgoing—sexy—lust for life. She was unguarded with Marty, she had given of herself completely and loved him openly. She still felt excited when they planned a night together, still loved getting tipsy, and acting the tease when they made love. With him, she was uninhibited. In doing so, she lowered the barrier she used to shield herself from the ugliness that would often hurt and scar others. There was no need to shut him out. Marty was sweet, genuine, caring and until today, she thought, honest.

"You know," she started, then swallowed to lubricate her throat. "This might sound stupid, but I could have handled being threatened by this asshole. I could even go along with your plan and trust you..."

"Maggie..."

"Shut up and listen to me! The hardest part of this for me is that you didn't trust me enough to tell me. I'm your wife, Marty. I don't keep secrets from you because I trust you with my life. Now, I am left with hours to decide what to do. Call work and bail on a major account, run and hide while you go off to some cold place and commit a crime for a man you claim is a complete psychopath. What is to stop him from killing you when this is over?"

"I won't let that happen."

Maggie studied him. Brought her hands up and clasped them together, her index fingers forming a steeple, and she was silent for a few seconds. Her silence was only outward. She was deciding what to do and he knew not to interrupt this thought process. A minute passed and then she stood, unclasped her hands, stood up and left the room. He waited and listened, expecting that she might start crying again, wounded by his dishonesty, but then she began speaking to someone else. He stood and listened.

"Garth, this is Maggie. I got some bad news, I have to leave immediately to tend to some family business. I can't go into it right now, but Marty and I are going on our way first thing in the morning." There was a pause as she listened to her boss. "Could you get Kelly to cover my accounts while I'm gone?"

Marty reached into his pocket and removed the mobile phone Crane had given him. As Maggie thanked Garth and assured him that she would contact him as soon as she knew more, Marty turned on the cell and waited for it to go through its loading process.

She reappeared in the doorway.

He looked up, placed a finger over his lips, then thumbed the contact list and pressed the only number there. It rang three times.

"Hello," Crane answered. In the background a diesel engine idled and he sounded out of breath.

"When is a good time to meet up?" Marty asked.

"Noon tomorrow sounds right. I'll call you around 9:00 am with a location. Bring the file folder and we'll go over it together."

3

Phil Crane hung up, placed the cell into his jacket, and then pulled a set of work gloves from his back pocket. Behind him an earth excavator tractor, its diesel engine purring, waiting to go back to work. Shamus would be happy. The Artist was not going to run. He'd initially thought that was what would happen. Running wouldn't do him a pinch of good, Shamus already had a contingency plan in place for that. In fact there were two holes already dug not far from this location.

He glanced down into the trench, still reeling from what he'd seen. The excavator made digging so much easier than using a shovel. Two, maybe three, scoops and you were done. In the trench lay was what was left of the body of the man who'd been pleading for his life only 15 minutes before.

Henry Reid was operating the excavator as Crane watched with deliberate fascination. He asked what levers worked the hydraulics and how to traverse the big shovel. Reid was a great instructor, talking Crane through each movement. There really wasn't much to it. "Just keep your movements slow and deliberate, Phil," Reid explained. "The machine does all the work, but the hydraulics should be treated with respect. If you're too hard on them, you'll blow a line."

"Slow and deliberate," Crane said.

Three scoops later, they had a seven by four trench that was five feet deep. Reid idled down the big Cat and hopped out of the cab. He was smiling and lighting a cigarette as he came around the front of the machine. He'd dug a few holes for Phil, they'd "shared a few scoops," he was proud of saying.

"What time is your man arriving?" he asked.

"Here he comes now." Crane pointed to the headlights of what he knew was a Lincoln MKV coming up over the horizon. They stood side by side watching Shamus's car wind its way up the gravel between the drifts of snow that shouldered the road.

Reid's face became a landscape of puzzlement. "What is Mr. Shamus doing here?" Then he turned to Crane, who'd removed his gun and pointed it at him. "Jesus Christ, what are you doing?" The Lincoln rolled up, snow and gravel crunching beneath it as it came to a stop. "Phil! What in the fuck?"

"Gordon will explain."

The rear door of the Lincoln opened and out stepped Gordon Shamus wearing a black track suit and sneakers. In his right hand, he held a .45. He grinned maniacally and marched toward them. Barely missing a beat, he raised the gun in a downward arch and fired two shots right into both of Reid's kneecaps.

Crane flinched and Reid, on slight delay, suddenly howled in agony.

"Ahhhh What the fuck! What the fuck!"

"Get him in the hole!" Shamus barked.

"Why did you shoot me?" Reid bawled.

"Phil!" Shamus was stomping forward, the gun still fixed in the same downward arch.

Crane came to life and grabbed the wounded Reid by the shoulder and tried to pull him into the trench, but Reid fought back, squirming out of his grasp. "No, Phil! Please," he cried, then his eyes bugged and there was a strangled gasp.

"Get him in the fucking hole," Shamus shrieked and kicked Reid in the guts again.

Crane holstered his gun and grabbed Reid with both hands now. No struggle ensued, he was wheezing, desperately trying to re-inflate his lungs. They dragged him the three feet to the edge and Shamus gave Reid another hard kick, sending him rolling over and into the hole. This ended with a dull powdery thump. Crane almost fell in with him, but released his grip in the last second. When he caught his balance he felt a hot sting on the side of his face, followed by a ringing in his ears. Shamus had smacked him.

"I fucking tell you to do something, you goddamn listen!"

Crane looked up, his eyes darkening, anger brewing in his belly, and he heard the driver's door open. The driver was named Donald. Crane had always thought of Donald's as four eyed pussies, but this Donald wasn't and he knew that what he did next could be a matter of life or death.

Just a slap, he told himself, *nothing worth getting killed over.*

"You better learn to pay attention, Phil!" Shamus growled.

Donald leaned over the Lincoln's door, pistol in hand and watched.

Don't let this Psycho Fuck bait you, Crane told himself.

Shamus's eyes bore into him, provoking him to do something. The crazy fuck was drooling like a mad dog waiting to bite. He`d seen this fucking maniac lose control. Seen and the wrong people killed as a result. Crane rubbed the stinging skin, which was now pinkish red. At that moment he promised himself that he would never let Gordon Shamus hit him again. *He does that and I'll go down swinging, but not today. Today we regroup,* he thought and felt the anger begin to slide.

From the hole, Reid was getting his wind back. His moans began to rise, capturing Shamus's attention enough to ratchet down the madness, but just a little.

"Please, Mr. Shamus. Why? Why are you doing this?"

Shamus turned his attention on the hole.

"Henry, how long have you worked for me?"

"What?"

Shamus shook his head, brought the gun up and shot Henry Reid in the shin, sending bits of bone and fresh blood splintering up into the air.

Reid screamed and let out a succession of moans.

"How long?" Shamus cocked the hammer back.

"Ten years!" Reid was blubbering now, his lower extremities a tangled mess blood and flesh. "Ten years, Mr. Shamus! Why are you doing this? I don't understand." His voice high and convulsive.

Phil Crane looked from Shamus to Reid and back again. He knew why Henry was down in that hole with his legs all shot up. It was Crane who had alerted the Shamus to the visit Reid had made. His contacts inside the force told him that Reid had been picked up on a trafficking charge. Seemed Henry was moving a bit of crystal on the side, unknown to Shamus. Not that Shamus would have cared, as long as he was getting his cut, but he wasn't. Then Reid got grabbed in a sting and that is when Crane's contact told him that Reid was getting ready to flip.

"You're a fucking rat now! A fucking rat, Henry!"

"No, Mr. Shamus, you got it wrong."

Shamus shot him in the other shin and he shrieked. Then he dropped the gun into the snow at Crane's feet and began to walk away. Crane took this as a signal to finish Reid off and pulled out his gun.

"Not yet," Shamus barked over his shoulder and climbed into the excavator.

"What the..." Crane started and stared from him to Donald. Donald had the same look of puzzlement. Then the machine lurched as he released the brake and started forward on its tracks.

Clack! Clack! Clack!

Oh shit, he's going to bury him alive! Crane got out of the way.

The shovel swung around over what would soon be Henry Reid's grave and the hydraulics whined as Shamus positioned the bucket above the now-screaming Reid. Crane felt his heart thud when he saw his boss's face twist up in a grimace. Then he hit the lever and down it came. Reid stopped making noise instantly, silenced in a bone-crunching glut that sprayed fresh syrupy blood up into the air.

"Jesus," Crane said.

But Shamus wasn't done. He hauled back on the lever and plunged it down again. And up, and down. Again and again. All the while Crane saw the maniac behind the controls screaming one word over and over as he mashed the remains of Reid into the soup of sand and bloody mud. Crane couldn't hear the word, but it was unmistakable. "Rat! Rat! Rat!" Then in one final thrust, Crane counted as number six, the shovel came down hard and held. The hydraulics protested under the strain and Shamus seemed not to notice. Climbing from the cab of the earth moving machine, he looked at a stunned Crane and yelled. "Get this fucking mess cleaned up!"

Donald swung around and opened the door, his face full of shock and revulsion. For a moment they shared in their duality of disbelief, and then Shamus opened the window and waved Crane over.

This is where he kills me, Crane thought, but went anyway.

Behind him the hydraulics of the shovel continued to protest.

"Phil, what's the status on Marty?"

Better than Reid's status, he thought, but said, "I'm waiting for his call."

"No fuck-ups, Phil."

How exactly would you define a fuck-up, Gordon? Does pulverizing a man with a excavator qualify as a fuck-up? Crane almost cracked a smile, but thought better of it. "No fuck-ups, Gordon."

"Better shut that thing down before it blows a line and you find yourself shoveling it in by hand." Shamus grinned, relishing the thought. Crane looked past Shamus and to his driver. Donald averted his gaze, visibly shaken by the episode, and while Crane couldn't blame him, he still thought less of the driver.

Not as tough as I thought you were. I'll keep that in mind.

"Get it gone," Shamus said, his smile curling into a self-satisfied sneer that supplemented the crazy, which swirled behind those eyes. Before he rolled up his window, Crane considered shooting him in the face right there. Instead, he hesitated and the opportunity, at least for now, was lost.

The Lincoln reversed and swung in a backward arc. Crane in his adolescence used to call that: "Doing a Jimmy Rockford" after the 70's television show: The Rockford Files with James Garner. In it Rockford would reverse his Pontiac Firebird, swinging the nose around and peeling out. This wasn't quite that, not so much urgency, but close enough. He was staring at the Lincoln, his mind in a muddled state of shock. He wondered if James Garner was even alive. Then his thoughts began to fragment, broken up by a high mechanical whine.

The hydraulics!

That broke his paralysis.

He bolted toward it, slipping in the snow and sliding right into the machine's steel track. Hot pain flared up in his shin, but he ignored it and climbed up the side of machine. As he fumbled with the door handle, he expected a hydraulic line to let go like a singing serpent and vomit hot oil everywhere. Thankfully, the latch clicked and he climbed and yanked the lever back, releasing it. The excavator gave a final shriek, then bucked and rocked before resuming into a rhythmic diesel purr. Crane waited a second—raised the bucket and swung it toward the pile of earth beside the grave. His face became flush, panic capitulated to fiery rage, and he turned his attention back to the Lincoln, which was almost out of site.

"Stupid mother fucker," he yelled. "What if it had blown a line? How would I have explained the flattened veal cutlet sitting below the bucket of this goddamned excavator, you fucking Psycho Irish fuck!"

He jumped from the cab, his shin reminding him of the collision with the unforgiving steel track. Crane ignored it, peering over the edge and into Henry Reid's final resting place. Only a foot contained inside a Kodiak work boot had survived the crushing weight of the bucket. The rest of Henry was a stew of pulverized flesh and bone intermingled with muddied dirt seasoned with plasma and body fluid.

"Couldn't just shoot him in the head and be done with it, eh." Crane glanced over his shoulder; the Lincoln was gone, but that didn't abate his anger. "Fucking asshole." Couldn't just do a clean kill, not Shamus. That would have been way too easy. There always had to be a statement. And what was the lesson in all this? "That the boss is a fucking psycho." He was shaking now, overdosing on adrenaline, anger receding, anxiety stealing his wind, and for a moment he thought he might have to sit down. There was a vibration in his pocket and he realized it was the other phone. It was Croft. He pushed the button and raised it to his ear, "Hello?"

"When is a good time to meet up?" Croft asked.

4

They lay side by side. The muted dark spoke volumes to the atmosphere in their bedroom. They'd argued late into the night. Marty wanted her to go to her Father's in New York, but she would have none of it.

"I am not putting my Dad in danger!"

"Jesus Christ, Maggie, if you're with family it will be safer!"

"I am not going to do to him what you've done to me!" The spite in her tone was deliberate and he wondered if he would ever be able to undo the damage. "I'll go to Montreal and wait it out. You can call me when this is over."

"Maggie..."

"No! I'm not doing it your way, Marty! I'll go to Montreal or I'll stay here."

"Please, Maggie, I don't want anything to happen..."

"You should have thought of that before... You… You shit! This is insane!" She started crying again and stormed out. He waited a few minutes, thinking she might return to scold him. Then, from the study, he heard the clicking of her fingers on the keyboard. When he entered the room she was already booking a flight. In her left hand she held her Visa, reciting the numbers aloud.

He watched, powerless; she was going to do it her way no matter what he said.

Now, side by side, separated by a thin invisible barrier of awkwardness, he listened to her breathe. He wondered if she would ever forgive him. Slowly he reached out to touch her shoulder and then, fearful she would pull away, he relented and said, "Tomorrow, before you leave, I am going to get both of us a throwaway cell phone so that I know you're okay." He took a breath. "If you decide to leave me when this is over I'll understand, but I need to know that you're safe."

"Is that what you want?" she whispered.

"Of course not."

She turned to face him—her eyes meeting his against the evening light of the sickle moon, which loomed outside their bedroom window. "I'm hurt and it's going to take a while to get over that hurt, but I think I can get past it." She placed both hands on his cheeks and held him steady. "Don't make me a widow, Marty, and don't leave me to live in fear that someone will come for me." Her grip tightened. "Promise me that."

"I promise," he said and she released him.

She turned over, her back to him again. "You better."

***

Chapter 5—Escape and Evasion

1

Maggie's flight was scheduled to leave at 1 pm and that made Marty's meeting with Crane a difficult task. She had to be in the airport two hours prior to departure, which gave Marty very little time to see her off and hook up with Crane for noon. He hated the idea of leaving her there alone but thought if he pushed off the meeting it would send up a red flag. Better to carry on as though nothing was up. After she was gone, he'd take his chances with Crane and Shamus. Getting her out of here was his first priority. The only logical plan was to get her through security and then he'd breathe a little easier. He doubted that anyone could stop her at that point, not without creating a major incident anyway.

They stopped in at Fowler Insurance and Maggie dropped off a couple portfolios for Kathy. Her boss, Garth, met them at the front door; sincere concern etched his face as he took the case files from Maggie. Garth was a decent guy and Marty liked him.

"If there's anything I can do," he started.

"Thanks, Garth, I'll get back as fast as I can," she said. Maggie had concocted a story about her nephew Kevin getting into a car accident. Kevin was supposed to be her Brother Jim's only son. The fact that Jim didn't have any kids and wasn't even in a relationship made the lie a real whopper. "He's in critical care," she told him this morning. "I'm heading into Toronto to be with him."

"What hospital?" Garth asked.

"Trillium, oh wait, St. Joe's," she lied, then began crying. "I'm sorry, Garth, my head is in another place. I'll have to double check that with my Dad."

"That's completely understandable, Maggie. You call me when you get it figured out and I'll send some flowers." She felt like a shit lying to him and hoped that, as silly as it seemed, karma did not deliver a return favor by making something happen to Jim.

Now, Marty stood at her side, wooden and uncomfortable. The morning had pretty much mirrored the evening. While Maggie had said she would forgive him, he wondered if that would ever be possible, and strangely he just wanted to get her out of here and get on with the job.

"Okay, we should probably get under way," Marty said.

"Umm, yeah," Maggie agreed.

"Okay, you guys take care." Garth gave Maggie a hug and shook Marty's hand. "Anything you need, just call."

"Thank you, Garth, you're a sweetheart."

"Thanks," Marty agreed and Maggie shot him a glance of disapproval. She didn't have to say what she was thinking; it was obvious. They descended the steps to the car. It was now 10:15 am. Forty-five minutes to get her to the airport and then back to meet Crane. He was still waiting for a location to meet up and hoped that the call wouldn't come at the airport. That's all he needed was a flight announcement while talking with Philip Crane. That would get him killed for sure. They climbed into the car and as he put the key into the ignition, he could feel her looking at him.

"I booked a room at the Comfort Inn," she said.

"Good. I'll send you a text when I get to Yellowknife. By the looks of it I'll be out of here in another day."

"How long will this take, Marty?"

"It's going to be at least a week. I have to go through the training and then one dry run north. Second run I get the package and before the third, I'm walking. Once I am squared with Shamus, I'll contact you that it's safe." He put the car in gear and they started for the airport.

2

Phil Crane waited for Shamus to show up. As usual, he was late. This drove Crane absolutely crazy, but he contained it. Much in the same way he contained his dislike of being smacked. It would have driven the old man crazy as well; a year after his death, Old Man Shamus's memory still lingered. Crane only knew the old man for a short while before his heart gave out, but what Crane did know of the old man was that he was organized, clear headed, and a hell of a lot less volatile than the prodigal son. Old Man Shamus had a loyal following, his men trusted and respected him. Gordon, on the other hand, instilled fear and as a result created a culture of paranoia. No one dared talk about the nutcase prodigal son or one might find oneself crushed beneath the bucket of a CAT Excavator.

"How's it progressing?" Shamus asked as he entered the room, startling Crane back from his thoughts.

"He's taking his lady to the airport," Crane said.

Shamus sat down behind his desk and smiled. “Good old Marty, I figured he’d do something like this.”

“You want me to pick them both up?”

“No, let her get on the plane. I’ll have someone meet her at the other end.”

“I’m meeting with him at one o’clock. I assume you want me to stay mum.”

“Yeah, no need to stir him up. I want him in Yellowknife by Thursday. Our friend up at Meanook tells me that the road will be open very soon.” Shamus lit a cigar and his smile faded. “How about that other business, all cleaned up?”

“Yes, taken care of.” Crane had buried the remains of Henry Reid and not long after one of Shamus’s men showed up with a flatbed to haul the big machine away. As they loaded it onto the float trailer, he noticed the sand turned to mud hardening in the frigid air. The truck driver seemed not to notice or care. Crane wasn’t sure of his name; maybe Evan. After the driver chained down, he walked around the big machine and could see frozen blood spatters against the mustard yellow paint on the main boom.

“Make sure this thing gets power washed by our people,” he told Evan or whatever his name was. “I don’t want this on a jobsite until it’s clean enough to eat off.”

“Sure thing,” he said, and then he saw what Crane had been referencing and added, “I’ll make sure they clean it up twice.”

“Do that,” Crane said and gave the filled hole a cursory glance. Fresh snow had already begun to blanket the disturbed ground. He climbed into his own car and thought once more about dumb ass Henry Reid selling crystal meth and getting ready to flip.

There was an internal pang of guilt.

What choice did I have, he thought. *He was going to flip. If Shamus goes down, I go right along with him.* Henry knew too much. Knew where the bodies were and god damn, there were a lot of bodies—more than Crane could count on two hands. He knew the risks and knew the golden rule. Live by the gun, be prepared to die by the gun or in Henry’s case, die by the excavator.

“Phil,” Shamus prodded, bringing him back. “Are you paying attention to me?”

“Yeah, sorry Gordon, I’ve got a bad headache.”

Shamus pulled the desk drawer open and shuffled around until he found a large bottle of Tylenol Extra Strength. He set the bottle down on the end of the desk and got up. “Migraines are a fucker, I can sympathize. Pop a few of those back and I’ll get you a can of soda water.”

“Thanks.” He opened the bottle and shook four into his hand.

“I put a couple more people in place to keep an eye on Marty when he gets up there. You’re not going to be able cover him 100% so I thought some more eyes and ears would be handy.” Shamus came back and handed him a can of club soda. “Sorry, I’m fresh out of bottled water. That mope Ricky was supposed to stock up my fridge this morning and his kid had some kind of incident at school. So I told him to go on. I’m too soft, Phil, people take advantage of that.”

“Who have you got watching him?”

3

They were inside the terminal. He was helping her with the bags, his head darting left and right for anyone suspicious. He couldn’t see anybody. Maggie, however, sensed his angst and that made her heart race. He stayed with her carry-on baggage while she checked in and got her ticket. He tried to tell himself that the anxiety he felt was not visible, but his heart was tightening in his chest and his hands were shaking.

She came back and he ushered her down toward the terminal at a very brisk pace. He wanted to get her through security. After that, he’d do whatever it was he had to do.

Get her safe, he thought. *Get her the hell out of here!*

When they reached the line-up and he could go no further, he stopped abruptly and took her hand. “I know I fucked up, Maggie. I love you more than anything and I am going through a living hell of worry. If something happens...”

“Marty...” she interrupted, but he covered her mouth with one finger.

Glancing left and right again, then pulling her in close, he whispered, “I need you to do two things while I’m up there. First, send me a text every day to let me know you’re okay. Just a quick note will do, something like ‘I’m seeing the sights.’ Or ‘Having fun.’ That will tell me you’re okay.” He took a deep breath, keeping his index finger pressed gently across her lips. “This is the most important thing. If you are in trouble, send me a text that says: I love you. Those are our three words, Maggie. I love you means: I’m in trouble. Her eyes glistened with fresh tears threatening to spill over, but she nodded just the same. “If you get into trouble, I will come for you, Mag.” He removed his finger and she fell into his arms, quivering.

“Oh, Marty, come with me, please.”

“I can’t. I want to. Believe me, I want to, but Shamus won’t stop until he finds us.”

She sniffed and wiped her eyes. “Okay.”

“Lay low, only go out when you have to, and remember what I said.”

She nodded again. “I’ll message you every day.”

“I may not be able to respond, but I’ll be checking often.”

Behind them a couple approached. She would have to get into line or step aside. Marty hugged her and moved her gently into the line. He gripped her arm and they held like that for a moment. All her anger melted away, replaced by a looming fear that she would never see him again. She tried to act strong and said, “Those three words are ours. I love you, Marty.”

“I love you too, Mag, but I don’t want to hear you to say that again until this is over.” He let go of her hand and his heart began to ache. She looked back over her shoulder. The line began to shuffle forward and he watched her pushing on toward the frosted doors—as he did this, he thought of his dead Mother and said, “Watch over her, Mom, please keep her safe.”

She turned back once more, gave a weak smile, then was gone behind the barrier.

4

Crane was waiting for him when he arrived at the old Quonset hut. The tin building located just west of Hamilton was used by Shamus’s people to cool off items that were too hot to move. The hut sat behind a chain link fence, floating in a sea of wild grass. It looked abandoned and though Marty had never been to this drop point, he understood that it was very active. In the past he had used similar buildings to unload stolen cargo.

“Ah, the legendary Dr. Hook arrives.” Crane was cutting up something on the work bench inside the building. He had a welder’s smock on and he held what looked like pieces of a hand gun. “Give me a second, Doc, and we’ll get at it.”

“Don’t call me that,” Marty said.

Crane opened up a Rubbermaid container, dropped the gun parts into it, and then proceeded to pour liquid toilet bowl cleaner over them. He snapped the lid on and pushed it up against the wall. "Don't like living up to the legend, eh?"

"Don't like being threatened or forced into doing jobs. Call me Croft."

"Alright, Croft it is. There's a fridge in the office with soda and beer. I'll take a beer and you can have whatever you like. Beside the office you'll find an old patio set on the main floor. I'm going to wash my hands and then we'll do our business there."

Marty waited a second to see if there was anything else and decided to get on with it. He wandered inside the building and passed a battered black stand-up tool box, which sat alone on the cracked oil-stained floor. Above him, a fluorescent light buzzed madly as one of its tubes flickered to hold on to its last bit of life. On the walls of the hut were hundreds of centerfolds from the magazine Hustler. Marty recognized the airbrush work done on each model to enhance the pink. This made him smile a bit. He had met an artist named Barry Monk who did this sort of thing for a living. Erotic airbrush was his specialty and Marty had joked with him about it. Truth be known, Monk preferred men to women and even remarked that staring at girls' privates all day only reinforced his love of cock. Marty had joked that maybe Monk should do only male photos, to which Monk replied, "No, thanks, I have no interest in coming back from the dark side."

He reached the office, which was really nothing more than a sectioned off cage of chain link and angle iron. The doorway was open and unlocked. Marty guessed it had remained that way for some time, as there were old cobs of web hanging between the door and the corrugated steel wall. Inside, an old avocado green fridge, which had lived well beyond its years, sung a noisy mechanical swan song. Marty looked at the desk. On it lay a tin ashtray overflowing with cigarette butts. He noticed three of the butts had lipstick on them and wondered whose lips they might belong to.

He stepped forward and opened the old fridge, revealing a case of Molson Export and three cans of Presidents Choice Cola. He considered the cola and thought that if he had a beer, it might put Crane a bit more at ease. As he reached for two cans, he wondered if Maggie was up in the air yet.

"Be there in a second," Crane called and there was an audible ripping noise, which could only be paper towel. As he stepped out with the two beers, he again examined the centerfold, trying to pinpoint the airbrush work. Little did he know that the man who had hung all of those centerfolds was none other than the late Henry Reid; in fact, Reid had even purchased the beers Marty now held in his hand. Marty had never met Reid, but had certainly met quite a few like him. People who died under the boot of Gordon Shamus.

Crane entered and he handed him a beer.

"Thanks," Crane said and they sat down.

"I gave it a once over. Looks like a pretty straightforward operation," Marty said, opening the dossier. "I really only have one question."

"Oh yeah, what's that?" Crane said.

"Why the dry run? Why not just go up there, get the package, and get gone?"

"Hydro-carbons."

"What?"

"Kristy Greenflag." Crane tapped a finger on her name in the dossier. "She's the reason for the dry run."

"I don't get you."

"This job has been in the works for over three years. We've covered every aspect of this, including recruiting people, such as yourself, to get it done. In fact, the package has been ready to go since last year, but Old Man Shamus dropped dead and that set us back a season. After Gordon buried his father, he started planning again. We missed our window last year. We have gone to great lengths to make this happen, but one thing we couldn't do was change scheduling, and Kristy doesn't come on shift until the second run. She is your contact. She will put a thermos into the valve control compartment of your lead tanker. This will happen while you're being unloaded. If you see her doing this, look the other way. At the Mine, there are more cameras than you'll find in a Las Vegas Casino, but there is a blind spot at Kristy's station. She'll put it in your compartment, but you give it no mind and wait until you reach the first portage outside Meanook before retrieving it."

"Portage?"

"You are going to be driving over frozen lakes, Croft. In those lakes are islands with roads and solid ground called portages. Each portage has a number. The first one south of Meanook is 59 and it has a fairly large pull off for drivers to check equipment. That is where I want you to retrieve it and put it into your cab. Then you get your ass to Corbett Lake, and when I hear you call in your convoy, I'll meet you and pull you over. Once I got the package, I want you to carry on until you get around portage 3 or 2 and then I want you to speed and get caught."

"Why?"

"Well, Mr. Croft, I'm guessing you won't want to be driving the entire season on ice. Therefore, it would be in your best interest to do something stupid and get a season ban. Driving 15 km hour over the limit should do it."

"I guess that beats just walking away."

"Yes it does. Our safety man at Chinook isn't on the inside, so he'll be tearing you a new asshole when you get punted, but that will keep things on an even keel. They usually boot two or three cowboys off the ice in the first few weeks anyhow, so you'll fit in nicely. However, I want you to play by the rules until we get that package. I don't think I have to explain how Gordon would react if you got kicked off the road before."

Marty could see something in Crane's eyes when he said that. "I guess you've seen Gordon's pleasant side a time or two, eh?"

Crane's face hardened. "Let's get something straight, Croft. Gordon Shamus is my boss. I've known him for over nine years. I've known you all of an hour-and-a-half, if that. So I'm going to do you a favor and drive home the point that we aren't going to share in any male bonding or become brothers of the ice. I'd also like to point out that if you start bad mouthing Gordon, he might just hear about it and that could be a bad thing for you and your woman."

This drove into Marty like a knife, causing him to stand up.

"Sit the fuck down, Croft. Sit down or I'll beat your fairy artsy fartsy ass to a pulp and tell Gordon that you are a liability." He didn't move, just sat there looking at Marty with a deadpan stare.

Marty sat back down.

"Good."

Marty's heart was pounding in his chest, adrenaline pulsing through his veins and causing him to shake. "Is there anything else?"

"Yeah, there is. You go up there, do what you're supposed to do, and this will all be a blip on your radar. Shit, you'll even make some money along the way."

"Anything else?"

"Yeah, we got you on a flight tomorrow out of Hamilton to Edmonton and a connector gets you into Yellowknife. The flight leaves at 7:00 am, so don't be late. There will be a guy at the airport to take you to the hotel, and you'll likely have a room until you're assigned a truck. The appropriate people will contact you once you're on the ground." Crane pulled out the ticket and slid it across the table. "Any questions?"

Marty snatched it up. He suddenly thought of Maggie, wondering where she was at this moment, and that curbed the anger a bit. "I guess we're done here then."

Crane took a swig of beer and smiled. "Yeah, we're done for now, unless you wanna finish your beer."

Marty glanced down at the unopened can. "You can put that soldier back in the fridge."

"Alright, I'll do that. Don't be late."

"I won't."

Marty turned to leave, and Crane called after him in an almost apologetic tone. "Do what you have to do, Croft." He took a large swig of beer, then cracked open Marty's can. "Pretty simple really, but then some guys need to be told."

Marty glanced back and walked out.

5

MONTREAL TRUDEAU AIRPORT
DORVAL, QUEBEC

Maggie was in the arrival terminal when she felt the phone in her pocket vibrate. She fumbled it out and pushed the button to read the incoming text.

It read: **Thinking of you.**

She looked about the terminal as a female voice announced softly over the intercom in French. "Maintenant au 46centi terminal quatre. Vol Air Canada 891 pour les Bermudes."

Maggie opened the keypad on the phone and typed: **Seeing the sights.**

Her phone chimed and the return text said: **Be careful. I miss you.**

Maggie thought for a second, then sent another. **Moi aussi, mon amour.** She waited for a response. Marty spoke very little French, but she was sure he understood the message, which was: "Me too, my love." Just as she was about to put the phone away, she heard it chime.

One word: **Soon.**

She closed the phone and went to get her luggage.

In the distance, a stranger watched and waited.

***

Chapter 6—Big Garney Wilson

1

The City of Yellowknife, (YK)
Northwest Territories (NWT)

Garnet Wilson climbed from the taxi, slung his duffle bag, and drew in the winter air. It was cold, but not as cold as it was going to get. Minus 35 Celsius was a treat for this time of the year. His faced widened to a big toothy grin as he took in the street before him. He was a big man, 6' 4", strong like an ox, but softening in the middle after a few too many fried egg sandwiches. He'd just turned 50. He looked somewhat like Johnny Cash, his face chiseled with hard angular cheeks bones and a square jaw, except Garnet (Garney to his friends) had a full head of blond hair tangled with grey. "It's good to be back," his gravelly voice proclaimed, followed by a low satisfied chuckle. This, his 10th Season on the ice, was split between working as a lead hand on a crab boat in the Bering Sea.

"Garney," a man's voice called.

He spotted the stout little man at the front of the hotel, just outside the glass doors, braving the elements to have a smoke. He tilted his head forward, pulling focus, and then the confused look on his face was replaced with one of recognition. "Sack? Jesus Christ, my brother, how the hell are yuh?" He tramped forward in long strides, his bare hand already outstretched.

Todd Sackman (Sack to his friends) flicked his cigarette away and walked toward Big Garney Wilson. "I see you managed to keep from drowning for another year, eh!"

Garney laughed, his voice booming against the biting wind. "Sack, my brother, you still crack me up. Yep, uh huh, yep." And with that, they shook hands. "How's the little woman, Sack?"

"Margaret left me six months ago," he replied.

"Aw shit, man. Oh, that's terrible. Why'd she leave?"

"I guess she wanted to be known as ex-wife number four."

This caused Big Garney to laugh in great thunderclaps. "Same old Sack."

"Same old Garney, some things never change."

“Ain’t that true, brother. Yep, uh huh… Yes, sir. Yep.” Garney rubbed his chin. “So give me the lowdown, my brother. How are we looking?”

“Looks like things will start hopping on Thursday. One more night in the hotel and then into the bread box we go.”

“Have you been down to the Talon for a cold one?”

“Oh yeah, I was down there the other night. Had my eye on a nice girl. She was hot, so hot in fact that I was going to give her the pleasure of tossing her salad, buddy.”

Garney wrinkled his nose. “Sack, my brother, how can you do that? I mean, aren’t you afraid she might…”

“Might what?”

“You know…”

Sack grinned. “You just have to take precautions, Big Garney.”

Garney grimaced and said, “Precautions? What kind of precautions?”

“I usually put a finger in to make sure there isn’t one in the chamber,” Sack grinned.

Garney broke into a fit of baritone laughter, and when he was finally able to contain himself, he asked, “Well, was there?”

“I’m not sure.” Sack frowned, and then brought up his finger and wagged it back and forth. “Give it a sniff and tell me what you think.”

Garney batted down his hand and guffawed. “You are a sick man, Sack—sick in the head, brother—sick in the head.” Then he laughed even harder as they entered the lobby. “One in the chamber, Jesus wept.”

“Good god, look at what the cat dragged in,” said a man loitering in the lobby.

“Pete, how the hell are yuh, my brother?”

Pete Walker sauntered up, hand outstretched, while behind him a couple rookie drivers watched as the two men shook and smiled. “I’m doing good, Garney, how about you? I don’t see any King Crab, where’s the shipment I ordered?”

“Aww shit, Pete, I done ate it on the plane. They just don’t feed you anymore on those airplanes. Can’t even get a bag of nuts for fear that some nose bleeder might inhale them and drop dead. Can I bring it to yuh next year?”

Pete Walker smiled. “Anyone else and I might call BS, but I know you’re good for it.”

"Thanks, my brother, I knew you'd understand." Garney winked and looked past Pete. Behind him stood two men he'd never seen. "You boys gonna introduce yourself?"

Each carried a binder, along with a red rectangular plate displaying their winter road number. These would be affixed to their windshield. The first man said, "I'm Scott Wright."

"Willy Anderson," said the second.

"This your first year on the ice, gents?"

"Yeah," both replied.

"Fucking new guys," Sack laughed and plucked the plastic plate away from the one named Scott. "Where's the chunk of Styrofoam for this winter road number driver?"

Garney grinned, so did Pete.

"This is all they gave us," Scott replied.

"Yeah, that's all we got. Did we miss something?" Willy said.

"Yeah, there's a piece of Styrofoam that goes on the back of these." Sack was shaking his head.

"Styrofoam?" Willy said.

"You don't know what Styrofoam is, son?" Sack asked.

"Sure, but wh…"

"Goddamned rookies," Garney laughed.

"No shit," Pete added.

"Listen, boys, if you don't have your Styrofoam backing, how are they going to know who you are?"

"I don't get you," Scott said. "They gave us a winter number, we put it on the windshield, seems pretty obvious who we are."

"Son, you're not thinking outside the box."

"Garney!" a woman in her mid-thirties interrupted. "How's my favorite driver?"

"Jennifer! How are yuh, sweetie?" Garney leaned down and hugged her. She was a solid little honey a foot below Big Garney. He had shared a bed with her last season.

"Better, now that I know Big Garney Wilson is going to be running the ice again."

"Yeahhhhhh," Garney laughed.

"Jennifer," Sack interrupted. "Why didn't you get these boys their Styrofoam backers for their winter number plates?"

Jennifer looked at Sack, then back to Garney. "Styrofoam backers."

Garney smile widened.

"I guess we didn't get something?" Willy added.

Jennifer sighed and pulled Garney close. "You guys are too much."

"Play along, Jen," Garney whispered.

"Me and Robby split up, so I expect some TLC payback if I run this errand of nonsense for you Veteran Ice Road Drivers." Jennifer's hand traveled down Garney's back where it found its way onto his buttock and squeezed. "Deal?"

"Mercy," Garney murmured. "Consider me there, darling."

"Jennifer," Sack started.

"Shut up, Sack. Don't tell me how to do my job." Then she turned to Garney and whispered, "I finish at six pm."

"Good grief," Sack complained.

"See you tonight," Garney winked.

"Okay, boys, let's go get your Styrofoam backers."

"What do we need this for again?" Willy asked.

"All in good time," Sack barked.

Another driver, a gruff man with a beard and shoulder length hair, said, "Buoyancy."

"Huh," Willy said.

"It's so they'll know who you are after your truck goes through the ice. The number will float to the top.

"You're fucking kidding me," Scott said, but he looked spooked.

"Am I?" He pushed past the two men and toward Sack and Garney.

"Merv, how the hell are you," Garney said.

Pete came up and stood beside Garney. "So much for that."

"Goddamn it, I bet they don`t even make it up the Ingraham now. Merv, you could have at least waited until they hit the ice," Sack said.

"Merv, my brother," Garney greeted and continued watching Jennifer's ample bottom.

2

Outside the snow fell slow against the night sky. Marty's flight had been laid over in Edmonton for five hours while they, the flight folks, decided on whether or not to resume air traffic. A lull in the storm opened a window of opportunity and they began sending out one plane after another. By the time he was up in the air, the sky had begun to turn dark blue, and when they announced final descent in Yellowknife, it was black and the winter storm had returned. Now, in the aftermath of a white knuckle landing, Marty was met at the arrival gate by a big man in his late-fifties.

"How are yuh? Name's Bob Stewman," he said, putting out his hand.

Planning, Marty thought and shook. "Marty Croft."

"I've been told you have tanker experience. Is that right?"

"Yeah, it's been awhile, but yeah."

Stewman looked around and then back at Marty. "You got baggage to claim?"

"No, I have everything I need right here."

"Good. I'll grab the truck, meet me at the main door."

Stewman walked away and Marty felt the cell vibrate in his pocket. He reached in, thinking it was Maggie and realized it was the one that Crane had given him. "Hello?"

"On the ground. Good. Did Bob Stewman get there yet?"

"He's grabbing the truck."

"Perfect. I'm flying in the day after tomorrow. By that time, you'll be in a truck and we'll hopefully be getting this show on the road. Until I get out there, I'd like a quick shout from you on a daily basis. Let me know you're okay or if you need anything."

Marty ignored the irony, but it was further driven home when Maggie's phone suddenly vibrated. He ignored it. "Alright, any particular time you want me to call?"

"Nah, just once a day will do. Bob will have a fresh phone for you today. Give him the old one and he'll dispose of it."

"Okay, anything else?"

"No, you won't see me until you're on the ice. I will be in Corbett Lake doing my part, but don't get any stupid ideas, Croft. I'm not the only one who has an eye on you."

Again Maggie's phone vibrated and he wanted desperately to check it.

"I know that," Marty said and thought that Stewman would be going through the phone for other numbers or even bugs, and this made his heart skip a beat. What if he found the other phone? "Look I better get going."

"Yeah, fine. Have Stewman exchange the phone and give me a shout from his vehicle to ensure that the numbers are good."

Maggie's phone vibrated a third time.

"Okay, will do." There was an uneasiness in his answer and Marty wondered if Crane could sense it. *What if Stewman searches me and finds the phone?* His chest tightened up and he felt almost ill. Crane used to be a cop, and he could sense when someone was lying or freaked out. *Knock it off!*

"Everything okay there?"

The phone vibrated a fourth time.

Marty clamped down on his left thigh with his hand and squeezed hard enough for it to hurt, sending a spasm of pain across the muscle. It also eased the tension in his chest and he said, "Look, Crane, I gotta grab my gear and head out into a bloody snowstorm. If you want me to call you with the new phone, I'll do that, but I don't even know what kind of truck Stewman is driving, so let me find him and then we can talk about the weather or Jessica Biel's tits if you like."

Crane laughed a little at this. "Okay, Croft, I'll let you get at it."

"Okay, talk to you in a minute." He hung up, not waiting for a reply.

Marty saw Stewman standing at the glass door waving him on, and he moved toward him. When he reached the door, it slid open and the vacuum sent a flurry of snow into the building. "Okay, we're ready to roll."

"Bob, I gotta use the John before we go. Could I give you my bag and waste five more minutes of your time?"

"Really? You can't wait? The hotel is only ten minutes away."

"I really gotta go, man."

"Uh, yeah, okay," Stewman said. Marty couldn't decide whether Stewman looked confused or skeptical and decided it really didn't matter. He held up the carry bag and Stewman took it. "Five minutes?"

"Four if I can help it." He turned to go and swung back around. "Oh yeah, Crane wanted me to give you this." He handed him the cell. "He said you got another one for me?"

"Yeah, I'll dig it out."

"He wants me to call him back as soon as we're mobile, so that would be good." Marty strutted off toward the washroom, not looking back. He guessed that Stewman would take the opportunity to check his bag, but wasn't sure if he was that kind of guy. Crane would definitely have him go through the phone, but Stewman didn't strike him as the gangster type. He was probably just a guy who owed Shamus a favor. Knowing Gordon Shamus, Marty wondered if Bob Stewman would meet with an accident after the job was done. *Worry about yourself and Maggie, fuck everyone else,* he thought.

He rounded the corner into the bathroom and went right into a stall. The other thing that had his nerves jumping was not being able to instantly see the message from Maggie. Once the stall door was closed, he pulled the phone out and read the text.

Seeing the sights.

He expelled the breath he'd been holding since entering the washroom. This was something he did often, especially when in a state of deep concentration, and it was something that few others noticed except Maggie. Sometimes she would lean down beside him as he worked on a particular piece. She wouldn't say anything at first, just listen intently, then she would say, "How do you forget to breathe?"

He'd think about the question, still holding his breath.

"Breathe, Marty, for God sake!"

He'd let out a breath and shrug.

They would laugh. God, he loved her.

Reality seeped back in. He typed: **In YK** –then: **With others. Txt later.**

He shut the phone down, unzipped his fly, and placed the phone in the only place he thought Stewman wouldn't want to look. His underpants. In any other circumstance, Maggie would have found this funny and would have immediately phoned him, calling gleefully, "Maggie to Marty's snake! Come in, Marty's snake!" He didn't think Stewman would search him, but he wasn't taking any chances. He zipped up and exited the restroom.

3

Angela drove and Scott watched the cab weave from one lane to the next through the city of Montreal. "These fucking frogs drive like maniacs," she complained and changed lanes.

"They're not all French, Angel."

"Don't call me that!" She swerved into the right lane, cutting off a car, whose driver honked his horn in anger. "Fuck you," she cursed at the impatient driver.

"That's my pet name for you, baby." He pointed. "They're going to turn right."

"I see that and I'm not your pet, so don't call me Angel."

"Speed up. We don't want to lose her."

"Sure thing, Scoot," she grinned.

He gave her an indignant look.

"What, a wife can't have a pet name for her man?"

"God, you're a bitch."

"That's why you married me, sweetheart. Everyone knows that the bitches are the best lays. It's all that pent up anger."

He thought about this for a second and laughed. They rounded the corner.

"When do you report in with Gordon?"

"I`ll call him tomorrow. Okay, there's the cab, keep your distance."

She tightened her grip on the wheel and eased off the accelerator. She hated driving in Montreal and Scott wouldn't. Scratch that—couldn't—he was a horrible driver. Once she let him do a pursuit and they ended up in a wreck. They'd gotten into the PI business almost a dozen years before and there couldn't have been an odder couple. Angela was overbearing, dominant, and large. Not fat large, but large as in Amazonian. Scott, on the other hand, was five foot nothing and seemed better suited to sit behind a computer monitor. He was the brains and she was the brawn.

A horn honked.

"Fuck you! You, you stupid, ignorant frog!" She swerved into the right lane, sending Scott reeling to the left and into her right shoulder. She seemed not to notice. "Maniacs, fucking maniacs!" The cab in front of them slowed, turning onto an off ramp, and this exasperated Angela even further. "Jesus Christ, why do they even put turn signals on their vehicles? It's not like they know how to use them." She clicked the turn indicator hard. Hard enough that Scott was thinking it might come off in her hand. They followed the cab up the ramp. "So, what did this bitch do?"

"Do?"

"Yeah." She slowed the car as they approached the top of the ramp. "Why does Shamus have us following her? Did she rip him off?"

"You know as much as I do. Crane didn't say. He just said that when he gives the word, we're supposed to pick her up."

"Come on, you dumb frog, you can do it, signal." The cabby turned right, ignoring her demand. "Moron." She clicked the turn indicator and followed, venting the occasional exclamatory sighs that Scott thought were more about drama than authentic displays of frustration.

4

As Marty climbed into the cab of the pickup, he caught the guilt on Stewman's face and immediately checked out his bag on the back seat. "Find anything?" he asked.

"No. It's not something I liked doing," he replied, staring out the window. "It's just…"

Marty wondered what Stewman had done to end up under Shamus's thumb. "Look, Bob, I know that you were told to check out my gear and probably my phone. I get it. So I'll be straight with you. I'm here to do a job and the people who sent me obviously don't trust me. So, if you want to check out my gear or go through the phone for anything that looks suspicious, knock yourself out."

Except the phone in my underwear.

"I don't like doing it, Marty."

Marty stared at him for a moment and said, "I believe that. The only thing I ask is that we dispense with the cloak and dagger. They tell you to check or if you have some agenda you're supposed to follow, please just ask and I'll open my pack or hand over a phone without an issue."

Stewman smiled. "I can do that for sure, Marty."

"Thanks."

Marty watched the snow as it drifted across the airport parking lot in lapping powdery waves. Stewman pulled the shifter into drive and it stumbled across the gears, bellowing in clunks. As they rolled, the snow crunched under their tires and Marty wondered if he would be able to work out a form of trust with this man. He thought he might.

When they got onto the highway, Stewman loosened up a bit.

"Have you ever been to Yellowknife before?"

"No."

"But you have tanker experience?"

"Yeah, some, been a few years. What kind of truck am I going to be driving?"

"I'm putting you into a Kenworth W900. It`s got a 600 Cat, more than enough power. It's not a brand new truck, but it's been a dependable rig on the ice for three years now. You should have no issues with it."

"Okay."

"Have you done any bush running, Marty?"

Marty thought back to his days of running stolen goods. He'd been down a few back roads, but this was definitely different. "No, not really. I've driven in crummy weather, but this will be a new experience."

"Well, once you get a handle on it, you'll do okay. You'll be running a section of the Old Ingraham Trail, that's the old route that you might have heard about on Discovery Channel. It's a main road, lots of twists and turns, hills and such. It's been fixed up every year, but you'll only be going up the Ingraham about 30 clicks and then you'll be on the Inuksuk Path."

"Inook shook?" Marty laughed. "Funny name."

"Yeah, that's the stone statue you see the all over the place up here. Some people call them cairns, I guess. Anyway, everything is kind of based around the native people up here. So the mines are using a lot of the cultural names when building the roads."

"How far does the Inuksuk go before it gets to the ice?"

"It runs 47 kilometers and the top speed you'll do is around 50 km hour. Anything faster and you'll be checking out the forest up close and personal. Running a super B up the Inuksuk is a real challenge. You won't be using your brakes that much, mostly gears, and there has to be a one km spacing between trucks."

"Sounds like it's going to be kinda hairy."

"We send loaded vehicles up in convoys of four, with 20-minute spacing between each convoy. You'll be following a veteran driver who knows what he's doing. Speed and spacing is the trick." Ahead was an intersection lit up by the orange glow of a sodium street lamp. Stewman started to slow down. "I'm going to pair you up with one of our best guys, and he'll keep you between the ditches."

"Does he know about the job?"

"No. That stays between us. His name's Garnet Wilson, most people call him Garney. Anyway, he's at the hotel already, so you might meet him tonight. I'm going to try and get you out on a local run around so that you can shake it out before you hit the ice."

"That would be good."

Stewman signaled and took a right turn a little fast. When they rounded the corner, Marty felt the truck slip a bit on the icy road. Stewman didn't say anything; he just kept driving and talking. "Marty, you listen to Garney. He's been doing this a long time and he'll keep you on the road, and that's what we want."

Marty nodded. Beyond the orange glow of streetlamps illuminating the snow, he could barely see the city of Yellowknife in the distance.

5

"Useless piece of shyte, that's what yay are," Jude Shamus growled. "I should have kicked yer Mother in the stomach. Maybe then she would have lived instead of ye, maybe I wouldn't be saddled with a fuck-up like you." Gordon Shamus stared at the picture of the old man sitting on his big desk and listened to the ghost berating him from the great beyond.

"Happy Birthday, Pop," he said and raised his glass into the air and smiled.

"You're a fucking Pariah!"

"And you're dead." He took a sip of scotch, letting it roll over his tongue, savoring the sweetness and holding it in his mouth a little longer than he should before swallowing. "Thanks for the business and the scotch, you heartless old fuck."

The old ghost fell silent.

They all loved the old man. Jude Shamus—hero-gangster, smart, considerate, pragmatic—but of course they forgot abusive and mean spirited. Gordon Shamus absently ground his teeth together hard, his eyes twirling, a leering madness fixed upon his face. Gently he touched the scar, which ran from his aquiline nose down to his upper lip. He traced along it with his index finger—drawing to the surface a memory from long ago.

6

March 8, 1981
Hamilton Collegiate

Hey, here comes the faggot, Gord had thought. *What's that in his hand?*

Beside him, Gill was laughing about something. Unaware that Jimmy-the Faggot-Poe was advancing on them carrying a sock filled with nuts and bolts. Swinging it like a pendulum. Actually it was two socks, doubled over. One sock would have come apart on the first blow, but that second sock had reinforced the membrane holding the jagged dangerous cargo together long enough to kill two and mutilate a third. Gord wondered how much time had elapsed? Two, maybe three seconds before it connected with Gill's lip, turning it into a mush of blood and tissue. Would that have been time enough to warn him? Probably not.

Gill fell to the tiled floor, holding his face. There was blood everywhere.

Beside him, Pat cried, "What the..." And then Pat was a dead man walking because a dirty gym socks filled with nuts and bolts obliterated his thought process in a single blow to the right temple. Pat took two steps, looking like he was mimicking night of the living dead; his left eye, wandering independently of the other, found Gordon for a second and then he fell face first onto the linoleum floor. Dead.

Young Gordon Shamus looked to his two friends still trying to process what was happening. "Gill," he said and then his face was on fire. It would be the last time his voice would sound normal. He fell back against the lockers, a white hot sensation blazing exquisitely as open nerve and raw bone lit like matchsticks across his face. They flared as they were exposed to the open air. His nose had detached from the gristle and flapped about, hinged only by the skin on the right side of his cheek. He brought his hand up to keep it from tearing away and thought. *I'm going to die.*

Gill turned his head to look up; below him was a pool of blood, broken bits of teeth protruding like jagged white pebbles from the expanding crimson pond. Blood dribbled from his mouth, plopping into the pool of blood. Gordon had no idea if Gill was turning his head to respond or if he was trying to get a bead on who had hit him.

As Gordon slid down the locker, he heard two things.

A girl was screaming. Soon there was a chorus of screams. Someone said, "Go get Mr. Todd."

And Jimmy Poe yelling, "Who's the faggot now, Gill?"

The sock oscillated in one deadly arc after another, mashing tissue, cracking bone, Larry Gill's face and head coming apart. Young Gordon Shamus closed his eyes, hiding from the carnage, waiting for his turn, listening to the wet sickening blows intermingling with the high shrill ranting of Jimmy Poe.

Thunk!

"Who's the faggot now, asshole!"

Thunk!

"Who's the faggot now!"

There was a liquid glut, trailed by the sour aromatic stench of stomach acid. Someone had vomited.

"James, stop this!" It was Mr. Todd. Mr. Todd taught social studies and gym. "James!"

There was a final whooshing arc, a liquid glut—cracking bone. Then, the familiar sound of something, Gordon thought marbles, clacking out across the tiled floor. The sock had come apart. And then, thankfully, the darkness engulfed him.

The next memory would come 20 minutes later through a fog of unconsciousness. He could hear the ambulance attendant calling to him, "Hang in there, Gordy. We're going to get you fixed up, buddy."

He ignored this, thinking. *Maybe he'll love me now. Maybe he'll treat me like his son instead of the person who took his wife. Maybe this is what I really needed. Maybe those guys were a sacrifice for me.* He wasn't thinking how Jimmy Poe had permanently rearranged his face with a single blow. He didn't consider how Gill and Pat wouldn't be stalking the hallways or boys rooms for victims anymore. He wasn't even thinking about what happened to Jimmy Poe. All he could think about was Dear Old Dad and that just maybe this would make him love him.

Poe had been a victim of theirs in school. Gill liked to call him a faggot and on that fateful day, they had trapped him in the bathroom next to the metal shop and slapped him until his face was as red as a lobster. No one thought that Poe would fight back. He never did before. No one thought he would wander down to Mr. Harvey's steel shop and fill a dirty gym sock with nuts and bolts. And certainly no one in their wildest dreams would have ever thought that Jimmy (the faggot) Poe would come up the main hall and kill two boys and permanently maim another. He couldn't see anything, only heard the tire rubber running along the roadway and the siren crying out.

The ambulance guy squeezed his hand. "It's gonna be okay, kid, we're going to get you fixed right up."

Then more darkness.

After he arrived at Hamilton General, he regained and lost consciousness a couple times. One minute he was awake, watching the rectangular fluorescents floating overhead to the metronomic click of the gurney`s wheel beating against the linoleum.

Was that gum on the wheel of the gurney? He thought so. It would be hard and tar black, filled with bits of dirt and rock. It probably still had some flavor. Gordon had kept a stack of used gum on his bed post after the flavor expired and he was always amazed at how a little of that sugary taste came back once it was left to dry and harden.

"We are going to need a plastic surgeon in here Asap," the attending doctor said.

Then there was more blackness, but before he succumbed, he heard, "Jesus Christ, this is Jude Shamus's kid." The voice floated away, fading to black.

He came awake screaming, vinaigrette pain coursing along every nerve receptor in his face.

"Peter, this kid is not under, increase the goddamned dosage."

His arm cooled, his mind numbed, the pain receded, and the world turned coal black.

Much later, he heard his father.

"Will he live?" Jude Shamus asked, but it sounded more like: "Willy live?"

"Yes."

There was a pause. Maybe it was disappointment. "Okay then."

"He was lucky." It was the voice of the man who'd given Peter hell about the dosage.

"One boy?"

"Pardon me?"

"One boy did all this damage?"

"Yes."

"Can yuh leave me with me boy, Doc?"

"Sure, I'll be at the nurse's station if you need me."

Gordon waited—unable to speak, but he knew. There was a storm of condescending proportion approaching. There was a moment of pause interrupted only by a machine beeping, an oxygen machine filling his lungs, and the door swung closed. His father sighed, and although Gordon didn't see it, he imagined the look of frustration. He'd seen that look so many times before. A chair scraped the floor and then there was the warmth of Daddy's breath puffing into his right ear.

"Got yourself in ball deep this time, didn't yay." Jude Shamus waited. "They're laughing at me because of this, you know. Sad excuse, you. Three of yuh beat down by one lowly kid with a sock of nuts and bolts. Yay better toughen up, lad, toughen or die, because up to this point you've been a basket of disappointment."

Behind the cloak of darkness, Gordon Shamus felt his heart sink and he wanted to sob, but instead he retreated deeper into the darkness, away from the sounds, away from his father.

I hate you, he thought. *I can't wait for you to die.*

8

The telephone rang, bringing him back. Somewhere in the fog of memory he'd finished his drink and poured another. He glanced from the now half full ball glass to the level of the scotch left in the bottle. It looked like he'd refilled it more than once. His head was swimming.

The phone rang again.

"Fuck," he said, reaching for the receiver and pulled it to his ear. "Yeah, what is it?"

"Mr. Shamus," said the voice.

Shamus thought for a second; it took a moment to recognize his voice, the scotch clouding his thoughts, but he remembered. It was Scott Turcotte: of Turcotte Investigations. "Yes, Scott, how are things progressing?"

"We are in place, Mr. Shamus, just waiting for the word."

"Good. Good. Be patient, Scott, I don't want her spooked."

"We are a safe distance back. No worries."

"Good. I don't want any fuck-ups." He replaced the cap on the Scotch. "How's Angie?"

There was a pause, one of disapproval, and this pleased Shamus. Scott Turcotte was insanely jealous and he had good reason for it. Shamus had slept with Angela, back when the old man was still in charge and even though she wasn't with Scott at the time; he knew. After her and Scott hooked up, he made a play for her, but she wouldn't go with him. Not long after the old man told him to lay off. He didn't know if it was Angela or Scott who had gone to his father, but while the old man was alive, he backed off. There were plenty of other women, and shitting where you ate was frowned upon. Of course, that didn't stop him from throwing out the odd dig Scott's way. These digs drove Scott nutty and made Angela uneasy. Scott didn't voice his jealousy, not to Shamus; he didn't dare, instead turning that jealous fury upon his wife. Crane witnessed a blow-up between the two after one of Gordon Shamus's pleasantries. Those dust-ups pleased Shamus. If he couldn't fuck Angela, he could at least fuck with her. Then again with the old man gone, he might just push a little harder and if Scott didn't like it, tough shit. She wasn't the hottest woman around, but she could screw like no woman he'd ever been with. She was aggressive in bed, rough and fast, and that made him want her even more.

"Angela is fine," Scott said.

Shamus smiled, uncapped the scotch again to pour another drink and said, "You give her my best, Scott. That woman of yours has a soft spot in my heart." His grin widened and as the scotch filled the oversize ball glass, he thought, *She fucks like a leopard in heat, too.*

"Okay, Mr. Shamus. We will be watching. Let us know when you're ready."

"Okay, Scott. No fuck-ups."

"No fuck-ups. Yes, Mr. Shamus."

Shamus set the phone back in its cradle then lifted his glass.

"Here's to you, yuh old fuck, and good old Jimmy Poe. See both of you in hell."

9

Maggie came awake with a start. She was dreaming, and in that dream she was transporting between the house back home and the motel room. *I'm safe,* she assured herself in the dream. I'm doing what I'm supposed to do, I am going to be okay. Then from inside her head, she heard it.

Someone's out there, a voice warned. *Someone's watching you.*

She sat upright, pushed the covers back, and rose out of the bed, slinking across the carpet to the window. She hooked a finger, eased the curtain back, and peeked through, her heart drumming.

Someone was out there.

She could feel them.

***

Chapter 7—Chocolate Milk Incident

1

ACADIA MINE
10:45 PM: Three Days before opening of the Winter Road

It was two weeks after the boardroom meeting that found Chase Fenwick briefing Damien Lars about the detection of a second pipe of kimberlite and the unearthing of a new allotrope. Allotrope was the scientific term for graphite or more specifically diamond. This particular diamond was entirely new, virtually flawless, and by all estimation would take its place at the head of the table in the gemstone family. Acadia, a French mining company, had everything to gain from this new discovery. In particular, the ease with which the new gemstone could be harvested.

The arduous task of mining diamonds in the north required thousands of hours from both machine and man. Up until this point, the Acadia Corporation for its 800 plus staff worked around the clock to yield approximately a kilogram of rough material per day. In layman terms, that was about the size of a Folgers coffee can. Once harvested, the rough diamonds would be shipped south to Yellowknife, cut and polished into single gemstones known as Polar Ice Diamonds.

Mining in the Northwest Territories was profitable business endeavored by five mines in the region. To the North of Acadia approximately 300 kilometers lay the Meanook Mine; to the East of that, Ekati; South of that were two other diamond mines known as Diavik and DeBeers.

Ekati, Diavik, and DeBeers were well known after being profiled in a number of documentaries, including a reality show on The Discovery Channel called: Ice Road Truckers. These media exposes brought new focus on the North and captured the imagination of people around the world.

Meanook and Acadia were new additions to the region. The Meanook Mine was only six years old, while Acadia was a mere four-and-a-half. Meanook and Acadia shared their own pathway, which ran parallel to the ice road that fed the three mines to the east. They were the new kids on the block and because of that, the roads and pathways that cut across frozen lakes and islands (known as portages) were still evolving. Acadia's recent discovery of a new allotrope was supposed to elevate its stature in the region. At least that is what President Damien Lars speculated as he put the dig into the hands of Chief Geologist Ron Fraser while under the watchful eye of his Chief Engineer, Chase Fenwick. It had been an upbeat meeting peppered with visions of grandeur and promises of rewards and bonuses.

That was then, this was now.

Again, four men found themselves in a closed meeting, this time in the company of a female. Allison Perch had been Ronny Fraser's pick as an assistant, and they worked overtime taking core samples from the dig while trying to isolate the source of energy emanating from the pipe. Lars had given them two weeks to come up with some answers and they delivered, but it wasn't what he had expected.

"Do you understand the ramifications of what you have told me," Lars said.

"Yes, Mr. Lars, but I don't see any way around it," Chase said. "We can't sit on top of this."

"Chase, this could end Acadia—shut us down—everyone could lose their job. Jesus Christ, folks, this is a fucking nightmare." Lars didn't raise his voice, instead opting to shift his eyes from Chase to the report, then back to Chase. He looked haggard, even old, and though Damien Lars was well into his sixties, he never looked old. At least not to Chase Fenwick, who held the man in the highest regard. Damien Lars represented pretty much everything that Chase Fenwick wanted to be once he reached his mid-sixties. And that didn't include money. No, Chase looked up to the old man, even admired him, but now...

"Dear God, it could be a fucking heritage site," Sal Godwin murmured.

"We haven't determined anything just yet. We don't even know if there is a connection to the aboriginals of the region. So let's not be hasty, gentlemen; as it stands now, there is a possibility that we may have stumbled onto some kind of an archaeological or even prehistoric finding, but this is just speculation at this point." Chase tried to assure them, but he sounded vanquished.

Ronny Fraser looked around the room. Only he and Chase had actually seen what was inside the new section of pipe, and while Chase was upset at the findings, Fraser was rather excited. He listened while his mind yammered: *Yes, this could mean the end of Acadia. Yes, people could lose their jobs, but this is a monumental find. Historical, in fact. Nothing like this has ever been found and you bums haven't even gone down into the dig to take a look at the newly discovered chamber.*

"How big is this chamber?" Godwin asked.

"Ronny?" Chase looked to Fraser.

"It appears the chamber has a circumference of 90 meters, and we think its depth is 600 meters. We lazed the distance and that is ballpark, but we can't be certain on depth, because we can't really see it. The laser could be bouncing off an obstruction."

"You have video?" Lars asked.

"Yes, we do," Allison Perch piped up and loaded the video on the laptop, which projected it onto a 42-inch monitor. "Say the word, gentlemen, and I will cue the video."

"Fire it up, Ally," Lars said.

She clicked a key and the media player started.

Their view of the chamber was seen through a fiber optic camera not unlike those used in surgical procedures. Of course, this camera was much larger and far more powerful, including a 1000 candle power LED light that could illuminate an area of about five meters. As it mapped the compartment with its bright white beam, Fraser gave narration to what they were seeing and how they had discovered the chamber.

"We were collecting core samples from the pipe to a depth of 1.76 meters in an attempt to isolate the source of energy we've been picking up. We drilled 19 separate holes and removed the samples. Yesterday, a decision was made to increase depth by an additional .24 meters and that is when the shell surrounding the chamber gave way." Fraser nodded toward Perch, who paused the video.

"Who made the decision to increase depth?" Lars asked.

"I did," Chase said.

Fraser waited, then, after ensuring Lars had no further questions and getting a nod of approval from Chase, he continued. "At first we thought that we might have broken the bit, because we have no data that would support a cavity inside the pipe. But then when we removed the sample, we found it intact. Both Allison and myself were present when we noted a sour smell, not unlike H2S, seeping from the freshly bored hole. We immediately vacated and I notified Chief Fenwick at the possibility of an H2S contamination."

The H2S gas, of which Fraser referred, was a lethal vapor that often occurred naturally below ground. Hydrogen sulphate had taken more than a few lives through history of mining and oil drilling. Education was used to identify the gas upon exposure, which often smelled like rotten eggs; that is, until it burned out the receptors in your nasal cavities and eventually knocked you down. Those working below ground had to be trained to identify the threat of H2S and where such a threat was imminent, the allowance for facial hair was strict, no beards allowed, because anyone working in proximity to H2S exposure must be able to put on a respirator.

"We vacated the area, even though the sensors did not indicate a presence of hydrogen sulphate. After alerting Chief Fenwick, we returned to the dig site in full environmental gear. Once we determined there was no H2S present and that the oxygen levels were not contaminated, we began to explore further." Fraser paused, then motioned to Allison to start the video again. "This is what we found."

Traversing from left to right, and tracing its hard white fluorescent beam across the chamber floor, the robotic camera unveiled the secrets held in the stale darkness. For how long? Who knew? They were jutting upward, like twisted claws of alabaster reaching for the top of the chamber.

"Bones," Sal Godwin uttered.

"Yes," Fraser agreed and the camera continued its inventory of the chamber floor.

"Prehistoric," Lars asked.

"I don't think so, could be caribou. They look like ribcages," Chase interjected.

At a glance, the bones did not seem that out of place for this territory. Maybe they were caribou. They could have easily drowned in a cavern or a lake and been preserved inside the kimberlite pipe, but the pipe wasn't what held this cache of fossils. It was the chamber inside the pipe, a chamber that was not a natural occurrence, but a structure, which had been constructed by someone. Or as Ronny Fraser speculated: something. There was one other thing that caught the eye of Damien Lars as the video continued its reveal, and that was the thousands of uncut allotropes embedded into the walls of the chamber. "My god, is it a tomb?" Lars asked.

"We don't know," Fraser said. "That is why we want to open it up for a closer look."

2

The Talon Hotel and Bar
Yellowknife, NWT

Every town of any significance has a bar like **The Talon**. It was what Spencer Hughes liked to call a HUG & SLUG. A place to pick up a lady and get into a fight all in the same night. Yellowknife had a number of bars, but The Talon was almost exclusively a native bar. That was not to say that local white folk did not wander in to tip a beer or two. All were welcome, but if you went into this particular drinking establishment, it was wise to exercise respect.

Spencer (Spence to his friends) was sitting with his two brothers. They were not his biological brothers, but they had adopted him as one of their own long ago. Sitting across from him were Billy and Danny Jack. Nobody called Danny by his real name, not for years in fact; most folks called him Axe. Billy was named after the half-breed Marine "Billy Jack" portrayed by Tom Laughlan. Their Mother, Sheila Jack, was a big fan of the Billy Jack series. The difference between Billy Jack on the big screen and Billy Jack of Yellowknife was that he was a full blood Dene' Indian.

"Mum gave him the cool name," Axe said, "named him after a movie hero."

"She named you after a celebrity, too."

Axe looked coolly at his brother. "That's not funny."

Spence laughed, because he knew what was coming, had in fact heard it on a number of occasions before, but was always amused when the brothers fired shots back and forth.

"Danny Partridge," Billy grinned.

"Shut up, Billy."

"He had freckles. Ever seen an Indian kid with freckles, Spence?"

"Can't say I have," Spence chuckled, finished his beer and then proceeded to fill all three glasses, emptying out the pitcher.

"You're an asshole," Axe said, but he didn't really mean it.

"Tell me, Axe, was Keith Partridge as dreamy in real life as he was on TV?"

"Jack-off," Axe replied.

Spence rubbed his cheek and watched bemused.

"Hey, boys, you want another?" asked the barmaid, who was now hovering just above Spence. "Do you want another pitcher? It'll be last call soon." She was a raven beauty who had shown interest in Spence every time they came by for a beer. He had taken her out once but hadn't pursued it much further.

"We're okay, Michelle," Spence smiled up at her.

"How's the Man of Steel tonight?" She smiled right back.

"Well, if I can keep the 'Brothers Jack' from scratching each other's eyes out, I'd say I'm ahead of the game," Spence said, which prompted Billy and Axe to stop their bickering long enough to simultaneously flip him the bird.

Michelle giggled, maybe a little too forcefully.

"Hey, we'd like another pitcher over here," a young man called from another table.

"Yeah, just hang on," Michelle barked, then turned back to Spence. "If you're not busy this weekend, Spence, I'll let you buy me dinner?"

"I'd love to, Michelle, but I'm going North in the next day or two. It's Ice Season."

"We're all going north," Billy said and gave her a wad of cash. "This should cover the tab and one more pitcher, Michelle."

"Jesus, Billy, I gotta be in for work," Axe muttered.

"This is too much," Michelle protested.

"Take the cash, Michelle, before Billy realizes what a tightwad he is and asks for it back," Spence said.

The young guy who had called for a pitcher stood up and came over, fixing his gaze squarely on Spence. "Who told you that you could talk to my girlfriend, white boy?"

"I'm not your girlfriend," Michelle sneered.

Billy tightened up, ready to step in, but Spence raised his hand and said, "I'm just sitting with my friends having a drink. What kind of beer are you drinking, my man?"

The young native man wasn't much more than twenty-four, a full decade younger than Spencer Hughes and the older Jack brother. But there was a cockiness that came hand in hand with liquor, and though the kid smiled, it was anything but pleasant. Nope, that smile told Spence that his kind wasn't welcome here, that this was an Indian Bar and that the Indian Girls were off limits to his white ass.

"What did you say?"

“I asked what kind of beer you and your friends are drinking. I’d like to buy you guys a round,” Spence repeated. Both Billy and Axe watched with interest, getting ready to step up if this Young Buck decided to tangle with Spence. It wasn’t the Buck they were watching, though, it was his three friends at the other table who looked ready to pounce. Spence was quite capable of handling himself.

“We’ll buy our own beer,” the Buck informed him. “That is, if we ever get any fucking service.”

Already lumbering toward them, like a great Buffalo, came Tony the Bouncer, and falling in behind him two smaller, but still tough-looking guys, wearing black T-shirts with the words **Talon Hotel** silk screened just over the right breast. Tony was a barrel of a man who’d come by his third chin the old fashioned way, chicken wings and beer. Even though he moved in a rather sluggish manner, snatching up and tossing troublemakers out the door was something he did very well.

“Okay, you’re cut off. Make for the door,” Tony ordered.

“What? This is bullshit. I didn’t do anything.”

Tony leaned in a little closer. “You have a choice. You go out on your feet. Or I drag your face across that carpet and turf you into the snow bank.”

“Things are cool, Tony,” Spence said.

“Spence, it’s out of your hands now.” He leaned into the young guy even closer. “I’m not fucking around here, man. You don’t mouth off to our staff and get to stay. Make for the door!”

Michelle took two steps back.

“Last chance,” Tony warned.

The young native man seemed to deliberate on his choices. His friends at the table stood up and Billy, Axe, and Spence waited to see if the hockey gloves were going to drop. From the table one of the young men nodded to their friend and he relented.

“We’re leaving, the service stinks anyway.”

“Have a good night,” Tony said crossing his arms.

The Young Buck shot Spence a dirty look, then followed his friends to the door.

“I always thought the service was pretty good,” Spence said, winking at Michelle. She smiled back. He watched the group of four head out the door and said, “He should have let me buy them a round.”

“One pitcher coming up for the Man of Steel and the Brothers Jack,” Michelle said and caressed the side of Spence’s cheek with her open palm. It was soft and warm. She'd been hitting on him for the better part of a month and he hadn't yet made a move. Just that one date. He thought he just might very soon, though, but not until he got back from the ice.

"Still smoking, Spence?" Tony asked.

"No, not really. Well, the odd one, I guess."

"Well, I'd stay out of the smoking area for tonight. That guy was giving you the stink eye; he might want to try something in the next fifteen minutes."

Spence looked from Billy to Axe and then up at Tony, a very large, toothy grin spreading across his face. "Are you my guardian angel, Tony?"

"Do I look like a guardian angel, Spence?"

"Nope, you look like a…"

"Like a guy that could toss your pasty ass out the door?"

"I was thinking Brontosaurus," Spence said.

"Nah, Java the Hut," Billy countered.

"Fats Domino," Axe tittered.

"Everyone's a comedian," Tony grunted, but he was smiling. He'd known the Jack Boys and their adopted brother Spence for over six years; he had, on occasion, even partied with them. "Just watch your ass, Spence, I can't help you on the street, liabilities being what they are."

"Thanks, Tony."

Michelle set a fresh pitcher down between them.

Tony looked around the bar and hollered, "Last call!"

3

They stumbled along through the snow under the orange glow of the streetlamps. All were a little more than drunk, wavering slightly, but not so drunk that they did not know where they were going. Spence could feel the cold pinching his cheeks. Each breath crystalized below his nostrils and mouth, leaving mini icicles in the web of his moustache and beard. It was Thursday night, so there wasn't the usual gaggle of drunks pouring out into the street this early in the morning. As he walked, he considered Michelle's offer of dinner and thought when he got back he might just take her up on it. She was nice and he liked her, but since his marriage went south six years ago, he wasn't really keen on getting hooked into another relationship.

"Getting colder," Axe exclaimed and pointed to the big red L.E.D. sign rotating in front of the Imperial bank. The readout exclaimed: IT'S -56 Celcius ! *** RENEW YOUR MORTGAGE TODAY! Spence wondered if it was -24 Celsius, if the sign would give the potential mortgage customer a few more days to renew.

"We should stop at the Macs Milk and warm up. I'll turn Old Betsy over so it's not a block of ice tomorrow," Axe said. Betsy was Axe's F150 pickup. It pretty much ran all the time during the winter months.

"Sounds good, I could use a chocolate milk," Spence said.

"Blah. How the hell can you put milk on top of beer," Billy grunted.

"I like chocolate milk, it settles my stomach."

"You're disgusting, Spence," Billy said.

"Chocolate milk is dangerous," Axe said.

Both Spence and Billy turned toward him, equal amounts of query in their faces, but it was Billy who asked. "Okay, I'll bite, how is chocolate milk dangerous?"

Axe stopped. A length of his long hair flickered about in the winter breeze as he engaged his two brothers. "Pay attention, grasshoppers, and I will tell you my secrets."

"Oh, shut up and get on with it," Billy said. "It's fucking cold."

Spence just listened.

"Chocolate milk, as Spence clearly pointed out, is the food, or should I say drink, of the gods. It has that chocolaty goodness that all people who walk the earth seek."

"You're fucked, Axe," Spence laughed.

Axe widened his eyes to feign surprise, then sighed before continuing. "Never disrespect your Sensei, Grasshopper."

"Yeah! Yeah! Yeah! It's fucking cold, get on with it, Chuck Norris." Billy waved his gloved hands impatiently.

"Patience, Little Grasshoppers," Axe said and drew a deep breath.

Spence knew that Axe was dicking around and the wisdom he was about to evoke was just drunken babble, but he also knew about the intelligence that lurked behind those brown eyes. Axe could have easily been a University Professor; he was a great orator and he spoke with an engaging tone that could make two drunks stop in the biting cold and listen to a bunch of nonsense about chocolate milk. He was smart, working in a job that was well below his intelligence. Axe was an avid reader of popular science, he had an appetite for knowledge and learning.

He should have gone to college and he would have if he hadn't become a Father at the age of 17. He could have, but his little girl came first. His mom offered to help out, but Axe refused. "There's enough kids out there being raised by Grandmothers," he told her. "My daughter is going to have a father who is there." He was thinking about his own absent father who left his mom to raise him and Billy on her own. He applied to Lupania, got a job, and married the girl as soon as she finished high school and turned 18.

"Can anybody tell me the biggest problem people face when it comes to milk? Be it 2% or the much respected Homogenized also known as: Homo milk," Axe said.

"Good god, we're a bunch of Homos standing out here. I don't know. Fascism! Or maybe freezing to death while your brother babbles on?"

"Sour milk," Spence said.

"Yes!" Axe cried. "Sour Milk, the very scourge that has plagued man since he first grabbed the cow's udder to taste of that milky goodness. Sour milk that has destroyed more than its fair share of meals, not including Corn Flakes, the vaunted Bacon and Tomato Sandwich, and A&W's World renowned Teen Burger. Sour Milk, Little Grasshoppers. Give me an AMEN!"

"Amen, Brother!" Spence could feel the cold nipping away the outer rim of his ears and pulled his wool cap down over them. "But what does that have to do with chocolate milk?"

"Jesus Christ, Spence, stop encouraging him!"

Axe ignored his brother and continued to pontificate. "The danger, little grasshoppers, lies in its sweetness, masking the dreaded scourge of sour before it is too late. Many a man, woman, and child have been fooled into thinking that all is well, chugging away unexpectedly until…"

"You are a numbskull! Let's go. I'm freezing my ass off!"

"Until barf-o-rama," Spence said.

"And that… is why chocolate milk is dangerous," Axe proclaimed.

"That's why you're an idiot!" Billy shook his head and started walking again.

They followed along in silence, mostly because the route they'd chosen was against an onslaught of wind and frozen ice crystals. Drunk or not, the harsh elements of winter showed no mercy and even if Axe was thinking of another sermon, perhaps the dangers of canned fruit, he kept silent. They trudged on through the night as the wind stirred up mini-storms of ice crystals that worked like an abrasive on the skin, turning it rose red and hard to the touch. In the distance, the parking lot to Mac's Milk loomed.

Waiting in the lot was Old Betsy.

As Axe pushed forward, he felt Spence tap him on the side and he lifted his wool cap, exposing his right ear. Spence leaned over, his breath warm and stinking of beer. "Great bit, Axe, but just so you know. I'm still buying a chocolate milk."

Axe smiled and gave him a glove-covered thumbs up.

"Danger is my business," Spence said over the howl of the wind.

Axe laughed out loud and covered his ear.

"Come on, lolly-gaggers," Billy ordered. "Pick up the pace."

"I've never gagged on a lolly in my life," Spence cracked.

Axe laughed and they continued to follow Billy's lead.

4

She was staring out the window, her heart thumping so hard she could hear it. Was there somebody out there or was she being paranoid? She really didn't know what had started her awake, whether the fear she felt was induced or real. Yet she held the cell phone, ready to key the message to Marty.

But what if she was wrong?

I could get him killed, Maggie, she told herself. *If I'm wrong, he could abandon the job and god knows what they'll do to him—or us, for that matter. I'm just being paranoid, a bad dream or nerves or fucking PMS.*

She stepped back from a window.

You had better be right there, sweetheart, her inner voice warned.

Yeah, easy for you to say.

Slowly she retreated to the bed, and though she couldn't decide whether common sense or stupidity had won out this time, she wondered how long she would be able to maintain her nerve. Climbing beneath the covers, her imagination ran rampant with thoughts that any moment the room door would bust open and they would take her. She fixated on the thin line of light beneath the door and watched for anything that would indicate that someone was out there.

She brought the cell phone up and scrolled to the only contact. She typed a short txt message.

"Marty, can i call you"

She pushed send.

She waited a minute—then two, and when it seemed there would be no response, a message came back.

Give me 5 min to get to secure place and ill call you

She let out sigh of relief; talking to him would help.

She sent him a quick: **Kk**

Biting her lower lip, she waited and continued watching the thin line of light below the hotel room door.

5

He was sitting on the stairwell, the phone pressed to his ear, attuned to any noise around him as he waited for the call to connect. Sitting there, he played his own game of paranoia. Wondering if one of Shamus's henchmen would suddenly appear and catch him in the act.

Unknown to Marty, Garney Wilson was just down the hall fulfilling his promise to Jennifer regarding some TLC. Simultaneously, the Jack Brothers and Spence were opening the glass door to the Mac's Milk. Even if told, at this point in time, Marty would not have considered the early intersections of these strangers to be of any significance to his present predicament. Truth be known, he would never know that all of these people were experiencing a brief benchmark in the history of their own lives. Not a significant marker, but for all, it would be the one they would recall in the instant when life and death seemed to dance in perfect harmony.

She picked up on the first ring.

"Marty, I'm really scared," Maggie cried.

"Did you see something?"

"No," she sniffed. "I woke up, I felt like someone was watching me."

He considered this. It could be stress. She had never been involved with anything like this and that could be playing hard on her nerves. "Do you want to change hotels? I know you're scared, Mag, but if I abandon this, and I will, we gotta be 100%, babe. There's no turning back if I book."

She sniffed again, and then blew her nose. This was followed by a brief silence, one which told Marty she was weighing her options. He could hear her gathering herself, imagined her wiping away the tears with the hotel room comforter. He knew the pragmatic Maggie was in control, overruling her emotional side. “No, I’m just… Just stressed out and I needed to hear your voice. As pissed off as I was… Or… I guess am, at you. I’m lonely without you. And that makes this all the more frightening.”

He smiled in spite of himself and said, “I love you, Mag. I miss you too and I want this to be over as soon as possible. I’m doing everything I can on this end to be safe. Watching when I communicate with you, keeping an eye for those who might be watching. I know I’m being watched, they might even have my room bugged, but I’m hoping that now that I’m here, Shamus isn’t really too worried about you.”

“Do you think that’s possible, Marty?”

He waited a second, then said, “I do, but I’m not 100% on it, Mag, and with that in mind we have to assume the worst. That means you keep an eye out for anyone suspicious and try not to venture out too much.”

She felt a little better. “Okay.”

“I’m sorry I got you into this.”

“I know.” Her voice was a little cooler now. “Just get this done.”

“I’m working on it.”

6

Spence reached into the cooler and pulled out a jug of chocolate milk. Outside Axe was warming up Old Betsy and Billy was in the bathroom disposing of the last beer he drank. When he closed the glass door on the stand up cooler, he heard a voice he recognized.

“Remember me?” the voice asked.

He glanced into the reflection in the glass and saw the three of them, and though he couldn’t quite make out their faces, he knew who they were. He recalled the sulky tone. It was the Young Buck from The Talon. Spence shifted the jug of milk from his right hand to his left and turned around.

“Hey, how are yuh,” he said coolly, now noting that Young Buck’s two friends were hanging back a bit, waiting to see what their valiant leader would do. *Where’s a fourth guy,* he thought.

“I was fine until you got us thrown out of The Talon.”

Spence stared straight into Young Buck’s eyes while searching out the bathroom and the front door to see where his brothers were. “I didn’t get you tossed out there, pal.”

“I’m not your pal.” He took a step forward.

"Fine, you're not my pal. I don't want any trouble. I just want to go home and call it a night. How about it?" Spence saw the bathroom door opening and Billy slipping out.

"Who the fuck do you think you are," Young Buck said.

Billy had spotted them and was moving in behind the other two. He stopped momentarily to see where his brother was and from the length of the pause, Spence guessed that Axe was busy with the other guy. "I don't think I'm anybody. You don't have anything to prove here, man. Let's just cool our jets and go our separate ways."

Young Buck took another step forward and said, "Why don't you fu..."

That was all Young Buck got out when Spence hit him below the chin with a quick upper cut. He stumbled backward and to the right, pulling down a display of Dorito's corn chips. He crumbled on the floor—didn't move—he was down for the count. Simultaneously, Billy stepped behind one of Young Buck's buddies and put him into a full nelson. What Spence did next, although comical, would seal his fate, at least for the next half hour or so.

Stepping forward, he uncapped the small milk jug and poured the contents onto the now unconscious Young Buck. As he did this, he stared at the one man standing, waited for that last of his drink to empty out, and said, "You can either go home or I can buy more chocolate milk."

That's when the police arrived.

7

Red and blue lights splashed across the brickwork of the Mac's Milk. In all there were three cars in the lot and another en-route. In the back of the first car sat Spence and the brothers Jack. In the other two were Young Buck and his buddies.

"I guess I might be late for work tomorrow," Axe mused.

"Axe, you were right," Spence said.

"About what?"

"Chocolate milk is dangerous."

Billy started laughing.

It didn't look good. Spence had laid out a guy in the store, Axe had laid a guy in the lot, and when the young constable came in, it looked as though Billy was getting ready to make short order of the third.

"We're going to jail, boys," Axe said.

"Maybe not," Billy said, watching a white pick-up marked Royal Canadian Mounted Police enter the lot and come to stop. The door opened and out stepped a much older cop.

8

"Good evening, Gents," Staff Sergeant Phillips said. He was looking around the lot into the backs of each cruiser and sizing things up. "What have we got here tonight?"

The constables looked at each other and after a moment, the first on the scene took the initiative and began a debriefing. "Looks like a bit of a last call hangover. In my car we have three males, two of them brothers, William and Daniel Jack, and their friend Spencer Hughes. Hughes, it appears, has a prosthetic leg, but that didn't stop him from KO'ing one of the guys in the other car."

"I'm going to stop you there, constable. I want you to cut Hughes and the Jack Boys loose. Then we'll talk about the rest."

The Constable looked confused. "Cut them loose? We have multiple charges here, Sergeant."

"Cut em loose."

"I don't understand," the Constable said.

"You don't know who they are, do you? Constable?" Phillips paused and glanced down at the young officer's name tag. "Constable Logan." The constable was still very new, fresh from Regina, in fact, and though Phillips had seen him around the detachment, he couldn't remember his name; although the name seemed vaguely familiar. "Logan, I know this name. You got family in the Mounties there, Constable?"

"I did," Constable Logan replied. "My father served 15 years. David Logan."

"Name sounds familiar, he retired there, son?"

"He's dead," Logan replied and by his tone it seemed that it was a subject that he didn't want to breach with the Sergeant. "With all due respect, Sergeant, these guys should be going to the tank at least. We have two assault charges, public intoxication, and the one named Daniel Jack was standing outside his truck, which was running, leading me to believe that he was drinking and driving as well."

Phillips was still trying to place the name Logan and equate it to this young clean-shaven kid in front of him. He didn't know; anyways it really didn't matter. "Constable Logan, this is your first posting and you will learn more here than you will likely learn the rest of your career. Consider this your first lesson. The three men you have in the back of your car are Daniel and Billy Jack and Spencer Hughes. Spence Hughes has a prosthetic leg because it was blown off in the southern part of Afghanistan. The older Jack boy along with Hughes were part of a Sniper Team and they were apparently very good at what they did. Unfortunately, six years ago they were on their way back to the base when the vehicle they were driving hit an IED. Everyone riding in the vehicle was killed except Sergeant Hughes and Sergeant Jack. That is how Hughes lost his leg and his career as a soldier. Sergeant Jack wrapped a tourniquet around his friend's leg and stood guard until a chopper was dispatched to extract them. Jack never got so much as a scratch in the attack, but when they gave Hughes his marching orders, Jack put in his release. Most folks here in YK regard these boys as heroes, except maybe that group of ass bags that called them out to challenge tonight."

The other two constables watched as the Staff Sergeant glanced from Logan to the men who were divided between the other two cars. During the pat down and emptying of pockets, a number of packets of crystal meth were discovered on the one Spence referred to as "Young Buck."

"Nigel," Phillips said. "Was he carrying?"

One of the two other constables, his name Fairbanks, stepped forward with an evidence bag. In it were five packets and a pipe. "We took this off of Nigel Tecumseh."

"What about the other three?" Phillips nodded.

"Nothing, well actually, the one that Jack socked in the parking lot had a roach in his cigarette package."

"Okay, Gents, this is where we use what I like to call: officers discretion. Everyone except Nigel gets cut loose. Let the Jack Boys and Hughes get a 15-minute head start, so the other three knuckleheads don't follow them and decide to pick it up again. Although I doubt they will. Get those sachets tested at the lab and prepare charges against my little buddy Nigel. Possession with intent to traffic," he said, then turned his attention back to Logan. "What's your first name, Constable Logan?"

"Howard," Logan said.

"Okay, Howard, your time here has just begun and I am not about to undermine the training you received in Regina. The law is to be observed and respected, but this is YK, and I guarantee you this. Over the course of your posting here, you are going to be faced with a number of judgment calls and you're going to have to pick your battles very carefully. I like to think of YK as the last throwback to the frontier towns, and North of 60, the rules are a little different." Phillips paused, considering the young officer. "You see where I'm coming from, Howard?"

"Not exactly, Sergeant, but I guess time will tell."

"Two months from now you will," Phillips smiled.

Logan smiled back, a little more at ease. "Okay, I'll cut them loose."

"Dress them down before you do. Tell them you're giving them a break, but next time they go to cells." Phillips unwrapped a stick of gum and popped it into his mouth. "Good work tonight, Gents."

There was a collective "Thank you, Sergeant."

And then they dispersed and headed back to their cruisers, intent on carrying out the directive laid down by the senior officer. As Phillips mounted his pickup, he glanced over at Spencer Hughes, who was now climbing from the back of Logan's cruiser. Their eyes locked and Hughes nodded slightly to acknowledge the Officer.

Phillips hadn't been on the same tour as Hughes and Jack; he was on the tour after. The RCMP often sent officers overseas to work in unison with the armed forces. Phillips did a six-month tour training the Kandahar Police Force. He gave Spence a cursory nod, pulled the gear selector into drive, and exited the lot.

***

Chapter 8—Angel

1

Corbett Lake Camp
Security and Dispatch

Corbett Lake was the halfway point between Yellowknife and the Meanook Mine. It was the safe haven for drivers to pull off and grab a hot meal before carrying on north to their destination. It was also the base of operations for security.

Standing alone, except for the chopper pilot who was warming up on the pad, John Pringle looked through his binoculars, waiting for the convoy to arrive. The portage on which he stood was littered with a number of structures, which included mobile trailers housing a kitchen, shower facilities, and sleeping quarters. There was also a Quonset hut that housed a grader, a dump truck loaded down with sand, and a very large generator that powered the camp. Beside the Quonset hut a microwave tower stood erect and ready for business. Beside that a large tank holding diesel intended to fuel the security and maintenance vehicles. The compliment of staff at Corbett Lake was 44, including the security, cooks, and logistics people.

It was Pringle's sixth year at Corbett as the head of security after transferring over from Lockhart Lake where he had been a 2IC. Pringle was a deliberate man, never ruled by his emotions, always basing his decisions on what he saw before him. The crew that was on its way was made up of retired cops. Among them were three new additions for whom he would extend a welcome and a warning. These men were not here to be cops, they were here to protect the ice and ensure that the mines, both Acadia and Meanook, got their supply needs filled over the course of the next six weeks.

As Pringle scanned the landscape, a northern breeze, cold and unforgiving, tightened the exposed skin on his face. The temperatures had begun to dip considerably in the last week. It was almost -56° Celsius.

2

The Aurora Hotel
Yellowknife, NWT

Marty awoke around six am, feeling the need to urinate. This had become the new reality when he hit his 40's, his bladder along with the ability to ignore its complaint of fullness were all but a memory. Still he lay on his side not wanting to get up, but knew eventually he'd have to and that once out of bed there would be no returning to sleep. Adding to the increasing pressure of his bladder, he could hear music coming from another room.

Who the hell listens to music at this time of the morning, he wondered and found himself concentrating on what exactly it was he was hearing through the insulation of the hotel room. There was a distinctive drum beat accented by a guitar and then a harmonica, and though he knew the song, he couldn't quite put his finger on it.

"Fuck it!" He tossed the covers aside and sat up. Depression fermented inside him. This was nothing new; he got this way when something troubled him or felt beyond the grasp of his control, and this surely qualified. He stomped into the bathroom and lifted the lid. Placing his palm upon the wall, he leaned forward slightly, taking aim and thought, *How the fuck do I get myself out of this mess?*

"Us," he said aloud, then thinking that the room might be bugged silenced him.

Yes, us out of this, he corrected and though he didn't want to think about it, the very real problem was not the job, but what would happen afterward.

You know what will happen.

And he did, or at least he speculated what would happen. Shamus would have Crane march him into a secluded area and put a bullet behind his ear. Once the job was done, it was always better to tie up the loose ends. Fourteen years before, he had done something very similar after a jewelry heist. There were five men lined up on that job: two were found floating in the Hamilton Harbor, the other three disappeared altogether.

If you knew that was how it would be, then why did you take the job?

Because he had to get her clear, that was priority number one. Get Maggie out of the way and then he could work on the rest of the plan.

So what is the plan?

I don't know.

That's great.

But he did know. Although he wasn't prepared to say he'd committed to his only alternative. The only way out of this would be to kill Gordon Shamus and very likely his right hand, Crane.

Can you live with that?

He finished his business, glanced sideways into the mirror, and gave his reflection a solemn stare. Standing in front of the basin, he ran the water cold, splashing a bit on his face. In the far off room, the music had stopped. This occurred sometime during his chitchat with his annoying self-loathing inner voice, but he had no idea when.

Can you, Marty? Can you live with killing two men?

"Yeah," he whispered through clenched teeth. "I can. And I will."

Then there was a knock at the door.

3

Corbett Lake
Security Briefing

Phil Crane was sitting at a conference table surrounded by ten other men who'd come north to Corbett for this briefing. The ride up from Yellowknife was an interesting one as the convoy of pickups sliced through the newly cut ice road and across the portages between. For the most part it was virgin trail and Crane actually had a bit of fun as they bah-hawed through the snow and ice. Along the way, they passed the occasional service vehicle or grader, but for today, at least, the ice road stretching from YK to Corbett Lake was theirs alone.

"Good morning, gentleman and welcome to the Lupania Winter Road 2015, my name is John Pringle and I am the Chief Security Officer here in Corbett Lake."

There were mumbles of "Good morning."

"I am, for lack of a better word, your boss. But with that said, I am a pretty informal guy who believes in the open door policy, so from here in, please call me John and know that you can approach me anytime." He paused, a smile creasing his face as he looked around to each man. "There is only one time I ask that you think very hard before interrupting me and that is during the time when my beloved Vancouver Canucks are setting up to bring home Lord Stanley's Cup."

This brought about laughter and a few heckles.

"I see that all of you have a law enforcement background. I myself was a Mountie for over 25 years. I am going to caution you about your duties as security. This job is not like running the 401, the Trans-Canada or any other highway. We're not out to nail these guys just for the sake of getting a quota, we're here to protect the ice and make sure that both Meanook and Acadia get the supplies they need in the very short window we have; six weeks is the average in my experience. So what I would like you gentlemen to do is start out slow and give the drivers some latitude. Pretty much all of them are running on GPS, but keep in mind we still have a few dinosaurs out there who have not embraced 21st Century technology. GPS gives us the most accurate reading for speed; it is our baseline. As the season progresses, they (the drivers) will have a 2 kilometer per hour grace. Anything beyond that heeds a warning and five kilometers over posted speed snags a suspension. In the beginning, I recommend that we go easy on the warnings unless someone is blatantly disobeying the posted limits. A lot of the seasoned drivers will ask for speedometer checks and that is what I want you gentleman to give them." Pringle lifted the water, took a sip, and continued. "Any questions so far?"

"So if we have a guy going over by three km/h in the first week, we just let him know to back it down?" the only native security man asked.

"Exactly," Pringle replied glancing down at his seating plan. "Steve has hit the nail on the head. We help these guys to find their baseline on their Speedo, match it up to the Speedo on the GPS, and as a bonus we get to calibrate our radars. If you think you have a cowboy, take note of his winter road number and keep an eye on him."

"Will that need to be reported?" Steve asked.

"Not at first," Pringle replied and looked out over his audience. "There are lots of old faces out here, men that are seasoned on the ice; take your cue from them and if you have a question, ask. The cowboys generally lynch themselves in the first two to three weeks, but we are not here to push them over. Our job here is two-fold; protect the ice and keep things running in a smooth and efficient order. We knock a driver off the ice without good reason, that's one more man that has to be replaced. So let's work with them as partners, not adversaries."

The man sitting next to Pringle looked up and said. "Can I interject here, John?"

"Yes, of course. Gentleman, this is my 2 IC, Ralph Ball. Ralph has been in this job almost as long as me and his only shortcoming is that he is a Leaf's fan."

There was more laughter.

"This is going to be the year," Ball said without much enthusiasm, then got on with his point. "As John said, I am old hat around here. I've worked Meanook and Acadia since they opened and spent a number of years patrolling for the Joint Ventures of Ekati, Diavik, and Snap. Speed and spacing is the key here, folks, the leader of each convoy sets the pace and the spacing between each truck is no more or less than half a kilometer apart. Loaded trucks passing each other on the ice in opposing directions must slow down to 10 km/h. We have a number of trouble lakes this year and the speed on those lakes is posted. Make sure that the trucks rolling onto the lakes adhere to the posted speed. As John said, we are not here to screw these guys, give them some latitude, but don't take any bullshit either. These drivers will be pulling long hours and when people get tired, they get bitchy. You men are in an authoritative role here. If a driver gets snarky, tell him to dial it back; if he continues, take his winter road number, issue him a warning and file a report. If you tune a guy up, write everything down. There will be grievances against us, claims that we are handing out warnings that aren't warranted. In the case of issuing warnings or suspensions, a paper trail is a must. That said, discretion is also a must; we are not out to screw these guys. Be courteous, but make sure that they know that you mean business. The other point I want to bring up is the environment. Under no circumstances are there to be any breaks given for littering or feeding wildlife. That goes for you gentleman here as well. Acadia and Meanook are under extreme scrutiny by a number of environmental groups and are hyper-sensitive about the eco-system up here. Littering is a season ban, no exceptions. The animals up here, in particular the ravens and foxes, will come begging for food. Drivers feed them, but if you catch someone doing that, he gets an automatic suspension. These animals become dependent on handouts and as a result forget how to forage. As they say in Yogi Bear's Jellystone, do not feed the animals."

"I second that," Pringle added and asked, "Anything else, Ralph?"

"No, that about covers it for me. I'll hand the floor back to you." He sat down.

"Any more questions?"

Crane raised his hand.

Pringle checked the roster for his name. “Do you prefer Philip or Phil?”

“Phil will do just fine. What sectors will we be covering, John?”

Pringle looked down again, checking his notes.

4

Montreal, Quebec

Maggie was eating breakfast. Picking at it might have been a better word. Occasionally she stole a glance around the restaurant, trying to justify the paranoia that had settled into her bones. This was madness and waiting around for this to be over was a nightmare. She didn’t even know who it was she might be looking for, if anyone at all.

Ghosts, I’m chasing ghosts.

But was she?

She took a sip of the coffee and pushed the poached egg around the plate, trying to consider what to do to pass the time. The boredom made it even worse, feeding the fear and paranoia. As she glanced down at the egg she knew she wouldn’t eat, she heard a women speaking a table over. The woman’s voice was rough and a bit on the husky side.

“Je suis de café avec crème de la Sucre,” the woman told the waitress, who giggled and the woman said in English, “What’s so goddamned funny?”

“Nothing, Madame, I will get your café.” The young waitress smiled and scampered off.

Maggie turned to look at the woman sitting alone. She was very tall, big boned, but not unattractive. She shook her head, obviously disheveled and glanced over Maggie’s way. When their eyes met, the woman laughed and said, “Okay, what did I say?”

Maggie giggled. “You told her that you are a coffee with cream and sugar.”

The woman closed her eyes, shook her head again and laughed. “I flunked French.”

“Just speak English, almost everyone in Montreal does. And it’s ‘je voudrais.’ That means I want. ‘Je suis’ is I am.” Maggie giggled again.

The woman joined her and said, “My name’s Angel.”

Maggie almost answered with her real name, but looked around again and decided to use her middle name. “Karen. Welcome to Montreal,

Angel," she smiled, while in her head she remembered Marty's warning about talking to anyone. This was harmless, though; in fact, it was just keeping up appearances.

"Do you mind if I join you for breakfast, Karen?"

Maggie felt suddenly uncomfortable. Small talk, now breakfast. She was doing exactly what Marty said not to do. Marty, who wasn't here looking over his shoulder, jumping at shadows. Besides, what the hell was she supposed to say? No?

"Sure, why not."

Angel stood up, and Maggie was amazed at her height. Over six feet. Her new acquaintance grabbed her purse and brought it over to the table. "You speak French fluently, Karen?"

"Enough to get by, but I stumble on a lot of words."

"So you're a stranger here as well. Cool."

5

Yellowknife, NWT

Standing before him in the doorway was a big man, sporting a full head of blond hair tangled up in grey. He was grinning, his teeth glistened in the yellow light of the hall, and when he spoke, his voice was deep, full of gravel. "My name's Garney Wilson. Bob Stewman said you might want to shake it up a bit today by touring around YK."

Marty opened the door a bit more and stuck out his hand. "Nice to meet you, Garney. I'm Marty Croft. And yes, I wouldn't mind taking a run around Yellowknife."

Garney reached out, his big mitt swallowing Marty's whole hand. He gripped firm, but not tight and that was good because he probably had the strength to crush a pineapple. "Good to meet you, Brother. I'm heading down for some breakfast with some of the other guys. You can join me if you like. I think they'll be booting us out of here today anyway. We'll be moving into our trucks and the YK yard. Stew said you haven't driven in a while and asked if I could take you for a run so you can get reacquainted with the gear shift."

Marty studied Garney, trying to decide if he might be working for Shamus. Stewman had said "no," but then who really knew? As far as he was concerned, everyone was suspect. "I'm going to grab a shower, how long you going to be down there?"

"Oh, go ahead and have a shower. I have to head out and brave the climate for a smoke anyhow. They serve a pretty good steak and eggs here, but I like my smoke and coffee first."

"Well, that works for me. I'll grab a quick shower and pack up."

"See you downstairs, Marty." Garney turned and walked down the hall, whistling as he went and Marty realized it was this man who had been listening to the music next door. He still couldn't place the song, though.

6

Shamus Contracting Yard
Hamilton Harbor

In a snow-covered portable trailer at the edge of the harbor, Shamus was sitting across from his driver/bodyguard Donald. Not that he needed a bodyguard. Gordon Shamus only used Donald as a back-up when administering a lesson to anyone he thought was in need of some education. That was the difference between him and his father. Jude Shamus rarely raised his hand and violence was below him; except when it came to his only son. Gordon Shamus took pride in doling out punishment. He used it as a relief valve, in fact. As Shamus made his way through each day, he could feel the madness cycling through his veins and knew that there were points in time when he would have to relieve the pressure. The madness was a final gift passed to Gordon Shamus from Jimmy Poe before his departure from this world.

Today was a good day. Crane and Marty were in place, the Turcotte's were getting ready to snatch Marty's wife, and within a month, he would have pulled off a heist that would be unknown to most, but spoken of in the hollows of the underworld. Gordon Shamus would have earned his own name and the legend that was Jude Shamus would fade to black.

This section of the harbor had become a ghost town after the Steel Plant shut down in the wake of the global recession. Shamus Construction, which was really a front for Shamus racketeering, Shamus Drug Trafficking, and a number of other illicit practices, owned this stretch of property and rather than sell it off, he hung onto it as a base of operations.

"What is the story with our friends over at the clubhouse?" Shamus said.

"They want a meeting on Saturday," Donald answered. "They think we could do business, but want to meet with you personally."

"Bikers, who would have thought we'd be working with bikers?"

"They're pretty innovative, Gordon. They gave the Italians a run for their money and I think that it's probably best to hear them out."

Shamus looked at his driver and smiled. "You think so, eh? You think a bunch of long hairs can put the run on me? Do I look like a Wop to you, Donald?"

"No," Donald said and fell silent. A second passed, then two. He lowered his eyes sheepishly.

"What's the Honcho's name again?"

"Henley, like the guy from that band The Eagles. First name is Stu."

"Stu Henley, that doesn't sound very bad-ass, does it? Okay, I've gotta take a piss and a smoke. You give this Henley a shout and tell him I'll meet with them, but on our turf. I don't trust these fuckers, they have no integrity." Shamus stood up and put on his jacket. "What about the other thing? Is that all set up?"

"Yes."

"Okay, call to confirm and set up the meeting. I'll be back in five." He opened the door, letting in a cold gust of harbor air accompanied by flurries swirling about his feet. Tightening his overcoat, he stepped out into the abandoned construction yard and let the wind bang the trailer door shut behind him.

Donald couldn't understand why he didn't just take a piss in the bathroom. Smoking wasn't the issue. Gordon lit up his stinky cigars in closed quarters all the time. Donald guessed it was just meditation; the crazy bastard would slip out into the dark, have a smoke, piss on the ground, and decide whose day he was going to fuck up next. The last incident with Crane and Henry Reid scared Donald, scared him bad. "It was brutal," he said later that day when talking to his brother. "The fucker is ruthless."

Shamus clipped the cigar, stuck it into his mouth, and lit it, cupping the flame against the wind. As he did this, he inventoried the yard. It was fenced in by corrugated steel sheets; they cried out in a ghostly warbling as the wind beat against them. He loved this old construction yard. It was where he cut his teeth in the business, learned to run various pieces of equipment, and it was the one place he felt at ease. When the big steel company packed up and went south, the old man wanted to sell it off, but

Shamus had rallied him to keep it open, had even offered to buy it. The old man knew why he wanted it and kept the place.

Littered about the yard was a long dead D9 Caterpillar bulldozer, an old electric bus from the 60's, and numerous other derelicts slowly decaying beneath the snow. At the corner of the yard was an old wrecking ball, rusted almost orange. He wandered over to it, looked around thoughtfully, puffing on his smoke. Opening his overcoat he reached down, unzipped his fly and pulled out his penis. A steady stream of urine splashed against the already yellowed snow and Gordon Shamus grinned. The ground here was foul with the smell of urine. It was even worse in the summer when the sweltering heat baked the earth and vapors percolated. That aroma was reassuring to Shamus; it was his scent because only he was allowed to piss in the yard. In fact, he'd beaten up a fellow for unzipping in the yard, beaten him pretty bad. Education, he called it. This particular lesson cost the fellow his left eye and a number of teeth.

The flow of urine slowed and Shamus puffed a little harder on the big cigar. Once finished, rather than shaking off, he stood there, his flaccid penis contracting from the cold and dripping onto the ground. Comfortable that he'd emptied every drop, he tucked it away, removed the cigar from his mouth and said, "Good afternoon, Jimmy."

7

"Big Garney Wilson, how are the balls of your feet, man?"

Garney was outside on his second smoke when that familiar voice called out to him. He looked down the walkway to see a familiar figure ambling toward him. He walked down the path, his big mitt stretched out. "Spence, how the hell are yuh, my brother? Then pointing toward his prosthetic leg, he added, "How's the Man of Steel?"

Spence smiled. "It's not the leg that earned me that reputation."

Garney guffawed loudly, snapping his head left, then right, to scope out any ghost who might be listening. "No doubt, no doubt about it! And how are Billy and Axe Man Jack doing these days?"

They clasped hands, shaking vigorously, both grinning ear to ear. They liked each other a great deal. Garney had mentored Spence when he arrived to live in YK after spending a year at a veteran's hospital while they rehabilitated him. That had been a tough year: his marriage disintegrated, he sunk into a deep state of depression, and if Billy hadn't come to get him out of there, he likely would have called it quits. "The Jack Brothers are good. Billy's going hunting and Axe is going to be the subject of a reality television show."

Garney straightened up. "Really? A reality show, you say."

Spence smiled. "Ice Road Flooders: The Unsung Heroes of the North."

Garney exploded with laughter and slapped Spence on the shoulder almost hard enough to knock him over. Taking a last puff on his smoke, he flicked the cherry off and stuffed it into his pocket. "You got me there, Spence, you're a funny guy, my brother. Let's go get some breakfast."

8

Inside a banquet room there was a buffet laid out specifically for the winter drivers of Chinook Tundra Transport. The owner of the company, a likeable down-to-earth fellow named Gustafon Orr took very good care of his drivers. Gus Orr had started out as a transport driver, founding Chinook Tundra 15 years earlier on a hope and a prayer. Back then the company hauled flat deck and was comprised of two weather beaten Western Stars that looked as though they'd been to hell and back. That is, if hell had frozen over.

Orr and his brother Brad ran those trucks hard and volunteered for every shit duty that came down the pipe. Back then, there was a running bet in YK that the Orr Brothers would either end up freezing to death when those jalopies gave up the ghost or ended up on the bottom on a frozen lake. But they had two things working to their advantage. First, Brad Orr was nothing short of a mechanical genius. In the world of diesel mechanics, he was to Chinook Tundra what Mr. Scott was to the Starship Enterprise. The second was that Gus was an extremely savvy businessman with a vision. He started with two trucks, but he had grander ideas, which in four years, Chinook Tundra grew from 2 to 42 trucks. While Gus took care of the business, Brad took care of the shop, and by its eighth year Chinook Tundra started hauling fuel in a fleet that now boasted 140 tractors and 200 super b tankers.

Now in its 15th year, Chinook Tundra was a premier northern company with a reputation for good pay, quality service, and a family atmosphere. The men of Chinook Tundra had little to bitch about, although on occasion some still did, but they were gentle bitches. During meal times, Gus Orr ate with the drivers, was always approachable, and aside from the fact that he was one of the richest men in YK, he never forgot it was these very drivers who gave him the comfort and luxury he enjoyed.

When Garney and Spence entered the buffet, they were met by an immense assortment of men, decked out in winter gear. Their heights and shapes were diverse, from short and plump to tall and lean. Many had beards, and those that didn't were sporting four and five days of growth. Silverware clanged against plates as men loaded up with waffles and pancakes, sausages, bacon, and scrambled eggs. There was more plaid in this room then you'd find at a lumberjack convention. There was laughter and barking of, "Hello how have you been?" And foul language sung out almost poetically. "She's got a face like a can of squashed assholes." Or, "My ass was puckering so hard I lifted an inch off my seat."

Among them, between the shoveling of food into his mouth and slurping coffee, Sack was trading barbs with another driver, who looked more like a biker than a truck driver. That was Merv White, who was bellowing about the grace of his flat top 379 Peterbilt. Merv was a tall drink of water, roughly 6' 3" with the usual truck driver belly, weathered hands that looked more like great big leather gloves, and arms painted with tattoos. Catching Spence out of the corner of his eye, he abandoned his soapbox and hollered. "Well, there's trouble if I ever saw it!"

Spence hollered back. "Well, if it isn't Mr. White."

Just then Marty entered the banquet room looking uncomfortable and out of place. As Merv and Spence shook hands, Marty walked up and nodded to Garney.

"Yuh made it. All packed up?"

"Yeah," Marty nodded toward the double door and pointed into the foyer where a pile of bags continued to grow. "I brought my stuff downstairs."

"Good deal, Marty. I was talking to Bob and your truck is almost ready for inhabiting. They're doing an oil change on it right now, but after the briefing we should be ready to rock 'n' roll."

"So, we'll be running my truck around YK?"

"Well, that would be the plan, my brother. Probably best you get acquainted with your own wheels. That work for you?"

"Sure, makes sense." Marty wondered how he'd make out after so many years away from driving. In fact, he was a little nervous and not looking forward to the scrutiny of another driver. The Kenworth was equipped with an 18 speed and until he figured out (if he figured out) the rpms, he'd be grinding a lot of gears. Then again, maybe his stick handling would suck so bad that Garney would tell Stewman that he wasn't up for the job.

"Marty, this is Spence and Merv and, oh, here comes Sack."

"Marty Croft." He shook hands all around.

"Ever been on the ice, Marty?" Sack asked.

"No, I'm an FNG. Hopefully I don't annoy you guys with all my questions."

"If you're here to learn, you'll do fine," Spence said.

"Yeah, uh huh, yup. Sure will, cus I'm training him," Garney said.

"Oh God, he's fucked," Merv laughed and the rest followed.

This made Marty feel a little better, and then Bob Stewman entered the room and that deflated this moment of normalcy. Marty watched Stewman, who returned his glance and moved up to the front of the banquet room where a table was set up for the winter road briefing. When he got to the front of the room, he set down some paperwork he'd been carrying under his arm, then flipped on a laptop and the projector. For a second there was a picture of a truck half submerged in frozen ice, and then it was gone. Stewman looked distressed and Marty wondered if it was over the job or if he was antsy about the impending meeting.

9

Both Angela and Maggie came out of the restaurant and stopped on the sidewalk to chat. Angela lit a smoke and turned her head to exhale. From a safe distance, Scott Turcotte watched the women interact. Angela towered over the other woman by at least six inches. She talked and waved her cigarette about; they looked like lifelong friends. Angela said something that made Maggie laugh, and this brought a grin to Scott's mouth. His wife, for all her coarse attributes, could be quite charming when she wanted. The only thing was, Angela had no lady friends, she only had Scott, and this was all business. The smile on her face had been sharpened specifically for this moment, and his Angel, for lack of a better word, would have no qualms with beating that little redhead bloody if the need arose. He'd seen her do it before.

"That's it, Angel, lay on the charm," he said and was interrupted by the sound of his cell phone. When he looked down, he saw the name Shamus and before he could press the button to take the call, it rung again, almost as if impatient. "Hello?"

"Are you ready?" Shamus asked.

"Whenever you are," Scott replied.

"Okay, I'm thinking two days from today, but be ready to move when I call."

"Alright, we'll be waiting."

"No fuck-ups."

***

Chapter 9—Look at the Bones

1

ACADIA MINE
48 hours before: Winter Road 2013

Ronny Fraser, Chase Fenwick, and Damien Lars were standing inside what they now surmised to be a room; or perhaps foyer was a better word. At least this is what Fraser considered it. It was definitely an entranceway of some sort. But, to what? The walls of what had been coined "The Chamber" looked to be made of a material that was porous, almost like sea coral, but not brittle like coral. In fact it was a hard as pig iron. The walls arched upward almost 16 feet, resembling that of a subway tunnel or station. As noted in the video, there were thousands, if not tens of thousands of allotropes encrusted in the walls and ceiling as well as littered about the floor. The diamonds gave the illusion of internal light as they winked back, catching the work lights in their prisms. It was entrancing, like a thousand random camera flashes.

And then there were the bones, grouped on the floor like demon fingers pointing accusingly upward. These were not caribou bones. Fraser had no idea what they were, but ringing in the back of his head was the Wizard from Monty Python's Holy Grail declaring incredulously, "Look at the bones!"

"Good God, Chase, there has to be a few billion in diamonds just sitting here," Lars gasped, and he was right. The loose allotropes were all over the chamber floor like broken glass literally ready to be scooped up with a shovel. "What do you make of this, Ronny?"

Ronny turned his attention away from the skeletal remains and to the two men who traversed the beams of their flashlights across the chamber walls, causing the encrusted gems to flicker even more. "It looks as though whatever created this… place, also created the gems as a by-product." Fraser shone his light at the wall and traced the beam downward to the floor. "Likely, the allotropes have fallen to the floor over time."

"We've tested these samples?" Lars asked.

"Yes," Chase replied.

"And they have the same hardness as the other samples. These are in fact the same diamonds?"

"Yes, Damien, they are the same diamonds."

Look at the bones, again cried the Monty Python Wizard in Ronny's head.

"So, what is it? A mine shaft from another time?" Lars turned his attention back to Ronny, although he wasn't focused—he kept glancing at the walls, at the floor, and in his head dollar signs danced. Ronny's head snapped up, thinking the old man might have had an epiphany of sorts, but realized it was likely a reference to something antiquated. Chase was beside him now and also looking down at the bones.

"I guess caribou is out of the question," Chase said.

"Yeah, this is foreign to me," Ronny whispered.

"Do you think it might be prehistoric?"

"I don't know, Chase. My guess is no, this is not my field. I'm a rock guy. If you want a firm answer to that question, you'll need a paleontologist, but even then I don't think what we are looking at here is in the dinosaur family."

"Why is that?" Lars said, joining them.

Ronny looked up from the bones. He swept his right arm out and, referencing the room they stood in, said, "Because dinosaurs wouldn't have built the chamber we are standing in. This would have taken greater intelligence than that, and this is most definitely not a natural occurrence. So…" He looked back down at the bones intermingled on the floor and traced the beam of his light across them. "My uneducated guess is that we are looking at a foreign entity."

"Extraterrestrial?" Lars chuckled uncertainly.

"You mean like The Thing? Something buried in the ice? Come on, Ronny, do you know how crazy that sounds?" Chase said.

"Look at the bones," Ronny said aloud and they all did. "You tell me."

The bones were scattered across the floor and it was more than evident that they had come from more than one creature, yet it was nearly impossible for them to separate what went with what. Then Chase knelt down and carefully pushed aside what he presumed to be a rib cage, revealing one of the creatures grinning skulls.

"Holy shit," Lars murmured.

No one responded, opting to stare morosely down at the basketball sized cranium that was smooth and round, and had it not held a large compartment of upper and lower teeth, they would have been hard pressed to identify it as a skull. There were no nasal cavities, no hollow eye sockets.

"Pac Man," Chase murmured.

Ronny snickered. "I don't think so, but definitely not something seen anywhere around here. Whatever these things are, I'm guessing that we are the first to find them, and my guess would be extraterrestrial, unless this is a species that was here long before man; but even then, I doubt it."

"Why?" Lars asked.

"The chamber, Mr. Lars, remember I said that we were picking up some kind of kinetic energy force? I'm guessing that this chamber was the source of that energy. These were intelligent beings."

Chase looked from Ronny to Lars and said, "I don't know what we are supposed to do here, Damien. Is there a protocol for something even remotely connected to what we've stumbled onto here?"

Damien Lars shook his head. "I'm pretty sure that finding alien life is nowhere to be found in the Miner's Handbook. This, gentlemen, is an unprecedented find; aside from the diamonds, there is really only one thing I am sure of."

"What's that, Mr. Lars?" Ronny asked.

Lars bit his lip and sniffed, something he did often before pontificating. "Once news of this breaks, Acadia as we know it will cease to exist in this region. With that in mind, I want work to begin immediately to harvest as many allotropes from the chamber as possible. I also want the remains of these creatures transported to the lab."

"I don't know, shouldn't we wait for some kind of direction on such a move? From Lupania Corporation, or even Environment Canada?" Chase asked.

"I am going to board a plane and seek the help of a few of our friends in the government. For the time being this is all considered property and mineral right of the Lupania Corporation, so I want it secured."

"Secured from what?" Ronny said.

"Let's start with loss due to accidental cave-in. I want a team assembled, I want all of these fossils crated up and moved to the lab. I want every allotrope collected from the ground and itemized. I want you, Ronny, to go over this chamber from top to bottom and itemize everything that you see. I want all of this done before the government dicks come in here and start pushing us out."

"We might be breaking laws here, Mr. Lars."

"I'm willing to take that chance," Lars responded and stared back down at the skull. "Remember what you see here, gentleman. Burn it into your minds."

"Why?" Chase asked.

"Because," Lars said. "—very likely this will be covered up."

"What makes you so sure?" Ronny asked.

"Roswell," Lars said. "Because they covered up Roswell."

"You actually believe that, Damien?" Chase said.

"I do now."

2

Chinook Tundra Base Camp
Yellowknife, NWT

Marty studied the instrument cluster on the dashboard, reacquainting himself with the many bells and whistles. As he did this, the diesel engine purred at 1400 RPM and according to Garney, it would only be shutting off to facilitate an oil change. Someone had already hooked the twin tankers up behind the tractor and for that he was thankful. His confidence wasn't exactly high. His gear was already stowed in the sleeper bunk, but it looked barren. This truck was decked out for the long haul: there was a wardrobe, overhead storage compartments, and even a fridge. Marty's gear consisted of one military duffle bag and an arctic sleeping bag he'd purchased before flying into YK.

Beyond the long hood of the Kenworth, men moved back and forth, readying their own trucks for the job to come. Beside him, Garney was going over his own truck. His was a burgundy Western Star. He could see Garney moving back and forth from cab to bunk, stowing gear, making his bed up, and Marty figured he should do the same. He stood up, moved back into the bunk, and rolled out his sleeping bag, and his work inside was done.

I'm only going to be a here a week, he thought, then said, "If that..."

A week, but then there was still the Shamus issue and much closer to that, his underling Crane. Who's to say that Crane wouldn't kill him after he handed over the diamonds? "That won't happen," he said and fell silent thinking that good old Bob Stewman may have planted a bug in the truck.

Don't be a goddamn idiot! These guys aren't the CIA, they're a bunch of asshole Irish gangsters from Hamilton. But that voice wasn't enough to convince him that the solitude of this truck was a safe place free of listening devices. He wouldn't chance it, Crane already had Stewman go through his gear. Better to be safe.

According to Garney, a trip to Meanook took around 19 hours with a 30-minute meal stopover in Corbett Lake. "They want to see your face," Garney told him. "Just to make sure you're not all goofed up." The return trip was somewhere around 13 hours. Coming south without a load gave the drivers an opportunity to step up their speed and make better time.

Thump thump thump!

Marty jumped and then realized it was Garney banging against the side of the sleeper. He leaned out of the bunk to see the big guy hanging off the side of his truck. He reached over and pulled the handle, releasing the door lock. Garney stepped down off the rocker and opened the door. "Permission to come aboard, Cap'n!"

"Permission granted," Marty said, feeling a smile creep across his face. As much as he resisted, he was starting to like this big galoot. Garney climbed in and slammed the passenger door as he sat in the driver seat.

"Shit," Garney looked around. "You got the big 600. Lot a power under the hood of this old girl."

"How much power are we really going to need driving 25 km per hour across frozen lakes?" Marty asked.

"You'll need it on the Ingraham and the Inuksuk trails, Marty. Once you got fuel in those tankers, you'll have to pull hard against some hills, but no worries. The big 600 in this baby will take you over just fine. Yep yep, uh huh, yes, sir!"

"So, when do you want to leave?"

"Let's do a walk around and then we'll take this sweetheart out on the town." Garney adjusted his wool cap and winked. To Marty he looked sort of like a longshoreman sitting there in his gear. Of course the long black overcoat had been traded for a bright blue fire retardant parka affixed with luminance stripes, but still. Marty had bought a similar coat, which was an even brighter blue, making him stick out like a sore thumb. He put it on and pulled a cap over his own mop of curly hair.

"Okay. Let's go then."

Garney stared at the new parka and laughed. "Man, we gotta dirty that thing up. It's burning my retinas, brother."

"What do you suggest? Should I roll around on the ground for a bit?"

"We'll think of something, my brother."

They climbed from the truck, and though the sky was wall-to-wall blue with sunshine raining down upon them, it was penetratingly cold. Marty adjusted his parka and pulled the cap down over his ears, feeling the cold bite at his earlobes. Garney came around the truck, rubbing his mitts together and shrugging—dramatizing his disagreement with old man winter.

Marty opened the jockey box on the side of the truck and peered inside. There were a number of tools and parts, including drive belts, an alternator, headlights, hose fittings. Garney looked over his shoulder and reached a gloved hand in to roll over the alternator, checking it. "Good, it's got a pulley."

"Don't we have mechanics here at Chinook?'

Garney guffawed. "Brother, where were going there's no mechanics. You blow a line or need to change your alternator, you have to be prepared to do that yourself."

"You've got to be kidding me."

"Nope, this is the North, my brother, not downtown Toronto. You get into trouble up here, you need to be able to sort yourself out and fast. Have you ever changed an alternator before?"

"Yeah, on my Chevelle, about 20 years ago."

"Chevelle, now that was a nice car. What year?"

"I had a 72. The Heavy Chevy."

"Ahhh, that was a muscle car. Yeah, uh huh, yep… Yes Sir… That tells me you have some mechanical aptitude. Uh huh." Garney scratched his chin. "Okay, here's what we're gonna do, Marty. We are gonna do a walk around the truck, make sure she's ready to roll, and then after you take her for a spin, we are going to switch out that alternator."

"Is that really necessary, Garney?"

Garney's demeanor changed. He placed a gloved hand on Marty's shoulder and frowned. "This is the north, Marty. Up here there is no AAA, no kicking your feet up and waiting for the Mechs to come out and fix your truck. When you break down up here, time is your worst enemy. Every second that diesel engine is not turning, the air in your tanks is not being replenished. In the cold the seals in your air system start to contract, your batteries begin to freeze, and if you don't get an alternator changed out and the truck restarted in record time, you will be dead in the water." Garney pointed out of the yard northward. "Up there we move in groups, and like the marines, no man is left behind, but all are expected to pull their weight. If you break down on my watch, I'll help you switch out a bad alternator or help you repair a blown line or even cage a brake chamber, but that courtesy comes with the understanding that you're not going to sit around and wait for me to come help. And if I'm in the same situation, I expect you'll be there with me, assholes and elbows, braving the elements. You get my meaning?"

Marty nodded. "Okay, well I guess we'll be switching out that alternator."

Garney smiled again. "This is the way of the north, my friend. The north doesn't forgive, so when we hit the ice, we have to be ready. You'll thank me for this when the day comes."

"Okay." But Marty wondered if the day would really come. *One week tops. Right?*

"Good." Garney's smile returned. "Now grab your hammer and we'll do a proper walk around."

Marty reached into the jockey box and pulled out a weather beaten hammer. As they walked, Garney pointed out things Marty should look for, loose lug nuts, blown wheel seals, flat tires, and while Marty knew most of these things, he listened as the big man schooled him on a proper pre-trip inspection. He popped open the box on the first tanker and flipped the switch. There was an audible sssshhhhhhhh from inside the tank. Then he flipped it off. "Good," he grunted. "Uh huh, yep, very good."

The walk around took a good thirty minutes and by the time it was over, Marty's parka no longer looked brand new after he was taken underneath the pup and shown how to free a frozen brake.

When they finally made it up to the other side of the truck, Marty's toes were cold and he was looking very forward to driving. Garney looked unhampered by the cold and his smile had returned. "We'll make an ice road trucker out of you yet."

"Do you think so?"

Marty climbed into the truck and loosened his jacket to compensate for the temperature change while Garney worked his way around the nose of the big Kenworth to the passenger side. As he did this, his head bobbed just above the front of the hood and this made Marty's smile.

3

Montreal, Quebec

Maggie opened her eyes and looked around the room. She sat up, wearing only a T-shirt and underwear. She stepped onto the carpet and walked softly toward the hotel room window. Had she been paranoid, was Marty okay? She thought she'd better get a note out to him let him know that everything was all right. Her period was coming and she felt bloated, along with occasional stabbing pains in her abdomen. She hated this stupid god damn bloodletting ceremony every month. It was messy, uncomfortable, and she wished to be done with the whole thing and worse, for five days it screwed up her sex life.

What sex life, she mused. The last night with Marty was cold and rightly so, but for Maggie, having sex with the man she loved was almost as important as food. Her bouts of lovemaking with Marty were excited, often noisy events that weren't immune to an odd laugh or cry of passion. Almost reminiscent of what you might find in a Harold Robbins novel. That was until she found out her life was in danger and her husband used to be a criminal. Although her initial reaction was hurt, she still wanted him. She wondered if the bad boy part played into that.

"Honestly, Marty, a bad boy." She giggled and picked up her cell. Text read: **Seeing the sights, miss you alot!**

Unbeknownst to Maggie, Marty was feeling like a complete idiot as he drove around Yellowknife with a giant of a man named Garnet Wilson. At the other end of this message, his cell phone sat dormant and shut off inside his kit bag. He would turn it on when he was alone.

Suddenly there was a knock at the door and that startled her. She peeked through the window and saw Angel standing at the door. In her hand were two Styrofoam cups, undoubtedly filled with coffee.

My God, she thought slipping into a set of blue jeans. "I'll be right there." *How did she find the room? Don't be an idiot, Maggie! You gave her the hotel name. I am an idiot, God. Karen is my name! Remember! Karen!*

She unlatched the door and peeked through the crack.

"Good morning," Angel said. "I am a coffee with cream and sugar."

Maggie laughed. "So you are."

"Can I come in or do you just want me to feed you your coffee through this little crack in the door?"

"Sorry, was still wiping the sleep out of my eyes."

Maggie stepped back and opened the door.

Angel stepped into the room and again Maggie was taken by how tall she was. She really was a pretty woman, but she had a quality that would likely scare the shit out of most men. Her voice was a little husky and she looked like she might be the scrappy type. Maggie had met a few women like that. Angel struck her as the type of lady who might give a beating rather than take one.

"I know I said I'd give you a call in a day or two, but then I thought maybe we could check out Montréal, see some of the artsy fartsy sites, and you could help me by being my translator so I don't make a complete ass out of myself." She handed over the coffee.

Maggie sat down on the unmade bed, stole a glance at the clock, and her eyes darted toward the cell phone. She was surprised to see it was almost 10 o'clock in the morning. Had she really slept that late? The stress and exhaustion must have been taking its toll.

Did I give her my hotel room number?

Angel sipped her coffee and studied Maggie.

Jesus Christ, what if she's a lesbian? Never thought of that.

"You got a guy, Karen?"

Jesus Christ, she's a mind reader too. This thought made her smile.

"Yes, I do. He's on business in Vancouver."

"Me too," she said. "Although he is so busy that I'm beginning to think I should just trade him in on a good vibrator." She smiled sardonically, then the look softened. "I'm just kidding, of course, he's a great guy. He's a cop, retiring next year after serving on the police force for 25 years. What does your man do?"

"He's a graphic artist," and then she almost said: *And a master criminal.*

This made her smirk.

"Something funny?"

"Long story. I have to get a shower and clean up. We could go down to the art district this afternoon if you like. Montréal is full of culture, it has lots of things to see, and I'd be happy to pass the time with you."

"Okay, that works. I have to get down to the bank this morning anyway to get some money if I can figure out how to use the bilingual ATM machine. Would one o'clock work for you?"

"That would be perfect."

"My man tells me that the Montréal smoked meat sandwiches are to die for. I doubt there is any sandwich worth dying for, but I like my meat, and if it's anything like pastrami, I'll give it a whirl. I'm guessing you can take us to a decent place."

"Sure, we can get some real Montreal smoked meat at Nickels or just about any sandwich shop. I'll tell you what, I'll meet you in the lobby then we can jump on the Metro or take a cab."

"It's a date." Angel stood up, coffee in one hand and fumbling a package of cigarettes out of her purse. "You know what I do like about Montréal, Karen."

"What's that?"

"These people still find smoking acceptable. I mean I know a lot of people are coming down on smokers these days, but Montréal seems to be one of the last places on earth where you don't get that look."

"Look?"

"Yeah, that look, like you're a baby killer or something."

Maggie grinned. There was something about Angel she liked, perhaps it was the direct manner in which she said things. But there was also something about her that seemed dishonest. "See you at one o'clock, Angel."

"Looking forward to it, Karen."

Angel stepped out of the room and even before the door closed, she was already lighting up. Maggie took another sip on her coffee, which she realized was loaded down with sugar, and set it on the table. Maggie didn't take sugar in her coffee.

With Angel out the door, she turned her attention back to the cell phone and was sad to see that there was still no response from Marty. Getting out and seeing the sights would probably be a good thing, and being in the company of another in public seemed a safe move.

She went to the window.

Angel was gone and there was nobody else out there. She took the still hot coffee into the bathroom, poured it down the sink, dropped the cup into the garbage, and disrobed for the shower.

***

Chapter 10—Old Whitey

1

Inuksuk Trail – Main Pathway to:
Lupania Joint Venture Ice Road

Billy Jack followed his brother's service vehicle as best he could, but it was only a matter of time before Axe pulled completely away from him. The F350 4X4 Axe was driving wasn't weighted down by a snowmobile and the gear Billy had packed on the sled behind his own Dodge Ram 4X4.

"Bluefish Lake, you have two pickups—one service vehicle and one civilian—heading north at kilometer fourteen," Axe reported over the VHF radio; then he added sarcastically, "The civilian vehicle is moving slow."

"Bluefish copy. Have a safe run north," a female voice said.

Billy smiled and though he was tempted to pick up his handset and fire off a retort, he didn't. The reason Axe was calling the kilometer numbers was to alert opposing traffic. The Inuksuk trail, not unlike the notorious Ingraham trail, was a dangerous stretch of road that boasted steep shoulders and offered very little room to accommodate two vehicles. Reporting his position by kilometer marker gave a driver coming the other way a heads up. Those who ran the Inuksuk understood the areas where two vehicles should avoid meeting. Communication was key to getting up and down both trails and onto the ice roads that would follow. Actually, the Jack Boys had it easy; they were driving pickups, and once the big rigs started north for the mines, this trail was going to be a hell of a lot more dangerous.

Axe was on his way to work while Billy was on his way to play. The trailer he pulled housed a mobile hunting cabin and behind that sat a snowmobile, a sled, and all the winter gear he was going to need to get his quota of caribou for the season. Billy could actually take more than three Caribou, but he only took what he needed, and what he needed was enough to be divided up between himself, Axe, and Spence.

The snow was light this morning, a confetti of flurries floating on an upward breeze, but the Inuksuk was another matter. Billy could feel his truck swimming around on the polished surface, and he adjusted for that lack of traction by easing off the accelerator and being very careful with the steering wheel. An over-correction or hasty move could easily send him sailing off the road, Billy knew this from experience. Never mind that he'd witnessed numerous vehicles in the ditch over the years, he had in fact done that particular dance himself. It was his first winter after leaving the military. The entire incident left him gun shy. The feeling of complete helplessness as his pickup careened off the road and into the ditch was unnerving. One minute he was driving along completely confident— the next he found himself out of control and afraid. The entire accident took seconds, but it stuck with Billy and when he felt his wheels begin to slip, he immediately removed his foot from the accelerator.

Axe liked pushing the limits, but then Axe had never known real danger, never been shot at. Axe had lived a relatively comfortable life free of any real danger. Oddly, Billy found it easier to deal with soldiering in Afghanistan than sliding around on the Inuksuk Trail. There, everything he did was calculated; even when the shit hit the fan, he was able to assess the situation and do something. When his truck buckled and slid off of the road, he was at its mercy and that scared the hell out of him.

Ahead, Axe's service vehicle began to pull away from him as they climbed a hill known as "Sally's Bosom."

He didn't know who Sally was, but he guessed she had huge tits.

"Have a good day, Axe," he said into the mike.

"Okay, Billy, see you in a week," Axe replied. "Service vehicle north at kilometer 20, pulling away from sloooooow civilian vehicle."

And then the white company pickup accelerated up over Sally's Bosom and was gone as Billy's 4x4 geared down and started pulling the hill.

Billy's destination was Corbett Lake. Even though his aboriginal status allowed him to hunt the land without a license or tags, he still had to check in with Corbett Lake Security so that they knew his whereabouts. It was good practice and he didn't mind. He checked in with Corbett, caught a free meal with the security chief, and on the way out he stopped at the game warden shack to declare his kill.

After Corbett, he would set up a base camp on an open plain about 40 km north of the Acadia Mine. In the trailer were all the accoutrements to set up a camp for two weeks. This was something that Billy did by himself. He had invited Spence along on more than one occasion, but

Spence wouldn't come. The problem wasn't even that damn prosthetic leg. No. The problem was Spence. Sgt. Spencer Hughes had no issue sighting in a human target and pulling the trigger, but he had no interest in hunting and killing animals. This didn't make him anti-hunting; he understood that what Billy did was within the natural order of things. He even ate the meat that was delivered after each hunt. Hunting just wasn't his bag.

As he drove, he wondered if old Whitey would be up there again this year.

2

It was three years ago when he first saw the big white wolf. Initially he thought it was an Alpha Male, likely a pack leader scouting for prey. It wouldn't be long before he changed his mind. It became clear that the big white wolf was getting on. Judging by a scar that ran across the bridge of its nose, Billy figured it had been bested by a pack member that was younger and stronger. He'd never seen it in the company of its own kind.

Lying in the prone position and peering through the scope of his 303, he set the cross hair just behind the caribou's front quarter, expelled half a breath, and squeezed the trigger. Its range was approximately 400 meters away. The report from the rifle was crisp, echoing out across the barren land, and two things happened. The herd suddenly bolted except for the animal he had engaged. It stood statuesque, then stumbled and fell.

Keeping his eyes fixed upon the target, he held ready to take another shot. He never had to, but this harkened back to his training as a sniper. The trigger clicked back into place and he expelled the second half of his breath. It was a clean kill. He got up from the prone position and shouldered his weapon. Then he mounted his snowmobile and descended on the kill. Behind the snowmobile was a battered old military toboggan and this was what Billy used to transport his kills. Just enough room for three disemboweled and dressed caribou. Usually what he did was: he disembowel the creature right on site, spilling the contents of its belly into snow. The fresh smell of blood would quickly attract the ravens, wolverines, and any other creature looking for a free meal. With that done, he would transport the carcass back to camp and hang them high in a tree he'd readied for his quarry.

As he cut open the belly of his first kill, he felt like someone was watching and that drew his eyes to the hill he had shot this animal from. That was when he saw the big white wolf peering down at him for the first time. Carefully, he reached for his rifle, thinking that maybe there might be danger, but the old wolf just stared, not moving at all.

An outcast, he thought. Perhaps too old to be the alpha, exiled after being beaten down by one of the younger and stronger of the pack. An older leader would have surely invited a challenger. That's what the pack does when it no longer needs you. They push you out. It was what they did to Spence when he lost his leg. Sgt. Spencer Hughes, a decorated veteran of Afghanistan, Spence the instructor, Spence the sniper, and then when the IED went off, everything that same decorated Sergeant had been seemed forgotten.

He was shipped off to a Veteran hospital and as he underwent multiple surgeries and intensive physiotherapy, they'd already begun processing him for medical release. Spence had been there when his country needed him, killed for them, in fact, and now after giving up a leg, they pushed him out. Thanks for your service, Sgt. Hughes, really sorry about the leg. Here's your hat, what's your hurry? It's what governments did to vets all the time. It was disgusting.

Spence and this old wolf had a lot in common. Both alpha males, both leaders, and both discarded once they outlived their usefulness.

When they pushed Spence out, Billy could no longer stomach wearing the uniform. Spence was his brother, some might even say blood brother. They had not had done the old Indian ritual, but they'd shared in spilling an awful lot of blood. Billy was up for promotion to Warrant Officer when he made his decision. He had been awarded a medal for bravery and they were grooming him for bigger things, but Billy had other plans.

3

The IED demolished the Armored Personnel Carrier. The Bison hadn't even been in a convoy; the vehicle was a loner—broken off to pick up Spence and Billy from a hunting expedition. The patrol was sent out to neutralize an IED team responsible for building some of the biggest improvised explosives to date. They found the team after being dropped in at night and waiting where the Intelligence section said they were working. Billy and Spence waited two days before their targets arrived and they dispatched the two men without fanfare.

The last thing Billy heard was the Bison's motor humming before the apocalyptic clap against grinding metal. He snapped his eyes shut, smelled the acrid dirty smoke, the rotten egg of cordite. His ears sealed up, a steady high-pitched whistle protesting against the decibel overload. When the explosion let loose, the driver and four other soldiers were killed instantly. Both Billy and Spence had been at the back of the armored vehicle when the detonation tore through the vehicle completely in half, and that was really what saved them.

"Shit, karma's a bitch," Spence gasped, staring out at his mangled stump, slipping from this world, but still he managed, "I bet these were our guys, Billy."

"Probably were," Billy agreed, trying maintain his composure while examining the mangled mess of tissue wrapped around the splintered nub of bone. Billy had used a cargo strap to tourniquet what was left and thankfully, the blood that milked out in great gluts slowed to a trickle. He wrapped a field dressing on it and surprisingly, his friend didn't even wince. It had to be the shock. "We'll be okay, Spence. The cavalry is on the way."

Spence looked morosely down at his leg, his face newsprint grey. His voice was shaky. "If we get ambushed… You got to bolt, man."

"Shut the fuck up, Spence, I'm not going anywhere and neither are you. The cavalry is coming." Billy removed the browning 9 mm he carried for close quarters and placed it into Spence's right hand, then said, "Watch your arcs."

Spence held the 9 mm weakly and in a labored tone he said, "Remember the Alamo."

"Cowboy fuck-head," Billy prodded back.

And then Spence passed out.

"Spence?"

The sudden fear of being alone washed over him. He pulled off his combat glove and placed his middle and index finger on Spence's neck to check for a pulse. There was a steady throb beneath his fingers and that eased his nerves enough for him to close the door on the looming panic. Spence was just out, and the pulse seemed strong, considering the circumstances, but Billy didn't know for how long. He retrieved the 9mm and leaned Spence back. "I got to get something, Spence, I'll be right back," he said on purpose, just in case he awoke. He stood up and began scrounging around the wreckage. He found what he was looking for and went to work.

4

Two hours passed and Sgt. Billy Jack was frozen like a statue, rifle at the ready, holding up an IV filled with plasma and scanning the crest for an impending assault. He fully expected he would die that day along with his friend and brother. Expected the Taliban fighters to mount an offensive and finish off them, or worse, take them prisoner. He'd already decided that he would use the 9mm on both of them before he'd let them be taken. He didn't want to end up on some fundamentalist website kicking and screaming while they sawed his head off.

No fucking way.

But the attack never came, and to his surprise, the Cavalry arrived. Even though the radios were destroyed and everyone was dead, it was the timeline that saved them. Headquarters kept a strict schedule of the logistics and vehicles that moved up and down the two main highways in Afghanistan. When their vehicle didn't show, the alarm bell started ringing. Nato had suffered numerous casualties along this stretch of road and even a single vehicle carrying one specialized sniper team returning from outside the wire wouldn't be missed for long.

A Black Hawk helicopter was dispatched for a look and once the carnage was spotted, the cavalry was there in no time. Billy and Spence were extracted immediately. A second chopper landed with a sizeable security force to protect the scene so they could extract the dead. Billy stayed with Spence all the way back to the field hospital in KAF and he watched with dismay as they flew his friend to Germany where they went to work on saving his life.

Their tour would have been over in three days.

5

Intelligence determined there were actually two IED teams working that section of road, and a drone found them. On the last day of his tour, a troop of tanks had been sent to engage that second team. Billy had asked to go, but the medical officer, along with his commanding officer, denied the request. He had been angry at first, but Wally Perkins, his Company Sgt. Major, calmed him down. "You did your bit, Billy, what good are you going to be to Spence if you're dead?"

Billy said nothing.

"You are heading to Cyprus for decompression tomorrow. In the meantime, I need an after action report for the Company Commander. So I want you to stand down and sharpen your pencil, Sergeant."

"Yes, Sir."

They set out that morning and Billy set up by the main gate with a field message pad recording the events of the ambush and the IED strike. As he did this, his mind swam back and forth between the events of that day and what he imagined Spence must be going through. He guessed he would be heavily medicated, but when he came through… What then?

6

The sun was sitting low against the sky and the air smelled of methane from the cesspool just downwind of the camp when he heard the familiar **click clack click** of tank track against drive sprockets.

Billy waited as the tanks rolled in and pivoted into the harbor set up for them on the South side of the compound. He was walking toward the whirlwind of dust when he heard a voice calling over the whine of the engines doing their post-trip cool-down. He spotted a dwarfish man climbing from the leopard, still wearing his crew commander helmet—his name tag read: McElheron.

"Sgt. Jack," Master Corporal McElheron said.

"Yeah."

"My troop commander said to give you a quick debrief before standing down."

"I'm all ears, Master Corporal."

"We engaged a small IED factory operating inside a small village called Galal. This was in the Southern sector, approximately 74 clicks outside the wire. We engaged it with HE and I don't mind saying that it was a hell of a show when their ordinance lit up. That factory is out of business."

"INT said there was a second team. Did you get them?"

Call sign 55 Charley engaged a light vehicle, I believe it was a Toyota Land Cruiser with two occupants, sex unknown, likely male LBG's. The passenger was loading 155 rounds into the back of the cruiser when it was engaged with 55 Charley's .50 Cal. It lit up on the first shot. No survivors! Payback's a motherfucker!"

"Anything else, Master Corporal?"

"No, Sergeant. That about covers it. Any word on your partner?"

"Not yet."

"Alright, well we got these guys, but I'm sure there'll be more waiting in line ready to go to paradise. I hope things work out with your man. If you don't mind, I'd like to square up my crew and see about some grub and a shower."

Billy stuck out his hand and the Master Corporal shook it. "Thanks."

"It was our pleasure."

"What's your first name, Master Corporal?" Billy said.

"Gerald, but most folks call me Mac."

"My name is Billy. I'll be sure to tell Spence Hughes who you are. Thank you, Mac." Billy squeezed and released his grip. "I'll let you get to your men."

McElheron nodded and went back to his crew.

7

"What's the matter, too old to hunt your own food?" Billy asked.

The Wolf stared back, unflinching, and for whatever reason, Billy felt sorry for it. Unsheathing his hunting knife, he reached down and cut away the front right leg of the Caribou.

If Axe saw me do this, he'd say I was an idiot.

Axe would never hear about the wolf or the offering.

He tossed the limb off to one side, away from the entrails destined to be picked over by the ravens. This kill would be his and if the old wolf decided to keep following him, he would again pay him the respect of leaving real meat. Billy loaded the kill onto the toboggan, covered it with a tarp, and started up his snowmobile.

"I'm leaving this for you as a show of respect," he said. "Don't come to my camp. I don't mind sharing a little, but I will not put up with thievery. You come to my camp and I'll set my sight on you."

He put the snowmobile into gear and spun the throttle.

Ten minutes later, from a distance he watched the old Wolf cautiously wander down and retrieve that gift he had left it. He expected that the creature would come for the rest, but it never did.

Over the remainder of the season, Billy Jack and the old wolf would occasionally cross paths. On his second and third kill, he paid tribute to the fallen pack leader with another gift of meat.

It was near the end of that first season, as Billy stared into the fire, when he again felt that sensation of being watched. When he brought his eyes up from the fire, he saw the shine of the Wolf eyes looking down on him.

He stood upright, grabbing his rifle, scolding himself for being so stupid.

Do not feed the animals. Goddamn it, I'm an idiot.

He started toward the creature, thinking he would have to put it down. It backed up, turned, and was gone into the night.

Walking to the edge of the camp, he shone a light into the thin woods. The beast was gone, but its tracks were still easy to spot, and he decided to follow. This is what Billy did; stalking was his forte. He was ready to pursue the white wolf, and then he saw something he dared not tell anybody about, especially Axe.

He kept this secret because no one would ever believe it, never mind that he barely believed it himself. This was the sort of thing that happened in a Farley Mowat or Jack London novel, not in real life. But there it was at his feet. The body of a scrawny white rabbit. Its neck was broken, but beyond that, the carcass was in good shape. He reached down to pick it up, looking around suspiciously.

The body of the rabbit was limp, not yet frozen, and there was no rigor.

"You've got be kidding me," he said. Then he laughed and called to the darkness, "Is this for me?"

He laughed again; nobody would believe this. He didn't believe this.

Billy could feel the Wolf's eyes upon him, but could not see it.

This was crazy.

"Okay then." He held up the rabbit. "I thank you for this tribute, good luck on the hunt, great white wolf."

A moment passed, and he waited for a response, an approving howl.

There was none. He returned to the fire, skinned the rabbit, roasted it on a spit, and ate it with great cheer.

By the second season when the Wolf returned, he named it Old Whitey.

***

Chapter 11—Jimmy Poe and Jude Shamus

1

Marty knew he was dreaming, even heard the purr of the diesel engine calling to him from the edge of his subconscious. It was, he supposed, a reminder that in the real world Old Man Shamus wasn't around any longer to protect him

"You're very talented, Marty," Jude Shamus said, his Irish accent rising and falling in waves. He was looking over a sketch Marty had done of a man standing at the edge of the harbor, his eyes looking up at the scruffy young man before him and then down again at the pencil sketch set upon his desk. "Is that me, Marty?"

"Yes."

"What will you do with it?"

"It's for you," Marty said.

Pleased by the answer, Jude Shamus smiled, came around his desk, and placed an arm on Marty's shoulder. This close, he could smell the fragrance of pipe tobacco permeating from the old man's suit coat. "I am going to have this framed up and put in my office. It's a wonderful piece, Marty."

"Thank you, Mr. Shamus."

"Nay boy, thank ye. Yay are far too talented to be wasting yer time stealing trucks. If ye were my son, ye'd be in school, getting an education." Old Man Shamus looked past Marty to the picture of Gordon sitting on the edge of his desk and disappointment tugged at his smile, pulling it downward into a brief frown... They stood there a moment, an uncomfortable silence suspended between them and then, as if coming back from a trance, Shamus shook his head and mumbled, "Much too talented."

A knock at the study door interrupted them.

"Dad?"

The source of the disappointment, Marty thought.

Jude Shamus sighed. "Come in, Gordon."

Gordon Shamus entered the room. "How's it going, Hook?"

"Gordon," Marty nodded.

"Everything ready for tonight?" Old Man Shamus asked.

Gordon looked down at the sketch on the table, then back up—his eyes narrowed slightly as he placed them squarely on Marty. "As long as old Hook here keeps his sketch pad down and his eyes open, we should have no problems whatsoever, Dad."

"No worries, Gordon," Marty said, while thinking, *You're the crazy one who acts before he thinks. The one who likes to wave a gun around. The crazy fucker who beat Mark Miller to a pulp when he told you to calm down and put the fucking gun away.*

Miller had been stupid in challenging Gordon, but Marty saw it coming. Gordon joined the crew on his 22nd birthday. Mark Miller was 31 and had been in the employ of Shamus Construction for six years. He didn't care for Gordon at all and didn't mind sharing that fact with anyone willing to listen. "Little prick is going to get someone pinched someday. Or worse, fucking killed."

The beating came after a culmination of events leading up to the eventual showdown. And though Marty wanted to say something to Miller, because he really liked him, he didn't. Marty was only 20 and as far as he knew, Miller looked at him the same way that he looked at Gordon.

Bullshit, Marty told himself. *You could have told him to back off. He might have barked at you, told you to mind your business, but it might have saved him from getting all busted up.* It took all of three jobs before Gordon got tired of the criticism. On the first job, Miller told him to sit down and shut up. Actually, the exact words were: "Sit down and shut your pie hole, you might be the boss's son, but today you're here to learn, so pay attention."

Aside from Miller, Gordon, and Marty, there were five others who witnessed the disrespectful way Miller spoke to Gordon. Five men who would laugh and joke about it out of earshot. Five men who thought that Mark Miller was one ballsy motherfucker talking to the boss's kid like that.

"And rightly so," Shane MacDougal said to Charlie Emerson over a pint. "Little fucker has gotta earn his stripes like the rest of us. Miller sorted him right the fuck out."

Marty kept his mouth shut. He knew better. Knew that Old Man Shamus would have sacrificed any one of these men for blood. Even if that blood was a crazy half-cocked lunatic like Gordon. When the second comment came, he caught the look on Gordon's face and thought sickly that he might pull out his Saturday night special and shoot Miller right in the face.

"Hey, Fuck-stick, put away those smokes," Miller growled as they staked out a drop yard in West of Toronto. It had been dark and while Miller had a point, his delivery of that point should have been driven home with just a bit more finesse.

Something Marty noticed Gordon doing in his spare time was pulling back on the hammer of the .38 he carried and spinning the cylinder over a chamber at a time. When he did this, his eyes grew wild and unpredictable. Marty didn't like being in the same room with Gordon when he got like that; he was dangerous.

As the saying goes, three's a charm, and it was after they had grabbed a load of Candy and were breaking it down inside a warehouse when Gordon removed his .38 from his waistband, pulled on the hammer, and began clicking the chamber over, using the thumb on left hand.

Click— turn—**click—** turn—**click**

Miller was telling Marty and MacDougal where to drop the truck and trailer when he saw Gordon pull out the gun. "Take the truck and trailer over to Cherry Street, have Lorry follow you, and leave it there. Don't forget to wipe it down and..." Miller turned his attention on Gordon. "Hey, Fuck-stick! Put that goddamned iron away!"

Gordon didn't look up. He just turned the chamber—**click**—his eyes staring downward—**click**—a weird grin on his face—**click.**

Marty backed up; he felt uneasy.

"Did you hear me? I said put the fucking iron away!"

Click.

Miller stomped across the floor yelling, "Jesus Christ, are you fucking deaf as well as stupid! I said put the fucking iron away!" Gordon didn't move, but the muscles on his neck tightened into hard bands and Marty guessed he was wound up like a spring ready to explode.

Marty took another step backward.

Gordon set the hammer back down and waited.

"What the fuck is the matter with…"

Then Gordon brought the gun up and smashed Mark Miller in the face. The sight on the snub nose tore open Miller's upper lip and then obliterated both of his central and right lateral incisors. Miller wheeled backward against the wall, having already swallowed the fragments of teeth, while his hand came up to his mouth and a befuddled moan of agony spilled out.

"Who you calling Fuck-stick now, ass wipe?!" Gordon never gave him a chance to respond. He moved across the floor full throttle and kicked Miller right in the nuts, and he doubled over, the pistol whipping began. "Call me fuck-stick again! Come on, I dare yuh!"

Crack!

A fine spray of red mist burst from Miller's cheek bone, painting Gordon's arm with fresh war paint.

No one dared move or protest. Marty was watched in horror.

"Well, aren't you going to tell me to put the iron away? Fuck-stick!" He brought the heel of a boot down on Miller's knee and there was a sickening crunch and then a pop. Miller would have screamed, but Gordon brought the gun around and smashed his nose in. This resulted in an even more sickening gristly pop.

Jesus, he's going to kill him, Marty thought.

Crack!

Then Miller was down like a rag doll, no longer responding to the beating, but this didn't slow Gordon down. He wound up and kicked the unconscious man again and again, shouting maniacally. "Fuck-stick! Who's the fuck-stick now? Miller, you piece of Scottish shit! Call me a fuck-stick! I dare yuh! I fucking double dog dare yuh!" Gordon Shamus was covered in Miller's blood from the waist up. He was panting like a dog, bits of spittle escaping his mouth, and that weird grin hung on him as his eyes whirled madly.

"Gordon, please stop," Marty finally cried. He was terrified, fearful of drawing fire. Somewhere deep down, he mustered the courage the others lacked and said, "Please, Gordon, he's had enough."

Gordon stopped, the gun hanging at his side.

Shane MacDougal looked from Gordon to Marty, his face also filled with horror. Marty guessed that MacDougal wouldn't be mouthing off about what a hero Miller was over pints any time soon. Gordon pulled back the hammer on the .38. Then he turned toward them and brought the gun up. "Anyone else think what this ass-bag said was funny?"

All of them looked to the floor, all except Marty.

"What about you?" He pointed the gun in Marty's direction.

Marty swallowed, his Adam's apple clicked. "We still have work to do, Gordon."

Gordon stared into Marty, his face angry, confused.

"What do we do, Gordon?"

Gordon looked around the room, from MacDougal to Scott Lorry and then Emerson, who caught on to what Marty was doing and said, “What do we need to do, Gordon?”

“The job’s not done,” Marty added. “Where should we take the truck?”

Gordon drew in deeply and exhaled, the gun floating downward. His breathing slowed—the labored pants of a man who had just finished a marathon. He wiped his mouth with his hand smearing the bloody spray across the scar that ran up his cheek.

The King is dead! Long live the King!

Miller was the man in charge. Gordon had bested him and he was now the man in charge. At least until Old Man Shamus had his say.

Gordon spoke. “Lorry, you and Shane dispose of the truck and trailer. Croft, you and Emerson get this mess cleaned up and then move the product to the other warehouse.”

“What about Miller?”

“Bury the fucker.”

He’s not dead, Gordon.”

“Oh, no?” Gordon Shamus walked over and pointed his gun into the face of the badly beaten Mark Miller and pulled the trigger. The gun clicked and Gordon brought it up to look at it. The cylinder was askew, having been dislodged during the pistol whipping. Gordon kicked the unconscious man one last time and said, “Get the warehouse sorted out, stow the product, and if and when that is done and if this piece of shit is still breathing, call Buddy King and get him to bring a doctor over. If he’s dead, take him up to the punchbowl and bury his ass.”

I’m in fucking deep shit here, Marty thought. *Deep fucking shit.*

Gordon walked out of the warehouse, pausing at the door long enough to drop the destroyed .38 onto the concrete floor. Before opening the door and heading out to his car, he said, “Get rid of the gun.”

The engine grew louder, pulling him back; he didn’t resist, he was happy to leave this horrific nightmare, even if he was only an entity floating outside the action.

When he opened his eyes, he saw a thin line of sunlight cutting through the bunk curtain. Reaching up, he glanced over at the LED clock, which read 11:30 am. He’d been napping for about an hour and a half. After his drive through YK with Garney, he decided to lie down. The drive around town was uncomfortable at first. He ground gears, swung the truck too wide on corners, and began braking far too soon when approaching intersections. Throughout this, Garney was quiet, watching and letting Marty feel his way. As time progressed, Marty felt himself getting more proficient with the gear shift and using the clutch less to shift as he became more accustomed with trucks rpms. By the time the drive was over, Marty's head was pounding, but that didn't stop Garney from showing him how to swap out the alternator and test it.

"Okay, uh huh, good deal, this one works," Garney said staring at the alternator's gage on the dash. "Tell you what, Marty, I'm going over to see the maintenance crew to grab a few bottles of fuel conditioner, why don't you pull that new one off and replace the original, and then we can call it a day."

Marty didn't want to pull the alternator off. It was -32 Celsius, but he didn't argue. He warmed his hands over the heater vent and said, "Yeah, okay. Are you going to check it when you get back?"

"Nope, my brother. You know what you're doing. Yes, sir. Once you get it switched out, close up the hood." Garney winked. "Warm up your hands first, Marty, and word to the wise: prepare everything in the warmth of the truck before you start. Know what tools you need and have them ready. The less time you spend out there jacking around in the cold, the less time you spend freezing your ass off."

Garney left, and after a few minutes he went out and switched the alternator back. The whole process took him 20 minutes and by the time it was all said and done, his fingers felt like useless twigs. Garney didn't return to check his work; he didn't have to, Marty understood that a poorly fitted belt or loose nut would only lead to further time spent working in these temperatures. He inspected his work thoroughly before starting the rig, then put his tools away. After that he climbed into the bunk, closed the curtain, and lay down. It wasn't long before he was sleeping. Not long after, he was dreaming about Mark Miller and Gordon Shamus.

Now, he fumbled his cell phone from the bag and turned it on. It seemed an eternity as he waited for the little Samsung throwaway to fire up. As it went through its tedious start-up, he considered the outcome of that day. Mark Miller survived the beating but would walk with a cane for the rest of his life. Marty initially thought that Gordon would pay for that beating at the hands of his father, but payment was never collected. Jude Shamus marched each man from the crew in one at a time and considered all versions of the story. Only Marty had sounded sympathetic to Miller, but even Marty didn't tell the Old Man what he really thought.

That his son was a certifiable psychopath. And the others? All cowards, who turned on Miller the minute they stood before the Old Man.

"Gordon was within his right," Shane MacDougal was said to have told the old man, a stark contrast to his tough talk about Gordon to Emerson. It was after that beating, Marty understood that there really was no honor among thieves. They would have looked on if he were being beaten and just as easily hung him out to dry.

The Samsung chimed and he began to text: **I am safe, I miss you very much and this will soon be over.**

He pushed send and waited.

The phone chimed, Maggie responded: **Miss you too, seeing the sites. Please be careful.**

He texted back: **I will. U2.**

He shut off the phone, placed it in his bag, and lay back on his pillow.

I'm in fucking deep shit here, the dream echoed.

2

At the same time that Marty was in the throes of a blow-by-blow flashback of Mark Miller's education, Gordon Shamus was also dreaming. In Shamus's case, he was dreaming of Jimmy Poe. Shamus's ghosts always came knocking when he got a little too deep into the scotch and nodded in and out of this world.

He'd turned 25 one week before Jimmy was released to a halfway house just inside the town limit of Niagara Falls. On the afternoon when he was tackled by ninth-grade geography teacher Mr. Todd, James Robert Poe began a mental downward spiral. He retreated into himself and although it was not complete catatonia, he became an introvert, his communication skills lessening each day. It would be some time before the psychiatric community would put a stamp of release on Poe's file, but it was an eventuality.

Old Man Shamus warned Gordon that he was not to go near Poe. "The police will be watching," he said. "They'll be waiting for something like this and they'll use you to get to me. Understand me, boy, if you go near him and get caught, I will cut you loose." The old man's eyes narrowed, his face hardening. And Gordon understood what he really meant. If Gordon Shamus went near Jimmy Poe and that resulted in Gordon being arrested, there was a strong possibility that he would meet with an unfortunate accident.

So he waited, and as the cliché goes: time marched on. From a distance he watched the comings and goings of his old pal Jimmy and he knew that the right moment would present itself. The scars, at least the physical ones, eventually healed, but on the inside, the anger was a gaping wound that could only be mended by retribution.

For six months after his release, Gordon followed Jimmy every day. Jimmy had become a creature of habit. He would eat breakfast at eight am, and just before nine, he would set out on an unsupervised walk. The post-war bungalow he stayed at housed three schizophrenics and was approximately 2 miles from Niagara Falls. Jimmy would wander down to the same bench that overlooked the horseshoe. He would sit there for three hours, staring out into the mist. Rain or shine, Gordon watched every day, staying a safe distance back, thinking that the cops might have Poe staked out. But as time went on, Gordon realized that neither he nor Jimmy Poe were on anyone's radar, let alone the cops. Gordon deduced that the numerous crack and meth houses had the police department's attention. His assumption was right. Gordon Shamus thought it was quite possible he could walk up and push Poe over the edge and into the cascade of water, but that wouldn't be good enough. Instead he schemed, watched, and waited, until the day came when he decided to move on his actions.

Gordon Shamus did not have the sanction of his father when he decided to make his move. But at this point in the game, he didn't really care if the he had it or not. There comes a point in every young man's life when he breaks away from his father's influence. If the old man wanted him dead after he did what he intended to do, he was willing to take that chance. He exercised restraint for a number of years and if he had his way, he would be digging two holes, one for Jimmy Poe and one for Jude Shamus.

He decided that Jimmy Poe would have to suffice.

On that morning the temperatures were dipping just below zero and the mist rising from the falls turned quickly to ice encasing everything it touched in a glassy cocoon. Gordon Shamus decided it was time. As Poe sat silently on the same bench he had for months, Gordon approached. He was wearing a long black overcoat, not unlike those worn by longshoremen; it looked a little silly on him because he was so thin, but he wore it just the same. Nobody would dare mock him now. After being called out by his father, "Toughen or die," Gordon learned to use his fists quite effectively.

Approaching the bench, he could see the back of Jimmy's head, which was shaded by a neatly cropped brush cut. He thought the schizoids at the halfway house probably trimmed each other up with a set of clippers when they weren't blowing each other or groping in the dark. This thought made him smile and he wondered if they'd done any shock treatment on Poe. He hoped they had. Along with the long overcoat he wore Kodiak boots, which clicked upon the frozen walkway, but this seemed not to alert Poe at all.

A foot or two short of the bench, he stopped and stared. For all his watching, and so-called planning, he realized he wasn't sure what to do at this point. Gordon intended to kill him, but wasn't quite sure how or for how long he intended on making it last. He pondered the broken young man sitting with his back to him, and as Gordon would later recall, that moment he might have actually walked away. Gordon Shamus lacked any real imagination, he was short tempered, violent and unremorseful, but he was horrible when it came to using his imagination. He couldn't push him over the falls or even shoot him in the back of the head. There were too many cameras mounted on light standards and railings. So what could he do? He'd have to re-think his options and come up with a better plan. He took in a breath and was getting ready to withdraw when Jimmy Poe spoke up and forced his hand.

"Hello, Gordon," Poe said. Shamus jumped a bit, completely caught off guard and before he could respond he said, "I've been waiting for you. Why don't you come and sit down."

Gordon moved around the bench, glanced down at the ice-encrusted seat, and wondered if it soaked through the clothes Poe was wearing. He didn`t think it would seep through the big wool overcoat he wore. Poe turned to look up at him. He was pathetic looking. Here was the shell of the young man who'd killed his two friends and unzipped the skin of his face with a stinky gym sock filled with nuts and bolts. Poe turned away, back to the falls.

"Are you going to sit down?"

"Sure, why not." Gordon sat down.

"What now?" Poe rubbed a droplet from the tip of his nose.

"What do you mean what now?" Gordon asked.

"You've been following me for a long time. You're not here to say you're sorry." Poe turned and faced Gordon him. "Are you?"

Gordon couldn't believe what he was hearing. "What did you say?"

"You're not here to say you're sorry, for what you did to me."

Gordon felt fire in his belly. "Did to you? Are you fucking kidding me?"

"No, I'm not kidding."

"If anything, you should be begging for my forgiveness or my mercy. You killed two of my friends, Poe. You disfigured me. Look at the scar on my face, you fuck." Shamus growled and reached out a gloved hand, placing it below Poe's chin, turning his head toward him. "Sixty eight stitches, my face was hanging off like a flap. The scar still tingles in the cold, it's hard, but the broken skin has never quite healed. Sometimes I get little infections that release pus. The doctor said that the nerve ends are tangled in the scar tissue and that it why I still get a tingling sensation. Oh, and I haven't even mentioned the throbbing I get where you cracked my cheek bone. That's a real treat."

"So, why are you here? Revenge?"

Shamus laughed. There was a razor edge in the laughter. "Well, I'm not here to apologize."

"You're here to beat me up? Kill me?"

Shamus said nothing.

"I see." Poe stood up. "Let's go then."

"Go where?"

"I'm guessing you're not going to do it here in broad daylight, so let's go."

"You're just going to come with me, no argument or struggles. Is that it?" His eyes darted around, then he reached over and began ruffling through Poe's jacket. "You wired up Jimmy, is that it?"

Poe's head jostled about as Shamus patted him down. "You think anyone gives a shit about me? I'm dead, Gordon. I've been dead since that day in the school. Nobody cares what happens to me, my parents stopped coming not long after the trial. Nobody gives a shit. In fact, I'll bet you're the only one who has anything invested in me."

"You're fucked in the head, Jimmy Poe."

"You could do it right here if it suited you. Push me over the falls."

"You're a fucking nut job." Shamus stood up and began to move away.

Poe smiled and yelled. "I knew you were a coward!"

"Fuck you!" Shamus was bounding away now, back up the path. His heart was racing, adrenaline coursing through his veins. "Fuck you, Poe!"

"I knew it! You fucking coward piece of shit!" Poe was laughing.

Shamus stopped and glared.

Not yet, he thought. *This is too easy.*

He strode up the path in long strides, making his way back to the car. This wasn't over: he would take care of this, but it would be his way.

3

Maggie and Angel were back at the hotel. They'd had dinner at a place called Schwartz. Both had Montreal smoked meat sandwiches piled onto rye bread with a large pickle as a garnish. The rest of day was spent having drinks, walking Saint Catharine Street in Montreal, browsing the shops and stopping along the way to have a drink or three. Angel had even dragged her into a sex store. "Come on, Karen, I need a decent toy and maybe something naughty for my man." Angel held up a package, which contained a very large dildo. "What do you think of this one?"

Maggie giggled, her cheeks turning red with embarrassment. She wasn't a prude, but she didn't talk with other women about her sexual appetite. Still, the mischief was contagious. "Is it big enough?"

Angel laughed aloud, then snatched up an even bigger one. "How about this?"

Maggie started to laugh uncontrollably. "Bigger."

Just then a male attendant came up. "Bonjours, vous cherchez quelque chose en particulier?"

Angel rolled her eyes.

"Un moment," Maggie told the attendant, then turned to Angel. "He wants to know if you're looking for something in particular."

Angel looked at the dildo, then with a deviant smile said, "Ask him if he's ever used this one."

The attendant smiled. "Madame, my English is quite good. I have never used it. Non. I prefer the real thing." Angel busted up and Maggie joined her. "If you need any advice, I will be happy to assist you."

"Merci," Maggie said.

"Mercy," Angel added and they both began laughing even harder.

"Pas de problem," he said and winked, then wandered off.

Angel purchased the toy and a few other things as Maggie watched in awe. She really had no shame, could care less what others thought and was extremely confident. They left the shop and carried on down the street. Along the way they stopped at an outside café and had a drink together. They caught the Metro back to Maggie's hotel and Angel saw her back to her door. In all, Maggie had had four drinks that afternoon and her head was buzzing. She and Marty occasionally drank, but only during vacation or on special occasions did she actually partake in such activity.

"Are you busy tonight?"

Maggie thought about it. She wanted to get in touch with Marty and see how things were going. "I have a few things to do, but tentatively, no."

"Well then, maybe you can show me around Montreal at night and we can have a few more drinks. Maybe have some dinner." Angel was leaning against the door jam, towering over.

"Alright, but I'll need to lay down for a few hours. Things around here don't start hopping until around 8 pm, so why don't we head out for dinner at seven and then we catch a show or have a few more drinks."

Suddenly, her phone vibrated in her purse and she felt hot panic.

"Alright, I'll be back at seven." Angel turned and began to walk away. "Have a good sleep, Karen."

"Thanks, see you at seven." She closed the hotel room door and dug for the phone. When she flipped it open, she saw the message from Marty. She sat down on the bed and began to text back.

4

Shamus swiped at the bit of drool spilling from the corner of his mouth. He was slouched over in his easy chair, tucked in beside him, the crystal tumbler still holding a finger of scotch. He must have jammed it in there when he felt himself nodding off. Pinching the glass between his thumb and index finger, he pulled it out and placed it on the table, then started to stand up.

His neck ached; the muscles had bound up in knots from the awkward position he'd been sleeping. He was in his office. Luckily no one had come knocking, seen him drooling like a four-year-old, or worse. No one had seen the fear he felt as he stumbled up the path to get away from Jimmy Poe.

That was the truth. Poe had scared him. Called him for what he really was.

Shut the fuck up, I'm no coward.

He brought his right hand up and massaged his neck. As he did this, he leaned over the desk and opened a book that held a number of business cards. In it he found the number he was looking for, and then reached into the second drawer of his desk. In that were a bunch of cell phones, Shamus had no idea how many. Donald brought a fresh supply when he alerted him that they were getting low; getting low was less than eight.

Holding the business card up, he pulled out a fresh cell phone, punched in the number, and pressed the call button. Placing it against his ear, he continued to massage the side of his neck. The phone began to ring.

"Hello, Chinook Tundra, Bob Stewman speaking."

"Bob, how are you?"

There was a pause, then a panicked, "Hello, Gordon."

"How are things progressing up there?"

"Good. Everything's set."

"When are you guys rolling?"

"Umm, we are setting up "T" times now. They're saying the road should be open by late tomorrow afternoon or evening, so I'm sending trucks over to begin loading up in the morning."

"What about my boy?"

"He should be in the fourth convoy."

"Good, glad to hear it. So things are progressing well. Thanks, Bob, I'll be in touch."

"Okay Gor…"

Shamus cut him off and pushed the end button. Then he snapped the flip phone in half and tossed it into the garbage. He placed the business card back into the flip book and pulled out a new phone.

5

When Angel opened the hotel room door, Scott grabbed her and pulled her in, kissing her full on the mouth. She reached down and cupped his crotch, grinding up against him, pushing her tongue into his mouth. In turn he reached up under her shirt and grabbed one of her breasts. They never spoke a word, instead pulling at each other's clothes and working their way to the bed. He could smell the liquor on her breath and this only turned him on further.

A half an hour later, they lay side by side, completely naked, the bedding crumpled on the floor. She was smoking, Scott was staring at her intently. The present she'd bought lay on the night table. "I love watching you work."

"Out there, or in here?" she asked.

"Both."

"I've got to meet her at 7 pm."

He reached over and grabbed a baggy off the table.

"You're going to need this."

Angel grabbed it out of his hand and held it up, just above her bare breasts. In the bag was a bottle, and on it was the word Rohypnol. Rohypnol, also known as Rufie, often referred to as the date rape drug.

"So tonight's the night."

"I got the call five minutes before you came back."

"We've got two more hours, lover, and I'm still very horny."
She climbed on top of him, crushed out her cigarette and got busy.

***

Chapter 12—Wormwell Theory

1

ACADIA MINE AIRFIELD
16 Hours before Winter Road 2013 Opens

Professor Nick Anderson climbed from the Bell 407 helicopter. When he ducked his head, the prop blast, hardened by the -45 degrees temperature, slashed at his face like a razor blade. As the snow churned, it bit into his skin abrasively, turning his exposed cheeks flush red. Protecting his face as best he could, he turned back and pulled his kit bag from the cargo hold, slung it over his shoulder, then his laptop and camera bag. Out of the corner of his watering eye, he could see a small pickup truck waiting at the edge of the airfield.

The prop whirred about, chopping through the air, exclaiming over and over in a baritone **Whup—whup—whup,** while the turbine whistled in a high contrasting whir. Nick closed the door on the helicopter and gave the pilot a thumbs up. The pilot returned the signal, said something into his mouthpiece, and waited for Nick to clear the props. Lugging his gear against the Western wind was a task. He tried to protect his face and keep from dropping the three bags he balanced on both shoulders; once he was clear, the chopper began to whine and lift off. In a matter of seconds it was up and gone, bound for god knew where.

Nick could care less if the chopper was heading for Santa's Workshop; he only knew that he had been plucked from a top secret research project in Worcester, Massachusetts and while he was wasn't heading up that particular venture, he was extremely pissed off to be here. Lupania had a hand in government projects, and it just so happened that the CEO of Acadia knew the President of the company Nick worked for.

For two years he'd been underground developing a smaller scale version of the Hadron Collider in Geneva. Smaller, yes, but far more powerful, and though it wasn't public knowledge, they had surpassed the Swiss and they weren't sharing, at least not yet. Nick was a physicist, who held numerous degrees, including three years as a bone hound working in Coahuila, Mexico. He had no idea why his boss, Doctor Lance Milgaard, came in that morning and told him to pack his gear, but he really didn't argue. Lance didn't take shit from subordinates, but Nick Anderson wasn't really a subordinate, at least not intellectually. Nick knew if Lance was sending him north, he had a good reason, but that didn't stop him from bitching a little.

"Did they say why they needed me, Lance?"

"No, but this came from the top, and I generally don't question the orders of those who hold the purse strings on my research projects."

"I can't tell you I'm happy about this. We're making great headway here. What the hell could be so important?"

"I don't know, Nick. When I say this came from the top, I mean the roof. All I know is that I was on the phone with the Executive Director of Lupania Corp this morning and he was very explicit that they needed someone with a background in both paleontology and quantum physics. You're the only bone hound I know. Maybe they found a big Mammoth in the ice or something that requires one of the Country's top scientists. Whatever it is, you need to get there and get it done, because we need your ass back here."

"Now you're just patronizing me."

"It's what I do best, Nick, but that doesn't mean it isn't true. I got you booked to fly in three hours. Dress warm."

Dress warm, he mused, stumbling toward the pickup truck. His face felt as though it were made of clay, and he could already feel his body slowing down. He wanted to run, but the kit back was roughly 60 pounds and the laptop and camera bag swung from his body haphazardly like opposing clock pendulums. He was doing everything he could to keep from landing on his ass. When he closed the distance, the driver opened the vehicle door and came forward.

"Professor Anderson." The man stuck out a gloved hand. "I'm Chase Fenwick, Chief of Operations here at Acadia. Welcome."

Nick took his hand. "Thank you, Nick will do just fine."

2

The laboratory was set up as a temporary home for the fossils they'd found and removed from the chamber. Each creature was set upon its own table, a plastic drop cloth laid out beneath them, and all skeletons were complete; Ronny Fraser had seen to that. He and Allison were waiting for the arrival of the man Lars had requested. Ronny was fidgety, nervous and half expecting the arriving scientist was going to tear them all a new asshole for moving the fossils out of the chamber. The allotropes were one thing, but these things were another matter altogether, and he was now absolute in his belief that they were not of this world. He wondered what laws they'd broken by moving this discovery out of its natural environment into the lab without alerting anyone. He waited, Allison a few feet away, tapping away on her keypad, completely oblivious to the sour malignance brewing in his guts.

3

"Normally I'd be inclined to give you a history lesson about Acadia, it's kind of been my SOP whenever I pick up a dignitary, but under the circumstances I think it might just be better to ask you what you know, then fill in the gaps." Chase was working his way up the road as he spoke, occasionally stealing a glance at his passenger.

"You want to know what I know," Nick chuckled.

"Yeah."

"Well, I know nothing. I was told that you guys found something. That you needed someone with a background in quantum physics and paleontology, which is about the tallest order you can make. That's what I know, Chase, nothing else. So, if you want to fill in a few of the blanks, I'd be grateful."

Chase stopped the truck at a stop sign and a giant mining truck, known as a 777, passed through the intersection. Just below the STOP sign, on the same post, a small red aluminum sign read: **MINING EQUIPMENT HAS RIGHT OF WAY.**

"That's a monster fucking dump truck," Nick said.

"It's a triple 7 rock truck, not the biggest, but it gets the job done." He gripped the wheel, sighed, and said, "I'll tell you what I can in the next ten minutes, after that we'll be below ground and you will have a pretty good idea why your presence was requested here."

4

The service elevator opened and Nick was still digesting what Chase had told him, which was, in his opinion, very little. As they walked down the corridor towards the lab, Nick noted the lack of staff anywhere in this section. The walls in the hall were covered with corrugated steel, the same kind used to make culverts and drainage pipes. Ahead, a set of double doors affixed with a crash bar waited on it, a sign read: **AUTHORIZED PERSONNEL ONLY!**

Just as Nick finished reading, the door swung open and out stepped a small man wearing a white environmental suit. Under his arm were two plastic wrapped bags, which Nick surmised to be environmental suits.

"Hi, Ronny, we're here," Chase greeted, then turned to Nick. "Nick, this is Ron Fraser, our resident geologist. Ronny, this is Professor Nick Anderson."

Ronny looked at him queerly, a flash of recognition crossed his face, and he stuck out his hand. "Professor Anderson, it's very nice to meet you. Didn't you write an article for 'Scientific Today' about dark matter?

"Yes I did."

"I still have a copy of that article. You put forth a fascinating theory, Professor."

"Thank you, and as I told Chase, Nick will do just fine. I'm a pretty informal guy, while the Professor thing bodes well on a resume, I prefer to be on a first name basis with the people I work with."

"Okay then, Nick, Chase told me you were around six foot so this suit should fit you just fine." He handed over the plastic wrapped suit and another to Chase. "I guess we'll start in the lab, then work our way down to the chamber, if that's okay with you, Chase."

"It's your tour, Ronny. I'll follow along with Nick here." Chase unwrapped the plastic package and Nick did the same.

"Joining us today will be my assistant Allison Perch. She's inside the lab now going over some of the measurements we've taken from the fossils."

"Okay, are we going to be wearing oxygen?" Nick was pulling the white environmental suit over his shoulders and felt it tug at his crotch when he slid his arms into the sleeves, but once that was done, the constriction in his groin area relaxed a bit.

"We ran a full scan for contaminants and everything came back clean, but on the side of caution, everyone is still going to wear full face shield and oxygen tank. If you'll follow me into the clean room, we'll kit up there and fit each other with masks and tanks."

Chase zipped up his suit. "I guess we're ready," Chase said.

Ronny nodded and pushed the crash bar on the double door, exposing a large plastic curtain with a single slit down the middle. Overhead fluorescent lights hummed against the drone of air exchangers. "Follow me," Ronny said, waved the heavy plastic curtain aside, and stepped through. The two men followed.

The clean room looked more like a locker room, but Nick guessed that they'd put it together rather hastily. On the wall hung four oxygen tanks fitted with harnesses and beside them wrapped in plastic were brand new full-face gas masks. To the right of that were a number of boxes that read: **Environ-Safe! H2S Ready!**

"I know I am probably telling you something you've heard a thousand times before, but safety protocol insists that I instruct you to ensure that your mask is air tight and properly fitted. You can do this by placing your hand over the air intake and inhaling. Continue to hold your breath for five seconds, keeping a tight seal on the intake to check for leaks." Ronny placed his mask over his face and demonstrated.

Five seconds elapsed and Ronny released his hand. "Good seal."

"No problem, Ron," Nick snickered. "And for the record: this is the ten thousandth time I've heard it." He unwrapped the mask, fitted it to his face, and then, raising a single thumb, added, "Good seal."

"Welcome to Acadia," Allison greeted as they entered the lab in single file, but Nick hardly heard her. His eyes were transfixed on the first table and the creature laid out on it.

"Holy fuck," he muttered.

"There are five complete fossils, as best we can tell, and two incomplete," Ronny said from behind. Nick moved in closer, examining the fossil on the first table. This one was approximately nine feet long from the tip to tip. Ronny continued, "Allison and I have spent the last 24 hours laying the bones out in what we think is the correct order, but you can be the judge of that. It also appears that these creatures were bio-mechanical, there are parts on them that appear fabricated. You'll notice the tubes."

Nick's eyes traced down the spine and on either side of the skeleton's back were two tubes, similar to that of a vacuum cleaner hose that stretched from the rear of the skull and into what looked like a plate on the creature's back. The 'tube,' as Ronny called it, had decomposed or rusted over time and had holes in it, but the intact fossil itself was in astounding shape. Nick had never seen a fossil in such good shape. "Why did you say bio-mechanical, Ron? How do we know this thing is not just a robot of some sort?"

"We ruled that it is bio-mechanical by the teeth on the skull and the nails. We took minor scrapings and found high concentrates of protein. We also found micro-organisms, long dead of course, in those samples, insect-like creatures. Allison, can you?" Ronny motioned to his assistant, who clicked on her laptop, which projected an image on a screen they had set against the far wall. On it, a magnified picture of what appeared to be an upside down dead insect, five legs on each side. To Nick, it looked somewhat like an aphid.

"I'd hazard a guess that it is their version of a dust mite," Ronny told him.

Nick rubbed his chin. "I'd guess that you are probably right and you've certainly won me over with the simplest proof that these organisms are certainly, or were certainly, living entities, not mechanical. Did your sampling bring up any other cosmopolitan guests?"

Chase laughed at this, Ronny and Allison did not, because they knew the term Nick was using was scientific.

"No, but we've only had a few days. As I said, Allison and I have been up for the last 24 hours laying out the fossils in the manner in which we think they are constructed."

"It looks as though you've done a good job," Nick said.

"The first was the hardest," Allison said. "It took us approximately nine hours."

"After we figured out where all the parts of the first one went, the others were a lot easier," Ronny said. "The incomplete ones are in the back of the room. Those are the ones we have been taking samples from, where we got the pictures of the mites."

Nick brought his eyes back down to the first fossil and felt giddy excitement dancing in his stomach. Only a few hours ago, he was angry that they had pulled him out of Worcester, now he was torn as to whether or not he would want to go back. "So we have five intact, two semi-intact. Any theory as to what might have happened to the remainder of the fossils, Ron?"

"Acadia Mine is built on a lake, as are most of the mines in the region. An uneducated guess is that the chamber we found them in was flooded by water and that maybe they were flushed out over time with the constant freeze and thaw."

"I'd like to see this chamber."

"You will," Chase said. "As soon as you're satisfied with what you've seen here, Ronny is going show you another room where we have stored the allotropes and then we'll go down to the chamber."

Nick smiled and looked around at all of them. “I’m going to say this right now and get it out of the way. This is exciting stuff, folks. Probably the biggest discovery of the 21st century.”

The smile was infectious.

Ronny sighed nervously and said, “I was afraid…”

Chase frowned at him.

“Afraid of what?” Nick asked.

“That we’d ignored some kind of protocol.”

“From what I see here, Ron, you and Allison have done a first rate job of getting these fossils into a stable environment. Although I would recommend that we use a lower level of lighting. The fluorescent lighting may or may not speed up the decay of these creatures. As to breaking protocol, I don’t think there is such a thing in a case like this.” He walked over and patted Ronny’s shoulder. “I’m impressed.”

Ronny glanced up through the shield of his mask. “Really?”

“Yeah, really, now how ‘bout you guys show me that chamber before I piss my pants.”

Everyone laughed.

5

The chamber, emptied of what content they could remove, now appeared the size of a school auditorium. They had not removed the thousands of diamonds encrusted in the walls. Truth be told, they hadn’t dared, but they had cleaned up almost everything from the floor. A crew had been brought in, more non-disclosure documents signed, and the work began. Chase oversaw the removal of the Allotropes, reassigned the ten-person work crew to the ‘F Wing’ of the Mine, which was designated for new digs that were considered sensitive. He also sweetened the non-disclosure contract with the same $10,000 bonus given to the crew sent on leave when they first discovered the pipe. The only difference was, this crew was here to stay, and any further work required would be carried out by them. None of them had seen the creatures. Those had been moved to the lab by Chase, Ron, and Allison before the crew was assembled and went to work.

When Nick Anderson saw the chamber, he couldn’t believe it. His work in Worcester seemed almost trivial compared to this and coincidentally he believed that there was a loose connection. He shone the light across the chamber and at the rear, something caught his eye.

Nick moved toward it and the others followed; his mouth hung open comically, his eyes wide and cartoonish. "Wow!"

"Any ideas?" Chase asked.

Standing at the back of the chamber were two rectangular shapes side by side to a uniform height of approximately 15 feet. Set against each other like dominoes only a few feet apart, the two plates gave off a mild blue glow that could almost be mistaken for a trick of the eye. Behind that, another thirty feet in, at the back of the chamber, the wall was etched in an octagon-like fashion.

"Do you know what this might be," Nick wasn't asking. "Holy shit. Do you know what this might be?"

"What?" Ronny asked.

"I think it's a wormwell."

"A wormwell?" Chase looked confused.

"You mean like a wormhole?" Ronny asked.

"Yes, but slightly different and, to be honest, completely theoretical."

"I think I understand," Ronny said.

Allison looked on.

"Okay, Nick, I'm lost," Chase said.

Nick turned toward them and as they gathered around him in a semi-circle, he took a deep breath and began. "All of you have understand what a wormhole is?"

Allison and Ronny nodded, Chase shook his head.

"A wormhole is a theoretical portal that connects two points in space. For a long time scientists have theorized that getting from one point to another in the universe does not necessarily mean traveling in a straight line." Nick stopped for a second and walked over to where a work cart sat with blank inventory sheets used. He snatched a sheet of the cart and resumed. "Think of this single sheet of paper as representative of the universe and at opposite ends are the two points in the universe you want to travel to. For the sake of argument, let's say the distance between these two points is 500 light years. This has always presented a problem for travel in space. The theory of wormholes is to abandon the preconceived notion that space travel must be linear."

Nick folded the sheet of paper over into the shape of a "C" and continued. "The two points in space are the same, but now the wormhole is a direct tunnel, which can run up or down and shortens the distance significantly. That in its shortest form is the theory of the wormhole."

"I thought you said wormwell," Chase said.

"I did and that is a theory I have been working on for about the last six years. Up until this point it has been pure hypothesis, but considering this discovery, I'd say that it is quite probable. I'll explain that theory to you, but how much oxygen do we have left?"

Ronny checked the gauge on his tank. "Fifteen minutes. We should get back to the clean room and discuss our next move after you view the last room."

6

The storage facility they'd built actually consisted of two 53-foot sea containers individually brought down into the mine on the back of a modified rock truck. Once the containers were set side by side, they were bolted together, then separating walls were cut out using torches. This storage area now held 17 crates, each being four feet square filled with the new precious allotropes harvested from the chamber.

Nick held one of the diamonds in his hand, turning it over and marveling at its beauty. "You think this is a natural occurrence, Ron?"

"I'm not sure. It is occurring inside the chamber, which we are pretty sure is artificial, so I guess it's not a natural occurrence of the core. But whatever that chamber does, perhaps it generated so much energy that diamonds are a by-product of that anomaly. They're not artificial, these are genuine allotropes."

Nick placed the diamond back into the crate and looked around the room. "How much raw product does a mine of this size usually yield in a day's work?"

"On a good day we harvest between 900 grams and 1.5 kilograms. To put that in layman terms, roughly around a large coffee can," Chase said.

"That's it? All these millions spent on manpower and equipment and you only take about a coffee can a day."

"I know it doesn't sound like much, Nick, but we are talking about diamonds and you can put a lot of diamonds in a coffee can."

"Then this is a hell of a haul."

"This is the mother-load."

7

He was standing at the front of the conference room. The same conference room used to brief Damien Lars on the discovery of the second pipe. Sitting at the table were Vice President Sal Godwin, Chase,

Ronny, and Allison. Chase was working with the computer, typing away until the projector cast the image upon the screen set behind Damien Lars. It read: **SECURE SATELITE TRANSMISSION TO OCCURR IN:** A counter was counting down from five minutes, 12 seconds.

Nick waited, feeling a little nervous and fidgety. He always felt this way before a briefing and this was probably going to be a benchmark in his career. He shuffled the papers, straightened and stacked them, then looked back at the countdown. Four minutes, 10 seconds. He wondered what Milgaard was going to say when he would ask to be transferred out of Worcester to head up this site.

He's going to shit himself in disbelief.

But that is exactly what Nick intended to do. The project in Worcester was called **THE CHASM PROJECT**. This might actually advance the science of Chasm, which had managed to create small black holes in the underground facility lasting milliseconds. Up until a few days ago, Nick believed that they were on the cusp of the greatest scientific discovery of all time.

Now?

He's going to shit himself. Nick smiled.

"Three minutes," Chase said.

Nick had gone back to the clean room, and he began formulating what he was going to need, what he had seen, and simultaneously, as promised, he spoke to them about the theory of the wormwell.

"A wormwell is basically a machine that gives us the ability to open up a wormhole and control it. In theory, going into a wormhole is an extremely dangerous venture, as we are unable to predict when or how they will open or close. If you get caught in a wormhole that is closing, you would be crushed by the gravity alone. Or worse, an unchartered wormhole could lead into the core of a sun or maybe to the bottom of a lake. This is all speculation, mind you, but let's say the creatures in the lab have the technology to use wormholes for travel. So they launch a machine, 'a wormwell,' into a wormhole and then use it as an anchor point. A seed of sorts that is now planted in the place they want to travel."

"Why would they come through and close it behind them?" Allison asked.

"Again speculation, because we haven't achieved anything like this, but my guess is that these beings are not able to control the wormwell remotely. My guess is that there is likely too much interference caused by the energy inside the wormhole and also taking into account that the destination could be 1000 light years away. So, maybe they have to send through a crew to set the anchor up. Maybe that's what these creatures did. Travelers who came through and found themselves submerged in a lake. Possibly they drowned."

"Who would get into a machine in the off chance they'd be killed?" Allison asked, while Ronny and Chase sat mute.

"You're thinking in terms of our society, our values. We don't know where these travelers came from, what their societal values are. They could have the same structure as a hive of bees or ants where the few are sacrificed for the many."

"The Spock theory," Ronny giggled.

This brought about laughter, even from Nick, but when it died down, he continued.

"So, you send out a probe or several probes each with a crew whose job it is to anchor itself at a point in time and create a functioning wormwell, which will open a doorway that can now be controlled."

"Unless you end up at the bottom of a lake and drown," Chase said and the group laughter echoed in the back of Nick's mind as he focused on the satellite countdown, which was now down to 10 seconds.

"Alright, here we go," Sal Godwin said.

The screen shuddered and then read: **Communication Established.**

Then before them, Damien Lars spoke.

"Hello, Professor Anderson, my name is Damien Lars. By now you have met my VP, my Chief Engineer, my Chief Geologist and his Assistant, so let's dispense with the formalities right off. Please call me Damien."

"Alright, Damien and as I have told your staff here, my first name is Nick."

"Perfect. So what can you tell me Nick, and what are your recommendations to this point?"

Nick looked around the room.

"I recommend that the mine be closed. That a team be assembled and that the appropriate authorities be contacted so that we can document and investigate this discovery further."

"What? Close the mine," Chase interrupted.

"Let him finish, Chase." Damien said flatly.

"I have toured the site, Damien, and I believe that this is going to change just about everything you could imagine in this world. I would say without a doubt that we have established intelligent life beyond our own world, intelligent life that has left behind a piece of its technology. I'd also say that the Acadia Mine has reaped a harvest of diamonds far beyond what it would have in a couple centuries, so from a profit perspective I'd say you folks are well into the black. So, that really leaves us with the task at hand and that task has to be a scientific one, which will include government officials. As I told your staff here, I don't know of any specific protocol laid down when finding extraterrestrial life, but what has been done to this point could very well violate a number of trade agreements."

Lars considered Nick's proposal, then said, "I'm afraid we won't be able to do that, Nick. Shutting down Acadia at this point in the season would be disastrous, not only for the employees who work here, but we are about to start the Ice Road Resupply, Even if I agreed with you, we are going to need the fuel and supplies to keep the mine operational, even for scientific purposes. Beyond that, I can't just hand out a thousand pink slips without some sort of preparation or notice. We'll need time to prepare, I'll need to consult with Lupania Corporation, and of course there will be lawyers and red tape."

"How long would it take you to start working toward a shutdown?"

"We could start consulting immediately, but until we know what we are dealing with and what action must be taken regarding this discovery, I couldn't give you a definitive answer. I am reaching out to government officials about our situation as it is, but this has to be done with a certain amount of sensitivity. All of this has to be handled quietly and everything said in this room must be confidential. Sal, I want non-disclosure contracts for everyone, including yourself, drawn up immediately."

"Yes, Damien." Sal scribbled on a pad.

"By tomorrow, there will be trucks coming north with supplies for Acadia and Meanook. We need the fuel most of all to keep this place up and running; it's our life-blood, Nick, and I can't stop that. Never mind all the contracts and negotiations we've made regarding the Winter Road. So, shutting down is out of the question, which leaves us to discuss alternative plans."

Nick looked over at Chase, who stared right back, his face red and angry. "You are an asshole," that stare said. "A two-faced asshole."

"How long does the re-supply take, Damien?" Nick asked.

"Between six and eight weeks, depending on the weather and the strength of the ice."

Nick glanced around the room. "Taking into account the

circumstances we find ourselves in, I would suggest that the management of Acadia start working toward a complete shutdown. Whatever, or however long that takes, should be at the discretion of management, but I suggest that it be done as expediently as possible."

"Okay, we knew this was a possibility. I will start speaking with Lupania Corp about that very thing. In the meantime, what do you need?"

"I am going to request my boss, Professor Lance Milgaard, assemble a team dedicated to investigation of both the chamber and the fossilized creatures. In the interim, I would ask that your original group be put at my disposal for immediate investigation."

"Consider that effective immediately. You folks now fall under the supervision of Professor Anderson until further notice. Any questions?'

Ronny and Allison both smiled and shook their heads.

Chase looked wounded. "So, I am working for him now."

"Yes, Chase," Lars responded. "Is this going to be a problem?"

"You're not working for me," Nick interrupted. "You are part of my team."

"Yeah, okay." Chase was unconvinced.

"Alright then, we all have plenty of work to do. I will sign off for now. I want a video transcript of this meeting sent via blast transmission to Lupania in Paris. In the meantime, Sal, you get to work on those contracts and Nick I would like a carbon of your personnel requests. You folks take care, I will be back there in four days. Anything else?"

The room was silent.

"Alright then, good luck. Signing off." The old man sat there expressionless for a second and then he was gone, replaced by the Lupania Corporation Logo and the words: **SATELITE COMMUNICATION CLOSED.**

Chase sat quietly in his seat, digesting what had just happened. Up until recently, he had been Damien Lars's right hand man. He could feel that shifting now and it stung. As the others got up and milled about, shaking hands and exchanging pleasantries, he stared into the distance.

"Chase?" Nick was standing over him. "I didn't come here to play politics or run over anyone's ambitions."

Chase glanced up.

Nick extended a hand and Chase took it.

"Alright," Chase said.

"This is a huge deal, Chase. This is going to change everything." Nick leaned in a little closer and whispered. "So, please understand me. If you get in the way of this, start trouble or attempt to play politics, I will crush you without batting an eye. You understand?"

Chase nodded and released his hand.

"Good."

***

Chapter 13—Working for the Man

1

Maggie had no idea what she was getting herself into when she agreed to go drinking with Angel, but there was a feeling of guilt, which had settled into the pit of her stomach. She tried to reason it away, but the idea that Marty was out there, possibly in harm's way, didn't help her case much. She was long past the anger and she had already forgiven him. Her reasoning was that passing time with Angel would only speed up the process and alleviate the boredom that was driving her insane and feeding the terror. So she shoved the guilt down and picked up her cell phone to send a quick text: Miss you a lot, seeing the sights, wish you were here.

She waited.

"Come on, Marty, I really need to hear from you."

Nothing.

It was 6:30 pm. In half an hour, Angel would be at the door and until she returned, any response, assuming he did respond, would go unanswered. This only added to her anxiety. *Maybe I should cancel,* she thought. *Yeah sure, I'll just stay in this room and go out of my mind waiting for a call that might not come for god knows how long.* This internal argument only elevated her anxiety. *Why is this happening? What the hell did I do to deserve this bullshit?* She went into the bathroom, set the cell phone down, and proceeded to get cleaned up before Angel arrived.

2

Garney was making his way back from the dispatch office when he met Sack coming in the opposite direction. He was on his way to wake up Marty. Dispatch had given him the go-ahead and he'd just gotten out of Bob Stewman`s office. Stewman, for reasons he couldn't explain, had some kind of special interest in Marty. As he was working his way down the hall with a dispatch bill in hand, Stewman stopped him.

"Garney, can I have a minute of your time?"

"Uh, sure thing, Bob. What's up?"

"In my office." Stewman looked serious.

"Sure." Garney followed him into the little office, which held a desk that was littered with seven separate piles paperwork; there was barely enough real estate left to accommodate a cup of coffee.

Stewman sat down behind the desk and motioned to the seat in front of the desk. "Take a seat and close the door." Stewman smiled thinly. Garney pushed the door closed and sat down in the folding chair, which groaned under his weight. He felt weary about being pulled into Stewman's office; Garney wasn't comfortable with the suits.

"Got your work cut out there for you, eh, Bob."

Stewman nodded. "If I had a match, it would be gone in a minute."

"So, what's up? I'm just going to get Marty up so we can head over to the tank farm to load."

"Carly told me you guys have a "T" time."

"Yes sir, we depart at 19:00 hours."

"Doing the Ingraham and the Inuksuk at night. Well, that should be a little easier on the new guy."

Garney laughed. "Well, what he doesn't see won't hurt him."

Stewman chuckled. What they were referring to was the fact that both the Ingraham and the Inuksuk could be very intimidating to a new driver. At night, the treacherous twists and turns wouldn't be as distinct, and that was a running joke for the Vets. Stewman's grin faded and Garney readied himself for whatever it was he was about to say. "I need a favor, Garney."

"What kind of favor?"

"I need you to keep an eye on this guy and nurse him along."

"Carly already briefed me, Bob, that's what I'm doing."

"Yeah, I know, but I wanted to make sure that this guy gets extra coverage. I know that we all have the best intentions, but when a driver chokes or acts like an ass, you guys usually cut them loose pretty quick."

"It's a closed track, some guys don't get that, but I think Marty will be fine. He handles a truck alright and takes instruction without problems. I'll do what I can. Okay?"

Stewman smiled again. "Ì appreciate that, Garney."

"No problem, we're all on the same team here. Yes Sir, uh huh, yep."

"Okay. Well, that's it, I just wanted to make sure we were on the same page. Go get your load. Who are you running with beside Croft?"

"Carly said Spence and Merv."

"Good, three vets and one rookie. Put him in the middle," Stewman said.

"That's the plan." Garney stood up. "No worries, Bob, I'll take care of the greenhorn. Uh huh, yes sir, yep." He gave Stewman one of his patented toothy grins. "Anything else, Bob?"

"Nope, that pretty much covers it."

That had been only a minute ago. As he strode toward Sack, he couldn't help but wonder what all the interest was in Marty. The first call he received came from Chinook's planner, Evan Jaffrey, who contacted him while he was still in Alaska. Jaffrey was the one who usually reigned in the wayward drivers every year and Marty certainly wasn't the first rook Garney had taken under his wing, but to call him up like this made Garney wonder what was so important. His thoughts were broken when he caught the look on Sack's face.

"Sack, my brother."

Sack looked up from the ground, a scowl hanging on his jowls. "Hey, Garney." He reached into his breast pocket, removed a cigarette, stabbed it between his lips and lit it. "They fucked me, Garney! Took away my Super B and put me on freight, for Chrissake. They got me pulling a goddamned van! A fucking freight hauler! What the fuck! I'm going in to tell dispatch to ram it straight up their ass. They even took me off Meanook and threw me on Acadia. That's a hundred and thirty less a trip! Never mind that I'll be dropping and hooking, which means frozen brakes. Well, fuck this!"

Garney reached out and seized Sack by the shoulder. "Hold up, my brother, You want to let some steam out of the tea kettle before you boil over and regret what you're going to say." Garney leaned over. "Can I have one of them smokes?"

Sack grunted and pulled out the pack. "Sure."

Garney popped a smoke into his mouth and Sack lit it. "Did they say why they switched you? Wasn't Jim Gillespie supposed to haul freight to Acadia?"

"Gillespie had to go home. His wife is sick or his kid or I don't know... Fucking freight, Garney, I don't do freight. I'm a tanker yanker!"

"That you are, my brother, and an asset to Chinook. So, let's finish our smoke and take a deep breath. How's that Lonestar of yours running these days?"

"Okay, but..."

"I saw you had it in the shop. Everything okay?"

"The rear diff is getting a little long in the tooth, probably be switching it out in the spring. What does that have to do with it?"

"Does dispatch know about that?"

No, just me and that kid mechanic, Walter."

"Well, my brother, rather than go off the deep end, I suggest you go in and negotiate a better deal. I bet if you ask to speak with Old Gus, they'll sweeten the pot a bit and in the end hauling a 53-foot van up and down the ice will probably see you through to the end of the season rather than blowing a diff pulling loaded tankers."

Sack took a puff on his cigarette. "You think they'd consider bumping the dollar amount?"

Garney smiled. "The Mine needs their shit, the Company needs you. Yeah, I think they'd play ball, why not? But you gotta play it cool, Sack. Go see dispatch, tell them you'll do the run after you speak with Gus, but only until. Gus will listen."

"I gotta tell Walter to shut his mouth, though."

"I'll talk to Walter. You talk to dispatch and don't threaten to quit. That shit only goes so far, Sack. Besides, you and I both know that you have too many ex-wives to quit." Garney winked and patted Sack's shoulder.

Sack smiled. "You sure have a way of talking a guy down, Garney."

"Yep, my brother, I should have been a marriage counselor. Think of all the dough I would have saved yuh."

"Okay. Thanks, and you're gonna talk to Walter?"

"I'm on my way right now." Garney crushed out his cigarette and took a detour toward the maintenance building. Before he did, he saw Marty was up and around, checking over his rig. That was good; it would save him the few minutes he was about to lose with Walter.

3

Evan Lake
20 Kilometers: North of Acadia Mine

The sun moved across the northern sky with the disquiet of a town stranger who didn't feel quite welcome. At this time of year, north of the 60th parallel, the sun rode the edge of the horizon and gave the impression—even in mid-morning—that it was late in the day.

Axe was out on the ice with his flooding crew. There were six of them in all, three were just kids hired on temporarily for the season. Then there were his two regular guys: Lonny and Vincent. Lonny drove the water truck, while Vincent cracked the whip on the young men. They were drilling holes in the ice, strengthening it before the first convoy was scheduled to cross sometime this evening. Evan Lake was the second largest crossing, approximately 95 kilometers from start to finish. The distance would take a northbound convoy approximately two hours and 50 minutes to cross at a maximum posted speed of 30 km/h. This section of the ice had been giving them trouble. The problem area they were working was called a pressure ridge. This was caused when opposing plates of ice butted against each other. When this happened, the intense pressure would cause the ice to heave, forming a ridge that looked like a miniature mountain range. These ridges could rise up as high as eight feet. As a result, the adjacent ice would become brittle and had to be reinforced and monitored regularly. While the others pulled out their ice augers and sump pumps, Axe removed the item that had earned him his nickname. It was an old fireman's ax. It was weathered, pocked, barely a fleck of its former fire engine red coat remained, but not a single flake of rust etched the polished blade.

As the workers positioned their gear, Axe surveyed the flood site and checked the holes they'd drilled earlier that morning. Vincent, his crew supervisor, was already barking out orders to the newbies. "Get those triangles out," he called to one man, then to another. "Romeo, get your butt over here with that auger."

Axe chopped away at one of the holes. The ice was too thick to penetrate, so he yelled back to Vincent, "We'll need the auger for this one."

"You can't chop it out? You losing your touch, Axe," Vincent prodded, then to another of the new guys. "You, Gilligan, what's your name again?"

"My name is..."

"Ah, forget it, your name is Gilligan from here in. Slide that pump over by Romeo and give him a hand on that auger. Forget about your woman and that water can! Today you're working for the man!" And with that, Vincent pushed the play button on the big boom box he had on the tailgate of the work truck. Suddenly their party was joined by the melodic voice of Roy Orbison.

Axe found a hole and swung in a downward arc, cracking through the membrane of ice in one hit. Water gushed up through the hole, then fell back again. "Okay, Vince, this one's open, let's get a pump on it!"

"You heard the man! What's your name, kid? Ah, forget it, I'm calling you Traffic. Grab a pump and get over to the Axe man, don't make him come to you."

The kid laying out the traffic triangles bolted across the ice toward the truck while the one named Gilligan complained, "Shit, man, that's old guy music. Don't you have any Eminem or Nine Inch Nails?"

"I have no M&M's or nine inch nails. What I have is a size 11 boot that will go straight up your ass if you ever take the name of Roy Orbison in vain again. Traffic, get your ass in gear, don't make the Axe man come to you. That, my little friend, would be a very bad move."

Axe grinned, having heard Vincent's song and dance a time or ten before. It never got old.

Vincent Gole was a tall thin native man of 55 who gave up the drink in his 30's after surviving a horrific car accident. That was the moment of his epiphany, he told Axe. "I wasn't even driving, but when I woke up I had a scratch on my nose while all three of my friends were dead. Imagine that, here I was with a scratch no worse than if I'd tangled with an old tomcat. I knew then, Axe, knew that the Creator had reached out with his powerful hand and cut me a solid. Didn't need any AA either, no sir. I got the biggest intervention when my pal Les wrapped his Delta 88 around a bridge pillar, killing himself, Duds, and Shoop."

Vincent was hired onto the flooding crew two weeks after Axe was promoted to supervisor and they hit it off immediately. Although Axe preferred Eminem to Orbison, he would never tell Vincent that. Besides, after a while, you got used to all that "Pretty Woman," "Blue Bayou" music, and just when he began learning the lyrics, Vincent switched it out for Johnny Cash. It wasn't long after, Axe learned the words to "Ring of Fire" or "Boy Named Sue." Vincent called the man in black one righteous dude.

Axe was moving on to the next hole; a can of fluorescent orange spray paint used to mark obstacles in the road bumped around in his parka pocket. To his right, the pressure ridge, which had been giving them so much grief, was a jagged, toothy three-foot wall of ice. It looked somewhat like a miniature rock cliff. Axe inspected the ridge for anything that might be suspect, new cracks or elevation. There didn't appear to be any change. It really wasn't his job anyway, but it always paid to be prudent. While the ice was considered extremely safe for the big rigs that were coming, building and maintaining the road was a different matter altogether. Last season a young girl who had just started driving a water truck went to the bottom of Wolverine Lake, which lay 37 km to the south. Below his feet, the ice cracked and ground as a reminder of the danger.

"It doesn't look that bad," Vincent said beside him.

"It doesn't hurt to keep an eye on it," Axe responded. "Anyway, the profilers will be by later this afternoon to take a look at it and take some depth measurements. In the meantime, we'll drill the holes, flood the shit out of it, and cone the area off. I don't want some jackass breaking up this new layer of ice before it has a chance to take." Lonny, wandered up just as Roy Orbison began belting out "Pretty Woman." "Lon, how's things looking at the other end?"

"There's two spots where there's about a foot and a half of heave. I marked them with some paint," Lonny said.

"That's might get a lot worse," Vincent interjected and barked. "Hey, Traffic, drag that auger of here!" The young man stared dumbfounded, then it suddenly dawned on him that Vincent had assigned him a new nickname and that snapped him out of it. He began dragging the auger across the ice. Gilligan, on the other hand, was oblivious, staring hypnotically into the jet of water gushing from the pump. This made Axe chuckle. They were always scared of Vincent in the beginning, but by the end of the season, the newbies loved him.

"Here comes a Jackass now," Lonny said, pointing in the direction of a white pickup rounding the bend toward them. "Here comes the law."

The pickup was driving too fast for the pressure ridge, but Axe immediately recognized that yelling at this cowboy probably wouldn't accomplish much. The fellow in the pickup was security, likely an ex-cop. These guys controlled the flow of traffic, handed out warnings and suspensions to speeders. Most of them were descent, but occasionally there was an odd asshole who thought he was still a cop. Axe tried not to rub these fellows the wrong way and work with them. He raised a friendly hand to the driver and walked toward the pickup. At his side, his fireman keepsake swung like a pendulum. When he was a little closer, he could see a bald man with a goatee behind the wheel.

"Jesus Christ, get a look at that," Phil Crane mumbled as he took in the big native man walking toward his pickup. He reached over and pushed the button to lower his window and it dropped sluggishly. The outside temperature was -45 Celsius, and Crane guessed that it was affecting the motor's ability to function. He disliked it up here already and unlike Croft, he was going to have to stay the entire season, so as not to raise suspicion. Shamus's orders.

"Hi, you going to be working this sector?" the native man asked.

"Yeah, it looks that way. I'm Phil, Phil Crane."

"Dan Jack, everyone up here calls me Axe." He removed his glove and brought a bare hand up. Crane took it gingerly, shook, then pulled his hand back in the window away from the biting cold. Axe replaced his mitt. "Is this your first year, Phil?"

"Yeah and probably my last. Man, it's fucking cold up here."

"This?" Axe smiled. "This is nice weather. It's going to get colder than this."

Well I'm not a fucking Eskimo, Crane thought, but instead said, "I guess you're more accustomed to the cold than I am."

"Yeah, very true. You'll get used to it, Phil."

Crane smiled. "I doubt it. Anyway, I'm just checking the area out. We should have convoys rolling through here after supper time. Anything you can tell me I haven't been told in the briefings?"

"Well we've been working this pressure ridge and prepping it. The speed through here is 10 km/h from cone to cone, all vehicles. My crew will be working on all the lakes from Acadia down to Corbett Lake, so I guess we'll be crossing paths regularly."

"Gotcha, guess I came in a little hot. Won't happen again. We've got a lot of civilians running around up here. I counted four pickups parked between here and Corbett."

"Yeah, hunters coming out for the caribou and folks coming up to play on their snowmobiles."

"That should make for an interesting mix when the big trucks start rolling."

"The hunters usually bugger off for a few days, they won't pose much of a hassle.

In fact, my brother's hunting on a portage just west of here. You won't see them until they get their quota. The other ones on the snow machines… Well, they'll definitely give you a run for your money."

"Yeah." Crane already knew about the civilians. Pringle told him that all he could do was warn them to slow down. Crane wasn't worried about that, he was thinking about the job and the hand-off when Croft got the package. All the civilians around here meant he'd have to be extra careful about witnesses. He didn't want to have to kill anyone unless it was absolutely necessary. The diamonds were already waiting to be delivered and as far as everyone knew, there was nothing missing, so he really didn't want to draw attention with a body or a missing person. Just the same, he'd have to keep an eye out. "Well, it's nice to meet you, Axe, I'm sure we'll see lots of each over the season. I'm going to check out the rest of my sector."

"Same to you, Phil. We usually brew up a pot of coffee in the back of the truck. If you can handle my 2IC's love of Roy Orbison, you're welcome to join us."

Crane smiled. Roy was now singing "Crying." "I'll catch you guys on the way back maybe."

"Sure thing, or we'll see you down at Corbett. Have a safe ride." Axe stepped back and Crane raised the window, which seemed to labor even harder when closing. The pickup pulled away, the dusting of snow on the ice road crunching beneath its tires. As he rolled past the flooding crew, he raised a hand in gesture and they returned the wave.

"Well," Vincent called, "is he a Barney Fife or a Roscoe P Coltrane?"

"Neither," Axe called back. "As far as I can tell, he seems okay."

"Time will tell." Vincent smiled, then turned his attention back to the crew. "Gilligan, pack up that pump and snap out of it. You look like a Lad who just seen his first set of tatas!"

Axe watched the pickup round the bend and work further north. Before long it was barely visible against the barren white landscape. That would come in handy as the Security lay in wait for speeders with radar gun at the ready.

4

Marty was skittish. In a very short while they would be heading over to the Tank Farm to load up on fuel, and while he was anxious to get this over with, he was also nervous about the job at hand. There were two treacherous roads ahead, the Ingraham and the Inuksuk, then there was the ice. No matter how much everyone proclaimed that the ice was the easiest part, he still felt uneasiness.

He was working his way around the truck and trailers, checking all the items Garney had briefed him on. As he did this, he saw the big man having a smoke with the fellow named Sack. Sack looked angry about something; he was waving his arms around and yelling, but Marty couldn't hear.

Marty watched the discussion break up and went back to banging the trailer tires with his ball peen hammer to make sure none had gone flat.

He could feel Garney looking his way, but when he turned back, the big guy was walking into Chinook's maintenance building. It was a hell of a lot colder today and the wind was whipping through the yard mercilessly.

He could feel that same depression taking hold and tried to shake it off, but that was getting harder to do. He felt so goddamned powerless. Why the fuck had he gone back to Hamilton with Maggie? He could have avoided all of this if he'd just stayed in New York or even Vancouver. Instead he had returned to his hometown to live in his parents' place. He stopped a second and used the back of his sleeve to wipe away the liquid snot dripping out of his nose to keep it from turning into icicles on the three-day moustache he was now sporting. When he did this, the sleeve snagged a hair, pulling painfully at the root. He removed his glove and used the nail on his index finger to scrape the ice out. He hadn't shaved since arriving in YK and the hair on his face, no longer under the threat of a razor, sprung with wild immunity. He supposed he would have a full beard and moustache by week's end.

Hidden inside the bunk, his phone sat turned off and he supposed he should send Maggie a text to let her know he was alright. He would do that before they headed out to load. He wished he could call, but that nagging paranoia about Stewman and the possibility the truck might be bugged was dogging him. It wasn't, but they had bugged his house, and he hadn't even considered this.

He replaced the glove and carried on toward the front of the truck; as he did, he checked the lug nuts on his wheels to make sure they were secure and looked for any indication that they might have loosened off.

How could they have loosened off, he thought. *You haven't moved since yesterday.* Then morosely, *I don't know, maybe they might want to get the fuck out of here just like me.*

He moved around to the driver side of the rig, put his hammer into the jockey box and closed it. The Kenworth rumbled in anticipation with all the other trucks in the yard. "A week, tops," he said aloud, then opened the driver door and climbed inside.

Reaching up, he flipped on the VHF radio, which was set to 13: Chinook's working channel. There was always chatter on this, drivers bitching about waiting, talking about the weather or discussing a favored pastime. He could hear the fellow who introduced himself as Spence chatting it up with another driver he didn't recognize. He listened as he hunted up the cell phone and turned it on.

"All set, Spence?" the unidentified driver asked.

"Yeah, got a T-time," Spence replied.

"Good deal, who you running up with?"

Marty waited as the phone went through an agonizing slow start-up and he scolded himself for not spending a few more dollars on better phones. As he waited, he continued to listen to the banter between Spence and the other fellow.

"Looks, like me, Garney, Merv, and Marty."

"Marty?"

"Marty Croft, Garney's ward," Spence chuckled.

Now Marty listened more attentively.

"Oh yeah, Marty Croft. Quiet fellow, doesn't say much."

"Yep. Garney's training him up. So, I guess we'll see what he's made of tonight."

The phone chimed and then beeped to alert him to an incoming message. He scrolled through the prompts while continuing to listen.

"Well, hopefully he doesn't choke. Herby Randall said that one of his drivers called it quits this morning. No warning, nothing, just up and quit."

Marty found the message and punched it up.

It read:

Miss you lots seeing the sights wish you were here.

Message sent at 6:30 PM EST

He checked the time. It was 5:01 pm. Montreal was two hours ahead of YK.

"Croft seems okay, just quiet. I'm sure Garney will get him up the road without much problem," Spence said.

Marty typed:

Heading North today. First run. May be out of signal for a day or two.

He pushed send.

"Okay, Spence, I'm heading over to the Tank Farm. I'll catch you up the road."

"Sure thing, Olly. Keep the greasy side up."

"You betcha."

Marty waited. A minute passed, then two. Nothing.

5

There was a knock at her room door. Maggie was wearing a black dress that hugged her figure favorably. She opened the door and there stood

Angel, dressed for a night out on the town. She was wearing a solid white dress with a grey sport jacket.

"Wow, you look sexy," Angel said.

Maggie blushed and then smiled. "So do you."

"Ready to go?"

"Yeah, let's go."

Maggie grabbed her clutch purse and followed Angel out of the room. As the door to her hotel room closed and the automatic lock clicked over, the cell phone she'd forgotten in the bathroom chimed to alert of an incoming message. It would be a message that Maggie Croft would never see.

***

Chapter 14—Check out Time

1

Montreal, Quebec

Scott Turcotte waited until the women had departed in a cab before he entered the room to begin his work. Getting into the room didn't require anything other than using the key card Angela had lifted from the bureau during her first visit to Maggie's room. Most hotels issued a second key card and while Scott had the ability to trip the electronic lock, Angela had saved him the hassle.

Standing in the hallway, he glanced both ways, then slipped the card into the slot and waited. The light on the brass plate flashed momentarily green, and then there was an audible click. Taking another quick look down the hall, he pushed the door open and stepped into the room. Before the door snapped shut, he reached around, grabbed the DO NOT DISTURB sign, and put it on the outside handle. The door clicked behind him and he went to work.

The first thing he did was go into the bathroom and relieve himself. As he reached over to flush the toilet, he surveyed the bathroom vanity. Scott stepped over to the counter, which had a number of items on it, including a makeup kit, a brush, a comb, some under arm deodorant, toothbrush, toothpaste, and to the right of those items lay the little flip phone. He was just laying his eyes upon it when it chirped.

"Hello there," Scott said picking up the little phone.

1 New Message, the screen prompted.

Scott pressed the button and read the incoming message aloud, in a mocking tone. "Heading north today. First run. May be out of signal for a day or two."

"Thanks for the update, buddy," he said and proceeded to scroll through all of the messages.

They were just short snippets. Miss you! Seeing the sights. Be safe.

Code, he mused and considered sending back a reply of his own. What could he send that would match this short acknowledgement? Maybe: Be careful, I Love you M. He thought about it for a second, his thumb hovering over the keypad. *Later,* he thought. Or maybe he'd have her send the message. He pocketed the cell phone. Next, he grabbed the garbage can from under the vanity and removed the clear plastic liner, which contained two sanitary napkins. He set the liner on the counter and began sweeping the items into the wastebasket. As he did this, he began to sing, "You are my sunshine, my only sunshine," just under his breath, which was more a humming sound with a smattering of words.

By the time he was finished in the bathroom, he was into the second chorus, "You'll never know dear how much I love you." He unsnapped her suitcase, revealing a neat stack of folded clothing that had not been removed since packing. Scott was always fascinated how people handled their belongings; it spoke to what type of person they were. Some people were slobs, dirty clothes mixed in with clean, their bags a torrent of unfolded chaos. Others were neat to the point of obsessive compulsive, everything having its place, perfectly folded in uniform fashion. Scott looked over these variations with forensic fascination, and in his line of work, going through the belongings of strangers was something he did quite regularly.

He reached around inside the bag, feeling for anything that could be used as a weapon. Checking now would ensure that nothing came back to haunt him later. After feeling around, he lifted out two sets of blue jeans and then below that, neatly laid upon each other, were six pairs of panties.

"What do have here?" he cooed and looked around as if someone were about to catch him running his fingers through a strange woman's unmentionables. He lifted the first pair up, which were a satin pink, and then looking about guiltily, he brought them up to his nose and smelled them. As he did this, he felt himself becoming aroused. He knew that Angela would go nuts if she saw him doing this. She'd slap him around something fierce for ogling over another woman's panties. The scent in the satin cloth had a fresh soapy fragrance. He had hoped for a musky perfume or maybe just musk. Regardless, the very thought of that redhead wearing nothing but these against her milky white skin was a definite turn on. Fully erect, he considered lying back on the bed and rubbing one out. After a moment, he abandoned the idea and began packing up the rest of her stuff.

2

They started the evening in a little Italian Restaurant called L'Italia Splendid. Angel ordered a large plate of spaghetti and a single meatball, while Maggie had a Linguine and Clam Sauce. It struck Maggie funny that Angel would order something like spaghetti while wearing a white dress.

"You sure like living on the edge," Maggie giggled.

Angel winked. "Danger is my business, sweetheart. If I get a drop of marinara on the duds, I'll just strip down to my bra and panties." Then she raised her glass, red wine of course, and clinked it against Maggie's, almost knocking it over.

Maggie reached across and caught it before it could spill. Both of them laughed.

"So, how much longer are you in Montreal for, Angel?"

"Well, Karen, it's funny you should ask. This is my last night." *And it's yours too,* she thought. Swallowing the last of her wine, she raised her glass and called, "More wine, toot sweet!"

Maggie felt an edge of sarcasm in Angel's response. She was also surprised at how fast they had burned through that first bottle of wine. *I can't get all pissed up,* she told herself. *I still have to be careful, just in case.*

A fresh bottle was brought to the table and before Maggie could protest, the waiter had already filled her glass and was working on Angel's.

"Madame," the waiter smiled.

"Merci buckets, sweet cheeks," Angel flirted and took another sip.

The young man smiled and moved along.

"So, you're leaving tomorrow? Where is it exactly that you're going?" Maggie asked.

Angel lifted the glass to her lips and stopped. "I should ask you the same thing." She took a sip, holding Maggie in her gaze, striking an uncomfortable silent moment that soured the flirtatious chemistry. Then Angel averted her eyes and frowned. "My husband, the cop, he was shot four years ago. He has a bullet lodged in the lower part of his spine."

"My god," Maggie said.

"Well, he was lucky. It didn't result in paralysis, but it ended his field career. He now goes from one city to another briefing Police Departments on gang-related policing."

"So, he's okay, from the bullet wound, I mean."

"Everything works, he has pain that is always there, but he's a real trooper." She fell silent, blinking her eyes, and used her pinky to dab away a tear. "Sorry, don't want to fuck up my makeup before we get past our meal."

"What's his name?"

"Phil," she lied, but there was a kernel of truth in that lie. She knew a cop named Phil, an ex-cop at least. Whether he'd been shot was something she didn't know. She and Scott had met with Phil Crane a little over a week before. They had in fact liaised at the same Quonset hut where Phil would meet Marty only two days later. Phil had briefed them on the surveillance job, putting bugs in the Croft place and would be on standby should they try and make a run for it. "I used to accompany him on all the lecture circuits, but I was just a third wheel when we got together with other cops, and they'd go for choir practice."

"Choir practice?"

"Yeah, when a bunch of cops say they're going out for choir practice, it really means they're going to get shit-faced." Angel smiled.

"Yes, I remember a movie about that. I think it was The Choirboys." Maggie took a sip of her wine. "So, where is he now?"

Angel ignored the reference, instead answering the question. "Up in Quebec City. I wanted to accompany him, but he thought I would like Montreal better, so while he and his fellow officers are out on the town doing god knows what, I am going to have a few drinks with you."

Maggie raised her glass. "To the Choir Girls."

Angel grinned, clinked her glass against Maggie's, and then sipped. When she swallowed, the grin deepened and she said, "Yeah, sweetheart. To the Choir Girls."

That was when the food arrived. Angel's Spaghetti dish was massive with a giant single meatball resting in a lake of marinara sauce on top of the noodles. Even she looked surprised.

Maggie giggled.

Angel peered up at the waiter. "Is he going to be okay?"

"Madame?" The waiter didn't understand.

"The bull you castrated." She waved her hand to the monstrosity on the plate. "Will he live?"

Maggie almost spat her wine out and the waiter laughed.

"Well?"

"Madame, I assure you that a bull only needs one good ball. Would you like Parmesan?"

Both Angel and Maggie cracked up.

3

Marty flipped the lever on his gear shift, switching the selector from low to high, released the accelerator and without using his clutch to assist, he slid the stick shift out of fourth into fifth gear, then accelerated again. The engine growled, accompanied by the high-pitched whistle of the turbo. He was actually enjoying himself a little. Away from the scrutiny of others, he was free to play with the gears and try shifting without the clutch. Garney was ahead, leading him to the Tank farm where they would pick up their first load. The VHF radio was now set to Channel Six, which was monitored by the Tank Farm. The road they were rolling down was just wide enough for two opposing trucks, and on either side of the road was a five-foot ditch. As Marty followed Garney's twin tankers up the road, he made sure to watch the position of his pup as it doglegged behind him.

"Tank Farm Bill, you got a copy," Garney hailed on the radio.

"Garney? Go ahead," the voice responded.

"Yes, my Brother. Two inbound tankers for Meanook, ETA 5 minutes."

"Okay, there's two trucks ahead of you. Clean off your placards, get your gear on and we'll call you when we're ready."

"Okay, good deal, Bill. Did you copy that, Marty?"

Marty picked up the microphone, pressed the transmission switch, and awkwardly said, "Roger."

He imagined big Garney nodding his head and letting out an enthusiast "Uh huh, yep," and this made him smile. He watched his tachometer; once the RPM's climbed to 1600, he grabbed another gear. It hadn't taken long to get accustomed with the transmission, and in spite of the fact that he didn't want to be here, he was actually enjoying being behind the wheel of this big truck.

Ahead, the left turn signal on Garney's pup begin to blink as the brake lights lit up. Above the tree-line to the left of the road loomed three monstrous fuel tanks. He hadn't noticed them until Garney signaled, but it was now quite clear that this was where they were going. As Garney turned left, Marty began downshifting in preparation for the turn. Beneath him he could feel the big rig slip a little on the icy road and this made his heart skip a beat. "Jesus Christ," he gasped and pushed in the clutch. He could feel himself regaining control, but this little slip was a preview of what he would be facing once they went north.

"Okay, Marty, my brother, it's a quick right after you turn left."

"Okay, thanks." Marty downshifted again, but this time was a little easier on the brake. It was funny, he had driven a tanker before, but never under these conditions, and this was going to be a challenge because he hadn't even put a load on yet. He flipped his left turn signal and, rounding the corner, he just caught sight of the back of Garney's pup trailer turning right. Once the tractor-trailer was straight, it was time to turn again and as he did, he could see two other trucks staged on the road ahead. He pulled in behind Garney, coasting to a slow stop. He reached down and pulled the truck's parking brake, which let out an exasperated **Puhshhhhhhhhh.**

4

The beat of the music pulsed repetitiously to the lights and Maggie had honestly never felt so out of place in her life. The young people, kids really, dancing around them, were hyped up on energy drinks and liquor. The music was a hybrid of techno-pop, rap, disco, and occasionally she even heard a song she recognized buried below the noise being spat out of the monster speakers on the stage. This was one of those places she had always detested, where you had to scream to have a conversation with the person across the table.

Above the dance floor hung a mirrored ball and she thought, *Disco isn't dead, it's just evolved into something else.* Across from her, Angel sipped her drink, checking out the hard bodies of young men strutting their stuff on the dance floor. One in particular had spotted her and was glancing over for a look. *I should have stayed at the hotel,* Maggie thought.

Angel finished her drink, stood up, and leaned across the table. "Smile!"

Maggie nodded and faked it as best she could.

"Good god, Karen, you need something to perk you up!"

"No, no, I'm okay," she argued.

"The hell you are! Sweetheart, I have just the thing to perk you up." Maggie started to stand and Angel gently pushed her down into her chair. "I'll be right back, sweetie." She hurried away toward the bar across the ocean of young people dancing to the beat of the music. Maggie watched her as she passed the young man who had been eyeing her from the dance floor. He said something and Angel stopped abruptly to converse.

"Bonjour," the young man said.

"Hi," Angel said back.

"Anglais?" He smiled. "You want to dance?"

"How old are you?"

The young guy glowed. "I'm 22."

"You're much too old for my taste. I like my boys around 18."

She turned to go and felt his hand reach out and grab her arm.

"Come on, one dance."

Angel turned back, her smile broadening. She leaned in and kissed the young man almost violently. Her tongue explored and twisted like a serpent; he tasted of beer and cigarettes. No matter. He ground himself against her and rolled his own tongue over hers. She cupped his head with both hands, bringing her thumbs to rest in the soft tissue just behind each ear lobe. Simultaneously she positioned her left boot just over the arch of his foot. She struck like a rattlesnake, digging each thumb into the soft tissue, clamping him like a vice. A bolt of agony shot through him.

"Hush now," she whispered. Her heel came down hard and spiked his foot, crushing the bone and tendon. She dug her thumbs in even deeper. She held him there like prey, her lips almost touching his. "Hurts, doesn't it."

He couldn't speak. Tears brimmed up in his eyes, spilled over. She wasn't done. Not yet. Her leg, hard and muscular, came up into his groin, crushing his left testicle almost to the point of rupture. His world exploded into a zenith of blinding white, and exquisite agony cut through him like broken bits of razor. She dug her thumbs in even deeper, touched her lips to his, then ran her tongue over his cheek across the trailing tear stream. It was salty—full of fear—and this stirred something in her loins. If Scott were here, she'd drag him to the bathroom and fuck him hard.

No one seemed to notice.

Maggie watched Angel release the young man. He stood dazed and statuesque as she moved away toward the bar. Then he staggered after her, enveloped by the sea of dancing bodies. He bounced off a girl wearing a bandanna and a Bob Marley T-shirt. She shot him an angry glance. The music stopped, and then a song Maggie recognized began to play. It was "Showdown" by Electric Light Orchestra. The young man staggered left, and then he began to shudder. His cheeks contracted—ballooned—a violent gush of alcohol spewed upward into the crowd. It was raining bile and Budweiser. He spun and fell, while others turned, confused as to what they'd been sprayed with. There was a sudden wave of revulsion that opened a hole in the dance floor.

From two different sides of the club the bouncers came.

What did she do to him? Maggie hadn't been close enough to witness the violence or black widow kiss.

The young man was up again, this time with the help of two men wearing tuxedos. They were ushering him to the door and as they held him under each arm, he vomited once more, but not as violently. The crowd opened a path and ELO sang: "Raining... All over the world."

"Oh my god," Maggie covered her mouth.

The door opened and the young man was ejected.

"Here," Angel said, thrusting a drink into her hand.

Maggie stared at the drink. It was red and orange. "I don't think I can drink anymore."

"This is low alcohol. Have a drink and we'll call it a night, too many kids around here anyway, that one almost barfed on me."

Maggie sipped the drink. She could taste orange, grenadine, tequila, and something else she couldn't put her finger on. "Tequila is hardly low alcohol, Angel."

"Drink up, Karen." Angel reached into her purse and pulled out a cell phone.

"What are you doing?"

"Calling us a cab. Drink up and we'll make for the door."

Maggie did as she was told.

5

Tank Farm
Yellowknife, NWT

"Next two trucks for Meanook, have you got a copy?"

"Go ahead," Garney responded.

"Okay, guys, if you got all your protective gear on and are ready to load, please proceed to racks 1 and 3. Shut off your engines once in place and chock your wheels."

"Copy that," Marty responded. He released the park brake and waited for Garney to start rolling. When they'd arrived, they cleaned all the excess snow off their trucks and trailers.

"Speed limit is 5 km/h inside the tank farm, guys," Bill warned.

"Copy that," Marty replied.

"Right oh, Bill, we got our PP and E on and a big old grin. Oh yeah!" Garney added.

Bill seemed not to notice. "How many trucks we have out there for Acadia and Meanook, not including the ones I just called in. Sound off, please." The radio came alive, buzzing with drivers walking on each other. Tank farm Bill finally cut in. "Stop! Let's try this again. First truck in line, report how many trucks you have behind you."

"Looks like eight or ten, Bill," a voice reported.

"Alright, one at a time, report in," Tank farm Bill said, and in an orderly fashion, the drivers began to sound off. The tank farm was on a five-acre property that was fenced in and wired with security cameras. It was here that they loaded the diesel destined for the mines and as Garney had explained, they would only be taking on about 15,000 liters. Each loading rack was set up to accommodate three super b tankers. At each rack stood a man decked out in blue fire retardant coveralls. Garney was rolling into the farthest rack, while Marty was going to the first. Set in behind the racks, looming over the site like white cylindrical titans, were the three massive fuel storage tanks. Behind that were three more.

Marty pushed in his clutch and waited as Garney crossed through the gate. Then a voice over the radio beckoned him. "Second truck for Meanook, keep coming." The man at the rack was waving his arm.

Marty picked up his handset. "Copy."

He released the clutch and moved slowly toward the gate. "That's it," the voice coaxed and he realized it was the man at the rack who was talking to him. "Pay attention to my signals, stay left, and when I tell you to stop. Stop right away."

"Copy." Marty wheeled the rig left and the twin tankers followed the turn. Once through the gate, he watched his ground guide, who motioned him right. He turned the wheel and the guide used both hands in a chopping motion to steer straight. Marty swung into the rack, following the direction of his guide. As Marty got closer to the man, he slowed and the guide stepped off to one side. Now from the right mirror, Marty watched the man as he continued to roll forward. The trailers he towed were almost straight now.

"That's good right there." The man dropped his arm.

Marty pushed down on the clutch and shifted into neutral.

"Stop."

He stopped the rig and pulled his parking brake, turned off the key, then put on his hardhat and safety glasses. When he opened the door, a blast of cold wind bit into his face. As he climbed from the cab, he could only wonder how these guys were able to work all day in such extreme temperatures. He stepped down onto the ground and followed the guide. It was time to go to work.

6

She could hear voices outside the enveloping cloak of intoxication. Against her cheek she felt something hard and plastic and there was a smell of perfume. She floated in the darkness, lapping waves pushing, then tugging, at her subconscious. Her body felt numb—prickly—she thought she might vomit. Then from far away, beyond the edge of night, she heard Angel. “You got everything?”

“Yeah, all you gotta do is check out.” It was a man’s voice.

“The night clerk hasn’t seen her?” Angel again.

Maybe this was a dream, a delusion conjured up by her paranoia.

How much did I drink?

She tried to move, but her limbs were heavy like clay. She was barely holding on to her consciousness.

“No, the night clerk hasn’t seen her, but I’ve been watching him and he skips out to smoke something every other hour. He’s clueless.” It was the man again.

Maggie tried to remember, but the black waves were turning her, pulling her away from the voices and down into an infinite purgatory. *This is where the drunks and drug addicts go when they black out,* she thought. *Down into the abysmal dark, beyond the edge of night.*

7

Angel stepped from the car, which was now parked in front of the motel lobby. She held Maggie’s clutch bag in her right hand when she pushed open the glass door. She had changed into jeans and a sweater after they got Maggie into the back seat of the car. She was small compared to Angel, but had become dead weight when the drug took hold. Angel had actually gotten one of the two bouncers to help in getting her out the door.

“My friend’s had a bit too much to drink,” Angel told him. “Can you give me a hand?”

"Oui, pas de problem. I will help you." He hoisted Maggie up and practically carried her out himself. Angel wondered if the bouncer would be so helpful if it had been a man trying to get her out the door in this condition. She doubted it very much. Women weren't considered predatory or dangerous. Angel was both. Outside the club, Scott idled the car, doors unlocked and ready for action. His phone rang and he answered.

"Karen's really drunk, can you open the door so I can put her in the backseat," Angel said, more for the bouncer's benefit than Scott.

"Okay," he said. He was just about to hop out of the car and open the rear door, but something caught his eye. A cop car was rolling up the street. He stiffened. "Angela, stall! I got a cop coming up the road."

Angela stopped. "Wait."

The bouncer stopped. "What is it?"

"Her phone, I think I left it on the table."

The big man went to set Maggie down in a chair. "I'll go get it."

"No, you stay here. I'll just be a second."

Angela cut across the floor, talking into her phone as she went. "Where is he?"

"Right here," Scott said and lowered the phone. "Good evening, officer."

The cop looked Scott over suspiciously. "You can't read?" He pointed to the NO PARKING sign. "Or you just don't care?"

"I'm picking someone up. They'll be right out."

The cop scratched his cheek. "Have you been drinking?"

"No, I'm the designated driver."

Then the cop said, "I'm going around the block, when I come back around, you better not be parked here."

"I won't." The cop released his brake and started up the block. Scott raised the phone to his ear. "Get her the fuck out of here Asap." He drummed his fingers on the steering wheel, staring at the police car as it rounded the corner. "Come on, come on."

Angel pin wheeled back and sprinted across the club, almost wiping out in her heels. "I just remembered she left her phone at home. Let's go." She lifted Maggie up and the bouncer resumed helping her.

As they approached the door, he hailed another staff member. "Rene."

Rene opened the door and they moved out into the street.

"I miss Marty," Maggie slurred, then whimpered. "I wanna go home."

"We're taking you home, sweetheart. You've had way too much to drink."

They set her down on the back seat and she slumped over. "Is this a Gypsy Taxi?"

The bouncer gave them a strange look.

"Thanks so much," Scott said and palmed him a twenty.

"Yes, thank you so very much." Angel wrapped her arms around the big guy and kissed his cheek affectionately. "You're my hero."

The look on his face melted away.

"Bon Soiree, Madame," he bowed and turned away.

Scott tossed a blanket over Maggie and closed the door. He was looking up the street to see if the cop car was anywhere. "Angela, we gotta get the fuck out of here."

Angel opened the door and climbed. "Well, let's go then."

That was 20 minutes ago. Now Angel was walking up to the counter and sizing up the night clerk. She guessed he was smoking something a hell of a lot stronger than pot. His eyes were red, but his teeth were terrible. Probably Meth or Crack. He was texting on a phone.

"Hi," Angel said.

"Bonjour," he replied, his smile revealing two stacks of rotting teeth. "May I help you?"

"Yes, Margaret Croft, Room 214, I'm checking out." *Must be the owner's kid,* Angel thought. *No way anyone else would hang onto this guy.*

He reached over and tapped the keys on the computer. "Is there a problem, Madame Croft?"

"No, no problem. I have been called away on business, so I have to shorten my stay."

"Do you want the room charge applied to your credit card?"

"No, I'll pay cash."

***

Chapter 15—Race with the Devil

1

ACADIA MINE
105 Miles below the Arctic Circle

Nick Anderson was back in the lab with Ronny Fraser at his side. They had spent the better part of the day measuring and cataloguing the fossils. Nick, Ronny noted, spotted a couple structural mistakes he and Andrea had made, but overall they has done a very good job. Nick was using a laser pointer to trace over the skeletal structure of the creatures while making observations and comments. "This is interesting," he said. At the side of the creature's skull a tube roughly the size of a drinking straw jutted outward for about four inches, then back into what could only be thought of as the creature's cheekbone. "I wonder what it does?"

"Maybe it's some kind of breathing tube," Ronny remarked.

"Maybe," he replied. "But I'm actually thinking that these creatures breathe through their back like insects." He traced the laser pointer over the large tube that protruded from both the left and right rear of the creature's skull into what looked like a dual motorcycle exhaust manifold. "You see how it runs into the back. I would say that this creature has a set of lungs. Perhaps it takes the air in through its mouth and feeds it through some type of filtering system inside the exoskeleton."

Ronny watched with fascination, following the path of the laser pointer as it traced the intake pipes on the creature. "This is amazing, Nick."

"Yes, it is, and we are going to do something that both of us will remember for the rest of our lives."

"We are?"

"Yes, we are going to do an autopsy on the other creature to see how it ticks internally." Nick turned to face Ronny, a grin of invite beaming through the face shield. "Do you think you'd be up for that?"

"Do the words "fucking eh" sound unprofessional?" Ronny grinned back.

"No, in fact they sound quite appropriate."

2

Highway 401:
Somewhere between Belleville and Hamilton

The drug that Angel slipped into Maggie's drink had finally begun to loosen its grip on her and although she couldn't see, she was aware of her circumstances. She had been kidnapped, most likely by the same people who had blackmailed Marty. There was something over her eyes and she was in a car or truck; the whine of the rubber against the pavement below told her that the vehicle was in motion. At first she thought she might have been abducted by a serial killer—this struck a chord of terror deep inside her—then she had heard Angel talking and knew. Once she got past the self-deprecation phase, there was a momentary lapse of relief, but as she digested this information, it became evident that her circumstances were dire.

My phone, she thought. *I need to get a message to Marty. Oh God, where is my phone.* If he knew she was in trouble, he might be able to save himself. Even if she could find her phone, it was useless; her hands, along with her feet, were bound.

This made her want to cry.

The pragmatic side of Maggie came forward and took control then.

What good will that do? We need to figure out where we are and how to get out of this. They hadn't gagged her. *I need to open a dialogue.*

Dialogue? Are you kidding? Maybe you can sell them some life insurance and they'll let you go, her inner voice, the emotional one that rarely thought through any situation, scolded.

Shut up, you whiny bitch, she mentally shouted back and the emotion ran out of her.

"Water," she said and her voice clicked.

Nothing, just the rubber grinding against the pavement.

"Please, I need something to drink."

There was movement in front of her, but no words. Maybe her captors were conversing in sign language. Then she felt someone moving over her, rifling around for something. There was a sigh of frustration; it was Angel. Maggie could feel the blanket draped over her head and she thought whatever it was that blindfolded her might be what was used to bind her legs and arms. It was cloth-like.

A hand fell on her face. It was cold, clammy, and she felt it pull at her face, telling her to open her mouth. There was a sound of a cap breaking its seal and suddenly, she felt the mouth of a water bottle touch her lips. Her captor tilted it slightly and she felt it scrape across her lower gum. A second hand knotted into her sweater, lifting her up, and she pulled away.

"You have to sit up or I'll spill it all over you," Angel said.

Maggie stopped resisting and sat up. She'd been on her left side for hours, pins and needles numbed her right shoulder and cheek. She could feel something digging into her left buttock, a loose seat belt perhaps. The plastic bottle was placed at her lips again and tilted. Lukewarm water poured over her gums and she drank as much as was offered. She felt hung over; her head pounded and she was extremely dehydrated. The bottle tilted up and she drank all of it. The last few drops spilled down her chin and into the cleavage of her breasts.

The bottle was removed, cap spun back on, and then Angel began setting her back down on her side.

"Please, no, I am really cramped. Can't I sit up?"

Angel said nothing, just pushed a little harder.

"Please, at least put me down on the other side."

"Oh, for shit's sake." Angel released her and began rearranging the seat beside her.

"Just put her back down," the man's voice said.

"Be quiet," she snapped and there was a thud of something being knocked from the seat. Then Angel's hands were on her again, pushing her down onto her left side. The cloth seat rubbed against her cheek, a muscle in her back twisted painfully. She turned slightly and Angel steadied her.

"I'm just trying to get comfortable. I'm not resisting you."

The grip relented, allowing Maggie to squirm a little until the muscle spasm loosened enough for her to relax. She settled into the seat and the blanket was set on top of her. As she lay there blind and bound, she took a chance and whispered. "Why are you doing this, Angel, I thought we were becoming friends."

The cool hand caressed her cheek, then a single finger touched her lips. "Hush, Maggie. I don't want to gag, but I will," Angel whispered. Then she was gone to the front seat. There was a click up front and then the sound of music, hard rock, maybe even heavy metal, started up. It was Ozzy Osborne and he was singing: No more tears.

Angel or her companion cranked the volume up even louder, drowning out Maggie's pleas from the back seat. She could not make out what they were saying, only knew that they were talking about her, and she prayed that she wasn't going to her death.

3

Chinook Tundra Camp
Yellowknife, NWT

One hundred diesel engines growled in defiance of the -40 degree temperatures. With their protest, they spat forth a steady stream of exhaust up into the clear evening sky. Above them, a curtain of northern lights stretched from one end of the horizon to the other, rippling like a ghostly blanket drawn out by the hand of god. The luminance of bright green shimmered against the starry sky. Marty looked into the heavens, taken by this hypnotic beauty. He had just finished banging his tires to check for flats, his walk around done; he stood in awe of the North's greatest wonder.

Maggie would love this, he thought.

A hand fell upon his shoulder. He turned to see Big Garney Wilson towering over him. "Some Natives believe that the Aurora carries the spirits of the dead from this world to the next. She's a beauty, ain't she?"

"It is quite a sight."

"This is why I keep coming back, my brother."

"Really?"

"Yeah," Garney grinned. "It sure in the hell ain't for the money."

Marty smiled.

Garney's smile melted away. "You ready for this, Marty, my brother?"

"Ready as I'll ever be."

This is going to be the hardest part of the trip. This road doesn't take kindly to those who don't respect it. Do you understand, Marty?"

"Trust me, I'll take it easy," Marty said.

"It will be like riding the top of a serpent. The edges can hook a wheel and drag you over. If that happens, there's no recovering from it. The road won't forgive you, it'll bite you hard."

Marty felt a rush of anxiety run through him. The Ingraham and the Inuksuk were the only way north. He didn't have the option of backing out. He had to make two runs up this god-forsaken trail and they had to be flawless. "I'll follow your lead, Garney."

"Ride the snake, Marty, ride the snake and get ready to race with the devil because he'll be out there waiting for us."

"The devil."

"Yeah man, the devil. He'll be running that track right alongside us, pulling our trailers hard, left and right. Pulling on you as you climb the hills and shoving you down the other side. I'm not saying this to scare you, but once we get onto the Inuksuk, you'll be riding the devil's serpent."

"Jesus Christ, thanks for the pep talk."

"Respect the trail, Marty, and listen to what I tell you over the radio. If you do that, we'll beat the devil tonight and before you know it, we will be cruising across the ice, eating our lunch."

"And if we don't?"

"Then you get to meet the ghosts who walk that trail."

"The ghosts?"

"The ones who lost the race," Garney frowned. "You'll be falling in behind me. The two guys running with us are Spence Hughes and Merv White, both seasoned. We're going to get you up that trail in one piece. If it don't feel right, stay off your brakes and back out of it with your gears."

"What do you mean if it don't feel right?"

"When the trail is icy, it shifts underneath you. That means you're on black ice, only use your brakes as a last resort. In this climate the transmission is your best friend, use the shifter to slow down and try to anticipate the conditions."

Marty stared up at Garney who was still taking in the northern lights. He felt ill. What the hell had he gotten himself into? "Should I be scared, Garney?"

"Yes." Garney looked down at him. "Let's saddle up."

4

The big rig lumbered from the yard into the night, the turbo whistling its constant rhythm into the night as Marty ran through the gears. Again, Garney leading. They were on their way to the Dispatch Yard to meet up with the others.

"This is it," he said and flipped the high range lever, while pushing the stick shift up into fifth gear. "All I gotta do is get up this trail." But that wasn't quite true. He had a long way to go. There were a lot of obstacles ahead and he still had no idea what he was going to do when he met them. What would stop Shamus from killing him and Maggie? They were loose ends, after all. The diesel engine called to him and he up-shifted once more. He tried to push it away, felt his chest tighten even more; this anxiety was going to get him into a wreck and that wasn't going to help his cause in the least. *Get up the trail, Marty,* he thought. *Get up the trail and onto the ice. After that you've got two days to figure something out.*

"Marty, my brother, you got a copy?"

He reached over, grabbed the radio handset. "Go ahead, Garney."

"How yuh doing back there?"

"I'm good. Just prepping myself to ride the snake."

"Uh huh, yeah."

"I'm not sure what you boys are talking about, but it sounds like something that should be talked over in private," Merv White interrupted and suddenly a set of headlights turned the corner behind Marty's, flashing against his side mirrors.

"Merv, my brother, glad you could make it. Where's the man of steel?"

"Bringing up the rear," Spence added and suddenly a second set of headlights poured out onto the road.

"Hey, Marty, Garney scaring the shit out of you yet?" Merv asked.

Marty smiled and suddenly felt a little better. "Yeah, a little."

"Good, scared is good," Spence interjected. "This is where the big boys play and once you get to the top of the Inuksuk you'll be over the worst of it."

"Yeah okay," Marty said.

"It's a tough road, but that's why we're here. Garney will keep you up to date on road conditions, oncoming traffic, and tourists."

"Tourists."

"Yeah, the Japanese come out here to consummate beneath the northern lights. Some spiritual thing or another," Spence continued. "Anyhow, you have to watch for them skulking about on the road with their cameras and girlfriends and wives because they pose a hazard."

"Are you pulling my leg, Spence?"

"He's not pulling your leg," Merv said. "Check out those lights, there'll be oriental jizz flying around like crazy tonight."

Marty laughed. "Merv, I'm pretty sure that oriental is considered racist."

"The fuck it is," Merv said.

"Attention, gentlemen, this is a working channel. If you feel the need to discuss such topics, take it to another channel," an authoritative voice broke in.

The radio fell silent.

Ahead, Garney turned the corner and Marty began to downshift.

5

Nick was all set—in his hand he held an air cutter a little larger than a Dremel rotary tool, and affixed to it was a diamond disk. Beneath him the creature's skull grinned back as if inviting him to open it. Imagined or real, he was all too happy to oblige the invitation. He pressed down on the trigger and the disk made a zinging sound.

He used a gloved hand to steady the skull and Ronny stepped forward to assist. On the table a digital recorder and video camera recorded the procedure. Nick turned to the camera. "My name is Professor Nick Anderson, assisting me is Geologist Ronald Fraser, and we are in an underground location at the Acadia Mine located approximately 105 miles below the Arctic Circle. Before us is a specimen that was unearthed along with five others during an exploration dig. This particular specimen is fragmented and incomplete while the others are intact. The procedure we will be carrying out will entail opening the skull plate on the unnamed creature. I will add that the creature appears to be bio-mechanical." Nick paused, then turned to Ronny. "I'll be making the first cut on the seam just above the mouth plate."

"Seems like a suitable choice."

He stared back at Ronny and mouthed the words, "Fuckin eh." Then grinned.

"Ready to proceed when you are, Professor Anderson," Ronny replied.

Nick pushed the button on the rotary saw and it let out a steady high-pitched whine. As Ronny held the skull, Nick leaned in carefully to place the spinning blade over the area he intended to cut. "Here goes nothing."

Weeeeeeeee! The blade cried as it began cutting into the skull plate. If they had not been wearing protective suits with fresh oxygen, they might have smelled the caustic stench of metal. The spinning blade sank into the skull right where Anderson set it, and then he worked his way up the seam toward the back. As he did this, the "***Weeeeee!***" morphed into a steady ***Brrrrrrr!*** Indicating that it was under a heavy strain, but the diamond tool was slicing through plate with greater ease than Nick had thought.

"Making some fine progress here," Nick said.

"Yes, very good so far."

And then the saw blade disintegrated.

"Guess I should have kept my mouth shut." He'd cut through eight inches of skull plate extending from the incisors up over the top of the skull. "Five more inches would have done it."

Ronny reached over, took the saw from Nick's hand, removed the air line, snapped the quick connect on another rotary saw, and handed it back. "This should cover it."

"Indeed it should." Nick leaned over and began cutting again. This time it sounded as if they were in a dentist's office. He carried on following the seam all the way to the back of the cranium until the cut was complete. He set the rotary saw down and examined his work. It was a nice clean cut, but the skull plate remained intact. "We'll probably have to pry it apart."

Ronny reached over and produced a wedge that had a tap on top of it. Nick had never seen anything like it before, but understood immediately the mechanics of the tool. It was used to pry things apart. The tap was threaded and the more you screwed it into the wedge, the wider it became.

"These should work."

Before Nick could ask, Ronny produced four more of the wedges and rather than discussing it, they placed each one in varied points in the cut. Once securely fitted, Nick slowly turned each tap a half a turn and moved onto the next. As he did this, the wedges bit into the cut and began to pry the skull apart. Inside the skull there was a second membrane that was dry and powdery, and as they opened the gap even further, he noted that the skull itself was made up of layers of tiny honeycombs. "Interesting, almost like carbon fiber or..."

"Kevlar," Ronny said.

"Yeah. Nice defense mechanism." Then he turned to the camera. "At first glance, the creature appears to be bio-mechanical, the exoskeleton looks more like an alloy, made up of interlocking honeycomb. The exoskeleton is also host to micro-organisms that presumably carry out the task of housecleaning." He turned attention away from the camera. Take a look at this, Ronny."

Ronny leaned in to see what Nick was pointing at. The exoskeleton was layered like a tree trunk. "The layers on this are in a state of growth. So, if we are looking at a machine or a suit, it has organic properties."

"Nanotechnology?"

"Maybe. Let's take a deeper look."

The skull was open approximately three inches and Ronny guessed the thin papery membrane encased whatever was left of the creature's brain. He was excited to see what was below that membrane, even though he deduced it would be nothing more than dust. His knees trembled. The exhilaration was almost overwhelming.

Nick picked up a scalpel from the tool tray, looked to Ronny, smiled, and then began the incision. He followed the contour of the opening as he sliced through the membrane. "Ronny, can you grab those tweezers? Once I'm done, I'd like to try and remove this piece intact."

Ronny said nothing; he grabbed the oversized tweezers used for examining gemstones and stood at the ready. Nick continued to cut in very short sawing motions and as he did, the membrane crumbled like burned newsprint. Ronny reached in and clamped the tweezers as gingerly as he dared while Nick completed the cut.

"There," Nick said and Ronny removed the papery membrane, then placed it onto a glass plate that seemed almost predestined for the sample. "Now let's have a look at what makes this baby tick."

6

The car stopped at least three hours after Maggie had been given water and put on her other side. Maggie timed it by the music. They'd listened to an entire Ozzy Osborne album, which she guessed at around 45 minutes and then the radio, which gave a time check every half hour. Maggie listened to a morning zoo show talking about what they did over the weekend. Mindless contrived drivel, but it helped pass the time. She needed the distraction; the muscles in her lower back were flexing and contracting in uncomfortable spasms. Maggie tried to zone out and ignore the pain by listening to the idiocy of the morning zoo. She was also listening to what her captors were doing. Then she heard Angel.

"This should do."

Then the car began to slow.

Maggie began to panic.

Then the car stopped and there was a metallic click from the front seat. She swore she smelled gun oil.

Oh my god.

The car door opened.

They're going to kill me!

They did not remove her blindfold. Angel leaned in and whispered, "This is the only chance you're going to get, sweetheart, I'm the only one watching, so get on with it." She hesitantly lowered her panties, squatted down and emptied her bladder. During this, she sobbed but refused to plead. Instead she waited, expecting to feel the cold barrel of a revolver against the back of her head—shadowed by a falling gun hammer and then there'd be nothing. She only hoped that she'd be allowed to finish her degrading pee before they did it.

Spare me that one dignity, she begged. *Don't let me pee all over myself as I lay dying.* And when that last squirt of urine spattered against the hard packed ground, she hoped they would allow her to pull up her panties before they did the deed. A new dignity to be negotiated. There was to be no execution. Only Angel's firm hand on her upper arm, clamping down like a vice and saying, "Pull up your shorts, sweetheart, we've got places to be." Maggie leaned right, awkwardly tugging her panties up with her one free hand. First hooking her thumb under the waistband, then tugging them lopsided and trying to straighten them out. Angel let out an aggravated sigh, then hooked the other side of the waistband, yanking them up into her crotch, purposely. "I said we didn't have all day."

And then they were on the move again.

Two-and-a-half hours later, the car came to a final stop and Maggie smelled the familiar acrid bite of the steel yards. She knew where she was, had in fact known before she'd arrived. She was back in Hamilton. Maggie knew what was coming next and she was terrified by it. They were taking her to meet the man. The psychopath named Gordon Shamus.

7

Lupania Dispatch
Yellowknife, NWT

Marty, Garney, Merv, and Spence were sitting around a folding table as the dispatcher entered their paperwork into the system. The dispatch office was located inside a portable trailer located in an open lot outside YK that was large enough to accommodate two convoys of eight trucks. They arrived half an hour prior to their departure time and were now getting close to kick off. Garney was glancing at his watch when the dispatcher appeared at the counter.

"Okay, Garney, your group is ready to go," he said, handing over their dispatch envelopes. "We've got some tourists hanging out at Giant Mine, so keep an eye for them. Traffic is pretty light, however you may meet a convoy of three coming south on their way back down the Ingraham. I know that you're old hat at this, gents, but keep the chatter down and remember to call your markers."

"Sure thing, Doug," Garney said, taking his envelope.

Doug the dispatcher handed over Marty's envelope and to each individual said, "Have a safe trip north."

Marty followed them out into the dispatch yard where the second convoy was already rolling in. When they reached the trucks, Garney stopped and turned to them. "Alright, my brothers, tonight we are going to be taking Marty up the Ingraham and the Inuksuk. I'm going to take it easy, there's no hurry, the ice will be there and they get their fuel when we say they get it."

Marty said nothing.

"Sounds good," Spence said.

Merv nodded in agreement, then looked to Marty. "Use your gears and listen to Big Garney. He's the point man, he'll alert you to everything."

Marty nodded. "Are we gonna do a group hug now? I'd really like to get this over with?"

Everyone laughed.

"Saddle up, my brothers," Garney said.

They climbed into their respective trucks and Garney did a radio check with each of them to ensure that communication was up to par. Then he pulled his truck from the yard and switched on his side lamps, making sure that none of his wheels were frozen. They weren't. By the time he exited the gate and was turning, Marty was in second gear and rolling forward. He did the same, looking at each of the yellow markers on his wheels to make sure they were spinning. Behind him he could see Merv beginning to roll and he felt his heart speed up just slightly. He thought about Maggie, hoped she was safe, but guiltily pushed the thought away. This was going to require his full attention.

"Tonight we are going to race with the devil," Garney had said. In the back of Marty's mind he imagined Satan himself might be waiting along the shoulder, getting ready. In Marty's head this devil was not a red fork-tailed creature of Christian theology or comic books. No, this creature was a dark apparition, little more than dirty smoke, talon fingers and blazing yellow eyes.

Five minutes later, Garney was at the T-junction where Highway 3 met the infamous Ingraham trail. Once they got onto the Ingraham, there wouldn't be much in the way of opportunity to pull over. With the exception of Giant Mine and Prosperous Lake there were no pull-offs to accommodate trucks this big. Garney signaled and turned left.

"Four north onto the Ingraham Trail," Big Garney Wilson's voice boomed across the airwaves.

"Three south at kilometer 30," someone, presumably another convoy, responded.

Marty began to slow the W900 in anticipation of an icy stop. Marty signaled his intent, crawling toward the stop, waiting for Garney to get ahead before rolling onto the trail himself. Marty brought his truck to a complete stop. From behind, Merv's headlights loomed, almost pushing him and with that he eased the clutch out and began his race with the devil. He rounded the corner, swinging wide and waiting until the truck was straight before up-shifting. He ground the gear slightly and the rig growled. Taking the corner wider than needed, he felt his stomach twist up into a rope bag of anxiety. It wasn't enough to worry about with fucking Shamus and Maggie out there on her own, he now had to deal with this shit. He shoved down the self-pity and put that into the back of his mind. This was no time to be dwelling on shit he couldn't control. He took a long, deep breath, held it, and exhaled.

"Here we fucking go."

Ahead, Garney was rolling downhill toward a hard left curve, as the lights from the Super B lit the night with crimson and amber. "Four north at kilometer two!"

Marty also rolled forward in a deliberate restrained crawl and rightly so. The road was slick and dangerous, adding to that, the gravitational slope pulled at the fuel in the twin tanks and they in turn began pushing him down the icy grade. The engine whined, the rpms were running high and, like it or not, he had to grab a higher gear. He shifted up and the truck increased speed. Garney had already rounded the left hand turn and was now making his way around another corner. The weight of the tankers shoved harder and Marty thought about the devil. Ahead a mustard colored road sign warned: **40 KM/H SHARP TURN** He checked his speed. He was doing 65. That may not have sounded like much, but the corner was icy—unforgiving, and his momentum was climbing. The rope in his guts loosened, a swish of angst ran through him. What if he couldn't get the truck to slow down? What if he lost it on that corner? He was going far too fast. Marty did exactly what Garney had told him not to do and got onto his brakes.

8

Hamilton Harbor

When the door opened, she considered struggling, maybe even making a dash. But what would be the point? Her hands and feet were bound and she was blindfolded. She'd have to hop like she was in a potato sack race and realistically, how far would she even get? Maybe ten feet before she bounced off some obstacle. If she was going to improve her odds at survival, she would have to accept the fact that for the time being she was at the mercy of her captors. Angel pulled her across the seat, and then sat her upright with her legs dangling out the door. As she did this, she placed one hand on her head to protect it from banging off the jam. The muscles in her left shoulder ached from being in the same position for so long.

"Hand me those," she told her partner.

Maggie could feel a hand impatiently spreading her ankles, then the zip tie binding them was cut and the cloth put in place to protect her from losing circulation was unwrapped. She felt Angel's hot breath against her ear, and the faint smell of cigarettes invaded her nasal cavities. "Here's how it's going to go, sweetheart, my friend and I are going to help you from the car. You're going to walk about fifty feet, then you'll have to climb a small stairwell. Don't worry, we'll guide you all the way, but I want to discourage you about something. Are you listening?"

"Yes," Maggie replied.

"I know you're scared, but you're in good shape. Sure you feel like shit, but when this is over you can go back to fucking people over on insurance claims and banging that good looking husband of yours. If, on the other hand, you try and run, I am going to beat you unconscious, break your nose, crack some of those perfect teeth, or maybe even dislocate your jaw." She paused to let it sink in. "Do you understand, Maggie?"

"Yes."

"Good, let's get moving then."

They were on either side of her, the snow crunched beneath her feet. She was still wearing the clothes from the club, but Angel had swapped out her heels for a set of flats. It was cold, the air stunk of steel and something else. Maybe urine? She was pretty sure they were down by the steel yards on the harbor. As she walked, she tried to remember what was down in this area. How far was she from Burlington Street?

"Okay, we are coming up to the stairs. I'm going to stop you right in front and then we'll take that first step." Angel's voice had an air of affection, like she was talking to a child or a disabled friend. Maggie wondered if she would have such a demeanor while she was beating her unconscious. "All right, sweetheart, you ready?"

Maggie nodded.

"Let's take that first step."

She lifted her foot and planted it on the first step. Once her footing was secured, they helped her with the next and the next. There were five steps in all. She counted and inventoried them along with the distance to the car. She might need this information for later, during a futile attempt at escape.

She could hear a door unlatch and swing open. Warm air rushed out against her face.

"One last step and you get to sit down in a more comfortable position."

She lifted her foot and treaded through the doorway. In the back of her head, she was trying to get a bearing on her location. She knew she was close to the steel yards, but more importantly she wondered where the police station was in relation to those yards. There was a third presence, one which didn't speak, but watched and assisted. This wasn't Gordon Shamus. She was pretty sure that Shamus wasn't the type to offer assistance. He hadn't arrived yet. This sort of thing would be below him.

Angel whispered in her ear. "Do you have to piss, Maggie? Now is the time."

Maggie almost said no, but felt the urge to do both. "Yes."

Angel led her across the room and opened another door. The room smelled dirty—chemical aromas hung in the air: bleach, industrial soap, toilet bowl cleaner. Below that intermingling fragrance, the pungent order of methane. Angel turned her around. They stepped inside the small room and Angel latched the door behind her. She sat down and relieved herself as Angel waited quietly.

"Can you unbind my hands so I can wipe?"

Angel sighed, but then she felt the zip tie being cut.

Maggie cleaned herself up.

Once finished, she was led from the room. Angel didn't bother to re-bind her wrists. And Maggie didn't dare struggle or run. She was still blindfolded and held out some faint hope that not seeing her captors insured her safety. It was a ridiculous thought; she knew what Angel looked like. They sat her in a chair and her hands were bound behind her back once again.

"Now what?" asked the man who had helped kidnap her.

"Now we wait," replied the assistant.

9

"Three south at kilometer 19," the voice on the radio announced.

"Four north at 17," Garney countered and added, "Looks like we get to meet in my favorite spot." The first 18 kilometers of the Ingraham Trail were really just a preview of what was to come for Marty. The Inuksuk Trail was far more treacherous, but from kilometer 17 to 19 the road snaked dangerously back and forth beside a frozen lake. On the northbound side, the shoulder fell away at a dangerous angle hidden by a layer of snow that camouflaged where the edge was. Marty was halfway between km marker 15 and 16. Occasionally in the rear, he could see Merv's headlamps and knew the big man was holding back to give him the space.

Garney turned the corner and was climbing the grade when he met the first southbound truck. "Hello there," he said over the radio.

"Hey, Big Garney Wilson! How the hell are you?"

There was a momentary pause, one of recollection and then, "Is that you, Brad?"

"In the flesh. Couldn't have found a better spot, could we?"

"Yes Sir, uh huh. Yep. Who yuh got with yuh?"

“Oh, Mark’s back there somewhere lollygagging and Heath’s our tail gunner, but he’s busy reading Mark’s book.”

Who the hell reads while driving, Marty wondered. *Was that a joke?*

To this was this was a snicker, presumably Heath.

“I’m meeting the first one now, Marty,” Garney said.

“Copy that,” Marty replied and saw the headlights coming around the bend. He moved the truck right along the snow covered edge as much as he dared, hoping and praying that he didn’t hook a wheel. In the meantime the conversation between Brad and Garney continued as if this were a stretch of dry interstate.

“Brad, are you boys still doing Ekati?”

“Yes sir, every year I say I’m done and I get sucked back in.”

Marty felt the muscles in his shoulders bunch up. His hands clamped onto the steering wheel and he pushed as hard against the seat as he could. He felt like he had a sudden paralysis of rigor when the trucks passed each other. He didn’t dare look over, terrified at what he might see, sure the southbound was close enough to touch. The air stream rocked the Kenworth and he gasped, thinking the ditch was pulling him over. Then the rig righted itself.

“Four north at 19.”

“Three south at 17. Okay, Garney have a safe trip north.”

“You too, my brother. Second one is coming at you, Marty.”

“Copy that,” Marty croaked, still reeling from the first pass and now prepping for the second. He was rounding the same corner Garney had and the southbound truck shut off his moose lights. Luckily he’d made the corner before they met and was climbing the hill, losing momentum, when they passed. The southbound truck had it the hardest. Below the corner cut into a hard left slope that banked downward to a drop-off littered with rocks and trees that waited mercilessly for a rig to fall victim. Marty hadn’t even considered that he would be coming back that way. “One to go! One more to go,” he wheezed and grabbed another gear.

“Evening Mark,” Merv said.

“Merv, how are yuh?”

“Living a dream.”

The third truck met him at the crest of the hill and they passed without incident. Marty let out a sigh of relief and shifted up again.

“Three south at sixteen.”

“Four north at 20. Have a good night, gents!”

“Same to you, Garney. See you at the Black Knight. Mark’s buying.”

"Sounds good."

"Meeting the last one now, Mark."

There was a click to acknowledge, but no words.

They continued north for another three kilometers, when Merv got on the radio and hailed Marty directly. "Marty, go to Ladd 4." Marty reached up and switched the radio over and then heard Merv say, "Did you make it?"

"Yeah," Marty replied.

"How are you doing up there?"

"I guess I'm not going fast enough, because you keep catching up."

"Nah, you're doing fine, but can I give you some advice?"

"I'll take anything I can get."

"Use the whole road. Unless we've got southbound, use the whole thing. Garney is up there bird dogging for you. If anything is coming, he'll tell you, so relax and use the whole road. It'll lessen your chances of buying a new mirror."

"A new mirror?"

"Yeah, the one you'll be laying on if you hook a wheel and end up in the ditch."

Marty moved his rig into the center of the narrow road, feeling some of his anxiety begin to ease. Then he exhaled a long exasperated gasp, and followed that with a convulsion of nervous laughter spurred by Merv's comment.

"Ride the snake," Marty said.

"Snake? What snake? You and Garney got some gay trucker thing going on?"

Marty reached up for his handset to explain, but Garney cut in.

"You're a funny guy, Merv. Marty, we'll be getting onto the Inuksuk in about two kilometers. I should have mentioned it earlier, but Merv gave you some good advice. Use the whole road when it's available. And don't worry about keeping up, my brother, I'm in no hurry."

"And stay the fuck off Garney's snake. You'll get the Aids," Spence chimed in.

"Too late," Marty snorted and felt a rush of relief. He also was surprised to realize that their conversation wasn't private. "Sorry, Garney, couldn't resist."

"No problem. Let these clowns have their laugh. When we hit Inuksuk, you'll see what I mean."

"Hey, Garney, shouldn't you be monitoring Ladd 1 for oncoming," Spence said.

"I'm already there," Garney replied.

"What does that mean," Spence asked.

"It means he's got two radios," Merv jabbed.

"And you call yourself an ice road trucker," Garney added. "How many radios you got, Merv?"

"Two, every winter driver worth his salt has two. Except Spence, of course."

"Yeah okay, whatever."

"Okay, my brothers, let's flip it back to Ladd 1."

Marty switched his radio back just in time to hear Garney announce. "Four north off the Ingraham Trail and onto the Inuksuk. Making a run for Sally's Bosom! Put your foot into it, Gents. The lady is slippery tonight. Keep her moving, Marty, she's wide open, there's no one coming."

Marty straddled the road as it twisted left and right. He was beginning to understand what Garney meant by riding the snake. Running on parts of the Ingraham was like balancing on the top of a ball that sloped dangerously on both sides; when you equated the twists and turns, it really was riding on the back of a snake.

"Marty," Merv said.

"Yeah?"

"Ahead the road forks, keep left and you're on the Inuksuk Trail. About a quarter of a click up you're going to start on a downward slope and at the bottom you are going to hit a right hand curve and then you'll be into a fucking hard left. After that you'll be running to climb Sally's Bosom. It's the biggest fucking hill on the trail. If you don't have the momentum, you'll be crawling over that hill, or worse, you won't make it and have to chain up. You don't want to chain up, Bud, so this is the one time I am going to tell you to put your foot into it. Use the whole road or ride Garney's snake, but get that big W900 moving, Bud."

Marty wondered why Merv, instead of Garney, was advising him about this, then understood that the big guy was probably too busy grabbing gears and steering to be giving advice.

Ahead, Marty saw the left hand fork.

Beyond that: **INUKSUK TRAIL – Keep Left! Notice to Public. Use at own risk!**

He took the left fork, leaving the Ingraham trail behind, but now the devil was hot on his heels. Ahead the road descended into darkness. The pavement was gone. Now he was running across beaten dirt and gravel track. Beneath him it shifted and bucked between ice patches and washboard. Marty took a deep breath and pushed down on the accelerator. His heart thudded—the turbo whistled, and the big 600 CAT engine growled with anticipation. The speedometer climbed as Marty sat on the edge of seat, searching the end of the headlight array for any change in the road. It began to curve as he pushed over seventy and the muscles in his chest contracted painfully. As he careened downward, he thought of nothing but the grey-brown icy corner that waited. Somewhere in the ditch, the devil waited eagerly. He didn't think he would ever again feel such terror and exhilaration for the rest of his life, but on this he was wrong.

When he hit the bottom he could feel the twin tankers being pulled hard by the gravitational pull of the curve and imagined Garney's devil riding the side, wrenching on the twin tankers, trying to knock them off their center of gravity. He turned the wheel as much as he gambled and shifted the big rig over and onto the slope of the road, riding the inside of the curve very much the same way a biker will lean into a turn. When he did this, the devil loosened its grip, but it wasn't over. The final approach to Sally's Bosom was met by an even harder bend, which cut hard left and he knew for this he would need to increase speed even more to make the hill. Ice crystals on the road scintillated and flickered in the dull yellow light—inviting him to come forth.

"Fuck it," he half moaned—half laughed. "Time to ride the snake!"

Then he pressed down on the accelerator. The turbo whistle rose, the engine roared, and the devil waited in the shadows just outside the arc of his headlamps. In the back of his head he thought he heard Ozzy Osbourne, screaming, "All aboard!" then laugh maniacally.

He rolled the truck over the snake's back and inside the curve. He leaned his body into the turn, as if his 164 pounds would make a difference once Lucifer climbed up the side of his rig. Inside the twin tankers, diesel sloshed, aiding in the tug-of-war with Big Garney Wilson's Devil. When he rounded the curve he felt the pull begin to release and moved the truck back up onto the middle of the trail.

Ahead, the two rock peaks jutted from the earth that had earned the namesake Sally's Bosom and straight off the cleavage, the Inuksuk Trail ran defiantly. Dancing behind them, a bright green curtain of northern lights twisted and turned erotically. Marty stamped down on the throttle and as he made a last push toward the hill, he wondered what awaited him on the other side. Heart pounding, sweat slick between his shoulder blades, he smiled and said, "The devil, of course. Waiting to race again."

10

At least an hour had passed since Angel sat her in the chair, binding her wrists to the armrests. An hour was her best guess, but it felt like an eternity and she wanted nothing more than to get this over with. That is, until she heard the vehicle come into the yard of the place she was being held. Then she decided that she wanted more time.

But that wasn't to be.

"He's here," Angel said nervously.

The vehicle engine shut off.

Maggie moaned. Her knees were suddenly shaking, and she had to pee again.

There was a pause, then a vacuous "Ca chunk!" of a vehicle door closing.

Footsteps clunked up the stairs, and then the door unlatched, followed by a gust of crisp winter air. He stamped his feet at the door and no one said a word. She could hear them breathing. Angel, her partner, and the assistant.

Were they afraid to say his name aloud, she wondered.

Footsteps moved toward her.

He leaned in close, the smell of aftershave, cigars, and some type of liquor. She could hear him breathing, feel him studying her. He stood in front of her, quietly waiting, for what she didn't know. She was terrified. Would there be a click of a gun hammer, the uncoiling of a spring loaded switchblade?

"You know who I am," he finally said.

She said nothing, instead fighting off the tears and urge to plead.

A hand came up and removed her blindfold.

No! No! No, she thought, averting her eyes and said, "Please don't."

"Don't what?"

"Please don't. I'm begging you, please."

"I'm not going to hurt you, Maggie."

She didn't believe him.

"Open your eyes. If I wanted you dead, it would already be done."

"I'm afraid."

"I know you are, but I promise you that if you open your eyes, nothing bad will happen."

"Okay," she said and with that she squinted, her pupils contracting against the dull yellow light and slowly the man's face came into focus. She blinked. He was inches from her.

"Do you know who I am?"

"Yes."

He was better looking than she had imagined. Except for the scar, which ran down the left side of his nose. His face was slim with hard, pronounced cheek bones pocked by acne scars from adolescence years, and he held a day's growth of stubble. His hair was blond, still winning the battle against the tangles of grey. He smiled and it was not unpleasant, but his eyes told another story, one that was conniving and dishonest. There were rattlesnakes in those eyes.

He turned back to the man who stood by Angel. "Cut her loose."

"Really?" the man questioned.

Shamus never turned his head back toward Maggie; instead, he held Angel's partner in his gaze. The man flinched and took what Maggie thought was a set of pliers from Angel. He looked afraid and remorseful.

He cut the zip ties that bound her hands to the armrests.

"Her feet too."

He reached down and cut the second ligature.

"Now throw that shit in the garbage." He took Maggie's hand in his own and in an apologetic business tone he said, "My name is Gordon Shamus, I used to work closely with your husband Marty. The fellow who just cut the unfortunate restraints is named Scott Turcotte, and the lady you already met is his wife Angela. The other fellow you see behind me is my personal assistant and driver, Donald Keefe."

Maggie glanced around at all of them, then back at Shamus. "Thank you."

"I am sorry for how you ended up here, Maggie, but Marty really left me no choice. You know what he's doing up there, you know how important it is that I keep tight control on everything, and sending you up to Montreal was too dangerous."

"Dangerous? Dangerous for who?"

Shamus didn't answer the question; instead he said, "If you had just stayed home and carried on, you wouldn't be sitting here today in this shitty trailer. Bad call on Marty's part, but I guess I can understand his concern. My reputation sometimes makes people nervous." At this he looked humble, but his eyes deceived the front.

As an insurance adjuster, Maggie made a career out of reading people. More than once she'd come upon an individual who set fire to a house, was feigning injury, and she would always look to their eyes. Those were the windows to the truth. In them she saw the truth and would know whether to start digging. She had a word for people like that. She called them Panda Bears. Garth Rogers, her boss, got a kick out of the analogy.

"What is a Panda Bear, Garth? A cute and cuddly creature that looks like a stuffed animal, but don't get too close or they'll tear you to pieces," she said in a matter of fact tone. "These people who burn down their houses or fake injuries aren't victims."

Gordon Shamus was definitely a Panda Bear.

"So, I have to stay here until Marty comes back?"

"No, of course not. From this point on, you're my guest."

11

ACADIA MINE
11:00 PM Pacific Time

The lab was a mess. White powdery fog hung in the air in the aftermath of the minor explosion that occurred when they removed the small pod from the interior of the skull. It wasn't an explosion really, not in the flash bang of artillery or that of a suicide bomber. This explosion was akin to but a similar reaction to dropping a bag of flour and having it split open, sending up spirals of white powder. The only difference was that they hadn't dropped anything. And the reaction based on the size of the pod seemed exaggerated.

From outside the skull, Nick traced the tubular straw-like thing that ran into the cheek. It was a direct feed into the pod in the roof of the creature's mouth to the pod. The pod was a little bigger than a computer mouse and had an eggshell texture on its outer skin. Nick had to cut a number of tendons to free it up before he could clamp onto it with the oversized tweezers and pull it away from the tube and remove it. Under the pressure of the tweezers, it collapsed slightly.

"What have we here," he said as he pulled it gingerly through the crevice. "It feels soft inside."

“A lubrication system? Like a saliva gland,” Ronny suggested.

“Maybe. The delivery tube looks organic.”

Ronny set a tray down beside the skull and Nick carefully lowered the pod onto it. They were both hovering over it, their foreheads almost touching when they heard the click of something. It sounded mechanical, spring-like, then poof. The contents of the pod blew upward into their face masks and filled the air.

Both men recoiled, but their face shields were hit with a force hard enough to push their heads back. Ronny was first to think that it had come alive and felt his heart skip a beat. Both men saw something in their mind’s eye, spots, moving, twisting, and then they were gone. When the air cleared, they looked down at the collapsed bag now emptied of its content.

“I certainly didn’t expect that.” Nick took a gloved hand and ran it over his face shield to clear the powder.

“No, never expected that at all.”

“You okay, any damage?”

Ronny wiped his face shield and couldn’t see anything that constituted a breach of his suit. “No, looks okay, no cracks, but the lab. There’s powder everywhere.”

“Yeah, bloody mess. I guess until it settles, we’re stuck here. We’ll need to vacuum up what we can, Ronny, then go through a complete decontamination.” Nick sighed. “I guess that settles it for today.”

He took an air gun and blew the powder off his suit and face shield, then did the same to Ronny. Neither man saw porous holes set into the face shields, nor did they feel the microscopic enzymes corkscrew into their corneas. Neither was aware, because at this point they could not feel the fluid contained in the anterior chamber of their eyes giving life to the microscopic organisms that were now embedded in the tissue of each man’s eye. They only saw spots in that instant and neither mentioned it to the other.

Now as they waited, the enzyme began its life-cycle, unfurling into worm-like organisms. They were half the size of a Paramecium, a mere 40 microns long. Twisting and spiraling in the eye fluid, their single purpose fired. Each micro-organism found its way into each man’s posterior chamber and corkscrewed through the membrane and into the vitreous fluid inside the eyeball. The tiny worm-like creatures were not big enough to complete their task, for now their journey was halted, until they were strong eat through the macula of the inner eye and into the optic nerve. In the meantime, tiny bits of lights fired at the macroscopic level; the worms had already begun to grow, absorbing enough vitreous fluid to feed themselves.

Ronny Fraser and Nick Anderson had no idea they'd been attacked by the parasitic organisms. They sat and waited for the dust to clear. As they did, changes took place. If each man were to gouge the other's eyes out in the next half minute, they might have saved themselves, but neither knew what was growing inside them.

But they would…

***

Chapter 16—Find the Thrombus

1

Portage 46
0500 HOURS

Phil Crane was driving the pickup across the portage, scoping out a decent place to park. This job reminded him of when he was a traffic cop lying in wait for some mope to push the speed limit. The speed on the portage was 30 km/h.

"Four North on 46," the convoy leader called out.

Crane was coming around the corner, trying to find a place to get out of the way when the first big rig met him head on. He turned hard up the snow bank and almost buried the pickup truck to avoid being run over.

"Holy fucking shit," he cried, watching the wheels of the trailer come dangerously close to his driver's side window.

"Boys, look like we got a security who doesn't like to call portages," the driver said.

"A newbie, huh, maybe looking to hand out some speeding tickets," another chuckled.

With the rig past him, Crane got on the radio. "That was pretty close, driver!"

"You're telling me, security. Might be wise to call your portage next time so I know you're there."

"You almost hit me. What's your driver number?" Crane barked.

"My driver number is 577, you can pass that on to John Pringle when you see him. Be sure to also pass on that you didn't call your portage and that I have three other drivers who are willing to back up my claim."

Crane held the handset, shook his head, and grumbled, "Never mind."

"Shit, he looks pretty stuck," a third man said.

And then the fourth rig went past and stopped on the trail.

"Chancy, I'm stopping for a sec." This driver had a British accent.

"Copy that, Willy, we'll wait up. Give a shout when you're done."

As Crane tried to rock the pickup from the rut, a big man, with red hair and beard to match, approached. Crane put the pickup in reverse, pretending not to notice, embarrassed at his situation. The bastard was probably just coming back to gloat. He stepped on the gas pedal, and the wheels spun. "Fuck!"

The driver tapped on his window.

Crane put the truck in park and opened the window.

"You're just digging in," the man named Willy said. "I've got a tow strap in my jockey-box. We could yank you out with a single tug."

"Okay," Crane sat up. "What do you need me to do?"

"Technically I'm not authorized to do this sort of thing. You'd have to call back to Corbett and get one of the Lupan Boys to come out with a grader. Pringle would hear about this, I imagine the other security guys would be busting your chops over it. I guess they'd probably give you a cool nickname. Something like Snowbank Hank." Willy smiled.

Crane smiled back. "Okay, so what's in it for you?"

"I was thinking that if I gave you a tug, no one would have to know. We let bygones be bygones. No harm, no foul, wink wink nudge nudge, know what I mean, Mate?"

"I could get behind that."

Willy broadened his smile and said, "I'll grab the tow strap."

Willy, it seemed, was well prepped for this sort of thing. He hooked the tow strap onto the eye-ring hanging from the back of the pickup, then onto a hook at the back of the trailer. He then told Crane to let the rig do all the work. "Don't need you piling into me when you break free. Just shout once you're out."

"Okay," Crane said, climbing back into the driver seat.

Willy ran up the side of the rig, disappearing the same way he had come.

Then on the radio: "You ready, Mate?"

"Yes."

The rig began to drive away, pulling up the slack on the tow strap, and then Crane felt a jolt as the pickup was pulled from the snow bank. In this instant, he dropped the handset and the rig was pulling him down the path behind it. He reached down and scooped it up when the rig stopped and began to back up. "Okay, all clear. I'm out."

"Okay, good show."

Willy came back, unhooked and rolled up his tow strap.

"Thanks," Crane said.

"You're welcome, Mate. See you on the trail."

All this was done in under five minutes.

Willy mounted up and called to the others. "Chancy, we're all finished up here!"

"Have a good day, Security," Chancy said.

"Yeah, you too."

2

Billy Jack was at his camp, unloading two kills from the toboggan. They had already been disemboweled and prepped for hanging. The trees surrounding the camp weren't very high. The tallest two were 25 feet, stunted by the unwelcoming tundra of rock and frozen earth. These two would suit Billy's purpose, though. Setting up a pulley-system that worked off his electric winch, he'd been able to suspend three caribou ten feet in the air without very little strain on the two trees. Before lifting them, he wrapped them in material to keep the ravens from getting into the meat.

He climbed into the Arctic tent and lit his catalytic heater, then the lantern. Setting them in the center of the tent, he stepped out to start a new fire. The clouds overhead sprinkled a confetti of snowflakes downward as he piled up wood.

Old Whitey had been in the camp today, leaving behind fresh tracks. But he hadn't seen the wolf since coming out to hunt. He wondered if age was finally catching up with him. Maybe his days were numbered. He considered this and though he had an affection for the old wolf, he knew that he would dispatch the animal if it came down to it suffering.

He poured a cup of gas over the kindling and lit it. The day was ending and the temperature would drop a little, but the overcast sky would keep it at an acceptable temperature for his purposes. As the fire crackled and popped, he added more wood. He'd brought wood out for the hunt. Trees and fallen wood were scarce up here and he tried to respect the landscape, so he brought his own in.

Reaching into his pocket, he felt for the baggy and pipe. As a rule he didn't smoke when he hunted, but when he was alone out here, he would partake in the herb. It made him relax, made him forget about the things he'd done, the men he'd killed. This allowed him to gaze up in wonder at the majesty of the night sky and its flickering lights. That wouldn't be the case today; the cloud cover blocked out the night sky, but that didn't stop him from glancing upward into the grey canopy.

He stuffed the cup of the pipe and lit it. Drawing it in, he felt it first burn, and then tickle the inside of his throat. He had considered buying a vaporizer, Spence had even suggested it, but he wasn't a serious pot smoker.

He exhaled, coughing a bit.

"If you're going to smoke, there's got to be a better delivery system," Spence, who occasionally shared in the ritual, said. "This shit is just too fucking harsh on the lungs, man. Why the hell did I quit smoking cigarettes if I'm going to beat the fuck out of my lungs with this shit?" He took another draw, leaving the memory of Spence's complaint behind and scanned the wood line for a voyeuristic silhouette.

Where are you, Old Whitey, he thought and exhaled.

He had a fresh piece of meat stowed in the toboggan specifically for the big wolf. Maybe he wouldn't return. Maybe their companionship was coming to an end after three years. "That's just the pot talking," he said aloud and giggled. The fire crackled in unison and he continued to smoke the contents of the pipe. As he did, he watched the flakes of snow swirl above the rising fire and the last light of day surrendered to the overwhelming night.

In the distance, beyond the obscuring trees, he could hear the thunder of diesel engines echoing out across the ice. He imagined that Spence would be rolling across that ice road very soon, or perhaps had already. Axe would also be close by, likely settled in at Corbett Camp, playing cribbage with Vincent or eating the crappy food that had put an extra 20 pounds around his little brother's midsection. He called Axe his little brother, but he was actually much bigger and far stronger than Billy.

He tapped the pipe on the side of his palm, emptying the ash from the bowl. That was enough for tonight; he still had to clean his weapon and eat. As he moved to the toboggan, he could feel the wolf watching him but did not know its whereabouts.

"Old Whitey," he said smiling. "I have something for you."

3

"Four North, off the Inuksuk and onto the ice," Garney announced.

Marty was just beginning to relax after the harrowing ride of twists and turns that not only elevated his adrenaline levels but left cramping in his lower back and arms. Now that it was over, he really had only two things to consider. Whether the stress of rolling across frozen lake would match the last 90 minutes, and the trip back down. He opened the window to let a bit of fresh air in. The last kilometer of the Inuksuk, thankfully, was flat and wide.

"Bring her on when you get here, Marty," Garney called back.

"Copy that." He was still a kilometer from the entrance to the ice road. In fact, instead of being a kilometer behind Garney, as he was supposed to be, he was a full two. His caution and inexperience led to multiple slowdowns, which also meant not having the momentum to pull the many hills. He guessed that Merv White was extending every ounce of patience, as he adjusted to his amateurish driving ability.

"Looking good, Marty," Merv said. "Just don't miss the turn. Unless you like backing up, cus there's no turn around."

Marty eased off the accelerator.

Ahead a sign read:

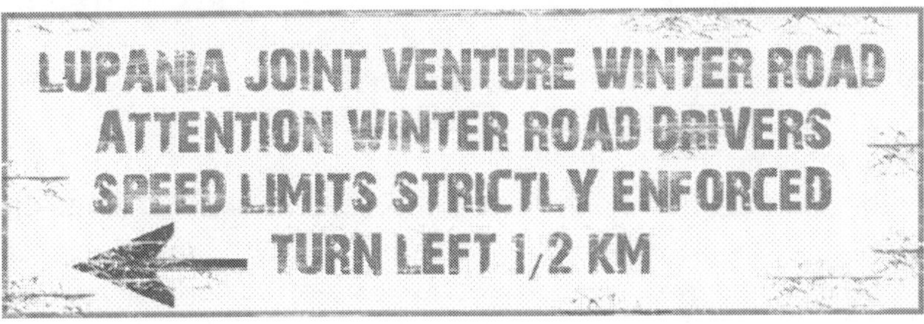

He shifted down; ahead a large sign with fluorescent orange arrow pointed left. He wasn't sure how he would have missed that. But apparently some drivers had, according to Merv. When he reached the turn, he was almost at a full stop. Flurries of snow danced in the beam of his headlights like tiny insects. He turned the Kenworth and crawled down the short bank that put him onto the lake bed. At the edge of the bank, a small blue sign bore the name: HANNON LAKE

Beyond that, a highway sign read: Maximum 25 km/h

In the distance, approximately a kilometer up the ice, he could see Garney's tail lights. Marty had fallen back pretty far. He wondered how he was going to close the distance at such a low speed. Then Garney piped up on the radio and he understood.

"Hannon Security, have you got a copy?"

"Go for Hannon."

"Good evening, I have four Super B's en-route to your front door. Here are the numbers. 956, 990, 901, and 999."

"Welcome back, Garney. Just to be sure, though. We have, 956, 990, 901 and 999. That's Merv White, Spencer Hughes, Martin Croft, and Big Garney Wilson. Not necessarily in order of appearance."

"Yes Sir, uh huh. That would be correct."

"Okay, Garney, you get your posse gathered up and once you're ready, we'll get you on your way."

"Thank you kindly. Once my brothers get here, we'll do a quick walk around and get this show on the road."

"Copy that. I'll wait for your call."

Marty rolled down onto the lake cautiously and once the truck and trailer leveled off, he sped up to the 25 km/h. As he followed Garney's tail lights, he could hear the ice pop and flex below him. He rolled down his window and it amplified the sound. He didn't like that, so he rolled it back up.

Then Garney called back to Marty.

"Marty, my brother, switch over to the other channel."

"Copy that," Marty said and flipped his radio over to Ladd 4. "Go ahead."

"Now that wasn't so hard, was it, my Brother?"

Marty laughed. "Yeah, a clean set of shorts and some valium and I'll be just fine."

"Can you hear the ice cracking, Marty?" Spence asked.

"Yeah. Is that normal?"

"Oh my god, no, it's not normal. Bail out, Marty! Bail out!" Merv cried.

"Quit fucking around," Spence said. "Yeah, it's normal."

"Marty, when you get to the portage, you'll be climbing a very short grade, but it will be icy so pick your speed up and do what you have to do. When you roll into Hannon's property, make sure you're only doing 30 clicks an hour. Last thing you want is to get an infraction on your first portage."

"Okay, Garney, no problem." He kept his eyes on Garney's tail lights.

Ahead, frozen into the ice, another sign read: **1/2 Km**

"What does this sign mean," he said into the handset.

"The half K sign? It means for the next driver can proceed onto the ice," Spence said.

"Coming on now," Merv called and rolled down the bank, falling in behind Marty.

Marty understood. This must have been the point when Garney told him to. "Bring her on when you get here." He smiled. "Sorry, Merv, I guess I should have figured that out."

"No worries, Bud."

"Just follow me onto the portage, Marty, and when you get into the Hannon's, fall in behind me and we'll do a walk around."

Garney's truck was veering left and disappeared up over the bank as it entered the portage. Marty followed him and it seemed to take forever to reach the base of the portage. Merv was 500 meters behind, calling Spence onto this ice.

"Bring her on, Spence."

"Copy."

When he reached the portage, he gave a little extra and rolled off of the ice and onto the hard pack. Once on the trail he backed his speed down and rolled into the Hannon Lake security yard. Which was little more than a clearing with a mobile trailer, a small structure that housed a generator and a pickup. The yard was lit up by a temporary street lamp that emitted a bright white glow. Ahead Garney's Rig idled, the tail lights glowing. Outside the rig, the big man waited.

Marty rolled up behind Garney and set his truck brakes.

Pu-shooooooosh!

Climbing from the rig, he felt the sudden change in temperature and wondered if he'd ever get used to it.

Garney seemed not to notice. He was grinning ear to ear, his lips pulled back from his giant choppers, bigger than life. He didn't even wait until Marty was off the step when he proudly put his arm around Marty and jostled him. "Well, you made it, my Brother! And all in one piece, too! Uh huh. Yep. I'm proud of yuh, my brother. Proud as punch!"

Marty smiled sheepishly. "That's a fucking scary road, Garney."

"Don't I know it," he said and winked. "Did you feel him?"

"Who?"

"Who? The devil, my brother! Did you feel old Beelzebub yanking on your rig?"

Marty nodded and laughed. "I felt the son of a bitch."

"I'm proud of yuh, Marty. That's the hardest part of the ice road. From here in it's a snap. You can relax now, crank up the tunes and put on the cruise control. I'll keep you up to date on what's happening, so you'll still need your radio on, but you just completed the hardest part of being an ice road trucker, my brother."

Marty beamed, filled with pride and then his face became serious because this wasn't the hardest part about the ice road. This was just the warm-up act. He knew that. The hardest part would be the second run, dealing with Crane, keeping Maggie safe and coming out of this alive. This? This was just a momentary vacation from the harsh reality of his circumstances. He needed to stay focused. Needed to remember that he wasn't out here to have fun or bond. He was out here to do a job.

"Is everything okay, my Brother?"

Marty pulled focus, looked up at the big man and realized his thoughts were being expressed outwardly. He smiled up at Big Garney Wilson. He pushed the thoughts of Shamus and Crane and even Maggie away for now. There was plenty of time and open ice on which to consider his predicament.

"Yeah, everything's fine."

Garney smiled and turned. "Here comes Merv. Get your walk around done and when Spence gets here, we'll have one more powwow. Meantime I gotta see a man about a horse, uh huh yep. Sure do."

Marty did a quick walk around, banging tires, listening for air leaks. As he did this, Merv hopped from his rig and did the same. Spence came rolling into the yard behind them and Marty approached Merv.

"Hey, how's it going?" Merv smiled.

"Well, I got up the trail without getting killed. I guess that's something."

"It sure is. I've seen a few calamities over the years, guys losing it on a corner. Even saw a guy freeze up in YK. You did just fine for a rookie. The Inuksuk is a dangerous road and as long as you respect it, you'll be fine."

Marty stuck out his hand.

Merv took it.

"Thanks."

"No problem, bud, that's what it's all about."

They shook and Marty waited for Garney and Spence to join them.

When they did, Garney gave a similar speech to the one in YK. That there were no hurries or worries. That they get their fuel when we damn well give it to them. Everyone agreed, Spence congratulated Marty on a job well done, and then they mounted up.

"Hannon Security, you got a copy?"

"Go for Hannon."

"We're all ready to rock 'n' roll."

"Okay, Garney, I've got you guys leaving Hannon at 21:32 Hours. There are no issues to report other than to say that Wombat Lake is still a trouble lake and has an All Trucks 10 km/h limit. You guys have a safe trip north.

"Thank you, Dave. We will do just that. Yep, and we'll catch you on the next one."

Garney's truck began moving and Marty followed, wanting to make sure he didn't fall behind as they rolled out of the staging area. Garney rolled onto the next lake. Marty waited to be called out. At the lake's edge two signs stood at the right.

The first a speed posting: Maximum 15 km/h.

Beside that: Wekweti Lake.

He scribbled down the name of the lake and the time of crossing. He thought this might be important, but wasn't really sure. The worry settled back into his guts as Garney got farther out onto the ice. At least she was safe up in Montreal and his biggest concern was watching his own back. But he knew she wouldn't be safe for long if this whole thing went sideways. He would have to work on a plan and think about what to do about Crane. Crane was his immediate concern.

"Okay, my brother, I'm at the half, bring her on."

"Copy that. Rolling on now." He pushed the shifter into second and rolled onto the ice. After getting his speed up to 15 km/h, he set the cruise, crawling at a snail's pace toward the 1/2 kilometer marker.

Two days, he thought. *Then I'm doing this shit for real. Two days.*

4

ACADIA MINE
05:10 HOURS

"*Find the thrombus! Skent! Find the thrombus! Skent,*" called the intermingling collective whispers. He didn't understand the demands, and even as they faded and he came back to the waking world, they insisted. *"Find it! Skent! Find the thrombus! Skent! Skent! Skent! Find the thrombus..."*

Then they were gone.

Nick heard a second sound, a minor tapping on his window. The winds had picked up and the silicone seal on the outside had developed a tail that thumped angrily against the glass pane. He sat up, pulled back the curtain, and looked down at the piece of rubber as it twisted and bumped against the glass. It was almost as if it was writhing in pain, wanting to pull away and escape. The thing had been a source of irritation since he'd gotten here. He was on the third floor and the window could not be opened. It was a sealed unit. All he needed really was a razor blade and the tail could be cut away. He hadn't bothered to report it to maintenance. Now, his third night since arriving and the fucking thing was driving him mental.

"Skent," he said aloud and thought. *I could go out on the ledge and pour a glass of water over it and it would be frozen until spring.* A blast of snow kicked up from the edge below the window and sent the tiny tail into a convulsive panicked dance. The edge below the window was approximately two feet wide and made of aluminum flashing. He followed the edge with his eyes to the West side of the building. *I'd have to get on the roof somehow and ease myself down onto the flashing.*

The tail twisted, tapping excitedly.

It's not that far, half a football field. The real trick would be dropping down from the roof onto the edge without spilling the water. He wasn't even considering the 40-foot drop or if he were to lose his footing and topple down to the steel grated walkway below, the glass of water would be the least of his concerns.

The phone on the nightstand rang.

He reached down and picked it up. "Hello."

"What did you say?" It was Chase.

"Huh?"

"What is skent?"

Did I say that?

Nick shook his head. "What can I do for you, Chase?"

"I'm calling to let you know that there is going to be a controlled blast in the pit today. I thought you might like to attend."

"Controlled blast?"

"What?"

"Do you have a hearing problem, Chase?" For some reason he was becoming increasingly irritated and though he considered Chase Fenwick somewhat of a lap dog to Damien Lars, it wasn't his usual approach to be confrontational. "Well..."

"No, it's just..."

"Just what," he snapped.

"You said it again."

"What?"

"Skent or maybe it was skentophyte."

The tail on the window flapped and twisted, demanding his attention.

Tap tap tap...

"I don't know what you're talking about?"

"Well maybe it's the connection. We've been getting some interference lately. I'll have the lineman look into it," Chase said defensively. "Would you like to attend the blast?"

Tap tap tap...

"Uh no, I've got business down in the lab."

"You won't be able to go down there during the blast, Nick. All active duty areas are restricted until the blasting is complete."

"Who authorized this?" Nick snapped.

"I did, it's been on the roster for weeks," Chase snapped back. "Look, in case you haven't noticed, my position here is Chief of Operations and until I get official notice from Damien Lars, overseeing the day to day operations here is still my job."

Tap tap tap...

Nick felt his temper flare and he was about to say something, but Chase kept going.

"So, there will be a controlled blast in the pit today and as a measure of safety, all work in and around the pit will be halted until the Explosives Team gives me the all clear. If you have a problem with this, Nick, we can take it up with Damien when he gets here the day after tomorrow."

Nick reached up and closed the curtain, then stuck his index finger into his left ear to muffle the sound. Taking a deep breath, he chose his words carefully. "I apologize, Chase, I had a sleepless night, migraine headache and I inadvertently took it out on you. Of course you have a job to do. I was out of line."

"Do you feel sick? Maybe you should report to the infirmary?"

"No, I've suffered migraines my whole life. I just have to ride this out. A couple of extra strength Tylenol should do the trick. Maybe some food too." He was lying, of course; there was no headache, but there was something wrong.

"Well I feel bad for barking at you. Grab some rest and let me know if there's anything I can do to help. Our resident nurse, Sheila, could stop in and check up on you, maybe prescribe something a little stronger."

"I'll just stick with the Tylenol for now. Can you call me when we get the all clear?"

“Sure, no problem. The blast is scheduled for 11:00 AM. Once I get an all clear, you’ll be the first to know.”

“Thank you, Chase.”

Chase hesitated, then replied, “Okay.”

Nick removed the phone from his ear and placed it back in the cradle, unaware that his final words to Chase Fenwick were, “Skent!” He moved away from the window, the flap of the tail and into the single toilet sink combination the small room provided. Above the sink a small rectangular mirror hung. He stared at his own reflection, trying to make sense of what was happening.

You’re just tired, he thought. *Jet lag and exhaustion coupled with extreme stress. Who the hell wouldn’t be irritable?* He reached over, unzipped his shaving kit, and pulled out his toothbrush. As he squeezed the paste onto the brush, he thought he heard another sound, not a flapping, but buzzing like mosquitoes. This sound did not emanate from the room, but inside his head.

“Find the thrombus!”

5

They were driving again, but this time she was in the back of Gordon Shamus’s Lincoln seated beside him. Before climbing into the car, he had allowed her to change into blue jeans and sneakers. His demeanor had been cordial, even affectionate, as if Marty meant something to him; and by proxy, so did she.

Bullshit, she told herself. *If you ran he’d beat you senseless.* Or worse, he’d get Angel to kick the hell out of her. She didn’t know why that would be worse, but something told her that it would. Maggie knew, at this point in the game there was a silent understanding between her and Shamus. He would treat her as a guest as long as she played by his rules. If she attempted to deviate from those rules, he would remove the tightly fitted mask. What lurked behind that mask was dangerous and unbalanced.

“Where are we going?” she asked.

“Tonight we are going to take you to a safe place to get cleaned up,” Shamus said, not looking at her, instead staring out the window. “You can get some food and sleep. Tomorrow we’ll have breakfast and I’ll bring you up to speed on what the plan is.”

The car was turning off Burlington Street and onto the Red Hill Parkway, which would take them up onto the Niagara Escarpment. Behind them, Angel or Angela and her husband followed in their car. She wondered why. Would they be guarding her until this was over? When she looked back from the window, Shamus was smiling at her.

She managed an awkward pleasantry and his grin widened.

“I’ll say this, Maggie, Marty has good taste. You are extremely pretty.”

“Thank you.” She felt her heart speed up.

Then he turned back toward the window. “You’re welcome.”

The mask had already begun to slip.

***

Chapter 17—The Day After

1

The home was a larger version of a Spanish villa, once inhabited by the late Jude Shamus. Gordon had inherited the place when the old man dropped dead. Maggie awoke that next morning to the fragrance of must and mothballs. The room was a time capsule of another era. This room had been a spare, and the bed on which she lay was the newest piece of furniture. The rest of the decor was a loose mess of oversized mirrors, bureaus, and chairs with hooked feet that resembled animal paws. Much of the furniture was gaudily wrapped in red and green velour prints. On the walls, photographic prints hibernated beneath an inch of dust. And there was a lot of that in here. Strands of light filtered through the gap in the heavy velvet curtains that covered the picture window. In that, dust particles floated like brine shrimp caught in unseen currents.

She was surprised how easily sleep had come the night before. How after the door closed and the lock clicked over, she had pulled back the covers on the bed, climbed beneath them, and fallen asleep. She guessed it was a hangover from whatever it was that Angel had slipped her.

Shamus had led her up the stairs and across an exposed hall to this room. A balcony that wrapped the perimeter of the upper floor overlooked the main foyer. "For tonight, you can sleep here. In the morning we'll have breakfast and talk about what happens next. It's not much, Maggie, but it has a working bathroom should you need it." He smiled.

"Thank you."

"Donald will bring up your bag." He turned to go, then stopped, his back still to her, and said, "Maggie."

"Yes."

"I know you're frightened and the way you ended up here was unpleasant, but I'm going to ask you refrain from any thoughts of leaving." He turned to face her. "I have Angela and Scott watching the house and there is Marty to think about." His face was expressionless, except for his eyes, which were far away, some unseen thought playing out behind them. What that was she didn't want to speculate. Marty had been right, this man was psychotic.

"I'll be here in the morning."

He stood that way, looking at her for a moment longer. Not hearing her, but looking through her. His chest rose and fell. She held him in her gaze, fearful that lowering her eyes would somehow indicate insincerity. For only a second, her eyes settled upon the old scar that ran down the side of his nose and wondered who had done that. Then when she brought them back up to meet his, he was looking at her instead of through her. "It happened when I was a kid."

She didn't know how to respond. "I'm sorry, I wasn't..."

"Don't be, it was a long time ago. Most people are afraid to ask." He grinned at this.

"Okay."

Beyond him, carrying Maggie's luggage, Donald was waiting. He was just a blur beyond the frightening figure who stood in the doorway. She understood now why they couldn't run, why Marty had been so adamant. She didn't think Gordon Shamus was capable of letting something go. What would have become of them had they been caught after mucking up his plans?

"I'll tell you about it some time." He reached out and touched her shoulder, his expression softened. "For tonight, get some sleep and we'll have breakfast." Then he let go and turned away.

Frozen in the doorway, Maggie watched Gordon Shamus glide past Donald, his left hand running along the balcony railing.

"Come down to my office after you get her squared away."

"Okay, Gordon," Donald said and began to walk toward her.

"Goodnight, Maggie."

"Goodnight, Gordon."

Now, she lay on her side watching the particles of dust rise and fall in the ray of light, feeling guilty for sleeping so soundly. She had to get up, but didn't want to. Afraid of what the day offered. Outside the room she could hear movement coming from downstairs. Not voices, but footsteps clunking about, water being turned on and off. She contemplated what the day would bring. This wasn't like her. She wasn't the type to sit in a puddle of her own self-pity and that infuriated her.

Oh, for shit's sake.

She threw the heavy comforter aside, hopping from the bed, almost tripping over her carry-on and stubbing her toe against the hard plastic edge of the bag. Hot vibrations of pain crystallized in nerves of her big toe, inviting her to cry out in sympathy. She sat back down on the edge of the bed, managing to keep her cry to a low and sharp, "Fuck."

She sat that way for a while, watching the floating dust, waiting for the pain to withdraw. She reached down, moved the carry-on aside, and stood. Moving across the room, she walked on tip toe, afraid movement might draw a curious knock at the door. Once reaching the window, she pushed the curtain aside and gazed out.

The landscape was blanketed by snow that rose in humps, concealing that which would sleep until spring. There was a patio, surrounded by stone edging, and a pillar at each corner. What would this look like in the summer? Did Shamus actually entertain on that patio? She couldn't imagine. Beyond that, the countryside fell away, leaving a panoramic view of city and the adjacent lake Ontario.

A knock came at the door.

She dropped the curtain and turned in panic, her voice a squeak. "Yes."

"Gordon would like you to come down for breakfast." It was Donald.

She took a step away from the window and strode back toward the bed as she spoke. "I'll need a few minutes to clean up and I'll be down."

"I'll let him know." There was an audible click as a key turned in the lock, then the footsteps she never heard approach clunked away. She had no idea how long Donald had been on the other side of that. She reached down, tossed the comforter back onto the bed, and lifted the carry-on up and opened it.

Breakfast with an Irish gangster. Oh, what to wear, she thought.

Stifling a hopeless cry, she cupped her hand over her mouth. How the hell did she end up here? What was it Angel had said? "You can go back to fucking people over on insurance claims and banging that good looking husband."

Really? Were they actually going to let them go back to their lives when this was over? She doubted it very much. The only reason she was alive now was because Marty hadn't completed the job. For now, she was leverage and that made her useful to Gordon Shamus. She wouldn't be needing to send Marty a message that she'd been taken, Shamus would be doing that, if he hadn't already. Her only use to him was keeping Marty motivated. After that? She didn't want to think about it. Grabbing her makeup kit and a clean set of clothes, she made for the bathroom to clean up.

2

"Come to me, Ronny," her voice, low—raspy and seductive, invited. She was inside the chamber, wearing her lab coat, glasses, and nothing else. Her hair hung loose over her shoulders, tangles of blond unbridled from the tight knit ponytail she usually wore. Overhead a light, blue and green, pulsed rhythmically like a heartbeat.

"Allison?" He felt a cool breeze and realized he was naked.

"Come to me, Ronny." She unbuttoned the lab coat, pulling it away and exposing her copper toned skin. "You know you want to."

The light continued to pulse above to an alternating electric hum.

"We can't do this down here," he said. "People will catch us."

"No one will know." She dropped the lab coat, and fully exposed, she ran a hand down between her ample breasts. "I want you, Ronny."

He stared at her, felt himself harden, and took a step forward.

Her hand pushed downward between her legs. "I want you inside me."

The blue green light pulsed.

He took three steps and reached out. She took his hand in hers and placed it upon her left breast.

"Yes," she cooed, reaching up, taking his other hand, leading it down to the place where hers had been. He came closer, brushing himself against the soft skin covering her pelvic bone. Simultaneously she led his free hand down into the warmth between her legs and he crushed against her. "Oh yes, Ronny, I have always wanted you."

"Really?"

With his hand now in the place it had been led, she let go and wrapped her fingers around him, squeezing him tightly. "Yes and this..." She squeezed again. "I want this inside me."

The light pulsed, green, then blue, humming, and her free hand ran down the arch of his back and onto his left buttock. He removed his hand from her breast and pulled her against him. When he did this he saw the two monoliths that stood between glowing white hot, fiery red beneath them. There was a smell of burning copper.

Her hand released him and the rock below his feet softened to foam, pushing up between his toes. Together they began to lie down as the light continued its pulse and hum and then there were the beckoning whispers.

Come to us. Find us. Feel us.

Allison wrapped her legs around him. Clamping onto him vice-like. She kissed him. First his lips, then his ears. “Thrombus,” she whispered. “Close your eyes.”

He did and felt the soft supple touch of her lips draw over him in a succession of kisses. As she did, her grip tightened and though he wanted to push up inside, he could not. “I want you,” he urged. “I want to be inside you.”

She kissed each of his closed eyes. “Do you?”

“Yes.”

“Come with me, Ronny.”

He pushed harder against her, and then his world became fluid and ethereal. Her embrace dissolving, he opened his eyes and the blue green light pulsed against a sudden succession of low hissing whispers.

“*Skent! Skent! Skent!*”

The light was blinding, overhead spokes turned, a clicking sound. Gears of machinery turned against the call of an electric hum. He felt himself being pulled upward into the light, still naked. Water droplets dripped upward. Inside his head there was a sound, like a horde of mosquitoes buzzing hungrily. Tiny needles of pain pricked from inside his eyes.

Allison called, “Come with me, Ronny.”

Her voice became static. “Come to me.”

Then her tone warped. “I’m inside you. Skent.”

Then there were low collective whispers. “We are Skentophyte.”

Ronny Fraser fell from earth into the light.

3

The convoy rolled across Corbett Lake at 25 km/h. In their path the sun was still behind the horizon, painting the sky in hues of cotton candy pink and blue. On the radio, Merv and Garney were talking about motorcycles. Spence was watching the movie “The Usual Suspects” on his laptop. Marty would have never believed someone could watch a movie while driving. Moving at this speed was mind numbing. He had to open the window twice and let a blast of fresh air in just to keep from nodding off. It had been eight hours since they departed YK and he was exhausted. He planned on filling his thermos with coffee when they got to Corbett Lake Camp, which was another thirty minutes away.

Occasionally, they passed a southbound convoy, which was met by greetings and the odd joke. Garney, it seemed, knew everyone on this track, or at least they knew him. Marty guessed it was that gravelly voice and cheerful demeanor that burned the bigger than life personality of Garnet Wilson into the memory of those he met.

"How's it going back there, Spence, anything to report?" Merv asked.

"Keyser Soze is just about to reveal himself," Spence answered.

"I was thinking more along the line of pickup trucks."

"No, Merv, no pickup trucks. Talk to me in five, this is almost over."

"Spence, my brother, how many times have you seen that movie?" Garney said chuckling.

"I don't know, Garney. I just know it's almost over, so I'll get back to you."

"How you doing, Marty? Still awake," Merv prodded.

"Yeah. Still awake, and learning the finer points of Harley Davidson."

"As you should, my friend. There is no substitute."

"So I've heard. I'm looking forward to breakfast."

"Once the sun comes up, you'll get your second wind, Marty. Best thing to do is just keep talking and don't let yourself zone out. We'll be in Corbett in about 25 minutes," Merv said. "Oh, and speak of the devil."

"She's a beauty," Garney said.

The sun crested the horizon, a thin arch of gold washing out in light pastels of vibrant pink and blue that defined the elegant arctic landscape. In doing this, it offered up a mirage of visual warmth.

From the radio Marty heard, "Corbett Lake, have you got a copy?"

"Go ahead for Corbett Lake," a female voice answered.

"Good morning, Kerry, we have five southbound empties looking to turn and burn. Here are the numbers..."

Marty turned the radio down and took in the morning sun. The exhaustion he'd spent the evening battling was now subsiding and he was getting his second wind.

Shadows deepened the rough edging of snow and ice.

In the distance, pushing up out of the ice, sat Corbett Lake Camp, accentuated by a cluster of buildings and 300-foot radio tower. Lights from the camp were drowning in the glow of the morning sunrise.

Halfway there, Marty thought.

"Good morning, security," Spence announced on the radio.

Marty glanced into the mirror. Saw the headlights bouncing up and down, a pickup following their convoy. This pickup, a ghostly shadow given away only by the glow of its halogen lights, was right beside Spence's rig.

"Good morning," Security responded. "How are we doing today?"

"Not bad," Spence said. "A hearty breakfast and some coffee will hit the spot. Can you give me a radar reading?"

"Sure thing," the security man said and moved his truck in behind Spence. "I've got you rolling at 25 km/h"

"Perfect."

"Hey, Security, can you give me a reading as well," Merv asked.

"You're the third truck?"

"Yeah, sure am."

"Okay." The pickup pulled out from behind Spence and proceeded past him.

"May as well check us all, Barry. Make sure we're all compliant," Garney interrupted.

"Oh, hey, Garney, I thought I heard you out here."

"Yes Sir, uh huh. How you been keeping, Barry?"

"Not bad. Another year on the ice. Third man, I have you at 25 km/h."

The pickup shot past Merv and moved up behind Marty's rig. "Second man, you are right on the money. Twenty five."

Marty picked up the handset. "Thanks, security."

"Not a problem at all." He pulled out from behind Marty and passed on the left, then got between him and Garney. "Garney, you are clocked at 25 km/h."

"Thank you, Barry. Well I guess my GPS is doing its job."

"Not a problem. Speaking of breakfast, I think I'm going to grab a little, so maybe we'll see you at Corbett." The driver wheeled out from behind Garney. "Going to bring her up your right side, Garney."

"Bring her on, Barry, I'll keep an eye out for yuh."

The pickup accelerated and shot past Garney. Two kilometers ahead, another southbound convoy was coming and that convoy leader announced a pickup was approaching. The sun climbed higher and across the ice road the morning breeze carried fine granules of snow that looked more like mist, in a continual wave across their path.

4

Ronny Fraser knew that what he was seeing was something between hallucination and lucid dream, but it did not make the sight any less frightening. They were the very skeletal creatures from the lab. Except in this state, they were living, breathing entities and he was among them. They moved about him in swarms. Like insects, each had a distinct purpose, but all were in service to the collective.

This is their world, he thought, taking in the strange buildings that were octagonal at the base and from them protruding upward were large porous towers that reminded him somewhat of termite mounds. These reached hundreds of feet into the air and from their peaks a green vapor expelled. There were thousands of these structures in this extraterrestrial city. Above the towers, the sky was lit by twin suns lighting the day not with Sunkist orange but emerald green. It would have been stunning, except for the clacking of teeth, the collective hiss as they moved past like cars on a city street. Each moved in uniform fashion, crawling on all fours, hissing those words. There was a stench as well, like rotten egg, and this caused him to gag.

In his head he could hear their thoughts. "*Skent! We are skent!*"

For a moment he watched from outside his body and they shifted left and right around him like busy worker ants coaxed by some distant signal transmitting their individual purpose. He saw his own body but knew full well that this was no dream but a vision of their city. Or was it a hive? Weren't hives in fact the metropolises of creatures lower on the food chain?

He snapped back into his body.

One of them stopped and stared at him, jagged teeth clacking.

Inside his head he could hear it say, "*Find the thrombus.*"

Then another joined the chant. "Skent, find the thrombus. Skent."

They were all stopping now, surrounding him by the hundreds, teeth clacking, hissing whispers becoming thousands. The smell of them was overpowering. They clacked their teeth in unison, like soldiers' boots on a parade square.

Clack clack clack clack clack clack clack clack clack clack clack!

"Find the thrombus! Skent! Find the thrombus."

Clack clack clack clack clack clack clack clack clack clack clack!

"Skent! Skent! Skent!"

Clack clack clack clack clack clack clack clack clack clack clack!

"Find the thrombus," they demanded.

Clack clack clack clack clack clack clack clack clack clack clack!

Ronny covered his ears as they crawled upon one another, singling him out.

"Find it!" Clack clack! "Find the thrombus!"

Then he was falling again, away from their world and back to his own. He felt his stomach churn as he turned helpless through the darkness; somewhere below he heard the clicking of the spokes. Below that, greenish blue light shimmered and pulsed.

I'm going to die when I impact, he thought, flailing about.

Ronny Fraser sat upright in bed, barely stifling a scream ripe for the darkness. He looked down, unable to see that he was clutching the blanket tight enough to turn his knuckles white on both hands. He was shivering and, worse, he realized that his bladder had let go and it had long since gone cold and damp. He'd forgotten about Allison, about the erotic dream, he could only think of them.

Suddenly he heard it again. **Clack clack clack!**

"Oh my god," he whimpered. His hand reached blindly in the dark, first batting the light and denting the paper lampshade, then reaching beneath. **Clack clack clack!**

His finger found the switch, then hesitated.

Clack clack clack!

There in the corner, behind the wardrobe, something was in here... In here with him and he was sure if he turned the light on, it would pounce upon him, clicking its teeth, making telepathic demands, or worse.

Maybe it's hungry!

The shadow moved slightly.

Dread ran through him like hot acrid poison.

Oh no! Oh no! Oh no!

It began to slip toward him.

At first a blue gray fog, then from out of the darkness a long boney hand with hooked fingers. **Clack clack clack!** Then there was a glint of light against the jagged teeth and Ronny felt his bladder deplete in a slow, hot squirt against his left thigh. This time he let loose a shrill terrified scream.

His eyes popped open to find himself lying in a pool of hot urine.

There was a knock at the door.

"Everything okay in there, Ronny?" It was Steve Petty from next door.

He looked over at the corner.

Nothing.

He reached over and snapped on the light.

"Ronny? You okay, man?"

Then from behind the door, a second voice. "What was that?"

"I'm okay, Steve," he said.

"You sure, sounded like you were being murdered in there."

He got out of the bed and moved toward the door, then stopped just short.

"I had a nightmare. Guess I must have cried out in my sleep."

"Okay, Ronny. As long as you're okay. I just finished my shift so I'm hitting the hay."

"Okay, sorry if I woke anyone up."

From there he went into the washroom to strip down and grab his shower gear. Glancing at the clock, he could see it was almost 7:30 am. He didn't start his shift for another three hours. He doubted he would be getting back to sleep, though. As he stripped out of his clothes and removed the bedding so that it could be laundered, he was unaware that two floors up and one wing down, Nick Anderson was watching a small piece of silicone tapping against the window and formulating a plan to freeze it.

Ten minutes later as he climbed into the shower, he thought about the strange dream and the creatures. Was it just a bad dream? Certainly he had not really seen their world or heard their calls inside his head. It was so real, as if something was reaching out to him, but what?

The collective of skentophyte, he thought.

5

"There she is," Gordon Shamus announced. They were all here, seated at the table, enjoying a little breakfast. Angel, her husband Scott, and, of course, the assistant Donald. They all looked her way as she entered the room dressed in blue jeans and turtleneck sweater.

"Good morning, Maggie," Angel smiled.

She said nothing. Looking instead at the buffet of food set out on the table, she wondered who had prepared it. Donald stood up and pulled out a chair.

"Come and join us, Maggie. I whipped up something quick, but I'm betting you could use some nourishment," Shamus invited.

Maggie took a seat, feeling their eyes upon her.

"Coffee?" Scott asked.

Maggie turned his way; this was the first time he'd addressed her directly.

He poured her a cup.

"I'm afraid that scrambled eggs is the best I can do for you this morning, Maggie. I have never had much luck cracking eggs without breaking the yokes. So when I cook them, everyone gets scrambled or omelets and I've always considered an omelet a fancy way of hiding the fact that you're too ashamed to admit you can't cook anything but scrambled." Shamus picked up the serving platter and held it out for her. "Eat."

Reluctantly she took it and spooned some of the egg onto her plate. This was followed by bacon and some fresh sliced tomatoes. Maggie took a little of everything, but quite a bit less than she normally would. She was afraid her nerves might get the better of her and she'd vomit all over the place. Then maybe Angela would lay a beating on her at the behest of Gordon Shamus. She lifted her fork and scooped up a helping of eggs and before putting it into her mouth, she said, "Thank you."

"You are quite welcome. Perhaps when all this business is done, you and Marty can come up for a Spring BBQ. The back deck doesn't look like much, but we do a Pig Roast in the last weekend of May each year."

Maggie watched Angel from the corner of her eye. Had there been a hint of surprise in her eyes? Yes, of course there was. There wouldn't be any BBQ invites when this was over. The look on Angel's face was more telling than the others who listened and smiled as Gordon spun his tale. Maggie took a sip of coffee and forced herself to eat a few more bites, feeling their eyes upon her, his eyes mostly. They had stopped discussing whatever business had been the topic when she had come down the stairs. Now it was Gordon who decided where the conversation went.

"So, I'm interested. Where did you meet Marty?" Gordon rested his chin in the cradle of his thumb and index finger. "You're an American, aren't you?"

Maggie looked up. "I met him in New York. At an art exhibit."

"Art exhibit. Oh yes, Marty is quite the artist. I've followed some of his work over the years. I think I've even got an old print he did for my father." This was a lie; he'd disposed of that print a few months earlier after cleaning out some of the old man's belongings. "Marty's done alright for himself. Every now and again, I'll flip open a magazine and see credit for his work. Thing I don't understand is why he chose to come back to Hamilton."

"We came back after his Father died. Moved into his house."

"Ah yes, I forgot Marty's Dad passed away a couple years ago. I saw it in the Obits, I was going to go to the funeral, but never had any contact info."

"Really." Maggie looked at him incredulously. He was making up his own version of events, speaking as though he and Marty were childhood friends. He did so with vigor and quite possibly, she thought, he believed his own lies. She didn't dare test him. "It was a small service, maybe ten people."

"Well, please accept my long overdue condolences. I lost my Father last year. Heart attack."

"I'm sorry to hear that," she responded almost mechanically.

"Thank you." Shamus smiled, lifted his coffee and sipped, never taking his eyes off her. "So, I guess the question you must have is what happens next."

She lowered her fork on to her plate. "Yes."

Scott placed her cell phone on the table.

"There will be no need for cloak and dagger," Shamus said. "Marty is out of cell range right now, beating his way up the ice to the Meanook Mine, so he won't get any messages until he gets back some time tomorrow morning. I want you to call him and leave a voice message. Tell him that you are alright. That you're my guest and that he is to call your phone back as soon as he gets the message."

Scott pushed the phone across the table.

Maggie touched it, and her hand began to shake. "What then, Gordon?"

"Then he does the job without the distraction of text messages saying that you're seeing the sights in Montreal. He knows you're with me and that I will be watching out for you while he does his job."

"Maybe you shouldn't tell him. Maybe it's best he thinks I'm still in Montreal."

"Oh no, Maggie. I want him to know that you're with me. I have a lot riding on him, but Marty needs to know that you're with me. Call it a motivational insurance." His grin receded, succumbing to the same hollow expression he had the night before. "He needs to know that you're with me."

"How do I know that once I make this call…" She stopped.

"That I'll have Donald take you to an undisclosed location and kill you?"

"Yes." She felt her throat knot up.

"You don't." He smiled again, letting it sink in. "But that's not the game plan."

"How do I know this, though?"

"What size coat do you wear, Maggie?"

"Coat? Why?"

"Because we are going to Yellowknife. This job is a big deal, Maggie, big enough that I am going to meet Marty personally when he delivers the package. And so are you. So pick up the phone and call."

Maggie lifted the phone from the table and began to punch in Marty's number.

6

3 km off the Ingraham Trail
West of Great Slave Lake, NWT

Carl Detki parked the Toyota FJ on a side road, then mounted his snowmobile, riding into the woods along a side road to the place he'd readied last spring. He could have brought the vehicle in here; it had good rubber and handled nicely off road. But that wasn't the plan, and he didn't want to leave vehicle tracks. The park roads were less traveled these days, except for the odd game warden. He doubted he would be bothered, and this would only take a few minutes, but why risk it?

The snowmobile whined as he cut across the trail, and then he saw the marker he'd left. It was easy for him to spot, but no one else would have given it much thought. Last fall he cut a chunk of bark out of a tree on the left side of the path, and 400 yards past that on the right was where he would stop and go back to the spot in the woods.

He pulled the snowmobile over and parked it beside the spot, removed his rifle, and slung it over his shoulder. Taking a passing glance up and down the trail, then stopping to listen, he nodded and started on his way. The snow in Yellowknife was light this year. He hoped that held, because it would make his life a lot easier. Snowshoes would have made the trek easier but would have left behind distinguishing tracks, and he couldn't have that. It didn't matter, walking in this snow wasn't too hard.

Fifteen minutes later he reached the spot and checked to see it wasn't disturbed. It hadn't been. When he dug the hole, he'd covered it with a thin sheet of plywood and then camouflaged it with ground debris. Beside it, a hump in the snow defined the pile of dirt, also covered with a heavy tarp and more ground debris. From the roadway, it could not be seen.

Most of his work came from drug business. He'd gotten the call from an associate to ready a hole. That associate had ties to someone out East. He didn't know who. He just dug holes for people and they filled them in. His rate was $1000.00 for a single and $1800.00 for a double. This was a double. Seven feet deep and four across. More than enough to accommodate two occupants. He'd never seen the people who were put into these holes, nor was he present during the burial.

Removing his GPS from his pocket, he pressed the prompt on the screen that read: **SAVE LOCATION.**

It beeped, then prompted. **NAME LOCATION.**

He typed in: **GROUND ZERO.**

Satisfied that everything was in place, he walked back toward the road. When he reached it, he would save that location as well and mark it as: **PARKING**. Climbing back onto his snowmobile, he drove back to the Land Cruiser and loaded it onto the trailer. This afternoon he would meet his cousin Nigel and give him the GPS with instructions. Nigel had already given him the cash up front. Nigel had also just been released from jail on bail after being picked up last week outside **The Talon** carrying enough Meth to catch him a trafficking charge. Nigel could be an idiot at times, but he knew better than to talk about their business. In fact, Nigel had a few holes of his own to worry about.

He shut off the GPS and plugged it in for a fresh charge before it would eventually end up in a manila envelope with a brief instruction. He put the vehicle in drive and headed back toward Yellowknife. His wife and son were waiting at her sister's. He promised his boy they'd go up to Prosperous Lake to do

some ice fishing. As he drove down the road, he forgot about the hole. The payment was made and sooner or later, there would be another. There would always be another. He pushed that away and focused on taking his boy ice fishing.

***

Chapter 18—The Kitchen Nazi

1

Corbett Lake Camp

Garney's booming voiced ricocheted out across the airwaves. "Corbett Dispatch. Nancy, my sister, you got a copy?" They were closing in now, the Quonset huts and portable trailers looking down on them from atop the portage. In the midst of these buildings, the radio tower adorned with microwave dishes, jagged antennas tied down by support cables, clawed skyward.

"Corbett copy, go ahead," a woman, presumably Nancy, replied.

"Yes, I have four Super B Tankers coming onto your property for a little breakfast." Garney read off the numbers and Marty watched his truck leave the ice and pull thc hill with lead to the lot. It was a large area, plowed out to accommodate at least 100 tractor trailer combinations. There weren't that many here now. Maybe thirty rigs, all running at high idle, lined up single file in groups of four facing back toward the frozen beach. "Marty, when I park, I'll throw my four ways on so you know where I am," Garney said.

"Copy."

At the base of the approach, a pickup truck sat watching as Marty closed in on the ramp. To Marty's right, a speed limit sign read: **Maximum 10 Km/h**. The driver of the pickup was clocking his speed with radar. He dropped his speed by doubling down on his shifts, causing the rpm on the Tachometer first to rise, then fall in operatic unison with the protesting growls of the engine. By the time he reached the speed limit sign, he was going 10 kp/h, but this left him to ponder how he'd make it up the icy grade at such a low speed. Then, as if reading his thoughts, Merv hailed him on the radio.

"Marty, go to the other channel."

He reached down and switched the radio to the alternate. "Go ahead, Merv."

"Okay, when you reach the base of the portage, you do what you have to and get up that hill. Put your lockers on and get your foot into it. Don't let Barney Fife there freak you out. If he pipes up, we'll take it up with Pringle."

“Copy that.”

At the base of the ramp, he did exactly what Merv advised. He flipped the differential switch, locking both drive axles—depressed the clutch—shifted up, and then put his foot into it. The rpms climbed up over 1800—engine snarling in protest, but he didn’t grab another gear. He could feel the drive wheels slipping, losing traction, and knew that any hesitation would cause him to spin out. Despite the engine protests, he held his foot steady, then the wheels dug in—finding their footing, consequently hauling the tankers with a bit more ease. When he was up over the hump and onto the flat, he eased off and turned on his four way flashers.

The security man in the pickup said nothing.

“I’m in the fifth line over, Marty. Bring her on, my brother.”

“Copy that, on my way.”

The sky, blue integrated with pink, was darkened by flowing smudges of charcoal gray. The source of the smudging came from a steady plume of diesel exhaust from the idling rigs. The color was exaggerated by the frigid cold. Two stacks per truck, Marty had no idea how many, but guessed at least 40, sent up dual plumes. The oily exhaust from each stack arched over into the eastern breeze, whispering across the landscape, only to be diluted and swallowed in the endless sky. It was rather anti-climactic, considering the drama with which the steady flow was born and cast out.

As an artist, the scene was not lost on Marty. At any other time, under different circumstances, he would been drawn to this majestic landscape—snapping pictures, saving pallets to use in his art. The panorama could easily be mistaken for an alien landscape and for the type of work he did, it would suit his purpose well. But that wasn’t why he was here, and this made him frown. He still hadn’t come up with any type of a plan and they were already halfway up to Meanook. Anxiety settled into his chest, tightening the muscles against his breast bone.

He turned after spotting Garney’s rig parked between the rows of trucks. He wheeled around and lined up. Garney shut off his four way flashers. Ahead, Garney’s door swung open and the big man climbed from the cab, wearing his weathered parka and oil man’s hardhat. He went to the side of the truck, opened up the jockey box, reached in, and removed a bottle of brake line anti-freeze. Showing Marty the ropes, Garney had explained that it was important to keep your brake lines from freezing up. It was his assumption that at every stop, a little brake line anti-freeze should be added to the Service lines to help dissipate any moisture. Marty took this as a reminder that he should do the same. So he put on his parka, buttoned up and climbed from the big rig. He took one last look at the sky, allowing himself the distraction. Soon enough there would be little time for such things.

2

ACADIA MINE
06:30 AM

The food, specifically the cereal, was tasteless. Nick was in the cafeteria, sitting by himself in front of a bowl of Honey Nut Cheerios. He had been craving sugar since leaving the confines of his room. Frosted Flakes was what he really wanted, but the plastic dispenser in the cafeteria only gave him three choices: Bran Flakes, Fiber One, and Honey Nut Cheerios. As a rule, Nick usually didn't eat anything with sugar on it. In fact, he considered sugar poison. A position brought on by the present epidemic of Type II Diabetes in North America. After getting off the phone with Chase, pulling himself away from the window, and getting the hell out of that room, he decided that he needed something to boost his energy. Halfway between the room and the cafeteria, cravings for something sweet hit him full force.

Maybe my blood sugar is in the toilet right now.

Injecting a little bit of sugar in his bloodstream certainly wasn't going to hurt. It wasn't like he ate this crap every day. But after filling his bowl with two easy twists on the dispenser, which reminded him of the knob on a gumball machine, he was horribly disappointed by his selection. Staring down into the bowl of floating life preservers, he couldn't help but feel cheated. He was sure it said Honey Nut, not plain.

Fuck me, I might as well try another bite.

He hoisted the spoon up to his mouth and inserted another heaping shovelful. Nothing, cardboard and another taste he couldn't quite put his finger on. Alkaline? Maybe? Or was it copper? He could taste ozone, that was for sure.

What he didn't know was that the twisting thing inside his eye was getting bigger and burning a hole through the macula and into the optic nerve. Outwardly, there was no sign of the distress and the pain he should have been feeling in the thousand nerve endings in his eye, dulled by an enzyme released concurrently with the prods and probes as it ate its way through the back of his eye. The only byproduct of this process was the loss of smell and enhanced taste in the roof of his mouth. And of course, there were the messages.

Find the thrombus.

Reaching over and grabbing the sugar dispenser, he turned it upside-down and allowed a mound of granules to grow atop his floating O's. If anyone were there, they most certainly would have stared. Nick gawked at the mound as it grew atop the cereal, absorbed the milk below, and melted away. As he did this, he wondered what that meant really. What was a thrombus? Why did he have to find it?

What the fuck is wrong with me?

Mental illness? Did the mentally ill know that they were sliding out of reality into the ethereal? He didn't think so. Perhaps if he were suffering from depression, he might have an inkling, but this...

Find the thrombus.

The container, once half full of sugar, ran dry, leaving in its wake a dissolving mountain surrounded by floating O's masquerading as sweetness. He set it aside, dug into the mound, and lifted another spoonful to his mouth.

Cardboard and alkaline.

He crunched mechanically, feeling the granules chewing away at the enamel of his teeth and settling into his gums. On his lower lip, a single droplet of milk clung– defying gravity–at least for the moment. There was a clicking sound as well, a distance breaker snapping on and off. Staring out across the sea of empty tables, he tried to identify its locale, but that was also from within. Then he heard John Lennon singing "I'm losing you," and wondered if the dearly departed member of the Fab Four was calling out to him from the great beyond. This caused him to smile numbly. Lennon faded and another voice was awakened; it was Sheila.

She said, "Why, Nick, why did you do this?"

This had been a 21-year-old Lab Assistant named Linda Quandry. He didn't know why. His dick knew, he supposed, but he didn't have feelings for her. That didn't stop him from inhaling the smell of her when she drew close. Nor did he draw back when she brushed against him. And of course when he mounted her in the solitude of his office, hours after everyone had gone home, he wasn't thinking love or relationship. No, not at all. And when the dirty deed was done, he did what every guilt-ridden husband would do. He zipped up his fly and eventually unburdened that guilt by saddling Sheila with the knowledge that her husband had traded her in for a fresh new young vagina to stuff his dick in.

"You're a bastard, Nick. A real bastard!"

Sheila filed for divorce and Linda found higher mountains to conquer. Harvey McLean had been his boss then and it seemed that Harvey's cock was the next rung on her career ladder. So while she latched onto Harvey's member, she stepped on his dick in the process. This was the analogy he had proposed to McLean after six very dirty Vodka Martinis, quite appropriately served at a meet and greet. The analogy was not well received.

"Knock it off, Nick. Not the time or the place," McLean warned.

It had been exactly the time and place, he thought. "I'm just trying to save your dick from getting stepped on, Harvey, old boy." Misery—after numerous vodka martinis—loves company, and Nick Anderson felt after eating a very costly divorce that the best dessert would be the ruination of his career. "I'll give you this. She has great tits."

"Get out!" McLean growled, which was really code for "You're fired."

He raised his glass in salute. Then said, "Here's to all the great titties."

"**Crunch crunch crunch,**" declared the cardboard alkaline O's as he converted them into so much mush with the assistance of his molars. Simultaneously, he wondered what became of Linda and how many cocks she'd stepped on in her ascent to the glass ceiling of academic excellence. He fell into a state of purgatory after his proclamation to "great titties." Purgatory lasted approximately a year. McLean had put the word out and the scientific community shunned him. Bitter and self-loathing, Nick took the next logical step; he drank his face off.

Then, one post-alcoholic hazy morning, the call came from Lance Milgaard. Milgaard was back from Geneva, putting together a team to head up a scaled down version of the Hadron Collider.

"I understand that you are the top man in your field," Milgaard said.

Nick was incredulous, never mind that he had four days of growth on his face, that he hadn't bathed in a week, and that the apartment stank of vomit and his latest buddy: Jimmy Beam.

Forget all that.

He was blown away that Milgaard had called him directly.

"I'm offering you a job, Nick. If you can get on a plane by this afternoon, I will have somebody pick you up in Boston and taxi you to

Worcester. There, we will discuss what I expect to be the most exciting project you've ever worked on."

"That's debatable, Lance," he said aloud.

"Who are you talking to?" Ronny Fraser asked.

Nick looked up from his bowl, now emptied.

Had he really eaten the whole bowl? He turned his eyes down again.

"Thinking out loud," he mumbled, still looking down.

"Can I sit down?"

He nodded, "Yes" and Ronny sat down across from him. There was an instance of silence while both men stared at each other, as if daring the other to speak first. Nick knew almost immediately that Ronny Fraser was suffering from the same symptoms as he was. He was quite sure of this, but not so sure that he would take that leap of faith and admit that something was wrong. Instead, he dropped his eyes to the milk in his bowl and considered pouring more sugar into it.

"Do you feel it?" Ronny asked.

"Feel what?"

"You don't know what I'm talking about?"

Nick said nothing.

"Come on, Nick. Nothing? I'm hearing voices, and... And having really bad dreams."

"What kind of dreams?"

Ronny took a deep breath, then exhaled. Resting his elbows on the table, he raked both hands through his hair. He stared at Nick, who was still staring into the empty bowl. This was pointless. "Forget it," he said and got up to leave.

"Thrombus." Nick didn't look up, but caught him by the arm. "Yes, I feel it."

Ronny sat back down.

"What the hell is happening to us, Nick?"

"I don't know. Maybe we inhaled something in the lab yesterday. Maybe it's long-term exposure to the chamber."

"We have to report this. There's something wrong with us. I feel like I'm going insane. Like... I'm not me!" Ronny's words were hurried, even panicky. "I'm scared."

"I've lost my sense of smell and it seems..." Staring down at the puddle of milk in his cereal bowl. "Taste."

"What is a thrombus?"

"An Easter egg, I suppose."

"What?"

"An Easter egg. The monoliths in the chamber. I think the thrombus is what activates them."

"We have to go to Chase and Mr. Lars."

"What will we tell them?"

"The truth!"

"You know what will happen then. They'll pull us off the dig. Maybe have us admitted for observation. Maybe we'll end up like those things in the lab. Being dissected in some warehouse."

"I'm willing to take that chance. I'm scared. No, scratch that. I'm terrified."

Well, I am afraid I am not.

This is insane. There's something wrong with both of us, something happened in the lab that day.

Nick was listening intently, but his eyes were following the veins of gold linoleum green table top. As he did this, Ronny's voice seemed to hang inside of his head, and while Ronny spoke of pushing back against whatever presence was possessing him, the truth was that the battle had already been lost.

Nick looked up. "We can't seek help. Whatever it is that's inhabited our heads will not allow it. I'm guessing any attempt to stop whatever it is will result in our death."

"Oh my God!"

"What is it?"

"Your lips, they're not moving, but Jesus Christ, I can hear you."

"Neither are yours," Nick thought and when he tried to speak aloud, all that came out was, *"Skent! We are skentophyte."*

Ronny's eyes grew wide and fearful. "Oh my god!"

"You try," Nick thought.

"Skent. Serve us. Serve the Skentophyte" Ronny reached into his pocket.

"What is it," Nick prodded.

"Wait." Ronny pulled out a battered note pad, clumsily dropped it onto the table, and then he fumbled for his pen. Taking a deep breath, he put pen to paper and tried to write something, anything, but what came out was a list of illegible numbers and letters. **Λσχχ00λσλσλγηϖδ** .

"What the hell is that? Hieroglyphics?"

Ronny's eyes widened, his mouth agape in horror. "Oh my god. It's taken away my, our, ability to communicate!"

Nick reached across the table and grabbed Ronny's wrist. "Calm down."

"How the fuck do I do that? How do we stop this? Oh my god! We're really fucked!" Nick tightened his grip, clamping down with his thumb and pressing the nail into the soft tendons on his wrist. "Stop it! That hurts!"

"Calm down, Ronny." Having made his point, Nick loosened his grip and Ronny pulled his hand away, massaging the affected area. "We aren't completely fucked. I have an idea."

"And what would that be?"

"We have to find the Thrombus."

3

Maggie watched the clouds below through the portal window of the 737. Sitting beside her were Angel and her husband Scott. She thought that Shamus would have liked to sit with her, even regale her with some anecdotes about the good old days with Marty, but for reasons of his own did not. Instead, he was a row back, charming a little girl of ten. She was going to see her Aunt Ginny in Fort Providence. They had a big back yard and a pet raven named Ravvy. "Ravvy can talk," the little girl insisted.

"Is that so? I thought only parrots could talk," Shamus said incredulously.

"No, ravens too. Ravvy says all sorts of stuff."

"Like what?"

Maggie could not see Shamus and didn't want to turn in her seat and interrupt the exchange. But she had a clear picture of his mannerisms. He would have a sincere smile that cloaked the real monster that lurked beneath his skin. The little girl would not see it, but perhaps if she looked directly into the vacant eyes of the sociopath, she would retreat back into herself.

"He says, I love you, Momma, Pretty, and a bunch of other stuff."

"Is that so? You are a very lucky young lady to know someone with a talking raven."

Maggie felt Angel's eyes upon her. She turned to meet them. Angel was studying her. She could only guess that Angel was trying to make heads or tails of her. Before they reached the airport, Angel had handed her a Canadian Passport and a couple other pieces of identification. The name on the passport: Karen Monchak. It looked authentic. "I thought that using the name Karen would prove an easy lie for you."

"What does it say on your passport?"

"You don't worry about that, Karen. Just smile for the attendant and security and flash the identification. No bullshit, this is very serious. Understand? You fuck this guy around and he'll spread parts of you all over the countryside." Angel leaned in closer. "Worst of all. While he's spreading parts of you all over the countryside, the best part of you might be sitting somewhere wondering where those other parts are being buried. I'm going to say this only once, sweetheart. Don't fuck with this man! He's wicked dangerous, some might even say diabolical." Angel didn't smile. Maggie thought there might be sincere concern in the warning. *Sincere concern? Really? This is the woman who threatened to beat you to a bloody pulp? Remember that?* And yes, she did remember, but she also sensed something in Angel's body language when being addressed by Gordon Shamus. He made her feel uncomfortable—maybe even frightened. Maggie wondered what it was. Then there was her husband Scott. He scurried about like an insect whenever Shamus addressed him. They were all scared of him.

"Mommy, I have to pee," the little girl said.

Shamus chuckled.

"Excuse us," the girl's mother said.

"Nature calls," Shamus said.

Then the click of safety belts unlatching to a chorus of "Excuse me's" followed by "No problem at all." When they passed, mother and daughter, Maggie was surprised to see that both were aboriginal. The little girl was very sweet, long silken black hair and almond eyes, her underdeveloped body riding upon slim coltish legs, a complete opposite of her mother, who was big breasted, short, and very plump.

Maggie wanted children. She and Marty had talked about having kids only a week before the revelation of his past. Now she wondered if she would live to see that day or if she would end up in a shallow grave somewhere in the territories. They were dead once this was over. Of this she was sure. This man wasn't going to allow them to return to their lives once the job was over. They would never see the inside of that old house in the country again.

So what am I supposed to do, she thought.

But she already knew the answer to that. She had to get closer to Shamus, engage him, but she'd have to be careful. If he sensed, even in the slightest, that she was patronizing him, that uglier thing that lurked below the surface would emerge and Maggie was quite sure that Angel's descriptive "Wicked dangerous, some might even say diabolical" was spot on.

4

Corbett Lake Camp

After doing some trip maintenance on their trucks, Marty, Garney, Merv, and Spence made their way across the parking lot and up the hill toward the main trailer that served as the camp kitchen. Marty was surprised to find out that Spence had a prosthetic leg. He came by this information when he noticed that Spence was limping and took it upon himself to ask if he'd hurt his leg.

"No, not now that it's gone," Spence replied.

"What do you mean it's gone?" Marty asked, thinking Spence was having him on.

"Left that baby somewhere in Afghanistan, didn't you, Spence?" Merv asked.

"Yep, sure did."

"Oh shit, I'm sorry." Marty apologized.

"Why, were you a supporter of the Taliban?"

Garney snorted, then unleashed a barrage of laughter. "Spence, my brother, you crack me up, man! Supporter of the Taliban. Yep, yep, uh huh, sure do!"

Spence smiled. "Don't sweat it, Marty, it's not that big a deal anymore."

Marty felt the sting of embarrassment, even with Spence's assurances. They continued on up the hill, Garney and Marty side by side, while Spence and Merv brought up the rear. The cold pinched at their exposed cheeks, comparable to the injections one feels when visiting the dentist. One of the rules at Corbett Lake Camp was that drivers and personnel had to wear full safety gear at all times when operating outside their trucks. The reflective vests and steel toed boots made perfect sense to Marty, but he couldn't figure out for the life of him why on earth they would want them to wear hardhats. Merv said that it was to avoid being killed by a raven.

"How on earth is a raven going to kill us," Marty laughed.

"You do feel the cold out here, don't you?"

"Yeah."

"Well think about this, we got a raven up there 300 feet above cruising and he decides to drop a big shit. Now normally, the worst thing that big shit's going to do is mess up your jacket. But this is the north, my friend, and you can pretty much piss ice cubes if you stand out here long enough. So by the time that earthbound present from our fine feathered friend finds its way to you, it's turned into a hard stone and falling with the velocity of a bullet. Hence the hardhat."

Garney guffawed.

Marty laughed.

"That's a good one, Merv, but you're full of shit." Spence tapped his hardhat. "This isn't exactly Kevlar."

"Take my word for it, Marty, back in the old days, two maybe three fatalities a year occurred up here in the north thanks to earthbound frozen shit." Merv lit up a cigarette, cupping the lighter with his hand and puffing between sentences. "It's all documented."

When they reached the door of the mobile trailer, Merv and Spence stayed behind to finish their smoke. Marty followed Garney through the door and into the trailer. The interior was separated by a mud room, and on the wall hung a sign that said: **All work boots and outerwear must be removed before proceeding beyond this point.** On the wall, numerous coats hung from hooks; above them on a shelf hardhats of all shapes and colors sat and below that were pairs of work boots and mukluks.

Garney was already stripping off. "Brother, I am some hungry. Yes sir, yep."

Marty found a hook and tried to take note of the spot. There was a sea of blue safety jackets here and he was miffed at how they didn't get mixed up. Once his jacket was hung up, he removed his hardhat and safety glasses and placed them on the shelf above the hook. He did the same with his boots, but to avoid confusion he set them side by side, switching both left and right. He figured that might make it easier to find them when he came back.

When the door opened behind them, Marty expected to see Merv and Spence enter, but was surprised to see that it was a man he did not at first recognize behind the hardhat and safety attire. Phil Crane looked almost as surprised as Marty.

"How yuh doing today, Sir?" Garney asked.

Crane removed his hardhat and turned his gaze to Garney. "Fine, thanks. And you?"

"Doing well. Right, Marty?"

"Yeah, doing fine," Marty agreed. Crane looked different. He'd begun to grow a beard, a goatee, in fact. It aged him somewhat, jutting from his chin like prickly grey straw. It also made him look harder–more intimidating. If that was possible. "Well I don't know about you, gentlemen, but I'm ready for some bacon and eggs. Uh huh, yep. Sure am. Yes sir." Garney pushed through the door, leaving the two behind.

Crane broke the uncomfortable silence. "Later," Crane said. "After you eat your breakfast, meet me in the smoking trailer."

"Anything else?"

"No."

The door opened again. Merv and Spence entered.

"Holy crap, Marty, I figured Garney would have you at a table shoveling the food in your mouth by now." Merv pushed past Crane, almost knocking him off balance. "Sorry about that, close quarters."

"Forget it," Crane replied and took one last look at Marty before exiting the mud room. Meanwhile, Spence sat down and removed his left boot, revealing his prosthetic leg. Stupidly, Marty made a concerted effort not to look at it while Spence pretended not to notice.

"I don't know why they don't hang up their own stuff in their own cloakroom," Merv commented. "It's not like the bastards like sitting with us in the first place."

"Hey, come on, John Pringle's a pretty decent guy."

"I'll give you that, but Pringle's been up here a lot of years. These other guys come and go. Short timers, that's all they are, rented cops looking to make a quota."

"They're not all like that, Merv."

"I know, but I'll bet you dollars to donuts that A-Hole is."

Marty smiled. He had developed a new affection for Merv White. "You're probably right." He opened the door of the mud room and stepped out into the main foyer to a smell of bacon, pancakes and something else he couldn't put his finger on. In sock feet, he moved into the dining area where better than 40 men sat at tables talking and eating. It looked like a lumberjack convention. Beards, unkempt hair, heavy sweaters, mostly men, of all shapes and sizes. Among them were two women drivers who looked just as hard and weathered as these men of the North.

"Marty," Garney called over to him. Marty picked up a tray and silverware as he stepped into the line. Garney leaned over and whispered in his ear. "Don't eat the eggs."

"Why?"

"Kitchen Nazi. She touches them. With her bare hands, and, my friend, that wouldn't be a big deal. But when you see her, you'll get to thinking about what she's been touching or scratching before putting her paws on your eggs."

Marty laughed. "So what the hell is safe to eat?"

"Go with the pancakes. Bill Cosby is cooking pancakes."

"Bill Cosby?"

Garney pointed, and behind the grill flipping pancakes was a black man who looked very much like the comedian/actor. "Bill always wears gloves. He's a way better cook than the Kitchen Nazi."

"I'm guessing the female cook is German?"

"I couldn't tell yuh, my brother, but believe me when I say that she's Nazi."

"This is one of those education moments isn't it, Garney?"

Garney grinned. "Yes, my brother, I guess you could say it is."

"Alright, well I guess we'll skip the preliminary back and forth and I'll just get right down to it. Why do you call her the Kitchen Nazi?"

Garney furrowed his brow. "If you take an extra cookie, or even an extra piece of fruit, she turns into Adolf Eichmann. Oh shit, take a look at this," Garney gestured toward the cook, who was a big woman, carrying a number of rolls around her mid-section that made Marty think more about the Michelin Tire Man than a goose-stepping member of the Third Reich. Her hair was pulled back in a neat bun, revealing a pudgy face with no real enduring features. She was rubbing her nose. "Now watch."

The female cook, aka the Kitchen Nazi, lowered the same hand she rubbed her nose with and placed two fingers on the yokes of the eggs she was cooking on the grill.

"You've got to be kidding me."

"Last year, seventy percent of the drivers got sick," Merv said as he and Spence fell in behind Marty. "I blame her. This place was just a big fucking petri dish last year. A hub of infectious disease. I like to call her Mistress Hygiene, digging and fucking scratching in all her orifices, touching the food with those bare fingers. Between that and her shitty cooking, I got sick as a dog."

"Admit it, Merv, you want her," Spence prodded.

Merv grinned ear to ear. "Spence, I just want to go on the record and say I wouldn't screw her with your dick."

A driver ahead of them, obviously listening, cracked up.

"What'll you have?" the Kitchen Nazi asked Garney.

Garney rubbed his chin. "You know, sister, I think I'll have the pancakes."

Marty snickered.

"Something funny?" the Kitchen Nazi asked.

Marty looked at the others in line, then realized she was addressing him. Worse still, he was on his own. He could feel the retreat of his fellow drivers, now onlookers as he faced down the bully. He felt like saying something. Maybe: "Hey, Sister, keep your mitts off the food! You want us all to get sick?" This would be met with the cheers of all drivers, maybe a standing ovation inside the cafeteria. Even the Security Head John Pringle would congratulate him with a hardy slap on the back. Yes, that would have been great, but all Marty really managed was an emasculated, "Pardon me?"

"I asked you what's so funny."

"Um, nothing."

"You're sure?" Her skin pulled back taunt against her pudgy face, producing a scowl that looked both inviting and menacing. *Come on, asshole, say something. I dare you.*

"Yeah, I'm sure." Marty felt like a tiny mouse.

"What'll you have then?"

The word fell out of his mouth before he had a chance to stop it. "Scrambled."

She grabbed a plate and scooped up a large helping of scrambled eggs from the steam table. Marty secretly wished that they were powdered and that Bill Cosby had prepared them. From behind, Merv poked him in what Marty assumed to be an acknowledgment of his cowardice.

"Sausage or bacon?"

"Sausage."

She held the plate up and he reached out to take it. She stared at him before releasing and he shuffled out of line. Behind him, he heard Merv order up pancakes just a little too loud.

In the corner of the cafeteria there was a milk dispenser and boxes of cereal. Marty made his way to it. Garney was already chatting it up with John Pringle and another man whom he assumed was the security truck they met on the road. Crane sat next to the two listening.

Breakfast lasted approximately 15 minutes. Marty had Corn Flakes and a large helping of crow as the others, Merv in particular, exclaimed how tasty the pancakes were and regularly asked why he wasn't eating his eggs. Adding insult to injury, the coffee was wretched. So foul in fact, that Marty wondered if an animal was decomposing in the bottom of the stainless steel urn. This was disheartening, because he knew he was going to need a caffeine boost for the second half of the trip.

"Add some hot chocolate to it, my brother. Kills the skunky taste," Garney suggested.

"You guys are pussies. There's nothing wrong with the coffee," Merv laughed.

"Would you like some of my eggs?"

"Nope, these flap jacks are mighty filling."

"I drink tea," Spence said. "I think tea has even more caffeine than coffee."

"Really?"

"Yeah, and it doesn't have the same road kill flavoring that Merv appears so fond of."

Merv raised his mug.

5

With the controlled blast completed, Nick and Ronny returned to the dig to look for the thrombus. Both men were well aware that their actions were no longer their own, but neither was in a position to change it. The worm-like creatures in their eyes were now growing at a rapid rate, thus exerting tighter control.

Ronny wondered if his thoughts were being monitored. Wondered what Nick's plan was when they found the thrombus, and if they would use it to turn the tables on whatever it was that was exhibiting control over them. He wondered if they were monitoring his thoughts now. Worse, he wondered if Nick could hear his thoughts. He didn't think so, otherwise Nick would have stared at him or perhaps the parasite within would have done something. Along with this, he wondered if all of this was just a chemical imbalance producing paranoid delusions. Maybe he was in an asylum somewhere being fed doses of lithium in an attempt to counteract a schizophrenic malaise.

They were suited up and in the service elevator. Thankfully alone. Nick was engulfed in his own train of thought. Even further gone than Ronny, his senses continued breaking down.

Can't smell, taste, gone.

The service elevator would take them a ½ a mile below the surface. From there they would mount a golf cart and drive ¾ of a mile to another shaft, which would take them to the dig.

"*If Allison is there. Send her up top,*" Nick transmitted.

"*How?*"

Nick stopped, realization dawning. *"Maybe it won't matter. We'll figure something out."*

Inside the eyes of both men, the parasitic organisms twisted and squirmed, a single glowing light no bigger than the head of a pin pulsed cyan, then flat orange, a dual purpose being undertaken. As they grew bigger, they released a pheromone into the bloodstream, taking over specific actions of their hosts. In this case, their immediate senses. Speech, smell, taste. Along with that, a pre-programmed directive.

Much as an addict has highs and lows from mania to self-loathing, both men were submitting to the organism that inhabited them. While Nick quietly reassured himself that finding the thrombus would offer them leverage, he really could not guarantee that he would not attempt to take the next logical step. Much as he could not fully guarantee that he would not kill Ronny Fraser, or Chase Fenwick or even the woman, Allison Perch, if she got in their way. At this point in time, nothing was off the table. Now that his ability to communicate was gone, he wondered if finding the thrombus would be his last act of self-worth.

When we find it. What then? Ronny interrupted.

First we have to find it, Nick responded.

6

"I gotta go back," Marty said. They were halfway down to the trucks. The wind had picked up from the south, sending wisps of snow up into the air in swirling, abrasive torrents. All four men, faces covered, pushed against the current of angry wind.

"What? What for?" Garney asked.

"I forgot my thermos."

Garney halted. "Okay, we'll go back."

"You guys go on. I'll only be a minute."

"I'll walk back with yuh, Marty. I don't mind."

"You going back to get her phone number, Marty?" Merv prodded.

"Fuck you, Merv!" Marty flipped a gloved bird.

Spence laughed.

"You guys go on," Garney told them.

"Garney, you go too. I'm a big boy." Marty lowered his voice. "I appreciate your helping me get this far, but I got this."

"Right." Garney nodded, then smiled. "Okay, my brother, we'll be waiting at the trucks."

"They grow up so fast." Spence removed his sunglasses and wiped an imaginary tear from his eye. Marty shook his head and rolled his eyes, but smiled just the same. He was really warming up to these guys. They liked busting chops, joking around, but all in all they were the decent sort. He felt like shit lying and leaving his thermos behind purposely so he could meet Crane. But he was actually protecting them. If they knew what was really going on, their lives would be in danger.

"You must be so proud," Merv said to Garney.

Garney guffawed and slapped his knee.

"Screw you too, Merv." Marty began backing up, middle finger still raised.

"You make me proud, Marty."

Spence giggled.

The group of three broke off and Marty turned with his back to the wind. The joy now would be making this trek back again. He picked up his pace and, two thirds of the way, almost wiped out on the polished pathway. He caught himself, wrenching a muscle in his lower back. When he turned between the two portable trailers, he saw Crane standing on the stairwell to the smoking trailer. He was holding Marty's thermos. He stepped into the building and Marty followed.

Once inside, his nose and eyes were assaulted by the stink of tobacco. He didn't have a big issue with smoking, had in fact smoked back in the day. But this building was like being inside an actual cigarette pack. It was in the walls. Crane was just inside the door, waiting for him. They were alone.

"There's been a change of plans," Crane said.

"What change?"

"Kristy Greenflag, the one in hydrocarbons, she'll be on shift when you get there."

"So I'm picking up today?"

“Tonight actually.”

“Anything else?

“Same drill, just a day early. I’ll meet you on the portage north of here.”

“Okay.”

Crane managed a smile. “This should make you happy.”

“Really?”

“Cheer up, Croft. Looks like this will be over sooner than anticipated.” Crane handed the thermos over to him. Marty took it, trying very hard to mask the sudden dread he felt. The game was really on. Instead of days, he was now down to less than 24 hours. “You better get moving.”

“How will you know where to be when we arrive?”

“I work for security, Croft. You guys are tracked on computer every step of the way.”

Marty turned and exited the building. He didn’t hold the door for Crane. He felt his pulse thumping inside his ears; swarms of insects rose and fell in his guts. He had to think. Think hard. The piercing wind blasted against him, flags flapping violently on the pole overhead. He barely heard them. He was doing math, calculating the trip north then back. He had less than 18 hours before he and Crane would rendezvous.

***

Chapter 19—Category 3

1

ACADIA MINE

The closer they got to the chamber, a current of hurried obsessive purpose ratcheted up within, overriding the consciousness of both men. Neither man was impaired, they absorbed everything that was happening around them, but neither was in control. They were simply passengers now, able to see and understand but in no position to rage against the machine that possessed them. When they reached the chamber, they found it deserted. Allison was not scheduled on for at least another hour. That was good. It would give them privacy to start searching.

Amplifying in both their heads came the order: **Find the thrombus!**

They turned to look at each other. Then they looked toward the two monoliths at the rear of the chamber and it all became very clear. "Take it to the sheekran. Skent! Thrombus, Sheekran," Nick was the first to say.

"Find the thrombus," Ronny concurred.

And with that, both men set out in opposite directions to search separate sides of the chamber. Turning stones, processing what they saw, their collective thought outlined what it was they were looking for. It was a disc, slightly bigger than a wheel rim. In its center, spokes, pitted with uniform pores, encrusted with a secretion not of this world.

The life-cycle of the parasitic organisms was now half expended. Without exterior control they would fade and complete their cycle by releasing a third enzyme into their host. That one would prove fatal.

They had to find it.

If it was broken or could not be found, all would be lost.

2

Ingraham Trail:
One km West of Prosperous Lake, NWT

They landed at noon, amid the beginnings of a coming storm. If they'd arrived a few hours later they would have been diverted to Edmonton, Alberta. Visibility and high winds would have proved a deadly combination even for the most seasoned pilot.

As they drove up Highway 3, then onto the Ingraham Trail, Maggie took mental snapshots of the route between Yellowknife and the log cabin. Most notably, Giant Mine, an abandoned Gold Mine that stood like a monument atop a hill beside the Ingraham, right beside the road. The sign hanging below wrought iron archway erected over the drive read: **Welcome to Tli Cho Manor.**

Log cabin was how Shamus described it. Definitely an understatement. The dwelling looked more like a ski chalet. The building was an exaggerated A-Frame with massive picture windows cut into the hard angles of the structure's cedar face. The roof was new, capped by overlapping jet black metal shingles.

This was where the rich came to play or lovers spent a dream getaway for a very large sum. Maggie estimated that the glass alone would be worth at least sixty or seventy thousand dollars. Maybe more, considering the remote location. It jutted arrowhead-like from the snow-covered earth, looking as though it were in a continuous state of growth. Halfway up the face sat a large balcony atop massive pillars of cedar that pushed out from beneath the hooded overhang of the roof. On either side of the Manor, indigenous trees, dwarfed by the building they protected, dotted the landscape. The drive snaked back and forth across the landscape for ½ a mile, freshly plowed snow on either side shouldering the drive.

"Home sweet home," Shamus announced and turned to face Maggie. They were seated side by side in the back seat of the Escalade. "What do you think?"

"It's beautiful. How old is it?"

"I think it was built back in the late 70's. A few celebrities have stayed here. I think Bruce Willis used it, but don't hold me to that. I'm not exactly up on tabloid comings and goings. There's seven rooms, your room has its own shower and toilet."

Angel and Scott were bringing up the rear in a second Cadillac Escalade. Maggie was supposed to ride with them, but specifically asked Shamus if she could ride with him. Angel's face soured at the suggestion. "You're riding with us, sweetheart."

"What difference does it make?" Maggie said.

"That's the routine."

Shamus watched the interaction with charmed interest.

"Routine?"

"Yeah, routine. You ride with us. Gordon has other things to do than worry about your skinny ass."

"Are you implying that Gordon can't handle me?"

"It's fucking cold out here. Just get in the goddamned car," Scott barked.

Angel took an aggressive step forward. "Don't get sassy, Maggie. I don't take shit off anyone and you're no exception to that rule."

"Fine." Maggie made a move toward their Escalade.

"Ah, fuck. She can ride with me. You two bring up the rear," Shamus smiled.

"Gordon, I don't think..." Scott started.

"You don't think nothing. Shut the fuck up and put her bag in my car!"

Donald opened the hatch, steering clear of the exchange.

As Scott lifted her bag and moved toward the back of the first vehicle, Angel held Maggie in a frozen stare. She was pissed. Maggie did not challenge that stare, instead averting her eyes to the snow-dusted parking lot.

"Any other questions? Bitches, complaints." Shamus was enjoying this. He loved throwing around his weight. "Angie, you have something you wanna say?" Angel didn't respond; instead, she pivoted around and got in the car. Scott scurried back and climbed into the passenger seat. Shamus continued to stare. "Never understand what she sees in that little bug. Fuck, he can't even drive."

He can drive, Maggie thought. *He was driving when they kidnapped me.*

Maggie felt his eyes upon her. She brought hers up to meet his, but did not return the smile. She considered saying something smart, maybe: "I bet they have interchangeable genitalia." But Shamus would see that as patronization, so she opted for, "I spent eight hours tied up in the back of their car, Gordon. I'm not exactly their biggest fans."

Shamus studied her momentarily. "Okay, Maggie, no problem." They started for the car and he placed a firm hand on her shoulder. "Angie is a tough broad, tougher than some guys, in fact. Me, I'm easy to get along with, but fuck me around and I'll make Angie look like Mother Theresa. Understand?"

Maggie nodded.

"Good. Maybe when this is over, we can all head down to Costa Rica for some sun. You, me, and Marty. I have a stretch of beach down there where I go to blow off steam and forget about my business responsibilities." There was that smile again.

"Maybe," Maggie replied. She would never be a guest of Gordon Shamus in some seaside resort. She knew this. Having grown up in Jersey, she knew what happened to liabilities when self-appointed businessmen finished conducting their endeavors. Many were never heard from again, others could be found floating in the river, sometimes minus their teeth and hands.

Inside the second car, Scott and Angela seethed, albeit for different reasons.

Who the fuck does she think she is, Angel thought. *Showing me up, like I'm the hired fucking help.* Her knuckles whitened as she gripped the steering wheel.

Scott's face was flush with disdain, tempered by hot panic.

Angie, he called her fucking Angie! I've gotta get her out of here!

Donald climbed from the vehicle and strode back to their car. When Angel lowered the window, he poked his head in and turned on their radio. Adjusting the squelch, he said, "Keep it on Ladd 1." Mounted inside each vehicle was a VHF radio. Not a requirement for the road, but a definite asset that many locals used to communicate with the onslaught of traffic. Especially during Ice Season. Tli Cho Manor was 15 kilometers up the Ingraham and now that the Winter Road was in full swing, it was a major truck route.

"Everybody ready," Shamus called on the radio.

Scott reached down and said, "Yes, ready."

"Good, let's get the show on the road."

Donald made his way back up to the Escalade. Shamus had been leaning over between the bucket seats, a little too close for Maggie, but not too much. He was a slim man, wiry and muscular beneath the suit he wore. With a change of attire, he'd easily fit in on a loading dock or melt into a construction crew. Unlike some gangsters, Gordon Shamus didn't succumb to bad habits, with the exception of cigars and scotch.

Now, they climbed out of the vehicles and gathered in between them.

"You boys get the bags," Shamus said and grinned. "Angie." He put out his hand and she obediently came to his side. Behind her, Scott turned away. Maggie didn't see his face screw up into a knot of jealous rage, but she felt it. And so did Angel; her eyes darted back to her husband.

He's screwing with them, Maggie thought. *And he's enjoying it.*

"Donald, the keys, please."

Donald fished them from his pocket and handed them over.

"Shall we?" Taking each woman by the arm, he led them up the path.

3

Targus Lake, Meteorological Station
140 kilometers inside the Arctic Circle

It was going to be a big blow but a short and sweet affair. A day at the most, but what kind of damage would it do? Harper licked her lips, comparing the computer model against the Norwegian data they'd received a few hours before.

"Yeah, Category 3 for sure," she said to no one but herself, then picked up the phone and called up to the communication tower.

It rang once and the individual answered, "Communications."

"We need to get a message out to Lupania Joint Ventures that we have a storm coming our way." She lifted the hard copy from her desk. "Looks like it will reach us somewhere around 21:00 hours. Let them know down south that all traffic should cease no later than 13:00 and be buttoned up before the storm's arrival."

"Oh, Harpy, you're going make a lot of people very unhappy with that news."

She set the paper down. "Listen, Chad, get the word out. I'll worry about the fallout." There wouldn't be any. If Harper Sherwood was putting out the word to shut the road down and get all their people indoors, that was reason enough. "They'll probably already be making the same preparations, but contact the station at Lac de Gras and give them a heads up as well. Doesn't hurt to be prudent."

"Alright. Anything else?"

"Yeah, stop fucking calling me Harpy or I'll climb up that hill and kick your scrawny ass." The communications command post was high above the rest of the camp. For Harper to march up there would involve climbing a significant grade that was better than a kilometer away.

Chad worked 12-hour shifts up in the communications outpost. When he finished his shift, Chad would come down to the main camp and if the timing was right, the two would eat dinner followed by a roll in the hay. Chad was five years younger than her, 37 years old, and he looked good. Of course everyone looked good up here after a few months, even the ugly guys. Chad was her winter thing, at least until he was rotated out to Corbett Lake or Lac de Gras. When the season was over, they'd part ways. She would be on her way to Greenland and he'd go back to his wife.

Chad laughed. "You wouldn't dare."

"I mean it."

"You can't get in if the door is locked, sweetheart."

"There's a big red fire ax right outside my office." She was giggling now.

"Don't you have work to do?"

"See you tonight."

She set the phone back in its cradle and looked over the data again. Yeah, this thing was going to come in hard and fast. The winds posed the biggest threat, cutting visibility and turning the landscape on its head. In 2012 Harper had been at the stick in Targus when a Cat 3 wiped out the entire northern half of the Winter Road. The head of road maintenance, Lee Bosworth, looked like he was going to cry. All their work blown away in the course of two days. "The empty lanes are gone, the loaded lanes are gone. What the fuck we supposed to do now?"

"Start cutting a new road," Lupania Director, Hayden Shaw, ordered. "Everyone's on shift, no downtime until we get it open again. We have two weeks of good ice left and the clock is ticking." Bosworth went to work and within four days they broke through, giving priority to northbound trucks. The mine had to get their supplies in, especially fuel. The approximate cost for shipping diesel via truck tanker was $33.00 a Liter, and if they had to fly it in on a C-130 Hercules, the cost would triple. Harper hoped it wouldn't come to that.

4

Sack was already on the ice when word came down regarding the incoming storm. He was well on his way and his convoy, consisting of two flatbeds and two dry vans, had passed the point of no return. He was still burned they had shifted him onto freight, not so much the job, but the fact that he would be running with drivers that were not from his company. For Sack, the ice was as much a social event as it was a job. He loved to chat it up with the boys, shoot the shit about music, dirty women, and if in the right frame of mind, he might even step onto a political soapbox.

Sack was in the lead, his metallic black International Lonestar cutting against the arctic landscape, its chrome winking and projecting stabbing beacons of hard light. Emblazoned across the bug deflector, which was also smoky black in italic silver, was the name: ***Midnight Rider***. Considering how dumpy Sack looked, small–fat–even a little dirty, his rig was the polar opposite. He took great pride in making the girl shine and would start each trip by blasting the Allman Brothers serenade out across the airwaves. When drivers heard Greg Allman declaring that he wasn't going to let them catch the Midnight Rider, they knew that Todd Sackman was rolling. Most joked that Allman probably hadn't envisioned Sack when composing the melody.

Glancing into the driver side mirror did little to raise his spirits. The wagon hooked to this polished rig was a white 53-foot Great Dane that had seen better days. Perhaps white was being duplicitous. It might have been white at one time, but now it was closer to cream and each rivet holding the panels in place bled rusty tears.

"She's a good trailer," Bob Stewman said.

"She's been rode hard and put away wet. Seriously, Bob, you're really going to send me up the ice with that piece of shit?" That was yesterday. Sack was standing in the office doorway, leaning on the jam.

Stewman said nothing. He looked preoccupied with something.

"Bob?"

"It's already loaded, Sack. I had the mechanics go over it from front to rear. It may not be the prettiest thing, but it's mechanically sound."

"I'd take your word for it, but I don't have a lot of faith in our mechanics."

Stewman said nothing, his mind elsewhere.

"You okay, Bob?"

Still nothing.

"Bob?"

"Yeah, I'm fine. I got a lot of shit on my plate. Up to my ass in permits and logs and drivers bitching about equipment. Check it over, Sack, if you're not happy we'll unload the fucking thing and find you another wagon." He removed his glasses and rubbed his eyes.

"No need of that." Sack suddenly felt defensive. "If there's anything wrong, I'll fix her up." Sack would have left it there, but he liked Bob Stewman. They'd known each other better than 25 years. "What the hell else is up with you, Bob? You aren't your usual hard ass self?"

Stewman picked up a pen from the desk and held it between both hands "Our daughter, Beth, she has multiple sclerosis, just got the diagnosis last month."

"Shit, MS, that's tough."

"Well, the Doc said she can live a productive life and they're prescribing drugs, but she was going to university... And now?"

"She can still go to university. Can't she?"

"Yeah, but she wanted to be a neurologist. Isn't that a kick in the fucking seeds? My daughter, who worked her butt off in school, accepted to UBC, put two and a half years in. She's a thousand times smarter than her old man, and she gets saddled with a fucking neurological disorder. She's devastated... We're devastated." He trailed off, tears welling up in his eyes, threatening to spill over. "We've invested almost a hundred G's."

"I'm sure everything will work out, Bob. Just think positive." Sack backed out of the doorway, into the hall. He liked Stewman but had no interest in watching him break down, and consoling was out of the question.

"Can we bump it up 1 or 2?" a driver in his convoy asked, bringing him around.

Fucking newbies! Asking to bump it up on Ladd 1. Didn't these retards get a briefing before they sent them up the ice? Everyone from the Mines to Security was listening and this shit stain was asking if they could speed up. "Where you from, kid?"

"Cape Breton. Why?"

"Oh okay, I thought you were from Retardistan."

"What's that supposed to mean?"

Another driver piped up. "I guess he thinks you're a retard for asking to speed on a channel monitored by Security." This was followed by dead air. Sack chuckled. At least one of the mopes he was running with understood rules and regulations of the road.

5

The farther north they pushed, the less defined the landscape became. The ice south of Corbett Lake was broken up by numerous portages covered in stunted trees stabbing from the tundra. All of that had fallen away now, replaced by an endless flat white landscape. Marty suddenly understood the term snow blind, but there was no snow falling from the sky, instead, there was an endless opaque sheet undefined by shadow or shape.

"Marty, my brother, stay in the middle of the road," Garney warned. "You get too close to the bank and you might get sucked in."

"Yeah, sucked in. Drivers get sucked into snowbanks all the time," Spence said.

"You have any orange sunglasses?" Garney again.

"No, I don't," he replied. "I have regular sunglasses."

"Those don't do shit," Merv said.

"Well, anyway... Give them a try, Marty, and focus on the back of my rig."

Marty slipped on his sunglasses, but if anything, it made matters worse. Garney's rig was a dot of black in the center of this canvas. Marty remembered what his old art teacher used to say. Black is a combination of all colors. White is the absence of color. At this moment, he couldn't have been more right. This was worse than driving in the fog, he couldn't see the edges of the road or if it curved. A thin layer of white powder coated the ice, camouflaging the cracks and imperfections and melting it into the emptiness, white. Marty was suddenly very aware that he could no longer see the four-foot snowbank on either side of the road and that filled him with anxiety. He pulled the sunglasses off and tossed them on the dashboard. He then rolled his window and listened to the wheels crunching on the road. Looking left, he pulled focus and to his surprise found he was dangerously close to the left bank. "Two feet," he said, spinning the wheel right. "Jesus, Murphy."

"A little close?" Merv called, but he already knew.

"Yeah, just a little." Marty left the window open. The cold air was good; it sharpened his senses, dousing the warmth of fatigue. Below, the ice flexed and popped in its continual protest of the rolling steel.

"Hey, Merv," Spence said.

"Go ahead, caller, you're on the air."

"You've got a friend coming your way."

Marty glanced in the mirror. He couldn't see anything.

"Ah yes, I see him."

And then Marty did. It was a bird chasing Merv's truck up the ice. A large black raven, flapping madly to pass him, then gliding playfully in front of the truck.

"Looks like we got some flooding going on," Garney called. "Dropping her down, my brothers. Marty, maintain your speed until you reach the 10-K sign."

“Copy.” Marty couldn’t see the flood crew, and he could barely see Garney. But then, through flat white light, silhouettes that were a lighter shade of grey began to form. They were nothing more than dots, but Marty aimed for that group of dots, glancing left and right, blindly searching for the edge of the bank. The wind sliced through the cab of the truck crossways—driver to passenger window—bringing with it glacial shards of confetti blown from cloaked edges of the road. Marty decided that he was awake enough and rolled up his windows. Now, traveling at three times the speed of Garney, it didn’t take long to close the distance to the flood zone.

“Hey, Garney, that old Western Star hasn’t given up the ghost yet?”

Marty had no idea who was calling at first, but quickly surmised that it must be one of the flooders.

“Hey! If it isn’t the World Famous Axe Man Jack! How are you, my brother?”

Now Marty saw him, a solid-looking native man standing on the ice road, a large fire ax twisting at his side.

“I’m good, Garney. Some might even say great!”

Garney laughed. “Okay then, where’s Billy?”

“My guess, he’s probably 35 clicks north of here, just finishing his personal quota.”

“Well, if you see him, you tell him I said ‘hello’ there, Axeman. Your Bro is a great guy. Salt of the earth, my brother, salt of the earth.”

“Sure thing, Garney. Spence giving you any trouble?”

“Easy,” Spence warned.

“Not at all. I’ve got Merv back there keeping him in check.”

“I see you got yourself a new fish.”

“Oh that’s my main man Marty. He’s practically a veteran now. Survived the Ingraham and the Inuksuk and you know what else, my brother? He had a showdown with the Kitchen Nazi and lived to tell about it. Marty fits right in here, Axeman. Yup, sure does, uh huh. Don’t be shy, Marty, say hello to the world famous Axeman Jack!”

Marty was crawling along at 10 km/h now, creeping up on the group of flooders who had drilled holes. Behind them, typhoon pumps sucked the water from the holes and sprayed the road with the same vigor as a fire hydrant. “Hey,” Marty said and waved from his window.

Axe nodded back, then keyed the radio on his color. “Kitchen Nazi, eh.”

“Yeah, I’m a real hero.”

"You took the eggs, didn't you?"

"I did," Marty said.

He was rolling past now; the native fellow was smiling and shaking his head.

6

Allison Perch rode the main service elevator from the lab down into the chamber. She was unaware that both Nick Anderson and Ronny Fraser were there scouring the room for an item they called the thrombus. As were they unaware that she was en-route. She was still reeling from a dream she had the night before in which she saw herself in a sexual affair with Ronny Fraser, and this disturbed her for two reasons. First, she had been carrying on with Chase Fenwick for better than a month. Second, she found Fraser completely unattractive. It wasn't that she didn't like Ronny; she did. Ronny was considerate and attentive, but he also had a quality that reminded her of a rodent. She could never see herself having sex with a man like Ron Fraser; he was too much of a wimp. She preferred men like Chase, whose ambition evoked an aura of power. Chase wanted their affair kept secret, mostly because of his position, but also because he thought it might upset Ronny.

"He's married," Allison said.

"That doesn't mean anything, Ally, I've seen the way he looks at you."

"God."

Chase laughed.

The service elevator shuddered, evaporating her thoughts. Then it clunked hard, and for a moment she had a terrifying premonition that it would suddenly break free of its cables and plummet downward. Her stomach fluttered, and she took a step backward. Panic with its single icy finger caressed her heart. But before she gave way to a low terrified cry, the ghost in the machine relented and the service elevator continued its descent.

What the hell was that, she thought. *Electrical interference?*

From above she could hear the rumbling of a 777 Rock truck rolling through one of the corridors of the main pipe on its way to pick up another load of kimberlite for processing. Allison got a chance to ride in one of those monster dump trucks with Chase, and that was before they started sleeping together. She was overwhelmed by its size and intimidated by the low ceiling of the corridors. The clearance wasn't much more than a few feet and instilled a claustrophobic anxiousness in her.

The elevator shuddered again, but this time stalled completely.

"Oh, for shit's sake," she said, trying to sound annoyed, but the panic was again settling in. The overhead light dimmed and retreated from the darkness, taking with it the brave front she had tried to display.

"No, no, no..."

Pitch black, distant rumbling sounds, thud, thud, thud went her heart. The shrouded solitude became claustrophobic. She placed her palm against the elevator wall and felt for the compartment that housed the emergency phone.

What if it doesn't work? Oh my god, there's no electricity. There was no voice of reason to counter the terror she felt, but just the same, her hand slid blindly along the wall, feeling for the seam that outlined the door of the compartment.

Come on, come on!

She didn't dare speak aloud; to do so would be validating the terror, and she feared that if she unleashed that genie there would be no putting it back in the bottle. Then she felt it, a straight line cut neatly into the stainless steel plate. Hooking a fingernail into the seam, she traced around it, dragging her thumb along, searching for the handle.

The elevator clunked, followed by a mechanical whine and for a second the overhead light popped like a flash bulb and then, darkness. In that second, Allison was able to spot the release handle and open the compartment door. She reached in for the phone.

7

At the same moment Allison Perch found herself trapped below ground, everything in the Acadia Mine came to a full stop. The crusher used to separate the diamonds from the kimberlite suffered the same debilitating interruption. All vehicles stalled and would not start again. Computers screens went blank. Lights popped.

Chase Fenwick, who was at the south pit working his way toward the main facility in his service pickup suddenly found himself three kilometers from camp without power. He tried his radio. Nothing. The temperature inside the vehicle began to drop rapidly. He'd been following a grader, which was also stopped. The digital readout on his dashboard was reading -57 Celsius before it went blank. The wind rocked the immobile pickup and his breath began to turn to vapor. From inside the cab of the grader, he could see the driver was donning his winter gear. He reached behind the seat and began doing the same.

By the time he got his parka on, the coffee in his travel mug had already begun to crystallize. He had no idea what had stopped his truck, and the fact that the grader was also dead in the water made him wonder what the hell was going on. Pulling a balaclava over his head, he knew that his only option would be to get out and walk. This didn't please him in the least.

When he climbed from the truck, the wind ripped the door from his hand and it swung out past the intended arch of the hinges. It made a metal crunching noise. He reached over and pulled it back and slammed the door shut. The wind pushed hard against him, sending up waves of fresh powder and making the outer material of his fire-proof parka crackle like paper. He could already feel the cold on the bottoms of his feet and knew if he stood in one position too long that no amount of movement would replenish the warmth the insulation was meant to keep. So with that thought, Chase Fenwick began marching toward the grader operator, thankfully with the frigid air current pushing him onward.

The muscles in his back tightened against the cold. Chase was dressed for the temperatures because they had already received notice that a heavy storm was coming. The grader operators were clearing a path between pits and making the roadway safe for the 777 rock trucks to get back to their depot. The first wave of inbound trucks were scheduled to arrive after dinner, but would be routed into Corbett Lake until the storm blew over. Communications from Targus were that the storm would be in full swing by 21:00. Right now the winds hadn't stolen the visibility, but the temperature was dipping to the point where metal was becoming as fragile as plastic. Soon, walking around in this, even with the best winter gear could prove fatal. He picked up his pace to that of a forced march. The muscles in his calves tightened as he walked faster, and he could feel the beginnings of shin splints, but if he didn't get to shelter, that would be the least of his worries.

As he walked, he pondered what could have caused two vehicles out here to conk out at the same time. Coincidence? Chase didn't believe in coincidence. The only thing he knew of that would shut down vehicles would be some kind of interference like an electro-magnetic pulse. The only thing he knew that caused such an event was a nuclear explosion. Last he checked, the powers to be were getting along just fine and doubted even the most hardened Jihadist would see any benefit in nuking the north.

He was now approximately 100 meters from the grader. Overhead the sky was flat opaque and it was eating away at the visibility. Looking back over his shoulder, the disabled pick-up truck was already starting to drift in. Clumsily he pulled back the sleeve of his parka to check his watch. The digital readout was blank.

"What the fuck is going on?" he said.

The grader operator climbed from the cab and dropped down onto the ground. He was a short fellow, not much more than five-foot-two, one of the many Inuit from the region who were employed at the mine. Chase remembered his first name, Lenny, which was good, because his last name, Aranuknuk, sounded ridiculous every time it crossed Chase's lips.

"It just quit," Lenny said.

"Yeah, mine too."

"I got nothing, no power at all," Lenny said. "It just quit, Chase. Kaput!"

Chase laughed. "Mine too. I think we're going to have to hoof her into camp."

"What would cause this?"

Chase looked out toward the main building. Beyond that lay the second pit and he guessed that if the entire camp was down, the source of the event came from the chamber. Ronny had mentioned about the energy source that they hadn't pinpointed. That was before Anderson showed up and took over. He could only speculate, but this had to be connected to that. He just hoped the rest of the camp wasn't down.

8

Preceding all this, Ronny Fraser's lifeless body lay at the base of the monoliths, the left side of his head caved in from the blow of a rock hammer. Above him, Nick Anderson stood paralyzed. In his hand, a blood soaked rock hammer dangled. Nick's right eye was completely gone, burned up by the fusion created by the parasite as it cut into his optic nerve. Once anchored there, its tail began to squirm, tearing through the outer skin of his eyeball, then retreating inside. And then the fire began; the parasite's tail began to light like element wire in an incandescent light bulb. The pain was hot and intense, and Nick Anderson screamed aloud as his eyeball cooked from the inside out. This happened after the fatal blow had been delivered. In the moment when they moved the thrombus from the rear of the chamber to its resting place between the two monoliths. At that very moment the parasitic organism in Ronny Fraser's eye malfunctioned and, holding the thrombus, he turned to Nick and said three words.

"This is wrong," he said aloud.

Nick looked at his assistant and at first said nothing. Together, they carefully placed the Thrombus Disc on the floor of the chamber and Nick smiled. Ronny smiled back, thinking that Nick was also in complete control now. They could stop this, stop whatever it was, before it was irrevocably set into motion. Then Nick said three words.

"I'm sorry, Ronny," and those words were sincere, he did not want to do it, but his hand removed the rock hammer from his belt and swung with deadly precision. There was a thud—a crack—bone splintered up into the air. This was followed by brain matter, and a geyser of that blood gushed momentarily with the ferocity of a garden hose. Nick's white neoprene suit became crimson and pink as the blood washed over it. Ronny dropped to his knees, still hanging from the hammer's hook. Nick shook him off. One more gush and then a thud. Lying on the floor, blood pumped from the hole in his skull and with each tapering beat of his heart, each gush became shorter until there was just a trickle. Then nothing. Ronny was dead.

Nick saw himself lift the thrombus, which as he earlier surmised, wasn't much bigger than a truck hub cap, and then place it between the monoliths. At first nothing happened, except of course the loss of his right eye, which at first cooked like a hardboiled egg, then began to burn and turn ashen. He did not scream aloud, but inside he felt the agony as each dying nerve sent pulses directly to the pain receptors in his brain.

"It hurts," he bawled internally. "Oh my god! It hurts so much!"

Now, with his eye burned out, his socket looked like some macabre fireplace. Tiny embers glowed and bits of ash floated from the socket out into the open air. Around his eye socket the skin was cracked and scorched, the bone below that already turning brittle. Deep within the socket, a pinprick of light glowed. First red, then blue, then green, sending out a menagerie of microscopic enzymes carrying a single message.

"Open the gate open the gate open the gate open the gate!"

Nick knelt down, lifted the thrombus with his left hand, and brought it up to chest level. As he did this, the disc began to hum. With his right hand, he felt for an indentation in which to set the disc, but there was nothing to hold it. He checked the left side. Still nothing.

"Insert it, skent! Insert! Open the gate! Open the gate!"

With three feet between the two monoliths, there was nothing to support the thrombus.

"Insert it into what?" he asked.

"Insert it, skent! Insert! Open the gate! Open the gate! We are Skentophyte!" Mob ranting!

He lifted it further, holding it between the two monoliths and it suddenly came to life in his hands. The hum was replaced by a clicking, and with his one good eye and his other disconnected mind's eye, he watched the spokes in the disc begin to turn and at its center a green light pulsated. He felt it begin to pull away. He released his grip and it floated magnetically away, first rising up three feet and then between the monoliths. The monoliths then began to glow as well, the thrombus turning between them like a gyro and humming electrically. Behind them, the rock face flashed, black allotropes formed in the walls, winking out energy and then falling to the floor. Bits of honeycomb glowed hot and from within the rock face, it brightened like a gridded heat element. Then the molecular state of the rock began to liquefy, warping, twisting.

Nick's left eardrum popped and broke, then his right; blood trickled from both canals. He turned, not of his elation, but because he was being moved from the site for his own safety. They were not done with him. Not yet. He walked from the chamber, zombie-like, the ash still floating from his burned out socket. Behind, the thrombus spun, blue green electrical arcs forking between the monoliths like a giant Jacob's Ladder. As he closed the door to the chamber behind him, he entered the clean room and stripped out of the neoprene suit, which pulled from him like so much taffy. It had begun to melt. He did not look into a mirror, but would have seen his right cheek bone protrude through the cooked skin, charred like a cut of meat that had spent all day in the oven.

During this event, the mine came to a full stop. Vehicles as far out as 10 miles fell dead in their tracks, their function temporarily disabled as the gate Nick had called the "wormwell" began to open.

He asked himself, "What have I done? What is it that I have let loose on the world?"

They answered: We are skent! We are skent! We are coming!

***

ACT II
THE INVADERS

Chapter 20—Finger Food

1

Telegraph Road
Acadia Mine

A silent hush whispered out across the tundra surrounding the Acadia Mine, stealing the power of all that was electro-mechanical. Those in the path of the undulating wave did not see the pulse burp upward from the pit and roll across the dunes of snow and ice. Like an invisible tsunami, it rolled outward, sucking the power from everything within a ten-mile radius. It was a chameleon tide. Neither Chase Fenwick nor Lenny Aranuknuk felt or heard the energy force move over them, taking with it the energy used to propel their machinery, from watch to vehicle. Nor did they feel the stolen energy being sucked back toward the pit, leaving in its wake disabled equipment. Workers began to abandon their vehicles in droves.

To the south of the mine lay the airfield where Boeing 737s, flown by Oasis Airways, regularly dropped off and picked up shift rotations every Thursday. Luckily, today was Wednesday. If the event had coincided with the scheduled landing, the jet liner would have lost power on approach and most certainly would have crashed.

The road they walked was called Telegraph Road, named because the low level wiring set on telephone poles that looked very much like the century old communication used on railroads. The wiring wasn't even for communication. It was actually an above ground conduit that provided power to the outlying buildings stretching between the two pits surrounding Acadia. When the mine was still under construction, someone named the route Telegraph Road and it stuck. The Telegraph circled the camp and pits. At the south end was a junction that connected it to a 5-kilometer gravel road known as the High Grade. The High Grade was the main route from the Winter Road. Northbound Ice Truckers could be heard calling their km markers after leaving the High Grade, alerting the mine and southbound trucks with the radio call, "Four northbound on Telegraph at kilometer 22."

But that wouldn't be happening today.

Chase cut his stride a bit so that Lenny could keep up. The little fellow could hardly keep pace with the Chief Engineer, who stood 6' 3". With the wind at their back, the trek back to Acadia was a little easier. They'd already covered a kilometer of the three click jaunt and they'd encountered four more vehicles disabled along the roadway.

"Guess everyone had the same idea as us, Chase?"

Chase nodded. "Guess so, Lenny."

The biggest vehicle had been a 777 rock truck which was on its way to the same maintenance facility Chase had just left. When they came upon the gargantuan vehicle, Chase spotted the driver working his way back to camp about 800 meters ahead. He was just a dot, bobbing along. Chase had driven one of these Goliath trucks in what seemed a thousand years ago. He'd worked his way through the ranks. Starting out as a Laborer and working his way up the ladder at an accelerated rate. Chase Fenwick wasn't just an administrator; he could operate almost every piece of equipment at the Acadia Mine. He'd run graders, snow cats, front end loaders, rock trucks, and even the big shovel used in the pits. Chase Fenwick knew what he was talking about when it came to equipment.

"That's gonna be a bitch, Chase," Lenny said.

"Don't I know it," Chase agreed.

"Another kaput."

"We'll be bringing out a fresh battery pack and some heaters to get this puppy up and running."

"As long as it ain't here too long."

Chase nodded. "Yeah, let's cross our fingers, Lenny."

The engine oil in the 777 was already turning into roofing tar from the extreme cold. They'd have to fire up a bunch of torpedo heaters and tarp it just to warm it up while they switched out the battery pack. The maintenance guys would definitely have their work cut out for them.

They moved past the 777 and followed the bobbing dot ahead.

"Anyone behind us?"

"Nope, just you and me, Lenny. I was the last one to leave the Sussex Building. How are you doing, anyway? Are you warm enough?"

"Shit, Chase, I'm an Inuit. This is T-shirt weather for my people."

Chase laughed. "Okay."

"Besides, even if I was cold, which I am not. What could you really do about it?"

"Well..." Chase grinned. "Sweet fuck all, Lenny."

"Exactly." And with that, they pushed on.

2

Old Town Yellowknife, NWT
Morrison Drive

Donald drummed his fingers on the steering wheel, eyes alternating between the clock radio and the street ahead. He already hated this place. It wasn't just cold here, this place was physically uncomfortable. From the moment they landed, he wanted nothing more than to get on the plane and head back to Hamilton. He'd done his fair share of freezing his ass off on an Artillery Base on the Prairies. He didn't show it, though, wouldn't show it. Working for Gordon Shamus did not afford him the privilege of complaint. No matter how crummy the circumstances, Donald conducted himself with quiet resolve and maintained a mask of practicality. This seemed the best course of action when your psycho boss was prone to pummeling someone into a flattened veal cutlet using a excavator.

"Where are you, little prick?"

The little prick was a local drug dealer named Nigel Tecumseh. Donald knew of him, but only through Phil Crane. Crane had been up here on more than one occasion setting things up and putting people into position for the job. He didn't like Crane much but respected his work ethic. Donald was much bigger than Crane and he thought he was tougher, but Crane had a reputation that almost matched Gordon Shamus. The difference being, Crane knew how to turn it off. Gordon didn't.

"Speak of the devil."

A battered black Ford pickup turned the corner and parked across the street. The door swung open and out stepped Nigel Tecumseh, a large yellow envelope dangling from his right hand. He glanced left, then right and strode across the street directly to the Escalade. He was of average height, shoulder length hair and to Donald, he looked like a two bit drug dealer. He might have thought he was the "Cock of the Walk," and maybe he was up here, but down in the Harbor he'd be eaten for breakfast. Still, he crossed the road in long vaunting steps, full of arrogance and ego, but as he got closer, Donald saw a chink in the armor. He had a dark swollen bruise just below the right side of his lower lip. Nigel had taken one on the chin.

Donald rolled down the driver window, letting in the cold.

"You Donald?"

"Yeah."

"You got the money?"

"Give me the envelope."

Nigel first offered, then pulled it back. "Three G's, that's the deal."

Donald sighed. "Get in the vehicle."

"What?"

He hit the lock release. "I said go around to the passenger side and get the fuck in."

Nigel suddenly looked worried. "Why?"

"Because you look like you're trying to sell me rock standing there, so go around to the passenger side and climb in."

Nigel looked around, then worked his way to the other side of the Escalade. He tugged on the handle, opened the door, and climbed in. Seated, he said, "Okay, now what?"

"Buckle your seat belt."

"What? Why?"

"You ever watch COPS?"

"Yeah."

"Ever notice that there's always some idiot who gets busted for a tail light or no license plate or not wearing his seat belt?"

"Yeah, okay, but why do I need a seat belt? I'm not going anywhere."

"You ask a lot of questions, Nigel Tecumseh. While you're putting it on, I'll answer, but do as I say or I'll kick your ass out of the car and go tell my boss that you are a fuck-up. He hates fuck-ups, Nigel. You don't want to know what he does to them."

Nigel pulled the belt across his shoulder and snapped it into place.

"Okay, we're going for a drive around the block for two reasons. The first is to make sure you weren't tailed."

"I wasn't..."

"Shut up, I'm not done. The first is to make sure you weren't tailed, and the second is to make our transaction." Donald put the Escalade in gear and pulled away from the curb. "Now, tell me what is in the envelope."

"A GPS and instructions on how to get to the site."

"Instructions. What do the instructions say?" Donald was turning the same corner the black pickup had come from.

Nigel tore open the envelope and pulled a piece of paper out. He began reciting the directions.

"What's on the GPS?"

"The location."

"So why did you guys write down instructions?"

"The GPS doesn't recognize half the roads up here. Until you got close, the GPS would be sending you cross country. The instructions will get you close enough, then you can use the GPS for the last leg."

"Alright, I want you to place that in the cubby hole."

"What's a cubby hole?"

Donald smiled and pointed. "The glove compartment."

Nigel opened the compartment, folded the envelope over, and then closed it. "What about the money?"

"You think I'm going to rip you off, Nigel?"

"No offense, but I don't know you. I only know Phil."

"No offense taken. Look in the back seat."

Nigel did and spotted a knapsack. "That's the money?"

"No, it's a bag of turnips."

Nigel frowned. "Did I do something to offend you?"

Donald was turning left again. "You holding anything?"

"Huh?"

"Don't play dumb. You carrying anything. Crystal, rock, a bag of weed, anything like that?"

"No."

"Don't bullshit me, Nigel."

"I've got a satchel."

"Toss it."

"What?"

"Look Nigel, are you fucking deaf as well as stupid? Toss the shit out the window or get the fuck out of the vehicle. Bringing a satchel of shit to a business exchange. Give your head a fucking shake. Now toss it. And if you have anything else, you better fess up."

Nigel reached into the breast pocket of his winter jacket and pulled out a single satchel of Crystal Meth. Donald lowered the passenger window and with great reluctance, Nigel tossed it. "Man, Phil isn't nearly as intense as you are."

"I'll take that as a compliment. Everything I need is in that envelope, right?"

"Yeah."

Donald turned the corner again; they were halfway around the block. "Okay, lean back, grab the knapsack and check it."

Nigel reached back, pulled the bag up between the seats and unzipped it. In it were several rolls of small bills wrapped with elastic. “Shit, you guys run out of fifties and hundreds?”

“No, big bills draw attention. Anyhow, it’s all there, $3000.00, in five, tens, and twenties. No need to count it, you won’t be in the vehicle long enough.” Donald pulled the vehicle over to the curb and stopped. “This is where you get out.”

“What’s this? My truck is a block over.”

“This transaction never happened. If word ever gets back about this, I will make it my business to come up here and kill everyone in your family. You get jammed up on something, you wear it. You know who my boss is and that’s good, but remember this, Nigel Tecumseh. We know who you are as well. We know who the guy is who dug the hole, your cousin, we know who his wife is and we know who his son, your nephew, is. You jam us up and all of them will suffer as a result.”

Nigel’s mouth dropped open as if unhinged. He looked scared. That was good. “Shit, man.”

“Shit, nothing. You picking up what I’m putting down here, Chief?”

“Yeah.”

“Good, now get the fuck out.”

Nigel’s face hardened, but just a little. Donald guessed he was deciding whether or not to challenge the order he was getting. He’d considered budging him, but instead frowned and gave him an unwavering, “I mean fucking business!” scowl.

It only took a second.

Nigel climbed from the Escalade, the knapsack slung over his right shoulder. Once the vehicle was around the bend he muttered, “Yeah, fuck you too.”

3

ACADIA MINE

Allison fought to maintain her self-control, only because succumbing to the terror she felt scratching at the outer reaches of her imagination was far too horrific. She didn’t want to think about what was going on out there; doing so would only intensify the claustrophobic dread. But she could hear sounds, some real, others imagined. Sounds of twisting metal, unwinding cables, crunching sounds that could mean cave-in. Dissecting these sounds led down paths to even worse considerations. She pushed this off.

Gotta keep my cool, she thought. *Panicking will only make matters worse.*

Of all those at the Acadia Mine, with the exception of Nick Anderson, she was closest to the source of the event. Although she really had no idea what was happening. The other sound she heard was a high electric hum rolling out in continual uniform pulses.

She pulled the phone from its compartment and placed it to her ear.

Nothing.

Oh dear God.

And as if her prayers were suddenly answered, the electricity came back on. She covered her eyes. The elevator shuddered, there was a whirring sound, and red LED panel displayed rotating zeroes. Another clunk and a whirr. She could hear other sounds as well.

Machinery!

The mine was coming back to life.

The elevator shuddered one last time and began to descend.

Allison took comfort in the noises. This told her that the worst case scenario had not happened. There was no cave-in and even better, she would soon not be alone. She fully expected to meet Ronny down there in the Lab and despite her dream, she was happy at that prospect. What she did not know as the service elevator ascended downward was that there was something far worse waiting to meet her.

The elevator stopped. She thought for a moment the door would not open and this stirred up the lingering dread, but then it did.

"Hello, Allison," Nick Anderson said.

Before she could scream, he pulled her out.

The door closed behind her.

No escape.

4

"Billy Jack," the voice over the radio called. "This is Chief of Security, John Pringle. Have you got a copy?" They were on a secure channel used only by security. Pringle had installed the channel on Billy's hand-held as a safeguard. He wasn't the only hunter out here, but he was the only one who operated alone.

Billy reached down and lifted the hand held radio. "Go ahead, John."

"What is your location?"

"I'm about 60 clicks north of the Acadia mine. East side of Portage 47."

"We have a blow coming in, Billy. I'd like to dispatch a driver to come and escort you back to Corbett."

"How bad is the storm?"

"It's a Category 3, set to hit us at around 21:00."

"They say how long it's gonna last?"

"Somewhere between 24 and 36 hours."

Billy looked at his kills and shook his head. He'd have to leave them, but he doubted if Pringle could get someone out to him in time. "John, if you send a guy out for me, there's a good chance you'll have two guys lost in a whiteout. I'll head on up to the old fish camp and sit things out there." The Fish Camp was a collection of abandoned shacks used by a scientific team six years before. They called it the Fish Camp because the so-called scientists appeared to do a lot of fishing and little else.

"Billy, I'd really feel better if I sent out a guy, or even if you went to Acadia."

"John, I got everything I need to sit this out. I'll charge my radio on the way up and park the pickup and trailer on the side of the ice road. I'll see you guys tomorrow after the Lupan Boys come and dig me out."

There was a long pause.

Pringle couldn't order him to do what he wanted, but if he had, Billy would have agreed to go, but only out of respect to Pringle. He didn't much care for the folks at the Acadia Mine. On his only visit to the Mine three years before, he was escorted everywhere. Better to head up the Fish Camp and hunker down there with his stove and his herb. "I've got everything I need, John."

"Okay, Billy, but I want a radio check as soon as you get there. And one in the morning. Even if you can't hear us, we can hear you on the repeaters." The repeaters Pringle mentioned were located every ten miles on the ice and kept communications between the mines unhampered by distance. Corbett, Targus Lake and both Mines were able to communicate over distances of 600 km thanks to those repeaters. They could also hear drivers as far south as Yellowknife, although the drivers did not have the range on their radios to reach out that far.

"Alright, I'm packing up now."

"Copy that. You give me a call when you're there so I know you're buttoned up."

"Will do." He placed the remote radio down on the sled and started gathering his gear. He stared up at the dull gray sky—wisps of snow swirled on the thermal current—it didn't seem that bad. He looked at his kills and hoped that none would be knocked over in the storm. If one fell, the wolves, or even a wolverine might make it into a meal. He shook his head. *The hell with it! If I lose one to the storm, I'll get another. There's plenty of Caribou out there, there will be plenty when this is over.*

He pulled down his tent and began folding it up.

5

The right side of his face was burned, but he was still recognizable. The horrifying thing, the thing that made Allison scream had been the empty socket. Nick looked as though he'd been in an industrial accident, transparent flesh, resembling the jelly surrounding canned ham, hung from the right side of his face. His right arm was burned and blistered; she couldn't imagine the pain he was in, but worse than that were the specks of ash floating out from the charred cavern where his right eye used to be. The ash seemed almost life-like, like tiny fleas swarming from a nest.

"Nick, what happened to you?"

"Skent." He attempted a grin, but only the unburned half of his face seemed to obey.

"What? Where's Ronny?"

He held her upper arm tight.

"Dead," he said. His tone was matter of fact. "Skent. I'm sorry, Allison."

Skent? She tried to pull away. "Sorry? Why? Let me go, Nick."

"I can't. Skent. I'm sorry, Allison. They're making me." He tugged her arm hard, almost pulling it from the socket. There was a pop. "It's almost time. We have to... Skent... Have to go back."

"Please, Nick, what happened to Ronny?"

"In the chamber. Skent. Dead. We have to go."

"Dead? What happened?" The self-control she had managed to maintain in the elevator was seeping out of her.

"I killed him. They made me do it. Skent."

"Nick, please stop this!"

"I can't. Skent. Can't stop this, Allison. They have control now. I'm sorry." He turned, and a fresh swarm of ash wafted out of the burned socket, fluttering into the corridor draft. He pulled her off her feet and began dragging her along the corridor.

"Please, Nick, please!" She was wailing now, begging for her life.

He seemed not to notice, his actions a stark contrast to his apologetic words. "I'm sorry, Allison. I don't want to do this. Skent. But they are, we are... We are skentophyte." He clamped down harder on her arm, causing the skin to bruise. Her shoe caught on the floor, came off her left foot and fell away, abandoning her. "It's almost time. We have to get to the chamber."

"Why?"

"Because they're coming."

"Please, Nick, let me at least stand up. Please, I won't fight, just let me stand up."

He stopped, turned his head again. She saw the dim glow deep inside the burned out socket and then saw something move within that cavern. Coiling itself, the light pulsed brighter, a fresh plume of ash expelled. She suddenly thought that if she could extinguish that light, she might be able to stop whatever it was that had turned him into a homicidal maniac. "Okay, stand up, Allison, and I will escort you."

He straightened her up, one sock foot resting on the cold concrete. He did not release his arm and she got an even deeper glimpse into the cavern. She saw the embers glowing behind the vagabond ash, burning like phosphorous and only now did she recognize the odor of protein.

If she could extinguish it, maybe she could stop this, maybe. She dug into her lab coat pocket with her right hand, feeling for the item she had there. Nick began leading her down the corridor, toward the double doors that led into the clean room. That electric hum intensified with each step. When they pushed through the doors, it was overbearing, spiraling toward them in pressurized octaves.

He's going to kill me, she thought. *He's contracted some kind of radiation poisoning.*

The double door clicked behind them.

On the floor lay a neoprene suit soaked in blood.

Clack whir clack whir clack, came the sound beyond the clean room.

Whose blood is that? Is that Ronny's blood!

Clack whir clack whir clack!

They pushed through the second set of doors.

Clack whir clack whir clack, and then: **Click—click—click!**

What is that?

Allison found what she was fishing for and wrapped her hand around it.

"Don't let him take you! If he gets you where he wants you, you're dead for sure," called a voice from the past. It was Danni Colpy, her self-defense instructor. She wished the 200-pound lesbian was here now. Danni was equipped to teach the average male a thing or two about fist-to-cuff brawling. Allison started taking the classes while she was getting her degree at the University of Michigan. In the spring of '94, a number of women had been raped in the area, although not on campus. Allison attended the class as a safeguard. "You gotta fight, sweetheart! Fight like you're going to die."

If I can hit whatever that light is in the back of his socket, maybe I can stop him.

"Fuck that, cut his throat if you have to. This is kill or be killed," Danni said.

Allison opened the multi-tool, using her fingernail to unfurl the four-inch blade. At first it snagged against the interior of the pocket. She pushed out on the material and freed the blade. It clicked into place, she reseated the handle, then tightened her grip on it. She was only going to get one shot at this.

"Nick," she said.

He stopped, turned toward her. "Yes, Allison."

"I'm sorry," she cried and swung her arm in a high, lethal arc. The blade entered his socket, there was a snap of gristle and bone, fresh ash exploded from the socket. She'd connected with something, but what? She hung there, holding the handle of the multi-tool, expecting him to drop.

Nothing. Just a steady, **Clack whir clack whir clack,** followed by: **Click—click—click!**

Nick stood statuesque.

Click—click—click!

She let go.

But he didn't.

Nick turned his head, his grip on her left wrist never loosened, his free hand reached up and pulled the blade out. As he did this, a second swarm of ash flowed out and she saw that the light was still glowing. If Danni had been here, there would have been an "I told you so," but she didn't need her to point out the mistake. Allison fully expected Nick to cut her throat with that very blade, but he dropped it to the floor and cocked his head sideways, dog-like, as if hearing some high-pitched sound.

Then he turned toward her.

"I'm sorry, Allison," he apologized. "I don't want to do this. Skent."

He grabbed her right hand, held it in his own.

"Please, Nick, I'm sorry. Please let me go. I don't want to die."

"I'm not going to kill you," he said. "Skent we are skent! Immobilize, skent." Nick released his grip on her forearm and held the offending hand with both of his. "I'm very sorry about this, Allison. I really don't want to do this." He opened his mouth, lips pulling back, and then he did the unthinkable. He started with her thumb and by the time he bit off her third finger, she fell unconscious, but that didn't stop him from finishing the remaining digits.

6

At around the same time that Chase Fenwick and Lenny Aranuknuk found their vehicles dead in the water, the convoy led by Big Garney Wilson was passing by the turn-off that led down to the Acadia mine. The distance was approximately 11 kilometers out from the 32-kilometer road known as the high grade. While they were too far out to be effected by the event, all trucks in the convoy experienced a minor electronic interference.

"What the hell was that?" Spence said.

"Shit, you too. I thought my rig was going to stall," Merv said.

"I don't know, my brothers. That was sort of strange. Did you get anything, Marty?"

Marty felt it too. His gauges dipped and he was sure the truck was going to stall, then it reset and the hiccup passed. "Yeah, what would cause that? A blast from the pit?"

"Aliens," Merv joked.

"A blast wouldn't do that," Spence said. "Not a conventional blast anyway."

"What would be unconventional?" Marty knew where Spence was going with this, imagined him rolling across the battlefield in Afghanistan under a barrage of artillery. Marty didn't know much about what went on over there; he equated most of what he imagined to war movies like Saving Private Ryan or Blackhawk Down.

"I don't know, electro-magnetic pulse? That's the only thing I know of that would shut down equipment like that."

"What are you saying, Spence, that somebody dropped a nuke?"

"No, I don't what just happened, that was really weird. Maybe some kind of magnetic field. If it was just one of us, I wouldn't be throwing this shit out there, but all four trucks? That's kind of strange, don't you think?"

"Any of you having problems now, my brothers?"

Each man walked on the other in a collective "No."

"Well, then we have three-and-a-half hours to talk about it while we cross the Dreamcatcher," Garney stated, then announced, "Four northbound at Portage 46!"

Dreamcatcher Lake was the largest lake on their route. Spanning 110 km across, it was also the most likely lake for a driver to nod off from fatigue and hit a snowbank. Garney climbed up the hill to Portage 46 and disappeared over the crest. Marty approached the Portage and accelerated. He glanced down at his GPS; his speed was around 40 km/h, ten over the posted limit, but he was learning quickly that the security had little regard for a driver who spun out on a hill. When he hit the hill, he kept his foot on the throttle, and the 600 rejoiced in a long turbulent growl. His heart sped up a bit; this was sort of fun.

Yeah fun, except for the psychotic who put you here.

"Marty, my brother, you have a pickup coming your way. Keep an eye," Garney said. The "pickup call" was the tip off to watch his speed on the portage. He rolled over the hump, waited until the lead trailer was on the flat, and eased off the throttle. The weight of the pup slowed him down to 30 km/h by the time the truck was level. Just in time, the pickup was coming at him.

"Who's the leader of this convoy?" the Security called.

"You're speaking to him," Garney replied.

"You boys don't be stopping for tea and crumpet. There's a wicked storm on the way, Lupan is gonna close the road until it's over. Get your butts up to Meanook and prepare to hunker down for a day or so."

"When is the storm supposed to roll in, Security?"

"They're saying that the winds will pick up around nine tonight, but we're not letting anyone else go north. All traffic is now being stopped at Corbett. You boys made it over the line, you're the last northbound convoy we're letting through."

"How many convoys in front of us, Security?" Merv interrupted.

"Two that I saw. Two groups of four. A convoy of flatbeds and hoppers. The second convoy was all tankers. They're about an hour ahead of you. That's another thing, the winds up in the barrens are polishing approaches to the portages something fierce. When you boys hit those last seven portages, do whatever you have to do to get up those hills. Last thing we want is a bunch of spun out rigs jamming up the whole works. If everything goes according to plan, you should hit the high grade at Meanook at around eight tonight. That will get you folks buttoned up and eating dinner an hour before the storm blows in." The pickup rolled past Marty, pulled off to the right, and stopped. "You guys keep her coming, I'll wait until you're all up the hill before I roll down. Do what you have to do to get up that hill, driver. My radar gun is taking a break."

"Thanks, Security," Merv said. "Here I come."

"No problem."

"Hey security, I have question for you." Merv again.

"Fire away."

"You experience any issues with your truck?"

"Issues? What kind of issues?"

"Interference. Like it was losing power."

"Nope, running like a top. Why?"

"Just wondering." Merv passed him.

"Alright?"

"I'm making a run for the hill now," Spence said.

"Okay, bring her on up. I'll wait for you."

Garney was already on his way down the other side of portage and rolling onto the big lake. Marty wasn't far behind. The Security man wished Spence well, and then headed south.

8

Maggie stood on the balcony overlooking the property, ignoring the cutting cold—focusing instead on the impressive scenery that enveloped this grand house. Ahead she could see the Escalade silently winding its way back up the drive, occasionally disappearing behind the snowbanks on either side of the long serpentine approach. Donald had been gone for about two hours, she didn't know where, but every action taken by these people, from her perspective, was a cause for alarm.

Inside the house, Shamus took a call and moved into one of the spare rooms for a bit of privacy. She guessed it might have been local or someone involved in this whole messy affair. Behind the door, she heard his muffled voice rise, but she found herself too afraid to eavesdrop. She only heard two words that she recognized. "How long," but beyond that, his words were a succession of animated ranting. She had not seen the insanity of Gordon Shamus, not yet anyway, but she could feel it swimming below the current like a predatory fish waiting to strike, so she went out onto the balcony to get away.

Scott and Angel were somewhere in the house, presumably fighting or fucking—or both. They were away from her and that was all that mattered. Their room was right next to hers, and Scott was a moaner. Prior to their session there had been words. Something told her that Angel and Shamus had history. It was obvious that he, Shamus, was taken by her, the other blatancy was that it drove Scott nuts. Aside from the fact that everyone, Maggie included, was scared shitless of Gordon Shamus, she thought that Scott's insecurity and Angel's discomfort might give her an edge.

Oh yes, you're going to turn them against each other, their entire reason for coming here completely forgotten. Sure, sweetheart, you'll just saunter out of here while the rabid dogs tear at each other's throats. No, maybe not that, but she might be able use that issue as a distraction to give Marty a chance to get them out of this. *Yeah, Marty's as scared of this guy as you are, maybe more.*

But she didn't think so. There were two Marty's, the quiet reserved Marty, the one who listened intently, and then there was that other Marty, the one who sat across from her and spoke of another place and time, the other person he had been. She hadn't asked him if he'd been involved in violence or killing, but that was probably going to be the Marty they needed. There was another alternative, one that repelled and disturbed her even more than killing, although it shouldn't.

You could just lay down for him. Let him have you and maybe when the sick bastard rubs Marty's nose in it, you could strike.

"Strike," she laughed at this.

"Hey," called Donald from below.

Maggie looked down, startled. How long had he been standing there?

"Yes."

"You might want to get inside, your nose looks a little frostbitten." She pulled off a glove and brought her hand up to touch her nose. The tip felt hard and numb. "Don't rub it, just go inside."

Maggie pulled her hand away and turned to go back in.

When she entered the main living room of the house, Angel was making her way through the room. She stopped and looked Maggie's way. Maggie expected her to come at her and hit her with a verbal beat down, but instead Angel's expression changed to one of concern. "What's the matter with your nose, sweetheart?"

"I don't know, I think I've got frostbite." Her voice was low and mousy.

The front door below opened.

"Let me see."

Maggie pulled her hand away.

Angel's eyes squinted, then widened. "Ouch."

Ouch was right. The warm air was sending pinpricks of pain through the tip and up over the bridge.

"Don't rub it," Donald warned. "You'll rub the skin right off."

Maggie suddenly felt like she was going to cry.

"It looks like candle wax." Angel said.

Donald was on the other side of her now, inspecting the tip. She wanted to get to a mirror, take a look at how badly she'd disfigured herself. She wondered crazily if she'd end up looking like a leper once the skin died. *Guess you won't be distracting Gordon Shamus with your sexual prowess after all. Unless he has a thing for lepers.*

"Why are you smiling?" Angel asked.

Maggie recoiled and hurried toward a mirror.

"It's superficial, Maggie, not deep," Donald reassured from behind.

"How do you know?" Angel asked.

"I was in the Army for 3 years," he answered, then called after Maggie. "Don't touch it, let it warm up on its own. It's going to be uncomfortable, might even peel like a sunburn, but it's not deep frostbite."

Maggie stood in front of the hall mirror. The white waxy spot on the tip of her nose wasn't bigger than an M&M. Angel was right, it looked like candle wax, but it was thawing, turning red around its outer edges and as an added extra, it was broadcasting pain out across her face and begging to be touched.

Donald came up beside her and said again, "Just don't touch it. White is superficial. You're lucky I came along when I did. A little longer and you might have a nice bout of deep frostbite."

Maggie turned toward him. He was a hard-looking fellow, not particularly attractive, but he was a long lean band of muscle. His eyes were deep green, his hair blonde with a tangled highlight of copper. "How do you know this? I mean superficial. How do you know it's not deep?"

"If it was deep, it would be black."

The door down the hall opened and out stepped Gordon Shamus. He didn't expect them there. "What's going on here?"

"Nothing serious, Gordon. Maggie was outside a little too long. Got a bit of frostbite on her nose," Donald explained.

"Oh, for Christ sake. Why was she outside?" he growled.

Angel hung back, not wanting a part of it.

Donald looked up defensively, about to say something.

"It was my own fault. I stepped out onto the balcony to look at the property. Guess I was out there a little too long," Maggie blurted.

Shamus turned his attention to her, inspecting the spot. "Does it hurt?"

Yes, it did. It hurt quite a lot, but she said, "It's not so bad. I guess I was lucky."

His expression softened. "You gotta be careful, Maggie."

"Yeah, lesson learned. I'm sorry, Gordon."

He turned his eyes to Angel. "Where's Scott?"

"He's laying down."

"Get him up. We need to have a powwow."

"Do you want me to go to my room?" Maggie asked.

"No, you can join us, Maggie. You're part of this."

Five minutes later, they convened in the living room where Shamus told them about the delay. "A big storm is coming," he said. "I guess they shut everything down up there when one of these blows in."

"How long, Gordon?" Angel asked.

"One or two days, add to that the travel time. I guess three is the magic number."

The look of collective disappointment was pretty hard to hide. Scott let out an exasperated sigh that caught Shamus's attention. "You got something you want to say, Scott."

"Gordon, he didn't mean..."

"I'm not talking to you, Angie, if I was talking to you, I'd be looking at you."

Scott cleared his throat, a nervous mannerism, then croaked, "I'm disappointed, but it is what it is."

Scott's answer, apparently insufficient, seemed only to infuriate Shamus. "It is what is?" He smiled sarcastically. "It is what is. Hmmmm."

Angel looked horrified.

Donald's eyes seemed to glaze over. The silence was deafening.

"I didn't mean anything by it, Gordon."

Angel was poised on the end of her seat. She was scared to death.

"If you didn't mean anything, why say it?" Scott was going to answer but Gordon cut him off. "You know what pisses me off? Do you, Scott?"

"No."

"When I deliver news of a setback and someone complains like I planned it, like it's my fault. That pisses me off. Do you think it's my fault, you little bug?" Shamus's face was reddening, rattlesnakes rearing up in his eyes.

"I was out of line, I apologize, Gordon."

"You apologize, that's good, but do you get it, little man? Because I'm thinking you don't really get it."

Angel was panic-stricken. Her eyes darted back and forth between Scott and Shamus, then they found Maggie. She looked like she was drowning, clawing out for help from anyone who would give it, even Maggie.

"Gordon, will Marty be in any danger?" Maggie interrupted. "Up there? In the storm?" She'd said what she could, didn't dare say anything else. From her vantage point it looked like Scott was in a world of trouble and she didn't want that rage turned on her. Shamus turned toward her, his face flush, the scar beside his nose hard contrasting white. His eyes were like steel ball bearings, angry spheres that mirrored an internal rage. He didn't like being interrupted and Maggie was already regretting opening her mouth. And for what, really? To save one of the assholes who kidnapped her and helped put her in this fucking house? With this fucking headcase?

God, I'm an idiot.

Shamus turned away, his attention back on Scott. "You better learn a thing or two about respect, little man. Understand?" And before Scott could answer, he brought his eyes back to Maggie. The madness in them was receding. "Up there? Nah. They'll be sitting on their asses at the mine until it blows over. Marty has nothing to worry about up there."

Not up there, but he has plenty to worry about down here, she thought.

9

Her right hand was a nest of fire ants, pinching and biting, discharging spasms of agony. The torment navigated up her arm like tiny broken pebbles of glass paring its way beneath the skin. She was strapped down on something. A gurney maybe? Whatever it was, she could feel one of the straps cutting into the undercarriage of her ribcage. She didn't want to open her eyes, didn't want to see the disfigurement left by the missing fingers and thumb on her right hand. She could only imagine it looked like a grisly bloated flipper. She'd passed out when Nick began chomping off her digits, but not before he took her index and thumb in two merciless chomps. Amazingly, he managed to take the first two off before spitting them onto the floor. Two was his limit before his gag reflex kicked in. Her only thought was: *He's going to eat my whole arm.* By the third chomp, she welcomed the blackness as it swallowed her up.

"Open your eyes! Open them, before it's too late," Danni commanded.

She did as she was told. If she'd listened to Danni and cut Nick's throat, maybe she wouldn't be strapped down. Maybe she wouldn't have to learn how to write or wipe after she did her business with her left hand.

Her pupils contracted defensively against the glaring light. Beside her, through sticky lids, she could see his blurred shape. Nick "the finger biter" was motionless, like a robot. But it wasn't Nick anymore; the thing beside her looked more like something from a horror movie. A rotted zombie came to mind. His skin was melting off around the burned out socket, his cheek bone protruding through the charred jellied flesh. He kept saying the same thing. "Skentophyte, we are skentophyte we are skentophyte we are skentophyte."

Whatever had happened was now in full swing.

She opened her eyes wider. She was propped up on a stretcher, bound to it by cargo straps. In front of her were the two monoliths and beyond that a giant swirling vortex of black that opened up onto another place. At the base of the monoliths lay a bundled carcass, baked almost black by whatever it was that was happening here. The carcass was a man, the broken yellow skull protruding from the lump of meat the only thing that gave definition to the heap.

Is that Ronny, she thought. *Who else could it be?*

Beyond the vortex, she heard something that conjured a memory. Danvers, Montana came to mind. Yes, the horse ranch in Danvers. Crooked Heights. That had been the name. Crooked Heights, but it wasn't the ranch that was stirring up the memories of her childhood. It was the clicking and clacking, the rhythmic continuance that was attuned to the steady beat of cloven hooves. It reminded her of the unbroken horses and the galloping cadence they carried when they broke into a run. The sound wasn't exactly that, but a close comparison.

Beside her, Nick mumbled, halted his rant long enough to say, "They're coming."

Her eyes flitted back to the vortex and she realized that the galloping sound was in the hundreds, perhaps thousands, and as Nick Anderson had announced, they were coming.

"I'm sorry, Allison," he apologized again.

She barely heard the hollow apology, focused instead on the muddy smoke swirling inside that vortex. She struggled harder as the steady **kathump kathump kathump** slowed as it approached the other side of that window.

She thought of the fossils in the lab. The creatures with their plated armor and large jagged teeth. *Was this them? It had to be. And what am I when they arrive? Dinner?* Terror cut through her. "What have you done, Nick? Why? Did they infect you?"

His head traversed mechanically toward her. His other eye, the good one, looked like a runny poached egg, while the hollow black socket burned like a pot belly stove. "They are Skentophyte—they need our eyes—I think they are blind."

"How do you know this, Nick?"

"I can see everything now. I am being absorbed."

"Why are they coming, Nick?"

"Skent, coming to harvest." He smiled.

"Why are you smiling?"

"Because this will be over soon. I do not want to... We are Skent. I do not want to live... I feel responsible." Nick stiffened, convulsed, more ash. "Get ready."

Ripples broke the steady whirlpool of smoke, making it look more like muddy water than gas. The first thing Allison saw was a long serpentine appendage push through the barrier. At first she thought it was a snake, then the fingers unfurled, revealing it as an arm. A second arm pushed through and next to that another. The bands of muscle in each arm were protected by an overlap of plating, which made her think of the insects. Then the rest of it came through, taking its first steps in this world.

"Please, Nick. Untie me, please," she whispered. "Please please please."

The lone creature, the thing Nick called Skentophyte, turned its head, left, then right, pivoting mechanically on its cervix. It snapped, teeth cutting air in a succession of long spastic chomps. It moved toward them, dog-like, snapping the air in bites interrupted by a low hissing snarl. The creature was how she would have imagined it from the fossils. Its skin beneath the armor plates was scaled and reptilian. It moved first to Nick, inspecting him, sniffing either side of his body, and then it stood up on hind quarters, and suddenly it was towering over him. Upright the creature stood almost eight feet.

"Allison, I'm sorry," Nick said again. "We are Skentophyte, serve us."

It reached down with one hand and caressed his shoulder as it turned its head. The tubing on its back gave a steady "**shhhh-hush-shhhh-hush**" as the air exchange filtered the oxygen it was taking in. Allison peered from the corner of her eye, not wanting to look, but unable to tear her eyes away. Tears flowed down her cheeks, hot and stinging; her heart crashed in her chest like machinery out of calibration.

Ahead, through the muddy vortex, more of them began to pass through, taking up defensive postures around the chamber. First one, then two, then four, they moved into the chamber, lining it. The steady humming of the gate fluctuated in alternating waves of sound.

Allison lowered her head, tears flowing, terror riding high as she waited for them to come to her. Nick stood paralyzed as the Skentophyte examined him. It stood over him, scaly hands on both shoulders, like a father having a heart-to-heart with a son before the big game. His left eye had cooked out, now bobbing inside the socket in tendrils of mucus and blood. "We are Skentophyte."

The Skentophyte's teeth began to clack and there was a buzzing sound, like swarming mosquitoes. The others took notice, turning in that direction. It released him from its fatherly embrace and lifted his right arm over his head. At first Allison thought it was going to pick him up for closer examination, but she was wrong.

The buzz intensified.

It pulled him forward and bit into his forearm, clamping down hard. Nick hardly flinched. Then the others came, surrounding him, biting into him, locking on snake-like. All of the creatures' cheeks began to inflate and deflate.

"We are Skent, we are skent, we are skent," Nick said weakly. Then he began to scream in agony. Something was happening to him; his arm, the one first bitten, began to lose structure, the bone within melting away, turning it to a loose bag of skin and muscle.

My god, she thought. *They're liquefying him.*

And with that final thought, Nick Anderson deflated before her eyes, no longer a man, but a massive bag of skin holding only tissue. The screaming stopped, he was dead, but the Skentophytes held on. There were sucking sounds—a drawing in the last of the liquefied bone.

"Coming to harvest," Nick's ghost echoed.

Allison thrashed about, but it was useless; the restraints held her. The first Skentophyte released its grip and rose up in front of her. It moved its skull-like face in close to hers, and a steady rush of hot stinking breath warmed the moisture in her tears. Instinctively she closed her eyes, waiting for it to clamp on and turn her into an empty sack of skin, muscle, and fat. When that didn't happen, she opened her eyes.

There was that buzzing insectivore sound again. The others disengaged and began to surround her. Allison Perch, never all that religious, began to pray aloud. "Our father, who art in heaven..."

The Skentophyte opened its mouth.

"Hallowed be thy..."

Took in a deep breath.

"…name. Forgive us our trespass..."

It spat, like a cobra, into her eyes. Not once, but twice, sending the same parasitic organisms corkscrewing through the tissue and directly to the optic nerve. Once there, they bit into the nerve and began to heat up. The somatic sensation, although only lasting seconds, felt like Hell's eternal damnation. Allison Perch's eyes cooked in their sockets, first hardening, then blackening, the elements inside them glowing white hot. As with the apologetic Nick, the nerves began dying—fluid vaporizing—tissue cauterizing, until there was nothing but black caverns and small flecks of ash floating out into the underground breeze.

Her eyes were gone, but she could still see. The organisms gave sight and as she now understood, plugged her straight into their collective. Perhaps even more than Nick or Ronny. She understood it all now, saw them searching for the Thrombus, opening the gate. Understood that she no longer had control, that she was simply an emcee that served them and there would be many more like her. Across the gateway, the wormwell led straight back to the collective, where high towers opened portals onto other places sharing one common denominator.

Harvest.

Allison Perch felt the restraining straps fall from her body. They were pouring in through the gate now. By the hundreds, like insects leaving a nest to wage war, pillage, infect, but mostly to harvest.

The invasion was just beginning.

“Skent,” she mumbled. “We are skentophyte.”

***

Chapter 21—First Wave

1

ACADIA MINE
17:45 Hours

They came in an endless wave, like army ants on the march, pouring into the subterranean chasm. Allison could see them streaming to one of the high towers of their world, entering at its base and climbing the spiral interior with unstoppable momentum. In the peak of the tower a great wheel spun, arcing electricity, sending out a signal that the gate was open The tower, one among thousands spiking the alien landscape, was a single portal anchored into this world; it was, as Nick Anderson put it, the wormwell.

She could hear them whispering madly, "Skent skent we are Skentophyte!"

They flooded in, lining up in long files on the floor and when they ran out of room on the floor, they dug into the walls and eventually the ceiling. Hanging upside down, like wingless bats, teeth clacking. She stood before them, fire burning in those cavernous sockets, ash floating out as the parasites dug in deeper, offering a direct line to her cerebral cortex.

I'm going to die from this, she thought. *I'm like an Aphid, but whatever is inside me is killing me.* And she was right. The life cycle of the infected depended on how long its body could withstand the fusion. *How long before my brain cooks off, before the bones in my face become too brittle to withstand the fire inside?*

Then a command overrode her thoughts, not language but impulse, flooding her brain chemically. She wondered if Nick got the same impulse before he bit off her fingers. It was time to leave the chamber, to take the Mine and begin the harvest. She turned and began to walk out of the cavity to the corridor that led back to the clean room and the service elevator. As she did, the creature that had spat into her eyes probed her brain, picking through it for information. She could feel it running its scaly fingers through the filing cabinet inside her grey matter. She knew what it wanted, heard the musings that resembled words, but weren't really. As it did, words popped into her head, then fell away.

Entry, exit, corridors, security, military, resistance, temperatures, landscape, strongholds, transport, and on it went as Allison pushed through the clean room. From behind, her escort moved deliberately on its hind quarters, using its front arms to propel itself onward, like a cross between a praying mantis and a chimpanzee. All the while it clacked its teeth.

When she reached the service elevator, she felt its thoughts being projected to the others.

Impractical. Another way?

Yes, there was. The chamber was annexed by a tunnel that led to the open pit. There, a road spiraled up and out onto the Telegraph Road. The distance was well over eight kilometers, but Allison would not be going. The Skentophyte would march out that way, while she would ride the service elevator with her escort. Once on top, a signal would be sent, then they would begin the first wave.

The targets were already being plucked from her head.

Central communications, the airport, security, and from there, the rest of Acadia. Estimates were already underway, temperatures considered and resistance measured, all from the mind of a single lab assistant. She would have laughed that their tactical assault was based on what she knew, but understood there would be others once the invasion began. Others like Chase Fenwick, like Damien Lars, like Rally Martins in communications, and Tea Riddick at the airport. These names were also being plucked from her mind, their mental pictures being distributed into the collective.

There was a ding and the elevator door slid open. She entered, her escort turned to the others, and they began to retreat back down the corridor, all except one, that is. It would be joining them for the ride up. They crowded in, bringing with them a chemical stench that seeped from their pours. Their teeth clacked and the hoses that extended from their backs continued a rhythmic: ***Shhhh Kaaa Shhhh Kaaa***.

She started to wonder if this was their version of a space suit, if the hard insect exterior coupled with the machines that filtered the air really only housed a smaller organism. She thought that was it, but her thoughts were clouded as another order came down the pipe.

Communications first, the order stated. Communications then the airport. From that, distant responses acknowledged the order as it fed into the skentophyte collective.

Skent—Skent—Skent

The two creatures pushed back against the walls, arching over her, obviously too large for the moving compartment. Her escort placed a hand on her shoulder, almost protectively.

It is blind without me, she thought.

Ascend, it commanded.

She pushed the button and the elevator began to climb.

2

ACADIA MINE
COMMUNICATIONS CENTER

Rally Martins worked the radio at Acadia. It was her job to maintain communications between the open pits, the high grade, the airport, and all traffic coming and going. Above her work station was a bank of six VHF radios, each serving a singular purpose. Before her sat a microphone that was hard-wired into the computer. When a call came in, the computer would alert her and switch communication on the mic automatically to the frequency and radio in question. Transmitting was a little different: she had to punch in the radio number using a touch pad set neatly by her right hand, propped up on a stand at a 45-degree angle. Rally wasn't her real name, it was Belinda, but Rally was her radio handle and it translated from on air to day-to-day. It was just easier to say Rally than Belinda, and truth be known, she preferred it. Along with Rally's many responsibilities, she also had a reputation as having the sexiest radio voice north of the 60th parallel. It was low, raspy, steeped with sex, and inbound truckers loved chatting it up with her.

Nobody from outside Acadia knew what she looked like, and there were arguments among the truckers whether she was blonde or brunette, Latino or Aboriginal, some even argued that she was white. It was anyone's guess, but that silky voice coming over the air waves warmed the insides of tired truckers like hot coffee spiked with Irish Cream. What's more, she flirted a little and that only added to the allure. Plenty of truckers wanted to know what she looked like, even inquired at the Information Desk or asked the folks at hydro-carbons or even security, but none would divulge who she was. Once in a while, someone would remark that she probably had a face for radio, in that she had an incredibly sexy voice, but would crack the lens of a camera. This would unleash the wrath of irate truckers who had their own mental picture of her, none too happy about anyone mucking with their fantasy.

Rally was a pretty lady, in her mid-thirties with long black hair that flowed straight and uncurled down over her shoulders. She looked a little like Sandra Bullock, except her eyes were slightly almond shaped, giving away the Dene Indian side of her heritage.

Rally had just come on shift when the power went out at Acadia. There was plenty of movement at the mine. Scores of people moving around outdoors on foot, leaving their posts without the ability to communicate, but Rally stayed put. For lack of a better word, she was the nucleus of this operation and while the engineers tried to figure out what went wrong, it would be her job to reestablish order once the radios finished firing back up.

Thank God there's no scheduled shift change today, she thought.

Thank God indeed, that was one less worry. Tea Riddick, Tea being short for Theissen, was the air traffic controller in the airport today. Tea was a panic button, and as the power restored, he was first on her list to square away. Rally had no idea how Tea managed to get his ATC license, but guessed that Acadia was the best thing to happen to him. One 737 every second week and the odd helicopter were about all Tea could manage without getting flustered. If not for the mandatory drug testing, Rally thought Tea should be entitled to smoke a big fatty before going on shift just to calm him down.

"Acadia to Corbett, have you got copy?"

"Go for Corbett," replied the male voice.

"Hello, Gene, this is Rally. We had a power outage up here, we are just reestablishing comms. How's my signal?"

"Clear as a bell, Rally. The entire camp went down?"

"I'm not 100% on that, but I think so. Anyhow, glad to have you up. I've gotta gather up all my call signs and do a check."

"Copy that, Rally. Call if you need anything."

"Will do. Acadia out."

At this point, she'd brought almost everyone back online, but she was still going through the list. She expected Chase to poke his head in at some point. He'd be looking for stragglers, applying pressure. This made her anxious. It wasn't that she disliked Chase, she just disliked the fact that he didn't seem to trust anyone to do their job. Well, her job anyhow. He made her feel nervous when he came around, like he was critiquing her. Chase never said much, so Rally figured he thought she was inadequate, but in higher circles he had said she was the best communicator he had ever seen. In fact, he had spoken with Damien Lars about promoting her out of communications into a supervisory role. Unfortunately, Rally would never live to see that promotion.

When the door to the communications room swung open, she didn't look up from her monitor, thinking it was Chase stepping in to see how she was making out. Then it occurred to her that Chase had been out on the Telegraph. She swiveled around and there stood a woman and on either side of her were two Halloween props. They had to be props because there was no way they were real. Then she saw the woman's face. She didn't know Allison Perch all that well, had seen her from time to time. The odd "Hello" was the extent of their interaction.

"Hello, Rally."

Before she could answer, the Halloween prop to her left stepped forward and spit into her eyes. Rally barely managed a scream when the scaly hand cupped her mouth. Then the short-lived eruption of pain subsided as her eyeballs began to cook off.

3

Chase and Lenny were still two kilometers out when the mine began coming back to life; they were actually the last two stragglers making their way in from the cold. Chase thought he'd be a kilometer out by now, but Lenny moved a little slower. Chase didn't mind; aside from the fact that he was anxious to find out what happened, he enjoyed walking with Lenny Aranuknuk.

The stacks on the main building were chugging away again. Good, that meant that the heating system was working and that also meant that the interruption had been temporary. Ahead, approximately 300 yards, an abandoned grader sat idle on the side of the road.

He had an idea.

"Let's see if we can fire that baby up, Lenny."

"Sure thing, Chase."

4

The Snow Cat cut a path across the freshly dusted road that led to the airfield, leaving a fishtail of powder. Behind the tillers sat Herb Crawford, beside him Allison Perch, and riding outside on the back of the vehicle was their escort clamped onto the machinery. It now held two people in its spell, but its main focus was on Herb. Below ground, the Skent were flooding the tunnel, pouring in by the thousands and waiting in reserve.

Communication was now locked up in the main building. There, an escort waited with Rally as she maintained her presence as radio communicator. Sitting behind the controls, she barely missed a beat after her transformation. Looking like some cadaverous hell-sent creature she continued her broadcast in that sultry voice, calling to the remaining call signs on her list. Herb checked in and alerted her that the Snow Cat was up and running.

Transport, Airport must be secured...

"Herb, I'll be sending you down a couple passengers who need to get out to the airfield Asap to perform communications maintenance. Can you meet them at the East door?"

"I'll be over there in a minute."

"Thanks for that," she said followed by, "Skent."

Herb ignored it and started rolling toward the East door.

Now, as they pushed toward the airport with the ghost of Gerry Rafferty singing, "Right down the Line," the two sat quietly, indifferent to the music. The music, as loud as it was, was muted by the anxious chattering of teeth and insectivore buzzing. The airfield would be the last communications stronghold. Guarded by the high strung, easily flustered Tea Riddick. Herb knew Tea well. It was his job to keep the airfield clear and he'd seen Tea all wired up and ready to explode like a box of clock springs. Say, when he had to coordinate inbound trucks with an inbound Oasis 737. Absently, beyond the thousand chants inside his head, he wondered how Tea would react to this.

Five minutes later, the snow cat stopped outside the tower on the airfield. The Skent detached itself and moved through the snow toward the building. Tea might have seen them, but he was preoccupied in the washroom and about the same time the main door opened, he was just shaking off.

Back at the communications center, Rally was following directions from her escort, passing information and directing people with her sultry voice. "I need a maintenance crew to head down to Level 9 to perform a check in the second pipe."

"I'll need a work permit, Rally," replied Kevin Halford. Halford was a by-the-book man, who considered standing orders to be even holier than the bible. Most of his co-workers thought he was a pain in the ass.

"I'll alert quality control, Kevin, and we'll get you a permit, but they need at least a four-man crew down there Asap."

"Is Chase on board with this?"

There was a pause.

"Rally, did Chief Fenwick authorize this?"

"Yes."

Within ten minutes, Kevin Halford got his crew together and they started for the same service elevator Allison Perch had used to bring her escorts up top. Through the Skentophyte Collective, an order was sent to dispatch four to meet them. They never had a chance.

"This is Acadia Airfield, checking in," Tea Riddick reported, somewhat more confidently, Rally thought. "Airfield is secure."

But Rally didn't need the report from Tea, the word went out across the collective in a chant declaring the same thing. The masses were waiting in that tunnel like Greek Forces inside a Trojan Horse.

Secure—secure—secure! We are Skentophyte! Move now!

Those men and women who worked the pit and found themselves stranded either below or above ground all found themselves walking back toward the camp. The pilgrimage out of the pit was taking much longer as they walked in groups of six and eight up the grade. As they did, the scourge hiding in the main tunnel let loose and began pouring out and into the open pit. They moved like giant dogs making bounds of 20 and 30 feet as they stampeded forth.

The clopping of their feet against the frozen rock and mud was comparable to that of a thousand war machines moving across any given battlefield. The sound was a rumble heard by the walkers as they poured out into the daylight.

"What the hell is that?" said one man.

"Run!" a woman screamed.

Others turned, the screaming started, and the group closest to them ran for their lives. But they could not outrun the scourge that was coming. Within a minute of pouring into the pit, they overtook the first group infecting all of them while the rest swarmed up the walls of the pit, climbing over one another to the next level.

And the next.

Then the second group fell and the third, and finally, the fourth. As they turned these people, the remaining skent, in the thousands, came bounding from the pit. They used the brains of those they had taken to direct them up and out. At first it was a handful, and those infected could feel information being taken from them. Out of the pit and onto the tundra they broke in different directions. Some jumped on the sides of buildings, easily scaling the hard red brickwork and busting through windows. Others opened doorways, holding them ajar like demonic doormen, charging through the doorway to operatic screams of terror.

Shift workers awakened by the alarms were just climbing back into their bunks when the Skentophyte came. One such fellow was just slipping back into a dream state when his room door broke off its hinges, and he opened his eyes only to have them burned out with venomous accuracy.

They were unstoppable, utilizing the element of surprise. The workers in the mine had no idea what was happening until it was too late and they'd been overrun. In the cafeteria where approximately 90 workers were drinking coffee and having a bite, they suddenly found themselves corralled inside the eatery. From every exit a Skentophyte entered and blocked any escape.

There were screams at first. Then uneasy questions amongst themselves.

"What are they? Where did they come from?"

Allison Perch stepped into the cafeteria, past the sentinel of skentophyte, and addressed the group. A woman working behind the steam counter screamed when she saw Allison, her fingerless hand swollen—infected, but it was the eyes, those hollow black caverns that set the panic alight in the female cook. She looked as though she had come straight from hell. Perhaps she had.

"Everyone please sit down. If you resist, they will take you." She smiled, which made her look even more terrifying. The skin over her right socket was turning hard yellow and her nose had begun to blister.

"What are they, Allison?" asked Roy Crenshaw, a maintenance man who worked in close proximity to her.

Allison turned in his direction, the smile still firmly planted on her face. "They... We are skentophyte."

"What do they want?"

"Us."

"Why?"

"Harvest."

Then they teemed into the room, seizing everyone, but not infecting them; these ones would be going back. A female cook pulled a ladle from the steam table as one of them crawled toward her. She swung, clanging the big gravy ladle off its hardened skull. It recoiled slightly, but not in pain, more in surprise. She pulled back her free arm and swung again. There was a metallic clink and the ladle's handle bent over. The Skentophyte, seemingly unimpressed, reached out with its four-foot long arm, locked onto her throat, then pulled her over the steam counter.

"Pay attention," Allison said. "Don't resist, or this will happen."

It spat into her eyes and she squirmed in agony.

When they began to cook, the screaming really started.

5

Acadia did not fall without resistance; there were attempts to stop the Skent as they pushed into the buildings. But most people became submissive and were taken with little or no fight. It would be a stroke of luck that saved Chase Fenwick and Lenny Aranuknuck's lives on the day the event happened. The two of them were crowded inside a cab of the grader that sputtered along Telegraph Road at a slow rate of speed –15 km/h to be exact. As far as Chase could tell, the grader's fuel filters were freezing up, a byproduct of sitting for too long in the extreme cold.

Lenny was at the controls, while Chase sat off to the side, his back pushing against the cab window. Both men had kept their sense of humor, sharing a laugh as the big machine almost stalled three times. Chase wasn't all that concerned; the power was on and that meant that they were taking care of business in his absence. Still, he had a responsibility as chief of operations. He was still puzzling over what had caused the event, speculated it had to do with the chamber, and hoped that Ronny and Nick Anderson hadn't blown the place sky high.

The stroke of luck that would save their lives was the busted radio inside a grader. When Chase noticed that it was an inoperable, he was plenty unhappy. The driver should have never taken a vehicle out of the machine pool with a busted radio. Out here, communication was everything and it frustrated him to no end that he was unable to touch base and find out what the hell was going on.

"Maybe it broke when everything happened," Lenny said.

"Nope, there's an out of service tag on it. Two days old." Chase flicked the tag with his middle finger. "Jesus, you talk to people and still they don't listen. Dumb—dumb—dumb."

Lenny said nothing. He knew the policy and there was no arguing about it. He figured the driver was going to be in for a shock when he found out that the Chief of Operations had commandeered his vehicle and found the busted radio. What Lenny didn't know was that the driver, along with about 90 others, was being corralled inside the cafeteria by an invading force.

The second thing that saved their lives was the clogged up fuel filters. Approximately 800 meters from the main building that housed the cafeteria, the grader started chugging hard and then lurched until the engine cut out. As they coasted approximately 100 meters, Chase and Lenny were in sync, calling out, "Come on, baby, you can do it!" The vehicle came to a stop—Lenny cranked it over—but it wouldn't catch, and on his third try, he felt Chase's bare hand fall onto his shoulder.

"Lenny, stop cranking it! Now." His voice was calm, but authoritative.

Lenny was focused on the volt meter, wondering how many cranks he had left. "It might catch, Chase." Chase didn't answer, but his hand tightened on Lenny's shoulder and before he could look up:

"Oh, dear sweet God."

Lenny brought his own eyes up, but he wished he hadn't.

From 700 meters out they could see the main building and the big glass entrance with the crash doors. The moment that Chase placed a hand on Lenny's shoulder was exactly two seconds after the front doors blew open and a stampede of people came running out. Chase had a set of miniature binoculars known as "Bushmasters" he sometimes used to check out the wildlife or just to watch what was going on when driving around the mine. He'd been using the Bushmasters when the group from the cafeteria made a break for it into the front lot. This was a pickup point for bussing workers to and from mine destinations.

Maybe there was a fire or an alarm, Chase thought.

Then he saw the Creatures crash through the glass and spill out into the snow. He wasn't sure what it was he was looking at. They moved like an insect horde, crawling over each other, through windows and doors surrounding those he realized were actually trying to escape. By the time he had processed this and equated it to the things in the lab, he heard himself telling Lenny to stop cranking, even felt himself squeeze Lenny's shoulder, but it felt ethereal. When he heard himself call out to a God he no longer believed in, those things were in the hundreds, surrounding the 20 runners. Chase watched, his jaw hanging open.

"What the fuck, Lenny."

"Chase, can I look?"

He didn't want to hand them over, afraid that what he was seeing might be a hallucination. That Lenny wouldn't see them and confirm that he'd lost his mind. Would that be so bad? Wouldn't that be better than the prospect at hand? Maybe. He lowered the Bushmasters and passed them to Lenny.

Lenny brought them up for a look. "What the hell is that, Chase?"

"We found something in the second pit. But... It was just fossils."

Lenny was entranced as he took this in. What were they doing? But that was a stupid question; he knew exactly what they were doing. Knew that the outcome was going to be tragic. The bloodbath was about to begin, so Lenny lowered the Bushmasters and handed them back to Chase. "I can't watch this."

"What?" Chase asked, but also knew as he took the glasses back and refocused.

Completely encircled, the 20, consisting of 13 men and seven women, huddled together. Backs to the center, they faced their attackers with a look of hopelessness, resigned to the fact that they weren't getting away. From their escape route, a woman walked through the door and stood atop the concrete patio. The creatures did not seem interested in the woman, but she appeared to be talking to them.

"My God, what the fuck did they do?" Chase said as he adjusted the focus and realized who the woman was standing on the patio. "Allison..." She looked like a snowman from here, with two chunks of coal for eyes. "What the hell is the matter with her?"

The first to be plucked from the circle was a woman. One of the things jumped from the wall like a dog and bounced into the circle; when it did, it latched onto her and yanked her out. She flailed about, her screams lost in the arctic vacuum. Now clear of the herd, six of them surrounded her and tugged from different directions, clamping onto each limb, pulling and yanking, teeth snapping, frenzied in the kill. Then they began to skin her alive.

The first Skentophyte snapped the woman's wrist clean off and then used the claw at the end of its thumb to slice up the side of her arm. She fought, twisting and kicking, but they held her. It peeled her forearm like a banana, crimson mist momentarily obscuring the slick wet bone.

"I think she's… My god! She's directing them, Lenny."

Lenny stared down at the instrument cluster.

The Creature clamped down on the protruding bone with crunching fury. Snapping its head back, it severed the limb, leaving behind a nub of protruding at the elbow. Another creature was standing on its hind quarters, holding the interior frame of the left forearm in its mouth. She fought to wriggle away as another Skent unzipped her leg. With her femoral artery opened up, she bled out and was dead before they took the calf bone and started onto the thigh.

They skinned the dead woman, taking only her bones, leaving the skin and viscera steaming on the lot while their teeth ground the bone down into workable bites. By the time that they were done with her, another Skent dropped into the circle and pulled out another. Unknown to Chase or Lenny, this next victim just happened to be the Grader operator who'd decided to ignore the rules and take a vehicle with a busted radio.

Limb by limb, they dismantled him.

"Lenny, we have to get the hell out of here," Chase said, still taking in the horror, understanding it was only a matter of time before they were spotted. There at the windows of the main building, the others who did not make a run for it were forced to stand and watch by their captors as the 20 were killed and eaten.

"Chase, the vehicle will not start."

"We got to go on foot, got to get the hell away from this place or we're going to end up like that."

"What about the storm, Chase?"

They were tearing apart another two, the frenzied circle of feeding increased to two. The snow-covered parking lot was now tarnished crimson. Chase was thankful he couldn't hear the screams; it would've been more than he could take. He assumed the other standing at the window was being made to watch. He had no idea of why they didn't touch Allison. Didn't care, because at this point, self-preservation was paramount. "I'd rather take my chances with the storm than be torn into fucking pieces. We have to get as far away from here as possible." He was suddenly thankful that the radio was busted and the vehicle had given up the ghost. Thank God he'd stopped Lenny when he did; the smoke from their stack could've given their position away. "Maybe we can find another running vehicle, get it going, and keep warm, but we got to get out of here, Lenny. Pretty soon what they're doing over there might not be enough entertainment."

The winds had picked up considerably, snow dust swirled, thankfully obscuring the horror show in front of the main building. Chase and Lenny used this cover to open the cab and climb out of the vehicle. Once out, they clung to its exterior, working up the nerve to begin walking in the other direction. The wind was merciless, but given the alternative, they really didn't have a choice.

"There's a trailer 7 km from here. We'll have to stay to the road, but if we can get there, it might buy us enough time to find a way to Corbett."

"That's a long walk in the snow, Chase."

"I know, Lenny. Maybe we can find a running vehicle that didn't conk out. If we can find that, maybe we can go for help. If we stay here, we'll be slaughtered like the rest." All along the ice road, vehicle left behind, by workers changing shifts, were left running. In fact, most vehicles on the ice were never shut off. Chase hoped this might give them an opportunity to get back to Corbett Lake and warn somebody about what was happening. The only problem, of course, was finding such a vehicle and not freezing to death during the trek. "We can't stay here." He looked at his watch, which had miraculously comc back to life. On the digital readout: 18:25 hours, but he really had no idea how long it had stopped working. By now it could be 19:30, and the full brunt of the storm was supposed to take hold around 21:00. "We've got about an hour and a half before the storm hits. I think we better take advantage of the weather and get the hell out of here."

Lenny nodded in agreement.

Chase took one last look through the binoculars. The herd of escapees had been culled to half. He turned his attention back to Allison. She was standing there, looking down, and he felt a pang of guilt for leaving her. It wasn't that he loved her—he didn't, although that did little to alleviate his conscience. He felt like a piece of shit for leaving her. It didn't matter; they were all dead and everything had to take a back seat. There was nothing he could do for her or them, but they were his people. If he and Lenny managed to get out of this alive, he had no doubt it would haunt him for the rest of his days.

"Let's get moving, Lenny."

6

The scene in front of the main building was even worse up close. The Skentophyte made the remainder inside the cafeteria line up at the windows to watch the horror unfold. The female cook, now transformed, gave the order issued by the Skentophyte. "Go to the windows." They were corralled in front of the big panes of glass and those who tried to turn away found themselves being held in place and forced to watch the macabre display. "Do not resist! Skent. Pay close attention! This is what happens to those who run! We are Skentophyte."

Those infected felt the orders passed across the collective. They were searching for leaders; those would be the ones they would want. Acadia had been taken, the bulk of its resistance overrun, but there were still things to do. Now they gathered intelligence, made lists of the missing, of who was coming, and of course, transport back to skentophyte would have to be made. This world was grand and would yield much, and this first raid was only the beginning.

In the main personnel office, Ross McNeil was sitting in front of his re-booted computer. On the screen, personnel lists along with pictures were being read through the black cavernous sockets and transmitted directly into the collective. Names, faces, positions, and head counts, all being considered. As he flipped through page after page, his escort acted as a conduit to the rest of the collective. How many? Here now? When does next wave return? And as these questions were laid out, Ross typed on the keyboard and brought up the information they required. Ironically, the brass plate hanging outside of Ross McNeil's office read: **Human Resources.**

Not far away, in the underground maintenance facility, vehicles and equipment were being inventoried by the machine pool operator and his escort. As with all the others, the information was being disseminated out to the collective, and a much larger picture was being drawn.

Over the intercom Rally Martin's silky voice alerted everybody in the mine. "Attention all personnel, we have experienced a minor disruption in power. Everything has been restored, but by order of Chief Operations, all personnel are to gather at their assigned muster points so that we may conduct a headcount. Please move now in a safe and orderly manner. Acadia thanks you."

In his office, Vice President Sal Godwin sat in front of his computer, while behind him an escort stood, teeth clacking intermittently. He was on the Internet, Google Earth to be exact; a big globe spun as the escort directed him. There.

The globe stopped at North America, then zoomed in. Then, information processed, it zoomed out again spinning on its virtual access. On a separate browser, populations were being tallied along with military strengths and vulnerability. Sal knew what they were planning; in fact, everyone who had the parasites in their eyes shared in that collective plan, but were powerless to stop it. These live parasites were far stronger in their ability to control than the ones that turned Nick and Ron.

There would be more entry points once this one had been secured. They would need to strike out and set up these new access points. Those not needed would be taken down into the pit and transported back for processing. Their bones would be harvested, some would be used for breeding. The wildlife in this area would be harvested as well. Creatures like caribou, wolves, and even foxes. Anything that lived or breathed, carrying in it the precious bones, would be rounded up and taken.

Back in the Human Resources office, Ross McNeil brought up two names on his list: Chase Fenwick and Lenny Aranuknuk. He highlighted these two names and copied them to a file that read: **Unaccounted.** That list was becoming increasingly shorter.

Acadia had fallen.

***

Chapter 22—Chase and Lenny

1

"We discovered them in the second pit. About a month ago. Lars wanted it kept secret until we got some outside help," Chase caught breaths between each sentence and steps as they pushed against a brutal cross-wind. The storm, it seemed, was coming in earlier than originally forecast. "That's when a scientist, Nick Anderson, from Worcester, Massachusetts got here and took over everything. Goddamn egotistical asshole and now..."

"These creatures lived down below?" Lenny pointed downward. "Underground?"

"No, I don't think so. Nick had a theory that they were travelers. He said a bunch of stuff about wormholes. He thought the chamber was a machine of some sort. Or a gateway..." They were only halfway to the building and both men knew that the four kilometers ahead were tantamount to 40 in this weather. They had to keep moving and they had to stay by the edge of the road because visibility was dropping quickly. Right now they could see 10 feet, but soon that could drop them into total whiteout. If that happened, they were done. The building they were hiking for was a gray steel structure made up of wood and corrugated steel plating. That plating would become invisible once the wind kicked up and even with the road as a guide, they might walk right by it. If that happened, they were finished.

Both men were turning over what they saw in their minds. Lenny considered the possibility that he was freezing to death in his grader and this was a hallucination resulting from his body shutting down and succumbing to the cold. But here beside him, Chase walked and explained the fantastic in a matter-of-fact tone.

Maybe Chase is dead too.

Chase knew he wasn't dead, but he was still having a hard time digesting the horror show they'd just witnessed. He wondered what the hell was the matter with Allison and why hadn't those things touched her?

What had Nick and Ronny done? What had they unleashed?

They had to get to Corbett, had to alert the military, but would the military be able to stop them?

Maybe, but Acadia was fucked.

Right now all they could do was get to that service building and hide out until the storm was over. Chase hoped the generator out there was in working order, because if it wasn't, they wouldn't be able to withstand the -50 degree temperatures for long. The building would be an ice box and when those creatures came along, they'd find Lenny and Chase as frozen as two sides of beef.

"So, what do you think happened?"

"I guess they must have turned it on and opened the gate."

"The gate?"

"Yeah, the gate, the gate to wherever the fuck those things came from."

Lenny face became serious; a frown tugged at either side of his mouth as he stared up, and between each labored breath, he said, "I don't want to die like that, Chase."

"Who the fuck does, Lenny?"

"Get torn to pieces like that, the poor people."

Chase said nothing. He was thinking about his son Jack who was going to college in Niagara. He was a couple thousand miles from this, but for how long? Chase knew they had to seek rescue and do something to stop this before they poured out of the north.

If this gets out, we are in big trouble, he thought, then said, "Let's focus on getting some shelter, Lenny. Can you pick up the pace a bit?"

"Yeah, okay, Chase." Lenny stretched his stride a bit, but the shin splints he was getting from the mukluks were agonizing. He might have had better adaptability in the cold, but he wasn't built for forced marching. He thought Chase must be annoyed with that, but he politely kept quiet. That thought wasn't too far from the truth, but the one thing Chase Fenwick feared, more than the storm or the cold, was the isolation and the possibility of being alone.

"We get to shelter, fire up the heater, and then we start planning a way to get to Corbett Lake and to help." Chase was counting his pace. He estimated they were well past halfway. "I think there's even a coffee pot."

"Really?"

"Yeah. Now coffee, that's something I can't promise." Chase looked down at his companion and grinned. "I'm guessing those creepy things will be riding out the storm just like us. So all we got to do is hunker down and when it starts to clear, we commandeer a vehicle to get to Corbett." Chase was speaking of the many pieces of equipment left behind by Lupania along the ice road. Those vehicles would be running, even when unmanned.

"They'll be kaput, Chase."

"Maybe, maybe not. I'm hoping that there's a range on what happened. Maybe there will be a vehicle that wasn't affected."

"How do you know that? Corbett Lake could be dead in the water. Even YK."

"I don't, but whatever happened in that mine, the interference was temporary. I'm hoping that means it only went so far and we are going to find a vehicle. Hell, we might catch a security on his way out when this blows over, maybe even an inbound convoy. Something, Lenny, we have hope."

"Hope is good."

"Damn right!" Yes, hope was good.

"Do you think anyone else made it, Chase?"

"At the mine?"

"Yeah."

"Maybe, if they had enough time to find somewhere to hide." But Chase really didn't think so. In fact, he thought they were the only ones who made it out, and on that assumption he was right. Both men fell silent for the next hour, following the jagged edge of snow that rose along the right side of the road, and as they did, Chase tried to keep count of his pace while scanning for the building. His body felt heavy and though he wanted to stop and rest, he didn't, nor did Lenny. The winds continued to pick up, painting their visibility flat white. They had to keep moving; time wasn't on their side.

Find a vehicle when this blows over, or even wave one down. That was his plan. If communications were lost at Acadia, as soon as the storm passed, someone from Lupania would be dispatched out of Corbett Lake to find out what the hell was going on. Of course, Chase had no idea that the Skentophyte had already taken control of the communications and as far as the rest of the world was concerned, everything was just fine. Damien Lars was already on a Trans-Atlantic flight back from France and would be catching the company jet back to the mine the next morning. Chase wasn't thinking about Damien, though; he was thinking about people who really mattered to him. His son, his sister in Vancouver, his cousins in Ypsilanti Michigan, and even his ex-wife Charlotte, in the town of Stoney Creek, Ontario. He imagined Lenny was thinking the same way. They, Chase and Lenny, had hope, but with hope came responsibility.

2

The line share of Acadia personnel followed the radio order issued by Rally Martins and found their way to designated muster points. Once there, they were collected by the Skentophyte and moved into larger concentrated areas. The numbers inside the cafeteria, minus the massacred 20, had increased by 45, bringing the number up to 100. The female cook, named Evelyn, stood at the steam table holding her deformed ladle, the sensors inside her cavernous sockets scanning the room for any would-be escapee. Most sat quietly, staring at the floor in defeat, while newcomers gazed out the window at the large blot of Indian red staining the snow. Beyond that, the pelts, stacked like cord wood, were already being swallowed in a growing drift of powder.

In the gymnasium another 150 were held, watched by two infected workers, perched atop the bleachers like vultures waiting for their prey to terminate. Skentophyte moved up and down the halls of the building pursuing tasks that served the collective, but all were wired into each of the infected. Every movement seen by a possessed individual was broadcast out across the telepathic web. Escorts stayed with each of the possessed, serving as a main conduit and protecting each as an ant would an aphid.

Allison led them through the bowels of the pit. There, they inventoried equipment, machinery, and the structure of the mine. There were two types of Skentophyte. The smaller ones, which Chase had called "Pac Man," had rounded skulls and stood approximately eight feet in height. The other Skent had come through after the initial invasion. These were the soldiers, twelve feet in high, armor-plated exoskeletons and their heads peaked on top almost like a swollen shark fin. It was the soldiers that leapt from the building into the circle, pulling the victims out with such ease. Tearing them to pieces. The Pac Man variety were less physical, clamping their victims like a snake, liquefying their bones with an enzyme, then sucking out the runny calcified marrow.

Every building, tunnel, and route had become a path for the Skentophyte, turning it into a hive of sorts. While the Skentophyte only had four limbs, they moved with the speed and agility of insects. Although physically they had no eyes, they navigated the corridors by smell and sound, maintaining an efficient pattern and flow. While the escorts disseminated information to the group, the soldiers massed in legion, waiting to set out on their first raid.

They were in the thousands now, like Centurions, and the intelligence collected about this new World via the escorts was absorbed by the massing force. Equipment was being readied by their new trustees. When the storm was over, they would push south and take the security camp. After that there was the city south of that. The cold did not seem to affect them; the Skentophytes' outer armor was equipped with a filtering system and also some type of antifreeze cooling ducts that warmed and cooled them in the most adverse conditions.

Sal Godwin had given them everything they needed. Using the Internet, they had maps, populations, military strengths and much more. This information was being transmitted back through the wormwell to the other side, and preparations were under way to send forth more anchors to be distributed across the land. Once the continent fell, they would push across the ocean. This plan was nothing new for the Skentophyte, as they had lain waste to numerous worlds before this one. Once conquered, they would dismantle the infrastructure and create an industrial world that served them. Essentially the earth, as man knew it, was destined to be converted into a global farm.

3

Marty concentrated on the crescent-shaped right edge of Garney's pup tanker, while watching for the snowbanks on both sides of the road. The winds had picked up considerably, turning their world into a pallet of chalky white, devoid of definition.

"How's it going up there, Garney?" Merv asked.

"Well," Garney started to say, then stopped. Marty had no idea how he was leading them. Marty could barely make out the back of Garney's tanker. The crescent suddenly shifted left and for a second he was able to see most of the truck, then as it straightened, it disappeared into the fog of snow. "Shit, my brothers, I almost kissed my first snowbank there. Oh yeah, uh huh, yep sure did."

"Don't do that," Marty said.

"Oh, go ahead and do it," Spence said. "We'll pick you up on the way back."

"Yeah, I'll bring you back some ice cream," Merv added.

"That's the team spirit, my brothers."

Marty laughed, pushing away the fact that in a few hours, he would be meeting with his contact, Kristy Greenflag, and taking possession of stolen diamonds. He'd thought he wouldn't be holding the package much more than eight hours, but with the storm, that could end up being much longer.

This added a new twist of anxiety to the deal. Not only did he have to worry about Crane and Shamus, but now he had an added bonus that security at the Meanook Mine might pull a random inspection during their uncertain stay. If he were caught, he'd never see the inside of a jail. And Maggie? They'd track her down and kill her without a second thought. Every now and again a group of bodies would be found after a heist, and that was always the last logistic worked out in a rip-off. Jude Shamus had done that a few times himself, but never to his regulars; those guys were in the circle, but outside contractors were fair game.

Marty was definitely an outside contractor.

Jesus Christ, he needed a friend, but kncw nonc of these men well enough to trust them with his secret, and really, even if he did trust them—was it fair to burden them with such responsibility? He could throw the dice and do the job, hope that Shamus didn't set about tying up loose ends. Maybe he and Maggie could bolt back to New York City, or Boston, or even some little Burb in New Hampshire. They had a bit of money, maybe they could disappear for a while, start over. Maybe they could disappear off the map for good and Shamus would get on with his own maniacal lifestyle.

"And maybe pigs will fly," he said.

"Everything okay, Marty, my brother?" Garney sounded tired, the gravel in his voice softening some. "You're very quiet."

He reached up and took the handset. "Yeah, it's all good, Garney. Just don't drive into a snowbank like these guys have been telling you to, because I'm following your every move and will likely be parked right next to you."

Garney chuckled.

"We'd bring you back a sandwich," Spence said.

"Uh uh, no snowbanks for Garnet Wilson. My Momma didn't raise me to be kissing snowbanks, uh uh no way, no how. We're on the straight and narrow, my brothers, across the Dreamcatcher and into the arms of the Meanook where the order of the day will be a hot shower and some much needed rest."

"Give me an Amen," Merv said.

"Amen," Spence said.

Marty smiled again, reached for the handset to chime in, then hung it back up.

There would be time to chat later. He had to think about what to do when they came south. His plan, what little there was, involved killing Crane, but he had no idea how he was going to accomplish that without these gents knowing about it. Even if he could get alone with the bald-headed asshole, he was pretty sure Crane could kick his ass. So, what was he going to kill him with? Run him down with the truck?

He shook his head and sighed.

"I gotta step out the porch," Spence announced.

"Alright, don't fall off," Merv said.

Stepping out on the porch was code for taking a leak. Drivers would open their door and step out onto the step of the big rig, holding their aim with one hand while steering with the other. The trick was not to hit a bump and fall off or you ran the risk of your truck hitting the snowbank. Or worse, getting run over by your own truck. There was a running joke about that. If a man fell asleep at the wheel, he usually said that he'd been distracted by something; a raven flying in his window or caribou running across his path was the stock excuse. But if a man said he fell asleep and hit the snowbank, most speculated he was out on the porch when he fell off and chased his truck into a snowbank. Stepping out on the porch was a regular occurrence, especially on the slower lakes. Yellow lines left by porch riding truckers were a testament to that fact. Marty hadn't found the nerve to do such a thing, instead opting to use a Gatorade bottle to relieve himself and empty out the window as they drove.

Suddenly, Garney was laughing hysterically, booming guffaws crashing out over the airwaves and finally he managed, "Oh, good golly Miss Molly, my brothers, check out the left bank when you go by." Then he was laughing again.

"What is it?" Marty asked.

"You'll see, my brother."

Along the left bank he could see a stick with a black piece of cloth flapping in the cross-wind. These flags dotted the landscape. Marty guessed they were put in place to give the drivers a reference or for wind direction. But this one was already behind Garney when the laughter started, so that wasn't it. Then he saw it; even at this snail's pace it wasn't long before he was rolling past a black bra and matching panties flapping frantically against the wind on pole. He didn't think this had placed there by anyone from the Lupania road crew. Someone had too much time on their hands.

"Do you see it, Marty?"

Marty began to laugh. "Sure do, Garney."

"What is it?" Merv asked.

"Patience, my brother, you'll see it soon enough."

Marty passed by the two ensigns still giggling. "At least now I can see the left bank."

"Yep, uh huh, yes sir."

"Oh, for fuck's sake. Bump it up! Now I really wanna see."

"You're like a little kid, Merv, bet you couldn't wait until Christmas morning," Spence said. "It's really kind of sad when you think about it."

"Kiss my ass, Spence."

Spence responded with a laugh.

Then Merv saw it and started to laugh himself. "I ought to stop and grab it up just so you don't get to see it."

"Why? I already know what it is."

"You do, do yuh."

"Yeah, bra and panties of the black variety."

"How the hell did you know that?"

Spence chuckled. "You'd like to know that, wouldn't you?"

"Spence, my brother, would the culprit happen to be a stout fellow who carries an instrument used for chopping down trees?"

"Could be, but even if such an individual had set out on such a mission, I would not be at liberty to discuss it without at least two or three pitchers of some fine Canadian Ale crowding the table I was sitting at." Spence knew that Axe man Jack had set up the bra and panties, because he'd mentioned doing it on the night they were detained for the chocolate milk incident. He laughed. Axe had a great sense of humor. "The only thing missing is a set of stockings and garters," he said.

They convoyed north, leaving the landmark behind. Moments after it fell into Spence's side view mirror, it washed away, bleached out in the squall of white, turning from inky black to gray, lighter gray, and then it was gone.

4

Yellowknife – Tli Cho Manor

Shamus was drinking. He'd killed his sixth scotch and was well into his seventh. Each drink darkened his mood in unison with the sky over YK.

The setback had infuriated him. It shouldn't have, he knew this, but it did anyway. He was seated in a big leather easy chair that was strategically located in front of the picture window that overlooked the grounds. He wondered if Bruce Willis had sat in this chair or if the story was just bullshit to make the place more appealing to suckers. Probably bullshit. He sipped the scotch, rolling it over his tongue.

The others had retreated, repelling from him the moment he uncorked the bottle and began pouring, even Donald. Fuck ‘em, bunch of goddamn cowards. Even the muscle bound Donald was afraid of him. He swallowed and a smile of satisfaction cut into his face, warping the shoestring scar slightly. He wondered if Donald would be interested in going toe to toe out there in the back forty. He was probably on steroids, just another idiot who couldn't do it the hard way. Shamus liked to push weights, he benched around 240, but he wasn't bulky like Donald; his body was sculpted with hard bands of meat that clung tight to his bones. He was fast and the punches he landed were unforgiving pistons that broke skin and tenderized the muscle beneath.

On occasion he'd throw on the gloves and do a little out-of-ring sparring. All his opponents were apprehensive underlings and only one had gotten the better of him, if only for a moment. His name had been Alex. Alex, along with his pal Glen, were tasked with doing blind cash drops in the Oakville/Mississauga area. A necessity of their Meth business.

Alex wasn't the intended victim that day; it was Glen who Shamus courted to go a few rounds. Everyone knew that going a few rounds with Gordon Shamus meant getting your ass kicked. It was about massaging the boss's ego and taking a few hits in the process. It all started out friendly enough: Gordon would ask the guy if he'd like to go a few rounds with the sparring gloves and reluctantly, his opponent, unable to decline, would step into an imaginary ring in the harbor yard and defend against a volley of punches. The exchange usually ended with a fat lip or a bruised eye or even a bloodied nose.

After the fight, Shamus would pump up his opponent every time he saw them. "Good fight! You almost had me. Watch this guy, he's got a mean left hook." But it was all bullshit. The challenges were about the pack leader solidifying his position by showing the group that he was ready to defend any attempt to take him down. No one dared win a bout with Shamus, and not one of them got the upper hand, except Alex, of course. Alex, who stepped up when Shamus was pushing his pussy pal Glen.

"Come on, Glen. I just want to see what you're made of. All my guys step into it sooner or later, it's a rite of passage here. Nothing serious." Shamus's eyes bore into the young man; this was going to be easy. Glen looked scared. That was good. "How about it? Just for shits and giggles."

Glen sighed and was about to say "Okay," then, out of his line of vision Shamus heard, "I'll go a round with you, Mr. Shamus." The voice was steady, unafraid, even a little irritated. "I'd like to show what I'm made of."

Shamus cocked his head right and said, "Would you now?"

Alex was a solid-looking young guy, maybe 26 or 27. He had a hard look, not cocky, but definitely confident. Shamus glanced down at the young man's hands and saw the web of scars that ran across the enlarged knuckles. Those hands had been used in more than a few punch-ups, the knuckles had been broken a time or two, but they were efficient looking tools that were weathered and worn. Put to good use, they were the hands of a man ten years his senior.

"No Alex, Mr. Shamus asked me. I'll..." Glen started.

Shamus raised his hand. "Done any boxing, kid?"

"A little," Alex said. "Mostly old school stuff."

"Old school, bare knuckle shit, you mean."

"Yeah, mostly. I'm nowhere near your caliber, but I'd still go a round with you. That way you'll know I can take care of business." Alex was massaging him.

"Okay, but are you gonna give it your all, kid? No taking a dive."

Alex glanced over at the horrified Glen, then back to Shamus. "No dives, Mr. Shamus, I'll bring you a good fight if that's what you're looking for."

Shamus took up boxing in spite of what the old man thought and it was the one thing he truly excelled in. He might have been hot headed, lacked imagination, and had poor people skills, but he could bust a head with the best of them. He only lacked one thing when it came to boxing: Gordon Shamus did not know how to turn it off. Over the course of 15 years, he had beaten four men to death with his hands. Two were killed during a tune-up, one ended after a punch-up, and the other had been Jimmy Poe.

Poe had died at the hands of Shamus after refusing to eat any more of what Shamus was feeding him. Seated in a chair in that trailer on

Hamilton Harbor, Poe was presented with a dirty gym sock containing 42 pairs of coarse 5/8 nuts and bolts. The very same type of nuts and bolts that had been used to kill Gordon's two friends and disfigure him for life. Before presenting this to Poe, Gordon Shamus pissed on the sock.

Shamus and Alex fought outside in the yard, a mere 50 feet from the grave of Jimmy Poe that was marked by the rusty orange wrecking ball. It was summer, Gordon was wearing an Adidas track suit, while Alex was wearing shorts and a white sleeveless undershirt often referred to as a wife beater. The audience consisted of Alex's buddy Glen, Phil Crane, Doug Favot, Rory Austin, and Jack Little. Everyone knew how this was going to turn out, or expected how, anyway. Alex would put up a defense against an offensive. He'd block punches, maybe plant a couple body shots on Shamus and eventually succumb, but that wasn't how it went at all.

"Okay, no low blows and let's keep it clean," Doug Favot said as the two men bounced around, loosening their muscles and readying for the fight. This was hardly an official fight; in fact, they weren't even wearing full boxing gloves, but open fingered sparring mitts used in MMA. Both men nodded and Favot stepped back before giving the go ahead. "Fight!"

Shamus didn't wait, he moved in and rabbit punched Alex in the left cheek twice, knocking him off balance. When Alex stumbled, Shamus should have moved in for the kill, but stepped off.

This is going to be easier than I thought.

Except it wasn't.

When Alex shook off the double tap, he came back up in full defensive mode, crowding Shamus and blocking the shots using his upper arms as shield. Shamus swung left and right and right again, but the young guy blocked each blow and once he saw an opening, he planted a hard right into the lower side of Gordon's left peck. The impact reverberated out across his chest and for a moment, Shamus thought that he might actually lose his wind. He pulled back from Alex, whose face was unafraid, but there was a determined look in his eyes that made Shamus regret passing on the pussy, Glen. What he didn't know was that Alex was also regretting getting into the ring.

Shamus's assault intensified, punches raining down on Alex, and he did his best to block them, but a few made it through, catching the left side of his chin and his right cheekbone. Unfortunately, the blows were slowed by their inaccuracy, and if Gordon Shamus were able to read Alex's mind he would have understood that the young man was hoping that his opponent would land a punch hard enough so that it wouldn't look like he was taking a dive. That never happened, and as Gordon Shamus continued with the volley of punches, Alex found himself fighting back, and then that final blow found its way. The punch hit the right side of Gordon Shamus's lower lip, splitting it open, sending a squirt of red syrup up his cheek and into his right eye. The cheering stopped and both men stood frozen in their tracks. There was a collective gasp from the minor audience as Shamus brought his wrist up to the stinging blossom, and then he saw the blood.

Across from him, Alex lowered his fists, horrified surprise dawning and that loss of momentum was what finished him. Shamus examined the damage, then his eyes traced over the audience and it dug into him. He had been bested by this "punk bag man" and they were watching, all of them, they had seen the vulnerability. In the back of head he could hear the whispers. "The kid socked the bastard right in the chops, split his lip open." That was what they would remember. The punk bag man who got the better of Gordon Shamus. "Guess he isn't as tough as people think," another voice spoke up.

Panic intermingled with anger rushed through him and as the adrenaline began flow, Gordon started to shake. His fists tightened, his shoulders bunched, and a smile pulled back from the cigar-yellowed teeth that were now tempered with pink and red. Phil Crane saw it before anyone else: a freight train of insanity was coming and there would be no stopping it. Shamus's eyelids opened ever so slightly, his eyes locking onto Alex, the smile plastered on his face like Heath Ledger's Joker.

Get your dukes up, kid, Crane thought.

But Alex couldn't read minds and Crane would never have said such a thing out loud. And even if the kid could hear the thoughts of those around him, Crane's inner voice would have been squelched by the inherently more dangerous thoughts of Gordon Shamus.

Kill you! Kill you! Kill you!

The first punch hit Alex in the nose; there was a crunch and a pop as the gristle snapped under the blow. Alex stumbled backward and then a right hook came around, compacting his left ear into the side of his skull. What balance he was reaching for ran out of his legs and he fell over onto his side. Before he could bring his arms up, Shamus was on top of him delivering more blows. One hit him in the left eye, pushing his eyeball back into its socket and ballooning the eyelid. Then the fatal blow hit him square in the windpipe. His larynx was crushed under that first blow and most certainly he would have died, but Shamus delivered two follow-up combinations that pulverized any hope that the young Alex might have had, if one of the henchman were capable of doing an emergency tracheotomy. None were, nor would any have dared. They just watched as their insane boss straddled the young man and kept on with the vicious beating. All the while, Shamus was grunting some incoherent language, spittle flying from his bloodied mouth while the almost dead Alex lay there like a rag doll. Through the bloody storm of rage, Shamus could hear screaming frantically. It was Alex's pal, Glen. Shamus couldn't make out what he was saying, but it must have been inappropriate because Crane grabbed the kid, popped him in the mouth, and yelled something at him. By this time, Alex's face had been reduced to a mash of blue, red, and pink.

"That's enough, Gordon," someone said. Then they were on him—Doug, Rory, and Jack. Clamping him from both sides and behind. He threw two more punches into the kid's body and as they dragged him off, he turned and planted an elbow right into Rory Austin's chin, clacking his teeth together and chipping his upper incisor.

"Shit," Rory cried. "Stop it, Gordon. The kid's dead!"

"Get your fucking meat hooks off me," he growled at them. They held him a second longer. "I fucking mean it! Get 'em off or I'll fucking bury every fucking last one of you. Laugh at me and I'll fucking bury you!"

"Let him go," Phil Crane barked. "He's done!"

They let him go.

He shrugged hard and spat on Alex's body, then looked around the yard. "Where's that other punk?"

Phil Crane looked at the others. "The rest of you get the fuck out of here!"

"Where is he, Phil?"

Crane turned to the others. "Go get a truck, we need to clean this up."

They happily shoved off while Gordon stood there huffing in great exasperated breaths while traversing his head back left and right. "I asked you a fucking question! Where the fuck is he?"

"I put him in the trailer! You just killed his buddy, Gordon. He doesn't need to be out here and see that." Crane cocked a thumb at the ground. "We need to get that under cover in case a helicopter flies over." The yard was self-contained, but Crane was right. Someone from CHCH News might be getting up in the air to cover afternoon traffic.

"Yeah," Shamus grunted. "I guess you've got a point."

They dragged the body across the yard and lay it next to a rusted out Sea Container. Crane grabbed an old tarp and pulled it over the body. "I'll have Favot take him out to the Punchbowl."

"Good. Get his pal to give you a hand."

"The kid?"

"Yeah. Then take care of it."

"Take care of it? You mean the kid in the trailer?"

"What the fuck do you think I mean?" Shamus didn't give him a chance to answer. He stomped off across the yard and said to no one in particular, "I need a fucking shower," then over his shoulder, "Call Donald and tell him to get his ass down here with a clean set of duds."

That night as they dug the hole and Glen cried emphatically as to how he should have just let Mr. Shamus beat him up instead of letting Alex step in, Philip Crane gave the kid a cigarette, then cut his throat from ear to ear. Neither of the two young men were ever found.

Shamus opened his eyes to see Angela standing over him, holding the empty scotch glass. "I'm sorry. I thought you were sleeping." She moved to replace it and he stopped her.

"That's fine, Angie, go ahead and take it. I'm not having anymore." She reached down to pick up the bottle from the table. She could feel his eyes upon her—he was looking at her ass—and she pretended not to notice. As she moved to stand up, he reached out and grasped her wrist, not hard, but had she pulled away, he would have fastened down. "Why didn't we work out, Angie?"

She stared at him, then looked around to make sure they were alone. "We were young, Gordon. You had other women."

He shook his head, smirked. "I cared about you."

"That was a long time ago."

He pulled her a little closer, close enough to kiss her. "What do you see in this guy? You're a tough lady, him, he's the polar opposite of what you are."

Angel's eyes darted around the room again. She was afraid, but not for herself, for Scott. If he came in on this, he might say or do something to light Gordon's fuse. Sure that no one could hear, she said, "I love him, Gordon. He treats me good."

"I treated you good."

"You were never able to stay with one woman. There would always be another woman. I knew that with you." She was bent over uncomfortably holding bottle and glass. She set the glass on the table and placed a warm hand upon his cheek. "I wanted to be the only one. With you that was never going to happen."

She slid her hand off his cheek and it fell away.

"I'm sorry, Angie. I guess I mucked that up, didn't I?" He released her wrist.

She smiled. "Thank you, Gordon."

"You're one fine woman, Angie." His right hand caressed the back of her thigh, finding her ass and his fingers probed up between her legs, then traced over the seam where her buttocks met. "Very fine," he finished, then pulled his hand away. He grinned, wanting her to protest.

She didn't. Instead, she snatched up the empty glass and pulled away with the same measured caution one might use to back away from a rabid animal. As she did this, her heart pummeled, turning her cheeks flush, she said, "Can I get you anything?"

His grin widened. "Yeah, but you won't."

She managed a weak awkward smile.

"At least not right now." He turned away and looked out the window.

Angel carried the bottle to the other side of the room and set it down on a large mahogany table that was assemblage for other containers of alcohol sitting uniform in front of a large slab mirror. As she did this, she stole a glance in the reflection to see if he was still seated and looking the other way. He hadn't turned; he was still staring off into the night. She glanced down at her free hand; it was trembling. When she looked up, she saw Maggie standing in the doorway, arms crossed, and watching her. Angel pivoted, working her way out of the room. When she was next to Maggie, she stopped, leaned over and whispered, "I'd stay out of there." Then she pushed down the hall toward the kitchen.

Maggie withdrew and followed Angel into the kitchen.

The kitchen looked industrial, like you one you would find in a restaurant or a hotel. Pots and pans hung on a copper ring above a stainless steel work station adorned with two large sinks and a single rack dishwasher. Angel was rinsing the glass underneath one of two goose neck faucets that sat in the center of each basin when Maggie walked in. She didn't look up, instead sloshing the crystal glass with water. She looked far too focused on the task at hand. Maggie stood there watching her, deciding whether or not to say something. Angel shut off the tap, grabbed a tea towel and began polishing the glass. Finally, she brought her eyes up to meet Maggie's.

"What?"

Maggie hesitated, then said, "Are you okay?"

Angel set the tea towel aside, sniffed indifferently. "I'm fine."

Maggie waited a second longer. "Alright then." She spun around to leave.

"Hey."

She turned back. "Yeah?"

"What you did earlier. I guess... Well, thanks."

"Sure."

"It doesn't change anything, Maggie."

"Of course not."

5

Chase and Lenny found the building they were looking for and none too soon. The winds, along with snow, stole their visibility in the last half hour of their trek. The two men held hands, for fear of losing the other as they plodded along. Lenny joked with Chase that no one should ever know that they were holding hands. "I have a reputation to maintain," Lenny said. "People find out we were walking hand in hand, they might get the wrong idea."

"You're secret is safe with me, Lenny." Then he saw it. A building constructed out of four sea containers with a peak made from aluminum siding. "Oh man, there is a god."

"Awesome!" Lenny agreed.

Left center of the peak was a stack that Chase hoped would soon be bellowing smoke, if they could get the heater running along with the generator. The sun behind the clouds had retreated to the east, riding low in the sky as it did. The outside temperature was dropping at a frightening rate and Chase knew they had to get to warmth as soon as possible. They climbed up the bank and worked their way across 120 feet of open field. As they did, Chase considered their tracks, but guessed they would be quickly erased away in the spate of wind-driven snow. The crossing to the building was slow and exhaustive, each of their steps swallowed to mid-thigh. Halfway across, both men could feel the sweat trickling down between their shoulder blades, a stark contrast to the rubbery feel of the exposed skin on their faces. Lenny was having greater difficulty, the snow up into his groin area with every step he took, which meant pulling free and swinging his other leg out. By the time both men reached the front of the building, they collapsed with exhaustion. The door was buried under a five-foot-high drift and they would have to clear it before they entered. They both sat side by side, huffing and puffing, wanting to succumb.

Just sleep a little, Chase thought. *Get my strength back and...*

A blast of cold brittle snow was mashed into his face followed by, "Wake up, Chase! Don't go kaput on me!"

Chase pushed Lenny back hard. "Get off!"

Lenny fell backward into the snow, but continued, "Don't fall asleep!"

Chase stood up defensively. "I'm not!"

"You were! We need to get indoors, Chase. We need to dig. No kaput!"

Chase got a grip on himself, realizing that he had been slipping in out of consciousness since halfway across the field. Lenny was right, he might have given up and not even realized it. If Lenny hadn't been there to wash his face with snow, he might already be halfway to dead.

God! I'm such an asshole. He shook his head and frowned. "Lenny, I'm sorry."

Chase put out a hand.

Lenny took it. "It's okay, Chase, but no kaput! We gotta dig."

They started by using their hands, but the wind was working against them, so Chase scavenged around until he found piece of aluminum siding. That made things a little easier and they cleared an opening in just under a half hour. Lenny secretly worried that the door might be locked, but he didn't say anything out loud for fear that such words might bring about bad karma. If he had mentioned it to Chase, he would have found out that it was Lupania policy to leave the shelters along the ice road unlocked for emergency reasons. With the entry clear, Chase turned the latch and pushed against it with his shoulder. After two abrupt hits to the ice sealing the door gave way and it opened up.

The inside of the structure was colder than it was outside and it was dark. Chase pulled out the mini mag light he carried and snapped it on. They surveyed the inside and found the generator in good working order in a separate room. Along with that, a Herman Nelson heater was parked in the generator room along with four Jerry cans of kerosene. "Things are looking up," Chase said.

They fired up the heater first and huddled over the output, greedily warming their hands. There was some concern about carbon monoxide, but the ventilation pipe on the outside of the building was clear. During the inventory of the storage building, they found a Coleman lantern and two cans of naphtha. Chase decided that firing up the generator might pose a risk of being seen from a distance, as the generator was hardwired into three exterior lampposts. They didn't really need the generator.

"Look what I found." Lenny held up a box of Lipton Cup a Soup, along with a steel cup—he was waving them triumphantly. "We'll be eating like kings tonight, Chase." Chase smiled back, nodded and continued rummaging around in stacks of debris piled in the corner of the building. "What are you looking for?"

"Anything, we can use as a weapon," he said, pulling back a piece of plywood and looking behind it. Lenny replaced the box of soup and joined him. He reached down and unsheathed his hunting knife; the glint of steel caught the red light on the kerosene heater and reflected. It was a hunter's knife with a seven-inch curved blade and a jagged edge. Chase reached into his own pocket and produced a four-inch blade and smiled. Lenny laughed and Chase said, "My dick is much bigger."

Lenny laughed harder and replaced the blade. Chase joined him and once the giddy nervous fear ran out of them, they went back to searching. Chase didn't think they would have a chance in fighting one of those things in a hand-to-hand fight, even with Lenny's big knife. The massacre in front of the canteen played out in his mind as he pulled back more debris looking for something, anything, they could use to even up the odds.

"God, I wish we had a gun."

Then Lenny found something they could use.

***

Chapter 23—Montreal

1

Meanook Mine – Misery Road
21:30 Hours

The storm, as predicted by Meteorologist Harper Sherwood, started to really pick up around eight that evening. The estimated time of arrival for the convoy led by Garney Wilson was slowed considerably due to ice, fog, and high winds on Dreamcatcher Lake. Instead of rolling off the ice onto the Misery Rd at 20:00 hours, they rolled off the ice a full half hour after the storm was predicted to take hold.

Misery road was a gravel route that snaked across and over the lunar-like landscape of the barrens. It looked like the surface of the moon. This far north there was no foliage of any type. Only rolling white tundra, peppered with specks of black rock cutting jaggedly from beneath iced over surface. Misery Road aptly was named by the drivers because to break down on that route could lead to nothing else. The Misery was wide enough to accommodate two passing tractor trailers, but that was under the best of conditions. Misery road ended at the Meanook Mine, after 45 kilometers of winding turns that rose and fell between the endless arctic dunes of snow. Under the best conditions, the speed limit was 60 km per hour.

"Four inbound Super B Tankers leaving the ice and onto the Misery road," Garney said, his voice was full of exhausted relief. No doubt brought on by the harrowing trip across the Dreamcatcher. All of them were exhausted, as the last two hours had garnered a combined focus that wore them down more than any physical activity ever would. "Alright, my brothers, we have lots of drifting across the roads. I'm going to creep along at about 30 K, Marty, so try not to run up my back end. If you have to cut your speed, let the guy behind you know. No point in hurrying, we've already missed steak night."

"I'm the guy behind you, Marty," Merv said. "Seems Garney has forgotten my name."

"And I'm the guy behind the guy behind you," Spence added.

"Sorry, my brothers, my eyeballs are bleeding from all that white. You copy what I said, Marty?"

"Copy that, I'm just getting off the ice now." Marty took in the approach. On either side of the Misery Road drifts rose up like great shoulders cut into arching angles by the blowing wind. To Marty, it looked very much like a gauntlet that towered well above the windows of his rig, and in some places, the roof. He flipped on his inter-axle lockers and accelerated toward the grade. The W900 growled in anticipation of this new challenge, its tires biting into the frozen gravel. He climbed the grade with little effort, centering himself on the road. Garney's tail lights disappeared over the crest, while from behind, Merv began to run at the hill, his lights bouncing as he started to climb. By the time he was off the ice, Marty was already cresting the first hill, his moose lights illuminating a cyclone of snow and ice swirling down from the great drifts. Garney's lights were lost in the blow momentarily and then Marty saw the beams of his headlights opening the trail ahead as Garney turned and climbed again. There was something whimsical in this, or maybe magical was a better word. From his seat in the Kenworth, as he descended down the grade of patchwork snow and gravel, he watched Garney's rig move with silent grace up yet another hill, and it looked animated. Marty felt the danger, knew that it would be easy to lower his guard and fall prey to this surreal landscape. He shook it off, shifted down, and readied himself for another climb.

"Four inbound on Misery Road at kilometer four," Garney announced.

At first there was nothing, then faintly across the airwaves came the reply, "Grader working at kilometer twenty seven."

"Okay copy that, we'll keep an eye for you, my brother."

There was no reply, leaving Marty to wonder if they had heard Garney's response. Marty also wondered how the hell Garney would know what kilometer marker they were at when everything on both sides of the road was buried in 8 feet of snow. He chalked it up to experience but didn't think in this weather even the most seasoned driver would be able to accurately pinpoint his position on the road. On this he was wrong; Garney knew exactly where he was.

"Four tankers inbound at Kilometer 5," Garney said. "How are you doing back there, my brother, Marty?"

Marty reached up and pulled the handset down. "I'm okay, Garney. I have you in sight." And he did, but only for short periods of time, between swirling cyclones of snow. They moved at a snail's pace over Misery Road, working their way toward the mine. For the most part, Marty could see both sides of the road, but the drifting across the trail resulted in occasional explosions of white powder when the moose bumper crashed through them. When this happened, his windshield became a crisp white haze, until the forward momentum of the rig and the enormous gusts of wind blew away the icy dusting. Perhaps Marty should've been frightened, but he wasn't. In fact, he was jacked right up. He knew this feeling; it was the same feeling used to get back in the day when he was Dr. Hook. His heart was drumming away in his chest, but he wasn't afraid, not of this anyway. Driving in bad weather was something that really turned his crank; he couldn't explain it, but it motivated him.

"Four inbound at kilometer six," Garney again.

From behind, Merv's headlights danced across his side view mirror. "I'm not getting too close, am I, Marty?"

He reached for the handset again, trying not to avert his eyes from the road. This might be exciting, but he was well aware that a moment of inattention could spell disaster. "No, Merv, you look far enough back." Then he hit a drift and fresh powder exploded into the air as the wheels were tugged to the right. "Oh, shit." He turned hard, riding the drift dangerously close to the edge and thought he was going to hit the bank, then his wheels caught the hard pack and he managed to straighten it out. "I got my hands full up here, Merv. I'll keep you advised."

Merv laughed. "Hands full, eh."

Marty didn't respond on the radio, but he laughed right along with him. He held the steering wheel in a death grip. Garney's lights disappeared behind the next hill and the banks of snow on either side seemed to climb even higher. "Yeah, got my hands full." He laughed again and hit another drift, sending up another explosion of powder. This time he held the wheel straight and rode it out. When his windshield cleared, he hit a bump in the road and his handset popped out of the bracket, almost hitting him in the side of the head.

"Four inbound at kilometer seven!"

"How's it going back there, Spence?" Merv called.

"Fine, I'm watching Hot Fuzz on my laptop."

"You're kidding, right?"

Spence answered with a laugh. "It's a great flick."

"How about you, Garney? You watching movies too?"

"No, my Brother. I'm reading a goddamned Harlequin Romance novel. Gee Goddamned Whiz, Merv." Garney went quiet, and then: "I think that security fellow was a little misinformed on the timings of this storm."

Marty giggled.

"What's that? I was watering my plants, I didn't catch you," Merv said sarcastically.

Another drift exploded.

"What kind of plants have you got, Merv?" Spence asked.

"Pansies!" Garney interjected. "Merv loves them pansies."

Marty cracked up.

"Mostly tulips, they make the cab smell nice."

Marty was laughing even harder now. He was giddy from lack of sleep and the amusing banter seemed to let loose a rolling barrage of nervous laughter.

"You related to Tiny Tim there, Merv?" Spence cracked.

"Hey cock jaws, you're missing your movie."

"I got it on pause."

Marty wondered if Spence was serious or kidding. He didn't think anyone could be watching a movie in this crap, but he wasn't willing to bet on it. Ahead Garney's headlights illuminated the hill he was now climbing.

"Four inbound at kilometer eight."

2

Acadia Mine
21:45 Hours

Allison Perch was moving up the hall. She was feeling sluggish, the signal inside her brain interrupted by electrical flashes and pops. When this happened, the pain receptors in her hand lit up. The grip of the Skentophyte was loosening. Her escort moved along behind her. It was close—teeth clacking, breath stinking—aware of the interruptions, alerting the others that it would soon need a new host. This one was expiring.

During the disruptions she was able to formulate thoughts that the Skentophyte were not privy to. This might have stirred excitement that maybe there was hope, maybe she could turn the tables on the collective, but there was only one problem. During the disruptions she was blind and, thanks to Nick Anderson, she only had one hand.

I'm dying, she thought when her world went black and the inferno of pain erupted from the severed stumps that used to be fingers. She stumbled against the wall, felt the claw clutching her shoulder, waiting for the lights to come back on. When it did, she fell into the milky white of their collective. Heard the overlapping rant of the thousands and they shared a soup of thoughts that overrode her own. Two steps, then three, then four, and out went the lights again. She stumbled against the wall, a fresh plume of ash emptied, dead skin falling away from the outer rim of her charred sockets.

Maybe it was the exposure. Maybe I was too close to the chamber when it happened.

She didn't know. She just want wanted it to be over. Nick's ghost agreed. The sooner the better. The Skent held her shoulder, holding on as a blind person does a willing guide. It was afraid. A main conduit into the collective, it did not draw off the others. She was the Creature's source, and from her the collective received its information. And from others, of course, she knew this, knew everything they knew.

Oh if only I could break away. Tell everyone what they were planning.

She could see what they intended. Knew what Sal Godwin had told them. About the plane that would be landing. Knew about the transport that was being arranged, about the disks that would open more portals. Across the universe or in that other dimension, they were waiting. Massing in the millions and when they came through, there would be no hope. If she could get that information to one of the uninfected, there might be hope.

The things inside her eyes came alive again. The hall ahead opened up in a fish eye perspective and she began to stumble forward, but now the color had washed out of her vision. She carried on, her escort close at hand. "Need replacement," it had said in its foreign language and still she understood. "Skentophyte, needs new host."

Then from a distant corner of her mind, she heard, "Replacement is coming."

She stumbled forward again, moving down the hall and they passed on left and right, teeth clacking, thoughts intensifying. "Expiring," they mused in their own language. Her escort tightened its grip. Her world began to swim and again the lights went out.

"Come on you fucking bugs," she muttered. "Let's get this over with."

The thing holding her hissed.

She just wanted to it to be over.

3

The Fish Camp
62 Kilometers North of the Acadia Mine

Snow climbed up the side of the building, layer upon layer drifting upward and burying Billy's snowmobile. Inside the shelter his Coleman lantern hissed and cast light against the retreating shadows that danced inside the solitary darkness of the building. In the circle of white light sat Billy Jack, sipping on a hot drink, a serious look crossing his face. He was concerned about his kills, of course, didn't want to leave them for the wolves and ravens, but he had changed his course of thought completely upon arriving here at the fish camp. Initially, he intended on setting up, cranking up the Drive-by Truckers on his Ipod and smoking a bit of weed, but that changed. Something told him that he needed to keep his wits sharpened.

Paranoia?

It wasn't that, intuition maybe, but Billy rarely experienced the anxiety of paranoia. He replaced the bag of herb in his pocket and took to cleaning his weapons instead. As he did, the snow rattled the walls with steady hollow sheets of sound. In usual military fashion, Billy set up as he would have when in the field. In the far corner of the building, his fuel was stacked neatly. Two red Jerry cans of gasoline and one green can of naphtha. In the other corner, a plastic bucket into which he would urinate and, only if absolutely necessary, defecate. Absolutely necessary was defined by becoming completely snowbound. The door inside the structure was not wide enough to accommodate his snowmobile, so he was forced to leave it outside. He'd be digging that out for sure.

So, why was he cleaning his weapons? Wolves was what he told himself, but he wasn't so sure if that was the case. Something had settled into Billy's guts since arriving at the fish camp. An intuitive feeling that he would need to stay alert. He'd heard a story about a pack of wolves surrounding a trucker the year before; he didn't know if it was true or not, but he wasn't about to take any chances. At any rate, he was no stranger to this intuition, had felt it eating at him when he was in KAF, usually the night before they crossed the wire into enemy territory. That feeling was an indication that something was coming, that he and Spence were going into the shit. Strangely, that feeling was usually right on the money.

"On the money," he mocked. "Every time we crossed the wire, we were in the shit."

And every time that feeling caused the hairs on the back of his neck to bristle, not long after the shit would hit the fan. He always felt it coming, knew before the bullets flew that something was about to happen. Except that last time when they hit the IED and that had completely disoriented him. It robbed of the belief that actually had an ability to see what was happening before it did. Even as he sat holding the IV of plasma and scanning his arcs for Taliban Fighters, he felt helpless. No sixth sense and he thought that the blast from the IED had shocked it right out of his system. Everyone thought Billy had left the Army because Spence was being tossed, and maybe that was true, but not entirely. He was worried that he had lost something in that blast, or that it was taken.

Spence knew about the intuition, called it his Mojo. "What's your mojo saying, Billy Jack?" And Billy always knew. The IED team they killed on that last day had been right where Billy thought they were; so had the sniper, and the ambush party, and all the others they were sent out to neutralize. But when the IED let loose and left him and Spence for dead, he never got that feeling again.

Until now, he thought.

He removed the bolt from his 303 and wiped it down some CLP, then laid it out neatly from left to right with the other parts on a roll of cloth. The gold jacket on his ammo winked in the light of the lantern's twin globes. He pulled through the chamber once, removed the swab, and inserted another, then dabbed it with CLP and pulled it through again. He sipped his hot chocolate and swallowed; it was chalky and artificial. Whatever the intuition was warning of, he'd be ready.

4

Meanook Mine
Misery Road 22:55 Hours

"Four inbound at kilometer 42!" Garney sounded exhausted and rightly so. The last 23 kilometers of their trek was a grueling pace in which they crawled along at speeds of 10 k/ph. Marty could barely see the road and the only evidence that Garney was in front of him were the reports he made every kilometer. There were two big graders out here trying to keep the road clear for them, and when he came upon the first one, it looked like something out of a Steven Spielberg movie. The vehicle's array of work lights cut through the currents of snow with blinding precision, camouflaging what it was.

"Come up my left side, driver," the operator told him on the radio. "I'll wait until you're past."

"Copy," Marty replied. The big lights clicked off and Marty saw the outline set against the towering bank. Inside, the driver was illuminated by the dash lights, making him look like he was a character in a science fiction story. Maybe Tom Swift moving across an alien landscape in his giant mechanical space suit that was more robot than suit. The right bank hung above them like a petrified tube wave waiting to be surfed. The banks were literally swallowing thc road from abovc, turning it into a tunnel. When he was past, the operator clicked his lights back on and though Marty didn't dare take his eyes from the road ahead, he reached up and grabbed his handset. "Thanks, you've definitely got your work cut out for you."

"We won't be out here much longer, just keeping it clear for you boys, then we're heading into camp," the grader operator said. "Watch out for the big drifts, driver, they'll suck you right off the road if you're not careful, and in this crap, recovery is not an option I want to think about."

"Copy that and thank you. I've got two more behind me."

"You're welcome and thanks. Next driver, let me know when you see my lights and I'll guide you past."

"Copy that, Grader, I can see your lights, I'm about a half a click out now," Merv said.

"Copy, I can see your big lights, keep her coming."

They were almost at the end.

"Four 'Super B Tankers' inbound at kilometer 43," Garney again. "One click to go, my brothers."

Beyond the grader, the sky began to lighten, blood orange brushed over with white haze. The lights from the mine punched through the storm and this perked Marty up. He could see the contours of rising moguls that reminded him of the ski hills in Whistler, BC. He and Maggie had vacationed there during the Winter Olympics. Maggie loved downhill skiing.

He smiled. "I wish you could see this, sweetheart."

The road was clearer and he picked up his speed.

"Bring her on by," the grader operator told Merv.

"Thanks," Merv replied. "You do nice work."

"Thanks. Fourth man, let me know when you're close and I'll drop my big lights."

"Copy that," Spence replied.

"He's probably watching porno," Merv jabbed. "Gay porno."

"Listen to the Bear," Spence shot back.

"Gentleman, this is a working channel. Let's keep the chatter to a minimum," a female voice intervened and they fell silent.

"Four inbound at 44! Meanook Dispatch, you got a copy?"

"Go for Meanook," the same female voice said.

"Good evening, Sister, I have four inbound tankers coming onto your property," Garney called out the numbers then said, "Can you have hydrocarbons meet us at the staging area?"

"Well, if it isn't Big Garney Wilson. Welcome back, and with you is Marty Croft, Merv White, and Spencer Hughes."

"Yes, uh huh, that would be us. The fab four. Uh, huh, yep, yep, four very tired truckers. Yes, Sister."

"Welcome to Meanook, guys, we've been waiting for you. Hydrocarbons techs are en route to the tank farm. Head into the staging area and they will call you up as soon as they're ready."

"Hydrocarbons will be ready in two minutes," another woman broke in.

Marty guessed it was Kristy Greenflag.

"Copy that, dispatch, and thank you, Hydro-carbons, we just want to get this load off and settle in for some much needed rest. Uh huh. Sure do."

"First two can come right up to the racks," this time a male voice spoke.

"Kenny, that you, my brother?"

"Garney, my boy, how's my favorite Nova Scotian?"

"Doing well, my brother. A little weary, but knowing that you're back from that god forsaken rock to share in some of this nonsense lifts my spirits." Garney sounded chipper now, an old friend bringing forth new energy. "How are things in Kippens?"

"We call that God's Country, my boy," Ken responded, his Newfoundland accent thickened purposefully, the word boy sounding more like "buy." "You better watch out, buy! Up here we are the majority!"

Garney chuckled. "You heard him, my brothers... The Newfoundland Mafia awaits."

There were snickers, but no further dialogue.

Marty assumed that he would be meeting up with Kristy Greenflag on rack two.

"First tanker entering your property now."

"Copy that, Garney, got you in my sights. Looking good."

Marty watched as Garney's rig slowed and turned off Misery onto the main service road that led onto the mine property. The sky was sodium orange now; thousands of lights ignited the evening sky through a steady current of confetti, making the mine look like a surreal arctic haven. Running across the last part of Misery Road was thc approach to the airstrip. Marty took it in as he descended down the last stretch of road and readied himself.

5

Maintenance Shed #32
23:00 Hours

They actually found three things. A flare gun, a propane torch, and a 24 of empty beer bottles. The beer bottles were a discovery that would have drawn scorn and even an investigation. Alcohol was prohibited on mine property. Acadia, like all the other mines in the region, were dry status. No alcohol or drugs permitted, and anyone caught breaking that rule was looking at immediate dismissal and a lifetime ban. Now, as Chase, with the help of Lenny, filled each beer bottle with naphtha, discipline was the furthest thing from his mind. In fact, a drink of just about anything would do well.

"Almost there." Lenny steadied the makeshift funnel. So far they'd filled eight of the bottles, converting them into Molotov cocktails. They went about this task away from the heater and just beyond the lantern. Naphtha was far more volatile than gasoline and worse than that, its vapor hung low to the ground and had a very low flash point. "Okay, Chase, that about does it for this one."

"Good." Chase righted the can and waited as Lenny stuffed the neck of the bottle with a piece of the dirty hand towel they had shredded. At this point, everything they found was a gift, especially the towel, because all of the clothing they wore was fire retardant. That's not to say it wouldn't burn if doused in naphtha, but it might not hold onto a flame in the heat of the moment.

Lenny came back with an empty, the label on the side faded, but Chase recognized it. Pilsner Old Style, he hadn't cared for the brand much, his father used to drink it all the time. "Nectar of the gods," he said.

"Huh?"

"That's what my old man used to call Old Style. The nectar of the gods."

Lenny chuckled. "No offense to your father, Chase, but I always considered Old Style mule piss."

Chase laughed and tilted the naphtha can again. "Oh yeah, what's your poison, Lenny?"

"Labatt 50, hard to get in the west though. Skunkier the better."

Chase considered this. They could have been sitting on a back deck or even around a fishing hole comparing tastes in beer, sports, and women, but here they were putting together an arsenal of cocktails best served up at an anti-globalization protest. Instead, they were getting ready for...

For what? The end of the world? Maybe.

"I wish we had some det-cord and maybe a few super-sacks of ammonium nitrate," Chase said.

Lenny looked up. "You're not thinking?"

"Launching an assault?" Chase laughed at the notion. "No, I'm thinking we could blow the road. Maybe slow them down."

"You think they'll be coming?"

Beer bottle filled, Chase lowered the can and frowned. "Yeah, I think we can count on it."

They finished filling the bottles at what Chase guessed to be just before midnight. He rolled his watch forward 45 minutes and Lenny did the same. The storm was supposed to last anywhere between 24 and 36 hours, but Chase wanted to be up before first light just in case. He was hoping that a northbound security might find his way to their front door. Shift change usually occurred around 5 am, but the damned storm was going to throw a monkey wrench into that.

The cup-a-soup was salty and having used melted snow, it was laden with granules of dirt or sand. Both Lenny and Chase drank every drop and treated it as the last supper. Lenny heated the cup on top of the lantern and it didn't take long to melt the snow and bring it up to a boil. Chase burned the tip of his tongue with the first sip, but he hardly noticed. He thought about his thermos sitting in the service truck and wished he'd had the foresight to snag it up. They used two of the four packets. If he'd had the thermos, he could have dumped the contents and filled it with the hot soup. That would have made traveling on foot a little easier.

They agreed to sleep in shifts, Chase taking the first watch, but Lenny couldn't sleep. When he closed his eyes, his imagination ran wild with skeletal creatures skulking outside the door, tapping on the roof and shrieking like the windigos and skinwalkers his elders prophesized of in talking circles. Every time he tried to push his thoughts away and embrace the darkness, he heard the mad click and call. Regardless, Lenny rolled over, away from the light, and tried to rest. Even if he couldn't sleep, his body demanded that he stay still. So he did.

The lantern hissed gently while Chase turned the flare gun over in his hands. Guilt had finally begun to seep in and a tear spilled down his cheek.

Allison, he thought.

Yes, but not just Allison. There was Ronny and even Damien. His people. His crews, the mourning husbands and wives, the crying kids. Was this how survivors of disaster felt? How the victims of 911 felt? The soldiers who lost comrades. He supposed it was. He looked across to Lenny, wiped the tear away, and gave thanks for the little Inuit man. It could be worse. Much worse.

6

"Second truck, when you're ready, come to rack two," the woman standing at the pump station called on the radio.

"Copy that," Marty was throwing on his winter gear. "Just suiting up."

"Copy."

Less than a minute later, he was doing just that.

"That's good right there."

He stopped, pulled the tractor brake, and left the rig running. When he climbed out, he tossed the wheel chocks between the drives and walked around the front of the truck. When he came around the corner, she was opening the second compartment on the trailer and glanced his way. She pulled a canister from her parka and slipped it into the compartment. He stood there watching, paperwork dangling at his side and she stared back, then pointed. “Put the paperwork inside the building! Then come back out and give me a hand!”

Marty turned toward the small building and climbed the stairwell. He pulled the door open and stepped inside. The room was just big enough for four people. The walls were covered in electrical control boxes with led lights and gauges that Marty guessed monitored the offload and controlled the pumping station. To the right, there was another door. On it, a sign read: Authorized Personnel Only. Behind that door, machinery sounds thumped, clunked, and whined. To the right of the doorway sat a single shelf and on that, Garney’s paperwork had already been placed neatly on the clipboard. He set his own paperwork under the clip and went back outside.

She already had the API covers off and had attached the two hoses to both the lead and pup trailer. The sight glass on both lines were filled with flowing diesel. She was standing beside the first line, leaning against the side of the big tanker. She was wearing yellow safety glasses over the top of the wire-rimmed glasses she regularly wore. She was much taller up close. She wore a black parka striped with reflective strips, on her head a hardhat and inside that a liner made of lamb wool. She was a big woman, standing almost six feet, with broad shoulders and wide hips. Even though the parka and winter gear added weight to this woman’s girth, there was no illusion that she would be walking down any Paris cat walks anytime soon.

She smiled. “Marty?”

“Yeah. You’re Kristy?”

“In the flesh. The first half of our business is done. All we have to do now is get this load off.”

“How long will that take?”

“The pump is sucking at 1900 liters a minute. I’m thinking 15 minutes and you’ll be on your way over to the parking area for some much needed sleep.”

“Okay.”

“Long day?”

“Yeah.”

"Almost over now." She pulled the scarf up across her mouth and nose.

Marty adjusted his hardhat liner. It was cold, but not as cold as he might have thought. He supposed the snow and low cloud cover warmed things up a bit. Everything had an orange tint due to the sodium lights overhead. Snow twisted and turned independently across the lot in micro-storms, and Marty looked around at his environment. Everything was covered in ice and snow. Beyond the giant tanks, a building with four stacks chugged away, sending chalky gray plumes up into the endless black sky. Even his tanker was carrying a heavy coating of snow in its undercarriage. Kristy Greenflag wasn't much of a talker. She wandered between the lines, checking the sight glasses. When she switched out the lines, she was sizing Marty up with her eyes. She nodded toward the pump house. "It'll be about another eight minutes. Let's get your paperwork sorted out."

They walked up into the pump house. Garney and his unloader, Ken, were already inside laughing and joking around. "You still plucking the guitar, my brother?"

"Not as much as I'd like too, but yeah," Ken said.

"Coming through," Kristy announced and passed both men to the shelf. "Hey, Garney."

"Kristy, how are yuh, Sister?"

She pulled the paperwork out of the clip and began signing it off, checking her watch and adding times. "I'm fine, but you keep knocking God's Country and I'll kick your big ass back to that jerk water little town in Nova Scotia you came from."

Garney chuckled. "You a Townie or a Bay girl, Kristy?"

Ken took a step back and covered a smile.

Kristy looked up from the paperwork. "I ain't no Townie." Then she proceeded to sign the papers.

Marty closed the door behind him and nodded toward Ken. "Hey."

"Hey." Ken smiled back.

"What part of Nova Scotia you from again, Garney?"

"Truro Sister. Land of milk and honey."

"Truro? Lot of inbreeding in Truro is what I heard. First cousin marriages. Stay out of Truro there, Marty. You'll end up like this big galoot." She sealed the paperwork in the envelope and passed it back to Marty. "Half-wit dick smacks come from Truro."

Garney laughed. "Mon crayon est grand."

"Oh, French," she smiled back. "Is that how a Truro boy acts romantic? Talks about how big their pencil is? Good god, Ken, you better watch this one."

Marty guffawed.

Ken joined him.

Marty looked on. He was thinking about the package she'd placed inside his control compartment. He wanted to look at it. He wouldn't, of course, not until he got to that first portage south of here and that wouldn't be until at least tomorrow or later. Maybe this would go as planned. He could hand the package off to Crane and go his merry way. Maggie was safe, why complicate things? Maybe that would be enough for Gordon.

"Okay, it's getting close, let's go," she said, interrupting his thoughts. "Throw your paperwork in the cab, then you can give me a hand unhooking." Marty followed her out the door and they parted ways. He tossed the paperwork onto the seat. When he returned, she was already removing the first hose. "Put your API covers back on." As he did this, she removed the second hose and nodded. "This one's done as well." She lifted the hose and dropped it into the big steel tub she'd dragged over when first hooking up the lines.

Marty put his covers on and closed the compartments. When he was finished, he felt her looming over him. She waited until he was finished before speaking. He clapped his gloves together, knocking off the excess snow. "All done."

"Good, you're halfway home, Marty. Don't approach me while you're here at the mine. Don't even wave. I won't talk about you to anyone, so pay me the same respect, okay?"

"Okay."

"One last thing. I have a message for you. I don't know anything about the message, in fact I don't want to know, but I was told to pass it on. The message was Montreal."

Marty's mouth dropped. His heart shuddered. "What?"

"I was told to tell you Montreal. I don't know what it means."

His heart was banging now, hard constricting thumps. "Anything else?"

I wrote a number on your envelope. We have payphones here. The number is a YK number so you should be able to call without long distance. I'm guessing if you call that number, there will be further explanation."

He felt numb, disconnected.

They had her! Oh my god, they had her!

"Lines here aren't secure. Be careful what you say."

"Is that it?"

Garney's rig was pulling away from the first rack.

"We're done. Remember what I said. Follow Garney over to the parking area." She reached down and keyed the handset on her lapel. "Next man for rack two. Pull up once the truck pulls away."

"Copy," Spence replied.

"Get going." She turned and walked back to her station.

***

Chapter 24—Start Packing

1

Meanook Mine – Driver's Area

The sleeping area was located a kilometer away from the unload area. Marty didn't absorb his surroundings; instead he followed Garney's tail lights through a veil of numb disbelief and the steady pumping of his heart. He could barely hear Garney telling him where they would park. The high winds whipped snow around the parking lot, erecting drifts like miniature mountain ranges that were engulfing the static vehicles on the lot.

They've got her, his mind yammered. *Oh my god, what if...*

But he couldn't... wouldn't, entertain the idea...

"Jesus, Maggie, I'm sorry," he moaned.

Ahead, Garney swung his truck and trailers in a tight U-turn.

"Swing in behind me, Marty," he called from far off.

Marty didn't say anything. He was reaching for the envelope, looking for the number she had mentioned. Where was it? He turned it over in his hand and he saw the neat script scrawled out in red ink and he heard her say, "Lines here aren't secure. Be careful what you say."

What would he say? And who would answer when he called?

"Marty, are you there, my brother?"

He reached up and grabbed the mic. "Go ahead."

"Swing in behind me, but leave enough space so that you can move up five feet or so."

"Copy." But he wasn't really paying attention. He was thinking about what he was going to say, what he was going to do. Who would answer? Would it be Gordon? Or one of his paid assholes? He banged his fist off the steering wheel, then, after a moment he turned the big truck and pulled in behind Garney. How did they find her? He was hyperventilating.

"Fuck! Fuck! Fuck!"

2

Acadia Mine

Bruce Phillips could hear a song turning over and over in the back of his head as he was marched down the hall by the skentophyte soldier. He didn't know where the huge creature was taking him, but he knew that the most likely scenario was that he was fucked. As it pushed him down the hallway on the second level, he could hear Leonard Cohen singing, "Everybody knows."

"Everybody knows that the war is over," Cohen sang. "Everybody knows that the good guys lost,"

Fuck you, Leonard, Bruce thought. *Get the fuck out of my head.*

The creature–it's teeth clacking–sensing his internal argument, shoved a little harder and hissed. Bruce lengthened his stride slightly. He'd been taken from the auditorium when that prick, take that back, eyeless traitor prick, Ross McNeil from Human Resources showed up and pointed to him like a fucking Nazi sympathizer.

"That one," McNeil said. "He is the one you want."

Bruce recoiled. "What? What are you doing, Ross?"

The others in the auditorium moved away from him, no doubt happy that they had not been singled out and adding to insult to injury, the eyeless traitor prick said, "I'm sorry, Bruce. We are skentophyte!"

"You're sorry. You're fucking sorry, Ross! You fucking piece of shit!" He bumped into one of his fellow sheep. There were gasps and some cried, but not one of them came to his aid, not a chance. There were two of them with McNeil, one small and one big. The smaller was hissing and clacking its teeth, giving orders to the larger. Little man syndrome. It responded by bounding across the auditorium floor and blocking his retreat. Before he could turn and run into the crowd, it plucked him up from the floor and carried him back to the little dictator and the eyeless traitor prick. Once there, it set him down and clamped its hand, claw, paw, whatever the fuck it was, onto his shoulder and held firm. He was facing them now, standing a few feet from Ross.

"You can't run," Ross McNeil said, but he wasn't just talking to Bruce. He was addressing all of them and the message seemed to be getting through. They looked to the floor in shame as he was held up before them like a prisoner about to go to the gallows. They were afraid; word had spread like wildfire about the massacre outside the cafeteria. It was purposely passed on by the traitors. "I'm sorry, it's just the way it is."

"The way it is? You son of a bitch!"

Bruce lunged forward and dug a finger into one of Ross's empty sockets. He felt something then, hard and coiled, the tip of his middle finger grazed against it, and it moved. He pulled his hand back and just in time. Out of the plume of ash came something snake or worm-like and he was pretty sure that the thing inside that cavern was ready to bite his finger. Even infect him.

The larger Skentophyte yanked him back, now holding him with each claw. Ross, on the other hand, stood motionless as the worm thing moved, searching outside its lair for the intruding force that had attacked. It slithered along the rim, leaving behind a trail of black ichor. Satisfied that the attacker was gone, it retreated back into the socket.

"Jesus Christ!"

There was a collective gasp, tempered with cries of terror and hopelessness.

One of the claws released and the thing gave him a nudge. They were leaving. Bruce looked back at the others. Not one of them would look him in the eye. This should have angered him, but instead it made him sad.

Fucking sheep, he thought.

Now, stumbling through the corridor away from the others and on his way to god knew where, he was afraid to think what fate was lurking in the not-too-distant future. In the hours since their arrival, information had circulated through the groups of uninfected about who they were and what their intentions were. The infected, like McNeil, communicated those intentions quite freely, and though each of the eyeless traitors was accompanied by an escort, the skentophyte seemed not to notice or care that its infected trustee was spilling out information.

Perhaps that was their Achilles heel?

Perhaps, but Bruce didn't know how that was going to benefit the remaining mine workers of Acadia who were easily outnumbered at 10 to one. The things were everywhere, crawling all over the mine like ants. But maybe it would benefit someone else. Whoever was going to be sent to clean up this mess after word finally got back to civilization.

Look at me, he thought. *Yesterday I was a mechanical engineer, now I'm pondering the future of all mankind. While jamming with the man whose voice has been said to be deeper than a Siberian coal mine.* A mordacious smile began to form and then the Skent nudged him with a clacking of its teeth and the smile fell away. They turned down the East Corridor, which led to Administrative section of the mine.

"Attention all Acadia personnel, we are looking for two unaccounted for personnel," came Rally's soothing voice on the intercom. "Their safety and whereabouts is important to us. If you have seen either Chase Fenwick or Lenny Aranuknuk, please have them report to the cafeteria."

Bruce shook his head. Chase must have gotten away. Or maybe he was dead. He didn't know Lenny Aranuknuk, but hoped the two were in Corbett getting them some help. What kind of help he didn't know. Army, Air Force, Nukes?

They're probably dead. Frozen somewhere out there beyond the mine, buried in ten feet of snow by now, he thought. *Probably, but maybe not. The Skento-fucks seem pretty concerned with finding them and their safety seems to be secondary to their whereabouts. Nope, I'm guessing that they are a tad worried, that their master plan is not completely in play and these two have them worried that the element of surprise might be lost if Chase and Lenny find their way to civilization.*

The creature halted him and turned him to a door.

He reached down and turned the knob. It opened and he was pushed inside.

"Hello, Bruce," Allison Perch greeted.

3

Maggie was watching the snow accumulate in the corner of her room window, light powder building a hard angular slope only to be blown away by an occasional cyclical gust. In the next room, the Turcotte's were engaged in a low inaudible conversation. She wondered if they were talking about Shamus's advances toward Angel. She guessed not. Something told her that if Scott got wind of that, little bug or not, he would go after Gordon and then he would be killed. No, Angel wasn't stupid, but she definitely had a problem. Maggie didn't think that helped her situation, but still, she wondered. A little palace revolt might even the odds.

She was hiding. Out on the balcony, Shamus was puffing away on his cigars. After leaving Angel in the kitchen, she cut back down the hall and passed the door that led into the recreation room. She saw him out on the balcony with Donald. Shamus was doing all the talking, while a visibly uncomfortable Donald was doing the listening. She stood there a moment watching the two until Donald glanced her way, and then she retreated.

Out on the balcony, Shamus leaned on the railing. Elbows set upon the wooden plank, he looked out at the light snow as it fell against the night sky. "This isn't a storm, goddamned flurries."

"I think it's worse up there," Donald said.

Shamus squinted. "How would you know?"

"They're 600 km north of here, Gordon, just under the Arctic Circle." Donald shifted slightly; it was cold out here. He wanted to say something, but the bastard wasn't finished his goddamned cigar.

"Yeah, I get it. But for fuck's sake."

Donald felt impatient. Gordon Shamus was six years older than him, but he acted like a spoiled kid half the time. "We should get an update shortly."

"You passed the message?"

"Yeah, I'm guessing he'll call soon enough."

"Good. I don't want any fuck-ups!" Shamus butted the cigar out in the snow and tossed it from the balcony. "This fucking place is cold and miserable. Sooner we're the fuck out of here the better." He tossed the spent cigar over the ledge and it fell away into the darkness.

Donald considered throwing in a "Hear hear," but he remembered how Shamus reacted to Scott Turcotte's impatient sigh. No need to tempt fate. "I'll wait up for the call if you want to grab some shut eye Gordon."

"You're a good man, Donald." Gordon turned and opened the door. "I think I will lay down for a while. Come and get me when it comes through, and be discreet."

"I will."

4

Meanook Mine
23:20 Hours

Dinner at Meanook was a bowl of vegetable soup and plastic wrapped sandwiches the cooks put out for the night shift. The soup was hot and welcoming, but Marty hardly tasted it. In fact he could barely hear the banter that went on between the four men who sat around the cafeteria table. Ken, the unloader, joined them at the table briefly. He was a slim fellow, bald who acted quite at home among these big burly guys. His smile was infectious to the others and they talked with the enthusiasm of friends who had shared years of life experience.

"Earth to Marty," Spence nudged. "You sure are quiet, man."

Marty smiled thinly. "Tired I guess. How long we looking at being here?"

"They're saying the storm should be clear by tomorrow, but the cleanup could hang you guys up a little longer," Ken said.

"Cleanup?"

"Yeah, that could be the real bitch," Merv said. "I was at Ekati in 2012, whole goddamned road got wiped out. We were stuck at the mine for five days. Kind of funny actually. The sun was out like it was summer, but we were stranded because there was no road to drive on."

"Ah, we'll be outta here before that, my brothers."

"Garney, always the optimist," Spence said.

Ken grinned.

"Best way to be, uh huh yep. Yes Sir… We'll grab us some sleep. A shower. May as well enjoy the down time while we got it."

Marty didn't share in the enthusiasm, of course. With each speculative report, he felt like the walls closing were getting a little tighter. Maggie was all he could think about. They had Maggie and he was up here. He considered approaching Kristy Greenflag, no matter what she said, and finding out if there was anything else. Desperation enveloped him, his legs were shaking, mind racing, and he wondered if they could see the panic in his eyes.

"I need to get to a phone," he blurted.

The conversation halted in its tracks, and all eyes were upon him.

"I've gotta check on somebody back home."

"It's almost 11:30 here," Spence said. "Where's home?"

He almost said Yellowknife, then realized that was going to draw more questions. "Hamilton."

"It'll be 1:30 in Ontario," Merv agreed.

Great, now they're going to want a debate.

"Everything alright, my brother?"

No! Everything is all fucked. They have my wife. They're in Yellowknife and I'm stuck here in a fucking snowstorm debating about time differences in the Country. Can't you guys just eat your soup and mind your fucking business.

Marty stood up. "Everything is fine, just need a phone and a piss. Not necessarily in that order." For shit's sake, all he wanted was a phone.

Why the hell were they making a big deal out of this? Their faces had changed, and he suddenly wondered if one or maybe two were in on this.

"There's payphones upstairs," Ken said. "Just go down the hall and you will see a sign for the First Aid Center, the stairwell is just past that on the left. Up the stairs and turn right. There's a bank of four payphones in one of the halls. First or second on the left, I can't remember, but it won't be hard to find."

"Thanks," Marty turned and got moving.

He reached into his pocket and felt for the paper he'd torn from the envelope. It was still there. The Mine was quiet at this hour, except for the odd night shift worker. The interior of the building looked like a school, hard square tiles mapped the walk, and on the walls hung notices and photographs of the site. He passed a display case with trophies, which was just outside an indoor gym.

And then he saw the First Aid sign.

His pulse pumped rhythmically in his ears; he took the stairs two at a time trying to think of what he would say or do. Terror and anger seemed to be at odds in his belly, making him feel like he was going to throw up.

What if they had killed her?

Shut up! Don't even think... "Shit!"

His toe clipped the step and he lost his balance. His right hand caught the railing and saved him from going down on his side and crashing against the hard edge of the steps. Then his ankle hit the step, breaking the skin and sending a hot reverberation of pain up his leg. Hanging there from the railing sprawled out on the stairwell, he half grunted something like a word, but he doubted it could actually be found in an English Dictionary. He hung there, staring down at his sock feet. They weren't allowed to wear boots or outside attire inside the mine. He wondered if this particular mishap would constitute a safety meeting. At Meanook, it seemed everything was about safety.

"Take a deep breath," he whispered and inhaled, then lowered himself down onto the step, sat upright and massaged his ankle. He knew that no matter the situation, he could not change what had happened, so that meant that he would have change what would happen. *How?* He had the diamonds. That was leverage.

Leverage? You're going to leverage Gordon Shamus?

I'll kill the motherfucker. For her. I'll rip his fucking head off!

Marty Croft rose from the stairwell, the internal struggle between anger and panic over.

Anger had won.

5

"Hello," Donald answered and there was a drawn out pause, followed by a buzz and crackle over the wire. The connection was bad, but he could hear the party on the other end breathing. "Is that you, Marty?" He waved at Shamus to come to the phone.

"Get her on the line!" His voice was a low guttural growl.

Shamus walked across the room and took the receiver. "Marty, good of you to call."

"Get her on the line or I hang up."

"Calm down, Marty."

"Get her to the phone, Gordon. I'm not fucking kidding."

"Are you threatening me?" His voice was hard, challenging, but there was also a hint of uncertainty.

Marty thrust a little harder. "I am beyond threats! Get her now!"

Shamus snapped his fingers and pointed to Donald. "I'm having someone wake her. No need to get all wired up, Marty. She's fine."

"Fuck you! If I don't hear her voice, you are in a world of hurt."

Gordon said nothing. He didn't like being talked to this way. Marty could only picture what was going on at the other end of the line. He considered pushing a little harder, then decided against it. He'd made his point. He'd played his hand, but all Gordon had to do was call his bluff and he was crazy enough to do just that. In the background he heard a minor commotion and then he heard her voice. He leaned against the booth, placed a hand over the receiver and let out a controlled exasperated breath that hurt. He was shaking.

Thank God, she's alive! Thank you God.

"Hello?" Her voice was tired.

"Mag?"

"Marty?"

"Yeah, it's me, Mag, you okay? Anyone mistreated you?"

There was a pause, not even a second, but he knew she was holding something back.

"I'm okay, Marty."

"Anyone hurt you, Mag?" Through gritting teeth he said, "Any of those fuckers put a hand on you?"

"No, I'm fine, Marty. Gordon and the others have been good to me. I'm okay, we're just waiting..."

"For me."

"Yeah, and the storm. Do you know how long?"

Marty thought back to Merv and Spence musing about storms from the past and decided to keep that knowledge to himself. "A day, maybe two. We're at the mercy of the weather here."

"You sound tired, Marty."

"I'm okay, Mag, I'll be coming for you. Remember that. No matter what."

"Do what you have been sent there to do, Marty. I'll be here when you're done."

"Yeah." He was waiting for the phone to be tugged away. "Okay, Mag, remember what I said."

"I do, Marty, I will and... I love you."

She's in deep shit!

He squeezed his fist hard, knuckles whitening, the fingernails digging into his palm and when he opened his hand, four crescent moons indented the skin. She was in serious trouble, but she was alive and up until a minute ago, he was debating whether or not to report to the head of security and turn himself in. She was alive and that gave him the incentive to carry on. But had he worsened the situation by threatening Gordon Shamus? Probably. He shouldn't have threatened him. That threat might have sealed their fate.

Fuck that! Our fate was sealed from the word go. She's in YK because he's going to tie up loose ends right here after the job is done. He could think about that after this was done. "Mag, I love you too, sweetheart, and I'll be coming for you as soon as this is done."

"Okay." Her voice hitched.

"Better put Gordon back on."

"Okay, Marty, be careful."

"I will."

Then she said, "He wants to talk to you, Gordon."

"Thank you, Maggie. Donald will see you back to your room."

The phone was passed, the exchange clunking out across the line.

Shamus let out a sigh, then said, "Feel better, Marty."

"No. But then that's not really relevant is it?"

"I'm not going to go into detail over the phone, but you left me little choice."

"Bullshit. You could have left well enough alone. But you had to up the ante."

"Poker references? You bluffing me now, Marty?"

Marty said nothing.

"Okay, well I'm going to ignore the disrespectful way you spoke to me because I know you only acted that way because you are under a great deal of stress. I'm cutting you some slack on that one. I don't have to tell you that I don't generally let disrespect roll off that way. But you know."

"Yeah, Gordon. I know that."

"Okay, so you do what it is that you have to do and I'll forget about the outburst and the other stuff you said as well," Shamus said and took in a long measured breath. Marty could feel the madness whispering out across the line. "This is your one freebie, Marty, you won't get another."

"When this is done, the second half... How will I know where to come?"

"Phil will tell you what you need to know. As soon as he has what he needs."

Marty thought about this for a second. If he handed the diamonds over to Crane, they would probably kill her on the spot. No probably about it, it was guaranteed. The only thing keeping them both alive were the diamonds. No, he couldn't hand them over, not to Crane, too goddamned risky. Marty got ready to double down. "Gordon?"

"Yeah."

"Change of plans."

"Marty, you're exhausting my patience." Shamus's voice ground down into a low snarl. "No change of plan. No fucking around here, Marty."

"Oh, that's exactly what is going to happen, Gordon. I was up here doing it your way and you pulled a fucking double cross."

Now his voice was even lower, but full of venom. "Do you have any idea what you're doing? I don't negotiate, you little cocksucker. You're treading on very thin ice here. Very thin indeed."

Marty's heart thudded in his ears. He clinched the privacy divider on the phone booth, his knuckles whitening, and steadied himself. "I know exactly what I'm doing and I know exactly what will happen the minute Crane does his end, so I am changing the game and you really have two options here, Gordon. Play it my way or pack a fucking bag!"

"Pack a bag? You can't be serious." Shamus laughed, but there was an edge of uncertainty in that cackle so Marty pushed even harder.

“Something happens to her, Gordon, and I’ve got nothing to lose. You understand what I’m saying here.”

“I’ll fucking... You little fucker, you don’t want to…”

“You or any of your fucking minions touch a hair on her head and you better pack a fucking bag, because I’ll bring the whole fucking show down! I’m not kidding.”

Silence, except for the inhalation of hot, angry breath.

“You fucking hear me, Gordon,” he growled through clinched teeth. “She better not have a mark on her or pack a bag, because there won’t be anywhere to hide. You couldn’t just let her be, well now I’m changing the game, Gordon, and you’re going to play it my fucking way.”

“You little motherfucker. I’ll...”

“You’ll what, Gordon! You’ll what? And keep in mind that this isn’t exactly a secure fucking line!”

“You’re making a mistake, Marty. A big fucking mistake.”

“No, you’re the one making a mistake. Take fucking heed. Something happens to her and after that I don’t give a fuck about anything, you think about that, Gordon. Think about the stakes here, because what I’m holding is minor compared to what I can do to you.” Marty’s heart wasn’t just pounding, it was cramping in long successive contractions. But the rage overrode it all. He pulled the phone away from his ear and spoke into the mouthpiece like a sports announcer. “You hear that? You psycho piece of shit!” He thudded it against the divider and brought it back. “Are you reading me, Gordon?”

Marty waited. The silence was deafening.

Any second now, the phone would go dead and his threats would be the thing that ended her life, and Gordon would do it himself. Just to make a point.

We’re dead already, he told himself. *This is the only way!*

Then something did happen.

Gordon sighed. “As long as she’s with me, she’s safe.”

“Straight up trade.”

“Marty, I’m not going to patronize you.”

“Yeah, I know what you’re thinking, but I’ve got some eyes on the situation too.”

“Oh, is that so? Why don’t I believe you?”

“You don’t have to. But I do. I made arrangements.”

Gordon chuckled. “Let’s cut out the bullshit, shall we.”

"Fine, I've made myself clear enough. You let your bald-headed pal know that the game has changed and once I'm south I'll come see you face to face. And one other thing. Give Maggie her phone back, when I'm back in signal I'll be calling to see how she's doing."

"Alright, Marty. We'll do it your way. It will be easier."

Easier, yeah, you can kill two birds with one stone, Marty thought and said, "I want her to answer when I call, Gordon, no texting. I need to hear her voice."

"No problem."

Marty pushed away the urge to call him a liar. There had to be some way to get to her before the inevitable happened. "Okay, Gordon, I've gotta get off the line, there are others waiting for me."

"I'll be waiting for a call from Phil then."

"Yeah."

"Anything else?"

"Keep her safe."

Gordon said nothing. The phone clicked and went dead.

Marty set the receiver in its cradle and stood there a moment longer, staring at the payphone, his eyes swimming in the murk of oblivion. Had he pushed too hard? Maybe Gordon would kill her just based on what he said tonight. He wasn't the kind of guy who liked being pushed and Marty had pushed harder than anyone had ever done before. Except for the Old Man. The Old Man would never have gone for this.

Oh Jude, why did you have to die?

"*Yee shouldn't have come back ere, Lad,*" Jude Shamus's ghost returned.

"God damned right on that, Mr. Shamus."

Gordon would probably wait for a call from Phil, then they'd march Maggie out into the woods and dispatch her before he even had a chance to come south. Maybe Phil would take the package and kill him and then whoever Donald was would kill Maggie. Maybe not, too messy. Easier to kill both of them at the same time.

Are you willing to risk that, Marty?

"Little too fucking late for buyer's remorse. This deal is bought and paid for." He'd have to be ready for Crane, just in case. He couldn't let him get his hands on the diamonds; they were the only leverage he had. He pulled focus and ambled back down the hall toward the stairwell. He was exhausted, physically and mentally, and still he didn't know how he could possibly sleep.

6

ACADIA MINE
23:45 Hours

For the moment, they had been left alone. Allison's escort had stepped out and left the two of them to sit together. Allison welcomed the company. Bruce, on the other hand, wasn't as enthusiastic. He tried not to look at her; he remembered how she'd looked before they'd turned her. Allison Perch was what Bruce called a "looker," blond, slim figure, and smart too. He remembered her smile. Her eyes would brighten when she smiled; it was infectious and though Bruce was 54 and well beyond an age of interest for the young pretty lab assistant, she still made him feel much younger.

That was then, this is now.

Now, Allison wasn't that bright sunny blond, but a turncoat collaborator lacking the blue eyes to animate her former sunny smile. She was seated in a chair in the corner of the room, her head canted to one side—a bit of drool spilling from her mouth. Besides the initial "Hello," accompanied by a weak smile, she'd gone quiet, her breathing erratic.

"What's wrong with you?"

She reached up and used her sleeve to wipe her mouth. "I'm expiring, dying, I guess."

"Do you know why I'm here?"

Allison did not look up; she was completely blind now. She only knew it was Bruce from the intermittent signals that came across the collective before the implants began to lose all power. "I think I'm supposed to have a longer shelf life, Bruce, but my exposure to the chamber has made me sick a lot faster than anticipated."

"The chamber?"

"Nick was really sick. When they came through, he looked burned and charred. He reminded me of..." She smiled. "The Toxic Avenger. Did you ever see that movie, Bruce? The Toxic Avenger."

"No, can't say I have. What chamber are you talking about?"

"Nick dragged me down there. He was a soupy mess. Bit all my fingers off. She raised a bandaged hand. Not him really. It was the Skentophytes that made him do it. Devils." She giggled. "The Devil made him do it. He even apologized between chomps. Kept on saying, 'I'm sorry, Allison,' as if I was going to say, 'Hey, that's okay, Nick, as long as you're sorry.' It wasn't him, though, not really, he was being ordered to eat my digits."

"Why would they want him to do that?"

"Because I fought back. I tried to stop him, tried to kill the thing in his eye. They see everything, Bruce, control you completely." The she lowered her voice to a whisper. "But they have a weakness."

"Why are you telling me this?"

"They don't have a hold on me anymore. I'm like sour milk, past my expiry date and now they have lost their grip on me. The worms are dead, I'm blind and dying."

"You said they have a weakness."

Allison coughed, and a mixture of mucus filled with tendrils of blood came out her nose and hung grotesquely, bridging the gap between her left nostril and her right breast. "Yeah, the bastards have a real weakness. It would be nice if there was someone to actually pass that tidbit of info onto, but it seems that they've pretty much taken out any threats." She coughed and this time a glut of blood splashed out over her lip and cascaded down her neck. "Shit, this can't be over soon enough."

Bruce slid his chair closer to Allison. He gripped her shoulder. "Please, Allison. Get to the point. What is their weakness?"

"They can't keep a secret." She snorted and scarlet mist sprayed onto his sleeve.

"I don't understand."

"They're very intelligent. They've mastered space travel by jumping from their world to others using portals. Chambers. Wormwells is what Nick called them. Smart enough to build machinery that will take them across the universe, but the fuckers can't string an individual thought without spilling it into their precious collective. They're like insects, but even better, they can't keep it from us. When they infect us, their entire thought process is open for examination."

"You're telling me you know what their plan is?"

Allison lifted her head. "The real invasion starts when they load up and head south. I'm dying, Bruce," she stuttered and in a whimper: "I had so much I wanted to do. I'm afraid, what if there is nothing after this? God, I'm scared." She lifted a hand limply and Bruce took it. He gazed into those empty sockets. Whatever life had been in there was now extinguished. The worm-like things that had coiled inside Allison's eyes were long expired. Poor kid, she didn't deserve this. None of them did. He felt bad for calling her a turncoat.

Then a chill ran through him.

“Oh, shit… I’m here to replace you, aren’t I,” he said sickly.

“Yes.”

7

Gordon Shamus set the phone down and fell back in the big leather chair that faced the picture window. His temples throbbed, adrenaline coursed through him like mercury, and he could barely hear Donald asking if he needed anything. “No, that will be all,” he said, but that was also distant, because he was slipping into a fugue. That little cocksucker had threatened him. No one had ever done that! He had never liked Marty, never understood what the Old Man had seen in him.

Because he’s everything you’re not, Jude Shamus reminded.

He smashed a fist on the chairs armrest.

Everything I’m not! Yeah, well, fuck him. He’s living on borrowed time now. Shamus seemed to forget that the hole had already been dug, that Marty and Maggie Croft had been living on borrowed time since the meeting in the pub.

He knows that too, Jude Shamus jabbed.

Yeah he knows, but that doesn’t matter, because he’s coming here. I ought to go in her room now, beat her black and blue, then fuck her. Right in the fucking dirty spot. Take her virgin ass and then when I’m done take a few snap shots to show Marty.

No, that wasn’t good enough.

The original plan had been to have Donald, Angel, and that Little Bug escort them into the woods and put ‘em both in the ground while he was somewhere else. But now? No fucking way! He’d go along for the ride, oh yeah. Marty needed a little education and Shamus intended to do it all himself.

Let the others watch.

That will reinforce things a bit, then they’ll be reminded that it isn’t wise to mouth off. Yeah, he’d kill her first, right in front of Marty, then a little education before he went to ground.

I’ll teach the little cocksucker a lesson.

***

Chapter 25—Ghost in the Machine

1

Ingraham Trail: Kilometer 3
Giant Mine, Yellowknife, NWT
2:12 Am

"Aw fuck, what now?"

The road coming south on the Ingraham between kilometer 5 and 3 was a winding icy stretch, unforgiving at the best of times. Neil Pratchett was driving an end dump gravel truck that early morning when the check engine light on his International Eagle lit up. The warning bell began to chime and whatever the issue was meant that he was going to be out of commission. He'd been hauling a load of gravel up to a section of the Ingraham they had been widening. If the light had come on a minute sooner, he could have diverted off the road into the museum at Giant Mine, where there was more than room to get out of the way. But fate or the Cat engine under his hood felt differently. Before he could limp it to a safer spot, the engine cut out and he rolled to a stop as far over on the non-existent shoulder as he dared. "God dammit," he grumbled and reached for his handset. "Perry, you got a copy."

"Go ahead, Neil."

"I'm dead in the water. I need a service truck up here pronto."

"What's your location?"

"Kilometer three."

"On the road?"

"Yeah, on the fucking road. Tell them to hurry and get the word out. I'm a fucking sitting duck out here." He had his window open, was listening for approaching vehicles. As far he could tell there was nothing, but he had to get his triangles out. Then some good news broke. Robby Mumford, the mechanic from Chinook Tundra, heard the call and responded.

"Neil, I'm on old highway three. I'll be there in five minutes."

Neil smiled. "Thanks, Robby, I'm not sure what the issue is but she's dead as a doornail."

"Okay, sit tight. Get your triangles out and we'll see what we can do."

Neil climbed from the truck, turned on his flashlight, and grabbed the warning triangles out of his jockey box. The truck was halfway into the crescent curve that snaked around the hill that the abandoned gold mine stood vigil on. From either direction he would not be seen, but it was a vehicle coming from the south that posed the most risk, so he decided to leave his flashlight on the ground behind the second triangle he laid out. When Robby arrived, hopefully the kid could work some magic and get the shit spreader moving again.

After marking the back, he hoofed it as far as he could to the north of the truck and set out his third warning triangle. He wished he'd had a couple of road flares, but for now this would have to do. He started back when he saw lights at the top of the hill coming from the south. "Shit, Robby, I hope that's you."

As he rounded the bend, he took in the four way flashers on the truck and hoped that the light could be seen from both corners. No matter, he decided to get on the vhf radio and announce himself just the same. That's when the cadence of amber blinks stopped and the truck went completely dead.

"Oh, come on!"

Neil sprinted back to the truck and opened the door.

It was dead.

He turned the key off and back on again.

Nothing.

"Sweet bloody hell! Come on!"

He tried the radio.

Nothing.

The lights from the south were winding down the hill toward him. He was glad that he'd parked the flashlight under the rear triangle. They'd be able to see that from a fair distance back. He turned the key on and off a few more times, if nothing but to satisfy himself that there was nothing within his ability to correct the issue. The approaching vehicle was getting closer now. Rays of light bounced off the low snow-dusted hills surrounding the chorus of diesel purrs that rose and fell.

It was Robby Mumford; this made Neil Pratchett feel a little better.

Ingraham Trail – South of Prosperous Lake

Peter Simmons downshifted as he readied himself for the curve ahead. The road was greasy tonight, but "Blue" was keeping her grip despite the constant shove he felt coming from the load of beaten concrete barriers he was carrying. Simmons was coming from the same site that Pratchett was heading for when he broke down.

Blue growled as he slipped the shifter into sixth gear.

"Easy girl," he patted the dashboard after lifting his hand from the stick. "We're almost home."

Blue was a Mack Vision that Peter had bought for a song after it was wrecked down in Fort Providence. Peter got it for a song because not only had the truck been wrecked, but the driver was killed and not many folks wanted to ride around in a rig that might be haunted. Peter picked it up for $10,000 and went about replacing and retro-fitting everything that was needed to bring the rig up to speck. The frame thankfully wasn't compromised in the wreck; otherwise, it would never have been road-worthy. Peter sunk $27,000 into the rig, and his brother Sandy painted the truck electric blue, giving the Mac Vision her namesake. He'd been running this road for two years and everyone who knew the rig called her blue.

"One south at kilometer five," Peter called on the radio. He was using the whole road as he rounded the bend, feeling the surface beneath him shift, and so he eased up on the throttle slightly. He was doing roughly 40 kph as he descended toward a left hand downward curve. The curve sloped to the right at the bottom of the hill, which made it an easy spot to lay a truck down on its side. Peter scanned the blind corner for approaching headlights, and satisfied there was nothing coming, he kept Blue into the center of the road.

Two kilometers ahead, Robby Mumford was underneath Neil's International Eagle, carefully tapping away at the ice and snow, trying to find a broken wire. He meticulously chipped away at road crud that reeked of diesel, trying very hard not to break anything other than the icy cocoon. In these temperatures, everything, including metal, was extremely brittle. A wire would snap like a piece of uncooked spaghetti.

"Find anything?" Neil asked.

Robby picked up his mitts, placed them on his chest, then removed his mechanic gloves and slipped his hands inside them. "Not yet, it's a fucking mess under here, Neil."

"Sorry about this, Robby."

"Forget it. I'll keep looking, but if I can't find something soon we're going to have to get you on a hook." Time was running out. The temperature was somewhere around -45 Celsius. As they tinkered, the engine oil was turning into tar, the air seals were contracting, and if they didn't get the Eagle started in the next few minutes, they'd be snookered. Robby scanned with his eyes, the LED headlamp he wore illuminating the undercarriage of the rig in hard fluorescent white. He was pretty sure he wasn't going to find it, then he saw a black plastic tentacle protruding out of the ice that encrusted a cross member below the battery box. "Well, what do we have here?" He reached up with a gloved hand.

Peter saw the amber strobes from Robby Mumford's service truck lighting up the rock face silhouette that obscured the breakdown. He reached up and pulled down his handset. "One southbound at kilometer four. Something going on at Giant Mine? You got a copy?"

At first there was nothing.

Peter eased up. "One southbound at Kilometer 3 and a half."

And then he heard Neil Pratchett on Robby Mumford's radio. "Southbound, there's a breakdown at kilometer 3, please approach with caution." He didn't know that Neil was talking on the service truck radio, would never know in fact; that would come later in the accident reconstruction.

Peter curved the bend and saw both the service vehicle and the crippled northbound truck. He was just reaching for his microphone to hail them when he saw a ghost sitting beside him in the passenger seat. The ghost was the nameless driver who'd been killed in Blue's other life before Peter made his bid on the wrecked truck and put it back into service. He didn't know the driver's name, had never inquired about it, but he knew this ghost sitting beside him was in fact the man who had died behind the wheel of this big rig.

"Where did you come from?" he asked.

The ghost didn't say anything, just sat there smiling.

Peter never saw the spots of white before the grand mal seizure sent him into the hallucinatory state. Never felt the tightening of his muscles, shooting his leg down on the accelerator plank stiff. He did not hear the protests from Blue's transmission as the RPMs red-lined, nor did he see the impending crash that would take his life and the lives of the two men ahead. He did not hear the crunch of metal when he hit Robby Mumford's service truck, killing Neil Pratchett, who was screaming madly into the handset. "Stop! Stop! Stop!" He only saw the ghost.

During this, Robby Mumford was pulling the wiring harness down, cutting the zip ties as he did. He'd found the culprit and thought with a little luck that he might just get this baby rolling before they had to resort to a hook. Then he heard two things that made him pause: the first was Neil repeatedly screaming "Stop!" and the second was the crunching sound of metal. In the last second of his life, the undercarriage of the truck above moved, yanking the harness from his right hand, a snag in the wiring ripping his glove away. Before he was aware what was happening, hot diesel rained down. Before the explosion, the steer wheel on a blue Mack Vision turned his head into a bloody pulp.

Darkness retreated from the detonation of amber. Liquid fire splashed upward into the night, then rained back down onto the frozen asphalt with hellish fury. As quickly as it retreated, darkness closed in, enveloping the surrounding silhouettes, turning them inky black. On the hill above the Ingraham, the tower from Giant Mine was lit in the aftermath of the carnage.

Before long, there was a chorus of approaching sirens.

2

Corbett Lake Camp
3:00 Am

John Pringle was drinking coffee and looking over the reports he'd gotten so far before the storm came along and shut the road down. One day in and they had already suspended two drivers—issued 12 warnings for a number of infractions ranging from speeding to spacing. This year wasn't all that different from any other; the usual idiots hung themselves, and then there were his own people to contend with. He always ended up with an overzealous guy that earned the nickname Barney Fife. He expected it every year. The Fifes of the world were cops trying to rekindle a little of that authoritarian magic that kept them down in real life. Traffic cops that enjoyed handing out tickets, because they knew that they weren't going up.

It was too early for breakfast, they didn't start slinging hash until 5:00 am, so he settled on some toast and jam. He was waiting for the word to come down from Lupania that the road would be reopening between Acadia and Corbett. Right now he had a yard stuffed with trucks running at high idle and along with that, tempers had already begun to flare. He peeled the foil wrapper back from the plastic square that held his strawberry jam and scooped the jellied square out onto his toast. As he did this, he initialed the last incident sheet and slid it into his log.

"Morning, John," Axe said, coming into the cafeteria.

"Hi, Axe. What are you doing up so early?"

"I just got word from higher. I'm taking my crew up to the pressure ridge." Axe had his back turned as he filled his thermos. "We're going to flood the shit out of it once Lonny scrapes it clear." The pressure ridge was 30 km north of the Acadia turnoff on Dreamcatcher Lake.

"Lonny going to be breaking trail for you boys?"

"That's the plan, I guess once the road gets scraped from here to Acadia, Lupan will be sending out some crews to widen the road so that you can at least unload the Acadia guys."

Pringle smiled. "Always the last to know."

"Sorry, John." His thermos and coffee mug filled, he sat and joined Pringle at the table.

Pringle shook his head. "No biggie, your brother is at the Fish Camp."

"Yeah, I figured he'd head that way. We'll swing by and see if he needs a tug. I'm sure he'll want to check on his kills. Probably buried below 10 feet of snow by now." He sipped his coffee, his brown eyes coming up to meet Pringle.

"Have him give me a shout so I know he's not out there frozen to the ground. I wanted him to go to Acadia or come back here, but he insisted on going to that Fish Camp."

"I can understand why. They're kind of dicks at Acadia. Escort here, escort there, escort to the bathroom. No wonder he wanted to go north. I hate that place."

Another man entered the cafeteria, a dispatcher who had just rotated in from Targus. He was slim, gray-haired, and looked like a throwback to the 60's. Vincent, Axe's pal, called him "Johnny Fever." He wandered up to the coffee urn, considered, then shook his head and reached for the tea bags instead. After pouring hot water into the cup, he did an about-face and approached the table. "This a private meeting?"

"Grab a chair, Mike." Pringle motioned with his hand.

"Thanks." The dispatcher set his cup on the table and pulled the chair back, legs scraping the linoleum in screechy protest. He set himself in front of the cup and began jigging the tea bag up and down with silent determination. "Rumor has it the road to Acadia should be open at first light. Storms already easing off."

"That's good news," Axe said and winked at Pringle. "You'll be able to get that overstuffed parking lot emptied out."

"What's the word on Meanook?" Pringle said.

Before the dispatcher could answer, Vincent entered the room and called out, "Johnny Fever! I got a request."

"Friend of yours," Mike asked of Axe and grinned.

"Yeah, my right hand man. Hey, Vincent, grab a coffee and join us."

"That's what I'm doing, Axe Man."

"Mike, what's the story on Meanook?" Pringle asked again.

"Late afternoon is the estimate." Mike used a spoon to squeeze the tea bag against the side of the cup. "We got lucky on this one, came in like a lion, but left like a lamb. The barrens took a hit, but nothing like last year, that's for sure. Targus already has its crews warming up."

"Sounds good."

"There is some bad news, John."

"Of course."

"There's was an accident this morning that resulted in three fatalities on the Ingraham down by Giant Mine. A Flatbed and an End Dump Gravel hauler mixed it up."

"Ah shit," Axe grunted.

"Shit indeed," Vincent added, pulling up a stump. "Anyone know who it is yet?"

"Not yet. The word is the end dump was disabled in the middle of a service call and the flatbed lost it on the turn. Both drivers got clipped along with the poor guy on the service call. Anyway, the road coming north will be closed for at least 24 hours while the Mounties do an investigation and get a crew in to do some roadwork. Apparently the fire burned the asphalt right out of the roadway. Must have been a hell of a blaze."

Pringle shook his head. No one said anything; there wasn't any need to. The mythology of the ice road was that the danger was up here, but the truth was the roads leading to the ice held the most danger with breakneck turns, whiteout conditions, and worst of all, human error. In the background, the clattering of pots and pans distracted from the silence as the Kitchen Nazi began her morning prep. "What about the road south? Is it passable?"

"Norman down at Halsey said they'll be digging out all day. Clearing drifts and sanding the shit out of the portages. They have their work cut out for them, but it could have been a hell of a lot worse," Mike said. "The accident down on the Ingraham, terrible as it is, will keep the outside world away long enough for us to get this mess cleaned up."

3

Acadia Mine
03:33 Hours

There is nothing worse than knowing that you are fucked. If Bruce were to write a philosophy paper, that would be the title. Not doomed—not destined to lose—just fucked. He was waiting for them, sitting across from the now deceased Allison Perch. Soon one of the Skento-fucks would open the door and infect him with their virus, and he would end up like the poor lifeless young lady across from him. Escape had been foremost in his mind, but there was nowhere to escape to. There was no duct work, conveniently found in most science fiction horror flicks, just four walls, a couple tables, a handful of chairs, and a corpse. Outside the room, they clattered up and down the hall, their breathing tubes inhaling and exhaling, their teeth clacking madly. Sooner or later, that door would open and they'd spit into his eyes and he'd become one of them.

"This fucking blows," he grumbled. "What the fuck did I do to deserve this?"

There wasn't even a garbage can to hide in.

He thought about putting up a fight. Going down in blaze of glory, maybe take a few of the Skento-fucks with him. He smiled. That would be great if he had a gun or a flamethrower, but all he had was a lousy set of needle nose pliers that he'd found after an initial sweep of the room.

"I know their weakness."

Yeah, he knew their weakness, but what good was that going to do him?

I'm fucked, but maybe not everyone is fucked. Maybe I can get that info out to the real world before these Skento-fucks lay a real fucking on it. Sure, that's it, I'll just go punch that radio whore Rally Martin in between her lookers and broadcast to the world. The Skentophytes are coming!

"Who's going to believe that shit?" First he let out an exasperated laugh, and then it morphed into a strangled whimper. "Oh god, I am so fucked."

Then something Allison said occurred to him. It wasn't about their lack of secrecy either, even though that tidbit might be useful for the Army or the CIA or whomever the fuck the government sent to fight invading alien forces. In her dying words, Allison had left him something that might be useful. "They're blind."

Yes, blind. He remembered being shoved down the hall by that behemoth. He also remembered that at every passageway stood one of the infected. They were the eyes and ears of these things. And of course, there was that asshole from Human Resources who pointed him out. "They need us to see."

Well, how the fuck did they see before they got here?

He shook his head. This was no time to have a chicken and egg argument. Those things would be coming back. When they did, he might find the answer to that question, but by then he'd be walking around with those lighted tentacles in his eyeless sockets and if it came to that, the answer wouldn't matter much anymore. Best to leave the science to the dicks that ate that shit up and focus on getting the fuck out of Dodge before the shit the fan.

"Everybody knows," Leonard Cohen piped up again.

"Ah shut the fuck up, Leonard, yuh fucking lefty bleeding heart."

Bruce began scavenging around the room.

He'd have to kill the lookouts.

4

MAINTENANCE SHED #32
0530 Hours

Lenny reached down and gave Chase a nudge. "Chase, wake up. There's somebody coming!"

Chase sat up with a start. "Get the cocktails!"

"No, not that, I hear vehicles. There's vehicles coming!"

Chase stood up and then almost fell over. He was still half asleep, and his balance still out of whack sent him stumbling to the left. "Cut the heater, Lenny."

"I already did. That's the vehicles you hear."

Chase listened. It was the steady rumble of diesel engines. Likely plows coming their way to clear the road. His heart suddenly raced. He smiled. "Come on, Lenny."

Lenny reached down, killed the lantern, and they bolted towards the door.

The vehicles were getting closer and definitely coming from the south. Chase yanked the door open and his heart sank. The doorway was buried in snow. "Fuck me! Fuck me! Dig!"

Both he and Lenny began clawing at the snow like dogs digging for unseen bones.

The vehicles were getting closer. Panic began to set in. What if they drive right by?

"Dig, Lenny!" Chase dug in with both hands, trying to clear the snow, but the cold was biting into his bare hands, turning them cold, waxen. Lenny was already putting on his mitts and Chase stepped away, barking at no one, "Come on come on come on!"

Lenny was back at the doorway, clawing into the bank.

Chase struggled to get his mitts on; his fingers burned as they rubbed against the material. "Jesus Christ, give me a fucking break!" Gloves back on, he joined Lenny at the door and the digging resumed. The vehicles were even closer.

"It must be Lupania clearing the road," Lenny said.

"Keep digging, Lenny." But they weren't going to make it. The vehicles were right on top of them now and the tunnel they were digging didn't seem to be breaking through. Then, by some miracle, the snow above the door collapsed in on them. Both Chase and Lenny crouched dumfounded below the small hole above, covered in white powder. The diesel engines were passing them. "No no no..."

Lenny scrambled up the incline and was out the hole before Chase could say anything. The little Inuit man was already struggling through the snow when Chase popped his head out and saw the red glow of taillights.

"Come back!" Lenny cried, waving his arms frantically. "Come back!"

But the vehicles were past them now, heading north, leaving behind a blaze of red taillights. A small convoy of vehicles were breaking trail up the road toward Meanook. They'd bypassed the Acadia turn-off. That was the responsibility of the Mine staff. Chase watched them disappear up the road. He might have been upset, but this meant that they were breaking through and that rescue was imminent. "Lenny. Come back inside."

Lenny glanced back, then toward the sound where the lights had been.

"There will be more. Come back."

Then there was another sound and it was coming from Acadia.

Lenny turned toward it. Saw the lights of a vehicle busting through the snow. "Lenny!"

But Lenny never heard him. He started running up the road toward the vehicle.

Someone had escaped. Someone with a vehicle had escaped.

"Lenny, no!" Chase screamed.

The lights of the snow cat bounced up in down in the morning light, tracks click clacking on the ice, powder kicking up into the air. Behind it, two more vehicles, a plow and a grader, cleared the road. Lenny only saw the headlights, he never saw the creatures riding on the vehicles, but Chase saw them and he scrambled back down into the trench.

The snow cat came to a stop.

In front of them, a little man waved his arms frantically.

Then he stopped.

The door on the snow cat popped open and out stepped Herb Aronson. "Lenny?"

Lenny realized his mistake. Saw them climbing down off the vehicles. Saw the caverns where Herb's eyes had been. He didn't turn his head to see where Chase was, although he tried to catch a glimpse of him from the corner of his eye. There were five hanging off the plow, all of them now dismounting onto the road. The grader moved up beside the snow cat, its massive lights drowning out the shadows and washing Lenny in amber milk.

The creatures were surrounding him now.

Chase covered his mouth in horror.

"We've been looking for you, Lenny."

"Well, I guess you found me."

"Where's Chief Fenwick?"

Lenny reached under his parka, unsheathed his knife.

"He froze to death. Up on the Telegraph."

They were closing in. He could hear the clacking of their teeth.

Herb looked around. He did not follow Lenny's tracks or see the building obscured by the darkness outside the circle of light they stood in. The winds were still up, polishing the surface of the snow, extinguishing his tracks. Lenny hoped there would be enough time to erase them permanently.

Herb turned his head, but Lenny, hoping to distract him, spoke up. "Herb."

"Yes, Lenny?" Herb turned his attention back to Lenny.

They were all around him now, no escape.

"Does it hurt?"

"Does what hurt?"

"Your eyes?"

Herb grinned. "A little, but not for long."

Lenny brought the knife up.

"What are you doing, Lenny?"

In one slick motion, he cut his own throat. There was a sting, sticky warmth, his knees buckled.

Better run like hell, Chase, was his last thought.

He was dead before they dismantled him.

5

Corbett Lake Communications
0600 Hours

"Corbett Lake, do you have a copy?" came Rally Martin's silky voice over the radio.

"Go ahead for Corbett."

"Hi, Mike, just calling to let you know that we are open for business up here at Acadia. The road in has been cleared."

"Copy that, we are still digging out south of here, but I'll be able to send a bunch of able truckers your way if you're ready for them." Mike released the transmit button and waited for a response. Behind him, John Pringle listened with some interest.

"Oh, we'll welcome them with open arms. Skent."

Mike cocked his head sideways. "Say again last?"

"Send them on, we'll have a party ready to meet them."

"Copy that."

John Pringle grabbed his parka and suited up. "Mike, get me a list and I'll have Ernie and Richard start waking up the Acadia truckers."

"Will do."

Pringle sat down and began putting on his mukluks when Phil Crane came through the door. "Hey, Phil, you're just in time."

Crane was just about to take off his gear. "Oh? Time for what?"

"Grab a bite of breakfast. I'm going to send you up to Portage 33. I want you to make your presence there known so that our overzealous truckers don't get lead feet running for Acadia."

"The road's open?"

"It's open to Acadia. They should have the rest of it cleared up by late today. Grab some breakfast, you've got 20 minutes."

6

Chase Fenwick thought he was going to freeze to death, and he might have had they come to investigate the building, but after they finished eating Lenny, they mounted up their vehicles and carried on about their business. That did not stop him from abandoning the building with a Molotov cocktail in each pocket and hiding out in the tree line to the west. He was sure they would have come to the building, but they didn't seem to notice.

It took ten minutes for them to eat Lenny's bones and discard his hide in the bank. Once the vehicles were gone, Chase went back to the building, slid down the hole, and began to gather up what he could carry. Carefully, he stuffed more beer bottles into each pocket. His fingers felt like hard waxy twigs from the cold. He looked at the Herman Nelson heater and thought better of it. *I'm not going to last out there if I don't warm up.*

"You're not going to last if you get caught here," he grunted.

He stared down at the Coleman lantern.

"Ten minutes."

He moved across the room and grabbed one of the pieces of plywood, dragged it over the floor and put it up in front of the open door. He would have just closed the door, but he and Lenny had created a real mess digging out. Besides, he didn't think his fingers could withstand any more digging before he warmed them up. He lit the lantern, wary of the flammable contents of his pockets.

He held his hands over the lantern, ears tuned to any sound of approaching vehicles.

Chase wasn't even aware that he was crying until one of his tears plopped onto the top of the lantern's hood and sizzled. He stared down at it incredulously for a moment, until more tears fell and evaporated. He brought a fist to his mouth in an attempt to mute the whimpers that escaped him. He felt like a coward.

"Jesus, Lenny, why didn't you come back," he said and then thought, *Why did you leave me alone?*

7

Todd Sackman, aka Sack, was dreaming about his third ex-wife. In his dream she was running up his credit card, something she had done, while wearing an extremely sexy piece of lingerie, something she had never done. Sack wasn't sure what to focus on. The fact that she was spending all his money online or that Theresa, devoid of any sexual drive, was finally doing something that turned him on.

She was seated at a computer desk wearing a black teddy, legs spread, telephone in hand, making purchases. "Yes, I'd like to buy the custom bedspread you have posted online." She was wearing a headset like a telephone operator too. She looked up at him. "Like what you see, Todd? Does it make you hard? Wake up. Time to get up! The road is opening."

Thumping.

"Huh?"

He turned, opened his eyes.

"Shit." He was in his sleeper.

More thumping.

He popped the vent on the sleeper, and cold air rushed into the bunk.

"What do you want? I was sleeping, yuh know."

"The road to Acadia will be open in an hour. If you want to get some breakfast before you go, you best get up now," said the man who had banged on his bunk.

"Yeah, yeah, okay," Sack said, but the man was gone, banging on another truck sleeper and waking another Acadia driver. Sack got up, feet dangling off the bed. He thought about Theresa, how she always seemed too tired to have sex. Maybe that dream meant things had changed. Maybe he'd give her a call, see what she was up to.

He lit a cigarette, pulled on his socks, and got dressed for breakfast.

8

Acadia Mine
06:30 Hours

They came for Bruce at 6:15 am.

The door opened, and one of the smaller skentophyte stepped into the room with him, blocking any chance of escape. His plans of revolt extinguished only a minute later when the creature spat the parasitic venom into his eyes. The embryonic worms corkscrewed in, immediately plugging into his optic nerves, and then their tails flared. Bruce's eyes became milky, like poached eggs, then hardboiled, and before long the flesh cooked off and became ashen. He had joined their collective.

His thoughts were now mired in the task at hand. There was much to do. Inside his head, a thousand whispers spoke with the same obsessive angst.

Harvest time! Harvest time! So much to do!

It was time to take all nonessentials back through the gate.

Time to harvest!

And Bruce understood this was their main objective. To rape and pillage the land for every bone that could be collected. Today they would strike out across the open tundra. Approximately 20 kilometers to the north, a herd of caribou, more than 400 strong, was waiting to be harvested.

Harvest yes. Skent! Harvest!

But there was much more to do. With the road now open, *more humans would be coming*, more humans with vehicles. More humans to harvest. Skent! We are Skentophyte! It was time to take out the second outpost.

Yes! Time to take Corbett Lake.

***

Chapter 26—Change of Plans

1

MEANOOK MINE
12:09 PM

Sleep had fallen upon him like a heavy blanket. First covering Marty, dissolving his thoughts and sending him headlong into an empty dreamless chasm. He was coming back to life now, listening to the steady purr of the engine, feeling small beads of sweat on the back of his neck from the heater. The curtains that separated the bunk from the cab kept most of the daylight at bay, but a thin, hard line of light cut through the darkness, stabbing into the upper wall of the sleeper.

Today I might have to kill a man, he thought and countered aloud, "Or be killed."

He sat upright, rubbed his eyes, and wiped away a bit of drool that had run from his mouth and across his cheek while sleeping. His face felt like sandpaper. Prickly hairs scratched the back of his hand. He wiped the moisture from his hand absently on the sleeping bag, then stood up and pulled the curtain apart.

"Shit." He squinted against the blinding daylight. His eyes slowly adjusted, pupils expanding with guarded clumsiness against the stabbing light. Reaching onto the dash, he snatched up his sunglasses and once on, that made things a little easier. As his eyes attuned, he took in his surroundings. The windshield held a thin layer of white powder, so thin he could still see the two-foot drift resting on the hood. He turned on the wipers and in one sweep, they brushed away the veil of snow, revealing a sky that was in fact blue. The storm had passed. He was surrounded by trucks, swallowed up in high drifts; carved into them by unseen fingers were shadows of aquamarine. The wind was still up, sculpting and reshaping the drifts, a northern god tending to unfinished business. On his right and left were trucks and to his front, Garney's Western Star. Behind him, Merv and Spence. He was boxed in with nowhere to go.

He pushed down on the window button and it whined before breaking free and falling sluggishly. Cool air whipped in, bringing with it tiny shards of snow that beat against his face and arm. The sounds of rumbling diesel engines now uninsulated was clear and crisp. He reached out and dusted the snow off his mirror.

Ahead, Garney's door swung open and out he climbed, wearing track pants and parka unzipped to the waist. He took a surveying glance and spotted Marty, so he stomped through the drift like a Yeti, his arm coming up in a half salute greeting. He was smiling as he came, and this raised Marty's spirits a little.

"Morning, Marty."

"Hey, Garney. I think it's more like afternoon."

"Yep, uh huh. Sure is, my brother. Feeling kind of hungry, gotta feed the machine, if you know what I mean."

Marty did; in spite of everything, he was hungry. "Me too."

From behind, Merv was lumbering through the snow as well. "Forgot my snowshoes. You order this shit, Big Garney?"

Garney cocked an eyebrow. "Merv, good morning, my brother. Yes sir. Old Man Winter and I are pretty tight. Is Spence up yet?" Garney had already spotted Spence walking up, but was baiting Merv into one of his usual smart-ass comments. Merv gladly took the bait.

"He'll be here in a minute, when he's done polishing his boots or whatever it is old grunts do in their down time."

"I heard that," Spence barked.

"Oh, look, here comes the pogo stick now," Merv said.

"Someone is looking at being buried in a snowbank."

Garney guffawed and Marty joined him.

Merv stuck a cigarette into his mouth and lit it. "Well, I'd say the storm has passed. I wonder what the damage is."

"Word on the radio is they'll be digging out all day long, my brothers. We can grab a bite to eat and a shower, I'm guessing we are stuck until tomorrow at least."

"Shit, didn't even get one trip in and we're marooned already. This usually doesn't happen until halfway through the season." Spence was lighting up now and offering a smoke. He tugged off his mitt and grabbed one from the pack.

"Well, could be this is it then. One big blow and clean running for the rest of the season."

"Wishful thinking, Merv, Old Man Winter isn't done with us."

Merv looked up at Marty and winked. Marty had no idea why, but he smiled and nodded back.

"Could be worse, my brothers."

"True," both Merv and Spence said.

Marty thought it could be as well. If anything, this was delaying the inevitable. Somewhere down the line, he'd be meeting up with Crane. What happened then was a definite unknown. Crane could pull out a gun and kill him on the spot and take the diamonds or send him on his way. Either way, he was headed into an ambush. The storm had, at the very least, bought him some time.

But what about Maggie, how much time does she have with that psycho brooding down there? The thought stole the smile from his face, wrenching his cheeks down into a frown. Gordon would wait. Either until Crane called and said he had the package or until Marty arrived with it in hand.

He hoped he was right.

"Let's get something to eat and find out what's happening, my brothers."

Marty looked down on the gaggle of men. "I'll be there in a minute."

"Sounds good, we'll save you a seat." Merv flicked the cherry off his smoke and stuffed the butt into his pocket. Spence took another puff and followed suit. "Lead on, Big Garn."

"See you inside," Marty assured and rolled up his window.

They cut to the left of the truck parked on Marty's driver's side and were gone. He waited, rolled the window back down again, and looked around. It looked safe enough, so he got his boots and parka on.

When he climbed from the truck, he heard Crane's voice in the back of his head.

"The place has more cameras than a Las Vegas Casino."

He took another paranoid glance around. He couldn't see anything, no light standards, no rooftops with cameras affixed. There was no way anyone could see down the corridor that ran between the truck and trailers. He stumbled through the snow. Kristy had put it in the front compartment. He made it to the first box and took another obsessed glance around.

Come on, let's get this over with!

He opened the box and inventoried the contents. There was a dull gray spill bucket, alongside that, hardened jugs of oil and antifreeze. Behind that and to the right was the package. Not so much a package really, but a large thermos. The kind most truckers carried. He reached in to get it, then nervously looked around again. In his head, he imagined touching the thermos and having security suddenly swoop in and arrest him. But such a thought was ridiculous. No one could see him. Just the same, he grabbed onto a jug of oil and pulled it out. The contents inside the jug was hard like clay.

"Just getting some oil to put in my cab so I can warm it up," he said aloud.

And let's not forget this thermos of stolen diamonds.

He snatched up the thermos and put it under his arm, purposely obscuring it with the oil jug. His chest tightened with each step, his lungs constricting until he found himself back at the driver door. He scanned around again. No one there. He opened the rig door and placed both items on the floor without climbing back in, then he closed the door. He turned to go, then stopped and decided that it wasn't good enough, so he reopened the door and climbed up onto the step. Reaching in, he grabbed the steel thermos and flung it into the bunk. It thumped on the carpet. He doubted anyone would be out and about burglarizing trucks for thermos's, but that was all the leverage he had. Satisfied, he stepped off and slammed the door.

2

Maggie was in her room when she heard Angel screaming frantically. She had no idea what was happening, hadn't even recognized the screaming until it registered that the only other female besides herself was Angel. At first, she didn't want to move. Why the hell should she? Whatever Angel was screaming about didn't concern her. She had enough to worry about after the blow-up that happened between Marty and Shamus. Even as Donald led her back to the room, she heard him yelling into the phone, making threats, and in a far off distant echo to that she could hear Marty's barely distinguishable voice snapping across the line in short sharp retorts.

He's coming for me, she thought. Donald gently tugged at her arm.

She didn't know if she would be alive when he got here, but she loved him just the same. She felt a weight lift from her shoulders when she heard him. He wasn't going to stop. Not her Marty, he was coming hell or high water and Shamus, for all the terror he instilled, had better worry.

"It's best you stay in here, Maggie," Donald said and gently pushed her into her room. She stood there staring back at him. His eyes said, "It isn't safe for you to stay out here. Not now, not when Gordon is like this." She wanted to ask if it was safe for anyone, but the door closed before she could muster the nerve.

Now she cowered behind that same door, listening to the muffled cries of desperation coming from Angel and she could only guess why. Was he raping her? Had he finally crossed that line and taken what he wanted? Maggie felt a pang of guilt. Although she had no idea why. This was the woman who first befriended, then drugged, then kidnapped her. She, along with her asshole husband, had put her life in peril. Why should she care what happened to her? Would Angel come to her rescue if she were on the other side of the door screaming frantically? No, of course not.

So, why should I give a shit? Why!

She knew the answer and it wasn't a high moral obligatory answer like she was better than them and held herself to a higher standard. She was, of course, but she didn't see herself rushing into any burning buildings to save anyone. Especially the likes of Angel Turcotte, kidnapper, bully, and maybe even killer. What made Maggie grab that doorknob was a question.

What if, after he's done with her, he comes for me?

The doorknob turned easily in her grasp, but she found it harder to pull open the door with Donald's previous warning ringing inside her head. "It's best you stay here, Maggie."

"It's best you fuck off," she whispered and pulled the door open.

"Stop it! Gordon, stop it please!" Angel's voice, now crisp and shrill—full of terror—pleading.

"I'm tired of talking," Shamus snapped.

Then there was a distinctive crack of flesh being smacked.

Maggie stepped through the doorway.

"Please, no more!"

Another crack.

She moved through this surreal state in someone else's consciousness, watching in horror as she crossed the hall into the main living area. She saw Angel, heard her cries, but what was happening at first didn't make any sense. Donald was standing back, farther than Angel, and he looked both confused and afraid. What was happening didn't quite sink in at first. She could see Gordon's back, his hand cocking upward as if on some imaginary spring. Then it came down and there was another audible crack. Followed by...

"Stop it, Gordon, you're really hurting him."

Hanging off the end of Gordon's left arm—his shirt bunched up in his fist—the rag doll that was Scott Turcotte. He was barely conscious, hanging from the Irish gangster's grasp drunkenly, his face strawberry red, splotched with purple marks.

Then there was another crack and Angel screamed again.

He was slapping him with an open hand.

Maggie was right behind Gordon now. Staring at the dark sweat stain between his shoulder blades, seeing the spastic shake of a man who was overdosing on adrenaline. She knew that this beating was for nothing, other than the fact that he, Shamus, needed someone to take his frustration out on.

Frustration with who? Marty, of course.

He cocked his hand back again and stood there, contemplating whether to strike.

"Please stop," Maggie heard herself say, but really couldn't believe she had.

And the cocked arm hung there, stiff and hard, every muscle cord filled to capacity with the blood of this maniac. Maggie was sure that if she were to walk over and hang off that arm, she could swing from it like a child on a tree branch. Shamus's head twisted slightly, his eyes turning in their sockets, straining to see her. Angel was only a few feet away. And she was crying. Donald stood a safe distance back. How could they not have intervened? Cowards, both of them. Maggie would never have watched Marty take a beating like this, she would have jumped on his back, hitting him—biting—whatever it took, no matter how futile. She opened her mouth and again, she said, "Please, Gordon, don't hit him anymore."

This was answered with a succession of short, abrupt inhalations and exhalations, but he said nothing.

His head turned back toward Donald, who was staring at the badly bruised Scott, not wanting to engage the fury that had brought about this mess. But when he felt Gordon's eyes upon him, he brought them up. "Come and get this little bug before I finish what I started."

Donald hesitated, then moved in and took Scott underneath the armpits. Gordon held on a second longer, then let go. Angel moved in to help. Gordon turned around and gave Maggie his full attention.

3

Portage 33
12 Kilometers South of Acadia Mine

Phil Crane was parked well out of the way on the north side of the portage, listening to the banter between the northbound drivers and thinking about the call he'd gotten from Shamus that morning on the sat phone.

"Things have changed, he'll be coming all the way."

"Okay, any reason why?"

"Not that I can discuss over the phone. Just tell him where to go when you see him. Everything else is the same. I'll take care of the other business personally." Gordon sounded angry, or at least off of one of his tantrums, but Crane knew better than to press him; never mind that this was a satellite phone and anyone could be listening. Nope, no point in poking the bear.

"Okay, so you want me to give him directions?"

"Yeah, don't fuck this up, Phil. I'm not in the mood for any more deviations. Meet him, give him directions, then send him on his way."

"Okay, Gordon."

"Alright, what's the deal up there, anyway? You guys in the middle of a big fucking snowstorm or what?"

"It's over, just digging out. The roads from the north are blown in, they're saying it's going to take all day. Maybe even until tomorrow."

"Perfect. Well, just get what I said done and once he's on his way, give me a call with an ETA."

"Okay. Anything else?"

"Nah, that's it. You know the drill."

The banter from the northbound truckers elevated and rather than telling them to knock it off, Crane turned the vhf radio down a bit and thought about this new change. What the hell was he up to? He thought it might be a double cross. Maybe they were cutting him out.

Who? Croft and Gordon? He laughed. But already knew what was happening.

"Gordon strikes again." He shook his head. "Couldn't keep your mouth shut, you stupid fucking mick, could you? Had to rub his nose in it, tell him that you got his wife." Yeah, that had to be it. Everything had to be a show. Now Croft was coming south with a package and quite possibly a death wish.

Well done, Gordon.

"Four north on 33," came the call on the radio.

Crane reached down, turned up the dial, and grabbed his handset. "Northbound, this is security, you have a copy?"

"Go ahead, security."

"Okay, just a heads up. I'm on the north side of the portage. Take it easy coming across, the graders have only done a single pass, so there isn't a lot of wiggle room between snowbanks. The road into Acadia is open, or so I am told, but I'm letting you know that folks are watching, so keep your speed within the limits. Do we understand each other?"

"Okay, security. We appreciate the heads up. Is there anything else we need to know?" The driver he was talking to was Sack, not that that would mean anything to Crane.

"Nope, I guess you should keep your eyes out for snow clearing equipment in the road, but beyond that just keep your spacing, pay attention to the posted limits, and you should have no problems."

"Okay, security. Thanks. Here we come."

The first truck in the convoy was in sight. A metallic black International Lonestar—the massive grill winked in the sunlight. It was an odd-looking rig, like an old retro fire truck from the 30's. It was an ugly thing, like that abortion the PT Cruiser, but if given enough time, it might grow on you. The wagon it was pulling was a sorry-looking piece of kit, a rusted out 53-foot tandem trailer that barely looked fit for the road. If Crane had still been a cop, he would have pulled that puppy over for an inspection in a heartbeat. "Nice trailer, Driver."

"Thanks, Security."

"You must be proud pulling that thing in your shiny new truck."

"If you talk nice to me, I'll sell it to you for a nickel."

"That's okay."

The first truck pushed past, kicking up a cloud of fresh powder, dusting Crane's pickup and growling as it did. He flipped the windshield wipers on and the second vehicle came around the bend. This one was a flatbed loaded down with super sacks. On the sides of the sacks were the letters ANFO and Crane immediately recognized it. It was prilled ammonium nitrate. The drivers just called it prill. Crane had never heard it called that, but he remembered the ANFO label. This was the stuff they used to do controlled detonations at the mines. Something Crane had learned in a discussion with Pringle. But he remembered what Ammonium Nitrate was because when he was a cop, there was a real buzz about it after an

American terrorist named Timothy McVeigh used it in the Oklahoma City bombing. Crane thought that asshole got off way too easy with the needle. Killing all those kids in that daycare. Scumbag asshole deserved to be kicked to death. The second big truck pushed by, dusting him again. Then the third and the fourth.

"Have a good day, security," said the last driver, and they were gone.

4

Chase stayed to the wood line, close enough to see the road, but far enough away to duck down. He was counting his paces again, using the road as a marker. By his estimation he had walked almost nine kilometers, but he wasn't 100% on that. He was hoping that he'd find a vehicle running somewhere along the line, but as of yet, nothing. Surprisingly, he wasn't in as bad a shape as he'd thought. Before leaving the shelter, he wrapped his mukluks up in rags to give a bit more insulation against the cold. It made walking awkward, but he adjusted and some of the wrapping had already fallen away.

Just have to keep moving. Keep the blood circulating, keep my body temperature warm.

The road pitched in and out of sight, almost 600 meters away. Its banks barely visible at times. He would have stayed right beside it until he decided that cutting a diagonal between the road leading into Acadia and the main ice road would shorten his travel time. Something in the back of his mind warned that he shouldn't abandon the road. That his chance of becoming lost would be greatly increased with no landmark, but then he thought about what happened to Lenny. He wanted to be as far away from the road into Acadia as he could possibly get. If that meant running the risk of getting lost, he was willing to take it.

In his pockets, weighted down by the Molotov cocktails, glass clinked as fuel sloshed back and forth in the beer bottles. In his right mitt, the lighter, between the outer mitt and a glove liner, was pressed against his palm. If those things came after him, they wouldn't be getting him as easily as they had Lenny. He'd barbeque a few of the bastards and anyone else, human or otherwise, that tried to stop him. It was obvious that no one at the Acadia Mine could be trusted. Those things had infected them some way. That must have been what was wrong with Allison. This gave him a thought.

He reached inside his parka and pulled out the Bushmasters. He'd forgotten all about them, even during the Lenny incident. He removed his left mitt and put it under his arm, then brought the Bushmasters up and scanned the landscape for the edge of the road. At first he didn't see anything, just white, then he adjusted the focus. He'd wandered a little farther away than he originally thought. The road was at least a kilometer away. Then he heard something. A far off rumble of diesel engines. He crouched down and pulled back his hood, trying to pin the direction of the sound.

"South," he said. "Shit, they're coming from the south!" He brought the Bushmasters up, tracing the landscape for them. The vehicles were still quite a distance off, but he was sure now, they were definitely coming north. "Where are you?" Then he saw them, distant specks on a broad canvas, bobbing up and down along the bank that shouldered the main ice road. And now he knew where the actual road was again. He lowered the Bushmasters and focused on the specks. They were at least a click away, maybe even two. He tucked the mini binoculars away and looked behind him. He'd never make it to the main road in time, maybe if he backtracked to the road.

No fucking way! That's how Lenny bought it!

"Fuck it!" Chase pulled up his hood and began bounding toward the main road. It was a long shot, but if he got there, he'd be able to wave them down and stop them. His feet thumped against the tundra and he could already feel the sweat beginning to build. Determined, he pushed harder. If he didn't make it, he'd still be farther south.

And them? The poor bastards in those rigs. What if you can't make it to them in time?

He ignored the voice and continued. The snow below his feet deepened, but he pressed on. The dots on the landscape were growing and taking shape.

It was a convoy. He picked up his pace.

5

Gordon Shamus held her in his gaze. Behind him, Angel and Donald helped Scott over to the couch and set him down. Maggie waited for him to say something, some explanation as to why he would slap around one of his own. He was catching his breath, his eyes twirling madly. She looked into this maniac's eyes and thought, *He got his kicks this way, beating people senseless, maybe even to death.*

Then it occurred to her.

Is it my turn now?

"I need a smoke," he grunted and pushed past her, plucking his coat off the easy chair.

Angel looked up from her husband, her mascara runny, intermingled with tears. Then she turned back to her husband. "It's okay, sweetheart."

The door below opened, then slammed shut.

"I'll grab a cold cloth." Donald stood up.

Maggie walked softly toward the front window and looked out. Below, Shamus was stomping through the snow and reaching into his overcoat pocket. She didn't say anything at first, thought of her first interaction with Angel after Gordon had touched her inappropriately. That was a polite way of putting it, she supposed. Inappropriately really meant foreplay for sexual assault! But that didn't change anything for Angel.

So why should this?

Because this was Scott. This was someone she loved.

Really? Notice how she jumped on his back and tried to defend her husband.

Donald returned, a cold face cloth in his hand. "What caused this? What did Scott say to him?"

"I don't know. I was in the other room when he started. Whatever it was is bullshit!"

"Shut up, Angela. You want to end up getting knocked around?" Donald warned.

"He's outside smoking," Maggie said.

They both gazed up at her.

"I asked him if there was any word on the storm," Scott mumbled.

"That fucking asshole. He's fucking nuts!"

"Shut your mouth, Angela." Donald sounded worried.

"He's taking out his frustrations on your husband because he can't touch mine right now," Maggie said, never taking her eyes off Shamus.

"Maggie, be quiet," Donald warned.

"Or what? You'll tell Gordon? You think I don't know how this ends, Donald? My husband brings Gordon his precious diamonds and you three, I guess now two..."

"Shut your mouth, bitch," Angel spat.

" . . . take us out somewhere and dispose of us. I'm not stupid. The question is, how disposable are you three? I already know what my fate is. Do you?" Maggie turned from the window and walked across the room with intention of going to the kitchen. Donald stood up and followed her, catching her arm just below the elbow.

"Listen to me. This divide and conquer shit… It ain't going to work. I'm not going to tell Gordon what you said, simply because I don't want to see you get that pretty face of yours bashed in, but you better check your mouth right here and now, lady, because no one here is going to stick their neck out for you. You're right about one thing. You're disposable and if you shoot off your mouth... I think the consequences go without saying. You'll be alone, Maggie. No one is going to save you, if you fire up Gordon Shamus. No one, not Angela, not even Scott."

"I'm already alone. I'll shut up. But that won't change your situation one bit." Maggie pulled her arm out of his grasp and turned for the kitchen. Donald reached out and grabbed her again. "Let go."

"Listen to me. You think this is bad. This is nothing compared to what he's capable of."

"Why are you telling me this?"

"Because the last thing I want to be doing is trying to figure out what to do with your battered body, just because you didn't have the sense to shut your yap." He really had no idea why he was bothering to tell her. She was right, everyone knew what the plan was, including Angela and Scott, so why was he patronizing this bitch? But Donald didn't think like that, he'd compartmentalized that other stuff, like the GPS sitting in his bag with the coordinates to the pre-dug grave out in the woods. The grave intended to hold the body of this woman and her husband. "I don't know what the plan is when this is done. You and your husband, for all his stupidity, could be walking out of here. But you go shooting your mouth off, I wouldn't count on it." He relaxed his grip and she pulled away.

Angel gently dabbed Scott's face with the damp cloth. His right eye was swelling up, as were his lips. It was amazing that Gordon had done all this damage with an open hand.

"All I did was ask about the storm," Scott mumbled again. "I didn't mean to provoke him, Angel."

She set the cloth down and stood up.

Donald was back at the window looking out on Shamus, who stood with his back to the house, small clouds of cigar smoke billowing up. He glanced over his shoulder. "Now what the fuck are you doing?" She stomped out of the room, past the kitchen and into the bedroom. "Angela?"

She lifted her suitcase and pulled out her Glock 17 pistol.

"The fucking bastard thinks he's going to beat up my man and get into my pants. Fuck that!" She racked the weapon's slide, chambering a round as she marched back out of the room. She passed Maggie, who stepped out of the way and started down the stairs.

"Angela, what the fuck are you doing?" Donald started after her.

She's going to blow the maniac away, Maggie thought hopefully.

"Stay out of it, Donald!" Angel marched purposefully, her finger already on the trigger.

"Are you insane? Stop, god damn it! This is suicide!" He was thumping down the stairs after her.

Maggie ran for the picture window. Shamus was turning around, heading back for the house.

She was at the door when she heard the hammer of his gun cock back. "I can't let you do this."

"He's a fucking lunatic."

"He's got connections, Angela. You kill him and there will be repercussions. Come on. I can't let you do this, Angela, don't make me. I'll shoot you where you stand. You know I fucking will."

She lowered the gun to her side and whispered, "What if she's right?"

"She's not."

"Yeah, maybe if it was your woman up there all banged up, you'd think differently."

"Angela, we don't have time for a debate. Put the gun away and get upstairs with your old man." He could see Shamus's silhouette approaching through the frosted glass. He released the hammer on his pistol and tucked it into the back of his pants. "Move!"

She hurried up the stairs, the gun still in her hand.

"Put that fucking piece away," he called as loud as he dared.

She was back upstairs in the living room. Maggie stood over her and Scott when the front door opened. "Help me get him into our room so I can lay him down." Maggie did as she was told and they helped Scott off of the couch.

Below, Shamus opened the door to find Donald standing there. "What?"

"We need to talk."

"Alright, then talk."

"Outside."

Shamus looked up the stairwell, then back at Donald. "Alright, you better get your coat on. It's fucking cold."

The two stepped outside at around the same time Angel and Maggie set Scott down on the bed. Scott's left ear was split open just above the lobe. There wasn't any blood, but the split was the hard cartilage of the inner ear. It might need a stitch, but wouldn't be getting one.

"Can you get him a glass of water?" Angel asked, fumbling for her purse.

"Yeah, okay," Maggie bolted for the kitchen. She fumbled a glass out of the rack and put it beneath the goose neck faucet and turned the tap.

"Hurry up," Angel called.

Maggie shut the tap off. The goddamned arrogance of these people. She walked back, with less purpose than she had come. When she got to the door, Angel had already shook a couple of pills out of the open bottle. Maggie wondered what it was. Oxy? Demerol?

"Come on, Maggie, bring the glass."

"Sure." She handed the glass over. "Not that it changes anything, right, Angela?"

Angel gave her an angry glance. "You don't get it, sweetheart." She placed the pills into Scott's mouth. "Take these, baby. They'll help you sleep and take the pain away." Scott opened his mouth; his eyes were closing up. He wasn't bloodied, but he still looked like Rocky Balboa. Angel poured some water into his mouth and there was a dry click as he swallowed. "Come on, lay back, baby."

"You're right, Angela. I don't get it."

She stood up and grabbed Maggie by the wrist and dragged her into the hall. In a low whisper she said, "He's connected. Shamus isn't just some nutty Irish prick, he's a real gangster and if he goes missing, there will be people who come knocking. People from Montreal, people from New Jersey, even Philly, he's their man in Hamilton. You get it now, sweetheart!"

"Seems that didn't matter a few minutes ago."

"Yeah, well cooler heads have prevailed."

"So, when he decides to come back and beat your husband to death because all he really wants is to get into your undies, will cooler heads prevail then?"

"That won't happen."

"Yeah, you did a great job of stopping him the first time around."

Angel grabbed Maggie by both shoulders. “Don’t sass me, you little bitch. I’m not in the mood!”

“Go ahead! Seems you’ve only got the guts to beat on the weaker of the species. If that had been my man in there, I’d have been all over him, biting, slapping, punching, you just stood there, like a fucking complet...”

The slap sent her head pivoting to the left, accompanied by a stinging buzz of cutting out across her face. Maggie brought her hand up to her cheek and scowled. “You should have shot him.”

“Shut your mouth, Maggie.” She lifted her hand.

“Hit me again, Angel, and I’ll tell him about the gun. That is, if Donald isn’t out there spilling it already.”

Angel dropped her hand, a look of horror dawning on her face.

Outside, Donald and Shamus were standing on the stoop. Shamus was waiting, reaching into his pocket, pulling out the remainder of the cigar he had been smirking. “Alright, Donald, why the fuck did you drag me back outside?”

Donald was trying to contain the anger he felt and searching for words that wouldn’t result in another blow up. “Do you trust me, Gordon?”

He didn’t. It wasn’t in his nature to trust, but he said. “Yeah, sure I trust you, Donald.”

“Do you trust my judgment?”

“Look, quit with the fucking preamble and get to the fucking point. And remember this, my man. You best go easy on the condescension because I’m not above kicking your ass.”

Donald sighed. “What the fuck? I’ve been nothing but loyal to you and you’re threatening to kick my ass. Come on, Gordon, for fuck’s sake.”

Shamus grinned. “Lighten up, Donald, I’m only kidding.”

Liar, Donald thought and said. “Why did you beat on Scott? We need him.”

“Ah, that little bug is an anchor. I need him like I need another hole in my dick.”

“We need Angela, you’re fucking with her when you knock her old man around. I know I’m probably out of line telling you this, but it was a mistake beating on Scott.”

“Out of line is an understatement.” Shamus laughed. “I’ve fucking killed guys for less, Donald.”

“So that must drive home how serious I think this is.”

The smile dropped away and Shamus narrowed his eyes. “Why are you telling me this?”

6

"Nooo, damn it! No! No! No! No!" Chase was down on his knees, beating his fists into the snow. "Jesus Christ almighty, why!" He'd missed the convoy, still 200 meters out, they'd driven by and kept right on going even after he reached the road, arms waving frantically in the air. They couldn't see him through the cloud of snow dust they kicked up. Now they were slipping away, headed for Acadia. He should have made his way back to the mine's inroad, where he would have caught them for sure.

He sat down on the ice, huffing and puffing, exhausted from the jaunt he'd made. The sweat on his back had moistened his inner layer of clothing and was now becoming cool. He closed his eyes. It would be so easy, just sit here and let the cold take him.

Yeah sure, I gave it the old team try. Why fight it.

"Fuck it." He leaned forward, rocking slightly.

Images flashed in his mind's eye. First Allison, then Lenny and then his son. He stiffened. "Gotta keep going," he said. *I can't just give up. I can still stop this. There will be northbound trucks, just gotta stay alive long enough to catch them.* He stood up, shook off the cold, and started walking south down the ice.

7

ACADIA MINE
13:00 Hours

"*The chamber has been readied,*" Bruce told Sal Godwin. *"They'll be taking the remainder across this afternoon."*

"*What about the inbound truckers, when do they arrive?"*

"*They should be here in approximately 45 minutes."*

The two of them were standing in the VP's office, behind each of them a Skentophyte. *I'm just a puppet now and these things hold the strings.* His mouth wasn't moving, communication between the two men passed telepathically and, as Bruce had learned from the dying Allison, out across the entire collective of Skentophyte. *"Herb Aronson is going to take a party of Skent out across the Tundra towards the Fish Camp, they're going to harvest a herd of caribou and bring them back."*

"That's a lot of bone," Sal sent back. Behind him, the Skentophyte escort clacked its teeth and let out a low whispery hiss that was a clear indication of pleasure.

"Yeah." Bruce could feel the worms twisting and squirming inside his eye sockets; the ash floated out with each twist of their tails. *What were they doing in there? Eating even further into the optic nerve?* The tissue and bone around his eye sockets felt like paper mache. The nerves had gone numb and he guessed that the tissue was pretty much dead. *Eventually my whole head will cook off, then they'll find another smuck to replace me.*

"Smuck? What is smuck?" The question rattled across the collective.

"Puppet, patsy, pawn," Sal responded.

"Yeah, what he said." Bruce added. Apparently, the Skentophyte didn't understand sarcasm and this made Bruce happy.

8

Portage 33
13:15 Hours

"Security, you got a copy?"

Crane reached down and lifted the mic. "Go for security."

"Yeah, we've got a spun-out tanker on the south side of 33. The road is blocked, we're going to need a grader here to unscrew this."

Crane sat up; he'd been dozing. He rubbed his eyes. "Okay, I'm on the other side of 33, I'll come down for a look and we'll see what we can do to sort it out. Is everyone okay? Nobody hurt?"

"Just a bruised ego. I'll get over it."

Crane laughed. "Okay, driver, sit tight. I'll be there in a minute."

"I'm not going anywhere, trust me."

He put the pickup and gear and started across the portage. A spin-out, well this ought to be interesting. He picked up the handset and got on the horn to Corbett Lake. "Corbett dispatch, be advised that I have a spin-out on the south side of Portage 33. I am en-route to assess, but the driver on the scene thinks he will need a tug to get up the hill."

"Copy that, I'll put a recovery on standby. Send the particulars when you get on scene."

"Copy." Crane was already halfway across the portage, driving a little too fast, but having fun all the same. "I'll get back to you." He was rather excited as he wheeled the pickup left and right, driving evasively.

When he arrived on the scene, he was greeted by an ugly spectacle. At the base of the hill leading onto the portage, a Super B was hung up, its pup twisted completely around in a jackknife and worse, the pup was almost touching the lead.

"Wow!" Crane muttered as he exited the pickup.

There were four drivers standing around. One of them smiled more than the rest. "And that is why you never back up when you spin out on a hill."

"Any fuel leaking?" Crane asked.

"No, I stopped before that could happen."

Crane examined the tankers; they were so close you could barely fit your hand between them. How the hell were they going to pull them apart without tearing a big gash in one of the two tankers? "Wait here," he said and ran back to the pickup. "Corbett, this is security on Portage 33, we have a tangled up Super B at the base of the portage. Hold all northbound convoys. The road is closed until we clear this."

"Copy that, security. I've got one more convoy coming your way. Northbound convoy south of 33, you have a copy?"

"We heard." The driver's voice was irritable. "We're just coming up to Portage 32, we'll sit tight until you clear the road."

"Thank you for your patience," Corbett dispatch said.

Crane laughed.

"Yeah, you're welcome."

"Corbett, I'm thinking we are going to need a grader and possibly a winch truck." Crane was getting out of his pickup again. He lit a smoke and joined the drivers. "Corbett is sending help. In the meantime, I'm going to need to get your names and winter road numbers."

"You writing me up?"

"No, but I have to have a report to give my boss, so let's get that out of the way."

The driver let out a sigh of relief. "Okay, let's get it over with then."

***

Chapter 27—Wolves

1

ACADIA MINE
14:30 Hours

"Four inbound at three." Sack was calling his kilometer markers as they closed in on Acadia. He and the other three drivers would be parting ways when they reached the mine. He would be heading for the main warehouse to unload the boxes of lubricants, while the flatbed driver was heading over to a drop yard and the two tanker drivers would be on their way to the tank farm. He called in the winter road numbers and told the radio operator the make-up of his group.

"Sounds good, I'll have escorts sent out to meet you," Rally Martins told him.

"God, that women stirs something in me," Sack said to no one but himself. Then over the radio: "Thank you, Rally. Four inbound at kilometer 2." They were clipping along at 60 kilometers an hour. The road had been cleaned up quite well, as opposed to the main ice road.

"It's our pleasure. Welcome to Acadia, gentlemen."

The road came to a T-Junction at the Telegraph Rd. There, Sack and the flatbed driver would be turning right to head for the warehouse, and the Tanker Yankers would be turning left toward the tank farm. The two tanker drivers weren't Chinook drivers; they worked for the competition. An outfit called: **Valley Run Bulk.** These guys were the competition and Sack looked upon them with a suspicious eye when his convoy was married up with theirs earlier that morning. The two freight haulers he originally had in his chock had opted to sleep in.

Good riddance, he thought. They had been nothing but mouthpieces anyway. Talking about bumping it up on Ladd 1. *Fucking newbies.* During the three-hour trip from Corbett Lake to Acadia, Sack had warmed up to the two tanker drivers. Stu and Kyle were their names. They weren't bad fellows, a hell of a lot more experienced than the twits he had been running with. Both of them were Easterners, economic refugees from Nova Scotia. There were a lot of Nova Scotians up here and Newfoundlanders as well. There was lots of down east jargon being thrown around. Sayings like: "Where's yuh too" and "Jayzus buy" from the Newfoundlanders. Which really meant: "Where are you?" and "Jesus Boy." The Nova Scotia riders didn't have the same thick accents, their tongue a little more refined to the main land. Tainted, a Newfoundlander might say. But then most Nova Scotians thought Newfies were dumber than the rock they lived on. At least that is what Sack had heard time and again.

"Well boys, this is where we part ways. Maybe we'll catch you on the way out." Sack was at the T-Junction. Here come our escorts right now. Beating up the Telegraph Road from opposite directions came two pick-ups with flashing Amber lights. The one coming for the tankers was still at least a kilometer out.

"Nice running with you, Sack," Kyle said. "And you too, Rory. Maybe next time you'll let us get a word in edgewise."

"Yeah, thanks." Rory was the flatbed driver behind Sack. He'd hardly spoke a word since they left Corbett Lake.

"Van driver, you got a copy," thc cscort approaching from the right interrupted.

"Go ahead."

"I'm going to pull a U-turn, follow me in, and maintain a safe distance. When we get to the warehouse, there will be a couple guides there to back you in." Before Sack could answer: "Flatbed driver, you got a copy?"

"Go ahead," Rory said.

"You follow along and... Skent... When I get your partner sorted out, we will carry on to the drop yard."

There was a pause, then Rory said, "Copy, what was that other thing you said?"

"What?"

Another pause, and then: "Never mind."

The pickup was into its U-turn. Sack lit up his beacons and four-way flashers. "Light 'em up, Rory."

"Copy." Rory turned his flashers and beacons on.

"Okay, driver, let's skent," the escort called.

Sack shook his head and chuckled. "Must be a Cape Bretoner," he mumbled. Cape Bretoners, according to Kyle and Stu, were Newfies with their heads kicked in. He released the clutch and turned right as the pickup took over calling the road markers. For this last bit of trip, he was only along for the ride.

Kyle and Stu pulled up to the T-Junction.

"Lead tanker driver, this is your escort. Switch your VHF over to Ladd 2."

Then they were gone from the airwaves.

2

Meanook Mine
14:45 Hours

The pulse of hot water beat down upon his neck and shoulders, numbing the skin. Eyes closed, Marty leaned forward, planting his hands against the cubicle wall, enjoying the heat and solitude. His hair was matted against his head, the prickly beard had run its course in itch and now was starting to fill in. He thought about shaving it off, but really didn't have the energy. He guessed he'd probably cut the shit out of himself if he attempted to put a razor on his skin.

During this, he deliberated that his tire thumper—a ball peen hammer normally kept in the jockey box—should be relocated into the cab. He'd need easy access to it, just in case the situation with Crane went sour. Using a hammer against a gun was a sucker bet for sure, but it was better than nothing.

And what about the others? What if they saw? How would he deal with that? If it came to that, all bets were off. He wouldn't worry about explaining himself, he'd make a dash south and get to her. If he had to call the cops he would, but he wasn't going to wait for them to kill her.

South where? He still wasn't even sure where Maggie was.

The fucker gives me an address or I'll beat his bald head to a pulp. This thought was accompanied by seething rage—tightening his muscles, increasing his heart rate. He didn't realize that he was gritting his teeth together hard. Later on, he would feel the soreness in his cheeks.

The door to the shower room opened.

"Marty, my brother, you in here?"

"Yeah, I'll be out in a minute. Weren't you going to use the shower down by the gymnasium?"

"I'm all showered up, my brother. I just got word. They've punched through. Single lane only, but they're going to be booting us south."

"Are you serious? What happened to being stranded for a couple days?"

"They punched through, my brother. They want everyone in the Cafeteria in 30 minutes. So towel off and hop to it, my brother."

Marty turned around and shut off the tap." His mind was scrambling now. This had happened a lot quicker than he'd thought it would. *Three hours. He only had three hours.*

3

THE FISH CAMP

Billy was drinking coffee that had been brewed up by Vincent on the Coleman stove they kept at the back of the flooding truck. They were digging out his pickup as Lyle Lovett sang, "The Girl with the Holiday Smile."

"Looks like we got off easy," Axe mused. "They're pushing hard from Meanook."

"Well, I probably lost my kills, I'm going to head south and see if there's anything worth salvaging." Billy took another sip of coffee; it was strong and bitter, but it was hot.

"Well, there's not much you can do if that's the case. Who knows, maybe it won't be as bad as you think. They sure overestimated the damage from the storm."

"True. Where you going from here?"

"We'll be working this piece of road all afternoon. At least without the traffic, the flooding will have a chance to set."

The plow was tugging gently at Billy's pickup. Normally when they hauled a big truck out of the snow, they used the kinetic snap of a hard tug, but in the case of a pickup, the plow would rip it to pieces before they unstuck it. Vincent was behind the wheel of the pickup. He'd insisted Billy get a hot drink while they took care of business. He liked Vincent—his black sense of humor, even the way he looked. He was the stereotypical native, long hair that turned and twisted in the wind, weathered face and a smile that was infectious to others. And as if Vincent had heard that thought, he peered out the driver window and grinned a big toothy smile. "Come on, Lonny, we ain't got all day!"

Lonny was behind the wheel of the plow truck and even if he could hear Vincent barking orders, which he couldn't, he would have ignored them. He wasn't about to pull the front end off Billy's pickup. He might do that to a tourist, but not Billy Jack. No way.

The pickup pulled free, Lonny throttled down, and then rolled forward, removing the tension from the big rope. He opened the door to the plow and climbed down. "You still hunting, Billy?"

"Yeah, why?"

"There a big herd up over the next hill. At least 300 head. Easy pickings."

Billy cocked his head right. "Where?"

Lonny pointed to the West. "There about a click out. You won't be able to see them from here, that mound is in the way. But if we got up on the flood truck."

Billy scrambled up the ladder on the flood truck and Axe joined him. Lonny, his work finished, stayed down below and poured himself a cup of coffee.

"Well, there you go. You could regain any losses in pretty short order."

"Yeah. I'll boogie back south and check my camp, if the kills aren't salvageable I might just come back this way with the snowmobile."

4

The wolf pack was 13 strong, the Alpha a big grey in the lead. Bellies full of fresh meat—fur lightly matted with blood—they were now moving northwest, following the scent of caribou. They'd been stalking the herd when they came upon the cleaned hanging carcasses. The snow drifts made it easy to pull down the kills and they ate this gift with frenzied delight. The ravens were picking over the mangled carcasses with equal delight.

The Alpha was watching the beast riding on its tracks across the open tundra. The big grey could hear the click clack of the track pads beating against the road wheels, could in fact smell the man inside its belly, possessing it to roll on. The rest of the pack was further back, moving along in a formation they'd used regularly while stalking prey. Three hundred meters to the left, another wolf set upon the mound, watching the same beast, and the pack took up positions, waiting for the Alpha to direct them.

The Alpha was slow and deliberate, calculating what the steel beast was going to do. The scent was overpowering. The steel beasts usually didn't come out by themselves, they came in groups, and they didn't always look the same. Unlike the caribou, the steel beasts varied in size and shape, but they shared a similarity. All of the steel beasts carried a man in their belly. It watched as the beast disappeared behind a low hill, but the scent, along with the noise, was still there and it was now moving in their direction. The big wolf sniffed the air, taking the scent into its nasal cavities, dissecting and processing it. It was a mixture of many aromas: there was the fragrance of its blood, sweat from the man, the poison breath that belched from the beast's back, and there was something else. Something it had never smelled before.

The steel beast crested the hill and came to a stop. Its side opened and out stepped the man. The wolf did not move. The man that lived inside the beast could see it, but they were still very far away. The Alpha watched as the man brought his arms up, holding something to his eyes. It was definitely watching him. It sniffed the air, processing intermingling smells and again that other scent, the one it had never known, rose up like a warning.

There was something else close by. It listened, a clacking, pattering sound.

Another herd? Not caribou. This smelled nothing like the caribou.

It turned each ear independently, listening for the herd while watching the beast and the man. There was another sound. Chattering teeth. Thumping of feet. Many feet. A herd of gallops that were coming from all directions. The Alpha could feel the unease in the air and turned to the scout to its left.

Danger! Something was coming! Something bad! Fear!

The Skentophyte moved in rank and file across the tundra until Herb spotted the wolf watching him from across the basin below the knoll where he'd parked the Snow Cat. He was ahead of them by about a kilometer. They moved out here on the tundra with great ease, sprinting on all fours and he could see that their outer shells changed with the snow, turning opaque. Perfect camouflage to their surroundings. When he spotted the lone wolf on the hill, his thought went out to the Skent.

His thought was: *There's a scout, they must be tracking the same herd.*

In response: Scout. Predator change formation.

Of course, Herb already knew what they were doing. He could see the advancing Skent breaking ranks and shooting in single file both east and west. They were encircling the wolves, cutting their escape. As he brought the binoculars up to engage the wolf, he saw through the collective eye that they had already surrounded them. As he and the wolf examined each other, they were tightening the circle. The wolf must have sensed them because it was looking around as if it had heard something.

"Too late to run," Herb said aloud.

Skentophyte came from all directions.

5

"Good afternoon, folks, my name is Roger Darby, I am the operations man here at Meanook." He was standing in front of approximately 40 drivers seated in the cafeteria. "I have some encouraging news regarding the storm and its effect on the road. If you haven't already heard, the Lupania Road crews have broken through and we will be able to get you folks headed south very shortly."

This was met with minor applause.

"Dispatch is already going over the lists of who came first, so you will be leaving in the order with which you arrived. It is my understanding that they are still digging out on the south half, but should have it cleaned up by the time you folks get to Corbett Lake."

Spence shook his head and snickered. "Guess we haven't got much to worry about."

"Guess not," Merv agreed. They had come in dead last, which meant they would be the last chock to leave.

Garney raised his hand. "What kind of interval between convoys, Roger?"

"We are going to separate you by 30 minutes. From what I understand, the road south isn't very wide and the hammer lanes are closed. So you'll be running loaded speed."

This was met with groans.

Empty trucks normally ran a separate lane south called the "hammer lane," which allowed for double the speed. The speed limit in a hammer lane was 60 km per hour, turning a southbound trip to YK into an 11-hour jaunt instead of 18. Southbound trucks still had to cross trouble lakes and pressure ridges with the same caution and speed as the northern loaded trucks, but the run south was much faster. Now with the hammer lane closed, they'd be reduced to an 18-hour run.

"I know, I know, don't shoot the messenger," Darby said, a gentle smile still fixed to his face.

Laughter.

Spence was counting the drivers, calculating the numbers in his head. *Forty two drivers, divided by four is ten, divided by two.* He tapped Marty on the arm. "We've got about four-and-a-half hours."

Darby wrapped up his briefing and the drivers dispersed, leaving the cafeteria empty. In the parking area, a plow and front end loader were already cleaning the snow away from the parked rigs. Marty made his way back to his own truck and climbed in. Once inside, he kicked off his boots and sat in the bunk. At his feet the thermos rested against the tip of his big toe. He stared down at it morosely. He was going to pick it up, look inside, that was for sure, but for now, he just bumped it with his big toe. He was trying to think of what he should do. What if Crane pulled a gun? The great thing about schemes such as this was that nothing ever went according to plan. He reached down and picked up the thermos.

He supposed that he could empty the thermos of its contents and give Crane the empty if it came to that. That might buy him enough time to get directions to where they were holding Maggie. He unscrewed the lid and looked inside. A wad of brown cloth was stuffed into the top of the thermos. He poked his index finger inside and snagged the cloth with his fingernail, pulling it out. Carefully, he tipped the thermos onto his sleeping bag and the uncut diamonds spilled out.

"That's it," he said. The contents of the thermos was full, but the diamonds themselves held little appeal. He hadn't expected them to look like those you'd find on a ring, but these precious stones could easily be mistaken for pieces of quartz or glass. He picked up one of the stones and held it in his hand. What was this haul worth? A million? Two million? How many people were behind this operation? It didn't make any sense to have so many people lined up for such a small take.

6

The wolves—now infected—led the Skent north, to the place where the caribou huddled. They too could hear thousands of collective whispers, but their understanding was less so than the human who had helped to trap them. He was in the belly of the mechanical beast again, following along as they ran across the open tundra. Eyes taken by venom, they now saw as the man, but their vision was less so, carrying out across the collective in reds, blues, and blacks. The Skentophyte, their new masters, adjusted to this, as they had done with many creatures before them. While their optic nerves carried less clarity, their hearing and sense of smell was far superior. And they held on to less independent thought, making them easier to control. Their scent had increased tenfold, going out across the collective wire feeding into the minds of all who were plugged in within proximity. Herb Aronson felt the animals' senses and could smell the urine and matted fur, breath that was pungent and dirty.

Closing in, the deposed alpha of the group thought and his pack immediately acknowledged, repositioning and moving in formation. The Skentophyte also repositioned out into an enveloping, forward V. When the time came they would spread out as the wolves herded the creatures the human called caribou into the advancing vortex.

Herb Aronson steered the snow cat up onto another frozen knoll and brought the tracked vehicle down to an idle. He knew advancing farther in the noisy tracked vehicle would only spook the animals, so he took up a vantage point and throttled back. Climbing from the vehicle, he stepped out with binoculars in hand and peered down upon the herd. The wolves were moving up either side of the herd, staying low to the ground as the Skent again began to encircle the large herd.

From up here, through the binoculars, even with the worm implants, he could barely make out the Skent, but the flurry of snow kicked up by their movement was unmistakable. A storm of snow dust raged upward, stirred from the ground by the galloping Skent and carried by an eastern breeze. The caribou herd could smell the wolves. It wasn't uncommon for the predators to move among the herds, taking the weak and sick. The caribou did not defend against these culls, they simply accepted their fate. They were not spooked by the wolves that closed in, but that other sound and scent was a different matter. Like the wolves, their prey did not recognize the danger until it was too late and they were corralled.

7

ACADIA MINE
Telegraph Road

The fate of Tanker drivers Stu and Kyle was sealed the moment they found themselves on the Telegraph Road being led to the tank farm by an infected guide. They did not see the escort as it trundled along the roadway beside them, using the snow drifts to move incognito. They did not know that they were in danger as they rolled into the staging and their escort told them to wait for a call from the Hydro-carbon techs.

Stu and Kyle did not see the Skentophyte standing sentry on the high points of the mine. Both men were suiting up for when the call came in. They were putting on insulated bib overalls, mukluks, parkas, and gloves.

"Lead tanker, do you have a copy?"

Kyle reached up and grabbed the mic. "Go ahead."

"As soon as you're ready, roll down to station one and we'll hook you up for unload."

"Copy that. I'm on my way."

"Second tanker, have you got a copy?"

"Go ahead," Stu answered.

"I'll take you at station number two."

"Copy that."

Kyle pulled away and seconds later, Stu followed. The staging area was a short jaunt uphill from the unloading stations. These were set up in front of the main tank farm, which housed three mammoth fuel tanks. Standing at each station was an individual wrapped from head to toe in environmental gear suitable for the extreme cold. As the two tankers approached, the men outdoors waved to them and gave hand signals. Kyle and Stu could not see the disfigurement of either of the men leading them in. That was hidden behind the safety glasses, hoods on their parkas and scarfs wrapping exposed skin.

Kyle rolled past his guide and used his right mirror to watch his hand signals. The unloading technician raised his right arm up in the air, held it, and then abruptly dropped it. Kyle put on the brakes and stopped the vehicle in alignment with the fuel hose. As he grabbed his paperwork and prepared to exit the truck, Stu, under the direction of his unloader, was coming to a stop as well.

Out of the corner of his eye, Kyle could see his unloader pulling a big tub toward the tanker, and hanging out of it like a tentacle was the hose they would attach to his pup. He put on his safety glasses and hardhat, taking in the bitter cold as he climbed down from the cab.

"Fucking nippy," he said to no one in particular.

On the rim of the center fuel tank, a group of 16 Skentophyte lay in wait. On the tanks to the left and right, even more were positioned. The tanks stood approximately 80 feet.

Kyle set a chock block behind his drive wheel, while holding tight onto his paperwork. The breeze tugged anxiously at the envelope, the cold turning the paper brittle, and it gave a crackling protest. He worked his way around the front of the rig and when he rounded the hood, he saw that the unloader was already hooking up the second hose. Sensing Kyle's presence, he turned and said, "I got this, put your paperwork in the pump house. Then come back out."

Kyle waved in acknowledgement of the order and gazed at the station to the rear, where it appeared Stu was being given the same marching orders. He bumbled along the path. His feet felt bloated and awkward inside the mukluks he wore. When he reached the short stairwell, he grabbed the handrail and climbed the six steps to the door. Once there, he grabbed onto the knob and opened it up.

The name of the unloader at Station #1 was Lance. He wasn't sure why he'd bothered to tell the driver to put his paperwork into the pump house. It wasn't like he was going to need it. In fact, the days of filling out forms and logging fuel tickets had long since gone by. That poor driver wouldn't be going back for another load. If he was lucky, the Skent would do away with him right here and now. This was certainly a better fate than the 360 Acadia employees who had been marched through the portal and into a Skentophyte version of a slaughterhouse in whatever remote part of the universe these things came from. He'd seen it all through their collective eye, heard the screams as they were marched through an elaborate grid that wasn't all that different from the beef slaughterhouse he himself had worked at in Porcupine Plains Saskatchewan. The stench of blood was higher than that place, though, but the mechanics were basically the same. They were funneled begging and screaming into a structure that looked much like a salt dome and then, one by one, they were killed and processed with precision. The only difference really was that the bones jacketed inside the human bodies were harvested while the tissue and organs were discarded. It was horrific.

Poetic justice, Lance thought. *Or maybe karma?* He remembered the many cows and pigs marched into that dark mill of death. He had only worked in the slaughterhouse for a month; that had put him off beef for almost six weeks and processed meat altogether. Industrial farmers, that's all these Skentophyte really were. "And we're the cattle."

He understood, was even disgusted by this, but could do nothing about it. While the Skentophyte did not interrupt his thought process, they controlled his actions, and saving the poor driver coming out of the pump house wasn't in the cards. He supposed he could apologize, as others had done, but what would be the point?

"Paperwork's inside," Kyle hollered over the mechanical whine of the pump and his diesel engine.

The Unloader had his back to him, was checking the hose, and when he turned he decided to say he was sorry anyhow, no matter how hollow it might see. "I'm really sorry, man."

He removed his safety glasses and Kyle thought his own eyes might be playing tricks on him. The sockets were empty, except for a pulsing diode of green light deep within each hollow. Before he could ask about this, he heard himself mumble. "Sorry about what?"

The Unloader looked up to the rim of the tank, then to the pump house and beyond: there were dozens of them. Kyle followed his gaze and he could only think of one thing when he saw them emerging from the shadows.

Grasshoppers, giant four-legged grasshoppers. He had to be dreaming; this wasn't real. *I've gotta wake up, I'm out on the lake heading for a snowbank. Shit, I better wake up!*

"About them," the unloader said. "Sorry, driver."

He turned his attention back to the unloader. This was a grotesque dream—they were scrambling on all fours—teeth clattering.

"Is this a nightmare? Am I having a bad dream?"

"The worst kind," the unloader said.

Acadia Warehouse

Sack had to wait around for almost 10 minutes before the ground guide opened the warehouse door and the barn doors on the 53-foot trailer, before he could back the rig into the building. After butting the trailer up against the interior loading dock, he started squaring up his logbook. He was thinking about a hot meal when he saw the flatbed go speeding across the lot through the loading dock port window.

"What the hell?"

It was just a glimpse, but he could have sworn that was Rory's flatbed; and it was hauling ass. He set his logbook down and prepared to climb out of the rig. He'd have to get directions to the cafeteria from in here. He expected that they wouldn't make him walk outside but grabbed his parka just in case.

He climbed out of the rig and went to the overhead door, thinking he might catch a second glance through the port window when from behind he heard, "Driver, we have a job for you."

A job? Sack turned away from the warehouse door, bringing his eyes up to meet the man on the dock. "What kind of j…" Sack shook his head. There on the dock was a man with no eyes. He might have had the same thought as Kyle before the Skentophyte took him, but Sack knew he wasn't dreaming.

They spilled down off the dock and he thought of Rory as they surrounded him.

He must have been high tailing it!

Sack turned around and then back to the only other human in the warehouse. "What is this?"

"Don't resist, driver," the eyeless man said. "It will be easier if you don't resist."

I wonder if he got away, he thought. Then they clamped onto him and put out his eyes. When the intense agony finally relented and the implants bit into the optics, he saw what they saw.

Down the Telegraph Road a flatbed rig—definitely Rory—was making a break for it, his trailer zigging back and forth, dangerously close to the sides. In pursuit, hundreds of Skentophyte hurled themselves along banks, pacing the rig. First two, then three, leapt from the banks, landing on the super sacks of prilled ammonium nitrate. One bag tore open, its substance wafting up into the air and catching in the chattering mouth of one of the Skent riders. The creature released its grip on the strap and fell from the flat deck into the snow. Sack could feel it spitting, not liking the ingredients it has tasted, but more so it had inhaled the substance and it was causing some sort of breathing issue. The Skentophyte twisted and turned, gasping, gulping, its oxygen exchangers clogging up. Sack could feel the panic and fear, as it strangled on the substance.

Dying, he thought, it's dying. Skent, we are dying.

Sack could feel the terror as if it were his own. The unrelenting desperation as it struggled to clear the breathing tubes in its back, but with each gasp it only pushed the poison deeper into its circulatory system. The collective eye was completely focused on the ordeal of the poisoned Skentophyte. Those in and around the mine, including the now-infected Kyle and Stu, shared in the spectacle. No attention was being paid to the fleeing Rory, who, by the way, had the accelerator of his rig pressed flat on the floor.

For whatever reason, the creatures that rode his rig fell motionless as they straddled the trailer behind him. He centered his truck on the Telegraph, trying to keep her upright. He had seen them coming from all sides as he opened the door in the drop lot. At first he had thought they might have been wolves, but he didn't wait to find out after the first one hit his fender, cracking it in half. He put the truck in gear and got moving. On his radio he heard the guide who led him in saying, "Driver, stop! Where are you going?"

Rory didn't respond. He just kept rolling.

Now making a run for the main ice road, he had one thought. *Get the fuck out of here!* He didn't care what those things were, where they came from, or why they were in a remote part of the north. He didn't analyze this as a dream or a nightmare. All Rory cared about was hitting the road because he was sure at the very least that if he stopped, they were going to eat him for dinner. He was wrong, of course. They just wanted his eyes.

Sack, along with the remainder of the collective, was frozen, but when the Skent strangled on the last gasp and the three chambers inside its heart seized, the view inside the collective refocused and the remaining riders on Rory's flatbed came back to life. A warning shot out.

Poisonous! Do not breathe! Skent!

Beads of ammonium nitrate fell from the hemorrhaged bag and created a chemical trail, which the advancing Skentophyte avoided as they worked their way up the trailer. They climbed over the super sacks, careful not to puncture them as they advanced toward the tractor.

Rory saw this in his right hand mirror.

"No! No! No!" He cut the wheel left, then right, desperately trying to shake them, feeling the center of gravity shift dangerously. They held tight. Beside him he could see more of them running parallel to his rig. He wished he had his gun right now. If he had his Dirty Harry special, that might even the odds. Except you weren't allowed to bring guns on the ice roads.

"Goddamned left wing limp-wristed, tree-hugging faggots," he screamed and cut the wheel again.

One of them fell off and he thought for a moment that he might actually make it until he heard the thump on the truck sleeper. A shadow fell across the skylight and then the plexus skylight blew in. Cold air gushed, intermingled with a confetti of snow that turned the semi's interior into a rolling snow globe. Rory only caught a brief shape, possibly a claw or hand. Then it hooked onto him and the lights went out.

The tractor trailer bowled into the snowbank with a walloping thump. There was a bloom of fresh white powder, and when it cleared, it was answered with silence. The truck had stalled, Rory was dead. The Skentophyte climbed over the rig, opening doors, tugging at limps and eventually, feasting on what was left. They dragged his body out into the snow, away from the rig, crunching the bones, peeling away the tissue, leaving no calcified morsel behind.

Sack was climbing the stairwell to the loading dock, thinking the same as Kyle and the Unloaders named Lance and Stu. Rory was one of the lucky ones. The man on the dock was climbing into a tow motor. They needed to get the lubricants out of this trailer. They had cargo to load, freight being brought over. This shipment would be going south, to Yellowknife.

Sack already knew what the cargo would be because the Skentophyte couldn't keep a secret. He would be taking that cargo once it was ready, once the road was open. That cargo had a strange name

Thrombus…

***

Chapter 28—Ten Little Piggies

1

Billy was taking in the carnage, while around him the ravens squawked in protest as he stomped through the camp. This was their domain now, their feeding ground, and he had no business here. At least that is what he interpreted from their angry cries. The bigger ravens didn't take flight, opting to move away when he approached, but only grudgingly. And those far enough away continued pecking at the mangled carcasses, pulling at bits of frozen meat with their beaks. The sky above was also flecked with ravens. These weren't as brazen and would wait for the human to leave before taking their place at the feast.

"Damn it," he grunted. He wasn't angry really, he half expected that the camp would be buried and by the time thc thaw camc, thc road would be too dangerous to drive on. This would have been the end result anyway. The ground was covered in tracks and he knew immediately. Wolves, a whole pack had taken his keep and left the rest for these black birds. He adjusted the rifle on his shoulder and turned to leave when something caught his eye. Ten feet away, beyond blanketed camp, out of reach of the feeding frenzy, he saw something else that made his heart sink. Just as he was about to mount his snowmobile, he saw the single raven hopping across a misshapen lump. A tangle of white fur fluttered in the breeze, cresting the embankment that didn't quite conceal it.

He climbed from the snow machine and barked, "Get out of there!" The raven lifted off and he made his way over to the lifeless body of the dead wolf. It was Old Whitey. Billy leaned down and brushed the snow from the wolf's face; its eyes were still open, but they were muddy, lifeless.

The wolf must have wandered into the camp while the pack was dining on his kills. The old fella didn't have a chance, they'd torn open his throat, but he hadn't gone down without a fight. The yellowing fur around his mouth was pink and red. The big wolf had finally been taken down by the group that had banished him. A tinge of guilt melted over him. If he hadn't been feeding the old wolf, maybe…

He sat down beside his sometime distant hunting companion and shuddered. "Shit, Whitey. You should have steered clear." He removed his glove and closed the animal's eyes. And though he tried to convince himself that he'd been helping the old wolf by offering up a bit of meat here and there, the truth was that his actions had probably led to its demise. He groaned. They'd made a real mess of him; the ravens would pick him apart in no time. If this had been a dog, he might be inclined to bury him, but up here it was pointless. Covering the body with snow was just delaying the inevitable. Once the snow retreated, everything went back to the earth. The white wolf would be gone to bones in no time. He stood back up.

"Goodbye, Old Whitey."

Billy took a last look at the white wolf and felt his heart pang. He mounted the snowmobile and fired it up, then revved the engine purposely a couple times to spook the black birds. Some took to the air, but most carried on feeding. He popped the clutch and left the encampment behind. He trekked north, leaving his pickup at the side of the road, cutting cross country toward the fish camp in search of the caribou.

2

Chase found the piece of equipment he and Lenny had discussed when they fled the Acadia mine. It was a grader encapsulated in a drift, the driver compartment was barely visible, but it was running and the exhaust chugged away. The vehicle chassis was completely buried and Chase knew that it wouldn't be going anywhere without a tug. He slowly dug out the driver door. His hands felt rigid, clay-like, and he was pretty sure frostbite had settled into his toes.

"No point in getting sentimental," he mumbled. "They're only toes." But he was worried. The scarf wrapped around his face had frozen like cardboard against his mouth. His eyelashes were also frozen beneath his safety glasses. At one point along his trek, he'd considered lighting one of the Molotov cocktails to try and warm up, then thought better of it. He unlatched the door and gave it a pull. At first it resisted, then with a crackling protest, it peeled away from the door seal and he climbed up in. The heater was on low. He pulled off a glove and turned it up to full. The hot air blasted from the vents and he held his hands over them; in doing so, he examined them for frostbite. They were splotched with pink around the knuckles, but overall they looked okay, and for this he let out an enthusiastic, "Yes." Then he closed his eyes and leaned his head back.

With the heat cranked, the circulation in his fingers began to return, but there was an arthritic ache in the joints. He unwrapped his scarf and unzipped the parka. He was dreading the prospect of what he'd find once he removed his mukluks. He expected to find his baby toes rolling around inside his wool socks like tiny frozen rabbit droppings. Black, dead and detached.

Fuck it.

He pulled the zipper up on his winter overalls, unlatched the Velcro straps on the right mukluk, and brought it up. He inhaled and exhaled three times, closed his eyes, and pulled it off. The sock came with it. Slowly he peeled open his lids and took in his bare foot. A smile tugged at the corners of his mouth, a laugh escaped him in short intermittent gasps. This was followed by a relieved cry. His right foot looked okay except for same discoloring he'd seen in his hands. He brought the foot up in front of the heater vent, but when the warm air beat on it, hot pain set the dormant nerves in his toes ablaze. He lowered his foot out of air flow whilst serenading, "Ouch! Ouch! Fuck! Ow!"

Slower still, he unlatched the second Velcro strap and pulled his left foot free. This time the sock only came halfway off, hanging there like Ebenezer Scrooge's night cap.

"Five little piggies," he said. "Show me five little piggies." He squeezed the hanging portion of the sock, feeling for pebbles, and after he found it empty, he pulled the sock free and let out a low exasperated gasp. All were attached, but the baby and its next-door neighbor were waxy white.

At least they're not black.

He thought about his cold weather training. He expected to find black, blistered digits, broken by friction of walking, but what he had was first-degree frostbite. The surface of the skin had frozen on the two toes, but there was still some feeling. There was an itch he felt beneath the surface and now, exposed to warm air inside the cab, the skin burned. He leaned his head back and closed his eyes. "Just gotta warm 'em up. Warm 'em up and all the little piggies will go to market. Thank you, God. Thank you, thank you."

Exhausted, Chase Fenwick brought his feet up onto the seat and leaned his head back against the glass. He needed to sleep, but when he closed his eyes, the vision of the creatures that dismantled Lenny haunted the solitary darkness.

He snapped back up, expecting to see one of the abominations scraping a talon along the windshield, but there was only ice and snow and blinding white.

"What the hell did they do?"

3

ACADIA MINE
PIT # 2

The road into the second pit spiraled downward like a frozen Victorian staircase. The caribou were being herded down the road by the Skentophyte, two members of the eyeless wolf pack, along with their escorts, shepherding them. Three quarters of the way down was the entranceway to a tunnel that led directly into the chamber. The area had undergone renovation since the arrival of the Skentophyte. Directed by their escorts, the infected used the equipment to clear debris and widen the path to the chamber.

From the conference room, Bruce and Sal sat at the table, watching the progress on the big screen monitor. Behind each, their escorts stood vigil, quiet except for the air exchange on each creature's back hushing in and out.

"There's a convoy underway," Bruce said and wondered why. Surely Sal knew this; all of them did. The collective eye saw and transmitted all. That wasn't why he said it. He was talking because that was all that was left; the fuckers controlled everything else. Had taken the rest of him.

"Yes. Rally told me the road coming north is still closed, some kind of accident." He stopped. The collective whispers were transmitting his words, deciphering them. Accident? Blockage? Delay? It wasn't an actual language, it was a series of clicks and chatters, but all of them understood, a byproduct of being hardwired to the collective. The two men fell silent, at least physically. Across the collective, the plans were being administered. Allison had said in her final moments that the bastards couldn't keep a secret, but that wasn't quite accurate. It was true that they couldn't keep a secret on the collective wire they used to transmit their plans. Anyone online would hear those plans, including the infected. For instance, he knew that the plan was to herd the southbound drivers coming from Meanook into Acadia and march them straight into the chamber for processing. He also knew that there was a raiding party on its way to Corbett Lake and everyone there would be taken except the communicator. Allison had said that the Skentophytes' Achilles heel was their inability to keep a secret, but she was wrong about that. The collective wire buzzed electrically with information, but only the collective heard that information. The skent were very effective at keeping secrets when it came to outside influence. Allison had only been able to talk because she was off the collective; had she still been infected, they would have shut her down.

But they did have an Achilles heel. They were blind. Or were they? They were in this world. Every action they'd taken required an escort. The escort was wired into an infected host and without the host? That wasn't exactly right either, Allison was failing, so how did they operate without her? Ross McNeil and Rally and all the others. So that was how they got around the mine, but they needed the infected to strike out into unknown territory.

The only way to stop this would be to warn those who weren't wired in, but the worms would shut down any attempt at that and hail the collective. So there was really only one way. Remove the worms, but with that came a new issue. If he removed the worms from his eyes, he would be blind. What a terrifying prospect that was. Bad enough he was living on borrowed time, but the idea of stumbling along the corridors of Acadia without sight while the Skent closed in was more than he could bear.

Still, he thought, closing his hand around the needle nose pliers that were still tucked inside his hip pocket, *it's an option.*

"What's an option?" Sal asked.

"What?"

"You said 'It's an option.'"

"It would be nice to have a private thought, Sal. I was thinking about my morning shit. Nothing is sacred, I guess."

"Sorry, I'm in the same boat as you, Bruce."

Bruce realized that some of his thoughts were still his own and that Sal had only heard his inner voice. The difficulty in that was separating the two. Thoughts and inner voice. He supposed if he could go to the Far East and study under a master of martial arts, he could use that second sight after he dug the worms out of his eyes with the needle nose pliers, then he could karate kick and punch his way the fuck out of here.

I'd be like a messiah then.

"What?"

Along with Sal's query, more Skent questions. Messiah? God. Leader? Myth Nonsense.

Get the fuck out of my head, Sal, Bruce thought, then deliberately changed the subject. "Herb has cleared the airfield. When is he scheduled to arrive?"

"Sorry, Bruce. It's not on purpose."

"Yeah, we're all real good at apologizing. Bunch of fucking enablers to the Skent. But hell, we're sorry, so that makes it all okay."

Sal ignored the complaint, opting to answer the question instead. "He'll be flying in on the corporate jet in the morning." Sal was speaking of Damien Lars. A mocking grin pushed his cheeks upward, beseeching an almost demonic presence. "He's going to piss himself."

"You sound pleased by this."

"Everybody loves Damien Lars, don't they?"

"He's a… a good boss."

"He was always an asshole to me."

"You're a fucking asshole, Sal."

"I never cared much for Damien. Always calling me Sally in front of the hired help. Making me the butt of his jokes. I guess the joke will be on him when he arrives. Maybe I am an asshole, Bruce, but what I'm really doing is making lemonade out of lemons."

4

Dreamcatcher Lake

The convoys came south from Meanook and across the barrens before the light drained from the sky. Separated by 20 minutes, each convoy of four rolled across the Dreamcatcher with the same 30 km per hour grind with which they had gone north.

"It's a prisoner exchange," the lead driver said into his handset.

"I don't get you."

"They haven't got the road south of Corbett opened yet, Carl. So we'll get as far as Corbett and then we'll be shut down until they punch through."

"Oh come on, Rob. They'll have it open."

"Nope, I'd bet a pitcher of beer on it. They just wanted to vacate us so they could get the rest of their northbound fuel. Sooner or later we are going to see more northbound trucks from Corbett and then we'll be sequestered to that fucking parking lot while being fed by that egg-touching ghoul."

"Prisoner exchange," another driver in the convoy laughed. "That's pretty funny."

"You won't think it's funny when you're shitting out both ends, pal."

"No swearing on Ladd 1, driver," an authoritative voice broke in.

"Who's that? Security?"

There was a chortle.

"Very funny, Axman," Rob the convoy leader said. "Boys, we have a flooding crew ahead. Slow her down to 10 clicks."

The other drivers in the convoy acknowledged.

"How are you, Rob?"

"Awesome, Ax. How's things?"

They could see the flood crew working, soaking down the ice road. The foreman, Axman Jack, was out front, leaning against his namesake. He keyed his remote radio. "Prisoner exchange, eh?"

"Heard that, did you?"

"I hear everything, Rob. Although, I haven't seen any Meanook bound trucks as of yet. There were a lot of Acadia boys chomping at the bit in Corbett when we left this morning."

"What's the word on the south bound road?"

"Well, the Ingraham was closed because of the accident. Not sure what the status is now. As far as the road south of Corbett. They're working it, but I think you'll be dining with a certain goose-stepping cook this evening."

He passed the flood crew, gave a two-finger salute, and they waved back. "If I get sick this year, I'm writing a letter of complaint to Lupania."

"Sure thing and who could blame you," Ax said, but he'd heard this same threat from numerous drivers and still the cook known as the Kitchen Nazi returned year after year. Truck drivers loved to bitch, but once the season was over, they found other interests: fishing, Vegas, women, Caribbean vacations. The idea of penning a letter to the head of Lupania seemed unimportant once the spring thaw came.

Ax watched the convoy pass; they were the first of many that would come and go at 20-minute intervals. A little over an hour-and-a-half later, the fourth had rolled by and they were packing up. The flood crew pushed further north to re-work the section of ice up by the fish camp again.

5

Phil Crane made a decision to deviate from the plan and drive north across the ice to the last portage before Dreamcatcher Lake. This decision would inevitably save his life and spare him from the fate of the southbound drivers he met along with his co-workers back in Corbett

Lake.

It was a call, not by Gordon Shamus, but some stranger that sent a chill of paranoia through him. When the satellite phone rang and when he answered, a male voice asked, "You ready?"

In retrospect, he was sure this must be the one Gordon had mentioned back in Hamilton. "I've got other eyes up there watching him, Phil. You can't be everywhere at once," Gordon had said, or at least words to that effect.

"Who is this?" he asked.

"Can't tell you that. It isn't safe."

"What?" Crane felt his heart shudder, as if dipped in ice water.

"Are you ready?"

He paused, unsure what to say, and then said the only thing he could think of. "Yeah, I'm ready."

"Good, he'll be in the tenth group. Make sure you're ready."

Then there was a click.

Phil glowered at the satellite phone. The hairs on the back of his neck prickled upward and he suddenly felt very nervous. "What the fuck is going on here?" Was this a double cross? Would there be somebody waiting on that portage to dump him into a hole? First, Shamus had changed the plan, and now there were cryptic calls coming from unknown participants.

Other eyes watching?

There was something very fucking wrong with this.

Phil Crane considered himself an astute man. That insight had been earned first as a Hamilton cop, then as security man for Jude Shamus. The insight had kept him alive all these years. He trusted his gut and his gut was telling him that something absolutely stunk in Denmark. He was going to meet Croft as planned, but not on the Portage they were suggesting.

No way, no how. Fuck that!

He reached over into his carry bag, pulled out the Desert Eagle pistol, cocked it and set the safety. When he replaced it in the bag, he didn't bother to zip it up. If there was an ambush on the horizon, he was going to be ready.

He put the truck in gear and rolled down the portage and onto the ice. He did not see the Grader that was buried at the side of the road and never noticed the single stack chugging cold white exhaust into the sky. Nor did the occupant, Chase Fenwick, awaken when his pickup rolled past.

Even if Crane had seen the vehicle stack and the almost camouflaged mustard yellow paint that would forever remind him of the excavator his boss used to pound Henry Carver into a soup of bone and tissue; it didn't matter anyway. He had no intention of stopping for anyone.

6

Acadia Mine
Ice Road Junction

Chase Fenwick jerked awake when he heard the vehicles—flying into a panicked frenzy as the last of the horrible dream he'd been having about Lenny began to fade. It had not been surreal, but ethereal. Lenny raising the blade to his own throat, asking, "Does it hurt, Chase?" Chase raising his hands to his eyes, feeling the heat from the hollows of his sockets, the serpentine coil.

I'm one of them, he thinks and before he can answer:

Lenny slices across his throat, an accusation of betrayal in his eyes.

"No, Lenny," Chase cries.

Then his knees buckle, his hand unfurls, and the clacks upon the ice.

They stand there face to face, the things still standing outside the light, teeth chattering.

Lenny's eyes roll back. Chase hears a solid gasp of air whistle from the open wound.

Then the creatures come to feed. Like ants dismantling a much larger insect. Cascades of blood spiral out as the feeding frenzy takes place. Oscillating out, slapping Chase across his cheek and into his mouth. The taste of iron. And then he heard vehicle engines.

His head snapped back, his eyes wide, and he realized he had no idea how long he'd conked out. In fact, he was confused as to where he was when he opened his eyes. He considered the dream, still dumb to his surroundings. Lenny hadn't thought the approaching vehicles would be unfriendly. But they had because they were from Acadia and everyone at the mine was now… different? Oh, they were different all right. He thought of Allison. And of course, Herb, who had really spoken to Lenny before he made the final cut. They were being controlled by the creatures, the things from the wormwell. Were they aliens, as Ronny had speculated? Probably, but he didn't know what to call them. Unbeknownst to him, that was a blessing. If he knew their name, it would have already been too late. His thoughts turned back to his feet, which had thankfully regained their fleshy pink color.

The vehicles called again. Far-off rumblings.

He tugged on his socks, buried each foot in a mukluk, then zipped up and reached to unlatch the door, but then he faltered. Lenny had thrown caution to the wind and paid with his life. Chase, on the other hand, had come too far to make the same mistake. He rubbed the frost from the window and brought his Bushmasters up for a look.

As he suspected, the convoy was coming from Acadia. Service trucks, three in all, straight jobs is what the drivers called them. They rolled across the junction and out onto the main ice road. Along with the three trucks was the Arctic Snow Cat. Once onto the ice, they stopped and began unloading equipment.

"What are they doing?" The question was answered moments after it spilled from his lips. They were setting out traffic cones, signage, and saw horses. *Detour! Son of a bitch!*

Chase scanned the landscape and saw the silhouettes huddled on the banks, watching, but staying well enough back so that anyone who wasn't looking would see them. The bastards were going to net the south bounders and take them right into Acadia. He reached up and turned the radio onto Ladd 1.

Voices boomed from the speaker, causing him to jump.

"Hello, security," a voice said.

There was no response.

"Oh, shit!" He turned the radio down. There were trucks coming and they'd met a security, probably north of here. He considered turning the engine of the grader off, but then decided against it. If he shut it down and had to restart it, the plume might give his position away. They would expect to see running equipment on the ice. He figured he was far enough away that he might not be noticed. And for now, they were focused on setting up their barricade.

Chase watched the men set up a saw horse and run traffic cones across the road. In front of the saw horse was a sign, but he was south of it and couldn't make out what it said. He assumed it was a detour sign and didn't have something obvious written on it like: **RIGHT THIS WAY TO BE DISMEMBERED AND EATEN.**

He closed a hand around the Molotov cocktails he'd carried all this way and thought that he might be able to throw a wrench into their meal plans when something happened that changed everything.

More vehicles came up the road from Acadia, but these weren't service vehicles, these were big rigs. And they weren't stopping. The driver of the first service vehicle waved the first big rig through as it turned south and Chase felt his guts churn with anxiety. South! They were going south! To Corbett. The first big rig was pulling a van behind it and behind that, three more super b trucks pulling hoppers. As the van approached, Chase breathed on the peephole he created and it instantly frosted over. His heart was pounding mercilessly. He fumbled for the flare gun and pulled out a Molotov cocktail. The big rig rolled by without slowing, then another and another, and then when the fourth truck rolled by, he rubbed away the frost and stared out. As the last rig disappeared into a haze of snow dust, he caught a glimpse of three creatures peering out above the hopper.

They were going south to Corbett! Those things were going south to Corbett! No escape!

And when Chase thought matters couldn't get any worse, he saw the convoy rolling south toward the barricade. And then he heard the voice over the radio. "South bound convoy, switch your radio to Ladd 2."

Chase flipped the channel over.

"This is the leader of the convoy. What's going on up there?"

"Sorry, driver, but we've had a major ice shift on Wombat Lake and it's created a five-foot pressure ridge. I'm afraid we're routing all traffic into Acadia until we can get a crew out there to clean up this mess."

"Oh man, this just gets better by the minute," the driver who'd conversed with Ax only an hour before said. "Any word on how long?"

"Afraid not, you'll be briefed when you get into Acadia."

Chase reached for the handset, put it to his mouth, even keyed it, and then released the switch. "Fuck me! Fuck me! This can't be happening!"

The first truck was already turning.

There was nothing he could do. Even if he ran over there now with his Molotov cocktails and set the whole fucking thing on fire, they would have him in pieces and just set up a new barricade. The last vehicle turned the corner and the driver lumbered toward his inevitable demise.

Chase sat paralyzed as yet another convoy came south. Then, twenty minutes later, another and another, and though he was powerless to save any of them, the overwhelming guilt was almost more than he could stand. He almost stepped out of the cab and ran toward the barricades, but with the realization that Corbett Lake would soon be under the control of these creatures, he knew he only had one choice. Find that security up on the Dreamcatcher and find a way to get to Meanook Mine before they punched through to Yellowknife. By the time the seventh convoy was routed into Acadia, Chase Fenwick could listen no more.

He switched the radio off and waited.

***

Chapter 29—Fall of Corbett Lake

1

Hotel 62
260 Kilometers south of Meanook Mine

Portage 62 was also called Hotel 62 because on a number of occasions, convoys found themselves trapped there for more than a few days during a storm. Marty didn't think that the insistence by Garney that he learn how to swap out his alternator would be of much use, but now here he was, along with Merv, doing just that. Except the failed alternator was on Merv's rig. It had happened just as they were getting off the last big lake that stretched between Meanook and Dreamcatcher.

"Ah, shit boys, she's pooched," Merv said.

"You got a back-up?" Spence asked.

"Yeah, but I'm going to have to dig it out. Fuck, why didn't this happen up at Meanook? At least there would have been coffee and a shitter."

"Laws of probability, my Brother. Okay, Marty and I will park side by side and leave you enough room to scoot in between. We'll act as a windbreaker. Where's your batteries on that jalopy, Merv? Driver or passenger side?"

"Driver side, but I got extra-long cables."

"Uh huh, yep. Right on, my Brother. Bring her on up and we'll get you fixed up. Marty, you jump out and give Merv a hand pulling the alternator and I'll hook him up and put a charge on his batteries."

"Copy," Marty replied.

"What do you guys need me to do?" Spence asked.

"You can go for coffee," Merv said. "Double double for me."

"Get your own coffee, bitch."

"That's not very nice," Merv said. "I've got feelings, you know."

Garney was the first to park in the infamous Hotel 62 parking lot, which was half the size of the lot at Corbett. Once parked, he got out and directed Marty to where he wanted him.

Marty suited up and as Merv parked, it was a tight fit. Once dressed, Marty revved the Kenworth up and set the RPM to 1400, causing the fan to kick on. Then he stepped out of the truck into the open air.

He walked around to see Merv getting dressed and without saying a word, he began unlatching the hood. Merv rolled down his window. "Marty, can you take the battery box cover off first so we can get some jumpers hooked up and throw a bit of charge into the batteries."

Marty gave him a thumbs up.

On the other side, Garney was pulling his own battery box cover off and readying it to hook up. The big aluminum cover clanged off the ice lot, barely audible over the chorus of diesel engines. Spence was rolling in now, adding to the symphony. By the time Marty spun the wing nuts off and inserted them in his pocket, Merv was climbing down and unlatching his hood. Marty pulled the cover off and set it against the rig's drive wheel, then went forward to help Merv with the hood.

"I'll get the moose bumper if you want to dig out your alternator," Marty said.

Merv gave him a toothy grin. "Works for me."

He left Marty to unlatch the bumper and began unloading his driver side jockey box in search of the replacement alternator. Spence was out of his rig, shambling over.

"Where's your cables," he yelled to Merv.

"Passenger jockey."

"I'll grab them."

Garney came around to check everyone's progress. "Ahh, my brothers, it's a wonderful day. The sun is almost down and what the fuck, Merv…"

Merv was unloading everything out of his jockey box. There was a mess of empty jugs, boxes, headlights, pieces of chain. He didn't bother to look back. "What?"

"My brother, there's a show I want you to watch when we get back to civilization." He winked at Marty. "It's called Hoarders."

"Fuck off, Wilson, you big Sasquatch!"

Marty cracked up and Garney joined him.

Spence came around with the jumper cables. Merv wasn't kidding when he said extra-long. The cables were at least 30 feet in length, maybe even 40. "How the hell did you get all that shit inside your jockey box?"

Merv jabbed a gloved thumb toward Garney. "I've already told him. Besides, I told you to get me a double-double."

"Where the hell would you fit it?" Marty added and all three men cracked up. Merv didn't respond, just kept digging stuff out and adding it to the pile.

Spence tossed the cables under Garney's rig and said. "I know this might be a no brainer, but we're dealing with Merv here. So red is positive."

"Hilarious," Merv snarled. "You should go into comedy, Spence."

Garney guffawed. Marty laughed along with him and Spence took a bow. Garney handed the cables to Marty and said, "Don't hook 'em up until I tell you." He worked his way around the rig and Marty felt a slight tug. Then: "Hook 'em up, my brother."

Marty made his way over to the battery box with Spence at his side. The batteries were flat black, but considering the state Merv kept his jockey box in, he was surprised at how clean they were. *Positive first,* he thought and clamped the red one first. Then he hooked up the ground, which caused a minor spark.

"We're hooked up!" Spence trudged back around the rig, throwing a thumbs up. "Looks good, Garney!" He climbed into Merv's rig and checked the gauge, then back down again. "We've got 14 on the volt meter, she's charging."

"Here it is," Merv pulled out an oil-stained cardboard box. No doubt a victim of its neighboring oil jugs and greasy tools. He set it on the catwalk behind the cab and opened it. Inside was a surprisingly clean brand new alternator. "Good stuff."

"Shouldn't you shut the truck off?" Marty asked.

"No, not yet. Not until we have all the tools ready and I better dig out a set of belts just in case. Now that Garney's throwing a charge on my batteries, it's all good until we're ready. We want to keep that oil warm, Marty. In these temps, it will be turning into roofing tar once that engine stops."

Five minutes later, on top of the engine compartment, Marty and Merv worked as a team to switch out the alternator. The biting arctic gale, in spite of the makeshift windbreak, swirled about them. Merv was smart to have pulled out his belts because the main alternator belt was frayed on one side and would not have made it across the big lake. Simultaneously, Garney was putting everything back into Merv's jockey box, much to Merv's irritated protest. "I'll never be able to find anything!"

"You just get that alternator switched, my brother. I'll get her back in the same orderly fashion with which you had it originally packed."

Spence cracked up and wandered back to his rig.

"Where are you going?" Merv barked.

"To put on a pot of coffee."

"I thought I told you to get on that earlier."

Spence flipped him the bird and kept walking.

The old alternator was off along with the belt. They'd been at it for almost 20 minutes, longer than Merv would have liked, but the adjustment bolt had been extremely stiff, and Merv, fearful that it might snap in the extreme cold, warmed it with a torch, easing it out slowly.

Marty was relishing the distraction. No matter what, he knew that he had less than 10 hours before he faced down Gordon Shamus and even less than that until he hooked up with Crane.

Marty clumsily looped the belt over the pulley on the idler wheel and then the drive wheel, and finally over the new alternator pulley. It hung there limp.

"Get the ratchet on that adjustment nut and start cranking until I tell you to stop." Merv put a pry bar behind the alternator and heaved it back, tightening the slack.

Marty began tightening the adjustment bolt.

"Good, keep cinching it down," Merv grunted and held the slack with his pry bar as the ratchet Marty was using gave a steady rhythm of ticks.

Marty marveled at what they were doing. The teamwork, the ingenuity these guys mustered for getting out of jams. He wondered if their northern ingenuity could get him out of the jam he was in. Not likely.

At the side of the rig, Merv's jockey box clunked shut and a rather bewildered Garney came around to the engine compartment. "I don't know how I did it, my brother, but I managed to stuff all that shit back into that little hole. Uh huh, yup. Don't be standing in front of it when you unlatch it, my brother. You'll likely lose that nose of yours."

"That would be an improvement," Spence barked.

Merv shook his head at Marty and smiled. "No respect."

"Nope," Marty grinned back and carefully climbed down from the steer wheel he'd been standing on.

"Let's get this thing fired up and I'll pour us a cup of coffee," Spence said. Merv gathered his tools and also carefully climbed down from atop the engine. Then he moved around to the cab and jumped in. He turned the key into the accessory position and the bells began to chime. His air had dropped, but not completely. He turned the key into the starting position.

The engine slurred as it rolled over, laboring, but there was plenty of charge in the batteries. It turned once, twice, and then Merv turned the key off and reached behind his seat. He brought out a small aerosol can and handed it to Marty. "Give two quick squirts of this into the air intake while I'm cranking, but no more."

"Don't use that shit, Merv. It'll fuck up your engine," Spence groaned.

Marty looked down at the aerosol can, which read: **QUICK START**; it was ether.

"Two squirts, Marty. No more," Merv said. "And wait until I'm cranking."

Marty nodded and stood by the cylindrical air intakes. At the top of the chromed barrels was an eight-inch wrap of honeycomb; this is where the air flowed into the filters. Marty adjusted the aerosol can and removed his glove. "Say when."

Merv turned the engine over.

It slurred a heavy 'Murr—Murr—Murr.'

"Now."

Marty gave it a squirt, and the engine responded by speeding up; shuddering slightly, it let out a heavy bang and then, with fire in its belly, it slowly came back to life. At first it ran slow, huffing and catching its breath, a slow succession of clicks and whirs, but its momentum was growing. The RPMs climbed and the Detroit Diesel in the 379 flat top Peterbilt gave a tumultuous roar and came back to life.

Merv grinned and Marty did too.

Once they had his hood buttoned up and battery box covers on, they stood between the trucks at Hotel 62, drinking coffee and smoking cigarettes. They were waiting for the air to restore in Merv's trailer—it had dropped slightly. Above them the color was draining from the sky, and the sun had sunk into the arctic rim, leaving behind a blood orange band of light that was fading by the minute.

This was to be their last gathering in good cheer. Marty was expecting to meet Crane in the coming hours and his focus was already on the ball peen hammer in his cab. As he stood in this circle, he felt like he'd known these men for years instead of days. Ridiculous as that was. The isolation seemed to thin the barriers normally thrown up between new acquaintances. There was a moment when he considered telling them of his predicament, but it was brief and to his estimation a foolish thought.

"Alright, my brothers," Garney said, tossing the last drops of coffee into the snow. "Let's get trucking before Merv's jockey box becomes unhinged and we have to spend another three hours cleaning it up."

"Get fucked, Big Garney!" Merv grinned and pinched off his smoke, pocketing the butt.

"Not until the spring, my brother."

They dispersed and mounted their rigs, preparing to cross the Dreamcatcher, and as they rolled onto the frozen sea, the final band of day succumbed to night and the aurora began to dance. For the next two hours, it would be a brilliant show, but would also succumb to the rising moon.

Like Philip Crane, the deviation in their progress would be what saved them from the fate of the other southbound truck drivers. The discussion between Merv and Garney regarding Harley Davidson resumed; this time it was Fat Boys versus Low riders. Spence turned his satellite radio to Ozzy's Boneyard, cranking up an Iron Maiden tune. Marty stared out across the ice, his mind racing, his grip wet on the wheel and his heart tightening. He put the truck in gear and released the clutch. Below the wheels the ice popped, crackled, and complained about the strain being put upon its shoulders.

"It's about to get bloody," he said to the solitude of the cab.

And on that he was right, but he was wrong about the circumstances.

2

Corbett Lake Camp

"Corbett Lake, have you got a copy?" Sack called over the radio.

"Go for Corbett," the male voice replied.

"I have four southbound trucks who wish to enter your yard for a bite."

"What are the numbers, driver?"

"The numbers are 222, 890, 867, and skent 909."

"Skent? Say that last number again, driver."

"Last number is 909, Corbett."

"Permission to land on our beach, driver."

"Thank you, Corbett. We will do just that." Sack released the handset and it retracted up the spring-loaded hanger. Behind him, in the sleeper, his escort hunkered on his bed. Far too large for the confined space, its elongated arms held fast to the interior of the sleeper. It hung over him—insect-like—head pressed up into the skylight. It had climbed in when they mounted up. The snow and ice that collected on its exoskeleton was now melting and plopping from its body in great splats upon the bedspread. Between liquid plops, its teeth clacked musically to the intermittent shushing of its air exchanger. Sack glanced back at the Skentophyte and the havoc it had wrought on his bedspread.

That'll never come out, he thought sadly. Then, considering his circumstances, he retracted the thought. Why should he care? It's not like he'd ever get to sleep in that bed again.

Then the Skentophyte did what Sack considered the ultimate insult. It began to urinate, a steady acrid stream of liquid that looked like a mixture of cranberry juice and milk staining the already soppy comforter.

"I hope that's piss and not spunk," Sack said and turned his attention back upon the approaching beach. He sat robotic, unemotional in every way. "You guys are kind of a pig race, aren't you?"

Pigs, Livestock, race, finish? The skent collective searched and riddled over Sack's insult and answered with their only true reality. Skent we are Skentophyte.

"Yeah, well you're skenting the fuck all over my bed, you fucking pig." Then he let out a low annoyed sigh. What was the use? He was already fucked and the fellow he was talking to on the radio along with everyone in Corbett were also already fucked. Sack understood how they were making him do what he was doing. It was the worms, of course, the ones squirming around inside his eye sockets, injecting some chemical that tapped whatever part of the brain it is that pisses away all your judgment. When he thought of pushing back, there'd been a pain that stabbed into the place where his eyes had once been. Then a plume of fresh ash followed by a hot syrupy haze. This came in unison with the firefly tails of the worms glowing hot in alternates of red and green.

As his truck climbed the grade that would take him into the Corbett staging area, he thought about the 80's. *I'm stuck in a fucking B horror film. Fucking Aliens! Fucking mind controlling aliens. Skentophyte? This has to be a dream. Or a movie.*

FOOD OF THE SKENTOPHYTE

Over the hump now, the truck leveled off and he was able to glance back at his escort again. The bed was sopping, stained, and it smelled terrible. Acrid copper.

"What a motherfucking shit show." The escort loomed over him, dripping—breathing—still pissing, but the steady hard stream that thudded against his bedspread now snapped in rhythmic squirts. "Race of fucking pigs. That's all you are." He turned the wheel and flicked on his four way flashers. The lot was empty except for two big rigs, a flat bed with super sacks tied down.

Powder, danger, poison! No breathe! No breathe! The skent collective telegraphed in the usual clatter of clicks and buzz that for some reason translated into language of the infected. Sack didn't know how he knew this, but the man who met him on the landing dock as they crawled in around him was hearing all of his Skentophyte translations in Polish.

"Don't like that stuff, eh? Pig Skent."

Then came a hot flash—that stabbing pain again, and Sack felt his will draining out of him. In its place, cold numb servitude. He lowered the sun visor and looked into the small mirror. What he saw looking back was a grinning man with pudgy cheeks, a fat dimpled chin, and two coal black caverns except for the diodes of light pulsing deep within. From his left nostril, a trickle of blood rolled over his lip and into his mouth. The pain was loosening, but the grip of control had tightened, leaving his mind drowning in hot thick syrup.

"We are skent," he heard himself say.

What is the use? We're fucked.

The second truck rolled up and parked on his right side. Then a third on his left. He barely saw the fourth truck through the cab on the right. When it stopped, he opened his door and climbed out. The skent followed, seemingly stretching out and slithering from the cab like a salamander. From the other trucks, the drivers and their escorts dismounted.

The targets and possible threats were assessed. The maintenance building with its rumbling generator. The main set of trailers connected together in an H formation. There was a small building, a shack really, that had a four-foot stack on top that chugged its toxins up into the sky.

The man to Sack's left, George was his name, began to walk at a forced pace toward the hill that led to the maintenance building. Then the one named Dennis got moving. His was the main building. And the third, Jack, started toward the back of the main building. From behind, the escorts followed at a safe distance, getting into position.

Sack had received no such orders; his came subconsciously. He moved to the back of his van, opened the barn doors, and latched them against the tug of the arctic wind. He heard Corbett's flag flapping hard in the squall. It snapped great rushing swoops, cracking against the dark of night and whisper of impending doom. He unsnapped the tarps on the first hopper and then the second. The skent crawled out and congregated between the trailers in military rank and file. Sack moved to the next truck and unlatched its tarp. More skent crawled out, joining the ranks, doubling their number to over 20. By the time he was pulling back the tarp on the third hopper, two men in the maintenance shed had joined the collective. The first squad of nine skent trotted up the icy path to meet the newly infected and take possession. Two broke from the nine to meet the men. The shack with the burning stack was nothing more than an incinerator for waste. Once they reached the main and front door, more skent bounded across the drive to join the raiders. Sack expected that he would be joining them, but his escort had other plans.

They again moved to the back of his trailer and he knew that there was something in there that his escort wanted. It was the first, he knew, an anchor of sorts. For some reason, the ghostly words "Worm Well" floated across his subconscious, although he knew that wasn't quite right. It was one word: wormwell. This was not a skent word, it was English and it had been coined or created, the word at least, by a man. "The word of a dead man," he whispered, thinking it sounded like the title of a folk song.

Sitting on the pallet was a disk as big as a manhole cover. A wormwell, anchor, the skent called it Thrombus.

"Find the thrombus," he said, more dead man words. "We're going wormwells," he giggled, but the clown's glee was a mask. Inside he knew that this was their "just in case insurance" and worse, they would be bringing more over. When the jet landed tomorrow, they would fuel it and fly it into Edmonton with another of these thrombus wormwells, and these were different than the one in the pit. Once they landed, it would activate right there on the tarmac. Creating a massive hole, not unlike the ones that Wile E. Coyote was known to order from the ACME Company in his quest to catch the Roadrunner. Except this hole would be huge, city block huge and once opened, they would overrun them in minutes. If that plan wasn't horrible enough, it got even worse because Sack was the tip of their spear. When they loaded him up with twelve of these intergalactic "fuck you ups," it would be his job, along with his new "piss wherever he feels like it" bunk buddy, to plant seeds in as many places as possible.

Oh yeah, it was worse.

He looked from behind the corner of the trailer and saw the shack. That is where they would put it. That was the "just in case," the fall back position. The Alamo or, he hoped, Little Big Horn.

But he doubted it because they were fucked.

"I'll need something to transport it," Sack said.

After, after the harvest, he heard it say. After the harvest move the thrombus, after the harvest is finished.

He felt his head being moved left and his line of sight was set upon the shack.

There.

"The just in case, we are skent."

As he climbed up into the back of the trailer and used the hand jack to move the pallet, a reprise of panicked screams was swallowed up by the wind. Not loud enough to travel the 400 meters, but the horror show came in stereo across the collective.

3

John Pringle's office was kitty-cornered by the main entrance to the cafeteria. He was going over paperwork when the front door to the building blew open and he saw the first man walk in with his boots on.

"Hey," Pringle said. "Take your boots and gear off, driver. No outwear in the dini…"

The man turned toward him and removed his safety glasses, exposing the empty sockets.

Pringle stood up, not registering what he was seeing. Not yet.

"Sit down."

Then the creature lumbered in behind the eyeless man.

Dinosaur, Pringle wondered. *Or insect?*

It stood behind the man, teeth clacking, then hearing Pringle's words, it pivoted its head his way. Behind it, clopping sounds as more of these strange dinosaur things poured in through the door.

"Sit down," the eyeless man said. "Don't run. They don't like it when you run." He turned then and entered the cafeteria, an entourage of the creatures following behind him, ignoring John Pringle.

The first screams came from the radio dispatcher, Mike, as the worms corkscrewed through his glasses and into the soft tissue of his eyes. Over him, his new escort waited as the fire in each socket flared and burned out. "It hurts! Oh my god, it hurts!" he cried, first falling from the seat, rebounding against the wall, then falling to the floor, writhing in misery.

He clawed at his cheeks, digging his fingernails into the soft tissue below his sockets, unable to actually touch the source of the agony.

By the time the skent entered the main dining room, his screams were reduced to a succession of moans.

In all, there were 13 people sitting in the cafeteria, mostly Lupania employees in for an evening meal break after a hard day digging out from the storm. Among them were two women, one a dispatcher, the other a dishwasher who was straightening up the food stations. The screams from the next room caused two of the men sitting at the big table to stand up. The bigger of the two was the head of maintenance, his name Miller Woods. He was 57 years old, but a hulking fellow with a thinning silken horseshoe of grey.

"Sit down, Gents," said a man standing in the doorway. "The screaming will end shortly."

"What in the name of god," Miller gasped.

The other fellow, a rakc of a man, said, "What is this?"

The cook, Ken Short, aka Bill Cosby, was frying bacon on the grill. His fellow cook Shawna, aka Kitchen Nazi, was by the walk-in fridge when the screaming started. Her first inclination was to come out and look, but her eye caught Ken's hand waving behind his back. It flopped fish-like and Shawna froze. He was telling her to stay there.

Ken Short was lifting the sagging strips of bacon from the grill with a long flat spatula designed to flip two eggs. He was just about to flip the saggy strips over when they poured into the cafeteria and lined the walls. Short set his spatula down and, being a man of few words, heard himself say, "Why are there animals in the dining area?"

"We are Skentophyte," said the eyeless man.

He heard Shawna behind him and motioned for her to stay there, but he was thinking. *Better hide Shawna, I think we are all in real trouble here.* Even if Shawna could read minds, she wouldn't have understood his warning, because he was thinking in Kenyan.

"Ladies and gentlemen, I am afraid that you are going to have to get your gear on and come with us."

"What is this?" said the rake of a man. "Who are they, and what is the matter with you?"

"My name is George Redford, and they…" He motioned toward the surrounding skent. "They are Skentophyte. We are Skentophyte. I'm afraid that everyone here is going to have to come back with us."

Miller stood up again. "I'm not going anywhere." He moved to leave.

George Redford shrugged.

A Skentophyte leaped across the room and wrapped a choking claw around Miller's neck. As it squeezed, cutting his oxygen, George Redford said again, "I'm afraid that everyone here is going to have accompany us back to the Acadia mine. I'm very sorry, folks, it's not my idea, skent, that's just the way it is."

The Skentophyte continued strangling Miller. His face was turning blue, snot discharging from his nostrils. He would be dead from asphyxia if it didn't release him. And, of course, it didn't; instead, it curled its other claw over the top of his skull and spun. His head twisted right off. There was a geyser of blood.

That ought to motivate them, George thought.

Yes, motivate Skent we are skent. Harvest.

Then the screaming really started.

Shawna opened the door to the walk-in fridge and slid inside. Short heard the door and knew what she was doing. *They'll hear,* he thought and knocked an empty pot from the cart behind the steam table. It clanged metallically and he barely heard the door click. When the skent pulled him over the steam table, he thought of his friend Shawna and said a prayer for her in Kenyan.

John Pringle was sitting at his desk, dumfounded. He could hardly believe what he was seeing and it had distracted to such a point that he completely forgot about his satellite phone. Why hadn't they herded him into the cafeteria with the others? Mike had stopped screaming, but there were more screams in the dining area. It was then that John Pringle went into survival mode.

As the skent corralled the remaining people in the dining area, Pringle slipped into his parka and tugged his winter cap over his head.

Gotta get out of here, he thought. The satellite phone caught his eye. *Gotta call for help.* But what was he to say if he got a call down to YK? *Hello, we are being overrun by monsters?* No, he'd tell them that someone had gone nuts. That there were dozens dead. That they needed the army. *Yeah. Bring lots of guns! Big fucking guns!* He was slipping his boots on now. He reached over and lifted the sat phone, tucking it into his pocket. He had three security men out on patrol. Crane was up around Portage 33, Rossey was at Meanook, and Jaffery was down south. Jaffrey would be the man to call. Yeah, if he could get a call in to him. Maybe, just maybe...

He was standing now, peering around the doorway. The things were still in the dining area, the eyeless man had his back turned. He glanced the other way and saw Mike sitting with his back to him and one of those things looming over him.

John Pringle crept toward the door, pulse thudding in his temples. He had to get to the pickup and make a run for it. Unless of course he awoke from this crazy nightmare. He eased the door to the mud room open, and thankfully, the hinge did not protest. Sliding through the door, he glanced out the window and onto the lot. He couldn't see anyone. His pickup was parked to the left of the building.

Thirty feet. Only thirty feet.

He could make that. Carefully, he pushed down the crash bar on the door. It clicked under the strain.

Come on! Come on!

He opened the door and the vacuum of arctic air sucked the warmth from the mud room. He squeezed through the crack and was outside.

Just a little farther. Once the door is closed, I can run.

Pringle eased the door closed and gingerly released the lock. He was out and taking the three steps to the path with equal measure, the snow crunching beneath his footwear amplified. When he reached the bottom, he took another look. Nothing. He could see the nose of his white pickup, already idling and ready for action. He ducked down below the dispatch window and broke into a monkey-like sprint.

Five seconds later, he had his hand on the truck door.

4

Shawna thought she would be caught when the pot clanged against the floor. Instead, there was a discord of terrified screams. Inside the walk-in, she felt her skin begin to pimple up from the cold. She removed the apron and wrapped it around her arms. What was going on out there? Why had Kenny motioned for her to hide?

Someone must have gone crazy, she thought and bit her lower lip to stifle a cry. *Calm down!*

Her head pivoted, as she took inventory of the wire shelving. There were steel pans, boxes of meat and veggies, prepped pots of soups and gravies, but what she really wanted was a knife. Above the door, the fan hummed musically to the chorus of muffled screams.

What if he comes in here?

She moved frantically. There had to be something she could use to protect herself. Then on the third shelf just above a large stock pot of green pea soup, she saw the meat hammer. She reached up and pulled it down. It was bigger than a regular hammer, like a mini sledge, but lighter, made of aluminum. On one side it was flat, but on the other was a grid of raised pyramids molded into the aluminum head. She swung it in an arc.

It would have to do.

5

"Where are you going?" Sack asked.

Pringle didn't turn around. He yanked the door open and attempted to get in. But then something clamped his shoulder. He was suddenly airborne and flying backward. He hit the ground with a thud, his head knocking against the frozen hard pack, lighting his world in pin pricks of black and silver.

Concussion, he thought.

The glow of the yard lighting was interrupted by the encircling silhouettes. There was that clicking, and the sound respirators. He heard the distant clunk of the crash bar and a succession of footfalls clunking down the steps. The he heard George Redford's voice.

"John, I thought I told you. They don't like it when you run."

Pringle looked up, the black and silver pin pricks receding, and silhouettes came into focus. He was surrounded by them. Within the circle a small man stood, his eyes also gone, but for the glow deep within the sockets. It was the driver everyone called Sack.

"Stand up, John," Sack motioned, then turned to one of the monstrosities. "He's the head of Security. He might be useful."

The monster said nothing, just clacked its teeth.

Across the collective: Spare this one from harvest.

George Redford stepped up beside Sack. Behind them, surrounded by the creatures, the remaining people from the dining area.

"It only hurts for a while, John," Sack said.

One of the monstrosities leaned over and plucked him from the ground. He heard someone cry out. Then there was a spitting sound and before he was able to wonder, black infernal pain. Cataclysmic agony enveloped him and when he thought he could no longer stand it, and that the pain alone would kill him, there came a milky numbness and with that, the whispers of a thousand thoughts all proclaiming:

Skent! We are Skentophyte! Serve us!

Corbett Lake had fallen…

***

Chapter 30—Paranoid

1

Yellowknife
Tli Cho Manor

In the aftermath of the day's drama came an undercurrent of dread as darkness fell over the northern estate. Neither Maggie nor Angel knew what words passed between Donald and Shamus, but when they re-entered the house, there was an indefinite wait. The stinging slap Angel planted on Maggie's cheek left no mark and both woman acted as if nothing had happened. Shamus sunk back into his chair and stared out the picture window while Donald went out and checked over the vehicles. Maggie retreated to her own room. She was terrified that Donald or even Angel might sell her out to the madman sitting in that chair.

These people were scumbags. There was no honor among thieves, no code of conduct. They screwed each other over like it was a game and would throw each other under the bus without a second thought. They were parasites and sitting in that big overstuffed chair was the king cockroach.

She sat on the edge of the bed, absently bunching the covers in both hands, her knuckles whitening. What would happen when Marty got here? What could he possibly do to save them from the impending storm?

If I could get my hands on Angel's gun, I could shoot him dead and anyone else who got in my way.

But could she really?

Not likely.

Maggie had never handled a firearm in her life.

2

Portage 34
North of the Acadia Mine

Chase Fenwick was coming down the other side of the small portage when he saw the silhouette of a pickup idling on the side of the road. Behind it a utility trailer and on that, a mobile shack.

A hunter, he thought and noted the gap on the trailer large enough to carry a snowmobile.

Must be out there somewhere? Hopefully away from this insanity.

He approached the trailer cautiously from behind. He didn't think there was anyone in it, but he didn't want to surprise anyone either. Especially if they were armed. As he rounded the trailer, he reached into one pocket and pulled out the flare gun. Clumsily he seated it under his arm and moved up to check the cab of the truck. There was no one inside.

Good.

He doubled back to the mobile shack, removed his right glove, and held the flare gun at the ready. Any sign of trouble, he was going to fire it. The way his luck had been, he figured that it would ricochet back and ignite the naphtha bombs he was carrying in his pockets. He tapped on the shack door.

"Hello, is anyone there?"

Nothing. So he tapped again.

"Hello, if anyone's there, please open up."

Silence.

Chase took a deep breath and held it, then reached out and turned the latch. There was no resistance and he hoped with all his heart that no one was home. His index finger wrapped around the trigger and he pulled the door open. It was dark, empty.

He stepped in and looked around. Inside the four-by-six shack was a small wood stove, a bunk, sleeping bag, and table. In the corner there were three folding chairs bungee corded to the wall. This hunter hadn't been here for at least a few hours. The wood stove was cool. He was probably set up somewhere out there, hunting caribou. Chase sat on the bunk for a second, putting down the flare gun and replacing his gloves.

He knew what he had to do. He could be screwing this guy if he took his wheels, and he'd be stranded here. He could leave him the trailer and at least he'd have shelter. The hunter could fire up that little stove and keep warm.

And if they come, he thought. The owner of this trailer had a snowmobile. That was mobility and there were four gas cans on the back of the trailer. If push came to shove, the guy could use the snowmobile.

What if they come, his inner voice nagged.

"Oh for Christ's sake, I just let 16 men go to their death. Now I'm getting a conscience?"

Better late than never.

"I'm not fucking walking anymore! I need this truck!"

The voice fell silent.

Chase stepped out of the shack, sealed the door, and climbed down off the trailer. He worked his way around and checked the driver door. It was unlocked. He was going to take the truck; his first thought was to turn south and make a run for YK, but his conscience was eating at him. He couldn't do that. Then he had another idea. He would stick with his original plan. Go north, find that security truck, and convince him that there was a…

He let out a strangled laugh. This was so fucking insane.

I'll figure that out when I get there. If I find that security man, I'll bring the truck back and ride with him. He was disconnecting the electric brake, winding down the landing gear.

"I'll bring it back," he mumbled. But inside he knew if it came down to life or death, the hunter would be on the losing end of this bargain.

3

Portage 35
Last Land Mass before Dreamcatcher Lake

Phil Crane was parked in the center of the portage when his Satellite phone rang. He turned it over and glanced down at the LED readout. He half expected it to be an unknown number, either coming from Gordon or his mystery man up on the ice, but it actually read: Corbett S1.

It was John Pringle.

He pushed the button. "Hi, John, what's up?"

"Hey, Phil, are you up on 33?"

"Actually no, I'm a little further north, cruising the lake, but working my way south," he lied.

"Oh? Something up?"

Don't tell me to come back, he thought. "No, just beating back a bit of boredom from sitting in one place, thought I'd do a little roving patrol and get the sleep out of my eyes."

"Good idea skent. So, what is your position exactly?"

What is your position exactly? Crane felt unease settle over him. Why did John want to know his exact position? In the back of his mind he could see security men and cops rallying—ready to take him down—Gordon Shamus being taken into custody in YK, Marty Croft sitting with

Meanook Security spilling everything. "What?"

"Where are you, Phil? Skent. Your position exactly."

Was there an accusation in that question? Was the jig up? Why hadn't Croft and his convoy come south yet? That had to be it, something had gone wrong. That had to be it! Crane pushed the panic back down, took a slow breath and said, "I'm on the lake heading south, back to 33." There was only silence, so Crane added, "What's going on, John?"

"I need you to head into the Acadia Mine and spare off Jeff Rossey. Skent. He's got a family issue that needs attending. I need you to do that now. Skent. You understand, Phil?"

Skent? What the hell is the matter with you, Pringle?

Phil knew he was being lied to. Jeff Rossey wasn't in the Acadia rotation, he worked Meanook. And then there was that other thing. That twitch, the word he kept repeating. "Skent." Phil had seen and heard enough nervous twitches in his day to recognize when someone was lying. Sometimes it was an aversion of the eyes, a repeated clearing of the throat before a sentence, and sometimes they focused on a word. Yeah, John Pringle was lying through his teeth.

"Sure, John, I can do that. I'll head over right away."

"Good. Skent. That would be good. See you soon."

See you soon?

"Yeah, okay." He set the phone on the seat and stared at it for a long time while considering his options. He couldn't call Shamus; if they had him in custody, it would only connect him. He wasn't going south to Acadia, it felt too much like a trap. So, his options were limited. Wait a little longer for Croft or…

Suddenly headlight beams bounced up the trail to his south. Someone was coming. Crane turned off his lights, threw the pickup into gear and sped up the trail. His daytime running lights still lit the way, and he wasn't too happy, considering the prospect that an eye in the sky might see him, but he beat it up the trail just the same.

They tracked me on the satellite!

He reached over and shut the phone off as he steered over the trail, haphazardly accelerating. On the other side of the portage was a high mound. He really had two choices: he could get onto the Dreamcatcher and make a run for it, or he could hide behind the mound and hope they blew right by.

Then what?

"Then we get the fuck out of here!" he said and rolled onto the ice.

The lights were still coming, but not as fast as he initially thought. Not fast enough for a pursuit? With that in mind, Crane opted for the latter and pulled the pickup around the mound and hid from the northbound vehicle. He reached over into his bag, pulled out the gun, and set it on his lap.

4

Chase Fenwick was driving northbound. The convoy ahead of him was comprised of nine big trucks from the Acadia Mine. They'd rolled up as he was unhooking the trailer. The first truck stopped, the passenger side window opened, and the driver popped his head out for a look. Chase only caught a glimpse, but that was enough. The driver had no eyes. Chase was hiding behind a bank of snow, Molotov cocktail in hand, flare gun at the ready. He hoped they didn't see the landing gear on the ground or the disconnected light cord. He prayed that they didn't de-bus for a closer look because the bank wasn't the greatest hiding place.

Come on, you bastards, he thought. *Move along!*

As if reading his thoughts, the driver pulled his head back in, rolled up his window, and reached for his handset. Chase hoped that he was alerting them that the truck was empty. The first rig rolled slowly on, then the convoy rumbled past one after another until they were gone. Chase recognized some of the trucks and, though he didn't want to admit it, he knew that at least some of these men were the ones he had failed to warn at the barricade.

Now, following at a safe distance, using their snow dust as cover, he knew exactly where they were going, although he wondered if his efforts to find the security man was futile. If the creatures inside those vehicles found him first, would they not just take him out? He hoped not, he was hedging his bets that the security man's satellite phone might offer enough of a deterrent until they reached Meanook.

Catch him on the way back? Maybe.

Maybe, and Chase was willing to risk that because he didn't know if there would be a barricade at Corbett, and even worse: he was afraid to face it alone. Besides, if he could hook up with the security guy, they could use that phone to call for help. He was almost across the lake and the convoy was climbing the last portage. That would be where the security guy was; if he was still alive, that was.

5

The Fish Camp

Billy Jack had spent the final hours of light trying to relocate the caribou herd he'd spotted while standing on top of Lonny's water truck. He wasn't having any luck; the herd had vanished, but to where? In the distance, he could see the lights of his brother's flooding crew out there on the ice road. Despite his poor luck in locating the herd, he smiled. Axe and the boys were racking up some serious overtime. Axe had been saving up to buy his son a snowmobile. Billy offered to chip in, but Axe was too proud; he didn't like taking money, not even from his brother. With the overtime, it didn't look like Axe would be saving for too long.

Good for him. Billy was proud of his brother, proud of the man he'd become.

The moon was full, a bloated sphere dominating the sky, washing the tundra in its milky glow. The camp was at a higher elevation than the road, making it a perfect vantage point for anyone looking to take in the splendor of this landscape. Axe's flooding crew was approximately 600 meters away, easy enough to distinguish from the landscape, but too far to actually make out who was who with the binoculars.

He scanned the road, following it north; it was an almost indiscernible shadow that snaked across the flattening sheet of snow and ice. Through the binoculars, he caught a flicker of amber cutting out across the lake, then another. Headlights coming south from Meanook.

Another crew, he wondered. Then he saw a second truck and a third. No, not another work crew, it was a convoy of four trucks. He set down the binoculars and picked up his rifle. He turned the adjustment dial on the Nightforce Scope up to full power and raised the aperture to his eye. Allowing his eye to adjust, he traversed the rifle in a slow right arc until he found the convoy. This was something he'd done quite often when looking for targets of opportunity outside the wire; in fact, it was common practice.

The trucks were inky silhouettes, moving slowly across the Dreamcatcher. Behind them, a floating stream of snow dust looking like a frozen comet tail. They had a long way to go, at least two hours before they hit the beach to the south. Billy wondered if he knew any of the truckers. Was Spence in that group? He'd laugh if he knew Billy was up here practicing target registration. He watched the convoy for a moment, then swung the sight back onto his brother's flooding crew. Axe was easier to make out now, wandering up and down the work site, his trusty fire axe swinging at his side. This widened Billy's smile.

6

Portage 35

Crane killed the engine and listened. He could hear the rise and fall of diesel engines and that eased his paranoia a little. Light danced across the surface of the lake when the first truck descended and rolled past.

"Just a convoy," he whispered. "Holy shit. I'm losing it."

The second truck trailed and Crane laughed.

They must have broken through down South.

The trucks kept coming and by the time the ninth had passed, Crane began to relax. He didn't consider how tightly spaced the rigs were and then he started to think about John Pringle. His glaring lie, the tick that manifested itself when he lied. No, this was not a time to relax, something was definitely wrong. And as if to put an exclamation on that thought, he heard another vehicle coming and this wasn't a rig. It was a smaller vehicle.

A pickup!

He turned and watched, dim cones of light bouncing up and down as the vehicle challenged the many twists and turns of the bumpy portage. It was getting closer, of this he was sure, but this vehicle was coming in the dark. Like Crane, the driver did not want to be seen. He only had his daytime running lights on. The vehicle came to a stop at the top of the hill and waited.

Crane began to panic. Maybe those were cops up there. He began to think about the satellite phone again. Was there a GPS tracking device in it? He knew that even a cell phone that was turned off emitted a ping that and that could be used as locator. He picked it up off the seat, turned it over, fumbled with it, and pulled the battery.

"Shit! Shit! Shit!" He pulled a plastic bag out from under the seat and wrapped it around the phone. Then quietly he stepped out of the truck and walked around to the box. In the back was a steel tool box; he opened it and placed the phone inside. Then he wandered over to the embankment and buried it in the snow. He had no idea if that would be enough to block a signal. Probably not, but why take a chance? He climbed back into the cab, his gun at the ready. The convoy of nine was vanishing into the opaque landscape, swallowed by the night. Above him, still out of sight, the mystery pickup continued to idle.

What are you waiting for?

Despite his parka, the interior of the truck was cooling off to an uncomfortable level. Either this guy did something soon or Crane would be forced to start his vehicle.

As if on cue, the vehicle began to creep down the grade, his daytime running lights barely pushing against the moonlight. Snow, sand, and ice crunched beneath the tires, as it rolled past and onto the ice. Crane checked out the truck: it was a black Ford F350. He didn't think it was a government vehicle; it was civilian.

Okay, it's not a cop. So, who is it? Shamus's mystery man? Why is he shadowing those trucks? Crane was sure of this and then he thought of Pringle again. "Where are you exactly, Phil?" The pickup continued on, keeping a safe distance back from the convoy. *Maybe he's not shadowing them, maybe he's waiting for me to be drawn to them.*

"What in the fuck are you up to?"

Crane considered turning tail and running for it, but there were so many unknowns. What if Croft was still coming with the shipment? What if that black pickup was going to meet him? What then? Face Shamus without completing his task? And the mother of all unknowns: What if this was all a large helping of paranoia? He couldn't just bolt, not without knowing for sure. He placed the gun back in his bag and waited until the black pickup was far enough out on the lake, and then took up a safe distance of pursuit.

7

The leader of the convoy did not see the pickup shadowing them. He was focused on the road ahead. He had four hours of driving ahead until they reached Meanook Mine. Occasionally, his escort would reach out an assuring claw and caress his shoulder. There was an almost maternal feel in that touch— after you filtered out the stink and clacking teeth.

He wondered if it was female.

Across the collective: Communications first, then the airfield. No distractions, objective must be secured, then harvest. Skent we are skentophyte.

There were workers on the lake. Flooders, to be exact. Pringle had given their location on the map. Approximately 45 minutes ahead on the pressure ridge. They would not be stopping for those people. They were but a handful, but still, there was a plan in place to collect them. The Skentophyte would harvest everything they could, leaving only the meek; they were an industrious race and bone collection was their stock and trade.

***

Chapter 31—Targets of Opportunity

1

Dreamcatcher Lake
68 km, North of Portage 35

Axe and Vincent stood side by side, watching the approaching convoy. They slowed to 10 km/h before reaching the flooded ice, crawling with deliberate lethargy.

"That's a big convoy," Vincent remarked.

"Sure is," Axe replied. "Nine trucks? I didn't think they were allowed to move in such a big group." His remote crackled and a voice called him.

"Flooding crew? You have a copy?"

Axe pressed the switch on his mic. "Go for flooding crew."

"Hi, flood crew, I assume you want us at minimum speed in this area. Anymore slow spots to consider?" It was the driver of the lead truck.

"No, this is your last flood zone on the lake. Take her slow until you guys clear the zone."

"Copy that. Skent. We're heading to Meanook, how's that road looking? Still a mess?"

Axe reached up again and keyed. "It's looking better than it did this morning, driver, but I'd use the middle on the portages and steer clear of the roads edges. You don't want to get bit by a snowbank."

The first truck rolled past and Axe could barely make out the driver's features. As he glided by, Axe could see his silhouette reaching for the hanging microphone and bringing it to his mouth. "Thanks for the heads up." Then he replaced the handset.

"You're welcome," Axe said. "Have a safe trip north."

Each driver brought up a hand as their truck rumbled past and Axe never saw a single face nor one single escort. But something felt wrong about this convoy. First off, they were all vans and that seemed unprecedented, but nine of them.

"Odd bunch," Vincent muttered while waving to the fifth truck.

"You can say that again," Axe replied.

"Odd bunch," Vincent snickered and turned to Axe.

"Oh, are we a tad on the punchy side?"

"Tell me to say that again, Axe man." Vincent turned his mouth, cupped into a big toothy grin. His eyes met Axe's in a dare.

"You can say that again."

"Tell me to say that again, Axe Man."

Axe laughed. "You're the goofiest old bugger I ever met in my life. Once the last truck is across, let's get this shit packed up for Corbett. I'm exhausted.

2

The Fish Camp

Billy watched the convoy roll through the flood zone. He was thinking about running the snowmobile down and grabbing some of Vincent's coffee. Then he caught a glint of light to the south. Two pickups almost a kilometer between them. He used the sight and spied the first vehicle. It was a black Ford F350, very much like his own, behind a Security vehicle.

Things are getting busy, he thought.

He turned his attention back to the convoy and watched as the last big truck rolled out of the flood zone. Ahead of the last truck, the convoy stretched almost 4 ½ kilometers. A big group, Billy thought. He wasn't even sure if such a thing was legal up here on the ice. *Maybe one group caught another,* he thought. *Maybe they just got bunched up.* North of them, another 10 kilometers up the southbound group of four was coming. Billy shivered. The cold was getting to him, even with his insulated coveralls and parka. He decided to boot down there on the snowmobile. Grab a cup of Vincent's coffee. That would hit the spot.

Then he saw something that put his thoughts on hold. The last big truck in the convoy of nine had stopped. Billy thought maybe they were having mechanical issues. He raised the sight to his eye—watched the brake lights blink, and then all the lights went out.

None of the other trucks stopped. Is this guy having *electrical issues? His radio not working?* They wouldn't leave him behind. It was against ice road rules to leave a truck stranded on their own. *Maybe they don't know he'd broke down.* Billy picked up his own radio, switched over to Ladd 1 and was about to call the convoy leader himself when something peculiar happened. The driver of the stopped truck appeared at the back of the trailer and unlatched the barn doors. He stepped aside and out jumped a dog. Then another, and it took a moment for Billy to realize they weren't dogs at all.

"Those look like wolves."

A third and a fourth hopped from the trailer and Billy knew they were wolves. They seemed to ignore the driver and trotted up and over the bank. There they lined up and waited. Billy didn't see the first creatures climbing from the van. He was focused on the wolves, trying to understand why they had been in the van to begin with. Why they seemed to have no fear of the man who had let them out. By the time the fifth creature clambered out and onto the ice, he caught it in his peripheral, but had no idea what he was looking at. More of them came out, climbing over the same bank the wolves congregated on. After that, with chameleon stealth they melted into the landscape.

"8, 9, 10, 11, 12, 13, 14," he counted as they joined the wolves on the other side of the bank. *They? What were they?* "What the hell is this? A circus act?"

The driver closed the barn door and worked his way back around the trailer. After a moment, the lights came back on and the big rig began to pull away. Billy shook his head, and even pinched his arm to make sure he wasn't dreaming. He swung the scope back onto the wolves: they moving south now, along bank. He couldn't see those other things, not clearly, but he knew they were in tow. Snow dust kicked up. They were working their way south along the frozen plain. Billy felt that sixth sense chirp again, the same he'd felt in Afghanistan.

"Got that Mojo fired up, Billy Jack," Sgt. Spence echoed.

And yes, that intuitive feeling told him that the shit was about to hit the fan. The hairs on his neck bristled, the pit of his belly tightened. He looked from the coming wolves to his brother's flood crew.

Heading straight for them. Ambush.

His emotions told him to fire up the snowmobile and make a beeline for the flood site, but the sniper knew that was wrong. He'd never get there in time, his weapon would be useless in such close quarters. Here he had the high ground. He reached over and unzipped the cover for his 303 and pulled it out. He glanced to the moon and adjusted the sight. He was calculating the range in his head, considering possible leads on moving targets. He laid out all his magazines. Began to control his breathing. He would be more effective up here, if his intuition was right. He followed the path of the four wolves, the tightly knit flurry of snow following behind them. As he readied himself, he swung his Nightforce scope back to the flooding crew. They were packing up. Pushing their pumps toward the truck. Lonny was doing another pass with the water truck.

"Come on, get into to those vehicles, boys," he muttered.

He swung the scope onto the northbound pickups. The security vehicle was gaining on the black Ford and wasn't even considering the possibility that the black pickup was his.

What the hell is going on?

Another chill rattled through him, stealing his collect, tiny involuntary tremors fluctuated between his shoulder blades. This was going to affect his aim. He stood and turned the handle bar on the snowmobile. He would need it to steady the weapon.

3

Chase stopped the pickup about 300 meters short from the flood site. He hadn't spotted the white pickup shadowing him, too engrossed in what was happening on the pressure ridge. He had his Bushmasters out, was watching the flood crew and determining whether or not they were infected. He'd caught sight of the rig sitting north, but the small sight glasses weren't powerful enough for him to see what was going on; although he was pretty sure he knew. And he wasn't going to sit idle this time. He had set his parka on the seat and stood with the pockets open, offering easy access to the four Molotov cocktails. On the dash, the flare gun was also ready. He was going in there, hell or high water, he wasn't going to sit by when they came this time. He considered calling on the radio, then thought of the other nine trucks loaded up with those things. No, better to just let them carry on north; there were too many. A warning would turn them around. If this was going to work, he'd need the element of surprise.

He placed his foot on the brake and pulled the gear selector out of park. He had the Bushmasters up again, watching the one man swinging an ax and giving orders to the rest of the crew. They were packing up. Maybe, if they got going, and started rolling south, the creatures that were coming for them would withdraw and rejoin the northern convoy.

That was too much to hope for.

Over the VHF radio he heard a booming voice. "Well, hello there, looks like traffic has resumed."

"The road is open, driver. How's it looking to Meanook?"

"What you see is what you get, my brother. Marty, I don't have to tell you that we got a whole hockey sock of trucks coming at us. Uh huh, yep yep."

4

Crane heard the name. Then heard the response.

"Okay, Garney."

Marty Croft, alive and well, coming south. Okay, so he wasn't with security, that was encouraging, but the black pickup was hanging back again and that merited an investigation. Crane decided to roll up for a chat; if it was a civilian who was just nosey, he'd play up his part as security. If the guy was here to scoop him, that would take things in a whole other direction. Crane placed the gun in his lap again. It was time to find out who was driving that black pickup and what his intentions were. He pulled out into the road and drove up the ice to meet the black pickup.

5

The wolves moved into position, taking up vantage points on both sides of the ice road. As Vincent pushed a cyclone pump across the ice, one of them darted behind him and climbed the opposing bank. Axe saw the first wolf silhouette on the east bank and knew immediately that they were being watched. "Vincent, get everyone to the truck. We got a wolf pack checking us out."

Vincent scanned the area. After spotting a second wolf, he let out a low authoritative bark. "Pssst… Traffic! Gilligan! Get your asses to the truck right now, we're being stalked by wolves!"

The young man nicknamed Gilligan started for the truck, while his friend "Traffic" was still processing what Vincent had said. He turned his head slowly and 20 feet to his left, he saw a grey wolf hanging over the bank. It snarled under the moonlight, looking like a demon from hell. Its eyes, cavernous black hollows with pulsing diodes of red and green.

Then, without mercy, they came.

From high above, Billy Jack expelled half of his first breath and squeezed the trigger. There was a click of metal hitting primer and the recoil in his shoulder. Across the tundra there was a brittle report of rifle fire. The first wolf fell, but the massacre was already underway.

Traffic, his name really Sandy, was pulled from the road, and sharp bony claws tore at him. His screams were shrill and high. He felt a thud against his shoulder, unusual warmth. When he turned to look, there was only a nub of bone. Before he had time to understand that, his head came off.

Lonny was driving the water truck up to meet Axe when the driver door seemed to disappear and he felt himself tumbling out on the ice. The water truck continued rolling forward toward the flood truck as four Skent unzipped Lonny from his pelt. He never had a chance to take in his killers.

There was another audible crack.

6

Billy fired at the creatures he saw scuttling around on the ice near the water truck, but they were hard to take aim on. He'd seen them attack the water truck, pull Lonny out, now reduced to a blotted stain on the evening white. He'd hit one but had no idea if he'd just winged it because it continued to rip and tear at the rag doll that was Lonny.

He swung the sight left, then right.

Where's Axe? Where is he?

Only two wolves stood now and Billy pulled his eye back from the scope and assessed the situation. Why weren't the wolves moving? Why had they not taken up in the bloodletting? And then it came to him, or so he hoped.

"FOO's," he said. "They're fucking FOO's!" And Billy Jack understood then, even though it shouldn't be, his mojo told him it was so. They were the eyes of the attacking force, whatever it was. Whatever was up with those wolves was key to what was happening down there. Foos, being the acronym for Forward Observation Officer. It had to be. He brought the Nightforce scope up—sighted in the third wolf—inhaled, let half out, and squeezed the trigger.

7

Chase was still looking through the Bushmasters when the pickup rolled up his right side. He hadn't noticed until the driver gave a toot on his horn. He turned to look. It was a security truck.

How the hell did he get behind me?

The driver motioned for him to lower his window.

Chase pushed the button down, the Bushmasters hanging halfway down his face. The massacre was just beginning.

"Hi, what are you doing out here?" Crane asked.

Chase stared, a confused look on his face. "How did I miss you?"

"You were looking for me?" Crane asked.

Chase's mouth hung open. His eyes averted to the pressure ridge, then back to Crane. "What?"

"I said, you were looking for me."

"Yeah," he brought the Bushmasters back up. "Oh, fuck! I gotta go. Now! Right fucking now!" He threw the truck into gear and stepped on the accelerator.

"What the…" Crane tightened his grip on the gun, taking his index off the trigger guard. Then the black pickup thudded into the driver side quarter panel, throwing Crane over in his seat, the muscles in his neck whiplashed. There was a complaint of crunching metal—grinding plastic, and then the black pickup was pulling away—fishtailing up the ice. Crane straightened, shook his head to see the truck peeling off.

They're cutting me out! "No fucking way," he growled and threw his own truck into gear.

8

The creatures encircled them and even though two of the wolves had fallen, the skentophyte were still overwhelming them. The kid Gilligan was the next to fall, one of the large creatures pounced into the open circle and as young Gilligan scrambled beneath the truck, it caught his ankle and dragged him out. He screamed, terrified and when they were on him, his screams became agonized wails.

Vincent and Axe were up against the cube van wall. One of the Skentophyte lunged in and Axe swung his namesake in a hard arc, catching the monster just below the jaw. It snarled and scrambled back.

Axe thought he heard gunfire.

Vincent saw the fourth wolf fall and suddenly the creatures stopped and began to twist blindly. "Something's happened," he whispered to Vincent and one of them twisted in his direction and spat hard twice. The first venomous wad splattered against the blade of his ax. He had just enough time to see the parasite twisting on the hardened steel, and then the second wad caught his right eye and set his world on fire.

Simultaneously, Billy was engaging the creature and looked for what he thought might be a weak point.

There's gotta be a chink in that armor.

Axe fell down, screaming.

The agony! Oh my god, it fucking hurts! His eye was cooking off, the prying voices touching inside him, trying to see, to regroup. We are skent! We are skent! We are skent!

The ax clanged on the ice. Vincent reached down, picked it up, and saw the armored worm still twisting in tendrils of mucous. Using his middle finger, he flicked it from the blade and brought it up defensively. But the creatures were twisting and turning blindly, as if trying to…

The things, they were listening.

Another shot rang out and the creature that had spat into Axe's face dropped. The others twisted defensively.

Axe moaned and rolled over, the fire in his socket burning down now.

I'm screwed, man, Vincent thought. Then something truly amazing happened.

A pickup truck skidded onto the scene, and not just any pickup truck, but Billy Jack's pickup truck. Except Billy wasn't driving it.

The creatures turned their heads in the direction of the sound and Vincent saw another pickup truck coming. It was Barney Fife! Then he looked down at Axe and saw the worm twisting in the socket. Without a second thought, he pulled out his knife and went to work.

"Get down," the guy driving Billy's truck screamed. He had a Molotov cocktail in one hand. Its wick was already lit, he pulled back his arm and tossed. It turned end over end, the flickering flame spiraling amber and then it exploded on the ice and there was a crackle of liquescent fire. Three of the creatures were burning. "Take that, you mother fuckers!"

More shots rang out!

Barney Fife, the security dude, was out of his vehicle now and he had a goddamned gun! He hesitated at first, then looked around and began shooting too.

Gotta get it out before it kills him. Vincent had his hands full, still digging into that socket, trying to get at the worm as it burrowed deeper. Axe's eye was completely gone. He struggled and tried to pull away, but Vincent dug in deeper.

Axe shrieked in agony.

Behind them, a snowmobile droned, and it was coming fast.

"Hold still, Axe Man. I gotta get it out!"

Axe couldn't hear him. He was being overloaded by the collective eye. **We are skentophyte!** He understood what was happening. **We are skentophyte!** Felt the will being drained from him. **We are skentophyte!** The fire was almost out, but Vincent would have none of that.

There was another crack of glass shattering, followed by a whoop, then the sizzle and fissure of even more fire. Then, to the delight of Chase Fenwick, an insect screech of misery. He'd bagged three more of them.

Billy dismounted his snowmobile and marched across the flood zone surrounded by body parts, both human and monster. He passed one of the things, turned his rifle on it and fired, but he was focused on his brother. Vincent appeared to be working on him. *Danny is down! Danny is down!* Another explosion! More screeches! Billy quick marched toward his kid brother. The security guy was firing a gun at them. The man with the cocktails had stolen his truck, but still, he kept moving. Questions were for later. *Danny needs my help!*

Billy knelt, overloaded on adrenaline, heart stammering, out of breath. "What's wrong with him? Is he hit?"

"Hold him down," Vincent barked. "He's got one of those things in his eye! I gotta get it out." Vincent put down the knife and dug in his pocket, looking for his Gerber multi-tool. Billy felt revulsion and terror sweep through him when he saw the empty socket. Then he saw the thing coiling like a snake, its tail glowing, bits of light arcing.

Then Axe began to turn.

"Skent! We are Skentophyte," Axe said.

The monsters surrounding them began to focus. The collective eye aligning them. Billy caught them in his peripheral and thought, *Foo, Axe is their Foo, just like the wolves.* Billy pulled out his own pliers. "Get out of the way, Vincent!" He clamped down on the worm and yanked it out. There was a spurt of blood, a gristly snap, and then, there it was, caught in the scissor grip of the pliers. Billy threw it down and it twisted on the ice. It was much longer than an earthworm, nine inches at least and covered in armor that looked almost medieval. Billy stood and brought his boot down hard. It crunched like a spring beetle.

Axe felt the boot come down on the worm, the crunch of its singular synaptic transmitter. He had been severed from the collective, but he knew everything. Who they were, what they'd done, and what their intentions were. He understood what was wrong with the wolves, felt the agony of his escort as it burned in the rain of fire. He saw something else, something they had. Something that would open up a huge portal. Bigger than the one at the Acadia Mine. He wanted to tell his brother and Vincent, but the pain was too much and coupled with an obsessive madness. He had to warn them, but he was tumbling away, into the darkness.

9

When it was over, there were four of the creatures left. Using their weapons, Billy and Crane dispatched them as Vincent packed the empty socket and put a fresh dressing on Axe's face.

With that done, Crane turned to both Chase and Billy and said, "Can anybody tell me what the fuck is going on here?"

"They're from the Acadia Mine. Corbett Lake is gone. And probably Meanook as well."

Vincent said, "That northbound convoy, they were the ones that set this shit storm on us."

"Yeah," Chase said. "Infected."

"The men in the northbound convoy were carrying more of these things? Why? Why would the drivers do that?"

"They infect you. Like your brother over there. Those men were under their control. Like the wolves you killed."

"So they can understand everything," Billy said.

"I don't know. I guess."

Billy caught the approaching convoy and suddenly bolted for the radio. He yanked the door open and lifted the handset and said, "Jackpot, this is Jester. Copy?"

There was a momentary pause, then he heard Spence. "Go for Jackpot?"

"Jackpot! No duff! Mike—Romeo—Sierra!"

There was no response. Billy ran across the ice and climbed up the ladder on the back of the water truck. Once up there, he pulled out his flashlight and gave it three short blasts.

The convoy stopped.

Good.

Billy climbed down and looked in on his brother. Vincent was cradling his head. He checked for a pulse. It was steady against irregular breathing. From behind him, Chase and Crane came up.

"What does Mike Romeo Sierra mean?" Chase asked.

Billy turned to meet Chase's eyes, then beyond his shoulder to the waiting convoy. “Maintain radio silence.” Then Billy shouldered his weapon and went out to meet them.

***

Chapter 32—Jackpot and Jester

1

"Jackpot, this is Jester! Copy?" Spence immediately recognized Billy's voice. And he looked ahead and saw the yellow glow.

Accident? He reached up and grabbed the handset.

"Go for Jackpot."

"Jackpot—No duff—Mike! Romeo! Sierra!"

Spence held the handset. *MRS? Why would Billy send him an MRS? Something was wrong, something that couldn't be discussed over the air.* He flipped his radio to the alternate channel. "Big Garney, copy."

"I just lost power. I need you guys to stop."

Four sets of brake lights lit up.

Spence put on his cap and grabbed his parka. He climbed out of the truck. Limping at a brisk pace up the ice toward Merv's truck was not an easy task; he was 500 meters back. By the time he was halfway there, all three men were climbing from their rigs. "Leave it to me to take up tail gunner. The gimp with the prosthetic leg," he grumbled. His stump was rubbing against the inner cup, but he ignored it. *No duff! What kind of trouble was Billy in?* They started back toward him, Merv in the lead, Marty, and then Garney.

Merv reached him first.

"Okay, what happened? Why can't we talk on the radio?" Merv said, a cigarette dangling between his lips, bouncing on every syllable. "And what the fuck is that?" He jammed a thumb toward the flickering light.

"I don't know. I guess we'll find out when I talk to Billy."

Then Marty was there. "What's wrong with your truck?"

"Nothing," Spence said and pointed to the glow of amber. "There's something wrong up there."

Marty had seen the flicker of yellow and thought it might be strobes from a recovery vehicle. He really hadn't given it much thought, but now it burned brighter, and he was beginning to think that there was an accident of some sort.

More delays.

Panic washed over him like ice water. What if Crane was in that accident? What if Crane was dead? What the hell would he do then? Then an even more terrifying thought occurred.

What if Crane had caused that?

They started back toward the front of the convoy to meet Garney. By the time they reached him, Billy Jack's silhouette appeared and was closing the distance.

2

The fires were cycling down, the naphtha expended, leaving in their wake a stench akin to burned hair. Fourteen dead Skentophyte smoldered in varied states, the wolves lay dead in the spots that Billy had dispatched them, and from the hollows of their sockets, an orange, yolk-like ooze spilled, but didn't freeze. The lights in their eyes blinked out.

Billy had told them very little. After all, what could he tell them? He was still reeling from the event himself. Still questioning his sanity. "My brother is hurt bad. More than half his crew is dead," he turned his eyes to Spence. Those deep dark brown eyes said, "There's more, Spence, but I can't say."

"What happened, Bill?" Garney asked.

"It will be easier if I show you. But I think we better be quick, I don't know if it will be safe to stay here."

"Why?" Marty asked.

Billy looked at Spence, then back to Marty. "This is a 'have to see it to believe it' moment. It will save a lot of time if I just show you. And to be honest, I still have a lot of questions myself."

"Okay, my brother, we'll mount up and follow you in."

"Wait," Marty said. "How do you know this isn't a trap?"

Spence grabbed Marty by the shoulder. "Listen to me, Marty, you don't know him. I get that, but this guy is my family. His brother is my family. So if he says he has to show us, we are going to take a look."

"Look, Spence, I…"

"You wonder how I lost my leg. It was an IED in Afghanistan. Billy here saved my life. Before that day, he was my fire-team partner and best friend. After that, he became my brother. If he says that Mars is invading, I'm going for a look."

"Okay, let's have a look then." Marty nodded.

"How do you want to do this?" Merv said.

Billy almost smiled. He hadn't told them about the creatures; Spence was in for a surprise. "Let's mount up on Garney's rig and roll in a little closer. I should have brought the snowmobile, I guess my head wasn't exactly in the game. Once we have a look, I'll bring the rest of you back to get your rigs with my pickup. Then we can figure out what the hell to do next."

3

When they rolled onto the scene, Marty saw Phil Crane standing there with the gun dangling at his side.

What the hell is he doing here?

Crane acknowledged Marty with a nod and placed the pistol into the hip pocket of his parka. The other man at Crane's side walked over to join them.

"Where's my brother?" he asked.

"We put him in the back of the flood truck," Chase said. "The old guy… Vincent? He's with him."

The others were taking in the carnage. The blood, the half-burned creatures, the smoldering remnants. It was surreal. They walked as a group in silence. Taking it all in, but not one of them was believing what he was seeing. Then Spence started laughing.

"I don't see how this is funny," Chase said.

"You didn't hear his Invaders from Mars speech," Billy said, half smirking, shaking his head.

"My brothers, what in the name of God's green earth happened here?"

"Those things. They were in the last rig that passed you. They attacked the flooding crew. I was up at the Fish Camp when it happened. This guy here was following him."

"Chase Fenwick," he said. "I'm the Chief Operations guy from the Acadia Mine. That is where these things came from."

"When they attacked the crew, I started shooting. Luckily, Chase here came on the scene and this other guy, I didn't get your name."

"Phil, Phil Crane." His eyes met Marty's, then darted away to the others. When he turned his attention, Marty made his move.

He didn't have the ball peen hammer. So he thrust his hand into Crane's open pocket and grabbed for the gun, simultaneously punching Crane in the nose. Marty felt the cold steel slip from his grasp, almost drop away when he reached into Crane's pocket. Then his middle finger hooked the trigger guard and he felt the trigger graze his knuckle. Later he would realize that the safety had been off and that the gun might very well have gone off in Crane's pocket. Crane went to his knees, a steady stream of blood discharging from his broken nose, into his mouth, and down his beard. He snapped a hand blindly for his pocket, but it was too late.

"Jesus, my brother! What gives?" Garney started.

Marty ignored him, bringing the gun up, placing it against Crane's temple and cocking the hammer. "Where is she, you motherfucker? Tell me or I'll kill you right fucking now."

"What are you doing?" Chase protested. "He's on our side."

"He's on no one's side! Where is she? Right now, Crane!"

Crane spit out a glut of blood. "I have no idea what he's talking about. I don't even… even know who are you? Why did you hit me?"

Billy reached up and slowly brought the rifle from his shoulder, but kept it in a neutral position. He didn't want to do anything to draw Marty's aim onto him. Calmly, he said, "What is going on here?"

Marty looked around at the others while keeping a trained eye on Crane. His finger was firm against the trigger, the cold steel biting into his skin, but he didn't care. "They've got my wife. This asshole and a guy named Gordon Shamus are holding her somewhere in YK."

"He's lying," Phil said. "I've never seen him before in my life. Somebody get this maniac off me."

Billy moved the rifle, swinging it in the general direction of Marty and Phil. He locked his eyes on Spence, who was already waiting for signal. "Everyone just take a breath here."

"I was blackmailed into coming here. There's a bag in the sleeper…"

"Shut the fuck up, Croft!" Phil whispered.

"You shut the fuck up!" Marty cracked him in the mouth with the gun, and then to the others, "Diamonds, from the Meanook Mine. They're in my sleeper. Don't trust this fucker. You let your guard down with him and we could all end up dead."

Crane buckled over, a tooth plopped onto the eyes, and then it was swimming in more blood. He wiped his mouth with his sleeve. "Idiot, you're going to get us both killed."

"If I didn't do it, they were going to kill my wife and me. Now they're holding my wife somewhere in Yellowknife. They're probably going to kill us anyway."

"Marty, my brother. Put the gun down, there's enough dead folks here. We can talk about this."

Billy turned to Merv. "Can you drive a snowmobile?"

"Sure, but..."

"Jump on my snowmobile and check out his sleeper. What color is the bag, Marty?"

"It's green," he said to Billy, then, "Where is she, Crane?"

Crane grimaced, "Keep fucking hitting me and you'll never know."

Then Billy brought his own weapon up and trained the sight on Crane. "Is this true? You're holding this guy's wife?"

Crane turned toward Billy, but said nothing.

Billy raised his voice. "Listen, my brother is really hurt, we've got dead people everywhere. Those things could be coming this way: either from north or south. So answer my question, Phil, or Crane, or whatever your name is, because at this point both you and this Marty guy are starting to look like a major fucking liability. I don't give a shit about any stolen diamonds. I just want to live to see another day and get my brother the fuck out of here!"

Still, Crane was mute.

"Merv, get going. Phil, if he comes back with that bag and I find out you're lying, I'm going to take it out of your hide."

"Fuck you," Crane seethed.

"Fuck me?" Billy said. "You know what, Marty, I'm going to take your word for it." He handed the rifle over to Spence, who immediately trained it on Crane. Then he pivoted with lightning speed and booted Crane hard in the guts. "Fuck you!"

Crane crumpled on the ice. Billy pushed Marty aside, but made no play for the gun. Instead, he knelt down, clamped his hand on Crane's windpipe, and began to squeeze. As Crane started to choke, he heard the Indian whisper in his ear, his voice a low, dangerous snarl. "Do you know what a honey pot is? That's when you use a wounded man to draw for targets of opportunity. Believe me when I tell you this. You're about to become a honey pot, my friend. I'm going to shoot you in in each kneecap and leave you for those things. If you're lucky, maybe you'll freeze to death before they find you. That you can hope for, but if they come back, well… I don't really have to tell you, do I? Convince me right now that I shouldn't do this. I've killed a lot of men better than you, so you better start talking."

Phil Crane's eyes became wide. He didn't know who this guy was, but he understood he meant business. He blinked and under the crushing hand of Billy Jack, he barely managed a nod.

He would talk.

Billy dropped him and turned. "Sounds like we've got something in common, Marty."

"You guys can have the diamonds or call the cops. I'll go to jail, I don't care. I just want my wife back."

"And I just want to save my brother, so how about we get on the same page. You hand that gun over to Big Garney and that will go a long way to building trust."

Marty bit his lower lip. He handed the gun to Garney, who took it uncomfortably. He glanced down at the bleeding Phil Crane then back up to the solemn Billy Jack. "I just want my wife back."

Billy nodded, then turned back to Crane. "Start talking."

4

Surrounded by the group, Crane spilled his guts. In any other circumstance, he wouldn't have opened his mouth. He could have been faced with a beating and he still would have kept his trap shut. But this was different. He was out of his element, this was a war zone and the soldier had the upper hand. Gordon Shamus, the money and jail all seemed secondary now. He told them about everything, except the grave that sat waiting in the woods.

"Stand up, Phil," Billy said.

Crane stood up.

"The question is: how do we deal with you now?"

"You gotta tie him up," Marty said.

"Fuck you, Croft! Nobody is tying me up!"

"He can't be trusted," Marty said.

"And you can," Spence interjected. "You've been lying to us from the beginning, Marty. Using us as cover."

Crane smirked.

Billy looked on, his brother's condition foremost on his mind. Behind him, Vincent was opening the door to the flood truck and stepping out.

Marty measured his response very carefully. "I didn't want to, Spence. I didn't have a choice, thanks to this asshole. Besides, I don't pose a threat." He pointed an accusing finger at Crane. "He does."

"Marty's got a point, Brother Spence," Garney said.

"Whatever we do, we need to get off this road," Chase said.

"Why? Do you really think that they'll come back?" Merv asked. "How do we know they just won't carry on?"

Chase turned to Billy. "These things aren't just animals. They are intelligent and organized. They've blocked the road to Acadia, they've taken out Corbett Lake, and now they are on their way to the Meanook Mine. I'm not a military man like yourself or Spence, but this is starting to look like a military operation." Chase leaned in. "We need to get off this road and figure out what we are going to do."

Then Vincent spoke. "He's right, Billy Jack. We gotta get out of here. If those things come back…"

"Any ideas where we can go to regroup?" Billy asked.

"The old Aquila Mine," Chase said. "I just hope the road is accessible."

Billy handed his 303 over to Spence and then he turned back to the others. "Gents, this is some fucked up shit. I am going to ask all of you to put aside whatever selfish thoughts you might have and focus on our present situation. That includes you, Crane… And you too, Marty."

Marty was about to protest.

Billy raised his hand and cut him off. "We need to regroup. Find a place where we can safely assess our situation and figure out the best way to get the fuck out of here. The Aquila Mine is probably our best bet. We can't stay here at the scene of the crime. Sooner or later these things will come back, and when they do, we will be lacking the one thing that let us get the upper hand."

"What's that?" Crane said.

"The element of surprise, Crane. We ambushed the fuckers, but next time it won't be a turkey shoot, next time we meet these fuckers—they'll be prepared."

"Okay, Chase, you're taking my truck. Phil, I'm riding with you. You going to give me any trouble?"

"If I said 'No," would you believe me?"

"No, but you can believe this. You fuck with me and I'll make good on my threat." He handed his other rifle to Garney in exchange for Crane's pistol. "Let's go."

***

Chapter 33—Big Girls Don't Cry

1

Corbett Lake Camp

Shawna couldn't take the cold anymore. Her lips were turning blue and her skin stretched painfully taut across the exposed parts of her arms, neck, and face. She had no idea how long she'd been in the walk-in fridge, only guessed it had to be more than an hour. Whatever the danger had been, she desperately hoped that it had passed, because she had to get out of here. She crouched by the steel door, trying to filter out the overhead fan, listening for a noise of any kind. She wanted to cry, but what would that do to change her circumstances really? *Nothing, cus big girls don't cry,* she thought, wiping her nose.

That's what her Dad first said when she was 10 years old and they called her "fatso" on the playground. She'd always been a big girl, always would be, and when Daddy took her pudgy cheeks in his hands and used his thumbs to wipe away the wounded tears, he said, "Come on now, Shawna! Big girls don't cry." She loved her Dad—he was a sweet man—bigger than life, and as he towered over her, he smiled reassuringly and repeated that mantra that would be her lifelong anthem. "Big girls don't cry, honey." He tapped her temple. "Never let them in here, this is your place and only you have the key."

She tightened her grip on the meat hammer and thought about what they called her.

Kitchen Nazi, how fucking dare they!

She used that anger to muster her courage as she pushed on the safety plunger. It clicked and there was an icy uncoupling kiss as the door seal released from the frozen jamb. Warm air collided with cold and cumulous clouds of vapor swirled in the meeting place. She cocked an ear. In the other room, a male voice was talking to someone. She stayed low, taking in her surroundings and crawled out of the fridge into the deserted confines of the camp kitchen.

The grill was smoking. The bacon on the grill was now dried jerky, having lost its sizzle, a mute witness to what had happened. Kenny had left it on. Not like him at all. A few feet away, the pan he'd purposely dropped was on its side. She crawled past it on all fours and moved toward the steam table. On the stove the two pots she put on the burners bubbled and spat. Whatever had happened, Kenny must have had to leave in a hurry. Even during a fire drill, Kenny calmly shut off everything in the kitchen before taking his place at the rally point.

The voice was still more audible now.

"They want the road south open as soon as possible, Don. Keep your crews working around the clock." It was Mike, the dispatcher.

Shawna peeked over the counter. The dining area was completely empty, then she saw the blood at the staff table and her stomach flip-flopped. There was a lot of blood, in fact there was blood on the ceiling. She ducked down.

Big girls don't cry, Shawna!

"I'm hungry," said Mike.

Who was he talking to?

There was a clacking sound.

"Come on, I just want a bacon sandwich and cold drink."

She reached up onto the counter and pulled down a meat clever.

They were coming.

2

OLD AQUILA MINE ROAD
42 Kilometers Southeast of Dreamcatcher Lake

The Aquila Mine hadn't been in operation for over 15 years. It wasn't a diamond mine either, it was a gold mine. In the late 90's, they closed it down when it became obvious that the cost of removing gold could not offset the mammoth cost of mining it in the deep north.

The group did not make it all the way to the Mine, but they were able to get far enough off the beaten track to obtain sanctuary. The road was being used as a staging site for the Lupania Corporation. A kilometer up the road on the right there was a large lot carved out of the landscape and in that an old D-9 Cat Bulldozer, and along with three flatbed trailers whose cargo were hidden by a tarp and four-foot blanket of snow.

The four Super B's encircled the smaller vehicles and as Vincent stayed with Axe, Billy asked Spence to watch over the group. He wanted to check on his kid brother, and if things looked glum he was going to put him in a pickup and take his chances. As he did this, Chase took the opportunity to tell them everything he knew about the creatures from

Acadia. He told them everything he could, but didn't tell them how he allowed the men from the seven convoys go to their demise. He couldn't tell them that. He didn't know if he'd ever be able to tell anyone about that.

Garney Wilson had become decidedly quiet. Occasionally he stole a glance at Marty, who tried to ignore it, but felt somewhat ashamed of himself for lying. Crane was also staring at him, but not with the same anger he'd projected during their encounter on the ice. When you came right down to it, they were all staring at him. He finally turned his attention to Crane and said, "Why didn't you guys just leave her alone? I was already committed."

Crane turned his palms over and shrugged. "Does it really matter at this point? I mean no offense, Croft, but in the general scheme of things, your wife is pretty insignificant to our present circumstances."

The others watched.

"Don't give me that shit, Cranc. You don't givc a flying fuck about anyone but yourself. Just answer my question."

He grinned, the missing tooth making him look less threatening, almost comical. "Gordon. He's the one you want to ask that question. I can't answer for his craziness. I would have left her in Montreal."

"And after the job?"

Crane didn't reply.

"You were going to kill us."

Crane stared blankly at him.

Marty stood up. "You were going to kill me and send someone to quiet her. Weren't you!"

Merv leaned over and tapped Spence on the arm. "Spence?"

"Yeah?"

"This has got to be the most fucked up day I've ever had north of 60. Security and lack of sleep was bad enough, but now… Aliens and gangsters? I think I'm done ice road trucking."

Garney broke into a loud barrage of howls. "Me too, Brother!"

"It just doesn't pay enough," Spence chuckled.

Collective laughter.

Even Crane cracked a smile.

Marty could not join in their distractive embrace of giddy humor. The desperation and isolation were strangling him. This wasn't funny in any way. How was he going to get to her? How would he save her? To them she might seem insignificant? But she was anything but. If he hadn't given Garney the revolver, he would have killed Crane for that statement.

3

"How is he?" Billy asked, touching his brother's shoulder.

"We gotta get him to a hospital, Billy," Vincent replied. "When he wakes up, he's going to be in a lot of pain."

"I'm working on it, Vincent. He's my first priority."

"I know that." Vincent stood up and squeezed Billy's forearm, his hand, now old and frail, shaking. "Mine too. He's the only family I got, Billy. What's going on with those other two? Marty and Phil?"

"Jesus, you don't even want to know. What a fucking Gong Show."

Vincent released his grip and Billy gazed back down at his brother. He didn't think Marty posed an issue—Phil on the other hand? He was a wild card—unpredictable, dangerous. He wasn't kidding when he said Axe was his first priority. He was seriously turning over the idea of killing Phil, just to eliminate that uncertainty. What would the others think if they saw him do that? Spence wouldn't say anything, he would understand the necessity, but the others? They would look at him like a rabid dog. Marty would probably help him, but the others would object.

And what about Marty? How do we help him?

Why should he care?

Because you don't want them to think you're a rabid dog. You don't want them to see what you really are. What you hide from every time you pull out that bag of weed and try to forget. You are a rabid dog, Billy Jack.

"What do you think our next move should be?"

"We could move as a convoy south, I'll put Axe in the pickup with me and lead us out."

"And if the road is still closed?"

"The snowmobile, I'll put him on the sled behind the snowmobile." *And the rest of you will be left to fend for yourselves.* "I'll go for the cavalry."

Vincent brushed the long strands of hair from his face, his grin tightening the wrinkles on his face. "You do whatever you have to do, Billy Jack."

Billy touched his brother once more and to Vincent, "Keep an eye on him and I'll get things ready."

"You know I will," Vincent said.

"Yeah, I do." He opened the back door and was about to step out when he heard his brother's voice.

"Billy?"

He spun around. A sudden hard ball of wax was in his throat. "Danny," he choked out.

Axe drew in a low raspy breath and swallowed. "Nobody calls me that, Billy. It must be bad, eh?"

Billy took his hand. "You can be the Axe Man with all these other guys, but you're still my kid brother. Still my Danny."

"I love you, Billy."

He barely choked down that hard waxy ball. "I love you too, Danny. And I'm going to get you out of here. Back to Rita and Scott, after they patch you up, of course."

"Oh my god," Axe moaned. His wife and daughter. What would become of them in all this? "I have to tell you something, Billy."

"I'm listening."

"We can't leave. Nobody can be allowed to leave." Axe Man Jack opened his one good eye; it was glassy, tiny spider veins crisscrossed the white portion. He focused on Billy and said, "You better bring the others."

4

Corbett Lake Camp

He was stumbling forward into the dining area, a bacon sandwich on his mind. Close behind, his escort trundled. After infecting the work crew, they had taken the rest back to Acadia. They were too far out for the collective to touch.

All alone, Dispatcher Mike mused. *Just me, my pal and the "Just in case."*

The worms were squirming, licking the outer rims of his sockets, kicking up ash, frantically looking for the collective wire to feed into. The Skentophyte behind him wasn't enough. It was here to protect him and the "Just in case" but it felt alone, even vulnerable.

"No worries," he said, slipping two pieces of bread into the toaster. "Nothing a toasted bacon and ketchup sandwich won't fix, my friend." The skentophyte did not reply. It had no access. No way to analyze the Human's words. It simply followed along and watched what he was doing. He pushed the plunger down on the toaster. “Okay, skent that’ll take a minute, so let’s do a little recce and grab us some bacon.”

He turned, a fresh trail of ash floated out into the room, the embedded worm chasing out after it, then retracting back into its lair. The Skent leaned over the toaster, sniffing the aroma, bits of yolky drool spilling downward onto the counter. Dispatcher Mike was already making his way across the floor toward the steam table. He stopped halfway, turned and grinned. “Are you coming?”

The Skentophyte turned in his direction and followed.

“The key to a toasted bacon and ketchup sandwich is, of course, the bacon, but ketchup is important too. I always recommend Heinz, but in a pinch a little Hunts will do as well.” It reached out and clutched the braided ponytail, gently tugging as it trundled along behind. He stopped. “Is that really necessary?”

It let go. So he continued on toward the steam table.

Behind the counter, Shawna listened as Mike made his way around the room. What ran through her mind was that Mike had been the one. She envisioned a scenario where he’d lost his mind and killed everyone in the room. If she were to go outside, there would be bodies everywhere. All killed by this maniac mumbling about the inner workings of a bacon and ketchup sandwich. It was obvious that he had gone completely insane. He was talking to himself. Never mind that he liked ketchup on toast.

“Gross,” she mouthed.

Mike reached the counter, but he didn’t see Shawna crouched behind it. His focal point was the grill and the dried out pieces of bacon jerky smoldering away. “Well, doesn’t that just suck ass.” Then he saw a flash of white and there was a sting of hot pain in his Adam’s apple.

When Shawna saw the tips of his fingers curl over the counter’s edge, she knew it was time to act. She came up like a spring and swung the cleaver across his throat. At first he did nothing, there was no blood, he just stood there gripping the counter. Then he lowered his chin and his eyeless sockets searched.

My god, he gouged his own eyes out!

Something licked out of the left socket; extending like a charmed snake, it twisted in the air. *Big girls don’t cry,* Daddy said and Shawna swung the meat hammer with all her might. When it connected, two things happened. First, the worm broke away from its anchor and landed on the grill, sizzling on contact. Second, Mike’s head spun on what little elasticity was left in his neck. She had cut him deep with the cleaver, severing his windpipe and almost every tendon. With his head gyrated around like Linda Blair, hands gripped the counter even tighter and the blood from his dying heart rhythmically squirted.

He fell to the floor, dead.

When he fell, Shawna heard the clacking and saw the thing standing behind Mike. It was turning its head, sniffing the air and listening. "Oh my goodness."

It turned toward the sound and spat.

Before the Skentophyte spat its infecting venom, Shawna dropped to the floor. She did not hear the mucous globs join their mature cousin on the grill, did not hear the sizzle as they coagulated like a couple of cracked eggs. For something born in fire, amazingly they cooked off on the grill until they split open. She scrambled away from the counter, as the monster came over and crashed into the pot cart. It toppled, pots and pans clanging left and right. In the mayhem, she slipped through the doorway into the main dining area as it blindly worked its way through the kitchen.

Spaghetti sauce, intended for dinner, gurgled and spat in a huge pot on the stove. Behind that, cream of mushroom soup ready to serve up also churned and plopped. The monster stood, sniffing the air, listening for the human. Hearing the sounds of liquids, it reached out, grabbing the spaghetti sauce pot for leverage then.

'Pain! Pain! Pain!'

But Shawna only heard it screech high enough to break glass and saw the big pot overturn and spill down the stove and down the side of the monster. It screeched louder.

I love you, Kenny Short!

The creature tried to scramble away from burning liquid and slipped on the linoleum floor. When it went down, it reached out, snagging the pot of cream of mushroom soup. Hot sticky magma showered down, coating its head, burning away the outer layer, and it screeched high in agony. Trying to reach the collective, to call for help, but they were out of range.

Now was her chance.

Still holding the meat hammer and the cleaver, she moved in to finish the thing off before it caught its second wind. There would be no second wind, though; it was writhing on the floor in agony.

It did not see her swing the hammer. Did not feel the cleaver cut through the honeycomb layer of its exoskeleton. It only felt the violent black thud. And then another and another and with each successive blow the synapses in its mind began to blink out. Another black thud, its consciousness reverberating out, spiraling into darkness. Far off, it heard a loud semi-metallic click, and then…

Nothing.

The toast had burned.

5

Aquila Mine Road

"We can't leave," Axe said. He was propped up, bundled in a sleeping bag in the doorway of the flood truck. Vincent stood at his side supporting him, while the rest of them were gathered at the back in a loose semi-circle looking on.

"Why?" Merv asked. "Why can't we leave?"

"Let him talk," Billy interrupted.

Billy was thinking about what Axe had told him privately. That no one could leave. That if any of them were caught by this collective, they would turn on the rest without a second thought. "I would have turned on you, Billy, they control your mind once they infect you. We can't let anyone leave, not you, not anyone."

"We have to stop them."

"That's insane," Marty mumbled. "Why do we have to stop them? We get south and we can call the army or the fucking air force?"

"Yeah," Chase agreed. "This is too big."

Billy lost his temper then. "Look! Everyone shut their fucking mouths and let my brother talk! Save your questions for when he's done." But Billy didn't know if Axe would have the strength to answer their questions. He looked so sick; his voice was weak and broken.

"When that thing spat into my eye, I saw what they were planning. They're like army ants, they overwhelm and destroy everything. If we don't stop them, they are going to bring even more over. They don't just want the north, they want everything, they are here to loot the earth. Harvest everything." He brought a shaky hand up just below the bandage over his eye. "Harvest…"

Phil Crane spoke then. "Okay, assuming you saw this and that it wasn't some hallucination brought on by what happened, I still don't understand why we can't run back to YK and call in the big guns.

Seriously, what have you got here? A handful of truckers, a couple of rifles, a handgun. This is fucking nuts, pal."

Billy withheld the urge to yell at the group again.

"It will be too late then," Axe mumbled. "They're bringing something across that will open more doorways. The word sounds like 'hombus' but that's not quite right." Axe concentrated; there was something else he couldn't put his finger on. *Justin Case? Who is Justin Case?*

"I've seen these things at the mine. They came through the chamber in Pit #2, but it would be suicide going back there. There were hundreds of them. Maybe even thousands. It would be like attacking a nest of giant ants! We wouldn't stand a hope…"

"Does it hurt?" Axe said, but it wasn't Axe's voice, it was Lenny voice—or his ghost—channeled through Herb Aronson. Chase Fenwick stopped in mid-sentence and stared. Axe stared back and said, "He did it to save you, Chase. That is why he cut his own throat. So that you could stop this."

"How do you know that? How?"

"Allison is dead. She said, 'They can't keep a secret,' and then she died, but she wasn't alone, Bruce was with her. She cried for you because she, she loved you."

"How do you know this?" Chase was shaking, his lower lip quivering. "Oh my god, how?"

Axe cautiously touched his cheek. "They can't keep a secret. They are the Skentophyte and they're coming to harvest everything. They took the caribou, Billy, the whole herd. The people at Acadia, Corbett, all being processed. For food. The people from Meanook will be next, but the machines they are bringing over will change everything. The gate at the mine is just small, but the machines, the hombus will open larger doors, and they will come through by the thousands. I saw them, god help me, I saw them and we won't stand a chance. Hombus? That's not quite right, but close enough. If they get into Yellowknife with even one of these machines, I don't think we will be able to stop them."

"I gotta get south," Marty implored. "My wife…"

"The road is still closed. They're working on it. My wife and my son are in YK too." Axe convulsed. "If we don't stop this, none of that will matter. They are waiting for the road to open and if they get out by the airfield, then the real invasion begins. This is their beach head."

"Axe, my brother, what are you saying?"

"If they, no… When they bring these things over. These machines, we won't stand a chance. They're bringing hundreds of them. One door can let thousands in. If that happens, they won't be stopped."

"You're sure about this?" Merv asked.

Axe leaned forward, pushing against the excruciating pain nesting inside the hollow of his empty socket. "If they get those things over here, we will be overrun. It's what they do, they are raiders. They overrun, they harvest."

"Food? They want us for food," Spence said.

"Our bones. They don't kill everyone. They farm as well."

"You saw all of this in the 20 seconds or so that thing was in your eye?" Phil Crane asked. "I find that hard to believe."

Axe reached deep down, pulled out a memory and in the voice of John Pringle said, "Send me your exact position, Phil."

"What?"

"That's what John Pringle said? Jeff Rossey needs you to spare him off," Axe said, then in Pringle's voice again, "I need you to go to Acadia." Then Axe again. "If you had gone, you would be dead or infected. John Pringle was calling you from Acadia. He is there now, helping them."

"Jesus Christ." Crane looked at Marty, seeming to forget that only an hour before the man had pistol whipped him and knocked out one of his teeth. "He's bang on, he's bang on. Oh, Jesus Christ. He's bang on."

"If they can't keep a secret, if they hear everything, why didn't they turn around when you fellas ambushed their buddies in the flood zone, my brother?" Garney was addressing Axe, but he was looking at Crane with voyeuristic curiosity.

"I don't know, there must be a range on their network." Axe brought a hand up to his head. A stabbing knife of pain twisted in his eye socket. Struggling, he said, "I… I didn't hear any distress calls, I was being overloaded." He closed his fist and held it, trying to push down the agonizing wave. "I don't think they meet a lot of resistance."

Billy stepped forward and blocked his brother. "Okay, that's enough for now" He leaned in. "You gotta lay down, Danny, and I gotta get you to a hospital."

"Bring Ch-Ch-Chase over here," Axe stuttered.

"Chase, come here."

Chase came forward. "Yeah."

"I… I got something else… Do you know a Justin Case?" Axe asked. His other eye was puffed up, irritated by the trauma to its neighbor. "That name, it's connected to something bigger. I don't know what, but if you remember something."

"I'm sorry, Axe, I've never heard the name."

He reached up and grabbed Billy's arm. "Spence, get Spence!"

Spence came forward. "I'm here, Axe."

"You have to close the gate. You have to block the chamber. If they get those machines across, we're done. Everyone we know is done."

"We go south, regroup and bring back the cavalry, Axe. We'll nuke the fuckers into next week," Spence assured him. "We got to get you to a hospital."

Now he grabbed Spence by the arm. "It will be too late by then. My boy, my wife. I don't care what happens to me, but we have to save them. You two are my brothers, please trust me, we have to stop those things even if it mean sacrificing everyone here."

Chase stepped back, his face gaunt and afraid. The others saw, but did not know what he was thinking. How many had he sacrificed to get here? His boy was in Niagara, his ex-wife, his sister. "How long, Axe? How long before they bring these machines over?"

"I don't know, soon. They might be bringing them over right now. You saw them, Chase. You saw what they did at Acadia." Axe leaned back then and begged, "Please don't run south, it will be too late. We have to close the chamber. Nobody can leave. Promise me, Billy. Spence, promise me. Please, my brothers, please."

"Okay," Billy said. "I promise."

"I promise, Axe," Spence said as his eyes locked with Billy. He intended on keeping that promise, but he had no idea how they were going to do it.

"Okay," Chase whispered. "No one can leave."

Billy covered up his brother and said to Vincent, "Watch him."

"Listen to him, Billy Jack," Vincent said. "I don't think there's any other choice."

"No one leaves," Billy whispered and knew that left three men to convince: Garney, Phil, and Marty.

"Chase, I'm going to need to build a rough model of the Acadia Camp. Let's gather up some things and we can look at this from a tactical perspective."

"Look, I'm in no matter what. I just don't think we'll stand a chance and we won't get close enough to that chamber with two hunting rifles and a pistol. They'll have us in pieces in no time."

Billy looked around, caught sight of the trailers. “Let’s see what we’ve got over there. Maybe we can increase our odds a little.”

***

Chapter 34—Rehearsals

1

Aquila Mine Road

"You don't understand! They're going to kill my wife! I can't stay here!" Marty was following Billy as he marched briskly across the open lot.

"No one is leaving, Marty. Too risky."

"Didn't you hear me? They're going to kill my wife." Billy ignored him, so he reached out and grabbed Billy's shoulder. "I'm not…"

"Get your hands off me," Billy growled. In one sweeping motion, he kicked his legs out and put him on the ground. Billy was over him, forearm pressed against his neck. "Get a grip on yourself. I'm not fucking around here."

"Please, I'm not a soldier like you or Spence. I'm just a guy who's been pushed into something I didn't want to do…"

Billy cut him off, "You think any of us want to do this? There's not a single man here that signed up for this." Billy removed his forearm from Marty's neck, remorseful he'd used such force. He extended a hand to Marty. "Come on, Marty. Get up."

Marty took his hand and allowed Billy to help him up. Once on his feet, he held the hand firm and looked into Billy's eyes. "I told her I would come. I promised her. No matter what I promised, surely your word must mean something to you? I promised."

"The road is closed. My brother says that if these things get through, nothing will matter. Your wife, the guy who's holding her, they'll be in the same boat as everyone." Billy went to pull away, but Marty held firm.

"I promised her I would come."

Billy glanced at Spence, then Chase, and then to Phil Crane. "This Shamus guy, you still in his camp?"

Crane pondered the question. Up until the flood zone, he was sure they were pushing him out. "What are you asking me? If I still give a shit about the diamonds?"

"Do you?"

"Not really, I just don't want to die up here."

"What about Shamus? Think he'll hold out for Marty and you?"

"You're going to believe him," Marty crowed. "He's part of the reason I'm up here!"

"Oh fuck off, Croft!"

"You fuck off, Crane!"

"Or what?"

"Both of you shut your mouth. This is bigger than all of us. My brother says… Ah, fuck it! No one is leaving! No one!" Billy pulled his hand free and stomped away. Chase followed, Crane turned and stomped back toward the flood truck. Leaving only Spence and Marty.

"Marty, I understand you're scared," Spence said. "But you're not getting south. At least not yet. You don't have any choice." He stabbed a thumb toward the flood truck. "Axe and Billy are my only family, if you help me get them to safety, I will help you with your problem."

Marty felt a faint tinge of hope. "How?"

"Whatever needs to be done, I will do it."

"Even kil…"

Spence cut him off. "I said, whatever needs to be done." He was gazing at Crane, wondering what to do about him. "How about it, we have a deal, Marty, or what?"

Marty followed his gaze. Crane was back with Garney and Merv, who were laying items on the ground for Billy's model. He spoke to them and they glanced up. The bastard was stirring the pot. "What did you do in the army?"

"Sniper."

"What if you get killed?"

"Then you go to Plan B."

"Oh yeah, and what's Plan B?"

"Do it your fucking self." Spence grinned and put out his hand.

Marty took it. "Don't get killed, Spence."

"I don't intend to."

2

"Things are looking up," Chase said, lifting the tarp up.

"That's what I want to hear," Billy said. "Now tell me how?"

"Prilled Ammonium Nitrate, a whole flatbed's worth," Chase said.

"Yeah, that's definitely a plus. All we need now is a little det-cord and a rocket to put it in." Billy looked glumly over the giant white sacks. "What do you know about this shit?"

"On its own, pretty inane stuff, but we use it for controlled blasts in the pits." Chase turned to Spence. "How much retain you think those tankers are holding?"

"Hard to say. Probably a couple pails each," Spence said.

"That won't be enough. We'll have to check the Cat, maybe even disable a vehicle and take all the fuel." Chase was looking around, doing the math inside his head. *1 gallon to 100, surround four, by nine.* "It could work. It could work."

"You want to fill me in," Billy said.

"Oklahoma City, the McVeigh bombing."

"You want to build a bomb, blow the place up."

"Something like that, but even if we do, we have other issues to consider."

"Like?"

"The chamber is in Pit #2. How do we get our bomb into Pit number two and close the barn door?"

"Spence, you and Marty rummage around and see what we can use on these other trailers. Metal barrels or containers would be good, but anything that will hold powder. I'd give my left nut for some c-4 or a spool of det-cord."

"I might be able to help you with that," Chase said.

3

It took two hours to build the model that was acceptable to both Billy and Spence. It consisted of canned goods, empty boxes, string outlining the pits, and orange and black spray paint from the flood truck. As they did this, Spence worked on Merv and Garney, who both reluctantly agreed to sign on. Billy took care of Crane.

Once the model was built, they covered it with a piece of tarp and both Spence and Billy went to his rig to start formulating a plan. The sky, once dark, was now brightening, rising low on the horizon behind a flat white curtain of clouds the morning sun came up.

Marty sat in his own rig as Billy and Spence discussed the outline of their plan. Chase joined them for a spell and eventually Big Garney Wilson made his way over to Marty's rig. He thumped on the passenger door and Marty hit the lock release.

He climbed in, shaking off the cold and gave a weak uncharacteristic grin. "How are you doing, Marty, my brother?"

Marty started to speak, then stopped. He didn't know what to say. There was a look on Garney's face. This was a mistake.

"Hell of a day." Garney shook his head and turned to go.

"I'm sorry I lied to you."

Garney turned back. "Family is important. I have a daughter, you know." He grinned now and pulled out his wallet and produced a small picture. In it a young girl in her mid-teens smiled brightly. She looked a little like Garney, his big toothy smile.

"She's pretty," Marty said, and then another uncomfortable pause.

"This is where you show me a picture, my brother."

"Oh, sorry." Marty reached into his own pocket and pulled out a wallet-sized photo of Maggie.

"Shit, my brother, she's gorgeous. A redhead too."

"She's my world." Marty thought he might break down.

Garney held up his own picture. "The picture is 20 years old, my brother. Her mom poisoned her against me, told a bunch of lies. Well, some of them were lies. Some of them were true. Yep, uh huh. Some of 'em were true."

Marty didn't know if he wanted to hear any of this.

"I was never a fellow who could commit. I tried being a partner and a dad, but it just didn't fit. I sent money and when I came to my senses, I guess it was too late."

"Do you know where she is now?"

"Seward Alaska. I did a google search. The internet is really quite amazing, you know. Her Mom passed away last year from ovarian cancer. Poor girl, she loathed me, but I guess she had her right."

"Did you contact her?"

"No, but I was going to when this season ended." He reached into his pocket and unfolded a piece of paper. It was a printout of a newspaper; in it a headline read: **SEWARD'S LATEST ENTREPRENEUR TAKES BAKING IN A NEW DIRECTION!** Below that, a more up to date picture of that same smiling girl holding a cupcake in each hand. She was roughly the same age as Maggie.

"Why are you telling me this, Garney?"

"I don't know, my brother. All things considered, I guess I want you to know that I understand why you did what you did. I'd probably do the same in your shoes." He glanced down at the picture of his little girl. "For her I'd do anything."

"Thank you, Garney. Kind words."

"Everyone here has someone. A reason to fight, my brother."

"Yeah?" Marty pointed out the window at Crane. "What about him?"

"That's a good question, my brother."

4

Billy went back in to check on Axe and this time took Spence with him. He was stable, in a great deal of pain, but that did not stop him from answering more of their questions. Vincent sat idle, listening as the three brothers conferred. Twenty minutes later, the back door to the flood truck opened and out stepped Billy, Spence, and Vincent. As the others watched, they unveiled the model and Vincent gestured for the others to come. The truck doors opened, each man stepping out onto the frozen ground, and there was a succession of clunks as the individual doors closed.

It reminded Marty of some silly Spaghetti Western as they walked toward them. As he looked to his left and right, he half expected one of them to pull out a harmonica and start playing. The four men, Big Garney Wilson, Merv White, Chase Fenwick, and Phil Crane also glanced left and right as they closed in on what would be a loose half-moon.

Spence lit a cigarette, standing at Billy's right. Merv and Garney followed suit, leaving Crane and Marty to do nothing but size each other up. Chase took in the model at their feet, marveled at its accuracy. These boys did this stuff for a living. The tank farm was simulated by two large soup cans taken from all of the driver's emergency rations. The pits were dug out of the snow and accented with spray paint. The main building was constituted from a Ritz cracker box, the living quarters from a condom box, which made Chase chuckle a bit. He had helped with this model, working from the tank farm out, and as they moved and arranged everything from the Telegraph Road. Billy and Spence studied the model, memorizing the landscape, pinpointing highs and lows.

"Look at that. All we need now is a train set," Merv said.

No one else said a word. They were waiting for Billy, who seemed lost in the diorama. He was breathing in low deliberate cycles that were purposely mechanical. To the others, it was unnerving, but Spence knew what it was about. Billy was finding his Mojo, seeking out that sixth sense. He knelt down and touched his gloved hand to the second pit. At its side a smaller Aylmer soup can sat. On its top, as with the others, he had used a sharpie to write Diesel. Then he stood up and faced them.

"Good morning," he reached out to Marty first and took his hand. "When I was a Section Commander, I always made a point of shaking the hand of every man I served with. I would ask that each of you take my hand now as I outline the plan we have made up, and when I am done, each of you can consider whether you want to sign on."

Marty took his hand, the grasp full of conviction.

"Marty, shake hands with my brother Spencer Hughes." He released and took Big Garney Wilson's mitt in his own. He smiled, "Big Garney Wilson, always a pleasure."

"Yes Sir, Billy Jack, uh huh yep."

Then Merv. "How's it going, Buds?"

A nod from Chase.

And the salutation continued until he reached Phil Crane and they clasped hands. "What I am asking you to do today is going to be very dangerous. This is not the army; in the army, you go where your orders take you, you don't question, you simply go and protect the one next to you." He released Crane's hand and after a brief shake with Spence, he clasped his partner's shoulder. "So, here is what I am going to do. I will lay out the operation and then I will ask you if you are in or out."

Each man nodded and Billy began.

"This is our objective." In his hand, he held a fifth wheel pin puller and used the long rod to point to the second pit. "Halfway down and underground is a place called The Chamber. This is the entry point where these creatures… Skentophyte, come through. It's also the place where my brother says they'll be bringing their machines through. This must be taken out. If we take this out, we stop their advance and cut them off from the rest of their force. If you've been paying attention, and I know all of you have, we've had a run of luck." He lifted the pin puller and pointed to the flat bed. "Over there is the payload, we are going to deliver to the objective. There is enough Prill Ammonium Nitrate there to level a couple city blocks, and thanks to Chase's ingenuity and experience, we have all the ingredients to bake one motherfucker of a cake."

Crane started to speak, but Spence cut him off. "Save your questions until after we get through this."

"In the base of the pit." He pointed to a CD case, where the mine stored its unused prill. "Luck would have it and we are going to need all we can get, that storage facility is approximately 150 meters vertical of the entranceway to the objective." He traced the pointer up the side of the pit, tapped it against the orange dot and continued tracing upward to the

Aylmer soup can. “This here, this is our catalyst. This is where we will drop the payload and stop these fuckers in their tracks. We blow that diesel tank and that should be enough to fuck up their plans. Questions so far?”

Merv started. “How do we get your truck bomb from the main road into the second pit without getting killed?”

Spence answered that one. “One thing will be on our side. We will have an element of surprise. I don’t think they are in any way prepared for an attack on their position. So we go in like any assaulting force. We use the whole road and come in as an armada, protecting the payload. The fuckers get in your way, you feed them your moose bumper. Everyone, except the man hauling the payload, will take out the threats.”

“I get it, like we’re escorting a bomber. We’re the Zeros,” Merv chuckled and the others joined in.

“That’s the basic idea, Merv, and if you want to call yourself a Zero, who am I to argue?” Billy grinned.

More laughter.

“What’s to stop them from overrunning the lot of us?” Crane asked. “Chase said there could be thousands.”

This stole the air of light humor and sobered everyone.

Billy took a deep breath. “They have a disadvantage. They’re blind. When they attacked the flood crew, they were using the wolves to direct them. I asked my brother and he said that is why they take the eyes of some. They need a host to see, so we are going to have to put their lights out.”

“How?” Marty asked

“Kill people,” Crane said.

“Yeah. When those things attacked the flooders, they were using the wolves, and according to my brother, they are doing the same with the people they infect.”

“That really stinks, my brother.”

“Yeah it does, but no worries, you folks will be too busy getting that payload to the objective. Spence and I are going to take care of the live threats and make your job a little easier. Chase, I’m assuming you can drive a big truck,” Billy said.

“Been awhile, but yeah. Sure.”

“Congratulations,” Spence said. “You’ll be driving the finest truck ever built.”

“Good grief, it’s a Kenworth for shit’s sake,” Merv prodded.

Billy didn't give anyone a chance to divert the discussion. "Spence, myself, and Phil are going to try and take the heat off you gentlemen as you bring the payload to the objective. Spence and I will be shooting, Phil will be spotting. That is, if you're up for that, Phil?"

Phil Crane cleared his throat.

"Don't answer just yet, wait until we're done here. Everyone please follow me."

They left the model and headed on over to the flat bed with the tarp removed. It was loaded from front to rear with Super-sacks of prill. Beside it, pails collected from each tanker, 12 altogether after they dumped the spill kits. There were two 45-gallon drums and spools of wire lying by the trailer. "Once we finish here, we are going to wire this baby up and give these fuckers a late Christmas present. I want to have this put together and delivered before last light today."

"Wouldn't it be better in the dark?" Chase asked.

"I've only got one night scope. It will be easier to spot targets of opportunity in daylight hours. Besides, they won't expect us to come in the daylight. We want you guys to come in hard and fast. Doing that in daylight will be easier. Spence and I will be moving to different vantage points. Phil here will be our FOO."

"FOO?" Phil asked.

"Forward Observation Officer. You're the spotter, Phil, so we are going to go over the mine layout together while Chase readies the payload with the others."

"You talk like I've already signed on."

"You have."

"Really?"

"Yeah," Billy grinned. "You're the one guy I can't let walk away, you're my wild card. You see, if I let you walk, I lose Marty because he's afraid that you are going to hook up with your buddy and kill his wife. I can't have Marty distracted by that if he's going to help us save the world."

Marty grinned.

"I don't give a fuck about any of that anymore."

"Good," Billy said. "Then you won't mind hanging around and giving us a hand."

Crane frowned. "I guess I don't have much of a choice."

"Trust me, Phil, this is better than the alternative."

"Yeah?"

"Oh yeah."

Billy turned back to Chase. "How many bullets will you need?"

Chase was doing math in his head again. "A dozen, maybe a few more."

"I've got three hundred rounds in the back of my truck. That is, if you didn't lose them when you stole it." Billy smiled. "And banged it up."

"I'll pay for the damage when we finish saving the world."

"Goddamned right you will. And you'll fill the tank up too. Okay, you guys give Chase a hand getting this thing wired up while me, Spence, and Phil go over the plan."

5

They went to work. First positioning the barrels under the direction of Chase Fenwick. The trailer was sectioned off, the super sacks pulled from its deck, cut open, and the barrels, and once the pails were positioned, they filled them with the powder from inside the sacks.

Chase used a pencil and paper to figure out the ratios that would turn the prill from an inert powder into a volatile explosive. Adding measured amounts of diesel fuel turned the powder in each pail into a semi-dry paste. Once they had filled each container to what he hoped was the right specification, he went to work on the bullets and converted them into crude blasting caps, using the copper wire they'd scrounged up. Merv and Marty went over to the D-9 Cat and removed the batteries. As Chase wired up the flat-deck bomb, they attempted to charge batteries. Two of the four began to charge. Garney, under the direction of Chase, removed the radio from Phil Crane's truck.

Back at the model, Billy, Spence, and Phil went over the orders that would be passing between them. "That's good, Phil. Now say it again," Billy urged.

"Reference tank one, 150 meters south east, one man in open."

"Right. And how about that?"

"Reference barracks, north side. Target of opportunity on roof."

"Good," Spence said. "Keep it mechanical. No emotion. It will be easier for us to understand and keep your orders short and sharp, so we can tell you who has engaged."

"Listen for the order or clarification," Billy said. "You have the easiest job here. You identify them and we drop them. We will be moving, but you are going to stay stationary with my truck on this knoll here." Billy pointed to a rise outside the model.

"What if they spot me?"

"They won't be looking for you. They'll be looking for us," Spence said. "Just keep your cool and keep looking for anyone who looks like they are out there acting as a set of eyes."

"I'd kill for some artillery," Billy mused.

"No thanks, the drop shorts would just end up fragging us."

Billy laughed. "Okay, let's go over it again."

6

Three hours later, their work was done, all except for a final briefing and commitment. The trailer was wired and ready to go. The radio harvested from Phil Crane's truck was tied into the battery pack mounted on the deck, beside it an antennae. Chase looked over the contraption with a certain amount of weird pride. He'd set the radio to Ladd 9 and turned it off. Garney dropped his cans and hooked up to the flatbed as they unfroze the brakes and checked it over.

Billy and Spence examined Chase's handiwork and nodded. This just might work. "Okay, last part of the plan. We roll in like thunder, the driver of the flatbed stops by the fuel storage tank and turns the radio on. Don't bother trying to unhook, just jump in one of the other rigs and you get the fuck out of Dodge."

"Who is going to light the fuse?" Marty asked.

"Before I say, Spence is going to ask all of you if you're in or out. Sound off."

"Garney, in or out?" Spence said.

"In."

"Merv?"

"In?"

"Chase?'

"In."

"Vincent?"

"In."

"Marty."

He glanced to Spence, who nodded, then looked directly at Billy. "I'm in."

"Crane?"

"Yeah, apparently I'm in," Crane grinned.

"Billy Jack?"

"Fuckin eh," he said, then to Spence, "Spencer Hughes?"

"Fuckin bee."

Billy wandered over to the back of the flood truck, opened the door, stepped up on the aluminum stairwell and leaned in. Axe was on his side, but he was conscious. "I'm in, big brother."

"Never had a doubt." He turned around and faced them. "Big Garney, am I to assume that you're volunteering to deliver the package?"

"Yes, my brother, you would be correct in that assumption."

"Good." He glanced down at his watch. "We've got about four-and-a-quarter hours of daylight left. Travel time to Acadia is about an hour-and-a-half. Chase, could you come up here and fill us in on this weapon of mass destruction?"

Chase came up, cleared his throat. "It's a simple set up, really. The caps are wired into the radio. Once someone transmits on that channel, the circuit closes and ignites the caps I've put in each pail."

"What if someone transmits on the way?" Crane asked.

"That's why it stays turned off. Garney, you get as close as you can to the Diesel tank, get out and turn that radio on. Whoever is closest, pick him up and then you guys make a run for the Telegraph and back to the ice. When you gents are at a safe distance, we'll light the fucker up and head for YK."

"So you guys will light it up?" Merv said.

"Once Garney turns the radio on, you guys head for the ice. If you don't hear a boom by that time, any one of you get on Ladd 9 and transmit."

"What about you guys?" Marty asked.

"Trust me, Marty, if that thing hasn't gone off, it means they got to us."

"What do you want me to do?" Vincent asked.

"You're going to take care of Axe for me. You're the ambulance driver, Vincent. Has everyone got the NWT1 channel on their radio?"

There was a succession of "Yes" replies.

"Good, that's our communications channel. I don't want anyone on Ladd 9 until Garney is sitting safely in someone else's rig. One of us will give the order to flip over. You will hear Phil calling out targets. Ignore this and get that package to its destination." Billy took one last look around. "Any more questions?"

There were none.

"Okay," Billy clapped Garney on the shoulder. "Let's go fuck these assholes up." There were a few grunts, a chuckle, and they made their way to their vehicles. Billy followed Marty back to his truck and said, "Give me the diamonds."

Marty climbed up into the W900 and pulled the cloth bag from his bunk. He stepped back out and handed them over to Billy. "What are you going to do with them?"

"Spence told me that he agreed to help you if you came along. Is that right?"

"Yeah."

"I go where my brother goes. I'm going to need these."

"Why?"

He gazed back at Crane who was helping Spence load the snowmobile. "Insurance, Marty. See you when this is over." He stuffed the satchel of diamonds into his parka pocket and wandered back to his pickup. There he conducted a radio check with everyone on NWT1.

Marty acknowledged the radio check. He hung the handset up and placed Maggie's picture on the sun visor. They formed up into a loose convoy and waited for the word to pull out. He touched the picture of Maggie, her smile sweet and genuine.

"Soon," he promised.

Then Billy gave the order, "Let's roll."

***

Chapter 35—Hornet Nest

1

Corbett Lake Camp

"Corbett Lake, you have a copy?" The radio buzzed away in the next room, yet she hardly heard it. She was standing over the monster's body— dripping meat hammer in hand—cleaver at the ready, prepared to strike if it came back to life. After three full minutes had passed, she tucked the bloodied hammer into her apron pocket and shut off the stove.

For those unfortunate enough to come across the Skentophyte, there was always the shock and belief that it wasn't real. A surreal nightmare within which they had become entangled. This wasn't the case for Shawna: she had known this day would eventually come. She was a longtime listener to Coast to Coast AM, but only when Art Bell had been the host. She hated George Noory, him and his stupid New World Order. She'd been so excited to hear Art was coming back to satellite radio. Then the assholes cancelled his show.

"Sons of bitches," she murmured, glowering at the reptilian thing lying dead at her feet. "What would you say about this, Art?"

"*Go ahead, caller, you're on the air!*"

"Hi, Art, longtime listener, first time caller. I just bagged a lizard-thing from middle earth."

"Well, I'll be," Art would say. "You got a picture?"

"Oh shit," she reached into her pocket and pulled out her iPhone and then started snapping pictures. First of the lizard man, then she stepped into the dining room and photographed the almost decapitated body of Mike. She had to dance a bit to avoid drowning her sneakers in the massive puddle of blood. His braided ponytail, normally shaded in grey, absorbed the life-force and bloated red like milk weed.

Shawna was unfazed; she knew she'd done the right thing and they'd taken the only friend she had at Corbett. *Where are you, Kenny?* She gave Mike's corpse a kick. *Where did these intergalactic assholes take you?*

She proceeded into the kitchen and snapped pictures of the fried worms on the grill. In the back of her mind, she thought she might never have to flip another egg or take anyone's shit again if she could get these pictures to a media outlet. Maybe Wolf Blitzer or the dreamy Anderson

Cooper. Oh yeah, Anderson Cooper. Shawna was sure if she could get alone with him for a bit of one-on-one intimacy, she'd bring that little man back from the dark side for sure. Her pictures taken, she moved through the building to see what else she could find.

2

Acadia Mine

Bruce walked the corridor, his escort lumbering along behind him, all around them Skentophyte moving left and right. Inside his mind, he heard their chants, ranting, and evaluations. His mind's eye animated each of their words, which rose and fell away to the steady clicks and clacks of skent transmissions.

MEANOOK—THROMBUS—READY—CONVOY—TRANSPORT—HARVEST—CROSS—SKENT—WE—ARE—SKENTOPHYTE—YELLOWKNIFE—HARVEST—SKENT—SKENT—SKENT—SKENT—SKENT—SKENT—SKENT!

To him, they were the ramblings of a madman, or a mad race.

How could something so obsessive compulsive find the patience to create technology that would bring them from such a far off place?

They heard his inner voice and began to evaluate.

OBSSESIVE—SKENT—COMPULSIVE—SKENT—NECESSITY—HARVEST.

"Psychopaths," he muttered and pushed the button on the elevator.

INSANITY—SKENT—WE ARE SKENTOPHYTE!

"Now you're getting it."

The elevator door opened and he stepped inside, his escort following, banging its shoulder against the outer frame with a thud.

"Klutz."

Once in, it moved behind him and clamored.

DOWN—INTO CHAMBER—NOW!

Bruce purposely took his time reaching for the button and even paused to look at his puppet master. "You sure?"

DOWN—INTO CHAMBER—NOW!

Bruce was the man now, but he wasn't sure for how long. Sal Godwin had expired. The worms had cooked him off. So, Sal Godwin wouldn't be around to watch Damien Lars shit his pants when his airplane landed in the morning. Tough break for Sal. They'd dismantled him before the last of his brain cooked off. It was quick, a second or two of unzipping him from his pelt, but the screams echoed through the collective in an endless tide of octaves. Worse, they were screams from inside, far worse than those you see in the horror films. Bruce felt sorry for Sal, but not for the fuck-stick from HR, who also happened to be degrading at a rapid rate.

What was his name again?

Bruce couldn't remember the name of the asshole from Human Resources, even though he'd given him up to the Skento-fucks in the first place. He assumed his own brain was failing. Cooking from the furnaces in his sockets.

They're turning my grey matter into a big old pot roast.

And he didn't even feel it. The analogy of the boiling frog came to mind. Where had he heard that theory, anyway? A frog swimming in a pot of water that is slowly warmed so that the frog doesn't know…

Then from the intercom came Rally's voice. "All underground personnel, report to pit two level four, please."

That cunt. Why isn't she affected?

Why did he hate her? He didn't know why he hated her, but he supposed the resent was born out of selfishness. It wasn't fair that people were dropping like flies and she got to carry on being a disc jockey for the Skento-Fuck Nation.

CUNT? VAGINA—REPRODUCTIVE ORGAN—WASTE DISPOSAL

He smiled, deriving pleasure from two things. One. That he had made the Skentophyte say the "mother of all words," and as a consolation, Rally probably heard the reference across the collective wire.

The elevator opened and Bruce stepped out.

3

25 Kilometers from Acadia Turn Off

They were pulled off to the side of the road for one order's group. To the West, a smaller road snaked out across the tundra. Billy had used this piece of road to make his camp. Thirty kilometers in, and accessible (he hoped) only by pickup, was an Indian Burial ground that was off limits to the mine. It was the only high ground in the region and it offered line of sight to both the High Grade and Telegraph road. That was where he, Phil, and Spence would be going.

"It will take us about 25 minutes to get into position," Billy said. "I'll call out to you guys on NWT-1 to let you know. I'll say, 'The hunting is good.' That means we're ready. We have to get that payload to the tank at Pit #2. If there are as many of these things as Chase says there are, it will be like running toward a stampede. Run the fuckers down and protect Garney all the way in."

"Yeah, my brothers, you heard the man. Protect me."

"Pay attention to what's going on around you. If I'm right, we won't have to shoot them, just the ones acting as their eyes."

"What about vehicles?" Merv asked.

"Anything that comes out of the mine is hostile," Spence said. "A pickup comes your way, mow it the fuck down!"

"What about us, Billy Jack?" Vincent asked.

"You get your ass down to Portage 33 and find a place to hold up. If you don't hear from us in an hour, you get my brother south and call in the cavalry."

"An Indian calling the cavalry," Vincent mused. "That just seems so wrong, Billy Jack. So very wrong." He smiled and wrapped his arms around Billy and gave him a hug. Then solemnly, he gave a half salute. "Wipe the fuckers out. You white boys pay attention to Billy Jack. He's a Dene Warrior."

"What about me?" Spence grinned.

"You're an honorary Dene Indian, Spencer Hughes and that should be enough."

"Take care, Vincent." Billy released him. "Now get the hell out of here."

Spence gave him a thumbs up.

"Kick their ass!" Vincent said, climbing into the flood truck. He drove down the road, disappeared around the bend, and was gone. Billy said a prayer for his brother and hoped he would see him again. Then he turned to the others. "There's four of you. Chase out front, Merv and Marty, you protect the sides. Like a spear. Move around if you have to, but protect that payload."

Marty could hardly believe he was doing this. He was suddenly very scared, but not that he would get killed while trying some hair-brained scheme to blow up a mine. He was terrified he was going to die and leave Maggie to Gordon Shamus.

"Don't make me a widow, Marty," she had said.

Phil Crane was standing by the security pickup, next to Spence. Marty walked over to him and for a long moment the two men stared at each other, then Marty said, “Why are you doing this?”

“Because I’ve been volunteered,” Crane grinned.

“After this is over, I just want my wife back.”

“Yeah, I know, probably won’t matter anyway, because I think that super soldier over there will probably get the lot of us killed, but if we survive this, you have no worries on my end. I’m going to retire from the business. Maybe do some fishing.”

“I hope that’s true, Phil.”

“I know you do. Let’s leave it at that.”

“Tli Cho Manor?”

“Off the Ingraham Trail, two kilometers south of Prosperous on the right. Steel gate. There isn’t another like it. There’ll be three other people there. A woman and two men. Aside from Shamus, the woman is more dangerous than the others.”

“I guess asking if you’ll help me is…”

“Asking too much? Yeah…”

Spence was on his way back now. “Saddle up!”

“Good luck Croft,” Crane didn’t put out his hand.

“Yeah.” Marty turned around and started toward his own rig.

Billy led them on, driving his black 4X4 while Phil and Spence brought up the rear. They were moving fast, winding their way up the road, trying to stay above the snow, bashing through the drifts. The remaining four men looked on, until they were all but gone. Big Garney broke the silence. “Okay, my brothers, from this point on, speed and spacing are out the goddamned door. Yes sir uh huh!”

Merv grinned. “Fuck the rules.”

Chase was quiet.

“How long?” Marty asked.

“Let’s mount up, they won’t be that long.”

4

Jackneetow Overlook Burial Ground
Northwest of Acadia Mine

Billy stopped his truck at the base of the hill. The cemetery was protected by a worn picket fence erected by the Lupania Corporation when it had first started mining the area. A blistered sign on the dilapidated fence read: OFF LIMITS! Other than the fence and the sign, there was no indication that this snow-covered hill was anything but.

Billy kicked the fence down and waved for Phil and Spence to proceed. Phil drove the white pickup through the opening in the fence and across the sacred ground. "Hope his ancestors don't mind."

"I think they'll make an exception in this case," Spence said. "Get it up on the crest just enough so you can see and reach the radio."

Billy jogged up the hill in front of them and stopped at the crest of the hill. When they got the truck situated, they joined him and looked out over Acadia mine. From this vantage point, they could see almost everything. Billy pulled out his binoculars and handed them to Phil. "Let's try this again."

Phil raised the glasses to his eyes and scanned the landscape as Billy and Spence followed along with their rifles. First, he identified the main building. Both Billy and Spence followed along, indicating: "Seen," when they acknowledged each landmark.

"Diesel Tank, Pit #2," Phil said.

"Seen," Billy and Spence both replied.

Billy reached in, grabbed the handset on Phil's second radio. "The hunting is good out here."

The reply came as a double click.

"They're moving," Billy said. "We've got about 25 minutes, maybe less, so let's do a dry rehearsal while we wait."

"Before we do, I have one question," Phil asked.

"Go ahead."

"You said I wouldn't like the alternative. What was the alternative?"

"The alternative was permanent."

Phil grinned.

Spence did and eventually so did Billy.

"Any other questions?"

"No, that should do it."

"Good, now start to identify those references, Phil, but this time, give us some references." Below them, to the naked eye, men as small as ants moved around the mine, behind them and all around were blurred images melting into the landscape.

Phil sighted his glasses on the first man. "Reference fuel rack, 2 o'clock, Man in open."

"Engaged," Spence replied.

"Reference Telegraph junction, two man on barrier."

"Engaged."

And so they continued their rehearsal, waiting for the convoy and its payload. Billy listened as Phil pinpointed targets, followed along, and was surprised to see how fast he'd picked up on the drill that he and Spence had worked out during their time in Sector South. Billy looked to Spence and nodded. They spread out and got ready as Phil continued calling targets of opportunity.

5

Acadia Mine

The **777** rock truck had been positioned outside the chamber as they brought the cargo through and loaded it. Bruce heard their excited calls as they worked in unison. Load the thrombus—Load the thrombus—We are skentophyte—Load the thrombus—Skent—Skent—Skent—Skent—Skent—Skent—Skent—Skent—Skent—Skent!

And so they did, and not hundreds as Axe had said, but thousands of the special discs were being passed in daisy chain from one worker skentophyte to the next. Three lines of Skentophyte extended from the back of the rock truck into the chamber and into the swirling vortex. On the other side, each disc was passed manually from one to the next with the efficiency of a conveyor directly to the box of the big mining truck.

Bruce watched, as did the others who were positioned at vantage points that would help the Skent in their work. He, along with others, were starting to fail. On occasion, he fell into a murky grey fugue that seemed to increase with each seizure. Blood trickled from both nostrils, as the worms were malfunctioning.

Or I'm malfunctioning, he thought. Then inside, away from their prying collective eye, he wondered if he should have released that onto the wire. Would they tear him to pieces once they realized he was shutting down?

Who fucking cares anymore?

Over the intercom came a voice he recognized. "Attention all Acadia… Attention… Acadia personnel… We have…"

Apparently the cunt was failing too. Whatever her name was?

It will all be over soon.

Bruce removed the needle nose pliers from his pocket and glanced down at them. *What was I going to do with these,* he wondered and dropped them. *Ninja, I'm a blind Ninja.*

On the surface in the main Gymnasium, the last batch of detainees were being infected to replace the failing ones. Their entry into the collective was heard, first through cries of pain, then obedience.

Load the thrombus—Faster-Skent—we are Skentophyte!

Good, he thought. *This job sucks anyway. They can have it.*

The grey murk resumed, turning his thoughts muddy—unreliable; he stumbled backward, embracing it.

Yes, let this end. I'm tired, let this end.

He heard something then.

Something over the cunto-com?

No, that wasn't quite right.

Intercom.

That was it. The cunt was saying something through the intercom.

Or was it the collective?

It was only one word.

"Intruders!"

6

High Grade Junction to Acadia

The barricade set up at the junction was abandoned. Chase turned off the main ice road onto the high grade as Garney followed close behind. Marty was on the right wing of the armada, his truck slipping both left and right. It was harder to control without the trailer, and he suddenly had a terrifying vision in which he hit the snowbank. He tightened his grip on the wheel and put his full focus on the road.

"Marty," came Merv's voice over the alternate channel.

He reached up and grabbed the handset. "Yeah, Merv."

"Is this some road warrior shit or what?"

Marty laughed nervously.

"It sure is, my brothers. Takes ice trucking to a whole new level. Yes sir yep, uh huh, sure does!"

Chase Fenwick didn't chime in. He was driving Spence's truck and it didn't have a second radio.

Chase was poised in the front when they ran the barricade. He was the tip of the spear, the point man on their armada. He glanced behind him. Garney was about two hundred meters back eating his snow dust, Merv and Marty flanking the flatbed by 20 meters each. Ahead a sign declared: **Telegraph Junction 3 Km**

They'd already passed the spot where Lenny cut his own throat, the storage container turned building where Chase had fashioned the Molotov cocktails. This was it, they were going in, hell or high water and as they did, Chase could feel himself being watched by the ghosts of the men he'd betrayed.

7

"There they are," Crane announced when he saw mini-armada break from behind the hill and turn off the High Grade and onto the Telegraph. This was it, they were really going in. "God fucking help us," Crane said.

"God help them," Billy said and brought his scope up.

"Phil, this is going to happen fast. Stay focused." Spence brought his rifle up, seated the butt into his shoulder, and waited. It felt natural there, as it always had. He brought the scope up and started controlling his breathing. Below, the convoy on the Telegraph was still out of rifle range, but closing in fast on the objective. All three men watched their progress, waiting for the resistance, expecting it would come the minute they were spotted, but it hadn't.

Approximately 800 meters from the camp, the alarm was rung. The alarm had been Rally Martins over Ladd 1. Barely able to stand, her sockets bleeding out mucus, the left completely dark, she leaned against the glass window in the communications tower. She'd only said one word, but that was enough. "Intruders!"

There was a moment of calm.

Then came a storm.

And with that a swarm of Skentophyte.

***

Chapter 36—Ballad of the Blind Ninja

1

Overlook Burial Ground

"Sweet mother of God," were the first words to transmit out across Ladd 9, and they had spilled incredulously from the mouth of Philip Crane as he took it in. At this moment, all of the drilling, the rehearsal and preparation, was lost in the awe of what he was seeing.

Billy heard the words, as did Spence, and so did every driver in the assaulting convoy. But Phil Crane saw it all and that is what froze him in place. From the main building, two people walked calmly side by side out across the snow beaten lot. Phil knew he was supposed to do something, identify them, but then the scourge or horde or whatever the fuck you would call it spilled out from every opening in what seemed an endless wave. Hundreds of them came down the stairs and filed out on the road. And that was just the beginning.

Vehicles raced up the spiral road out of Pit #2, behind them the creatures came holding speed. Hundreds more. And from the maintenance building, even more, and the airport. Vehicles were rolling and the things were all heading in one direction, and far off he heard…

"Phil! Phil! Phil!"

Rifle fire exploded on his right; suddenly he was being kicked and he looked up dumbly. It was the super soldier and he was pissed. "Get a grip on yourself and start calling those fucking targets!" He grabbed Phil by the shoulder. "Now, or I'll fucking shoot you myself!" He stomped back down the hill to the nest he had set for himself.

Crane brought the glasses back up, swinging the lenses left and right, the silhouettes bouncing in and out of his sights. Then he saw the first one in the parking lot fall.

"Second target down," Spence's voice called, an invitation to an actor who'd forgotten his lines.

Crane held his breath. Watched the reaction of the creatures when the man dropped. They were scurrying, as if confused. He raised the glasses and spotted a man climbing the side of one of the big diesel tanks. "Reference Tank #1. Man climbing ladder."

"Engaged," Billy called and took the shot.

Phil heard the report, then saw the man fall. He started to search and called, "Reference staging area—3 o'clock—target of opportunity."

"Seen," Spence called back, fired, and that man fell. "Move to the next target, Phil. Don't wait for us!"

"Reference main building, at 6 o'clock. Two men in open."

Crack! Crack!

2

Chase could see the main building now, but they had not come out to meet them. Not yet. Then he saw the pickup truck and behind it a whirlwind of snow dust. "Here they come!" he yelled to the inside of his Spence's truck and pushed down hard on the accelerator. His speed climbed from 69 km/h up to 90 and the diesel engine growled hungrily as it ingested and regurgitated the unspent fuel. "Here we come, you mother fuckers!"

"Jesus," Marty gasped. They were on a collision course. The lone pickup was coming full speed, behind it a cyclone of snow dust. He leaned over the wheel, then to his right, he caught Garney staring at him.

"What do you see, my brother?" Garney asked on the alternate.

Marty shook his head. They were slowing down.

Merv was also watching in horror at the collision course coming at them. "This has got to be the stupidest idea I have ever signed up for in my life!"

Meanwhile on the radio: "Reference Telegraph. Pickup truck!"

Marty watched as the distance was closing. 300 meters, 200, 100, and then when they were almost close enough to see the driver, the windshield washed out and frosted over. At least that was how it looked to Marty, but it was actually being peppered with shots.

"Pickup engaged!" The truck suddenly swerved right, then hard left, and then it spun out of control and hit the bank. The cyclone behind it was still coming. "Take it out!"

Marty didn't recognize Spence's call and was still computing it when Chases Rig cut left and finished it off with his moose bumper. The pickup truck exploded, its occupant vaporized. Chase swung back in front of Garney. The Skentophyte continued coming forward.

They'd been wrong. They weren't blind! They were still coming, at least 100 strong. *Oh, we are screwed!* Marty looked up at the picture of his wife. The cyclone of dust rolled forward. They were on a collision course, they could see them galloping now in legion. "I'm sorry, Maggie, I did my best."

"Put on your seatbelts, boys," Merv yelled over the air.

The collision came as a surprise to everyone.

Crane continued calling targets.

Chase connected with the first rank and the creatures exploded on impact, looking at first like a vapor, then revealing itself as muddy goop across the side of Spence's Kenworth. They cracked and crunched, bouncing off the big steel aluminum bumper and those that did not connect hit Merv's bumper and Marty's, but made no effort to flank or get out of the way.

They continued like stampeding cattle, blind to the danger, blind to this world—running forward into death. Those that weren't mowed down kept galloping past them, teeth clacking, searching for the collective eye so they could regroup. They could not see the intruders on the Telegraph, the human in the pickup was gone, the man scaling the tank extinguished.

Blind—Reestablish—Blind—Reinforce! Skent! Skent! Skent!

As quickly as they had met the first wave of Skentophyte defenders, they were through them and moving in past the air strip. Marty stole a glance in his side view mirror and caught a quick imprint of the carnage. The remaining creatures were out of sync, running in circles and over banks.

Jesus Christ, this just might work!

"Keep moving, boys, you're almost there," came Billy's voice across the airwaves.

"Reference Maintenance building, two more pickups heading for the Telegraph," Crane interrupted. "And shit, they've got a lot of company."

Overlook Burial Ground

Billy tracked their progress. They were 500 hundred meters from the objective, just half a kilometer. Billy fired, Spence fired, and Crane kept the orders coming as the truck armada continued its advance. Four minutes had elapsed since the first shot rang out. What happened in the next few would determine the failure or success of the assault. Two, three minutes at the most. Three minutes might seem like nothing in the real world, but in the heat of battle, it was an eternity. For Billy, each second drew down—a painful click at a time—gut wrenching lethargy.

"Crane, put your focus on the second pit, we have to protect that approach," Billy called and inserted a fresh magazine. So far, they'd been lucky; the convoy was drawing all attention away from them. The chaos created by the Skentophyte actually offered them cover.

Guess these motherfuckers have never been in a firefight.

Crane called more targets.

Billy and Spence continued dropping them.

The convoy kept making ground.

Billy engaged the first pickup from the maintenance building.

Its windshield thudded inward and, although the bullets did not hit the driver, the imploding glass put out the lights in his sockets. The pickup swerved and bounced off the bank. The second one passed it, and the Skent rolled over it 200 hundred strong.

Ponk! Crunch! Ponk! Crunch! Ponk Crunch!

Came sounds of steel denting under the feet of the skent. They were following the collective eye, which was now focused on one objective.

The inbound convoy.

The Telegraph circled the camp and rather than take the convoy head on, the driver took a cross road and cut the distance in half. Neither Spence nor Billy could get a bead on him and it became increasingly apparent that they weren't going to get a shot. To make matters even worse, they were coming from the rear and gaining distance.

They heard it then. Over the air. "Listen, boys, one of you is going to have to break off. There's a pickup coming up your back end and he's bringing a whole fucking bunch of his friends. Take it out!"

Chase wouldn't have time.

Marty turned to Merv, who smiled. Then he was gone.

Merv eased onto the brake, kicked on the Jake and to a steady, ***Brap-brap-brap-brap-brap!*** He spun the 379 Peterbilt with the precision of a figure skater. The engine continued its machine gun report until he was straight, and then he punched the accelerator, giving the hungry Detroit the fuel it was demanding. Black smoke chugged from her twin stacks as the RPMs climbed and propelled Merv and his 379 Pete toward the second wave.

"Been a pleasure, boys," Merv said. "Big Garney, you get it done, old boy!" When he saw them, he didn't hesitate; instead, he cut the Jake, grabbed a higher gear and punched the fuel. He watched the RPMs drop and grabbed another gear. "Here I come, Motherfuckers."

3

Bruce was receiving intermittent signals across the collective wire. They had loaded the 777, and the driver was idling the mammoth truck up. The stink of diesel exhaust flooded the interior. Apparently the Skento-fucks were getting a taste of their own medicine. Now the panic was on to get these bad boy thrombus things to the surface. Bruce's left eye was out of service, the right failing fast. He couldn't hear the cunt anymore. But from the Gymnasium, a whole slew of new recruits had joined the fun.

Get to the surface! Skent! Get thrombus to the surface!

The fuckers were afraid.

Good!

He'd seen the big rigs rolling into the camp. Between static interruptions, he'd even seen them mow down a few of the bastards. He was seeing the vantage points being knocked out one by one. The virtual television screens that floated through his subconscious, through Skentophyte collective, were blinking out. As they indoctrinated newcomers, new screens appeared, but they weren't in place. A crowd of virtual monitors being herded down the corridors of the mine.

Bruce laughed. *You fuckers are losing! A big old Skento-fuckerooney!*

But were they?

At the airport was their man. The one called Sack. He was told to wait, his escort and him. They had to get the cargo to the surface, but he was there just in case. He was parked behind the hanger, Herb was fueling up his rig. Moving through the building was a new addition to the puppetry of Skentophyte. John Pringle would be their main man here at the mine. Bruce's replacement. He had already put a call out to his security forces, urging them to come to Acadia. So far, none had arrived and now it looked as though none would.

One could hope anyway, Bruce thought.

The 777 was rolling out of the tunnel, fifty Skentophyte rode in the giant rock box, protecting their precious cargo. Ahead, the outside light beckoned, and beyond the base of the pit was the spiral pit.

Faster—Skent—Faster to the surface—to the airfield.

Bruce leaned over, feeling his way along the wall, the last spark of electricity in his right socket arced, then he was in darkness. He expected they would jump on him, tear him piece by piece, but they had other priorities: intruders took precedence. He stumbled, feeling along, hearing the drumming of feet and clacking of teeth, but not one of them bothered with him.

"I'm a blind fucking Ninja." He cackled and continued on toward the surface. "Now watch me karate kick my way the fuck out of here." He knew he was fucked, he just wanted to get out of this hole, breathe in one last gulp of fresh air, before the bell on his crock pot dinged and turned out the lights.

One last breath of fresh air. That wasn't too much to ask for, was it?

Then he had another thought…

4

Billy and Spence dropped three more targets in the general vicinity of Pit #2. The armada only had 200 meters left to cover; fifteen seconds at best. Merv was closing the distance with the pickup that was attempting to ambush them from behind. There was little the two could do for him. This was his show. They could only hope that he took out the pickup and got back out alive.

No one saw Todd Sackman's rig waiting at the airport. His intended cargo was ascending from Pit #2, following the spiral road made of ice and rock. If Axe were here, he might have cried out, "Justin Case, stop Justin Case!" But even to Axe, it made no sense.

In the last two hundred meters, Billy and Spence let the hot barrels of their rifles' air cool, as Crane continued scanning for targets of opportunity. They watched Merv set a collision course with the pickup. It was like watching a silent movie from up here. When the Peterbilt and the pickup collided, there was no sound. Even when it exploded. And instead of bouncing off the moose bumper, the big rig rolled over it and suddenly Merv`s rig was careening toward the bank.

"Oh no," Spence said.

The Skentophyte in tow went into a mass of confusion, turning and twisting blindly. Merv's Pete stopped on the bank, his left steer wheel on the ground behind him.

Crane stopped scanning long enough to watch.

The Peterbilt was completely surrounded, 200-plus skulking creatures moving, searching and smelling the air. There was no movement in the rig and Billy hoped that he was dead. Then he heard it and his heart sunk a little deeper.

Telegraph Road

Merv White heard the whistle of the wind and felt the cold breeze against his face. The driver door window had imploded. Square jagged pebbles of safety glass were everywhere. He shook his head and tiny pieces fell from his beard and hair. The dashboard was covered, but he was amazed to find that he had not even gotten a scratch in the impact.

Imagine that, not even a scratch, he thought.

The Peterbilt, on the other hand, hadn't been as lucky. The driver side fender was ripped nearly off and the driver steer wheel gone. Beyond the long, sleek hood was a greater source of concern. "Damn it."

He was surrounded by skentophyte, blindly circling, seeking his scent. One of the creatures bumped against his step—then another—then he saw the claw curling up over the moose bumper. He could hear the hushing of their air exchangers, the clacking of the hungry teeth. There was nowhere to run. Merv White calmly reached over and removed the frame holding a picture of his wife and son. The adhesive he used to glue the frame to the dash refused to budge, and the plastic frame cracked. The sound caught the attention of the marauders on the ice so he left the frame and he took out the picture. Another bumped against the truck. He reached up and took the radio handset. "Spence, I'm going to step out now. You make it count, Bud." He pulled on the handle and it creaked. Skentophyte heads swung in the direction of that sound.

Closing in.

Not even a scratch, he again mused.

He pushed open the door, scrambled up what was left of the beaten fender, over the hood and onto the roof. The creatures were all around now, teeth clacking hungrily. He stood erect, eyes drawn to the picture of his wife, Mary, and their son, Frances, and waited. He waited, head tilted as they climbed up from all sides. He didn't look their way, fearful he would give up their position. He focused on his wife and son and hoped Garney was getting to where he needed to be. "I love you," he told his wife and son, and then his world went black.

The report of rifle fire didn't follow until after Merv's lifeless body fell sideways into a fetal position on the roof of his 379 Flattop Peterbilt. It was a crisp sound, cutting out across the tundra in defiance of its shooter's cry. When he thumped lifelessly down, the Skentophyte drew back, and then they were on him.

5

Spence lowered the rifle sight and glanced Billy's way. Merv White had been his friend for over three years. Billy gave him a solemn look and repositioned his weapon. Spence took another look: they had his body off the roof of the truck and onto the ground, but he could not see him below the sea of creatures blindly ripping and tearing. He took up a firing position and shot a couple of them down, but he was just wasting ammo.

Then over the radio:

"Jesus Christ," Phil Crane called. "There, there, something coming out of Pit #2! Something big!"

Both Billy and Spence swung their sights onto the pit, searching until they saw it winding its way up the path. It was the 777 rock truck and it was moving up to high speed. In its box they could see the creatures riding atop the cargo.

The machines, Billy looked Spence's way.

Spence lowered his sight again, glanced back, and gave a thumbs down.

It had to be! From their vantage point, they could see three layers of road that spiraled out of the pit. The 777 was on the second layer. *How long would they have?* Billy swung his sight onto the convoy. *One hundred meters!*

The armada was already slowing down.

"There won't be enough time," Billy said.

Spence couldn't hear him, but he nodded in agreement.

He turned his head, glanced back at Crane, who was standing behind the truck door. He brought the binoculars up. Then dropped them and looked to Billy. Then up again.

"Is that what I think it is?" Crane asked.

Billy nodded.

Behind the 777, legions of skentophyte trailed.

The armada was at the objective, idling away.

It was coming fast. Too fast for a clean getaway. If they abandoned the truck, chances were the Rock truck would blow past before they were far enough out of range to detonate the ruck prill bomb.

Garney's door opened.

"We gotta blow it," Phil yelled. "They'll never make it!"

Billy turned from Phil, and then to Spence.

Spence nodded. The 777 was too far off to take a shot at.

6

Bruce was completely blind now, and barely alive, but he continued to stumble toward the beckoning cold of the tunnel's mouth. The tunnel leading back to the chamber was barren, not a click or a clack and even better, his mind was a free. Free of their insane chants. A burden this blind ninja could do without.

If I had my eyes, I could get over to the stockpile in the storage building and light the place up. But he didn't have his eyes, so he stumbled out of the tunnel, hoping he could remember the lay of the land based on memory. "Of course I can, I'm a blind fucking Ninja." Then that idea came swirling back. It was a long shot, but what the hell else did he have to do with himself. He reached into his pocket and pulled out a Zippo lighter and then fumbled for his cigarettes. He hadn't had a smoke since…

Since they took him out of the gymnasium. He stabbed the smoke between his lips and then he tripped, falling down hard. He skinned his hand on a piece of rock.

He chuckled. "The blind Ninja isn't all that nimbly bimbly."

He stood up, removed the broken cigarette from his mouth. The heat exchangers were pushing against the cold air in the tunnel, dust coated the hairs in his nostrils. He pulled another smoke from the pack, placed it between his teeth, and stopped to light it.

The heat exchangers. LNG, he thought. *Maybe, just maybe.*

7

Big Garney pulled the air brake on the tractor and reached for the door handle. They were alone, the things had not gotten this far, and it looked as though he might be able to abandon ship. When he pulled the door handle, he heard the call come in on the radio.

"Boys, I got some really lousy news." It was Billy Jack.

No one responded. They just listened. So Billy continued.

"It looks like those things are bringing their machines out of the pit on one of those monster dump trucks," Billy said. Marty was staring though his driver window right into the cab at Big Garney Wilson. "There isn't enough time to get clear, boys. That big truck is going to be on top of you in a minute and that won't be far enough to get out of range."

"Garney, get that thing rigged up," Chase Fenwick interrupted.

Billy swallowed. "Hook her up, boys, and get the fuck out of there. I'll wait until…"

Garney was already out of the rig, moving to the front of the trailer. When he got there, he flipped the radio on and started up toward Chase Fenwick's truck, but stopped dead in his tracks.

"Until it's right on top of the trailer before we light it up."

Chase pushed in his clutch, slammed the gear selector into fourth, and released his brake. In his side view mirror, Garney stopped and he continued, leaving him behind. "Marty, you and Garney get the hell out of here." He shifted from low into high range, picking up momentum. "I'll see if I can slow the bastards down."

"Oh my god," Marty whispered.

"God speed, Chase," Billy said. "Get the fuck out of there, boys!"

Garney turned confused and mouthed, "What the hell?"

"Get in! Get in!" Marty yanked the air horn, frantically waving for Garney to hurry. Big Garney came alive then—bounding in great big strides, and then he was climbing into the cab.

"Where the hell is he going, my brother?" But Marty was too busy spinning the W900 around and upshifting to answer. Then it dawned on him and he said, "Oh no, my brother. Oh no! Damn!" Marty wasn't sure, but he thought that Garney might have been on the verge of tears. "Why is he doing that, Marty? Why didn't he just come with us?"

Marty glanced over between shifts. "I don't know."

8

Bruce had found what he was looking for and as a result, he crushed out the cigarette. Funny how those things tasted like shit after a day or two of being off of them. Regardless, he was going to have another, but not until he was finished. He placed his hand on the cool pipe and felt the stinging cold of the frost. In what was left of his mind, he could see the letters: LNG. Liquefied Natural Gas. The tunnels were still heated by diesel, but this year they had started experimenting with LNG. It was much cheaper and easier to store.

Bruce grinned. "That's the one," he said and began to follow it.

Above him, the Skent were trying to get their precious cargo to the surface before the intruders fucked them up. He wondered who it was. Maybe the army? God, he hoped so. He didn't know, but he knew what he was going to do even if the Skent was facing eventual defeat. He found his way into the maintenance room and almost tripped over the acetylene pack. He reached over the pack, fingers scrambling for the striker and closed his hand around it.

"Time for that smoke," he said and began opening the T-valves. "Acetylene to 7, Oxygen to 30," Bruce said, then opened the rear valves approximately half a turn. He began unraveling the lines from the hook. "Not bad for a blind Ninja." He moved back to the wall, felt again for the LNG pipe, and then opened the acetylene valve on the torch and hit the striker. There was a **fwap**, a **pop** and a warm **hiss**. "Eureka." Bruce began adjusting the knobs on the torch, listening as the hiss tightened and became more disciplined. Oxygen was what he needed, oxygen was the key to cutting. He adjusted the flow, and the sound became even more refined. "Yes, almost there," he said and lit the smoke between his teeth. Then he moved toward the natural gas line and went to work. Under the heat of the torch, the frost on the line melted, sizzled, and evaporated. Bruce hoped he had the ratio correct. It was only going to take a few seconds to find out as he lay the inner cone against the pipe.

9

As Marty and Big Garney Wilson made a break for it, Chase Fenwick was driving the Kenworth down the road into the pit. On the opposite side, the 777 was coming around to meet him, bringing up the rear, hundreds of the ugly bastards.

Chase grabbed the stick and shifted into eighth gear. The road into the pit, littered with rock and ice, snapped—crunched and banged—road debris banging beneath his wheels and undercarriage. And it was slippery. He almost lost control, the rig sliding dangerously near the edge. For a moment, Chase had the horrible vision of toppling off the edge and bouncing down the rock face into the pit. He backed his speed down and tightened his grip.

This is going to have to be enough.

10

Marty swerved the truck through carnage of dead and dying Skentophyte from their first encounter on the Telegraph. Those who hadn't been taken out trundled blindly along the road toward them, thudding against the moose bumper—crunching beneath the wheels. He couldn't see the front of the truck, but knew the bumper wouldn't withstand much more. After a few seconds, they were past the carnage and the high grade loomed ahead.

11

Billy, Spence, and Phil were enthralled by the bobtail rig careening down the spiral pit toward the monster rock truck. It looked miniscule compared to the mining rig.

It's just going to run right over him, Billy thought. He had the radio in his hand, the channel switched over to Ladd 9, waiting to press the transmit button.

Ballsy guy, Spence thought. *Too bad we didn't get to know him better.*

In their peripheral, Marty's rig slowed and turned onto the high grade. Were they far enough away to ignite the explosives? Billy didn't know. Nobody knew, in fact, the explosion could kill them up here for all they knew. They were backing up the hill now, to join Crane. There would be no more radio communications, no calling of targets. They were just waiting to see if Chase could slow it down to buy them just a little more time.

12

Chase was now locked into a head on collision, and he pushed down on the throttle, increasing his speed. As the seconds of his life wound down, he did not think about the giant coming toward him. He turned his thoughts to his son in Niagara, to the men he'd let go to their death, and he hoped that if he were to stand and be judged for all that he had done that this would be enough right to balance out the wrongs.

The rolling house of steel and rubber bore down on him, then the windshield turned cat yellow, black, and then nothing. When the truck exploded, Chase Fenwick thought he heard Lenny Aranuknuk calling to him. "Wake up, Chase. Wake up!"

13

Bruce tasted the steel as it melted and splashed onto the leather of his work boots, sizzling as it did. He was smiling, and why not, a man should be happy in his work and this would be his finest hour. The smoke between his teeth was only burned a quarter way, the ash clinging in a downward arc. He adjusted the oxygen knob and the torch hissed like a snake. He was getting through…

Although Bruce couldn't see it, the ash on his smoke came off, but it didn't fall, but went sideways.

Then the gas line ignited...

14

At first they thought that the 777 had won and rolled right over the rig. Then, from beneath, there came a cloud of black smoke and a flash of orange. Debris burst in every direction, spilling down the rock face, fire and smoke trailing behind. The 777 rebounded off course and into the rock wall, but continued rolling up and out of the pit.

"No, no, no," Billy grunted.

Then it stopped.

Billy turned his attention to Marty and Garney. They were on the high grade now, slipping behind the ridge from which the armada had first appeared. "Spence," Billy motioned and the two climbed the hill.

When they reached Phil, he was looking through the binoculars.

"Phil, we better get that truck behind the hill," Billy called.

"Pringle," Phil said. "Oh shit, Pringle."

"What?" Billy didn't understand. Didn't see the Skentophyte massing in the open lot. Didn't see the man standing in the communications room holding his own set of binoculars, staring right back at them.

"Oh my god," Crane said as he met John Pringle's gaze and realized they'd been spotted.

"Better get behind the hill," Spence warned.

Billy brought his rifle sight up and saw the Skentophyte all turning in their direction. How many were there? 300? 500?

"Jesus Christ," Billy cried and as if he were announcing the word "Go!" the Skentophyte started toward them in a lethal stampede. They stood mesmerized, Crane with his glasses up, Billy with the rifle sight, and Spence seemed the only one who was not caught in the shock. He raised the rifle up and sighted in his target, took in a full breath, relaxed his muscles, expelled halfway and squeezed the trigger.

The shot found its target a second later, first shattering the window in the communications center, then piercing John Pringle's heart. He fell dead instantly, but the Skentophyte kept coming. Charging toward them and they saw the others. Some were on the roof. Others behind vehicles. What Bruce would have called new recruits looking in the direction of their O.P. The Skentophyte were 400 meters out now, there wouldn't be enough time to take out all the observers. "Move the truck back!" Spence was screaming. "Blow it now, Billy! Blow it now!"

Crane yanked the gear selector into reverse and backed the truck up.

"Holy shit!" Billy cried and hit the ground. Spence also hit the snow, and then Billy keyed the radio.

At first there was nothing, and the seconds it took for the signal to light up the radio and close the circuit between Chase Fenwick's homemade blasting caps and the pails of prilled ammonium nitrate seemed an eternity. The Skentophyte were 300 meters out now, coming strong.

"Fuck," Billy said and keyed the radio again. "Come on!"

15

The first explosion, and there were many, catapulted Big Garney Wilson's Western Star 300 meters out across the lot, leaving the fifth wheel still attached to the trailer's king pin. But that would only be a microsecond because the rest of the trailer was vaporized thereafter. Snow, rock, dust, and shrapnel blew outward in every direction. The first fuel storage tank crumpled like a giant dented soup can, its double bulk head breached. Inside the pit, a second before Billy keyed the radio and a full two seconds after Chase stopped the advancing 777, an indiscriminate flame licked out of the tunnel, which led to the chamber. No one bore witness to the explosion inside the chamber, but for Bruce it was a small victory.

A last "fuck you" to the Skento-fucks.

A tempest of debris bowled out across the camp, uprooting equipment and vehicles—sandblasting paint—grinding the metals and plastics in fibrous dust, swallowing them and becoming a tsunamis rolling barrage. Both the living quarters and main building were flattened. The Tank at Pit #2 ignited then and flared, a river of burning diesel decanting from the hole that looked remarkably like a jagged smiling mouth.

The river of fire cascaded downward into the pit, raining upon the skentophyte who were not blown from the spiral road in the initial blast. Across the collective, agonized cries went out in a succession of clicks and clacks with only one call that made sense.

Just in case—get to the just in case!

Then the Ammonium Nitrate stored in the main pit ignited, and seconds later, the main tank farm caught fire. Following that, an operatic succession of quaking thuds walloped the arctic landscape that seemed to go on forever.

16

Marty almost lost control when the mine exploded. The W900 veered sideways and almost got sucked into the bank, but he was able to correct and kept going. He stole a glance in the side view mirror and saw the grey cloud billowing upwards, staining the white horizon. Then he looked forward.

"They did it, Marty," Big Garney said. "My brother, they really did it!" Then he sat back in his seat, thought about Chase and Merv, sadness filling his big heart. "I wonder if Billy and Spence are okay."

And Crane, Marty thought. *Did he make it?*

"Should we wait for them, my brother?" Garney asked.

"No," Marty replied. "If they made it, Billy will be heading for Portage 35. Let's get there, Garney."

"Yeah, uh huh. That's sounds good, my brother. Portage 35. Yes sir!" They rolled onto the ice, leaving the high grade behind and headed southbound for the last time.

17

Billy Jack stood and worked his way back up to the ridge. Behind him, Spence and Phil followed. Using the rifle scope, he surveyed the aftermath. The Mine as they had seen it was gone. The earth was scorched by a mammoth spiral snowflake of grey scarring the ground from Pit #2 out. A waterfall of diesel poured down into the pit, liquid flame dripping, black smoke billowing from its edge up into the air. The main tank farm was burning as well.

"It worked," Spence said, gazing through his own rifle sight.

"Yeah, not bad for a couple of grunts." Billy was still surveying the sight, looking for the advancing Skentophyte, and then he saw movement. Only 250 meters out, they scuttled insect-like amongst the rubble, like ants whose mound had been obliterated by a child's angry kick. They had hurt them, but there were still plenty down there. "I'd say we leave the rest for the cavalry."

"Yeah." Spence lowered his rifle.

"Are we done yet?" Phil asked.

"Yeah, we're done." Billy reached down, touched the satchel of diamonds in his pocket.

"Can we get the fuck out of here?"

"We've got one more piece of business," Spence said, and looked to Billy. "You ready?"

Phil Crane suddenly recognized the voice and understood.

You ready?

Who is this?

Are you ready?

Yeah, I'm ready?

Good, he'll be in the tenth group. Make sure you're ready.

Spence removed the satellite phone from his pocket.

Billy Jack raised his weapon. "Yeah, I'm ready."

***

Chapter 37—Doc

1

Five Hours Later
Yellowknife, NWT

"Hello," Gordon Shamus said.

"He'll be coming to you in about half an hour."

"How did it go up there?"

"It's all good. There's been trouble at the Acadia mine, but it has no bearing on us."

"Trouble? What do you mean?"

"Should be all over the news in no time. Everything else is fine."

Shamus came in off the deck. "Half an hour? He's coming alone?

"That is what you wanted."

"Yes."

"Do it off site."

That sounded like an order, but he let it go. "Anything else?"

"No. Everything has been taken care of on this end." The phone clicked off. He closed his own cell and stared at Donald, then he picked up the remote and turned the television on.

2

Lupania Corporate Jet
Somewhere over the Pacific Ocean

Damien Lars was drifting in and out of his afternoon nap when the steward gently touched his shoulder. He opened his eyes and looked up at the young man. "Mr. Lars, you need to see something."

He stood and followed the young steward to the back of the aircraft to the conference section of the plane. Sitting in the chairs, his special assistant, Jaimie Watts and his secretary Andrea Carr. They didn't look up. They were entranced by the news report.

"What is it?" Lars asked sitting down.

"Listen," Jaimie said and turned up the television.

Damien Lars sat down to see a newscaster from CNN. Beside him a satellite map showed flashes repeating over and over again to the news commentary. "We are now receiving confirmed reports that there has been a major explosion north of the 60th parallel at what our sources say is the Meanook Diamond Mine." Below that, a scrolling ribbon: **MASSIVE EXPLOSIONS PICKED UP ON WEATHER SATELLITE.**

Damien looked at the map. Saw the contracting flash repeating again and again. He turned to Jaimie, then back to the television screen and said, "That's not Meanook. That's Acadia."

3

Acadia Airfield

Todd Sackman regained consciousness, not because he wanted to, but because his escort was shaking him, screaming madly inside his head. Just in case—Skent—Just in case—Skent—Just in case. He turned the windshield wipers on and it smeared the mixture of dust and snow from the windshield.

What the hell had happened?

Intruders—explosion—we must leave—skent—just in case.

"What happened?" he said again, this time aloud. He looked through the windshield, saw the smoke rising beyond the hill that enclosed the mine from the airfield. Sack saw it then, through the collective eye. The Mine was gone and so was the chamber, while across the wire there was a chorus of panic and cries of agony. Whatever had happened had wiped a lot of them out and severely hurt the rest. He wondered if anyone else who was not a skentophyte had survived. *Probably not.* A smile began to rise, but that evaporated when his escort clinched down hard onto his shoulder.

Sack moaned.

Skent—we must get to just in case—Corbett—now.

Sack started his rig and pulled from behind the hanger. The sweet smell of burning diesel hung in the air. He looked to the Telegraph ring road. The high shoulders of rock and snow had been flattened. The place was burning, the stink of charred flesh intermingled with scorched earth. He didn't think he was going to be able to navigate through the carnage, but he crawled on.

Mount St Helens, he thought. *That's what this looks like: the aftermath of Mount St Helens.*

Drive—get to just in case—we are skentophyte!

“Don’t know how far I’ll get,” he pointed to a large pile of debris blocking their advance. A call went out across the wire and from all sides, the Skentophyte appeared and began to move the debris out of their way. They dragged away a burning pickup, a steel support beam from the Main building. They cleared the way, making the advance passable. Before he knew it, Todd Sackman was driving obstacle free across the telegraph toward the high grade on his way to Corbett Lake.

4

They rallied at Portage 35. Vincent came out, a smile on his face until he saw the missing vehicles. “Where are the others?”

“Merv and Chase never made it,” Marty said.

“What about Billy Jack and Spence? And Phil.”

“I don’t know, they sure as hell lit up camp.”

“They’re probably not far behind, my brother,” Garney said. “How’s the Axe Man doing?”

“He’s out, but we really need to get him to a hospital.”

Marty looked to Garney. “Let’s put him in the sleeper. He’ll be more comfortable on the bed. Then you guys take him south to the hospital in YK.”

“I’m not leaving here until Billy Jack arrives,” Vincent insisted.

“Marty my brother, we have got to stick together.”

“Both of you listen. Take Axe south. Garney, you can drive while Vincent looks after him. It will be warmer and more comfortable than him bouncing on that frozen seat. I’ll wait for Billy and Spence. I’ve still got to get my wife. I need Phil for that.”

“I don’t think…” Vincent started to say.

“What will Billy say if he knew you waited around for an hour or two while his brother was dying? What if they don’t arrive at all, Vincent? Take him south, I’ll wait for them and tell them where you went.”

“Marty, my brother, I don’t want to leave you out here. Not after all of this. It just ain’t right, my brother. No sir, not right at all.”

“You gotta drive the rig, Garney. I’ll get a hold of you.”

Big Garney Wilson looked back at Vincent, then to Marty. “He’s right, Vincent, let’s get Axe to a hospital. If Billy was here, he’d tell us that is what we should do.”

They popped the sleeper escape door on the W900 and both Marty and Garney transferred him from the back of the flood truck into the waiting bunk. The transfer only took a minute and as Vincent secured Axe in the bunk and wrapped him up, Big Garney Wilson stared out at the vacant road. Where were they?

"They'll be here." Marty stuck out his hand.

"Yeah, uh huh. Okay, my brother." Garney took his hand and pulled him into an embrace. "What happens on the ice, stays on the ice, my brother." He handed Marty Phil Crane's gun.

"Sure thing."

They mounted up and took off across the portage. Marty got into the cab of the flood truck and waited. It wasn't until they were out of earshot that he realized that he'd left Maggie's picture in the sun visor.

Fifteen minutes later, he saw the approaching pickup trucks.

5

Four Hours Later
Tli Cho Manor—Kilometer 17 on the Ingraham Trail

The phone rang once, then twice, and then he heard her voice. "Hello?"

"Maggie," Marty said.

"Marty, where are you?"

"Coming to get you."

"I don't think that's a good idea, Marty. I…" Then she was gone.

"Marty," Shamus said. "Where are you?"

"Walking up the drive to meet you."

Shamus stepped toward the window, saw him coming, cell phone to his ear. "So you are. Did you come alone, Marty?"

"Yeah, I'm alone." Marty had left the flood truck parked on the Ingraham trail. He was alone. "Bring her outside, Gordon, I want to see her."

Shamus snapped his fingers, signaling and pointing outside. "I'm sending my man, Donald, out to meet you. I gotta make sure it's safe to bring her out, Marty. That you aren't going to do anything stupid."

"I'm unarmed, Gordon." And he was, he'd left Crane's pistol under the seat of the flood truck. He hadn't wanted to, but he probably would have gotten both of them killed if he brought it. No, he had nothing, just a cell phone and he hoped that the diamonds would be his leverage.

Gordon raised a hand. "Well, let's just make sure, okay?"

"Whatever it takes," Marty said.

Maggie strode toward the window and Angel caught her arm.

"Better stay here, sweetheart."

Maggie gave her a dirty look. "Get your fucking hands off me."

"Come to the window, Maggie. He needs to see you too," Gordon Shamus said.

Angel released her and she dashed to the big picture window and saw him standing down there. At first, she didn't recognize him. He was wearing a bright blue jacket with reflective striping and he had a beard. He stared up at her and they locked eyes. He smiled, she smiled back, then brought her hand up to her mouth, stifling a cry, but she couldn't stop the tears.

He came! Of course he did. She knew he would.

He raised a hand to wave.

She waved back and let out a short cry and covered her mouth again.

Then his arms went out to his sides.

5

"Okay, pal, put your arms out," Donald said as he approached. "I'm going to have to pat you down."

"You must be Donald."

"Let's just get this over with and then you and your lady can be reunited. Bring your hands up over your head." Donald ran his right hand under his arm and kept the gun in his left out of reach. He checked him over thoroughly, even grabbing his crotch just to make sure.

Donald stepped back, turned, and gave a thumbs up.

Shamus raised the phone to his ear. "Come on inside, Marty. It's too cold out there to chit chat and I'm sure Maggie would like to see you."

Marty turned to Donald. "He wants us inside."

"Okay, Marty, you lead the way." Donald gestured with the gun.

Marty walked to the doorway and thought, *I'm about to enter the mouth of madness.* Behind, Donald followed, his boots crunching in the snow. Overhead the sun was descending behind the cloud cover. In an hour and a half, or maybe two, day would surrender to night.

He stepped through the doorway and climbed the stairwell, slowly scanning for sudden movement. There was none. From above, Gordon Shamus called cheerfully, "Come on upstairs, Marty."

When he caught sight of them, he heard Phil Crane's warning.

The woman is almost as dangerous as Shamus.

She was tall, blonde, athletic-looking, and she watched him closely as he entered the main living room. Beside her a short guy was standing, his face banged up. No one had to explain what happened to this guy. Marty already knew. Gordon happened. To the left of them, the lanky maniac stood smiling and beside him, Maggie.

Marty stopped abruptly and Donald almost bumped into him.

"Welcome, Marty," Gordon said, and then to Maggie, "Go ahead."

She hesitated, but only for a second, and then dashed across the room and into his waiting arms. He enveloped her and she buried her head in the crook of his neck, shaking—convulsing and whispering, "I knew you'd come." She cried then, because she loved him so much and was sure their time was almost up. "I love you, Marty." Warm tears smeared against his neck and face. He held her protectively, smelling her, loving her and never wanting to let go.

"I love you too, Mag." He squeezed her tight and brought his eyes up to meet Gordon Shamus, who was grinning ear to ear, but his eyes were wild and unpredictable. The grin was a painted smile, like Heath Ledger's Joker, window dressing on an insane asylum.

"You have something for me, Marty?"

Marty straightened Maggie up and eased her to his side. "Yeah."

"But not here, right?"

"You have to let her go first. Then I'll take you to it."

Marty heard the click of the hammer on Donald's gun cock and then the barrel pressed against the back of his head.

"I think we need to go for a ride, Marty."

"What are you doing? I said if you let her go, I'll give you what you want."

Angel drew her own gun then and pointed it at them.

Maggie gave her a look of disdain.

Angel pretended not to notice and said, "Let's go, sweetheart."

"I don't feel safe here, Marty. Let's go somewhere where it's a little more private, then he can discuss your proposition," Shamus said and drew his own gun. The guy beside the blonde looked too dazed to be of much good to anyone. "Both of you put your hands out."

They put their hands out in front of them and the man beside the blonde walked over and zip tied their wrists. "Just being cautious."

"Gordon, this isn't necessary."

"It's absolutely necessary, Marty," Gordon Shamus said and then his world exploded into a zenith of pain, followed by Maggie screaming. The gun butt caught just below the right cheek bone and after splitting the skin, he felt one of his molars crack in two. Then there was a punch to the stomach, emptying him of his ability to breathe. His legs became rubber.

He collapsed, but Gordon was hoisting him up. Still, Maggie was screaming, but that was a hundred miles away. The coppery taste of blood ran down the back of his throat, wafted up into his nasal cavities. His vision swam in a pool of tears and he thought he might fall down, except far off, he heard Gordon say, "Grab him, Donald, before he falls down the fucking stairs."

Far off, Maggie screamed again, "You bastard! You fucking bastard!"

Then Donald was hoisting him up and Shamus brought his face in close. "Stay with me, Marty." The stench of cigar smoke was sweet and stale. "We're going for a ride and I'm not done with you just yet."

Then the blonde was pulling Maggie away. She was struggling, and Marty felt the cold steel push into his temple. He was using everything he had to hold on, though his body was insisting he should just let go.

"Maggie, I want you to calm down," Gordon said and cocked the hammer back. "Can you do that for me, Maggie?"

The room went quiet.

"Okay, then, let's all go for a ride."

Then they were clunking down the stairs. The hall, swinging like a pendulum, light, wall, stairs, floor, and still Marty hung on. He knew that if he capitulated to the darkness, he would never see Maggie again. Then they were at the door of SUV and he felt himself being pushed inside by Donald. Slowly, he was clawing his way back, the double vision amalgamating into one-and-a-half. Then it was tunnel vision.

"Move over, Marty," Donald said. He hooked his tied wrists over the headrest of the driver seat and dragged himself over. Then they pushed Maggie in beside him and he knew that this was the plan all along.

We're going to the execution spot, he thought. *He probably already has a hole dug.* The door closed and he felt Maggie's hands upon his own, squeezing tight. He leaned against her. Took in her warmth.

The front and passenger doors opened, then shut with a successive "Ka-chunk! Ka-chunk!" Then the engine started and before he could steady himself, he felt the vehicle back up and turn. He thought he might vomit then, but held back.

Just a little longer, he thought.

"Where are the diamonds, Marty?" Gordon asked.

"Let her go and I'll tell you." His cheek stung with each syllable.

“You must think I’m fucking stupid.” Gordon held up his phone, then dialed. The blue tooth kicked on.

A female voice announced, “Dialing unknown number.”

Then it began to ring.

“Hello,” it was Spence.

“It’s Gordon. You have the package?”

“Yeah, I got it. We’re all good on this end.”

“Meet you at the rendezvous.”

“Sure.”

Gordon smiled. “Sorry, Marty.”

Marty tightened his grip on Maggie’s hands.

Suddenly, at the end of the drive stood a man. Donald eased up on the gas; he was blocking the drive. The man was dressed in a parka; he pulled back the hood and Donald said, “Phil?”

“What? Gordon turned his head and saw Phil Crane blocking the road, but that couldn’t be. Phil Cranc was supposed to be dead? Gordon grabbed the microphone for the VHF radio. “Angel, there’s something going on here.”

Then Marty said something.

“The hunting is good,” Marty said and pushed Maggie down onto the bench seat, shielding her. He never heard the shots, never heard the glass from both the front driver and passenger sides exploded inward. He only heard the horn from the vehicle behind, ringing out as Angel’s lifeless body collapsed upon it. Then he heard Gordon Shamus.

“Donald, get us the fuck out of here!”

Suddenly, gunfire exploded inside the cab of the Escalade and blood splashed up and over the head rest, a single drop landing on Marty’s hand. Then there was a rush of cool air. “Stay down,” Marty whispered and wiped the drop of blood on the carpet. Maggie responded by squeezing his hand. She could hear his heart beating in his chest. Footsteps approached, snow crunching beneath boots.

“You guys stay down for now,” Donald said. Marty opened his eyes to see Crane was approaching. “Stay in the vehicle until I clear up this other matter.” He moved to the second vehicle and leaned in the driver window.

“Stay down, Mag,” Marty said.

“Okay,” she whispered back. “Is he…”

“Yeah.”

He waited for more shots, but none rang out.

6

Billy and Spence walked in from separate sides of the property toward the lead vehicle. They did so with weapons tucked into their shoulders and at the ready. The kills had been clean. Marty and his wife were out of the vehicle now. She clung to him like a life raft and who could blame her? Donald was walking back to the second vehicle with Crane.

Before they reached him, Donald called back, “All clear!” and gave a thumbs up.

Billy stopped and returned the thumbs up, then lowered his rife and approached Maggie and Marty.

“You folks okay?” Spence asked Marty.

He was shaking, full of adrenaline. “We will be.”

Maggie whispered, “Are they police?”

Spence nodded. “No, Maggie, we’re friends of Marty’s. He told us you were in trouble and needed help.”

Maggie broke away from Marty then and hugged Spence. “Thank you.” She was crying. Then she grabbed Billy and hugged him too. “Thank you so much.” She continued to cry. “Oh my god, what are your names?”

“My name’s Spence and this is my brother Billy Jack.”

“Spence and Billy, I’m never going to forget you.” Then she turned to Marty. “I thought we were dead, baby. I thought we were dead!” And she collapsed into his arms, shaking, convulsing, and the sobs came out in great long painful hiccups.

“Thank you,” Marty said and he was tearful as well.

“I gotta talk to those two,” Billy said. “And then I gotta get over to the YK Gen and see about Axe.”

“Sure.” Marty squeezed Maggie tighter. “I’ll never forget this.”

“We’re square, Marty,” Billy said over his shoulder and walked back to meet Crane and Donald.

When Billy reached Donald, they hugged each other.

“How the hell are yuh, Doc?” Billy asked and grinned.

“Doing well, Sergeant Jack. How about you?”

“Good.”

Spence reached out and shook Donald’s hand. “Good to see you, Doc.”

“Sergeant Spence.” Donald, aka Doc, grinned ear to ear.

Crane looked on, outside this brotherhood, abandoning his own when he became a dirty cop.

Donald said to them, “You tell him the deal?”

“Yeah. He knows the score.”

“Phil, we are going to deal with that and then we go our separate ways.”

“You copy that, Phil? It’s over.” Billy placed a hand on his shoulder. “The only reason you’re alive is because of what you did up there. Remember that when we part ways.”

“I understand.” Phil Crane cocked a thumb back at Marty and Maggie. “Like them, I just want to get the fuck out of here.” And he did. He didn’t give a shit about the diamonds. He just wanted to get the cash he’d saved up for a rainy day and disappear.

“First we deal with that. And then, well, then you get your walking papers, but understand me, Phil. I hear a word about this and we will track you down and put you in the ground.” Billy leaned forward. “You think you have gangster friends, I have people everywhere,” Billy said.

Crane looked over at Donald. “Apparently.” He wondered if things had been different, if the thing hadn’t happened up north, if Croft and his wife would be on their way to place where they would soon be disposing of Shamus, Angel, and Scott. Was the double cross always on the agenda, or had the super soldier suddenly grown a conscience?

Billy’s phone rang then, so he stepped off to take the call. “Hello.”

It was Vincent. “They have him in ICU, he’s stable, but he’s asking for you.”

“I’ll be there soon, Vincent. Just have a bit of mopping up to do.”

“Okay, Billy Jack. Big Garney is here too. We’ll be waiting.”

“Sure, be there as soon as possible.” He shut the phone off.

They broke off then.

After retrieving her personal belongings, Marty and Maggie walked out to the Ingraham and jumped in the Flood truck. She didn’t want to go back in the house, but Marty insisted. She could leave no trace that she was here. Billy told them to get down to YK and catch a plane, he’d be in touch, but for now they needed distance. When they reached the flood truck, Maggie got the first aid kit and put a large butterfly bandage on Marty’s cheek. The bleeding had stopped and she cleaned him up. The ride into YK was quiet. There was so much she didn’t know; he really had no idea where to begin.

She thought about the things Angel had said. How Gordon Shamus was the man in Hamilton, that there were others that would come knocking, people from Jersey and Montreal.

Leave it for now, her inner voice said. And the pragmatic Maggie was right; that could all be talked about later. For now, they needed to distance themselves from this place. She bought the tickets as Marty waited on a nearby bench. He was quiet, looking out the window.

Three hours later, they were in the air.

She held his hand tightly, never wanting to let go. He had come. Come and saved her just as he said he would, but was it over? She leaned in and asked, "Is this it, Marty, are we safe now? Is it over?'

He brought his eyes up to meet hers. "I don't know, Mag. I really don't." He didn't have the strength to go into it. Not now. It was too incredible. He turned away then, looked out the window at the darkness below.

Not long after, the exhaustion took him to sleep.

***

FINAL ACT
JUST IN CASE

Chapter 38—One More Silver Dollar

1

Ingraham Trail – Kilometer 3

Todd Sackman had to use every bit of his strength to keep the International Lonestar centered on the Ingraham. Behind him, his escort watched as they wound south, around Giant Mine and toward the city of Yellowknife. He wasn't bleeding anymore, but he'd lost a lot of blood.

"Crazy fucking bitch," he mumbled. She'd come out of nowhere, chopping into him with a meat cleaver when he opened the incinerator hut to access the "just in case." "A fucking meat cleaver. Of all things, a fucking meat cleaver. Crazy fucking bitch."

It hadn't happened exactly like that. He opened the door and saw her hiding just behind the Thrombus Disc. He was as surprised as she when he opened that door, and rather than step aside and let his escort do the talking, he said, "Holy fuck, it's the goddamned Kitchen Nazi!"

That must have pissed her off, because she came flying out from behind that Thrombus Disc and swung at him. There was a sick wet thud and he looked down to see the meat cleaver embedded in his right hip.

"You crazy bitch," he said.

Her eyes darted madly, and then she screamed and ran past him and past his escort, who apparently was too dazed to stop her. It let out a series of chatters and clacks that did not translate into English, but were, Sack thought, a mirror of his own thoughts. The Skentophyte turned its head, regarding her, teeth clacking. She was still screaming insanely, running for the main building. It lost interest, turning back toward him. He guessed it decided she wasn't worth it, because he heard the command.

Load the just in case—Skent—we must go south—time is short—we are dying.

"Well, I am anyway," Sack said and looked down at the embedded cleaver. Syrupy warmth flowed from the wound inside his bib coveralls and into his boot. The escort came closer, examined the wound, and it knew. What happened next, Sack would have never dreamed in his most psychotic nightmare.

The Skent reached down and pulled the cleaver free. Sack wanted to say, "That's only going to make matters worse." Because the trickle of blood was now a cascade, and his boot was filling up. Or maybe it would be better. If the blood continued to flow, he would become sleepy and this would be over.

He stumbled against the doorway.

Yes, let it flow, let go. Yes…

No—Skent—not finished—must deliver just in case!

"Come on, pal, it's done. I'm done. We're done."

NO—WE ARE SKENTOPHYTE!

Sack felt himself being spun and lifted. *You can't stop Mother Nature, big guy. Even the great and all powerful skent can't rewind the clock when its spring is broken. Just let it flow…*

SKENT—NO—WE ARE SKENTOPHYTE!

Then it was digging into the wound and the cascade became a waterfall, his sock warm and spongy. He was swimming now, not toward any light, but down into the abysmal dark.

Yes, let it flow! Then there was light, pulsing light of red and green, swimming in the dark liquid. A ball of serpentine madness rolled over through the abyss, unfurling, gathering strength. Then he saw the elements flare. First one, then two, then three. And it seemed the almighty skent would have its way as Mother Nature released her grip and he fell back to earth.

No, no, no…

The odor of cauterizing flesh wafted upward, his thoughts doused by the agonized screams that he did not realize were his own. He could feel the puppeteer's strings being reattached, the pain was dulling from the enzymes the worms released, and though he was weak, it seemed that there was still a ways left to go. He heard his escort call to the others, the ones who waited inside the trailer.

Just in case—Load the just in case!

And they did.

2

When he passed the McKenzie Highway turnoff and carried on toward Yellowknife, he knew that it wouldn't be long. From his stereo, his swan song pulsed, Greg Allman singing how he had one more silver dollar and wasn't that just so damned true. The track rang loud and wasn't there just a hint of death wish in the melody this time? This last time. His escort seemed not to notice the rhythmic pulse or Sack's obvious embrace of the inevitable. He was expiring and there was nothing the Skentophyte could do to stop that. They could put another set of eyes in him, but he already had two in his head and three in the gash in his hip. Feeding the collective here and in the trailer, a camera view of his dashboard. Their collective was small, protecting the just in case, they too had one more silver dollar.

He was on 48th street now, ahead the city loomed, and still, they pushed him. But Mother Nature was winning.

God love her.

No! We are Skentophyte. Just in Case! Come back! Come back! Not finished!

The music began to fade, darkness was coming and Sack began to slip.

The last thing he saw, before the lights went out, was the skywalk that crossed over 48th street and a giant bucket of the Colonels finest rotating atop the KFC just beyond. That wasn't so bad, he loved KFC, especially the drumsticks. He never heard the panicked car horns, or shouts and screams, or even the crunch of metal as the Lonestar destroyed a line of parked vehicles on the right side of the street. He was dead before the big truck stopped. In the aftermath, the street fell silent, except for the serpentine hissing of antifreeze squirting down onto the snow-dusted concrete walk to the beat of Sweet Melissa.

3

Constable Howard Logan was the only car dispatched to the scene after the frantic 911 call came in. Almost everyone in the detachment had been called out. Something had happened at the Acadia Mine. A team of officers, along with rescue workers, were being dispatched to the scene. They were even mobilizing the Reserve Unit to help out. The Canadian Unit, Joint Task Force North, was also on the move. He didn't know what had happened, but wished he was there rather than here. That sounded exciting, they were going to a major rescue.

And I get to do traffic control.

He rolled up 50th avenue and saw the crowd.

"Dispatch, I'm on the scene now."

He turned left onto 48th street and saw the mess of smashed up cars and the big rig half on the sidewalk.

"Copy. Send status report after you know what's going on."

His red and blue strobes glinted against the chrome grill of the big truck. The grill looked like a joker's manic smile. Steam poured out from underneath the rig. Logan gave the siren two quick squawks before pulling off to the side.

"Will comply," he said and got out of his patrol car.

He surveyed the street; everyone was standing well back. The angry hissing from beneath the hood had spooked them, he guessed. He crossed the road, walking over to the crowd first. "Anybody see this?"

"I saw it," an old man said. "He just came barreling down the street, smashing cars left and right. Then just stopped."

"Anyone hurt? Where's the driver?"

"Still inside," the old man said.

Heart attack, Logan thought, then keyed his remote radio. "Dispatch, I'm going to need an ambulance to the scene, a couple tow trucks, and also a heavy hook."

"Copy that. Dispatching to your location now."

"Copy. I'll update you as I know morc."

He removed his Mag-lite, aimed it at the carnage, and strode across the street to the big truck, then traced the beam over the trailer for dangerous good placards. Nothing. That was good. When he reached the truck, he saw a motionless form slumped over the wheel.

Yeah, must have been a heart attack. Poor bugger. Then he heard something. *What was that? Chattering teeth.*

The truck cab shifted slightly.

Someone else inside!

"Is somebody there?"

Yes, somebody else. Trapped inside!

Then from the trailer, more movement.

What was that? Logan felt his heart speed up.

He heard his father's ghost, calling from the grave. "Don't do it, Howie! It isn't safe."

Logan paused, he was suddenly afraid, but he pushed it down. He had to check; someone might need help.

He switched the flashlight to his other hand…

Took a deep breath…

And reached for the door handle. When he did this, the cab shifted once more and the glass from the driver's windows detonated, then rained down upon him.

Reactively, Logan fell backward, on his ass, ready to scramble away—thinking the big truck was exploding. Then from behind him, he heard a collective gasp. He turned to look at the audience lined up on the sidewalk and as a result did not see the elongated arm come out to hook the remote radio handset attached to his shoulder. But he felt the tug and the snap of the cord whip back into his face, stinging him like a snake. Then he heard the clacking of teeth.

The crowd began to scatter, gasps turning to panicked screams. Logan tried to find his balance, tried to stand and flee whatever was happening, because he still didn't know. He only knew he was in trouble and that he had to get away. He was halfway up when the ice beneath his feet betrayed him and he toppled, coming down hard and breaking the wrist on his right hand. The pain was excruciating. He let out an agonizing howl, but it was cut short when he took in what had tried to grab him and understood immediately why the crowd was screaming. The truck door thumped and thudded, thumped and thudded, then unhinged, crashing down beside him. Then the driver, who was most assuredly dead, fell in a heavy wallop. But Logan wasn't looking at that. He was scuttling away, because that thing inside the cab was now slithering out. Teeth clacking, sniffing the air, looking for someone.

Not someone! You, his mind screamed. He crawled on one arm, his broken wrist tucked defensively underneath. His gun was on his right hip. That thing would be on top of him before he could reach it! It was on the ground now, on all fours, crawling toward him, head pivoting left and right.

Oh my god, what is that?

It kept coming, only feet away. Teeth clacking, spitting. Something hit the snow beside Logan's foot and powder kicked up. He had to get up! Had to get up! It was almost on top of him.

Then the trailer began to rock back and forth. Its cargo restless.

The creature twisted its head toward the trailer, teeth chattering, and let out a screech. It was calling to whatever was in there. The trailer rocked harder, the panels began to warp and swell with denting outward.

Logan struggled up on one knee, reaching clumsily with his left hand for the snap on his holster. At his right foot, something twisted and glowed beneath the blanket of powder. Something that had spit at him. He tried to unhook the snap and failed. The thing began to turn back toward him.

"Run," someone cried.

He had to get up! It was almost on top of him.

"Get down," someone else ordered.

Logan hit the ground mechanically, hoping what he'd heard meant what he thought. Hoping that his training was serving him in this moment of panic. From that point on time slowed—stretching out each moment in a succession of frozen frames. The creature took another step, zeroing in on him, readying itself to spit once more. To Logan's right, the trailer rocked violently on its springs, the aluminum shell popping in different spots. The spring groaning against the strain.

There's a bunch more of those things in there! Oh, dear god! If they get out... He brought his hands up defensively. *I don't want to die. I'm not ready.*

The creature drew in a gulp of air, preparing to strike. Suddenly, the back of its neck burst open, spraying mucous up into the morning air. It teetered for a moment, then it collapsed onto the ground, its teeth chattering a snare drummer's solo of clicks and clacks. Its body quivered three times. The sound of gunfire exclaiming each convulsive spasm. **Crack! Crack! Crack!**

It was dead.

"Stay down," the voice ordered and this was followed by even more gunfire. **Crack! Ping! Crack Ping! Crack! Ping! Crack Ping! Crack! Ping!** The fuel tanks on the truck clanged, morphing into a spaghetti strainer and from newborn pores, fuel began to spill. Logan, who still couldn't see the shooter, managed to unsnap the holster of his service weapon and drew it up awkwardly in his left hand. There were even more shots! **Crack! Ping! Crack! Ping!** The diesel splashed down onto the road and began to flow into the gutter, turning the dusting of snow buttery yellow. The pool of diesel widened and rolled back beneath the trailer tandems.

Logan turned, left, then right. Where was he? Where was the shooter? Then he saw him. A lone man, rifle in hand, limping toward him. He knew this man, had met him only a week before. The fucking one-legged chocolate milk guy! The chocolate milk guy had saved his life!

"I know you," Logan said. "Spencer Hughes."

Hughes said nothing at first, pushing past Logan toward the trailer. Then he pulled out a Zippo lighter and struck the flint. He turned back toward Logan, catching him in his gaze, tossing the lighter into the pooling diesel. There was a momentary pause, a hesitation before the diesel ignited. Then the street was ablaze and Hughes became a silhouette against the growing inferno. Hughes was coming back, hooking his free arm under Logan`s, lifting him up. He was yelling as he did this. "Get fucking moving, Constable! She`s gonna blow!"

Logan found his feet and they ran for their lives.

The End

Afterword

Back in January of 2012, I was invited by my friend Brad Hardy to drive the world's longest ice road as an Ice Road Trucker. I have had a long career behind the wheel of different rigs and pulled everything from freight, to flatbed and even oversize dimensions. I considered myself an experienced driver with an iron will, but this new trek was going to be totally different. For starters, I had next to no experience pulling "super b's" and my off road experience was very limited.

So, when I signed on to be a Winter Road Driver, I was about as green as you can get. I can certainly identify with Marty Croft as he races the devil up the Inuksuk, because I'd raced the evil bastard up the infamous Ingraham Trail and like Marty, I had to peel my fingers off the steering wheel and swallow my heart which was up in my throat.

After every trip up the Ingraham I rewarded myself with a ham salad sandwich prepared by our camp cooks: Tammy and Linda. This was my reward to myself, for not getting killed. Some 21 trips later, I put on 20 pounds and finally found my nerve and my second season went a little smoother; at least on the Ingraham. There was a calamity that second season which I'll address another time.

By the time that first season on the ice ended, I snapped over 10,000 pictures and I also found my muse, who insisted that this landscape, this frozen paradise, was the best setting for my new book.

And as they say, the rest is history. I am not going to regal you with my adventures on the ice. There's a rule that Big Garney makes quite clear to Marty when he hands over the gun. "What happens on the ice stays on the ice." And I have already told you much in this book, but rest assured. I haven't told you everything. I haven't told you what docking is. Haven't spilled secrets best unsaid and only spoken of over pitchers of beer and only in the company of other ice truckers worthy of keeping the secret. I can't and I won't.

But there is always something else to say. Do you want to talk about the story? How it ended? Does this mean sequel? First answer is: It ended where it did, because it did. You are the one to draw what conclusion will happen after Spence yelled at Constable Logan to move his ass and get the hell out of there. You can draw whatever conclusion of the remaining Skentophyte and if their collective will regroup or fall at the hands of the cavalry. **Piss off Preston! Does this mean sequel? Or not?** I have no intention of writing a sequel, but I will not take that possibility off the table. For now I will leave the outcome to your imagination. I have other business. A new book to get back to, one that is calling to me. For now, the world as we know it, the one where everything has changed, is suspended in the mind of the readers. This author is exhausted, his brain cooked off, his eyes burned out.

But, never say never.

One last thing.

Please, if you liked this book, tell other people and by gosh drop me a review. I love the art of storytelling, and if you think I am a worthy storyteller I implore you to help me get the word out so that I can continue to do what I love to do. I'm not looking to get famous—screw that—I just want to write stories for the rest of my life without the burden of a day job. If you think I am up for that, help a brother out and pass the word.

Okay, enough pandering.

I will say goodbye for now. I have to thank a number of folks in the coming pages for their help in getting this project into print. Thanks for tagging along down the rabbit hole.

M.J. Preston
January 16, 2015

Acknowledgments

A project of this size does not get to print without the help and cooperation of a number of people. Undoubtedly, someone will always be missed in such an acknowledgment, so before naming names I would like to thank everyone involved in the Winter Roads of 2012 and 2013. The drivers, most of all, who filled the gaps during long tiring hours as I asked endless questions. They are the Men of the North, the ones who sign on to endure the elements and yes, the adventure. The cooks in our camp, Tammy and Linda, who fattened me up that first season and fattened me up a little less my second season on the ice. The dispatchers, who put up with our bullshit when we're tired. Yes, we appreciate you. Sort of…

And now on a more personal note:

Karen Preston (Stormy)
My love, my life and my reason for being. Without you, I don't know where I would be, but I know it wouldn't be the same. Thank you for being by my side all these years.

Robert James Steel (Jim)
What I said in the beginning I meant. Without him, I wouldn't have found the courage to write that first book. Jim again read the first draft of this book, stumbling through a minefield of typos and double words.

R Bradford Hardy (Brad)
Brad has been a longtime friend and will remain so for the rest of my life. His invitation to run the ice is but a fraction of contribution he has had in the writing of this book. *"Hey Brad! Nobody's coming man."*

Michael B. Steward (Big Mike)
The five days I spent with Big Mike trapped at Ekati mine after a category 3 storm wiped out the ice road was the beginning of a lifelong friendship. Following that I spent hours with him, getting into trouble, but most of

all telling stories. Mike's talent is music, but he is also a wonderful storyteller. "Hey Mike! Nobody's coming!"

Jacob Anfinson (Jake)
Jake acted as a beta reader and also offered up a critical eye for rogue comma's and unruly clichés. I would refer to Jake as my long suffering first editor. Thanks Jake. Visine is good for bleeding eyeballs. Ask any stoner.

Dan McKeown (Sam)
Sam also stepped up as a beta reader and gave me his insights on Acadia and where he thought it needed shoring up. Dan is also an administrator for the Writing Forums where I occasionally drag my sorry ass to watch the masters and learn. Thanks Sam.

Todd Quinn (The Codfather)
Todd offered up insight into some of the aspects of hunting. Todd has done his fair share of trucking on the ice and has no idea I'm giving him a nod, but he gets it deservedly so.

Roger Gysel (Just Roger)
Roger also a hunter, and I guess by marriage he's sort of my nephew, although he's never called me Uncle Mark. Roger also gave insight into hunting.

Philip Perron
Phil acted as a beta reader, but he also supported this project by helping to get the word out. His Podcast, Dark Discussions, is a must for anyone who has a love for horror fiction and all that's fantastic. Check em out: http://darkdiscussions.com/

Dan Hunter and Eric Webster (The Askancity Boys)

The Askancity Podcast has also been a great supporter of my craft and deserves credit for bringing a spotlight on my work. They are irreverence at its finest and I mean that in a respectful way. Check them out at: http://askancity.com/

Artwork

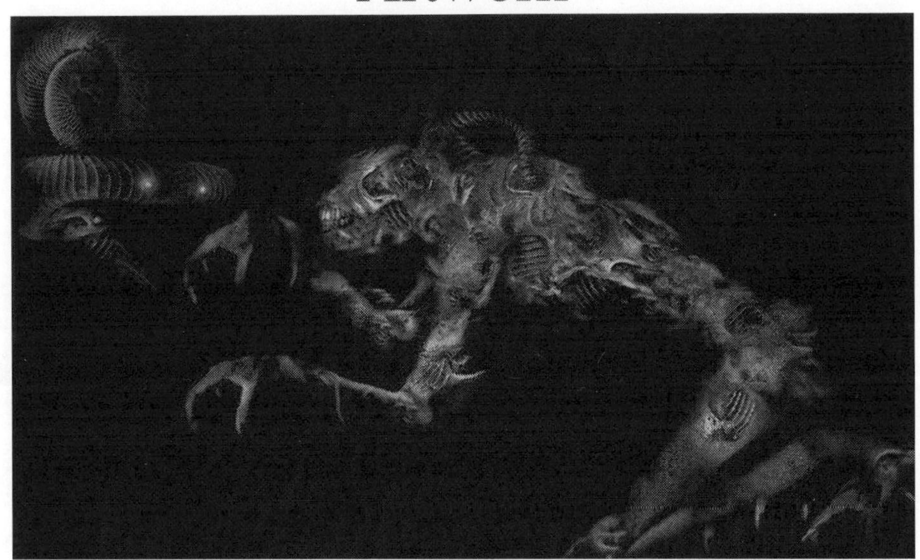

THE COLLECTIVE OF SKENTOPHYTE

The Players

Photos from the Ice

The following photos were taken when I ran the ice in 2012. I thought I might share some of them with you. It is near impossible to present the majesty of the north through black and white photos, but I hope that this short presentation gives you some visuals as I saw them.

To view many of these photos in full color you can visit my website http://mjpreston.net and link to my flickr page.

Above: Vehicles staged on the Misery Road outside the Ekati Mine after a vehicle broke down. I spent a morning broke down on this very road in temperatures that were around -50 Celsius and that really drove home the name of the road. I decided to use both Misery and High Grade in the telling of Acadia.

Above: This raven was prone to riding the mirrors of northbound trucks.

Below: A Raven leads the way as I trek southbound to YK for another load.

Above: Landlocked at Portage aka Hotel 49 after a storm left us stranded.
Below: A Category 3 storm left us stranded at the Ekati Mine for 5 days.

Above: Flooding crew reinforces the ice road.

Below: A Typhoon Pump is used to draw lake water up to flood the ice road.

Above: Standing in front of one of the big mine shovels at the Ekati Mine.

Below: A 777 Rock truck heads toward the crusher with a fresh load of kimberlite.

Above: This picture was taken in The Barrens 150 km below the Arctic Circle.

Below: Another shot of a convoy leader moving across a frozen lake.

About The Author

M.J. Preston hails from Canada, where he pursues writing fiction, creating digital art, and dabbling in photography. He is now hard at work on his third novel: 4

Visit him on the web at:

M.J. Preston Author and Artist at Large

http://mjpreston.net

MORE FROM M.J. PRESTON
SKINWALKER PRESS

Anthologies with other Writers
Great Old Ones Publishing

Skinwalker Press

Made in the USA
Charleston, SC
11 March 2015